From A. Persac, "Norman's Chart of the Lower Mississippi River" (New Orleans) 1858 as reproduced by the Pelican Publishing Company, New Orleans.

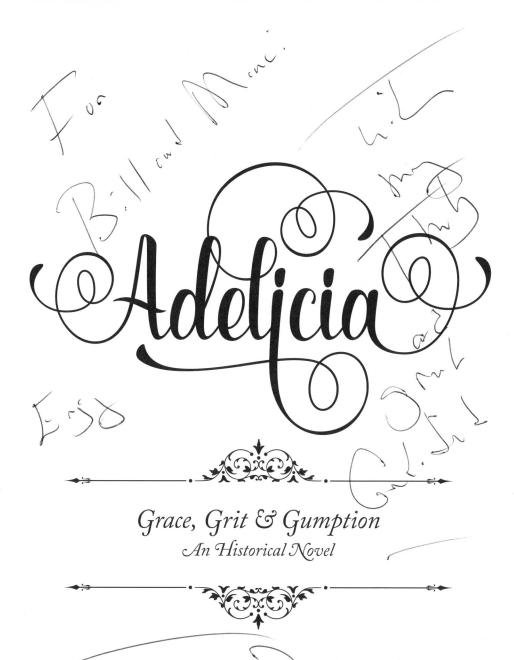

Adelicia

Grace, Grit & Gumption

An Historical Novel

Joyce Blaylock

ISBN 978-0-9982760-0-7

Library of Congress Control Number: 2016918049

Cover and interior design: Bill Kersey, www.kerseygraphics.com

Printed in the United States of America by Pollock Printing, Nashville, TN
10 9 8 7 6 5 4 3 2 1

Second Printing
Revised Edition 2017

DEDICATION

My parents,
Roberta Virginia Francis and Gilbert Freeman Carvell
(1908–1983)   *(1903–1985)*

Sola virtus triumphat

Contents

Part 1

Adelicia Hayes and Isaac Franklin

1838–1847

Nashville
1838

ATOP ONE OF THE LOW ROLLING HARPETH HILLS THE GRAY gelding lifted his head high, sniffing the early morning air, then shook his mane and whinnied before Adelicia galloped him down into the valley below and onto the Natchez Trace. She could not resist venturing onto the Trace's forbidden turf, despite her father's warnings of murder, robbery and harm to unescorted ladies. And she would never tell how far she and her best friend, Camille Perkins, had pursued its shadowed bends that wound along the Little Harpeth River.

Before leaving the Trace, where a large Beech hangs over and shades a brief stretch of the narrow lane, she rested one hand on the pommel and stroked Mozzalpa's sleek, firm neck with the other. Then giving him a familiar nudge with her knees, she cut across Hillsboro Pike to follow the bridle path home to Rokeby.

Horse and rider paced a handsome trot back to the stables where she quickly slid from the saddle, handing reins and gloves to Uncle Ben, before racing up the back stairs, crossing the gallery to her room. She impatiently dropped her clothes about her before stepping into the bath Essie had already drawn in the oval copper tub that perfectly fit her petite body. Sinking into the cool water that soothed away the August heat, she leaned back and rested her head on white linen that lay folded on the tub's rim.

Rumor had it that Sam Houston was going to be at the White's ball that evening in Gallatin, and she and Camille were determined to have him all to themselves. From the artist's rendition in the *Nashville Whig*, he was probably the handsomest man in the Union. More importantly, he was President of the Republic of Texas! It *was* a long way from her native Tennessee, but she would willingly sacrifice living in the nation's sixteenth state to become the First Lady of Texas. And since Camille was practically engaged to her brother Joel, they could always visit her in Texas.

She thought about the coming evening as she patted herself dry, then powdered her whole body with the soft scented sachet her father had brought from New York, before stepping into freshly ironed pantaloons that Essie had laid out. Parties in Sumner County were such fun, never boring like most Nashville ones. Her cousin, Emma White, liked fiddling music and fast dancing. Once, at the Whites, Adelicia and some school friends had danced until the sun came up, stayed the day and danced again that night until the moon faded into the first streaks of dawn. And she was in a mood to dance all night— with Sam Houston—as long as her father did not find out. He had twice cautioned her about the former Tennessee governor not only being too old for her, but divorced as well. A scandalous affair about which everyone knew.

Adelicia paused in front of the long gilt framed mirror to take another look at her new ruffled organdy dress. The pale pink complemented her smooth ivory skin, while the contrasting rose satin ribbons, tied in her long dark hair, added an additional luster. She tossed her hair back, pleased with what she saw. She could not remember a time, not even her very first party, when she had not been the most sought after girl there.

She expected every man she met to fall in love with her, and it bothered her not at all to break their hearts. She sometimes wondered if that were not her intention. There were moments, however, when she wished she could be more like her mother, fondly remembered by all, not only for her grace and beauty, but for her quiet and gentle spirit as well. But, as she continued to gaze at her own reflection, she regretfully supposed she had never wished for it long enough. Lingering a moment more, she blew a kiss to Telemachus, who always seemed to be gazing directly at her from the wallpaper, then went to find her father.

She loved the library with its myriad of books lined on dark mahogany shelves from floor to ceiling. When she was a child, she thought all of the books in the world must be in this one room, a room that smelled of old leather and sweet tobacco.

Adelicia leaned over the Morocco hide chair, kissed her father's forehead, then picked up his pipe and began refilling it with the cherry blend tobacco that lay on the table beside it. Oliver Bliss Hayes was handsome at fifty-six, a man who had come to Middle Tennessee from Massachusetts as a young lawyer and married the beautiful Sarah Clements Hightower from Williamson County.

"My Adie," he said reaching up and taking her hand. "I am a blessed man. I have the smartest, prettiest daughters in the county and the finest sons. Run along now, Uncle Will's had the carriage waiting far too long, and your brothers are in a stew. You have thirty miles to go and it's already past midmorning."

It was not the first time her older brothers, Joel and Richard, had been in a "stew," and it would not be the last.

"By-the-way, Adie, if Mr. Houston does show up tonight, which I highly doubt, keep in mind, that I shall have no flirtations from my eldest daughter with the former governor."

She put the pipe in her father's hand and blew him a kiss, as she gracefully twirled out the door closing it behind her.

It was no secret that Oliver Hayes spoiled and adored all seven of his children. It was also no secret that he indulged Adelicia. She reminded him so much of her mother…in all but temperament. Even as a small child, she had been a challenge, how be it, a delightful one, and now, although she tried his patience at times, he could not help but admire her. He liked saying that she was as keen as one of "Old Hickory's" thoroughbreds. And when he was at Balie Peyton's race track in Lebanon, just across the river, with Andrew Jackson and the usual crowd, watching some of the finest horses in the nation run, he was reminded of his spirited daughter. He loved the spiciness she brought to life at Rokeby.

As the Hayes carriage turned onto the Nashville-Gallatin Pike, the threatening cloud overhead turned into a late summer's downpour. "It's your fault," Joel instantly snapped. "If you had been on time, we would not be caught in this torrent."

"Snit, snit, snit. If Camille were in the carriage, you would not care a tidily about being late." Joel was such a bore. She never understood what Camille saw in him. Perhaps opposites did attract. She could not imagine him as a lover for her high-spirited friend. Adelicia almost said aloud what she was thinking, but bit her tongue just as Uncle Will called out, "Mr. Richard, I spects we better stop somewheres. The chain done broke on my lead horse, and these elements ain't making it no better, and I's gettin' drenched."

"For goodness sakes, Richey, the rain is no more than an August cloudburst," she said exactingly. She understood what the girls saw in Richard. He was strikingly handsome, very charming and not quite the bore as was Joel, but far too sensible. However, he was a sweet and loving brother, except for his overprotectiveness—that, she abhorred.

"Now listen to who's worried about being late," Joel snapped.

"Both of you be quiet. If the chain is broken, it is broken. Do whatever you need to do, Uncle Will."

"We's near Mr. Franklin's place now, if that's all right with you, Mr. Richard."

Adelicia's eyes brightened at the mention of Franklin's name, and as she flashed them toward her brothers, she saw their instant looks of disapproval. Could they possibly suspect what she was already thinking?

Since she was very young, Adelicia had been fascinated with the controversial Isaac Franklin and the mystery that surrounded him. Once, after her mother had died, he had called at Rokeby, and Essie had insisted that she and her younger sisters stay confined to their rooms.

Will slowed the carriage to let it pass between the granite posts, and Adelicia got her first glimpse of Fairvue Plantation.

It was grander than the tales she had heard; grander than she had imagined as they rode beneath century-old walnut trees that wound through lush green pasture. Thoroughbreds grazed on either side and beyond lay hundreds of rich black acres crowded with tall stalks of corn as far as she could see. And as they rounded a bend, Fairvue, in its columned splendor, rose to full view, encircled by a low cinnamon brick wall, laid in Flemish bond to match the Georgian mansion, reminding her of pictures she had seen of grand English manors.

It was obvious that Mr. Franklin had spared not even the smallest detail when planning his country estate and its immaculate grounds. It was grandeur set in sheer elegance!

She could no longer conceal her awe as the carriage stopped in front of the scrolled iron gate. "How I would love to meet Mr. Isaac Franklin!"

"Adie, sometimes it's hard to believe you're our mother's daughter."

"Oh hush, Joel. When you come back from your honeymoon you'll probably still have your virginity." Then she teased, "I shall discuss it with Camille this very afternoon."

Joel blushed, "Do you know what you need?"

"Please! Both of you be quiet," Richard interrupted. "Adie, I'll speak to you later."

An elderly gentleman walked through the gracefully arched entrance with its fan-shaped glass panes and symmetrical side lights, greeting the unexpected guests with umbrellas. He accompanied Adelicia inside, then had a house boy take her brothers and Uncle Will to the blacksmith's beyond the stables. It seemed an eternity before her brothers were out of sight.

"I'm Uncle Sugart. Please take a seat, Missus. I'll be back with freshments."

It felt right for her to be standing inside the enormous hallway, to step onto the magnificent Aubusson rug with its rich colors of Prussian blue and deep wine red, to place her hand on the handsome mahogany stair rail. No wonder the girls at the Nashville Female Academy had for years whispered and made dares about Isaac Franklin. Adelicia had learned French and history, prosody, mathematics and rhetoric, art, music, orthography and etymology—all those areas in which young ladies were expected to be well versed and adept. But she had learned nothing of life and marriage, certainly not about things 'never mentioned,' nor asked, nor questioned, all of which she found fascinating.

Not one of the girls had actually met Isaac Franklin, but some of their fathers had made visits to Fairvue—after a Sunday's race at Balie Peyton's track, or to smoke Havana cigars and sip specially blended Bourbon over business. The girls had repeatedly told tales of grand extravagance they had overheard, but not until now did Adelicia know that none of the stories were exaggerated.

The identical parlors on her left had matching black Irish Kilkenny marble mantels, and the prisms dazzling from the Venetian chandeliers reflected so much of the midday's light that their spectrum of colors danced on and off the tall ceilings.

Each room was furnished with the finest pieces from the Louis XIV period: gilt tables and chests, and chairs and sofas upholstered in ivory and mauve silks, their arms and legs carved with acanthus leaves and roped with garlands of flowers. Ispahan carpets in the medallion and vase design, blended the mauves, ivories, greens and blues. "Splendor!" she whispered. "Absolute Splendor!"

In the music room to her right was the loveliest of grand pianos, and although an accomplished pianist, she was hesitant to run her tapered fingers over the delicate ivory keys. The silence was as awe-inspiring as the room itself. And as she continued to gaze about her, her eyes stopped above the exquisite, deep green Sevres figurines on the portrait above the mantel, a portrait that could be none other than Isaac Franklin. He was extraordinarily handsome—strong cheekbones and strikingly beautiful blue eyes that appeared to be looking directly at her. Her pirate, her Paris, her Odysseus, her King Arthur, her heroes from epics and myths of an eternal age.

Uncle Sugart interrupted her reverie when he came into the room bearing a silver tray laden with freshly picked strawberries and a crystal bowl filled with soft, powdered sugar. "Mr. Franklin sure be sorry he miss the young missus. He gone to Nashville today."

"And I regret not being able to meet Mr. Franklin. Perhaps…"

"We wish you to express our regrets to Mr. Franklin," Joel interrupted, walking into the room. "Adelicia, the carriage is ready." She gave him a devilish look, but decided to hold her tongue.

"We'd be mighty pleased to have you sign the guest register. Mr. Franklin take a heap of pleasure knowing the quality folk who come to Fairvue."

"We shall be delighted," Adelicia immediately offered.

"I'm pleased to do so," Joel responded, but not taking the quill in hand.

"Sugart, Sugart Jacobs," a shrill voice called from somewhere at the rear of the house.

"Scuse me, that's Aggie calling, and when she call, I goes. Be sure and eat all them berries".

Uncle Sugart reappeared almost instantly to inform Joel that Richard had asked for him to return to the stables. Joel had probably made it up about the carriage being ready, she thought. He was obviously checking on her.

Adelicia walked toward the rear verandah while dipping a ripe, red berry into snow white powder. Biting into it, she licked the pink juice from her lips as she watched a parade of peacocks strut across the lawn, before putting another ripe berry to her mouth.

Alone again, her eyes returned to the portrait her thoughts had never left. Once more, she ran her delicate fingers silently across the keyboard, then moved quietly into the large foyer playing make-believe, resting her hand on the brass newel post, smiling and bowing to imaginary guests when suddenly, she froze.

Her eyes fixed on a beautiful olive-skinned woman standing at the top of the stairs, exquisitely dressed in lavender silk, a gown that seemed designed to accent her perfectly portioned body. Adelicia blushed. Her interloper stood statue-like for a moment as the two women stared at each other, then quickly turned and disappeared behind the soft sound of a closing door.

Adelicia's thoughts raced from astonishment to embarrassment to awe. She and friends had whispered such things, but to actually see, to know that Isaac Franklin kept such a person—in his own house!

She continued to stare up at the open balcony, her thoughts racing. She had decided from the moment the carriage had stopped in front of the great house that she would be mistress of Fairvue, to have all she had seen and all she had not yet seen. Isaac Franklin was a wealthy forty-nine year old bachelor. What difference did it make how he had at first made his fortune? And as she glanced back to the portrait, it was with the assurance of a woman who knew what she wanted and how to get it.

She turned to observe her own slender figure in the beveled-edge mirror, cupping her hands beneath her breasts making mental comparisons when Richard came in. "What in heaven's name are you doing?"

Looking at him with an impish grin, she answered, "I am wondering how to make my bosoms larger."

"If I did not know you were my own flesh and blood, I'd think you no better than a common street girl. Uncle Will is waiting."

"Richard, sometimes, I have no idea why all the girls flitter over you, except you are handsome."

Joel watched in disbelief, "Papa will hear how Precious Perfect has flaunted herself!"

Adelicia could not care less what either of them were saying or thinking. She had more important things to consider.

The sun was shining as they stepped onto the front portico where hundreds of monarchs were fluttering and circling, creating a dazzling spectacle. Appearing fairy-like, they seemingly floated from where she stood to the circular ice house in the midst of a walled rose garden.

She had stayed about two paces behind her brothers, and just as they reached the carriage door, she quickly turned and rushed back inside.

She signed the guest book beneath the signature of Richard, then hurried past Uncle Sugart, still standing in the doorway. With a smile of assurance she stepped into the carriage, tucking her skirts about her.

AUGUST 22, 1838
ADELICIA HAYES
ROKEBY PLANTATION
NASHVILLE, TENNESSEE

"I like this house and I have set my cap for its master."

Aunt Aggie, pipe in hand, leaned over the curved rosewood chest, squinting her eyes to make out the most recent signature in the guest book.

"Yes sir. Yes sir!" Aunt Aggie exclaimed, slapping her husband on the back. "If ever the moon did come up, Sugart Jacobs, we gonna get a mistress at Fairvue!"

"Don't just stand there a shouting, woman, reveal me what it says."

Aunt Aggie read aloud to Uncle Sugart while he peered over her broad shoulders.

CHAPTER 2

IT WAS MID-AFTERNOON BEFORE THE HAYES' CARRIAGE REACHED Gallatin, and it was all Adelicia could do to conceal her excitement until she saw Camille. After greeting the Whites and explaining their delay, Richard and Joel went into the library to smoke with Judge White and the other men. Uncle Will went to the kitchen, toting baked goods for Louisa.

Adelicia followed Emma upstairs, her thoughts, singular, with no trace of adventures with Sam Houston. She made certain to be out of hearing distance before turning to Emma. "May I have a word with you, please, Cousin Emma?" she whispered.

"Of course, dear."

She had always been fond of her cousin Emma. "Do you know Mr. Franklin well?"

"He and the Judge have been friends for years, Adie. You know how my husband loves horses, and Fairvue breeds some of the best. There's not a Sunday when half the men in Sumner County don't show up at Cloverbottom for the races, General Jackson, when he's well enough, included."

Adelicia's thoughts flashed to the magnificent thoroughbreds she had seen earlier, and her eyes sparkled with mounting enthusiasm. "Does he go to Nashville often?"

"When he's in town."

"Where is out of town?"

"Louisiana, Adie. Most of Mr. Franklin's property is there, with the exception of Texas. According to the Judge, he grows enormous amounts of cotton along the Mississippi River bottom in West Feliciana Parish. Surely you've heard your father speak of him?"

She was so intrigued by the talk of land and horses and cotton, and the power she imagined it brought, that she had unconsciously dug her nails into the palms of her hands. "Yes, but, after seeing Fairvue today...." she remarked, thinking of her next line while speaking. "His servants were so gracious; I feel badly, not being able to thank Mr. Franklin in person for his kind hospitality, and because we are no more than four to five miles distance, I thought perhaps..."

"Adie, dear, I know just what you're thinking, and your formality doesn't fool me atall. It hasn't been that many years since I, too, was a maiden in all the circles, and almost as daring as yourself. If you are so intent on meeting Isaac Franklin, we shall call on him tomorrow. On second thought," she said, "it may be best to invite him here for a late breakfast."

"That is wonderful," Adelicia answered, hugging Emma and kissing her on the cheek. "Wonderful!"

"But, Adie, I would not set my bonnet for Isaac Franklin. He's not a young lady's—let us say, it would not be agreeable."

Ignoring Emma's last remark, Adelicia tiptoed quietly into the room where the Perkins' sisters from Williamson County were already resting. She slipped out of her pink organdy and lay across the half-tester bed beside Camille. "Are you asleep?" she whispered.

"Of course not. I was pretending, to see how long it would take for you to try and wake me."

"Do you know who Isaac Franklin is?"

"Who?"

"*Shh*. Isaac Franklin."

"No more than you. Why?"

"I am going to marry him."

"You're what?"

Lindy, in the bed beside them, turned over. "Will ya'll please, *shush*?"

They lay quietly. "His mattresses must be made of the finest down. They would have to be, to match everything else."

"Will you please stop gibbering and tell me why you've suddenly retreated to loony land?"

The thought of mattresses reminded her of the exquisite woman on the stairway, and she began telling Camille the story from beginning to end. Neither of them had ever seen a fallen woman, however an acquaintance's brother whose bachelor friend in New Orleans actually kept such an enigma had, to their dismay, related only a few scant details, forcing them to use their imaginations that were based solely on limited knowledge.

"Do I get Sam Houston all to myself now?"

"What about Joel?"

"Only teasing, only teasing," Camille responded.

"Sam Houston is a memory. I shan't even flirt with him, I don't think. Cousin Emma is inviting Mr. Franklin for breakfast in the morning."

Planning the following morning, Adelicia finally dozed off thinking about her meeting with the controversial Mr. Franklin.

As a young man at the beginning of the century, he had begun accumulating wealth through the interstate slave trade, but having reconsidered, began to invest wisely in bonds, land and banking. He was now a prosperous gentleman planter with vast holdings. In fact, her cousin Emma had further related that folks said he had saved, on average, twenty-thousand dollars per year for every year of his life, since he had turned twenty-one.

All too soon it seemed to her, that Lizzy was at the door announcing, "Rising time."

Adelicia stretched from her favorite sleeping position, a valley formed in the middle of the bed so that she could feel the luxury of puffed feathers all about her. She moved one leg over to let it sink into the mound of softness as Lizzy gently shook her. "Miss Adie, you gotta hurry. The others done dressed and down stairs."

Adelicia opened her eyes to find that she was alone in the room except for Emma's house servant, Lizzy. And according to the shadows streaking across the floor, she knew it was later than she had intended it to be. She stretched once more, making new valleys in the feathers, then quickly got up to dab her body with the blend of cool water and dried lavender that Lizzy was pouring into the bowl.

It was true about Adelicia's untimely approach to social affairs; she enjoyed making a grand entrance. Camille once said it even amazed her how everyone snapped to attention whenever Adelicia swept into a room. And Adelicia was well aware that women admired her talents and envied her for having them; that men adored her and envied the man she favored. Her genuine friends were few and those who loved her even fewer.

When she sat on the cushioned bench in front of the mirror, her thoughts returned again to Fairvue and its master, if indeed they had been elsewhere, as Lizzy helped with her hair.

"Miss Adie, I do believe the good Lord bless you with enough hair for three girls. It's like Absalom's in de Bible," Lizzy said, pinning the right side back with a melon silk butterfly clip.

"Papa says I have hair like my mother's. When I was very small, I would watch him brush it for her in the evenings, and after she became ill, holding it close to him as he brushed…"

"Adie," Emma called. "Camille asked me to say that she is with Joel and to hurry."

Lizzy tied the long crinolines, fastened the tiny pearl buttons in the back of Adelicia's bodice, straighten the layers of silk and finally fastened her mother's onyx brooch around her neck.

"I declare, Miss Adie. You gets prettier all de time."

"Thank you, Lizzy. Are you coming down?"

"And who else you think Miss Emma have do her fancy serving?"

Adelicia felt radiant in her soft melon silk gown that draped from her shoulders, barely revealing the tops of her breast. From the upstairs gallery, she could see Joel standing with Camille and nearby, Adelicia's assumed beau, Grainger Caldwell, talking with Randall McGavock and Margaret Donelson.

Poor Grainger. He could never mean anything more to her than a friend. He was her first escort after the death of her fiancée, Alphonso Gibbs, four years before when she was seventeen. Her family was fond of Grainger, but he was not the ideal match that her father had supposed Alphonso to be. And although Grainger continued to be her primary beau and called at Rokeby on occasion, there were others as well. She did not even flirt with him and actually discouraged any advances, except for an occasional polite kiss on the cheek.

Candles were lit throughout the ballroom and from her vantage point, it was like being above the stars and looking down upon them. A glorious array of multicolored ball gowns reflecting in the candlelight and the beginning strains of the evening's first polka.

After two hours of steady dancing to country reels and polkas, Adelicia welcomed the intermission for the traditional eleven o'clock supper. She felt ravenous, as well as lightheaded from the fast paced dancing and the restraint of her binding waist corset. Hastily drinking a cup of Madeira punch, she sat on the moiré Hepplewhite sofa, sipping a second one, speculating with Camille and the others about Sam Houston, what they would do if he walked in the door. Of course, Emily Dyer was rattling on about how when he came she would excuse herself and not be caught in the same room with him... as if Sam Houston would give her a second look in the first place.

Adelicia heard one of the ladies asking for someone to play the piano, then her cousin Emma's voice, "Find Adelicia, she plays beautifully."

"With hands like those, I'm sure you play very well." The voice was deep, mellow and clear. She looked up to see the unmistakable blue eyes peering down at her, even more captivating than in the oil portrait. She first stared, then blushed, deaf to the sound of her name being called from the other room. Isaac Franklin bent toward her, "I believe someone is asking for you."

Attempting to regain her composure, she rose, back straight, feet positioned. But with the unexpected, magical touch of Isaac's hand, she became warm and flushed and spilled Madeira onto the front of her gown. When he proceeded to dab the rosy liquid from her skirt with his linen handkerchief, she blushed even more, frustrated that one man's presence could have such an effect on her; it had never happened before.

And moments later, she found little relief while sitting at the rosewood piano playing the latest ballads with everyone gathered around singing. It was not until Camille leaned forward, turned the page in the music book and whispered in Adelicia's ear, that her dauntless spirit resurfaced and she began the chorus of an old favorite, "Roses of December Forever Bloom in May." Isaac was near enough that she could hear his humming a smooth tenor to the familiar tune.

At the call for supper, she walked into the dining room with Joel, Camille and Grainger, and was looking for her place card among the tables when Emma took her by the arm and said, "Adelicia, your playing was beautiful; you must entertain some more before the evening ends. I'd like you to meet Isaac Franklin. Mr. Franklin, I believe Adelicia and her family were your unexpected guests during the rain showers today."

"Yes, Miss Emma. Miss Hayes was thoughtful enough to sign the guest book." He lifted her hand to his lips. "The pleasure is mine."

Fortunately, the soft glow from the low-burning tapers prevented either of them from seeing the scarlet flush she felt in her face, although she was certain Isaac knew it was there and was enjoying it.

"You know her father, Oliver Bliss Hayes."

"Matter of fact, I saw him in town today along with Sam Perkins and James Polk. Polk's going to be our next governor, you know, and then to the White House. Must keep Tennesseans in Washington."

"He and Mrs. Polk are lovely people," Adelicia responded, "Do you think he will, indeed, be President?" She felt her nervous comment embarrassingly lame.

"If Andy Jackson has anything to do with it."

They walked through the buffet line together, Isaac commenting on each dish, the aromas, the colors and piling his plate high with some of everything, and she barely realizing what she was putting on hers, or where Camille and Grainger were. Isaac escorted her to her seat at the long mahogony dining table, then found his place at a table for four diagonally across the room. She stood behind her chair, enduring what seemed an eternally long blessing by Judge White, and when they were at last seated, she looked up to find her eyes in direct contact with Isaac's. The glow of candlelight, the soft sound of the mandolin, and the look in his eyes, created a moment she would like to have held forever.

And any attempt to make conversation with her dinner companions was stifled by the certainty that whenever she glanced up, Isaac was looking attentively at her, as if he were examining her every feature, her every gesture. She flirted with her eyes and her lips, fully aware, and in spite of the fact, that Grainger and Richard were seated across from her, and knowing Richard saw her every glance to Isaac's table.

Her usual ravenous appetite had long since vanished, as well as any thoughts of Sam Houston. But when Lizzy served a tempting lemon chiffon desert, she brought the spoon slowly to her lips to taste the tart lemon topped with freshly whipped cream that melted upon contact with her tongue. She wished that Isaac could dab the cream from her lips, and in her fanciful dreaminess glanced over, only to discover, he was no longer there.

The starched linen napkins removed from the lap, folded and returned to the table, signaled the end of supper and the beginning of the second half of the ball. As Sam Perkins removed her chair, she looked about the room. How quickly he had disappeared, she thought.

Adelicia almost refused when Grainger asked her to be his partner for the quadrille, but having second thoughts, she decided Isaac should learn to act with more finesse. She would make him dreadfully jealous by twirling about the floor with another man and after the first few moments, he would cut in.

However, her prediction of Isaac Franklin's behavior proved more unsettling when half an hour later, she glimpsed him sitting, steeped in conversation, not even glancing in her direction. She was certainly aware that men sometimes only appeared not to notice when they were actually aware of a girl's every move. Her only consolation was that he was not dancing with anyone else. "Perhaps he does not dance at all!" she almost said aloud.

She loved the fact that Cousin Emma, on her mother's side, dispensed of the formality of dance cards, which allowed a girl to have so many more choices. It certainly made the evening more interesting, permitting one to flirt ever so much more.

An hour passed before she saw Isaac again, this time standing by the oversized sterling bowl filled with delicious concoctions of iced punch, talking with Judge White.

"Adie, is something wrong?" Grainger asked.

"I feel faint," she said, putting her hand to her head.

"Would you like to rest and have some punch?"

"Graingy, darling, how thoughtful. That is exactly what I need."

With her hand in his arm, Grainger escorted her to the refreshment table, and from a chilled crystal pitcher poured her a cup of seasoned cider.

"Hello, Judge, Mr. Franklin. Miss Hayes was feeling a bit lightheaded and we stopped for some refreshment."

"What a shame, Miss Hayes," Isaac said. "I was hoping you'd give me the honor of a dance before I go."

"You are leaving? Must you?" she asked, unable to stop her anxious words from spilling out.

"I've a great deal of business to attend to before leaving for the City of New Orleans next week, and my days begin early."

"Will you be away long?" she asked, wishing she could conceal her obvious disappointment.

"I'm never sure how long I'll be. Do you feel well enough to dance with the *Master of Fairvue*?"

She put her hand in his, not caring what the Judge, nor Grainger, nor anyone thought, or would think.

She found being in Isaac's arms more tantalizing than she had dreamed. He was a marvelous dancer, and her frustration quickly disappeared as they twirled around the floor to the rhythm of a polka. He held her, almost lifting, suspending her, her feet feeling as if they touched nothing at all; that she was spinning, gliding through the air with him.

"Your recovery is remarkable," he said, taking deep breaths.

"You keep my secrets well," she parried, flaunting her sophistication.

His blue eyes sparkled. "Have you been to New Orleans?"

"Papa says it is wicked and no place for any of his children…but I would love to." She answered between breaths, as he drew her close to him.

"Love to what?" he laughed as he spun her to the rhythm at arm's length.

"Visit the wicked city."

He laughed again.

"You are laughing at my naiveté," she lightly scolded.

When the music ended, he did not release his hold from either of her hands.

"My dear, you may be a lot of things concealed in innocence, but naive, you're not. The blushing is very becoming," he added. "We'll see if we can convince your father that New Orleans is quite a decent place and plan a trip for you and your family. Perhaps you can visit my West Feliciana' plantations as well."

She hoped the disappointment that he was inviting everyone did not show in her face, although she knew that it could not be otherwise. The thought, however, was truly wicked, and she was enjoying thinking on its complexities.

"Are you as fond of New Orleans as of Nashville?" She asked.

"It's a city like none other. I'm never sure if New Orleans reminds me of Paris, or if Paris reminds me of New Orleans. The chicory coffee and Creole delicacies can be found nowhere else in the world." Isaac looked at her, smiling, "To answer your question, I'm very fond of New Orleans, but my heart will always be in Middle Tennessee."

Adelicia was thankful no one had cut in during the polka, and even more grateful that they were still uninterrupted as they stood talking on the ballroom floor when the minuet was beginning. Although she found it odd that no one had.

His touch was tender, yet firm, captivating. And she found being in his arms wonderfully warm and comforting, unlike that of the young men's she had known. She delighted in the appearance she was certain they were making, but as the mandolin sounded its closing chords, Richard was there requesting the next dance, and there was little she could do but accept.

"Thank you, Miss Hayes, for two memorable dances," Isaac said, bowing. "It's time for me to leave."

He added what seemed to be an afterthought. "You're even lovelier than Uncle Sugart described you." Then he nodded politely to Richard and left.

How subtle and engaging, she thought, in a full state of fascination.

Furious with her behavior, Richard gripped her waist so tightly when the waltz began that she purposefully crushed the heel of her slipper onto the top of his foot. She knew, however, that he would not cause a scene and continue the dance.

"I am shamed, embarrassed! Do you realize how foolish and absurd you looked with him?"

"And do you realize how foolish you sound reprimanding me? I shall dance with whomever I please and flirt with whomever I please. I am not overly concerned with appearances, nor Mr. Franklin's reputation—perhaps none of it is true."

Richard looked at her with what she interpreted as apparent disgust. "Did you see anyone else dancing with him? Young or old? He is a friend of the Judge's, *not* a social equal. You need a good whopping, and don't think you are too old for one! This will prove humiliating for Father."

"When you and Joel tattle to Papa, I shall say you are exaggerating as usual. You are such a snob, Richard. Now dance with me and smile as if you are enjoying it. My honor has not been tainted."

Fortunately, the waltz was ending, but not too soon for Adelicia to peer over Richard's shoulder and see both Judge White and Isaac Franklin walk to the front door, then step outside. When they were out of view, she closed her eyes and tried to imagine Isaac in the saddle, galloping away. He continued foremost in her thoughts the remainder of the evening, and she found that none of the young men waiting to dance with her mattered at all. "You know, Richard, a man does not even become charming until he is past forty."

Chapter 3

ISAAC DID NOT GALLOP AWAY ON HIS MAGNIFICENT STEED, AS Adelicia had fantasized. Instead, he had paced Imposter at a slow walk while the light from the full moon cast its shadow on the two of them as they followed the winding bridle path back home to Fairvue. His thoughts were uneasy, as entangled as the brambles about him.

He could not ignore the directness of a woman who would sign her name as Adelicia had, and when he had looked over the guests gathered at the Whites, it had been unnecessary for anyone to point her out. The posture, the face, the gown fit perfectly with the signature. Her eyes fascinated him, as did the way she held her head, the way she moved, her voice, the light touch of her fingertips on his arm, but it was the daring of her spirit that intrigued him the more. He did not doubt he could have her, but that knowledge was tempered by the certainty that he would have to give up Lona de Bloviere.

He had come close to marriage on a number of occasions, but there had been more reasons for remaining a bachelor than becoming a husband. Tonight, however, the idea had new appeal. The flush on her face when she had spilled her Madeira, not embarrassed that it had happened, but angry that she had committed the unpardonable sin for a southern woman: the loss of her composure. He smiled to himself. She seemed everything a man could want.

He was acutely aware that Adelicia was interested in his money: that had been her introduction. And he was sure she realized all too well that with money came power. But she had what his money could not buy, nor his power sway: a position in society. She was the daughter of one of Nashville's most prominent and respected families.

His instinct about women made him certain that she was capable of passion. By that same instinct, he suspected she would never give the unconditional love that was Lona's.

He did not wish to hurt Lona, nor did he want to think about hurting her. However, that afternoon when he had returned from

Nashville, they had again exchanged harsh words over Aunt Aggie's behavior towards her. Lona had again complained that his old mammy referred to him as "Mr. Franklin" in her presence, never with the more familiar, "Mr. Isaac," and that at meals Aunt Aggie continued to behave as if Lona were not present, never addressing her directly. His having come to Aunt Aggie's defense had prompted more anger; it was then he had hurriedly dressed and gone to the Whites.

It was no secret that Aunt Aggie loathed Lona's presence at Fairvue, and it was also no secret that her presence in Sumner County had caused a stir from the beginning. Although his friend and neighbor, Eli Odom, had said little, it was obvious that he and the other neighbors politely ignored it. In New Orleans, such relationships were accepted among the upper classes, if not expected, but it was, to say the least, not expected in a more conservative Middle Tennessee.

Before bringing Lona to Fairvue, Isaac had given lengthy explaintions to her about Aunt Aggie and Uncle Sugart. That they had come as slaves from Virginia with his father across the Appalachians' to the virgin Tennessee Territory, and were in their teens when he was born in 1789. He could not remember a time, he had told her, when they were not members of his household. That Aunt Aggie was like a mother to him, Uncle Sugart like a father, that he had built Fairvue as much for them as for himself. Nevertheless, Lona had not understood, nor he, the impact her presence would present.

He loved Lona, in his way, cared for her and had generously provided for her from the beginning; he would continue to provide for her, but he had known, even before having met Adelicia, that he must return with Lona to New Orleans, to the house he had purchased for her on Esplanade.

Isaac entered Lona's room where a single flame from the bureau lamp cast a faint glow of light upon silk curtains that fluttered in the evening breeze. His favorite whiskey with two glasses was on the marbled-topped chest beside the bed, and her white cotton gown lay in folds upon the floor. He watched for a moment the careful stroking and brushing of her long silky hair at the dressing table, this evening's ritual enhanced as each soft movement was accented in the filtered shadows. Then he filled the glasses and came and stood behind her.

"Did you have supper?"

"Della brought me a tray."

"I'm sorry about this afternoon..."

She reached up and put her fingers to his lips, permitting the fullness of her exquisitely shaped breast to reflect in the mirror. "You need say no more."

She opened the tiny enameled music box he had given her when she first came to live at the house on Esplanade. And it seemed that she was hearing "When Love Never Ceases" for the first time.

He placed his hands on her bare shoulders, gently traced his fingers along her neck and removed the one remaining emerald ear bob.

She stood facing him and began loosening the onyx studs in his shirt, while he lightly moved his fingers down her bare back.

"Are you unhappy here?"

"Unhappy? I am happy wherever you are, Cherie."

"I think we must return to New Orleans soon."

"Are we not staying for the turning of your leaves? How do you say it...'They become a hundred different shades of reds, oranges and yellows?'"

He smiled, "Another autumn, perhaps."

Her lips were warm, and Isaac loved the way they made him feel. He slowly moved his hands over her soft olive skin watching the reflection in the mirror until they reached, then held her thighs. And as he drew her closer to him, she felt the urgency in his touch.

"Oh, Cherie, I wish for us always to be like now."

The lamp's wick burned lower, then went out, leaving the full moon as the solitary light to cast soft shadows across the floor.

Isaac awoke, easing his arm from beneath Lona's head and slipping out of bed even before the peacocks had come down from their roosts, knowing he must return to New Orleans with her sooner than originally intended. He stepped outside onto the long gallery, his cotton robe still in hand, before striking a match between his fingers and watching the blue flame flicker in the early morning air. He lit his cigar, took a deep puff, then held it between his teeth, as he put on his robe and walked to the rear verandah, silently looking toward the river.

He loved this sight of the Cumberland with her hard limestone cliffs and sloping hills beyond, and from his vantage point he could observe the activity all the way to the river and the bustle already taking place aboard the *Tribune* that had docked the previous afternoon. He quietly stepped back inside to dress, then quickly walked towards the landing, as the *Tribune's* great paddlewheel glistened against rippling waters in the first rays of early morning sun.

His former partner, John Armfield, who piloted the *Tribune* on her runs from New Orleans to Nashville and back, was directing the unloading of molasses, hogs heads of sugar, flour, coffee, medicimals of every sort and sundry other cargo, and already perspiring in the humid August heat. His man, Pompy, a high yellow who had been with John the day Isaac first met him on a stage coach in Virginia, was standing beside him.

"Got anything to drink on here?" Isaac asked.

"Anything you want, pardner...mighty early."

John, like Isaac, was a product of the frontier, but his quick mind for business, combined with good judgment, had caused Isaac thirteen years earlier, to make him a full partner in his profitable slave trading establishments in Alexandria and Natchez, a business in which neither were any longer involved.

Isaac went aboard and walked into the cabin, where his younger brother, William, was leaning back in an elephant hide chair, sipping coffee. John followed.

Isaac poured straight bourbon.

"What's wrong?" John asked, scratching his black beard while keeping an eye on Isaac. "I keep telling you, you ought a leave the women alone. They ain't nothing but trouble."

"My big brother never learned the delicate art of handling the delicate creatures," William Franklin said, stretching his hands over his head until his fingers touched the frame of a clipper ship painting above him.

"One of these days, I may listen to you, John," he said, ignoring his brother's comment.

"A sight better off you'd be if you did. What you grieving about?"

"The conflict between Aunt Aggie and Lona has been constant since we arrived…now there's a new development. I have got to take Lona back to New Orleans."

"What's wrong with that?" John's indifference toward women never ceased to amaze him.

He watched as Isaac drained the glass and poured himself another. "I have to end it, John, not just take her back."

William looked intently at Isaac and straightened up in his chair. "I told you not to bring her here. That it was no good."

"You were right." Isaac stood up and for the second time emptied his glass before setting it on the table. "She's the first woman, I suppose, I've really cared about." Then he asked half-heartedly, "When are you going back down-river?"

"Four or five days, soon as we finish this and get the corn and hogs loaded," John answered.

"We'll be on board," Isaac answered. And as an afterthought added, "We'll stay at Lochlomond briefly, then take a packet from Bayou Sara to New Orleans."

William walked to where Isaac stood and put his hand on his shoulder. "Lona's an extraordinary woman."

"I brought her here to see if it would work. It didn't. It's an uneasy situation, Will, she's better off in New Orleans. Thanks," he said, "I don't want to talk about it anymore."

The two brothers and John walked out, cups of strong coffee in their hands, leaving the directing to Pompy, and stepped onto the dock where the trees had begun to give shade and a cooling breeze could be felt stirring up from the river.

Lona would know the change in him without a word. "A woman can tell by the way a man touches her when his feelings change, almost as much as by his eyes," she once told him. "Touches, also, do not lie."

CHAPTER 4

DEEP IN THOUGHT, LONA WALKED ON THE FRONT LAWN AMONG the peacocks. From the moment Aunt Aggie and Uncle Sugart had seen her, she had felt their disdain and was all too aware that their approval was of great importance to Isaac. This friction between his favored slaves, a term never used when referring to them, had kept her from fully enjoying the Sumner County that Isaac loved so well. Only Della, whose place was in the kitchen, had been civil to her. She was actually the only one on the plantation who behaved as if Lona were a guest.

Lona was a free person of color and resented the coolness, the aloofness from the servants at Fairvue. It was different in New Orleans. At the grand house that Isaac had purchased for her there, Bess and Moriah cared for her just like the Creole governess with whom her father had left her in Natchitoches before he returned to Paris after her mother died.

When Isaac had returned to her room later that morning, his indifference had been obvious, so unlike the night before. She felt the tenseness as he removed his shirt and boots and lay beside her. Even so, she turned to put her face on top of his chest and partially entwined her legs around his, but when she began to touch and kiss as she had done on so many mornings, he quickly got up. He was the only man she had known, and for three years she had been his mistress; she loved him more than she had understood love to be.

She sat in the east rose garden watching a delicate petal bend beneath the weight of a bumblebee, remembering her first meeting with Isaac and wishing reality allowed her to be more to him than what she was, that for which she had been reared. Her mother, first, then her governess had explained her place. It was obvious, that to Aunt Aggie and Uncle Sugart, Lona could never be a suitable mate for their master.

Suddenly the peacocks scattered, their eerie cries breaking her austere reverie, as Chance Hadley stepped from behind a tree and rested his heavy work boot on the gray-streaked marble bench beside her now-tense figure.

"What are you doing here?" she questioned, attempting to conceal her fright at seeing the hired hand, and repulsed by his suffocating odor.

"Followed you to maybe give you a little comfort." He spat tobacco juice into the rose bushes and moved his boot closer to the folds of her skirt, his ginger hair partially hiding his beady eyes.

"Mr. Hadley, I have made it clear, and I shall make it clear again; I want nothing to do with you!"

"You can cut out all them airs and that mister stuff, honey. Niggers don't take to you too much around here, do they? I know what goes on," he said, pushing back his straggled hair with his sweaty shirt sleeve.

Her mouth agape, she put her hand to her lips and gasped. "It is not your business what happens here or elsewhere."

"Maybe I'm making it my business. He don't appreciate a woman like you." When she stood to leave, he pressed both his hands on her shoulders.

"Take your hands off me!" she screamed.

He released her, then stood laughing, resentfully, after her. "You ain't never gonna be nothing to him but a whoring nigger—you hear that—just a nigger." He continued laughing and sneering. "You think a hired hand's not good enough for you? Just you wait!"

When Lona did not appear for the noonday meal, Isaac, supposing she had sensed his uneasiness, was not overly concerned by her absence. Aunt Aggie was delighted. She had prepared some of his favorite dishes, simple garden vegetables grown on his own land, sugar cured country ham and deep-dish apple pie, a meal he preferred to any city's finest cuisine.

As dinner ended, Isaac leaned back in the informal dining chair. He liked this small room off the kitchen where he usually took his first two meals of the day. "You've outdone yourself again, Aunt Aggie."

"Don't that Sugart cure the best ham in Sumner County?"

"In any county. Tennessee ham...nothing like it. Don't know why Virginians even bother. Won't be long before he'll have that sweet aroma coming from the smoke house again."

Isaac took a cigar from its silver case and struck a match against the sole of his boot. He toyed with it between his fingers, oblivious to Aunt Aggie's movements clearing the table, thinking of Lona and knowing what he must do.

As William and John had warned, Aunt Aggie and Uncle Sugart loathed her from the day she arrived. She had wished to see his Sumner County; he had wanted to share it with her, and took full blame for his poor judgment and the uncomfortable circumstances in which he had put Lona, as well as, the aggravation it caused Aunt Aggie and Uncle Sugart.

Lona had been the most beautiful and sought-after girl at the New Orleans' Quadroon Balls in the '35 season. He first saw her as she sat with three other young ladies of color on the opposite side of an elegant ballroom on Rue Orleans. She was holding a delicate silk fan below her dark, fascinating oval eyes. It was then he told his best friend, Crawford Benedict, that he would have her. Later, after watching her dance with, and be courted by some of New Orleans' most prominent and wealthy citizens, he introduced himself to her and her guardian and asked if he might call the following day. He was known for getting what he wanted, and with so many desirous of her hand, he knew the bargaining would be difficult.

Not only was she daunting in beauty and grace, Lona's education and training were obviously perfect for her destined role, a wealthy planter's mistress. Isaac had been faithful to her longer than he had any woman. She had fulfilled his needs and made him feel much younger than his forty-nine years.

"Mister Isaac, I keeps telling you, what you needs is a fine Christian wife and raise a fambly," Aunt Aggie said, setting a cup of strong boiled coffee in front of him. "Ain't none of us getting no younger, and it sure be a happy day to see little childrens running around this big ole house. I gets tickly just thinking about it. I does. Like that nice Miss Hayes, who visit with her brothers two days ago." She stopped by his chair, then reached for her pipe on the mantle. "Mister Isaac, you listening to me?"

"I always listen to you."

"I wish it was the truth...you hear, but you don't do."

"Thank you for a lovely dinner, Aunt Aggie, he said, pushing back his chair. He made a great gesture of bowing and walked out onto the verandah.

"You's impossible, Mr. Isaac, that's what you is!" Aunt Aggie struck a match across the fireplace brick and held it to her pipe bowl.

CHAPTER 5

Rokeby Plantation

IT WAS MID-OCTOBER, AND THE LEAVES HAD ALMOST COMPLETED their seasonal changes. Two months had passed since the White's ball without hearing a single word from Isaac, his promised invitation to visit New Orleans, or any sort of invitation. She was furious with herself and with the captivating Mr. Franklin; she had never been anxious over a beau before; it was *they* who had been anxious over *her*.

At most, his trip to New Orleans and back would have taken no longer than three weeks. And although he had not specified a time, he had indicated it would not be *that* long before calling on her. Why had he not returned and immediately done so, or sent an immediate invitation? A letter would have been in order. There was no reasonable explanation.

She and Camille had discussed the situation while cantoring through open pasture, while stopping in the middle of creek beds watering their horses, while pacing at a slow gait back to the stables, and found none of their explanations for his behavior plausible.

The Perkins' driver brought Adelicia home as the last rays of sun reflected on the window panes. She unhitched Mozzalpa from the back of the buggy and led him to the stables, allowing him to nuzzle her face as they walked. She was an accomplished rider before most girls were taking their first lesson, and the bond she felt with horses, beginning when Uncle Ben had held the reins and walked her in the ring, and later cantering through the fields with the wind in front of her, seemed to be understood only by herself, her father, and more importantly…the horse.

Still dressed in knee-high leather boots and her dusty brown riding habit that smelled of the marvelous blend of horse and trodden clover, she dashed into the dining room.

"Liza," she called, "What a marvelous aroma! Roast beef?" She lifted the top of a large china tureen. "I am famished! For whom is the extra place?"

"Now, how can a body answer so many questions with one breath?"

Adelicia heard voices in the next room, and upon turning around, found herself facing Isaac, who stood beside her father in front of the drawing room mantle.

"Come in, Adelicia. I was in the process of thanking Mr. Franklin for the hospitality he extended to my children at Fairvue." Her father's voice was too formal, not at all like his usual, easy manner.

"Hello, Miss Hayes. Your father tells me you're quite the equestrian."

"I enjoy riding," she answered, hoping her feigned humility would be convincing. "How nice to see you again."

"I was in New Orleans much longer than expected, but I'll be home for a while now. You must come to Fairvue and ride one of my thoroughbreds."

"A racehorse I have not ridden, but," she said flirting with her eyes, "I would love to, however, Mr. Franklin, I am not so sure I can depend on your invitations."

"Well," Oliver Hayes interrupted, clearing his throat, "I believe Liza is ready to serve supper."

Nine-year-old Laura, three-year-old Corrine and six-year-old Henry had eaten earlier, leaving Adelicia to dine with Joel, thirteen-year-old Oliver Bliss II, her father and Isaac. She rued the absence of Camille to divert Joel's attention, but was grateful that Richard was away at his law office, forty miles south in Columbia.

Had Adelicia known Isaac was coming, she would not have ridden with Camille all afternoon, but would have spent hours dressing. On the other hand, she was pleased for him to see her in her favorite attire, and assumed the smell of horse and trodden clover would prove pleasant enough if he were the horseman everyone said he was.

As the evening progressed, she felt more comfortable in his presence and delighted in their secret glances across the banquet-sized Duncan Phyfe table. Being in the company of all males was quite ordinary at Rokeby; in fact, she preferred it unless it were one of her best friends. She made certain her flirting was not too obvious to her father, and was thankful when her brothers excused themselves soon after dessert and were no longer there to observe her. However, this meant no invitation would be extended to Isaac for smoking and libation after supper...it also most probably meant that it released her father from the obligation.

During supper, while eating heartily, she had pretended to listen as the men discussed politics and the economy, but all the while was conjuring ways to be alone with Isaac; she decided on inviting him to the stables.

Liza was a marvelous cook and tonight was no exception, as she had served tender roast beef stuffed with garlic, oyster dressing and small new potatoes smothered in a delicious white wine sauce, sprinkled with fresh parsley. The culinary perfection was only excelled by her dessert specialty, chilled chocolate mousse made with fresh shaved chocolate and rich whipped cream.

Isaac complimented Liza and asked if she might share a recipe or two to take home to his Aunt Aggie. Everyone who dined at Rokeby bragged on Liza, who took great pride in her cooking, but like Aunt Aggie and all cooks of the wealthy classes, Liza's recipes remained confidential. She had great difficulty remembering 'xactly how much of this goes into 'xactly how much of that.'

As Liza was completing her removal of the dessert dishes, she asked if Oliver would like coffee served in the parlor. Adelicia quickly turned to her father and asked if before coffee she might invite Isaac to see the horses.

Oliver Hayes looked at his pocket watch and told Liza to serve the coffee at precisely nine o'clock. Adelicia did not like the look of disapproval in her father's eyes; nevertheless, she was excused to escort Isaac to the stables. And at least her papa had invited Isaac for coffee.

The Hayes' groom proudly showed the stabled horses, including two prize stallions, the saddlebreds and Adelicia's gelding, who whinnied when she handed him an apple from the barrel. He nuzzled against her as she ran her hand along his sleek muzzle. "You need to be sleeping, Mozzalpa...you have had a tiring day."

"How in the devil," Isaac asked, "can a five-foot-two woman, who could not possibly weigh more than ninety to ninety-five pounds control a fifteen-hundred pound horse?"

She looked at him cunningly, "I have never known an animal I could not control."

When they were near the last stall, she gave a slight shiver and Isaac asked if the night air were too chilling. Without waiting for an answer, he placed his brown merino coat around her shoulders. The warmth from his hands made her blush and she did not want him to take them away. It was eight-forty-five, Adelicia noted from the stable clock. "Goodnight, Mozzalpa."

She put her hand in Isaac's arm as they walked to the garden gazebo, then sat among late-blooming autumn flowers. Isaac looked thoughtfully at her for a moment, then teased, "I couldn't wait to meet the woman who could so shamelessly sign her name. Thus, I changed my plans for the evening, and hurried to the Whites."

"Is it necessary to remind me?" she asked, as if embarrassed.

"I liked it. I liked it very much, and it doesn't bother you at all. I'm curious to know, however, if you sign your name like that in the guest books of all unsuspecting bachelors?"

"You are not being fair," she flirted. "You said you liked it."

"I did say that, and I like you, too."

"Like?"

He laughed, "It is a good thing to like. Do you ever tire of being told you are beautiful? That eyes could be as tempting as yours?"

"It depends on who is telling me," she flirted.

"I shall never forget your captivating eyes peering across the room at me, neither brown, nor blue, nor green, perhaps changing colors in the glow of candlelight. I could not remove mine from yours, or my thoughts."

She melted into his words, but would not tell him that she had felt the same that evening at the Whites in Gallatin, that he had been paramount in her thoughts from the moment she had first glimpsed Fairvue. She wanted him to kiss her, a real kiss, a worldly kiss.

He looked at her pensively and took her hand in his. "I think we should return to your father. Let's not forget his twenty-one year old daughter is unescorted in the night with a man of questionable reputation, the latter of which I regret; he set a time limit and that I respect."

She could hear the rapid beating of her heart, affected by his words, her desire to be kissed, and of the question she was about to ask.

Adelicia put her hand gently on his arm, "Isaac?" she began, hoping the unconventional use of his first name would make him more responsive. "The day my brothers and I were at Fairvue, I glimpsed a beautifully dressed lady at the top of the stairs."

No sooner had the words slipped out than she wished they had not. He rose and stood with his back to her—his hands deep inside his breeches pockets.

"I'd prefer not to discuss it." Her directness had obviously taken him by surprise. And just as obvious, he was unaware that she had seen Lona.

"I am sorry," she said sincerely.

"It must wait for another time."

"I am sorry," she repeated, softly.

"It's all right," he said turning towards her and removing his hands from his pockets. "Will you come to supper next week at Fairvue?" When she did not answer, he asked again. "Will you come?"

"I can think of nowhere else I had rather be, or anything else I had rather do."

They returned to the house just as Liza was carrying the tray into the parlor where her father sat with his pipe. After a brief conversation, Adelicia excused herself, but not before it was arranged that on the following Friday evening, she and her father, along with her brothers and their ladies, would dine at Fairvue.

CHAPTER 6

Fairvue Plantation

"AUNT AGGIE, YOU'VE BEEN IN THIS KITCHEN FOR A WEEK NOW, fixing and messing and cooking," Isaac teased. "Della says you're running everyone ragged, not to mention Uncle Sugart."

"There ain't no messing to it. You done told me what a good cook their Liza is, and your Aunt Aggie not gonna be outdone by nobody in the cooking line."

"No one can hold a light to you," he insisted, putting his arm around her wide shoulders.

"I reckon with you on that, but we's having quality folk tonight, and I intends to show them we's quality folk. Now go shush it on up and get out of my kitchen," she said, shooing him away. "You gonna make my apple layer cake fall for sure."

Isaac had watched his old mammy and Uncle Sugart bustling about all week in preparation for his guests, knowing full well their intention. They had questioned him about Oliver Bliss Hayes, a prominent lawyer, staunch Presbyterian and member of one of Nashville's best families. They wanted Adelicia as mistress of Fairvue.

The imported English silver was polished and shining; the damask cloth and napkins, with their delicate cut-work were in place. For a center-piece, Aunt Aggie had meticulously arranged late blooming asters with deep green magnolia leaves in a silver epergne, and to either side, she had put her own hand-dipped, burnt orange candles into two six-pronged sterling candelabras, complementing the rust and golden tones in the asters.

Each place was set with heavy cut-glass goblets, monogrammed sterling flatware and bone white china bordered with wide platinum bands. Aunt Aggie stood with her large arms folded, making a final inspection of her elegant creation. Being fully satisfied, she said, "Yes sir, if this ain't doing it right, there ain't no doing it right."

Smiling, Isaac left Aunt Aggie's kitchen to make his usual afternoon rounds over the plantation, visiting the quarter and stopping occasionally to speak with the slaves. The children, wondering at the presence of the large man on the roan stallion, heralded his coming as he always managed to find a treat in his saddlebag to please them. He liked to know that all was well, and to see for himself the tranquility that he hoped existed on his land.

Streaks from the fading sunlight stretched over the Cumberland's cliffs as he galloped back through rich clean rows of corn. Suddenly, Imposter reared as Chance Hadley appeared out of the thick stalks.

"What the hell are you doing?"

"Sorry Capt'n. I..."

"Sorry, hell! You almost caused me to break my neck! What's wrong with you?"

Isaac saw Hadley sway as the corn stalks bent beneath his instability. "You've been warned about drinking on the place."

"Just had a couple," he said staggering and coming nearer Imposter. "Need to talk to you," he continued, pushing his thin ginger hair back from his eyes, attempting to focus.

"You can take it up with the foreman, or it'll have to wait till morning," Isaac answered. "I'll talk to you then when you're sober."

Hadley reeled unsteadily in front of him blocking the way. "I been thinking how I'd like to work on one of them Louisiana places, with winter coming and all. Maybe you'd send me down there to be overseer, and maybe I could get a little spot of my own like Strawn has here."

Just that morning, he had discussed Hadley with Jack Strawn, and had agreed that the recent unrest among the fieldhands was due to Hadley's influence. As soon as the harvest was over, he would be dismissed. Isaac took great pride in the contentment exhibited among his Negroes. Although slave unrest was not that uncommon on some plantations, it was a rarity at Fairvue.

"I said it would have to wait till morning. Now, get out of my way." He reined the roan to the right and pulled around Hadley.

"Heard about the uppity folks coming from the city," he called with a drunken snicker. "Got a good-looking white gal coming. Don't reckon you'll be needing that nigger whore no more so..."

Isaac suddenly wheeled Imposter around, swung to the ground and knocked Hadley into the dirt with so direct a blow that he appeared unconscious as he lay penned beneath Isaac's heavy boot.

"You get off my place before this sun gets through going down!" Isaac shouted. "I don't like to kill a man, but if I ever see you again, I'll kill you." He released his foothold, kicked Hadley over onto his side and mounted Imposter.

As Isaac dressed for dinner, he could not remove Chance Hadley from his mind. He wished he had dismissed him when Della reported a comment she had overheard when Lona first came to Fairvue. Again, he wondered if Hadley had ever spoken to Lona. She had not told him about seeing Adelicia. Perhaps she had encountered Hadley as well.

Aunt Aggie's call from downstairs interrupted his reverie. "Sugart says he hears wheels rumbling!"

Isaac smiled. Aunt Aggie and Uncle Sugart were more excited than he had seen them since they made the move into the big house that they had assumed was built with a mistress in mind. Six years had already passed.

Adelicia intrigued, fascinated him as no woman had, and the difference in their ages was of no concern to him. He was confident that his own vitality and strength were greater than that of men half his age. He expected to enjoy good health for decades to come, to see his children grow up, perhaps even his grandchildren. He was certain that he could satisfy her, and for the first time, he would ask someone to be his wife.

The sun had just dropped behind the cliffs of the Cumberland when the Hayes' carriages arrived, and the peacocks flaunting their long exotic plumes strutted over the lawn, cocking their heads as if listening in the twilight.

Adelicia was splendid as she stepped from the barouche onto the limestone carriage stand, lifting her skirt slightly above the tops of her small lavender satin shoes. Her fashionably cut emerald-green taffeta dress was trimmed in green velvet around the vee neckline and waist, and her matching green cape was lined with lavender satin. Isaac greeted her with a low sweeping bow and took her hand.

"Welcome back to Fairvue."

She answered with an exaggerated curtsy, adjusting her cape. "I am delighted to find its master at home." At the same moment, she caught Richard's eye just in time to see his look of disapproval as he and Lindy Robertson stepped from the second carriage with Camille and Joel.

Controlling an urge to make a retort to her brother, she instead strolled between Isaac and her father up the brick walk, her hands lightly touching each of their arms. She looked back over her shoulder at Richard and Lindy, satisfied that she was making an awesome show.

"The peacocks are beautiful, majestic," she said. "Especially the white one. It is even more magical. We have never had them at Rokeby. Essie says they are bad luck."

"Luck is something I've never believed in," he replied. "They are proud and stately beings, aren't they?" Isaac stood in the wide open doorway, greeting each of the men with a warm handshake and their ladies with a gentle bow. "Welcome to Fairvue," he said.

The dozen lit candles on the dining table made an inspiring spectacle of silver, cut glass and candlelight. Adelicia was seated on Isaac's right and her father on his left, with her brothers, Camille and Lindy making up the remainder of the table. She sat in fascination. The Venetian chandier, holding eleven lit candles, had been lowered and hung between the sterling candelabras, its prisms dancing in the glow. Wall sconces lent additional light that lit up the shadows around them, enhancing the rich wallpaper and furnishings. Suppers at Rokeby were never of this scale, she thought, never. Then she wondered if it were the usual at Fairvue. She supposed so.

The food was excellent, broiled leg of lamb, turtle soup, pompano that had been wrapped in brown paper and baked in hickory ashes, and roast duck with Creole herbs that Aunt Aggie had prepared from a recipe Isaac had brought from Boudro's Restaurant in New Orleans. When questions were asked about the unusual dishes, whose deliciousness and scents were intoxicating, Isaac had taken great care to make them feel comfortable and to answer each one carefully. Her father had remained in reserve, but conversation was light and easy, as everyone commented on the marvelously prepared dishes and the extraordinary Chateau Lafitte. Perhaps, she thought, Isaac had planned for conversation to center upon food and wine.

"Isaac, your wine is exquisite!" Oliver Hayes exclaimed.

"It's opened for very special guests, on very special occasions. 1820 vintage," he said, looking at her father and then at Adelicia. He held the crystal goblet in his hand, slowly rotating the red liquid as he spoke. "It has a taste, unique to itself. Serving good wine is a great pleasure."

"The wine is excellent, indeed, along with all else," her father reaffirmed. "You're a man of exceptional tastes."

"I wish to make a toast to the Hayes' family and their lovely guests, Miss Camille and Miss Lindy," Isaac gestured, standing.

"And I," her father said, after graciously accepting, "toast our host, Mr. Franklin, and the cook."

Adelicia took the compliment as a positive affirmation on the part of her father, who had had been reserved in discussing Isaac with her since his visit to Rokeby the previous week, and had been less than enthusiastic about bringing his family to dine in Isaac's home. However, the toast was far from his usual ones filled with great adoration.

She held the long stemmed wine glass in her fingertips and looked down the long table, imagining herself as mistress of Fairvue sitting at the opposite end, sharing the splendor with its master.

In the kitchen, Aunt Aggie beamed. "Lawsy me, Sugart, did you see the way she look at him, and did you see the way he look at her? I tells you, in our old age, we's gonna have childrens yet. And purty! Have you ever seen a young missus any purtier? This house gonna have little ones, Sugart. I's tickly all over, I is!"

"This house gonna have trouble. I sees the way she look at him too," piped Della.

Aunt Aggie gave her a quick look of disapproval, as Uncle Sugart said, "She's a looker all right, and them sure quality folk. But she a awful lot younger than Mr. Isaac."

"If that ain't the truth, nothing is," Della agreed.

"It's better that way," Aunt Aggie haughtily replied. "Miss Adelicia be so good for Mr. Isaac and he be so good for her. Women folk have ways of taking to mature gentlemens and the other way around."

Then slapping Uncle Sugart on the back, she proclaimed, "We's gonna have a weddin!"

"Iffen so, I sure hopes you don't work me to death like you did for this supper. I won't be able to stand much more."

She handed him a small silver pitcher. "Now you be careful when you pours this brandy over my apple cake. You member how we hearsed it?"

"I member, Aggie," he said, taking a deep breath.

When Uncle Sugart lit the brandy, the blue flames spilled perfectly over the lush cake, enhancing its flavor, and after the scrumptious dessert had been devoured, Isaac directed his guests into the parlor, where a light liqueur was served to the gentlemen and milk punch to the ladies.

After the initial theatrics, it was obvious that Richard and Joel were so charmed by their own ladies and by the captivating evening that they had given little thought to Adelicia and her flirtations.

She loved sitting in the parlor, from where she could glimpse the grand piano over which she had silently run her fingers upon her first visit to Fairvue, sipping warm punch that had a generous touch of nutmeg, but also, a smooth, soothing taste unfamiliar to her. After having had a second cup, she returned the sterling mug to a nearby tray, and seeing Camille and Lindy absorbed into their beaux, thought it the ideal moment to make her request.

"Papa, if you will excuse us, Mr. Franklin promised to show me his thoroughbreds."

"Mr. Hayes, on my visit to Rokeby last week, I promised Miss Adelicia to show her my stables. I hope you and your family will join us."

When her father said he thought the suggestion an excellent one, she instantly decided that she would pretend to be alone with Isaac. She walked close beside him, ignoring everyone else, even Camille. At the moment, she did not care if she ever saw another horse, and she was infuriated that her scheme to be alone with Isaac had failed.

She wished Camille would lead them all away…to where she had no idea…nor did she care.

In the darkness, she felt Isaac's fingers brush across the small of her back, a sudden, tantalizing reminder of being in his arms while dancing, and of the evening at Rokeby when he had put his coat around her shoulders, and she had not wanted him to take his hands away. Then she breathlessly imagined how it would feel to have them encircle her waist.

As they strolled across the spacious lawn, she was suddenly startled by a shrill cry.

"What is it?"

"The peacocks, it's their mating call."

"Where are they?" she asked, lingering on his words

He tilted her chin with his right hand and raised the lantern with the other. "See," he said, holding the light higher. "They roost in the trees." Another moment that she wanted to embrace, this time, his touch against her face. He reached down and picked up a turquoise feather that had fallen from one of the plumed tails and handed it to her.

"How extraordinary," she said, running the plumage through her fingers. "The white one is ethereal. Is it rare?"

"It is a pleasure in itself to be in the company of one who is delighted by so many things."

She looked up at him in the soft lantern's glow, wishing her father held the lantern instead of Isaac. Not only would it cause the light to be farther away, it would free Isaac's other hand, that she wanted to be touching her. She was certain that Richard and Joel were taking advantage of the darkness, although Joel did have a lantern. She never understood why it was acceptable to have a man's arms around you while dancing, but an abominable sin at any other time.

They had reached the stables by the time she could concentrate on the surroundings, with which she was more than a little impressed. Both the physical quality of the animals and the magnificence of the brick stables and stone barns were unparalleled. Two stables each housed twelve prize stallions, and another two, the mares and their foals. Outdoor lanterns attached to the barns were lit, now leading their way to a world of horses she had not known.

The oversized stalls were also far from ordinary, with each having its own sleeping quarters in an overhead loft for the groom, an unprecedented luxury in Tennessee, perhaps anywhere. His horses were better cared for than most humans, she thought. No wonder her cousin Emma had said that Isaac had the finest brood mares in the south, and just as she had whispered to Camille that August afternoon, she had had no doubt that everything Isaac Franklin had would be the finest.

When they returned to the house, the ladies were served rich hot chocolate before the fire in the music room, and the men, aged brandy as the remainder of the evening began with Adelicia, Camille and Lindy taking turns on the piano and singing popular songs of the '20s and '30s.

Just before the evening was ending, Isaac removed a worn and faded paper from a chest drawer and put it on the music stand, then asked that Camille do the honors. As she began playing the beautiful French melody, he explained in a soft whisper, that the music had belonged to his grandmother, a Huguenot who had fled France with her children during the 1730's. It had been sung at his grandparent's wedding years before in a small village outside Paris. Isaac's mother, Mary Lauderdale, had cherished the music and had it played at her own wedding to Isaac's father, James. "Plaisir d'amour."

As Camille's fingers graced the ivory keys, Adelicia beamed. He was in love with her! This was his way of telling her family! There was no doubt! How subtle. It did not seem that even her father took notice.

As the evening closed and farewells were made, Isaac reminded his guests of the favors beside their place cards: small straw West Indies cornucopias filled with miniature chocolates in vegetable designs. "Miss Hayes," he said, walking out to the carriages, "I hope I may call on you when I return from the City of New Orleans."

If Isaac's quest had been to impress Adelicia, he had definitely succeeded. She and her father said little on the ride home as she reflected over the evening, nibbling on the petite candies. She was also thinking what fun it would be when they got to Rokeby to discuss every detail with Camille.

In the dark of the carriage, her fingers touched what seemed to be a piece of paper folded near the tip of the horn. Thinking it to be filler, she forgot about it until later, just after she and Camille had finished recreating the evening and were climbing into bed. She picked up the cornucopia and saw a bit of gold foil protruding out. Curiously tugging at it, she read in the candle's light.

"I have set my mind for a girl like you, who knows what she wants. Will you do me the honor of becoming my wife?"

Isaac awakened in the middle of the night to the cry of frightened peacocks. Uncle Sugart was already on the lawn when he arrived at the rear door. Isaac watched as the old man bent over the white peacock and held its broken neck in his hand. He remembered what Adelicia had said about the white one, and understood that Chance Hadley must have been watching and listening in the darkness as they walked to the stables.

CHAPTER 7

IT WAS THE FIRST OF DECEMBER WHEN ISAAC SAILED THE *TRIBUNE* into New Orleans' busy harbor. Over three months had passed since he had left Lona at the house on Esplanade, and he missed her much more than he had foreseen. Afterwards, he had immediately returned to the West Feliciana plantations to attend to business, as well as in Mississippi and Texas, before returning home to Gallatin. There, he had seen to both business and pleasure in October—when his life changed forever.

It had been necessary to make a brief, December trip back to New Orleans and the plantations; he also wanted to see Lona one last time before traveling up the Mississippi to Loch Lomond, where Fanny and Brutus were expecting him before Christmas. Jim Clack, overseer of all his West Feliciana plantations, Brutus and Fanny, at Loch Lomond and Alfred, Rufus and Lucy at Bellevue were among the people he trusted most on earth.

Lona had preferred Loch Lomond to his other five plantations in the Parish. The Lake of the Cross was at its center, a site with which she had fallen in love at first glimpse, and had asked if they might make the small dwelling near its crystal waters their country residence. He had granted her request.

They had spent two days at Loch Lomond upon their arrival from Gallatin the first of September, and it was there he had told Lona of his intended marriage. He had revealed no details; he had spoken of Lona's welfare only, that she would be well provided for, that a trust was set up for her, that she would be contacted by his banker. Afterward, they had taken a packet from Bayou Sara to New Orleans.

The light was fading when the driver turned onto Esplanade with its elegant townhouses competing in grandeur with one another.

"What number was that again?" asked the driver.

"Sixteen," he called out.

With some hesitation, Isaac climbed the graciously curved stairs and put the key in the brass lock of the heavy wrought-iron door. As he stood in the darkened hallway, a chill ran through him, affecting all of his senses, the quiet and cold diffused and eerie.

Bess interrupted the silence when she called from upstairs, "Who's there?" She peeked around the enclosed banister holding a lamp in one hand, "Oh, Mr. Franklin! I's so glad to see you." Bess, as broad as she was high, walked with a pronounced waddle. "I gots the miseries in my back and the miseries in my head. I gots the..."

"Hold on, Bess," he interrupted. "Where's Lona?"

"That's why I got the miseries. She in my keep and all. Well sir, she just up and left day fore yestiddy with lots her stuff. I ask her where she going and she say she don't know. I tells her I's watching out for her, she my sponsibility, and you won't like it none, and she say she don't care what you don't like cause nothing don't matter no more."

"Damn! How did she go?"

"In the carriage you buy for her."

"Where did Moriah take her?"

"My Moriah don't take her nowhere. That red-faced swamp rat, who been hanging round here all last week, hitch up the horses, load her, baggage and all. Off they went, me begging her not to the whole time."

"Do you know his name?"

"Moriah run him off, but he come back, called him Hadley."

"Hadley! The son of a bitch! I'll kill him." The blood rushed to Isaac's face as he slammed his fist against the door facing.

"I hear him say he going to faraway places of the world on your filthy money. He talking real loud."

"What money? It's in a trust for Lona along with the house and... Oh, my god," he said, as if to himself. "Sinclair wouldn't advance her money on the trust!"

"That's all I knows, Mr. Franklin. Day fore yestiddy, and I ain't seen or heard from her since."

Isaac looked at his watch, hurried down the steps and ran up Rue Chartres to where it intersects Toulouse, and hailed a cab to drive him to his banker's house two miles outside the city on Canal Street.

Andrew Sinclair was enjoying his second glass of bourbon when Isaac pushed past the butler into the library. The banker extended his hand, "I was hoping you'd get down soon. Coincidentally, I mailed you a letter yesterday."

"Has Lona been to see you?"

"That's why I mailed the letter," Sinclair drawled. "Lona wanted to know about getting an advance or selling some other properties, and when I explained it was in a trust, she became upset, and began taking off her jewelry. 'What about this and this and this?' she asked. 'He doesn't own these?' She emptied a small bag of some really nice pieces and asked if I were going to give her the money or not. So, I let her draw ten thousand on the estate. I certainly would not take her jewelry."

"Damn it to hell! Ten thousand!"

"I asked where you were; she only shook her head."

There was something about Andrew Sinclair that Isaac despised at that moment. He reached for Sinclair's collar, then dropped his hands to his side. "I can't believe a man can be so damned stupid. Don't you know if something weren't wrong, she wouldn't have been asking you for money? I don't suppose you thought to ask why she wanted it or what she was going to do with it?"

"Look, Isaac, I'm sorry. After she left..."

"I don't give a damn what you did after she left," he interrupted. "I don't know how you've managed to be my banker for twelve years, but you can be sure as hell this is your last day."

"Now, Isaac, we go back a long way."

"Go to hell, Andrew."

The cab driver was humming a plaintive tune, unique to New Orleans, as he waited beside his patient horse. At any other time, the hauntingly soothing sounds of French Haitian would have pleased Isaac, but tonight it only magnified the mounting apprehension he felt. "Take me to the St. Louis, and stop the damn humming."

The evening had been a nightmare, and he knew little more now than he had three hours earlier. Surely, Lona was not with Chance Hadley, he reasoned. It made no sense to him why she could not have stayed in New Orleans with her house, money and servants. While at Loch Lomond, when he had told her of his impending marriage, she had behaved as if it were no surprise, that she understood. It was when he was saying good-bye at the town house, that she had said, "...but I always hoped."

A fifth of whiskey was not enough to relax him, nor dull his senses. He tossed and turned all night in his bed at the St. Louis Hotel and rose at daybreak while the street cleaners were still making their early morning rounds. With such a large sum of money, he thought Lona must be leaving the country, as Bess had suggested. She had often spoken of going to Paris and he had considered taking her there; he would begin his search with the passenger lists on ships bound for Europe.

He walked past the French Market, its fruits and vegetables still covered from the night before, on his way down to the wharf crowded with its mixture of steamboats, barges, flatboats and freighters. It was an early morning scene that any other time would have given him a great sense of pleasure, the grand vessels resting before the busy docks were overrun with workers loading and unloading their cargo, and before the vendors began their familiar chants. He was standing on the levee, staring into the muddy Mississippi, when Crawford Benedict came up behind him.

"Isaac! When did you get into town? And what the hell are you doing out so early?"

"I was hoping you would be here," he said, shaking his hand. "I need to check passenger lists for the past couple of days. Lona's left the city."

"You must have told her about the filly in Nashville. Lona is different from..."

"Just show me the lists, please. She may not be traveling alone, that's the issue."

As they walked up the stairs to Crawford's office, Isaac felt more at ease, more confident in the presence of his best friend. They looked over the long list of passengers on departing ships for the previous week and for two weeks forward, but none of the names were even vaguely familiar.

"Why don't you go back and get some sleep? You look terrible, my friend. I'll ask around, then come by and get you for dinner, say around one o'clock, tell you what I find out."

The idea appealed to Isaac, as the whiskey and lack of sleep had dulled his senses. He walked back to the St. Louis and asked to be awakened at noon, and this time he rested comfortably until the butler woke him to say it was twelve-thirty. He dressed hurriedly and walked over to Boudros's where Crawford was waiting, and had already ordered both food and drink.

"I must say you're looking better, though you can still stand improvement."

"What did you find?"

"Thank you," he said to the waiter. "I ordered you a double."

"Tell me what you found out."

"I asked around and one of my employees who takes reservations remembered a foul-looking fellow who gave the name of Finley and wanted passage for himself and his lady aboard a freighter bound for Denmark. But when he asked for identification papers, the man made some excuse and said he'd be back. Well, he didn't return until yesterday afternoon right after the freighter had gone, so he asked what other ships were leaving for, "across the waters." This time, he brought papers for himself, as well as for a free person of color, and paid in large bills. I had an employee check out the address just a while ago. He went up to the door with the pretense of asking directions, and as far as I can tell from the description, the woman he glimpsed was Lona."

"Let's go."

"Finish your dinner first. The ship doesn't leave until in the morning at six."

Isaac drank much more than he ate. They took a cab to Poydras Street, and Crawford rang the bell while Isaac stood to the side with his hands in his pockets. After some time, a large woman with spectacles opened the door. "Yeah," she answered. "A woman something like that was here for a few days, but she was leaving on a boat for somewheres, and I ain't got no idee where."

Isaac heard the reality of what he had not wanted to hear; Lona was leaving the City of New Orleans, perhaps with Hadley. He had spared no expense in providing for her welfare. She had often told him he did not understand women; for certain, he did not understand her now.

A door closed somewhere in the rear of the house and Isaac, uninvited, stepped inside. He heard footsteps ascending the back stairs, and quickly started up those in the front. "Now just a minute," said the matron, "You can't do that."

Crawford pushed past her and took a position behind Isaac. "Wait down here," Isaac told him.

He reached the top of the hallway in time to see a bedroom door close. Without knocking, he quietly opened it and found Lona standing with her back to the fire, looking tired and worn.

"What are you doing here?" she asked, startled.

"Where's Hadley?"

"Leave me alone. Please. I do not wish to see you."

"Where's Hadley?"

"How did you find me?" Although she was angry, she had the same, unmistakable look in her eyes—love without condition.

"Why did you do this, Lona? Why with a man like Hadley?"

"I don't suppose it would matter if it were a man of stature and position, like you?"

"Damn, Lona, Chance Hadley is filth, scum! I set up a trust; you can live as well as anyone in the city, better. Why would you do something like this?"

"Yes, Cherie, you set up everything for me—except yourself."

The anger in her voice subsided, and she spoke softly. "And that is all I ever wanted. I never cared about the house, the jewelry, the clothing. They never mattered. I cared only about you."

"But you knew...we always knew," he said firmly.

"You are right. We always knew. But there is a time when a woman tells herself one thing on the outside and convinces her heart of something different on the inside, and when she loves like I loved, the hoping...the wishing...the believing, never goes away." The words came slowly, her thoughts seeming to linger on each one. "I understand now, it is over." She stood trembling, with tears streaming down her cheeks, her hands clasped beneath her chin. Isaac walked over beside the waning fire and embraced her gently.

"Lona, please stay here. You'll never want for anything. You can marry, have a family."

She lifted her head from his shoulder. "You do not understand, Cherie. It can never be the same with anyone else. I cannot stay in New Orleans. There are too many memories. I'll repay the money..."

"Hell, I don't want the money. I want you to stay. Please don't leave with him. He's not fit to be in the same room with you."

"Chance Hadley came to Esplanade; Moriah led him to the carriage house as he said he had news for me concerning you," she said dabbing her tears. "I allowed him to come inside, into the kitchen, then he told me of the lady whom you are to marry. It became real to me as he described her and her family. I was angry at you, at my situation, my *place*. I hope you understand...I gave him money to leave the country."

Isaac nodded, as Lona wiped the last of the tears from her face and eyes.

"Cherie, I cannot imagine a time that I shall not love you," she said, "But from this day, I shall make it on my own, without you or anyone else."

The determination in her voice echoed in his ears, as he released her waist, stood back and looked at her in the diminishing glow of the fire. "If you ever need anything, will you ask?"

"What I will need, you cannot give me...Adieu, Cherie," she said, lifting his hand to her lips. "Do you really believe I would be with him? You do not know me very well."

He lingered in the doorway for a moment, then turned and hurried down the steps. Crawford had charmed the housekeeper and was having a second sobering cup of chicory.

"Let's get out of here."

They wandered silently in the Vieux Carre, stopping here and there for a drink. The inevitability of endings, he thought. How does a man tell a woman he no longer feels the same about her? It never seemed right, he thought, one person continuing to love, the other knowing it is over.

It was late when they settled into the Old Absinthe Bar on the corner of Bienville and Bourbon. And, again, Isaac could not find the escape that comes with strong whiskey.

In the early morning hours, Crawford walked back to the St. Louis with him. "I had to know that she was all right, you know." He shook Crawford's hand, "Thanks, my friend."

CHAPTER 8

Nashville

OLIVER HAYES HAD NOT FELT AT EASE SINCE THE EVENING AT Fairvue. He knew Adelicia all too well, and her behavior was causing him grave concern. She spoke of Isaac in every conversation, whether to probe into his past or to fill everyone in on his present status and wealth. The servants at Rokeby were disturbed that their master would permit his daughter to be called on by such a man and mumbled among themselves as to the "goings-on." Essie was distraught.

In the late evening, Oliver sat in his large morocco hide wing chair in front of the brightly lit fire thinking about his eldest daughter. Toying with a small brass Christmas bell that Adelicia had left lying on his desk, he wished what he hoped was an infatuation would pass before all Nashville found out about it. If indeed, he thought, the news had not already passed among the servants. Adelicia flirted with everyone, it was her nature. But with Isaac, whom she had seen on only three occasions, it was different. He was not pleased with the attention that Isaac, who was only a few years younger than himself, had given Adelicia; this older man of the world was not a candidate to be a part of his family. And Oliver especially abhorred the tasteless note stuffed inside the straw cornucopia that Essie had shown him.

Adelicia was expected to marry within her class. Alonso Gibbs had been an excellent match, but sadly, had been taken by the fever at age twenty-six, when she was only seventeen. She had no intention of marrying Grainger Caldwell, another young lawyer, another excellent match, according to her father.

Isaac was a business associate, recognized in Nashville as a man with an extraordinary talent for making the right investments at the right time and always ending up with considerable profits. However, a business friend was one thing; a suitor for his daughter's hand was another. And although Isaac was now a prosperous planter and his Alexandria slave trading establishment of Franklin and Armfield had long since dissolved, it was still rumored that he had *indirect* interest in the scandalous business in Natchez. Slave traders were a common breed, no matter how respectable they became, and there was no way Oliver Hayes would permit his daughter to marry into such a class, if indeed she were seriously considering the idea. He knew she was intrigued by Isaac's wealth; he also realized how advantageous the marriage would be for Isaac in providing the social status he had never attained in Middle Tennessee.

Oliver had just dozed off with his thoughts, his head resting against a wing of the leather chair, when Adelicia tiptoed into the room and placed an afghan over his lap.

"Papa, Papa," she called softly, stooping down and kissing him gently on the cheek. "You'll catch your death of cold. Remember Dr. Freeman's warning about getting chilled."

"Why aren't you sleeping?" he asked, as the clock on the mantle rang its chime for half past eleven.

"I was finishing ornaments for the tree and wanted to kiss my papa good night before going to bed."

He took her hand and looked up into the precocious face that reminded him so much of her mother's. "What is it you want at this late hour? The three dresses I ordered from New York are in. Uncle Will's picking them up in town tomorrow."

"Oh, Papa," she said, hugging his neck, "You do spoil us so. There will never be anyone ever like you."

She sat at his feet, her legs folded beneath her on the floor, her robe pulled tight, as they silently watched the flickering soft flames together. He smiled down at her, knowing this was her favorite time of year, and that she too was missing her mother.

The house smelled of rich spices and fresh cut evergreen. On every table, on every flat surface, in every corner, there was a reminder of the festive holidays: out-of-season fresh fruits, nuts of every kind; pine, cedar, and magnolia leaves covering the mantles and stair rails with strands of dried cranberries and popcorn draped beneath; apples stuffed with cloves and petite bags containing freshly grated nutmeg hung from the chandeliers, filling the large rooms with irresistible holiday aromas. It was that time of year when guests dropped by unexpectedly to leave small remembrances. When good food, parties and dancing prevailed, all encompassed with a spirit of peace and good will.

"Well, Adie," he said, just before the mantle clock struck, "I believe we had better turn in for the night."

"Papa?" she asked sweetly. "Why does Mr. Franklin stay away so long? I had invited him for the season's opening ball, and he said this trip to New Orleans would be brief. Tomorrow is December second. Do you suppose he has returned to Gallatin and not called on us?"

"Adelicia," a name her father seldom used unless he were perturbed or very serious, "First, I do not understand the attraction you feel for this man old enough to be your father. Secondly, he has shown the poorest taste in his conduct toward you."

She wondered to high heaven why he had begun this tirade so late in the evening.

"The wealth you find so fascinating was accumulated in a manner, in an occupation, in which decent people do not engage. He's widely traveled and sees many women who are not the sort in our circles. He is a different class than we are…a separate class."

"You have taught us to treat and respect everyone the same. Have you changed your beliefs on that?" she asked quickly.

"Treating everyone with respect and knowing where you belong and from whence you come does not have the same interpretation. One does not breed a thoroughbred with a cart horse."

"People are not horses, and I do not care how he made his money," she said beaming. "The point is, he has so much of it. He is no longer a slave trader, and he is extremely handsome and charming."

"Adelicia, you are making no attempt to understand. A man, a respectable man, does not give a young lady a note, no matter how unique you think it to be, asking her to marry him and obviously avoiding speaking to her father of his intentions."

"Mr. Franklin does things differently than the *boys* we know," she said.

"You have not heard from him. It has been more than five weeks since the night we were at Fairvue. Is that the way a man behaves when his intentions are honorable? Mr. Franklin has not formerly asked for your hand, nor does he probably intend to do so...Your mother could say these things so much better than I...He is a bachelor; there are rumors concerning the women he sees."

Her thoughts momentarily raced to the beautiful woman on the stairs, and she felt "the truth hurts," apparent on her face; her father spoke more firmly.

"I find it difficult to believe you could possibly have more than a school girl's infatuation for him. It is high time it should pass...you are no longer a school girl."

"It is much more than that, Papa." Adelicia stood facing her father in front of the mantle looking defiant. "I intend to marry him!"

"Adelicia, I shall not have you speaking in this manner. No daughter of mine will marry a man with a past like his! Perhaps the present! We shall discuss it no further!"

He stood with one hand on the carved walnut mantle and watched Adelicia charge angrily out of the room and up the stairs. The manner in which he had handled the situation was obviously the worst he could have projected. When, he reasoned, had this eldest daughter been told "no" that she had not found a way to make it "yes?" In truth, saying "no" ignited an ember into a full flame.

He sat back down, feeling like a defeated man. How he missed her mother, the love of his life, an endearing relationship he had wished for each of his children. And tonight, he longed to share another Christmas season with her.

Uncle Bob was making his nightly rounds through the house, humming "Silent Night" as only he could do, with a word slipped into the melody here and there. "Mr. Oliver, you asleep?"

"No, no, just thinking." He was tired and felt old. He got up, scattered the embers across the grate and slowly went up the stairs to bed.

Adelicia, alone in her room, vowed to attend the December ball with Isaac and not Grainger Caldwell, with whom she had attended all the autumn parties, beginning with the Harvest Ball in September.

She imagined making her entrance on the arm of her handsome older suitor, causing all the ladies to be envious and wishing they were in her place, whether they would admit it or not. Most women, she told herself, did not have the gumption to admit what they really wanted, and she could not care less what they said or thought. However, disappointing her father did bother her, but in time, he, too, would see things her way.

With only a few days remaining, she knew that she must find Isaac and have him back in Nashville in time for the ball. He had to have returned from New Orleans by now! No man had ever ignored her, and Isaac was not going to be the first. As she unfastened the bodice of her chemise, a smile of assurance came across her face. This was a game all new to her, one that she would play and—win.

Adelicia was the first to the breakfast table, and in the best of moods. She kissed her father, gave him an affectionate hug, apologized for having been disrespectful the night before, and chatted incessantly in her usual manner. Joel and Richard were discussing the upcoming ball along with politics, and Bliss was teasing Laura. She reveled in the camouflage of morning. Adelicia knew her father was enjoying the gay, family conversation and extremely pleased with everyone's attitude, especially her own.

"You will always be the dearest, most special man in my life," Adelicia said, reaching over for his hand.

"Laura, if you and Corrine grow up to be like your older sister, I haven't a chance," he laughed.

Adelicia excused herself when Richard came in telling her father that Uncle Will was waiting with the horses, and left to find Essie.

"You promised to go with me to Judge White's this morning," Adelicia said, walking into Essie's room. "If you do not, I shall be forced to go by myself," she declared. Her mammy, sitting beside her sewing box, was taking tucks in Corrine's organdy pantalets.

"Child, I knows I said I would, but I wish I'd said I wouldn't, cause I knows it's got something to do with what I don't want nothing to do with."

"We have an open invitation with Judge White to drop by anytime, especially if we might need something, and it so happens, I need something—and it *is* the Christmas season."

"I don't know what it can be, but I gots my imagines. I been knowing you too long to not know when you up to no good." Essie laid her handwork aside and reached above the armoire for her broad brimmed felt hat and scarf, then peeked into the mirror to smooth her hair beneath it, before putting on her coat. "One of these days you gonna be the ruin of me," she said.

Uncle Will had the carriage waiting according to her instructions, and Adelicia stepped in followed by her mammy. Essie was tall and slender with straight black hair that she wore pulled up into a small knot on top of her head. She was proud her father had been a member of the Cherokee Tribe in East Tennessee. Orphaned when both parents died in the fever epidemic, she had grown up on Mrs. Hayes' childhood plantation near Franklin, where Adelicia's mother, Sarah Hightower, was born. When Sarah had come to Rokeby as Oliver's bride more than twenty-five years before, Essie had come with her, and when her beloved Miss Sarah passed, she had been entrusted with full care of the seven children...Oliver Hayes never courted for another bride.

Thirty minutes later, the carriage pulled up to the two-story brick office on Church Street. "Wait here for me, Essie. I shant be long." Adelicia hurried out of the carriage, gathering her skirt in her hands in order to hasten her steps, and carrying a Christmas basket filled with seasonal baked goods.

Judge White was seated behind his large cherry desk, pipe in hand, when Adelicia came bursting through the door.

"Why, Adelicia, what a pleasant surprise! What brings you to town?" He took both her hands and gently kissed her forehead. "You get prettier every time I see you. Your cousin Emma was asking about you just last evening. We haven't seen you since the ball in August, which is much too long."

"It is always good to see one of my favorite relatives." She handed him the miniature Christmas cakes Liza had made, and took the chair he had pulled out for her beside the fire.

"Judge, I had no idea that I was missed," she said beaming, "Everyone knows that you and Cousin Emma give the best parties in Middle Tennessee. I am anxiously anticipating the next one."

"Thank you, dear. My wife loves a good party, I must say. We look forward to Liza's cakes," he said, still holding them in his hand and taking the chair opposite hers.

"Judge White," she asked, "I know Mr. Franklin is your neighbor, and oddly enough, we've not heard from him since we dined at Fairvue in late October. Do you suppose he is still in New Orleans?" Already knowing she had failed in her effort at subtlety.

"Adie, dear. Why this interest in Mr. Franklin's whereabouts?"

"Papa and I were discussing Mr. Franklin last night, and I had thought of inviting him to the December ball." Judge White looked astonished. Perhaps he had considered her having danced with Isaac nothing more than being polite, she thought. Or most probably, the Judge had more important things on his mind than her dancing, after all he was married to her cousin.

"Adie," he said hesitating, "Mr. Franklin most often spends September through April in West Feliciana Parish. I was aware he had returned briefly in October, but I believe he left shortly after for Louisiana. I am curious as to your interest in this older gentleman."

"Judge," she said, cunningly, "I do not want to out stay my welcome. I know you are a busy man—and an important one. Please give my love to my cousin Emma," she said, rushing to the door.

Judge White took her hand, "And please give my very best to your family."

Essie was all too familiar with Adelicia's 'minutes.' According to the carriage clock, she had been sitting in the buggy for more than a quarter of an hour. And although it was an unseasonably warm December, she had begun to feel chilled.

Just as she was preparing to go inside to replace the embers in the brass foot warmer, she saw three men approaching on horseback: Sam Perkins, Richard and Oliver Hayes. "I's like a rat trapped in a water hole," she mumbled. "When you been seen, you been seen, and there ain't nothing I can do about it. I knew that child would be the ruin of me." She watched the men hitch their horses, and saw a look she did not know how to interpret on Oliver's face.

"No one said anything about coming into town today when I left this morning. Are some of the children with you?" His tone was friendly, although there was edginess in it.

"Yes sir. Miss Adie, she have some errands she need to run with the season and all. We stop in here to give Judge White his Christmas cakes."

"Why, you're trembling, Essie. Adie's not being very thoughtful to leave you and Uncle Will out here in the cold. I'll go rush her up."

"Yes sir, I was just fixing to go in and get some new embers for the foot warmer, cause it is a mite cold."

"Let me have it. I'll have the Judge's boy to do it for you."

"Thank you, sir."

When, the men went inside, Essie was more frightened than ever. "Forgive me Lord, for having to use the birth time of your dear Son as a excuse for my reasons. And now Lord help that child to get herself on out here without gettin us both in any more trouble. Amen."

Seeing her father had taken Adelicia by surprise, but she felt confident in having, perhaps, charmed her way out of the Judge's office. She had intended to be more cautious in questioning the Judge, but had happily gotten some of the information she wanted. He had told her it was not unusual for Isaac to spend long periods in New Orleans, that he often spent the winters there. He also informed her that when Isaac was not on the plantations, he either stayed at his townhouse on Esplanade or at the St. Louis Hotel, where he had an office. Most probably, he had not returned to Gallatin.

Isaac was becoming as mysterious to her as the sound of his name had once been. And although she found his patterns of unpredictability perplexing, perhaps that was also a part of the intrigue he held for her. He was smooth, knowing all the right things to say to a woman, and was a man of experience with a questionable reputation both of which she found almost as fascinating as his money. Her strict Presbyterian upbringing had sheltered her from knowing the things of 'the world' as Essie and the minister called it, and she was certain Isaac knew everything there was to know. She would continue her quest to find him.

"Lordy, child, what did your papa say? I done froze to death from the cold and shook to death from the frights. Will, you head this buggy home!"

Adelicia teased her mammy. "You have passed on twice in the last half hour, and you are still as sassy as ever. Papa was pleased I had been thoughtful enough to bring Christmas cakes for the Whites, although earlier than usual. Uncle Will, head the carriage for Union Street. I have one more errand." Will obligingly turn the horses west.

The town was festive for the Yuletide, with all the shops and stores displaying their finest. Rubens Toy Store' windows appeared to bulge with every imaginable play-thing: large and small drums, clowns with china heads, dolls with painted faces dressed in velvet, ice skates, sleds with shiny runners, everything to tempt the wonder of a child. The German meat market advertised in large letters that they had the choicest of geese, duck and venison that one need not go elsewhere. The clothing stores displayed their latest fashions, as well as fabrics, for all passers-by to admire. Colliers even had two gowns from Paris in their large rectangular window. The town was filled with gay shoppers and businessmen alike crowding onto plank sidewalks to avoid the potholes caused by the previous night's downpour, and carolers stood singing at the corner of Summer Street and Spring.

The joy of the Christmas season was difficult to ignore, and Adelicia was delighted to see Essie forgetting her recent experience and becoming caught up in the holiday spirit as the horses trotted up High Street. At Adelicia's request, Will turned the corner onto Union and stopped in front of a building where a sign in large print was tacked over the door.

"No sir, no sir, I'm not being no party to no telegrams," Essie objected. "You keep this buggy moving, Will," she said, sticking her head out the window and making a clucking sound to the horse.

Adelicia was already on the sidewalk. "You are not being a party to anything. I shall not be long." She spoke more softly, "Please Essie, I am doing what I must. Papa will not blame you. Besides, he will never know." She quickly went inside, and this time was out just as quickly. "Now, Uncle Will, you may head for home."

They rode back in silence, Adelicia deep in thought, until on the outskirts of town, just before they were ready to turn off Broad Street onto the Hillsboro Pike, when Adelicia asked Uncle Will to, again, stop the buggy. She stepped down, taking her carriage blanket and putting it around two children huddled close to their mother. The woman, thin and gaunt, appeared to have nothing but a small, faded shawl for warmth. Giving her a five-dollar gold-piece, Adelicia asked her name and where she lived. The woman's troubled eyes saddened her; the poor, saddened her. Was this mother a widow, was her husband ill, unable to find work, was there a husband? She spoke only of more children as she stared at the gold piece in the rough palm of her hand. The address she gave was in an area called "Trash town" by some, "Poor town" by others, a site Adelicia had visited only once with her mother, but she had never forgotten the picture of poverty. She could at least provide temporary food and comfort, she thought, if nothing more.

The legacy her mother had left her of kindness for the less fortunate was a sincere, tender aspect of Adelicia that few people ever knew, nor had she allowed them to know. Human suffering troubled her greatly, but she had no answers, no remedies, for the inequities.

As Essie watched and noted the tenderness with which Adelicia spoke, she wondered, as she had for so many years, how Adelicia could be so definite a blend of both demon and angel.

"Miss Adie," she said as they turned into Rokeby's drive, "Promise me you won't have nothing more to do with that Franklin fellow. That man not good for you or no other respectable lady. He not like your papa or the gentlemen you been brought up around."

"How well I know that, Essie! I like Mr. Franklin. I like him a lot. And I am going to...never mind now. Have Liza put some things together for a family of six, and Uncle Will is to deliver them to this address," she said handing Essie a piece of paper. "Be sure to put in a ham, two hams…and some blankets," she called back. Adelicia hurried inside the main entrance, while Essie took slow steps toward the kitchen.

"That child's so good hearted, Liza. You ought to see her putting her blanket around them childrens. She wants food, lots of it, for them and their mother." Liza took a crate from the corner and set it on the thick wood table. "She never could stand to see nothing in want, whether animal or human. But goodness me, put more apples in there, goodness me, I's gonna be the one in want," Essie said, pulling up a stool near the fire.

"You making too much of it, Essie," Liza said, "Mr. Oliver ain't never been mad with you. How you know it got something to do with that Gallatin fellow?"

"Cause I knows that child." She handed Liza some salt pork. "We didn't talk about it directly, but I knows it's all to no good, and getting her to change her mind is like changing a turnip into a watermelon. She never been no different. If she got her mind set on Mr. Franklin, you can bet it's gonna be Mr. Franklin."

Liza was filling the two crates as they talked, and Essie was chewing on dried sassafras root. "Maybe he won't come back from down south," said Liza, "Maybe he just stay there."

"You really talking like a silly now. You ever knowed a man yet that stayed away when he thought he had a pea vine's chance? And I has a feeling he knows he got one."

"Then maybe you better tell Mr. Oliver about the grams."

"That's what I wants to do, but then if he don't know already, I be getting Miss Adie in trouble. Course if I don't tell him, I might be getting her in worse trouble. I just don't know."

"Well, the good Lord will think of something."

"I may be in trouble with Him, too."

CHAPTER 9

A COLD FRONT MOVING IN FROM KENTUCKY BROUGHT RAIN mixed with ice across Middle Tennessee. It was the morning of December fifth, and Adelicia had received no word from Isaac, not a reply to her telegram or her note to Fairvue. She was in no mood to attend the ball with Grainger Caldwell, but considered her options; after all, she could not refuse Grainger at this last minute, even if Isaac were to appear.

The glimmering lights in Cleveland Hall could be seen from the main road long before turning onto the oval shaped drive. And there were no more appropriate hosts for the season's opening ball than the Donelsons. The Hayes' carriage arrived with Adelicia, Grainger, Camille and Joel, and as it stood in line, waiting in turn for their passengers to be delivered to the front portico, they heard in the distance the soft, solemn carols sung by a chorus of Negroes.

"Camille, listen." A woman with a falsetto voice was singing a solo to "The First Noel," while others hummed softly in the background. "Have you ever heard it sung more beautifully?" Adelicia loved Christmas for the servants at Rokeby, the feasting, the holiday gifts; their understanding of Jesus and His birth seemed far more real than her own.

"I could enjoy it a lot more if we weren't sitting in this cold carriage with freezing rain beating down," remarked Grainger.

"You complain more than anyone I know. If the weather were perfect and our carriage next in line, you would be complaining because we have not had any real December weather to make it feel like Christmas," Adelicia snapped.

"Aren't you being a little tough on Grainger?" said Joel. "After all, it is uncomfortable, and it's not getting any warmer."

"You do not hear Camille and me complaining, and what about Uncle Will sitting out in all this?" She stuck her head out the window and called, "Are you all right, Uncle Will? Does the pail still have plenty of embers?"

"Sure do, Miss Adie. All's well."

Camille smiled. "The singing is beautiful. The discomfort almost goes unnoticed when one can listen to that." She recognized what an evening this was going to be for poor Grainger, who really did not deserve it. She had been almost as disappointed as Adelicia when she learned Isaac was not attending and nowhere to be found. She looked forward to seeing him again with her best friend. They made a divinely charming couple, both at the Whites and at Fairvue, she thought; an older man, wealthy, handsome, and with one of those reputations no one dared discuss. "Adie, you have all the luck," she said.

"Now why do you say that?" asked Joel.

"I was just thinking how lucky Adie and I are to be here with you and Grainger tonight." Camille put Joel's hand inside her muff, hoping he would forget her indiscretion.

It was a gala evening. Adelicia's cranberry silk gown that her father had had shipped from New York was outstanding, and she received the usual attention to which she was accustomed. But beneath her outward appearance of gaiety, she was inwardly wishing for Isaac, shrouded in disappointment, and angry with him and herself. She did not understand his absence nor his indifference towards her. She remembered how happy she had been at last year's ball, flirting and teasing and dancing until two in the morning. And although she appeared to be doing the same thing tonight, her heart was elsewhere. She wanted to be with only one man now, and she did not even know where he was!

"Adelicia!" Emily Dyer called as she approached Adelicia and some friends who were gathered talking in the enormous front hallway, the echo of her high-pitched voice seeming to bounce from wall to wall. "Tell me it's not true. I mean I just could not believe it, and my mama always says, 'Now Emiline, you go right to the source. Remember, ladies do not gossip.' So that's just what I'm doing. I heard you were supposed to be," her voice rose higher, "escorted right here, tonight, by Mr. Isaac Franklin, but like I said, I know it's not true."

She never had liked Emily Dyer.

When Adelicia offered one of her most charming smiles, Richard, who was joining the group, looked at his sister awaiting a discreet answer. Fortunately, Grainger was not among the gathering.

"Actually, Emily, every word is true. Mr. Franklin was detained in New Orleans and therefore unable to attend tonight. Your mama was absolutely right; it is best to go directly to the source, and just so everyone will know you are a lady, I shall tell you a secret." She leaned in toward Emily as if she were going to whisper in her ear, but continued in the same clear voice. "I shall be marrying him in the summer."

Richard's face turned deep scarlet, while in contrast, Emily turned ghostly pale. Camille bit her bottom lip to keep from bursting into laughter and asked to be excused. Joel immediately followed her, thinking she was embarrassed to tears by his sister's behavior. And before Richard could say anything, Adelicia walked away from those still gawking to find Grainger and tell him she was ready to dance.

For the remainder of the evening, Adelicia made certain that neither Richard nor Joel could get her alone, and she felt quite wicked with the looks and whisperings directed at her. It was not unusual to be the topic of conversation, but she knew that tonight's topic was quite different from any before. She appreciated Grainger's chivalrous behavior towards her, even though it had only taken a matter of minutes before he had heard of her comment. He was indeed a gentleman.

In the morning's wee hours, when the Donelsons were bidding their guests good-bye, they kissed Adelicia affectionately and asked her to give her father their warmest wishes. The rain had now turned to sleet mixed with snow, and in the silence of the drive back to Rokeby, the only sounds were the horses' hooves and the soft crystals of falling ice.

CHAPTER 10

New Orleans

ISAAC AWAKENED FROM A SOUNDLESS SLEEP. ALL NIGHT HE HAD tossed to the signals of ships' horns—the long low sounds that in the past he had found so restful. The early morning streets were hazy from the river fog as he walked down Chartres toward Esplanade, the collar of his camel's hair coat turned up to protect him from the chilly dampness. He arrived at the foot of the familiar stairs all too quickly and stood staring at the door that he did not want to open. He thought it an eternity since he had stood in the extensive hall within, yet it was only the day before yesterday that he had learned Lona was no longer there. He turned the key in the brass lock and felt the emptiness from deep inside. Lona would not be there to greet him with "Cherie!"

The smell of Tennessee cured ham was coming from the downstairs kitchen. He hesitated for a moment, then walked down the narrow curved steps and found Bess sitting at the table sipping coffee.

"Mr. Franklin!" said Bess, "Lord me, is it good to see you! Tell me about Lona. I ain't eat or slept since you was here. I just cook for Moriah who's always hungry." She gathered up her dress to show how loose it was. "But me, I can't eat a nibble, and Moriah say I might just disappear, and he always like me a good size. Tell me about her. Where is she? Is she all right?"

He sat down at the cypress table while Bess poured him a cup of hot chicory.

"Lonas leaving New Orleans; I don't know to where."

"Why she do such a thing? I don't understand. Though she been acting a might peculiar since she come home from Tennessee."

"Andrew Sinclair advanced her money, and she left yesterday morning aboard a ship." He ran his left hand through his thick graying curls. His eyes stung and felt more blurred than they had the long night before.

"But you ain't said why. Lona love you better than anything. I ain't knowed another woman who love a man like that. It don't make no sense." She carefully laid the fat trimmings in the black iron skillet to fry so they would leave the perfect amount of grease for the savory ham.

"I am going to marry a lady in Nashville."

Bess became almost too careful with her cooking as she listened intently. "I'd made every provision for her through Sinclair, you know that," he said. "She could've stayed with you and Moriah for the rest of her life if she'd wanted to, and have anything money could buy, yet she leaves with someone who's not good enough to be in the same room with her—at least she left this house with him. Now you tell me why?"

Bess removed the fat, now curled and brown, from the heavy skillet, and the slices of ham sizzled when she laid them in the rich grease. She whipped the eggs and cheese and put a tablespoon of drippings into another hot iron skillet. Then she put the tender meat on a plate with the omelet and set it before Isaac with beaten biscuits dripping with butter.

"You didn't answer my question."

She had not faced him directly since he had mentioned marriage, but she turned from the wood-fed stove and looked into his tired eyes. "Women are about the strangest creatures God ever made. On the outside, they may act like they don't care or when the time comes for their man to leave, it'll be all right. But see," she said slowly, "inside, they's hoping against hope that that time ain't gonna come, and when it does come, ain't none of us knows zactly what we'll do. If another woman take my Moriah, why Lord me, I don't know what would happen. See, God made a woman's mind double where He make a man's mind single. That's why it so hard to figure 'em out; they say one thing and all the time are thinking something different," she sighed. "Lona just love you, that's all."

Isaac made no response, but kept his head lowered. Bess turned away to remove the cooking utensils from the stove and after a short silence, asked, "What's she like, the lady you marrying?"

"I'll tell you some other time."

"You hardly eat a nibble."

He put on his coat. "Fix me some ham between the biscuits; I'll take them with me. I'm not hungry right now."

She wrapped the biscuits in cheesecloth, then brown paper and slipped them into his coat pocket. "If you need anything, send a message to the St. Louis."

He hesitated at the door. "You and Moriah always have a home here."

The fog had lifted and the warmth of the late morning sun caused Isaac to remove his coat before reaching Crawford's office.

"Good morning, my friend. I would say how well you look after a good night's sleep, but I'd be lying. You look awful."

"Let's go have a drink."

"It's not even noon yet."

"What difference does that make?"

Isaac was silent as they walked to the corner of Bourbon and Bienville. He did not know what he had expected from Lona—probably that she would stay in New Orleans; that he would know she was well and safe, that he would continue to look after her.

They took a rear table at the Old Absinthe House and discussed Adelicia, Lona, the stakes involved. This time, the morning liquor brought him relief; things appeared clearer. He, too, wanted something money could not buy, and he knew that to get it, he must forget Lona and return to Nashville. He would be faithful to Adelicia. He loved her, differently than he had loved Lona. He loved Adelicia very much.

CHAPTER 11

Nashville

AFTER THE LATE AND INFAMOUS NIGHT AT CLEVELAND HALL, Adelicia and Camille did not come down for breakfast till past noon. The house that should have been bustling with activity was unusually quiet. When Adelicia checked the dining room, she found Liza sitting by the fire mending a linen table cloth with stacks of damask napkins about her.

"Where is everyone? One would think someone died."

"Good morning, Miss Camille, Miss Adie. I'll turn ya'lls hot cakes." They sat at the breakfast dining table and Liza poured their warm milk-coffee.

"Where is everyone?" Adelicia repeated.

"Miss Laura and Master Bliss, they gone into town with Essie." Liza yawned and returned to the kitchen. Mr. Richard, he leave by sun-up for Columbia."

Things were too quiet, and Liza's manner too passive. Adelicia supposed the strangeness to be in direct proportion to her behavior the prior evening.

Camille filled her mouth with milk coffee till both cheeks were protruding and let it trickle slowly down her throat. "Mama has one fit when she sees me do that. 'Young ladies do not engage in such habits. For that matter, no one does!'" She said imitating her mother. "Wonder what Emily's mother would say?"

With impish glances, they refilled their mouths with the liquid and tossed back their heads. But the loud banging of a door caused them to sit up abruptly and swallow quickly. Liza came through the swinging door with the steaming cakes at the same time that Oliver Hayes appeared in the opposite doorway with gloves in one hand and a yellow paper in the other.

"Put the cakes down, Liza."

She hurriedly did as she was told and left the room, making the sign of the cross with one hand and pushing the door open with the other.

"Adelicia, you can have your breakfast later. Camille, if you'll excuse us, Joel will join you after he takes the horses to Uncle Will."

"You," he gestured to Adelicia, "can come with me to the library."

She glanced at Camille out of the corner of her eye and respectfully rose to join her father, who closed the large double doors.

While sitting with Camille, she had felt like a child anticipating a stern reprimand from her father. But as the doors closed, she felt once again a woman who intended to have what she wanted.

"Adelicia, I never thought I would have to say this to a daughter of mine, especially to you." He paused. "You have disgraced our family." His pace quickened. "It is inconceivable to me how you could possibly have been responsible for the despicable behavior that took place last night. Had it not come from the lips of your own brothers, I would have thought it to be a complete falsehood. Do you realize the foolishness of such a statement, or the consequences?"

She stood with her arms folded, looking amused. "Papa, you sound as if you are trying a court case before a jury."

"Pay attention to me, young lady! To have publicly announced an engagement to a man—was shameless enough, but to one you hardly even know—that anyone hardly knows—who is more than twice your age, and whose money is considered ill gained by the better families, is more than I can comprehend! The tasteless proposal stuffed into a cornucopia, his lack of position, suitability, his…" He poured himself a glass of water from the pitcher on his writing table.

Thankful for his pause, she took advantage, "No one *hardly* knows him? His name and fortune are household words, and all of the *better* families are eager for his donations to their causes whether political, new roads, city improvements, or whatever the like. They place bets with him at Cloverbottom, and they're equally eager for his business. I wonder if he is aware of the deep sentiment and appreciation the populace of Nashville has for him."

"You're making no attempt to look at this sensibly or realistically."

"And you still sound as if you are in court! Papa, can you not try to understand?" She lowered her voice and moved close to him. "I am sorry about last night. I sincerely am, and I apologize, but I care about Isaac in a way I have not cared about anyone, ever...it is a feeling, Papa, that is very different. If I know what love is, Papa, I love him, far beyond the fascination for Fairvue and what it offers. I should not have said that to Emily, but you know how she runs on and on. I'm sorry, dearest, dearest Papa...What is that?" she exclaimed, noticing for the first time the folded papers in her father's hand.

"Telegrams that never arrived at the St. Louis Hotel in New Orleans, or Fairvue in Gallatin," he answered triumphantly.

She reached for them. "How could you?" she accused through angry tears. "You had no right!"

"And you've had no right to behave as you have, Adelicia...throwing yourself at a man, chasing after him, if I must use those disgusting words. Ladies do not send telegrams to gentlemen!" He stopped and looked directly at her. "What has happened to you? You can have any eligible, well-positioned young man you want!"

It was then she realized that Emily's father, Hugh Dyer, who owned the telegram office, must have intercepted her messages to Isaac and had been holding them for two days. Her anger subsided, replaced with defiance.

"You are right, Papa, but I see the situation differently than you. I do not want *any* man. I want one particular man, and I intend to have him!" She stood looking at her father like a judge who had just informed the jury that the case was closed.

Her father stared at Adelicia, tight lipped. "Your brothers and I shall speak to Isaac on that matter."

"I have a feeling, Papa, that I shall be more persuasive." She placed her hand on the door-knob. "May I be excused?" Without waiting for an answer, she left the room.

Adelicia was sad as she undressed for bed that night, reflecting on her words to her father. She had never overtly defied him, nor spoken so disrespectfully. She knelt to pray.

In the early morning, before the sun had stretched out of the dark, Adelicia leaned her head back against the chair, as heavy tears rolled over her cheeks. The morning before, while she was still sleeping, her brother Richard had mounted his horse and ridden forty miles south to Columbia, Tennessee. Late that evening, he was borne home lying in a wagon bed, his horse hitched to the rear. Uncle Will drove; her father and Joel followed.

The senseless duel had been fought over a remark her brother had made about William Polk's fiancée. Richard was challenged, and a gentleman must accept. That was his honor. She would have preferred to have her brother.

At the burial, she would place a red rose atop his coffin, and she would paraphrase a poem by Catullus, "Take this, soaked with your sister's tears, and forever more, my brother, good-bye."

The servants had quickly removed all holiday decorations, and in their places had draped black muslin. Mourning wreaths were hung on the exterior doors, the columns on the front portico, wrapped in black crepe paper. Rokeby was in mourning.

CHAPTER 12

January 1839

ISAAC LOVED THE RIVER AND ITS SOUNDS. HE FOUND THERE A quiet, a peace, seldom equaled elsewhere. The Mississippi was the widest, muddiest river south and north of the Ohio, and east to the Atlantic, and he loved following her graceful form and bends. The *Tribune* pulled out of New Orleans' busy port and traveled west before turning northward for home. Steep levees on either side, protecting the plantations along the river, appeared as great, grassy green mounds in contrast to the flat low countryside of South Louisiana. And gracious homes with their widow's walks stood meticulously spaced on grand plantation sites along either side of the river's path.

The *Tribune* followed the Mississippi north toward Memphis, then on to Cairo where an artery of the great river merged with the Ohio. At this point, the steamer would change course south, and eventually flow into the winding Cumberland before passing through Dover and reducing her speed for home port.

After Memphis, the waters had changed from moderately cool and smooth to cold and choppy, with small waves lapping at the ship's sides. By the time they approached Clarksville, heavy snow had begun falling, and Isaac was glad to be nearing home.

The skies thickened with white falling flakes as they rounded the bend to the Nashville Dock, Isaac standing on the bridge, peering through the snowy thickness, trying to discern the apparent confusion on the banks. Makeshift rafts filled with Indians were being shoved into the icy water, and the piers were crowded with hundreds more awaiting their turn.

As they neared the scene, sounds of chaos and wailing became more apparent, and he asked John to request clearance to dock rather than continuing to Fairvue.

"What the hell's going on down there?" he called from the bridge from where he could now see women and children huddled together with nothing more than light clothing to protect them from the elements.

"Shut up, you reds, can't you hear the Captain?"

"What in the devil's name is going on?"

"Just Indians moving west," said the uniformed man.

"Who's in charge here?"

"I'm in charge for right here. But if you mean for all this, you'd have to say General Jackson hisself. Of course..."

"Look soldier, I want to know who the officer in charge is," Isaac said, with mounting impatience.

"Like I was about to say before you interrupted, it's Lieutenant Roberts. Call him 'the Moose.'"

Isaac had stepped onto the icy pier among the mass disorder, unsure of what he could do, but the sight sickened him. He had strongly disagreed with Andrew Jackson's orders to move the Cherokee Tribe from their homeland in North Carolina and Tennessee, knowing their land would be divided up for grabs or lotteries, for settlers.

A man, head and shoulders above everyone else, came weaving his way through the crowd.

"I'm looking for the officer in charge," Isaac said.

"You're looking at him, and we're a sight busy right now with all these injuns, so if you'd hurry up and tell me what you want, I'd be obliged."

"Who's responsible for moving these people in this kind of weather and under these conditions? "

"Nobody ordered the weather and we're a month behind schedule. Government can't go around pacifying redskins. If I had my way, we'd shoot 'em all and save ourselves the trouble. Furthermore, I ain't got no more time for no Indian sympathizer."

He turned to go, roughly pushing a small boy aside who was standing in his path. When an aged Indian woman stooped to help the child, Roberts shoved her with his foot; Isaac moved quickly, stunning him with a blow just beneath his chin. Roberts stumbled backward, then pulled a sharp blade from the side of his boot. With the knife in his right hand and his left arm raised, he moved cautiously, deliberately towards Isaac.

With his back to the hushed crowd, he never took his eyes from Roberts. But the towering man lunged forward with his knife before Isaac could dodge.

There was a shot in the stillness, and Isaac raised his head to see John Armfield standing over the slumped body of Roberts, a smoking pistol in his hand. Then Isaac felt the gushing of his own warm blood before losing conscious.

It was no more than midday, but visibility was poor as they helped Isaac into a coach and drove the short distance to his office-townhouse on Market Street. The town appeared deserted as the horses cautiously made their way through the iced streets toward the two story brick building just around the corner from Judge White's. John and Pompy carried Isaac into his bedroom, shocked at the loss of blood as they removed his heavy coat, shirt and woolen underwear. The flesh of his left shoulder lay open, exposing bare bone amidst blood that still gushed from the wound.

Pompy returned quickly with Dr. Chester Freeman, who administered a dose of morphine, then just as quickly examined the wound and used a mixture of sugar and turpentine to hasten the clotting before closing it. The flesh had been torn away from the muscles and tendons, he explained. The sharp blade had sliced beneath the left clavicle, striking an artery.

Isaac rested easily for a few hours until the soothing effects of the drug began wearing off. He had been wounded before: once during the War of 1812, when as a young man of twenty-one, he had served in the Tennessee Regiment and again by a drunken slave trader in Alexandria. The first had been a musket ball near the groin, from which he quickly healed; the second, a pistol shot that grazed his kneecap. But this time, the wound was serious, the pain more severe. His fever had risen, and Pompy had gone for Dr. Freeman a second time as the afternoon shadows lengthened across the snow that had continued falling throughout the day.

"Doc, I'm hurting pretty bad," Isaac managed to whisper.

"There's good reason why you should. It's lucky you dodged when you did or you might not be here at all. Roberts knew what he was doing. I'm hoping you'll be able to use your arm all right again."

The thought of disability had never occurred to him. "What do you mean by that?"

"It's a nasty wound. I tied off an artery. That's why you bled so much. That muscle's messed up pretty bad," he said, pointing to the upper left shoulder. "I'll probably have to go back in after a while." He stopped short of further explanation. "But knowing you, you'll recover where the ordinary man wouldn't. I've told John to keep you in bed for at least four or five days."

"That's almost a week! I can't do that!" A stabbing pain that caused his body to tremble, was concurrent with the blood that trickled from his mouth after biting his tongue. Dr. Freeman gave him another dose of soothing morphine and left a powder potion to be mixed with water, when the pain became too severe.

The news had traveled quickly in Nashville, especially among the Negroes. The carriage driver and the workers on the wharf had wasted no time in spreading the tale of "the heroic fight of Mr. Franklin, who against the gravest odds, had taken on an armed man twice his size, and had braved it all to protect pore red men who'd been took from their homes by the government."

The winter's first heavy snow fell as Oliver Hayes had travelled to his law office earlier that morning. The news about Isaac had reached him by way of his boy Dobbin, who had heard it first-hand from the public coachman who had taken Isaac to 205 Market Street.

The plight of the Cherokees being forced from their homes in East Tennessee and Western North Carolina, had troubled Oliver Hayes for some time, as it had other Nashville residents. But he, like the others, had looked the other way.

Nashville's old guard chose not to buck the campaign that for years had been Andrew Jackson's call: to resettle the Indians—voluntarily if possible—but if not, to resettle by force. Although he had succeeded in getting Martin Van Buren elected following his own term, to Washington Democrats, the old general was no longer a political threat. However, in Nashville he still had a loyal following, despite the fact that the Whig Party's, Hugh Lawson White, had carried both Tennessee and Davidson County over Van Buren. If too much were made of the march West that had begun in '37, Jackson's political enemies would not let it rest, and would affect his plans for James K. Polk to be elected the second president from Tennessee.

Feeling vaguely guilty to hear that Isaac had been wounded attempting to defend the conditions of the Cherokee movement, Oliver thought it his duty to visit.

Dobbin brought the gray mare from the stables, the horse stepping with special caution as Oliver slowly guided him through the blizzard-like snow toward Isaac's office.

"Good morning, Doc, how's the patient?" Oliver asked, spotting Chester Freeman standing on the front steps, wrapping a wool scarf around his neck.

"Greetings, Oll, I was just leaving. He's worse than I cared to tell him. It's possible he could lose the use of his arm, if not the arm itself. Isaac's lost a lot of blood, and the wound's deep, awful deep. I tell you Oll, not many would have done what he did…not many"

They continued to stand outside the doorway with the dry snow peppering around them, turning their hats white. "Do you know what happened?" Oliver asked.

"John can tell you more than I can, but from what I gather, he was trying to get some straight answers on the fate of the Cherokees when…."

John interrupted when he opened the door, "Well, if it's not Oliver Hayes." Oliver extended his hand.

"I'll be going on, John," Chester Freeman said. "If you need me, don't delay." The doctor tipped his hat. "Good day, Oliver."

Moments later, the bearded adventurer and the impeccably dressed lawyer-minister-aristocrat stood in contrast beside the heavily carved bed where Isaac lay listless. As John related the early morning events, Oliver listened with growing concern. Protecting the rights of others was a major issue when the country was formed some sixty years before, and the fact that this same government could drive Indians from their homes, divide their lands among the white settlers, and feel justified in doing it, was becoming more intolerable.

He was embarrassed to have closed his eyes to the miserable conditions the Indians were forced to endure on the march to Oklahoma. For how long, he asked himself, could humanity close its eyes to vile indignation and continue each day beneath a facade of truth? For how long could slavery endure?

Isaac turned and asked for water, that Pompy quickly poured and held to his lips. John elevated him with pillows and mopped the heavy perspiration from around his face and neck. He opened his eyes. "I've got to get back to the dock. How long has it been?"

"Old partner, you can't go nowhere. The doc says you got to rest like this for a week, you heard him, and me and Pompy intend to see you do just that."

Oliver came near the bed and put his hand on top of Isaac's. "I'm proud of you, Isaac, for acting on your conscience." Oliver tightened his grip. "Now tell me what the others and I can do to set the course in another direction."

"Thank you, Oliver. There are many wrongs that takes more than one man to make right. But improving their present conditions will be a good thing."

Word had gotten to John that the stabbing incident, or murder, as it was being termed by some, had halted the operations at the dock. The fifteen hundred or so remnants of the Cherokee Nation had been herded into unheated, waterfront warehouses, where they waited. Stripped of their pride and broken, Isaac had said they appeared a different breed from the majestic race about whom books were written and tales told. This was a peaceful tribe, he had said, who had been repeatedly lied to and filled with broken promises, the result of which was what he had witnessed: being transported twelve hundred miles from their homes to a flat grassy plain, opposite from the mountains and green valleys they loved.

The sound of horse's hooves crunching through the icy layers came after the clock had struck seven. The group on horseback was made up of Perkins, Harding, Caldwell, White, McGavock, Wilson, Murdoch, Polk and Hayes. Oliver felt fortunate with the number assembled, given the treacherous weather.

Although in immense pain, Isaac had charted the proposed action and tentatively planned to meet with the men in Governor Newton Cannon's office the following morning. The men agreed there was no way they, nor anyone else, could stop the atrocity begun years before. But they could see it delayed until better provisions were made.

Isaac did not attend the early morning meeting. John sent word to Oliver Hayes that Isaac's fever had risen during the night, that he had again lost consciousness, and realized much sooner than expected the doctor's prognosis of having to reopen the wound.

Governor Cannon had sent a telegram to Washington denouncing the maneuver and the conditions on the river. He received a hasty reply stating that the transporting would not resume until Friday of the following week, with new and better provisions. However, Oliver and the others discovered the visible proof of that promise would not be realized until Memphis, where the goods were to arrive from Fort Pendleton, Kentucky, just before the Cherokees would cross the Mississippi and again set out on foot. Meanwhile, they had two hundred and fifty miles to go by freezing river. An era was closing. The Cherokee Nation would pass as the last of its people boarded the rafts on the Cumberland.

Adelicia had learned of the incident the same afternoon her father had visited with Isaac, and she convinced Uncle Will the very next morning, without her father or Essie's knowledge, to drive her into town.

It was a beautiful Wednesday morning, and the sun shone on the day-old snow with a glistening glow that stung her eyes, as the horse trotted in the melting slush with his nostrils blowing smoke into the icy air.

When Uncle Will turned the carriage onto Market Street, Adelicia's heart beat rapidly, feeling the same tenseness she had experienced earlier upon hearing the news. Surely Isaac would be pleased to see her, surely he was in love with her, regardless of how it had appeared, and surely her father could say nothing to the contrary of her wishes to marry him. She checked the address, then signaled for Uncle Will to stop the carriage, with further instructions for him to return to Rokeby without her. She watched him turn back onto Spring Street toward home, before she pulled the brass bell beside the door.

"I'm Adelicia Hayes." She put out her gloved hand which remained untouched as John stood gaping. "May I come In?"

"Yes, ma'am," he stammered, stepping aside to let her pass. "Pompy, take the lady's wraps." She removed her other hand from her beaver muff, and smiling, handed the muff to John, who in turn gave it to Pompy, never once taking his eyes from her face.

"How is Mr. Franklin?" she asked.

"Not well, not well atall. He's been in a fever since yesterday."

"Do you have any hot tea, any sassafras root?"

"Oh, excuse me, ma'am, for not offering."

"Not for me," she smiled. "Hot sassafras is the best remedy for reducing fever, and when it breaks, we shall need honey."

She stood beside the bed and looked at Isaac in his uneasy sleep.

"Pompy, go fix the tea and bring it to Miss Hayes."

"Please, Mr. Armfield, call me Adie, and I shall prepare the tea when the water is ready."

Adelicia followed Pompy into the kitchen, took the root, split it three ways and expertly cut the tips as John watched. She dipped the ends quickly into the crock bowl and removed them just as quickly. Waiting a moment, she repeated the procedure that Essie had taught her until the water became a dull, reddish orange. Then she slipped an herb from a tiny pocket pinned at her waist and dropped it into the colorful liquid.

With John supporting Isaac, she put small drops of warm tea into his mouth, and soon after, a cold sweat began to appear. Pompy brought some honey, and Isaac swallowed a teaspoonful.

"Nashville is proud of you. How do you feel?" She leaned nearer and put her hand on top of his. Emily Dyer would pass out for sure, she thought.

"How did you come here?" he asked, dazed, trying to make sense of Adelicia's presence at his bedside.

"Uncle Will brought me."

"I mean, how did you know?"

"Everyone knows."

"The meeting. What time is the meeting?" Isaac asked, suddenly remembering.

"This morning," answered Pompy.

Adelicia looked up at John, "What happened? I know Papa was there and…"

John put his fingers to his lips.

"Well, damn it! Excuse me, Miss Adelicia. What happened? Where's William?"

"Mr. Franklin," Adelicia said, stroking the top of his hand. "I am sure they have not had time to finish. You must know how long-winded Papa is, especially when he is with Mr. Perkins and the others. We have bothered you with too much talk. Lie back and rest." She touched his face with the tips of her fingers. "I shall be here when you awake."

He settled back easily onto the pillow after she spooned more tea into his mouth and slept, taking deep, exhausted breaths.

John related the morning's events to Adelicia, how Dr. Freeman had administered a heavy dose of morphine, probed deep into the torn flesh and swollen tissue, and again cleaned the wound, hoping to prevent further infection. He also related the dramatic information that Isaac could lose the use of his arm, if not his life.

"Who is William?" Adelicia asked John.

"Isaac's younger brother—got here shortly after it happened—left just fore you came."

She liked the way John looked at her and his easy simple manner. The night at Fairvue, Isaac had mentioned to her and her family that his friend and former partner, John Armfield, thought women were generally mindless and had little use for them. She had found the comment rather amusing, thinking it useful at times to be underestimated, and now found him a charming host and conversation companion.

"Does he have other brothers?"

"Two older, but one has passed, five sisters and one brother younger than William. All the Franklin men have plantations in Gallatin."

She loved learning about Isaac, but she would inquire no further for now. She wondered how long it would be before her father either sent for her or sent Essie? She also prayed that Isaac would be well, and that there would be no further need to discuss the loss of his arm, or his life.

It was almost six-thirty when Adelicia went to prepare a second draft of tea. Pompy had been busy in the kitchen cooking a delicious-smelling something or other that made her realize she had not eaten since breakfast. She discovered it to be seafood gumbo that had been simmering for hours, made with fresh fish brought aboard the *Tribune* from New Orleans. She sampled it, pronounced it delectable, praised the cook and told him she could hardly wait for supper. She was going to be one of them and fit in. She would eat at the kitchen table with John and Pompy.

Adelicia stayed at the combination office and townhouse on Market Street through the end of the week. Uncle Will, however, had driven Essie into town late that Wednesday evening. Her father had insisted that if she were determined to stay there, that it must at least appear proper, having some semblance of respectability.

Adelicia was pleased to have Essie with her, although she detested her father's reasons for having sent her. She disliked anything done for the sake of how others perceived it, and liked living in the coziness of the townhouse, with no interest in anyone's opinion as to how it looked. She liked the masculine furniture, being enshrouded by its strength that reflected Isaac's. She liked all things stronger that herself.

As she slept upstairs on the down feather bed, with Essie sleeping on a smaller one in the same room, she thought about the many women Isaac had known before her and wondered if they could possibly have felt the way she did now. Was she infatuated? Was she in love? Whichever, she liked the feeling. "For certain," she said quietly to herself, "there will be no one else for Isaac, ever."

On Saturday morning, Pompy drove Adelicia and the steadily recovering Isaac to the waterfront so they might view the Cherokees' final departure. The sharing of sense and purpose over the bleakness of the situation cast new horizons on their relationship as they watched the end of an age. Riding the short distance from the river back to his office, Adelicia knew Isaac was everything she wanted. She had liked being needed by him when he had lain ill with fever, and although still quite unwell, she liked the power and warmth he generated as they rode in the carriage together. She straightened his coat over his arm, and instead of putting her hand back into her beaver muff, she slipped it into his. He rubbed his fingers gently over hers.

"This is a great catastrophe," she said. "It isn't fair."

"Most things are unfair," he answered. "Life is not a promise of fairness. I'm not sure I know what justice is anymore." He paused, staring out the carriage window. "One day this will surely be lamented by future generations as a demeanable error in the government's judgment."

"What about slavery?" she asked.

"One man's justice may be another man's injustice. I've heard the word freedom till I'm sick of it. No one seems to understand there's no such thing. The Abolitionists and people who talk about it the most have the least idea of what it means. What is freedom? I'm afraid I don't have any answers. I once thought I did. I'm sorry," he said, looking at her. "I don't intend to bore you. It's like you said; the whole thing ought not be."

"I asked the question."

He looked over at her. "Adelicia, the importing was outlawed in '07. Major agriculture in the south depends on slave labor; the north, England and France depend on the cotton. It's simple economics. It's the world in which we live. Ambiguity prevails."

She looked pensively at him. "Will Mr. Armfield be all right? I mean, will he be arrested because of the shooting?"

"He's fine, my sweet girl. There has already been an inquisition, and there will be a formal hearing, but it's a clear–cut case of self-defense, our lawyer says. Roberts had already drawn his pistol when he fell. Thank you for asking."

"I like him," she said.

Adelicia felt oddly detached. She had never doubted any of the concepts he mentioned, or felt she had not, but had taken them for granted, a part of life. She remembered her father and the other men discussing Montgomery Bell, who just the year before had freed fifty of his slaves. He had conducted a ceremony on their behalf at the First Presbyterian Church on Spring Street, then walked with them down to the wharf where they boarded a ship for Liberia. She was not sure how she felt about that; she was not sure how other members of the gentry had felt or what they had thought. Her father had simply called it a noble gesture. Obviously, most, if not all, did not approve of the trafficking of slaves, however, they used slave labor.

They stopped in front of the office-townhouse, where Pompy helped Isaac out of the carriage. John had not argued over Isaac taking this first outing, providing he not hesitate in promptly returning to bed. Isaac admitted to feeling tired and by the time Uncle Will came to take Adelicia and Essie back to Rokeby, he was resting comfortably.

While Essie stood nearby frowning, Adelicia leaned over and kissed Isaac lightly on the brow. "John," Adelicia said, "Do not let him forget, he promised to be in church Sunday morning, next. I wish you would come too."

"Not me, ma'am. But if he told you, I'll remind him if he's feeling up to it."

Adelicia put her hand in his. "Thank you for everything, John."

"Pompy," Adelicia said, "when I tell Liza about those marvelous dishes, she'll turn every shade of envy. But you did say you would share your recipes."

Essie spoke up. "He done done it. While you gone this morning, I had him say 'em to me while I write 'em down, and I don't like it none a tall when I say I can write and he don't believe me. He don't know class when he's looking at it, Miss Adie, and he better not left out none of the gredients."

Pompy and Essie had become instant rivals from the moment Essie arrived. Pompy shared his master's sentiments toward women and was especially intolerant of anyone in his kitchen giving instructions. Ever since that first morning at the townhouse when Essie complained about the way her eggs were fried, he had shown contempt for her authoritative voice. He did not want her in the kitchen preparing her own food, nor did he want her to tell him how it should be done. Thus the days had passed: Essie feeling her superiority to the "field bred" Negro, as she called him, and Pompy disliking the "bossy woman."

Essie's voice was kinder for John. "And I thanks you, Mr. John. Hope Mr. Franklin be feeling tolerable well mighty soon. Believe Sunday next, though, too early for him to be about."

John watched them get into the carriage and stood in the doorway until the wheels were out of sight. "If all women was like Miss Adelicia, I might even get used to one. Believe Isaac's got hisself trapped this time. She's some kind of woman."

"That mammy of hers is some kind of woman, too, but if it's all the same to you, I can shore get by without having her around." Pompy continued muttering into the kitchen.

The December sun was disappearing behind heavy clouds as the carriage wheels rolled toward Rokeby. "Essie, why in heaven's name did you say that to John?" she snapped. "It is high time you realize that I am going to be seen with Isaac."

"Child, can you imagine what a stir it'll cause if Mr. Franklin walk in and sit in your Papa's pew? The heads that'll turn, the tongues that'll wag, won't nobody pay no attention to Reverend Edgar. They all be watching that pew to see what's going on."

"Good goshen, Essie! Wagging tongues come from bored minds. I hope all the old biddies get cricks in their necks from the strain. The major shock will be before the service when I wait in the vestibule for Isaac, walk down the aisle with him, then sit in Papa's pew." The impish grin and sparkle in her eyes were the same with which Essie was too familiar when Adelicia was planning some sort of mischief. "I think it will be marvelous, and there is little now that Papa can say."

Essie knew there was little that anyone could say. As she had told Liza, "When Adie's mind's decided, it's decided. Only the good Lord Hisself can handle that child, and sometimes I wonder if He could if He was right here on earth."

CHAPTER 13

THE FIRST SUNDAY IN MARCH BROKE WITH A CHILLING RAIN, BUT Adelicia's victorious smile beamed warm and radiant as she proceeded down the aisle slightly in front of Isaac, with him touching her back ever so lightly as they entered the pew marked, "Hayes." Indeed some heads did turn and low rumbled whispers were heard, but no one could deny how extraordinary they looked together. His six-foot lean ruggedness was complemented by his thick graying curls that touched the top of his collar and his blue captivating eyes; eyes that penetrated, not only causing one to want a second glance, but causing one to want to continue glancing in their direction. In contrast was Adelicia's petite, well-proportioned figure, dark hair parted in the middle and pulled up on the sides, allowing her curls to cascade around her shoulders, and thick dark brows that enhanced her large hazel eyes.

Essie's seat in the balcony was empty as she had feigned a sudden attack of the gout and had taken to bed. Five were in the Hayes' pew: her father, Joel, Bliss, Isaac and Adelicia.

After the services, most of the men in the congregation made it a point to greet Isaac, commending him on the stand he had taken on behalf of the Cherokees and extending their pleasure in seeing him out, only weeks after the incident. But Adelicia sensed the lack of sincerity in their voices; the well-defined arrogance that said, "You don't belong." She hoped that Isaac did not also sense it.

Her friends and acquaintances gathered around her to meet the handsome visitor, disregarding their mothers' disapproving glances, and Adelicia was enjoying every moment of it. "Mr. Franklin, you remember Camille Perkins."

Isaac gallantly bent forward and took her hand. "A beautiful woman isn't easily forgotten, Miss Camille. I hope we'll be seeing more of each other."

"I'm sure we shall, Mr.Franklin. I'm certain of it," she said, glancing at Adelicia.

"You have met Margaret, and this is Susanne Murdoch and..." She looked near the door to see Emily Dyer standing with her parents. "Emily, darling, do come here for a moment." Emily approached, blushing, as the girls made way for her in the circle.

"Isaac, you must meet Emily Dyer. She has simply been dying to meet you, asking me every sort of question. Why, Emily, why ever are you fanning on such a cold day? You did ask me all about him, remember, at the ball? Isaac, I do believe you have rendered her speechless." She hoped Isaac found her impishness as much fun as did she.

"I'm delighted to meet you, Miss Emily," Isaac said into her flushed face. "Perhaps you'll do me the honor of saving a dance for me at the next ball?"

"Emeline, the carriage is waiting. Come right now!" Mrs. Dyer called. Still glowing red, Emily turned and obediently followed her mother out the door. Adelicia and Camille were about to burst into laughter, thinking for an encore they would suggest that Isaac ask Mrs. Dyer to dance at the next ball.

Pompy was waiting for Isaac outside the door and helped him down the steep stone steps and into the carriage. If anyone had had any doubts concerning Adelicia's rumored infatuations, they had been put to rest that morning. Adelicia knew she would be the topic of conversation for the day, over Sunday dinner, at evening supper and around the fire before bedtime. She could hear the old biddies now: "Have you ever? It's disgraceful, that's what it is! Why, you know that's probably the first time he's set foot in a church door in his whole life."

Adelicia took great satisfaction in the fact that she was causing more gossip and speculation than anyone since the time Eliza Allen had divorced Sam Houston.

CHAPTER 14

As long as Adelicia could remember, it had been customary to celebrate the Eve of Ash Wednesday with a dinner and ball. As she dressed for this year's grand affair, she reflected how as a child, she had watched her mother don the latest fashion for the gala, and how her father's eyes would light up whenever she walked into a room. "Sarah doesn't need jewelry. On her, it's a distraction," her father would say.

Adelicia had kept Isaac waiting over twenty minutes, and she hated admitting how nervous she was. "Essie, tell me once more how I look. Is my dress centered in the back?"

"Child, you never looked bad a day in your life, even when you're a mite poly you look better than most. Your Papa done called up here two times. Now you go on down them stairs and greet your Mr. What's-His-Name."

"Essie! Would you please..."she stopped abruptly, after putting her hands on her hips, and gave her mammy a quick kiss on the cheek.

She turned to go, taking one final glance. "See that piece of hair. Essie, do something!" Essie patiently tucked the few misplaced strands into the finger curls piled high on top of her head, and Adelicia went down the stairs with a confident smile.

Isaac, her father and she rode in Isaac's plush barouche to Harpeth Hall. "Isaac," her father began, "winning a case in court against the strongest opposition is like taking an egg from its nest in comparison to tangling with my daughter. I accepted, years ago, that I was no match for her."

She reached up and kissed her father's cheek. It had thrilled her that morning when he had asked her to come into the library and talk with him. And as he sat in his favorite chair, he had expressed his positive feelings for Isaac, telling her that he felt him a good and decent man, regardless of his past, and how impressed he had been with Isaac's sincerity and integrity the Sunday afternoon he had asked him for Adelicia's hand. Isaac had spoken to him with a kindness and concern for her and her future that any father would have found touching and gratifying. And after he had told Isaac that he would be proud to accept him as a son-in-law, Isaac had said, "Oliver, I promise you, you'll never be sorry...and I hope we can be the best of friends." And strangely, Oliver told Adelicia, he was looking forward to the promised friendship—he trusted him.

He had also been extremely impressed as Isaac had laid his life and wealth before him, concealing none of his business ventures or assets: it was not the ordinary for a prospective son-in-law to declare. Oliver believed that Isaac cherished and loved his daughter...and he did not think himself a man easily fooled. He would join forces with the two of them and announce her engagement to the forty-nine year-old bachelor that very night at the ball.

Friarson Murdoch met them at Harpeth Hall's great entrance; "Oliver, it's good to see you." His old friend warmly took his hand and reached with the other one to take Adelicia's. "Adie, child, it is a sin, yes it is, for a girl to be as pretty as you are! You're a lucky man, Isaac Franklin," he said, and shook his hand. "And we're awfully glad to have you among us tonight, we certainly are. Now come on in and join in the merry-making."

Adelicia was more radiant than ever before. She knew she was outwardly dazzling, and she felt inwardly dazzling as well. She was so happy, so exuberant, that she thought the butterflies fluttering in the top of her stomach would come floating right out of her mouth. As she danced and twirled in her deep blue satin gown and matching slippers, looking up into Isaac's eyes, she delighted in the passion of the evening, knowing they were the envy of everyone there.

The clock in the great hall had just struck eleven when Friarson Murdoch stood before the orchestra and called his guests to attention. He and Oliver Hayes stood side by side as the latter began to speak. "Dear friends," he began, "On this gala occasion, on the eve of remembering and celebrating the days before the resurrection of our dear Savior..."

"Oh dear, Isaac, Papa sounds as if he is going to preach a sermon," Adelicia whispered.

"He'll be all right."

"I want to announce to you gathered here this evening—just a moment, Isaac, would you and Adie step forward, please." They stood on either side of her father. "I want to announce the engagement of my daughter, Adelicia, to Isaac Franklin Esquire, whom most of you know, from Sumner County." He turned to Isaac... "A gentleman, a planter and a shrewd businessman."

It had been done. Isaac had been proclaimed by one of the most respected men in the city, before his friends and family, as his future son-in-law.

Momentarily, the crowd was hushed. Then it broke into what Adelicia thought were sincere applause...sincere from her friends for her genuine happiness, or sincere from her enemies that she was getting just what she deserved. They could even be sympathizing with Isaac. Regardless, she was ecstatic, the room was ecstatic!

"I want to be the first to congratulate Isaac and kiss the bride-to-be," said Friarson. "Let us have a toast, yes sir, let us have a toast to Isaac and Adie!" Everyone raised their glasses and mirthfully proclaimed in unison. "To Adelicia and Isaac." He shook Isaac's hand and scooped Adelicia up and kissed her. "Now let us dance everybody! Let us dance!"

The officially engaged couple led the O'Cain polka, with the men cutting in every few seconds to dance with Adelicia, and Isaac taking their partners. Despite the pain in his shoulder, he managed well with one arm as he took his turn with the ladies, even Matilda Dyer.

This was an evening Adelicia did not want to see end, and one she would never forget; everything was just as she wanted it to be. After the polka, the men all gathered to congratulate Isaac while the girls fluttered around her. "Adie, Adie, has he kissed you? Do tell!"

Adelicia winked. "We must not speak of such things."

It was past midnight when Isaac freed himself to rescue Adelicia from the well-wishers. They slipped unnoticed onto the rear verandah and stood in the partial moonlight, listening to soft songs coming from the Negro quarter. They watched as a small cloud covered the upturned moon, causing the distant stars to appear clearer.

"Adie, I had a little something sent down from New York." He reached into his coat pocket. "I hope you like it, but if you don't, we can always return it." He handed her a small velvet box. "Go ahead, open it."

Her fluttery fingers unfastened the tiny gold clasp and she raised the lid. Her astonishment at seeing the sapphire inside was even greater than her first glimpse of Fairvue.

"Oh, Isaac! It is the most beautiful ring I have ever seen. It is the most beautiful anything I have ever seen."

"The moon must have known precisely when to have gone behind the clouds," he said. "Your eyes are brighter than the stars."

She responded as if she had heard nothing he said, "Oh, Isaac, you should not have, but I love it."

"Well, are you not going to put it on?"

"You are supposed to do that."

"Oh, am I?" He asked mischievously.

The ring fit perfectly as he slipped it onto her third finger. The flawless sapphire with diamond baguettes was so large it reached her knuckle.

"Oh, it is so astonishingly beautiful!"

"You said that already."

"Stop teasing and let me enjoy it. No one in Nashville has ever seen a ring like this! No one in Tennessee! Does it not look extraordinary on my hand? May we go inside and show everyone?" Almost as an afterthought, she asked, "Isaac, after we are married, can we have Chateau Lafitte every evening while dining?"

He laughed. "My dear, you may have anything you wish except—" He stopped short, not wishing to mar a beautiful moment of girlish glee. "Let's hurry and go show everyone."

He found her childlike excitement and selfishness amusing, refreshing. She was a delightful blend of little girl and what he had no doubt would be all woman, but he was well aware of that part of her on which he would always keep a watchful eye, the part that wanted control. She could have anything his money could buy—but not his empire.

She walked back into the ballroom with her right hand in Isaac's arm and her left hand in front of her with obvious intent. The deep blue stone could easily be seen through the candlelight from across the room on her ivory hand. "Papa, have you ever seen anything like it?" she asked, beaming into her father's face.

"No, Adie, I must confess. I've never seen anything quite like it. Isaac, I'm afraid you're starting her out on the wrong foot."

Unfortunately, Adelicia heard jealous whispers spoken behind gloved hands. "Hmph, starting her out on the wrong foot! She has been on the wrong foot ever since she was born, and that ring is the most vulgar piece of jewelry I have ever seen."

"Now, Matilda Dyer, you know Adelicia is a very sweet girl, and talented. No one can deny her that," said Francis Murdoch. She thanked God for Mrs. Murdoch.

"Oh, Adie," said Camille, admiring the ring, "Do you suppose he has a friend who…Whatever am I mumbling? Joel, isn't it simply gorgeous?" she asked, as he walked to where they were standing.

The night was a long brilliant one, but finally the last dance had been danced, the last songs had been sung, and the last good-byes said.

"A merry farewell to you, Mrs. Murdoch," Adelicia said, gently kissing her on the cheek, "and to you, Mr. Murdoch. It has been the grandest of evenings."

"Goodnight, Fry. The night couldn't have been any better. See you very soon, and thank you," said Oliver.

Isaac held Francis Murdoch's hand. "You are a charming and gracious hostess, Mrs. Murdoch. I hope to repay the hospitality at Fairvue."

"We mustn't keep your driver waiting any longer, Isaac," declared Oliver. "A warm goodnight to you all."

Later, as Adelicia lay in bed, she replayed the evening in her mind, her thoughts focusing on the sapphire. She touched the enormous stone with her right fingers and held it up to take another look by the bit of moonlight seeping through the closed curtains. It was without a doubt the most beautiful ring she had ever seen…but then Isaac could afford such luxuries and would always be able to afford such luxuries. He was extremely handsome with marvelous eyes, and she could easily see why all women were charmed by him…she certainly admitted that she was. His past conquests did not matter to her.

Very soon, she would be mistress of Fairvue. She knew that she loved Isaac with the infatuation with which one loves in the beginning, or perhaps even like her mother had loved her father. It was definitely different from the girlishness with which she had loved Alphonso. But, as she lay there in the darkness, she asked herself, "If Isaac did not have so much money, would I still feel the same?" She found that her answer was an emphatic—"No!"

CHAPTER 15

O N JULY 2, 1839, ADELICIA HAYES MARRIED ISAAC FRANKLIN Esquire in the drawing room at Rokeby. Carriages lined the graveled drive as well as either direction on Spruce Street as far as the eye could see. The lawn and gardens were magnificent with summer flowers and roses, their sweet scents greeting the guests as they ascended the front steps and made their way into the lavishly decorated and crowded rooms within. Oliver Hayes had spared nothing for the wedding of his eldest daughter.

The house servants, along with Uncle Sugart and Aunt Aggie, were seated in the parlor adjoining the drawing room with family members. The rooms were so filled that the last guests to arrive had to be ushered to the rear verandah. Ladies were seen tucking and holding their hoops close to them to make more room.

"Dang it, partner," John Armfield said, as he and Isaac stood well out of view amidst a bed of multi-colored zinnias behind the brick kitchen. "I never wore one of these things before, and I never intend to again," he continued, as he nervously fingered the onyx studs that were a gift from Isaac.

"One of these days, Martha's going to catch you in a weak moment, and I'll be serving as your best man," Isaac taunted, referring to his niece, who'd had her eye on John for some time.

"It's not going to happen, I tell you. Pompy and me do just fine... dang it, will you fix this?"

Isaac walked closer and fastened the last stud in place and looked at his friend. They had come a long way together...from buying their first auction house on Duke Street in Alexandria, "Franklin and Armfield," to controlling a larger part of the business in Natchez. They had also acquired the reputation of being the fairest establishment for both slave and buyer. And after selling their interest in an enterprise, with which both had come to find extremely unsettling, through wise investing; each had become millionaires.

"I just want you to know," Isaac said, "it wouldn't have been the same with anybody else...The times we've had!" The two held each other's arms for a moment, and it was John who broke the sentimentality.

"And now you're gonna become a man of the cross, going to church every Sunday, squiring a wife around town and raising a family," John complained, as he and Isaac walked toward the house, perspiring in the July heat. "I just can't see you fitting into all that, but I guess if you gotta do it, you picked about the best looking one around. I wouldn't be surprised if she don't turn out to be pretty smart too."

"I wouldn't be surprised at anything, where Adelicia's concerned."

The bridesmaids were lovely in soft pastel organdy gowns, with garlands of baby's breath in their hair, as they proceeded slowly down the spiral staircase in the drawing room, one behind the other to the strains of "Plaisir d'amour." Adelicia's younger sisters, Laura and Corrine, preceding Camille, as they took their places in front of the carved walnut mantle near Reverend Edgar of the First Presbyterian Church.

"Papa, I love you. I would not have exchanged you for any father in the world," Adelicia said, reaching up and kissing him on the cheek, as they stood in the upstairs hallway. He bent down and kissed her on the forehead, blinking back his tears, knowing all eyes would soon be upon them.

Handel's "Sonata in F Major" swelled throughout the rooms; two small flower girls straightened the long satin and lace train, and Oliver Bliss Hayes escorted his Adie down the stairs of Rokeby into the drawing room.

The wedding guests and family, later followed the bridal party onto the lawn for the grand festivities, where Friarson Murdoch offered, "Yes sir, I don't even care for weddings, but this had to be the prettiest there's ever been, outside of my own Susannah's last month."

Rokeby displayed its finest for the occasion: French champagne had been shipped from New York. Isaac's brothers had insisted on supplying the reception with every sort of fresh seafood from New Orleans, John Armfield had insisted on supplying the roast beef and mutton, and earlier in the week had delivered it to Rokeby. Liza, with much additional kitchen help, had prepared the delicious dishes, including ices, creams, cakes and exotic fruits made abundant on each of the four festive serving tables.

The July sun could still be seen above the hills as the guests showered the newlyweds with rice just as they stepped into the gaily decorated barouche driven by Pompy. At the wharf, they boarded Isaac's newest steamer, *The Tennessee,* that would take them North to where the Cumberland narrows at Bristol. From there they would go by stage to the Virginia Springs, then by rail to Alexandria, Washington City and finally New York.

Pompy carried the luggage aboard into the large elegantly furnished suite, designed by Isaac for Adelicia. Then he removed two silver goblets from a fine leather case, followed by a bottle of champagne sealed with old wax, and carefully unwrapped two-cut glass cologne bottles. "This all compliments of Mr. John. He know you need a new case, and he figure you buy Miz Franklin all that smelling stuff, so he have the bottles made up special for her. He too tell me to say when you get to New York, he done paid the hotel for two weeks; I guess if you stays longer than that, you has to pay yourself."

"Thank you, Pompy, you're a good man. Give your master our best and kindest thanks." Isaac put a gold piece in his hand and Pompy backed out the door, bowing mockingly in his usual manner.

Isaac picked up the case to see his initials embossed in gold on the rich dark brown leather. "It is handsome," Adelicia said, then turned to the cologne bottles, recognizing the quality of the Venetian glass. "He must have paid a fortune for these!" she exclaimed.

"Knowing John, he probably did."

"Isaac, look, your initials are engraved on one and mine on the other," she said, holding up two silver goblets. "I like it, I like it very much, AHF, Adelicia Hayes Franklin. What a beautiful name!" She twirled around the suite into his arms.

He held her for a moment, resting his chin against her forehead, then easily, gently, kissed her eyelids, her face and lips and removed the goblets from her hands, never taking his eyes from hers. Again, he kissed her.

Her first *real* kiss, so different from Alphonso's gentle pecks to her lips. She stayed in his arms waiting for more, melting into a oneness unknown to her.

"I love your holding me, kissing me," she whispered in his ear, "Do not let go of me, ever."

The sloshing of the paddle wheels began, as the knock at the door signaled dinner, eaten in partial silence...silence immersed in smiles and glances of the expectations of new lovers.

After Adelicia excused herself to go into an adjoining dressing room, Isaac donned his silk smoking jacket, lit a cigar and stood watching the Nashville dock become less and less visible behind him. He was filling the second glass with vintage champagne when Adelicia appeared standing just inside the door, wearing an ivory silk and lace peignoir that bared her shoulders and chest, partially revealing her youthful breasts, virgin breast that had never been held, nor kissed, nor made love to.

Isaac walked to her, put both hands beneath the fullness of her dark hair that hung loosely over her shoulders, and held her face for a moment. Her eyes were filled with a look he had seen many times in the past, that of other women, other places, but this time his feelings were as if there were no past. This was lasting, eternal. He loved her, and he wanted her more than he had ever wanted anything or anyone, ever. He wished he could let her know how deeply he loved her.

He lifted her in his arms and carried her to the peau de soie down sofa, where the silver goblets sat on a small tea table beside. "A toast to you, Mrs. Franklin, that life may always be as you wish it, that our life together will be fulfilled beyond what either of us can suppose; Adelicia Hayes Franklin, I am in love with you." He filled their glasses with champagne.

"A toast to you, Mr. Franklin. I hope that I shall always be what you want, more so, what you need. That years from now, we shall feel the magic that we feel today." She paused, misty eyed, "That I shall enrich and fulfill your desires...please you."

Isaac took a satin box from his pocket and opened it.

"How exquisite!" she exclaimed.

Taking the small gold locket in his hands, he fastened it around her slender neck and both read the inscription, "Amo, amas, amat."

He kissed her once more and as they stood, he removed his jacket, then unfastened the tiny silk loop which held the robe over her negligee.

CHAPTER 16

New York, August 1839

HE VIRGINIA SPRINGS HAD BEEN SOOTHING, NOURISHING, AND there Adelicia had learned more of the joys of love making, the natural divine, desire of it.

Washington City amazed her, so beautifully designed, she, unable not to think about how few years it had been since the British had burned the Capitol, yet how all structures were now in excellent shape, its avenues and homes lovely.

But it was New York that she found exciting, exhilarating, fascinating: the theater, the opera, the museums, the extravagant boutiques. Theater in Nashville, as well as the opera, was limited to the traveling companies that made infrequent appearances, and there were no museums.

She delighted in the late suppers following evening performances, as well as Isaac's pleasantly surprising knowledge of the arts, as well as fine taste in dining.

He knew people wherever they were—important people. She was more impressed than she had imagined she could be with him, and also with his investment banker, Harry Stone, whom she found brilliant. At first, Isaac had apologized for having to conduct business on their honeymoon, but discovering her genuine interest, as well as her having a basic understanding of finance, he invited her to sit in on a business meeting with some associates, a meeting that was to be her first glimpse into Isaac's empire...that stretched from New York to Haiti to Louisiana to Texas to Tennessee.

She was well aware that there was a part of Isaac he never shared. Even before they were married, he had told her that her love of life, her quest for life itself, was sometimes greater than he understood. Also, it was the same quest that had drawn him to her. She wondered at moments—when she would see him looking at her with his extraordinary, captivating eyes—if she would ever know the force that drove him—that also held him in reserve.

"Darling, I especially loved today's meeting," she said as they undressed for bed one evening. "And I adore Rivers Thurmond. Are we really going to Haiti?"

"He adored you, too."

"Silly, I did not mean it that way."

"They all adore you," he said, playfully taking her in his arms. "That's the trouble with you."

"I cannot imagine what Haiti would be like, the voo doo, and seeing all those things he talked about! Do they really wear nothing at all?" she asked, excited.

He laughed at her large questioning eyes. "Tell you what. If the sugar cane deal goes through, I'll let you see for yourself. If not, I'll tell you about my experiences there."

"I am not sure I want to hear. On second thought, I do, I really do," she said, pulling him beside her into the soft down. "Thank you for asking me to attend."

She lay silently beside him in the dark, listening to his soft, steady breathing. She had loved their first night together aboard the *Tennesse*e, and all the nights and days that had followed, but an inward restlessness remained, forever torturing her to examine, to seek, to see each new experience, each new awakening, as a stepping stone to another. She wished to know the contentment that should by all rights be hers, but it remained ever elusive.

Making love with Isaac had been extraordinarily wonderful, awakening feelings all new to her. From that first night, he had been gentle and tender, rich and bold, the blend of which excited her. He taught her how to touch to please him; it also pleased her, and she longed for his touch. She felt his love for her, and she loved this handsome, enchanting man, twenty-eight years older than she. She could not put her feelings into words, not even to share with Camille.

She was overwhelmed with the things he bought for her, and she quickly learned that he could afford whatever she wanted.

Although Isaac was pleased to have her sit with him at a business meeting, she quickly understood that she was nothing more than an object on display. Whenever she had spoken of being more than a listener, later in the privacy of their suite, he either became edgy and changed the subject, or laughed and teased her. She sensed a secret, but she would concern herself no further with that now.

"Isaac?"

"Mmm?"

"When will you know about the island?"

"Don't you ever get sleepy?"

"I am thinking about sugarcane. Thousands of acres of sugar cane, and all ours! Divided between Rivers and John and Harry, but still so much of it. Ours! I cannot imagine having so much land. Can we build a house there?"

"My dear, you can imagine having anything that can be bought." He yawned. "How do you know you're going to like Haiti so much? The mosquitoes are as big as Tennessee rats, spiders as large as your fist, vipers the size of a man's body, the voo doo is shrouded in evil spirits, and the weather is so sticky one can hardly breathe."

"It is the voo doo I am dying to see. Rivers says the Louisiana voo doo you described in Congo Square is nothing compared with that in Port-au-Prince." She moved closer to her husband, "You must know by now, I do not frighten easily. The way he spoke of the drums, then the eerie silence." Her eyes widened. "Is it truly scandalous? Wicked?"

"If you don't let me get some sleep, I'm going to be too tired to work out the calculations with Thurmond in the morning." He put his arms beneath her, "It's been almost two months, and I'm still in love with you. That's a near record for me," he teased, kissing her tenderly on the lips.

"After you, I can never love another woman. You know you bewitch every man you meet? And you have cast a special spell on me."

She nuzzled closer to feel his strength beneath her as they made love once more.

Adelicia slipped out of bed and opened the window to hear the early morning sounds of New York. It seemed no one ever slept here.

She certainly had not wanted to sleep or to miss a single moment. She watched as the lamplighter went from one post to another, extinguishing the gas lights, then stopping beside one to take a long draw from his pipe before continuing on his rounds. She liked this city bustling with life, and she felt so alive, she wanted to shout or run or sing, or do all three together!

She looked over at her husband sleeping soundly and a surge of delight passed through her body. He brought feelings from within her that she never knew a woman could have, and the more she experienced, the more she wanted to experience. She pulled back the covers, and bending over him, kissed his face and neck and slowly ran the tip of her tongue over his lips and ears.

"Adie, I have to sleep," he said, barely moving his lips. "What time is it?"

"The sun is not quite up yet," she said, softly in his ear.

He moved his fingers down her back, "Just because you don't need to sleep doesn't mean no one else does."

She had succeeded in arousing him, and he began teasing her as he sleepily pulled her to him, slipped her negligee off her shoulders to the floor and ran his warm hands over her body.

It was late morning when they awoke, and Isaac hurriedly dressed while Adelicia lay in bed stretching and admiring her husband. He sat on the bed beside her, brushing her hair back away from her face, "We start for home tomorrow," he said, kissing the tip of her nose. "These three months have been a dream, as if this is the only world I've ever known." He looked at her decisively, lifting her hand, gently putting her palm to his lips, "I wish it were."

Chapter 17

Gallatin, September

"Hurry up, Sugart! They's a coming, they's a coming! Goodness to me, you gets slower every day. I's gonna start calling you, uncle, like everybody else. You acts old enough to be my uncle."

Uncle Sugart came into the kitchen, tottering on his cane and out of breath. "I's here, Aggie."

"I knows you here, Sugart," she said taking one more long draw from her pipe before putting it on the kitchen mantle. "I told you how I wants you to be and how I wants you to be standing when Mr. Isaac and Miss Adelicia come up the hill, just like we hearsed it."

"Aggie, they ain't got off the boat yet. You been rushin' me 'round all mornin,' with do this and do that."

"If I didn't rush you, you'd be meeting night in the morning."

"You being smart with me, Aggie, and I don't think I likes it one bit."

"Listen to the shoutin! What a great day, with Mr. Isaac bringing home his bride and her a fine lady." She paused. "Let's bow our head, Sugart." She folded her wrinkled brown hands and spoke softly. "We want to ask you to bless 'em with lots and lots of childrens to bring joy after all this time into this house, in the name of the dear Lord, Amen."

"That's them for sure," said Sugart, as he watched the entourage of Negro children dancing around their master and his bride as they walked up the sloping hill from the landing. They, too, would have a celebration.

"Get in place, Sugart. Get in place," she whispered out of the corner of her mouth, standing erect as her two hundred pounds were capable of doing, and putting on all the sophisticated airs she knew.

She curtsied as they stepped into the grand entrance hall, "Welcome home, Master Franklin, Mrs. Franklin. We delighted you arrive safe."

"What's happened to you, Aunt Aggie? You never called me master in your life. If you don't get that kink out of your back, you won't be able to walk for the next month." He put both arms around his mammy and hugged her. "We're glad to be home," he said as big tears welled up in her squinted eyes.

"I am glad to be home too, Aunt Aggie," said Adelicia, reaching for both her hands, following Isaac's example.

Isaac stood resting his arm around Uncle Sugart's bent shoulders. "Has Aunt Aggie been good to you without me around to take care of you?"

The old man grinned. "Tolerable well, tolerable well. We sure glad to have you home."

Adelicia took his hand. "We are glad to be home, Uncle Sugart. Isaac, tell the secret. You are the very first to know."

"Adelicia wants me to tell you, that come April, they'll be a baby at Fairvue."

"Lord have mercy, Lord have mercy!" Aunt Aggie said, fanning herself. "Did you hear that, Sugart Jacobs?" she asked, shaking his shoulder. "We're having a baby!" She raised both arms. "Thank you, Lord, thank you. Please sit down, Miss Adelicia. Let me hurry to the kitchen and get you some refreshment," she said, leaving the room, while congratulating herself about the baby.

"Della, didn't I tell you? I knowed she was quality. They already gonna have a child."

"Quality, quality, that's all I been hearing. She interested in one thing and only one thing, and that's getting Mr. Isaac's money."

"Della," Aunt Aggie sharply reprimanded. "That's enough and all I's gonna hear of it."

Glancing around the front parlor to her left, Adelicia rested her hand on the brass newel post of the grand staircase, savoring the moment of her arrival at Fairvue as its mistress.

"Uncle Sugart, remember what I wrote you about?" Isaac asked, walking over to Adelicia and putting his arm around her.

"In all the 'citement, I clean forgot." He slowly walked to the door opposite the entrance, leaning on his cane. "Everything just like you ask," he said, as Adelicia and Isaac followed behind him.

They stepped onto the rear portico to see the stable boy leading a beautiful sorrel gelding.

"What a magnificent animal," she exclaimed, "He is gorgeous!"

"Welcome to Fairvue, Adie. He is yours."

She and Isaac walked towards the stable boy, "Thank you, darling!" She kissed Isaac, then nuzzled her face against the horse's nose.

"You better be careful, Missus, this one mighty spirited," volunteered the stable boy.

She continued to stroke his long forehead and feel the massive jaws, "What is your name?"

"Luke, Ma'am."

Looking at him, she explained, "Luke, a horse is only as spirited as his rider permits. It is not necessary to even touch the animal for him to know who is in command." Luke let go of the tight rein, and the horse stood still and calm with Adelicia's hand touching only the harness. "Go saddle him, Luke. I am dying to ride over these wonderful acres and see Fairvue as its mistress!"

"Mr. Isaac, I don't know if it so good a idee for her to do no riding with the baby coming, and after that long trip," Sugart commented.

"Adie, we have had quite an excursion today. Wouldn't you like to rest a while, then ride later, together?"

"Isaac, darling, you know traveling does not tire me. And I want to ride...now." She paused, considering her strategy. "Uncle Sugart, what do you think would be a good name for this extraordinary creature? Think of a good one."

Isaac smiled as he lit a cigar, watching her flatter the old man.

"Well, Miss Adelicia, this animal strong and powerful, and the strongest name I can think of is Samson in de Bible. You say there ain't no such thing as a spirited horse, which I always thought there was, so I guess Samson's a good a name as any, cause everybody thought he's strong but a woman knowed better and tamed him, too."

Adelicia laughed, "I like the name, Uncle Sugart. Samson he shall be."

She turned, "Now, Luke, you take Samson and put a saddle on him, and I shall be ready..." she hesitated, "Better still, I shall walk to the stables with you. If I go inside, Aunt Aggie may not let me out again."

"Adie, are you sure you don't want to rest, just for a while?" Isaac asked, more persuasively.

"Yes, I am sure," she responded quickly, and just as quickly saw the flush in Isaac's face and thought she had best appear more compliant.

"Goodness gracious, darling, you gave me the horse, did you not? And I have no intention of letting the three of you make an invalid of me. This will be our baby's first ride."

She tossed her head, shaking her dark curls away from her face. "Will you come with me?"

"I'll be along in a minute. Saddle Imposter for me, Luke."

Adelicia, leading Samson, followed Luke to the stables. She would make no mention of riding boots, that would bring further delay. She would ride in her slippers.

Uncle Sugart went into the kitchen where Aunt Aggie was helping Della prepare the evening meal and sat down at the table. "What a woman, what a woman!" he said, shaking his head.

"What you talking about, Sugart Jacobs?"

"You know that gelding Mr. Isaac order and you say there ain't no woman could ever ride him? Well, that horse stand still as midnight when Miss Adelicia come near him. Then she say there ain't no such thing as a spirited horse, and she out there riding him right now."

"I don't believe it! She too well bred to go flaunting on a horse and her with child."

Della was slyly grinning as Sugart continued with his story. "Well, you may as well start believing cause she out there riding. Don't think Mr. Isaac like it a little bit neither, but you be seeing them come in after a spell. She asks me to name him, and I say Samson." He thought for a moment. "You know, I believe she got just a little bit of Delilah in her."

"She got more than any little bit. Just you wait," piped Della, still grinning.

Isaac rode behind her through the tall rows of corn, fascinated by the skill with which his wife handled the large mount and how gracefully she cantered. They had looked at horses together and talked about them endlessly, but he had no idea she rode with such expertise. Every movement was perfect, and Samson knew it was perfect.

When they had previewed prized stallions and mares in New York, Adelicia had been elated, looking over the horse flesh as if she were an experienced buyer. However, she had made no suggestions on purchases, just comments of delight as she viewed them in the ring. Isaac had made a number of selections for Fairvue, including the gelding.

"Come on, I'll race you to the river." She gave Samson full rein, jumped the gate, and had time to dismount before Imposter reached the Cumberland's banks and came to a halt beside her.

"You're sure full of surprises. Don't you ever stop to open a gate?"

"Not when it is in my way," she said, smiling.

Isaac looked at her thoughtfully, and after a moment said, "I sure as the devil knew you rode, but nothing like that. Five feet, two inch, ninety pound female, controlling a fifteen hundred pound gelding she's never ridden!"

She put her arms around Isaac's neck and kissed him lightly, "A girl is not supposed to reveal all her secrets at once," she teased. She looked up at him with flirting eyes, "Thank you for this beautiful creature, and thank you for being you." She kissed his face, his neck, then lightly closed her teeth on his ear lobe. "Do you think anyone would see us here?" she whispered.

"I don't think so, but I'm not concerned. Are you?"

"What do you think, darling?" she answered, running the tip of her tongue along his jowl line to his lips.

The horses made ripples in the cool water as they drank side by side on the river's edge, waiting for their masters.

By mid-October, the changing leaves had lost most of their glorious colors and lay crisp upon the ground. Adelicia was proving to be a competent mistress of the household, displaying firmness, expertly combined with genteel kindness, that kept things in proper perspective and order. Although some of the household servants complained that Adelicia was "working them like field hands," they willingly attended to the chores in making ready for the coming winter. The third floor of the country mansion had five small rooms on either side of the central hallway that were being restocked with clothing, bedding and provisions for the one hundred and fifty slaves. After taking a brief inventory, she had quickly ascertained that it was not to her expectations, thus additional labor was necessary to up-grade the quality as well as the quantity of each room's storage. Adelicia's tongue was seldom sharp, and the Negroes quickly learned the rewards for a task well done.

She had not felt like an intruder at Fairvue, and had easily and confidently slipped into the role of a planter's wife. She continued Rokeby's practice of Negroes making requests for clothing or bedding beyond that normally provided. She, herself made inquiries to see if those requests were valid. Wise mistresses knew that well cared for servants, kept in good health, proved the most efficient.

Dr. Kenneth Mentlo came from Gallatin to make monthly checks on the health of the Negroes, reporting directly to Adelicia if anyone needed care in the infirmary. Riding Samson, she made by-weekly trips to the small hospital located near the river's side of the brick slave houses to check on the ailing and disabled and make certain of their care. She also insisted that field hands with child be relieved of their regular duties beginning with the seventh month and continue until their babies were two months old. She kept a discerning and watchful eye on all the Negroes and their activities, as well as the business of the plantation itself. Isaac had permitted her that. In a short while, Adelicia had become a much respected and admired mistress.

But, to the chagrin of those on the plantation, Adelicia had also secured the services of Dr. Thomas Lawrence, a new dentist in Nashville, who had contracted on an annual basis to examine everyone's teeth on the plantation and make the necessary repairs. Dr. Lawrence had explained that the cool weather in late autumn would help keep down infection if extractions were necessary.

It was the first of November, and Adelicia was preparing everyone for Dr. Lawrence's visit at the end of the week. Most had never heard the word, "dentist," and the ones who had, knew little more of what to expect than wild rumors of having their teeth yanked out, leaving them to gum their food. But because of the trust they placed in their new mistress, it was unanimously accepted that their mouths would be checked.

"Aggie, I tells you one more time," Uncle Sugart said, clenching a cup of coffee between his hands at the far end of the kitchen table. "I don't have many tooths left, and what I does have I wants to keep. The good Lord never intended for no denny, or whatever she call him, to take no person's tooths from him, and I got no idee to be left gummin' till the Lord sees fit, and that's that," Uncle Sugart said, looking firmly at his wife. "It's hog killin time and curing time, and no time for tooth checking."

"Now, Sugart Jacobs, Miss Adie done honored us by having us two checked before the house servants, alongside her and Mr. Isaac, and I says you not going to cause her no trouble, or upset her none, or that baby, and I too says you going first, like all gentleman husbands would do, and like the brave person I is, I'll be next, then they check the in charge of operations, as she call them, then the field hands. And you, Sugart, is going first!"

Uncle Sugart sat stiffly in the chair moved out from the kitchen table where Dr. Lawrence had set up his examining instruments. The old man was so frightened, his jaws seemed locked together as his clenched muscles showed in the strain of his face.

"Now, Uncle Sugart," the dentist began gently, "this is just a small reflector mirror. Here, hold it," he said, putting the mirror into his hand. "All it does is help me see the back side of your teeth and gums that I can't see without it."

Uncle Sugart looked at the strange instrument in his shaking hand. "Now give it back to me, and I'll take a look in your mouth."

Aunt Aggie was staring along with Della, Daniel and the others, while Adelicia and Isaac smiled patiently as Uncle Sugart returned the tiny mirror and slowly opened his mouth.

"Why Uncle Sugart, your gums are some of the healthiest I've seen. Got some pretty bad stains from tobacco chewing, but I don't see a thing here that can't wait. Tell you what, I have another little tool that's just to probe around with, now if I touch any place that hurts, you let me know and I'll stop. All right?" The old man nodded approval and never flinched until Thomas Lawrence had completed his examination. "Tell you what, Isaac, if everybody's teeth and gums are as sound as Uncle Sugart's, my stay will be cut short to a couple of days. He has a few that could be tended to, but as long as they're not giving him any pain, we'll leave well enough alone." The old man gave a sigh of relief, grinned, stood erect with his chest out and readied the chair for Aunt Aggie, who no longer behaved as bravely now that it was her turn.

Dr. Lawrence's annual visit came to be known as the time of "wailing and gnashing." Caleb, perhaps the strongest field hand on the plantation, had been chosen to operate the drill, set up on the porch just outside the kitchen door. And it did not take him long to develop his natural rhythm in peddling the strange-looking machine beside the dentist' chair. He boasted that Dr. Lawrence could not have performed his work without him, and he was right.

The only relief was the liquor that flowed freely to help ease the pain of the much-feared drill and the pliers used for pulling. And two weeks later when Thomas Lawrence returned to Nashville, there was great joy that another year would pass before they would be subjected to his services again.

Chapter 18

Although the winter had been a cold one with more than the usual ice and snow, spring of 1840 had dawned early and Adelicia had continued to ride Samson, much to the despair of Isaac and the household at Fairvue. Her independent will refused to be countered. It was she who decided to ride more carefully, mostly allowing Samson to walk in his usual smooth gait. But at the beginning of March, she at last became a spectator, watching Luke exercise Samson in the ring each day.

"Spring is glorious," she said aloud to herself while sitting in the East garden waiting for Isaac among the diagonal rows of jonquils and hyacinths, tulips, sweet peas and snapdragons. She took deep breaths, inhaling the sacred aromas wafting about her and the soft scent of lilac, whose leafy branches hung so near that they touched her shoulders. She stretched her legs in front of her and leaned back in the white wood rocker, delighting in the sun's warmth and remembering.

However, her exuberant joy of expecting had been marred by the loss of her Mozzalpa, whom she had first ridden in the ring when she was four, and he a young three year old. The beloved horse had been her constant friend, her dearest friend; there had been no fear or distrust between them.

As a child, her mother almost gave in once and allowed Adelicia to sleep in his stall. Regardless, she had sneaked out to his stable many times in the early morning to feed him an extra carrot or apple and to hold his horsey face in her small hands. He knew to bend his long neck over so that she could pat his forehead. Uncle Will kept her secret as she slipped away and back into the house unnoticed. After breakfast, she would don her riding habit and head back to the stables. Uncle Will also alerted her to "washing time," and although her mother had thought Adelicia's desire to groom and scrub her own horse unladylike, she permitted it.

Adelicia loved Samson, but she did not believe she could ever love him as much as Mozzalpa. She had cried herself to sleep the afternoon that Isaac had received word from her father at the Virginia Springs where they had stopped on their way back from their honeymoon. The letter simply said that Mozzalpa did not get up one morning when Uncle Will had brought his oats, that he had not awakened from his sleep. They had buried him on the grounds at Rokeby.

Still resting her head against the back of the white wooden rocker, it was a happier thought when she reminisced about the Twelfth Night ball that she and Isaac had hosted in January at Fairvue, when Camille had told her that everyone trembled with fear their names might be omitted from the guest list, the same ones that the year before were in shock over the announcement of her marriage to Isaac. And she would never forget how lovely and radiant Camille had looked when Mr. Perkins announced her engagement to Joel that evening and all the merry-making that followed.

Her father had walked among the guests beaming, obviously pleased with his future daughter-in-law, his son Joel's election to Congress, his present son-in-law and the prospect of soon becoming a grandfather. She smiled with pleasure recalling her father standing between Camille and Isaac, telling them how happy he was that they were a part of his family.

Adelicia looked down at her bulging figure and at her large bosoms shadowing over her abdomen. Dr. Mentlo had said she was made for having babies, and she admitted that she did not mind it at all, providing her waist measurement would be twenty-one inches again.

Isaac found her in the garden, dozing with both hands resting beneath her protruding middle, as if she were already cradling their child in her arms. He stood behind her and gently straightened the gold locket she had worn since the night he first gave it to her, then bent over and kissed the tip of her nose.

"I am resting," she said dreamily.

"An unusual thing for my Adie," he teased, taking her by the hand.

"Spring must be God's favorite time of year," she said, as Isaac helped her up from the low-set rocker. They strolled down a winding lane at the rear of the house beneath strong oaks and maples, some of whose branches, sprouting new green leaves, touched the ground. "Life renewed, and new life, as if we, too, are contributing to spring," she said, stooping to pluck a deep pink peony.

"When I was a little girl," she continued, "I used to walk in the woods like this with Papa and as we walked, he would stop and have me feel the texture of each leaf and its veins; he taught me the names of the trees, how to recognize them by their leaves and bark. After I repeated the names, he would tell me stories..." She put her hand on the lower part of her abdomen and bent forward, still holding the flower in her hand.

"What's wrong?" Isaac asked anxiously.

"Nothing alarming. Perhaps we should return to the house. I am feeling hungry."

"After the breakfast you ate! Three thick omelets, six slices of bacon, four biscuits dripping with butter, two cups of cocoa."

"How you do exaggerate, my husband." He put his arm around her shoulders, as they strolled slowly back to the house.

"What in the devil's name are you doing now?" he asked sometime later, walking into the nursery. Isaac set the tray of sliced roast beef and fresh fruit beside her and watched.

"What does it look like?" Adelicia was sitting on the floor tacking another row of yellow satin ribbon with petite rosettes on the skirt of the baby's walnut poster bed. "And when I finish this," she said between bites, "I am going to add more netting to the canopy."

"I'm not leaving your side for the rest of the day. The next thing I know, you'll be galloping on Samson!"

"Mmm," she teased, "I so miss riding him. He is a fine horse, darling."

Adelicia woke Isaac in the middle of the night, again holding her lower abdomen, to tell him she was feeling strange.

"Probably indigestion from what you've eaten today," he teased, putting one arm beneath her pillow and wrapping the other around her.

"It feels different from that. My stomach is cramping like when—it is my time," she blurted.

He sat up immediately. "Are you having pains?"

"No, just cramps. But they are getting stronger. Why are we whispering?"

"I'll send Luke after Doc Mentlo," he said, hurriedly dressing.

"I do not think he will have time to get here."

"What do you mean not have time? You're supposed to have...do you mean it's ready?" He pulled on the last boot, ran down the steps and soon had the entire household frantically running and fetching. Just as quickly, he was sitting beside her on the bed again. "Luke's on his way. Tell me what to do."

"I am fine, really I am, just stay with me. I feel much better when you are here. The cramps are much stronger now."

He held her hands in his and did not let go until the doctor asked him to leave the room just minutes before Victoria Hayes Franklin was born.

"Is she not the most precious three-day-old baby you have ever seen?" asked Adelicia, as the infant nursed at her breast.

"She's the most precious, beautiful, any-day-old there's ever been," said Isaac, gazing adoringly at the child in her arms. "I wired Benedict to buy a cask of the best Port available and send it up river with John. We'll store it in the cellar till Victoria's wedding day."

Adelicia laughed, "I am anxious to meet Crawford Benedict. Are you going to do this for each of your daughters?"

"I certainly am," he said, bending over and kissing her. "Are we also having sons?"

"I think we can manage," she flirted.

"Are you sure it wasn't that bad?"

"I am sure. I enjoyed...that is, if I do not stay fat. April, May, June," she counted on her fingers. "June will be a perfect time for us to go down to New Orleans, then on to Haiti."

"It will be ungodly hot, my love. One does not go in the summer heat. And what about little Victoria?"

"She will go with us, of course. Essie can be her nurse now that Papa has Jenny for Laura and Corrine. Besides, Laura and Bliss are both in school. I mentioned it to Essie at Christmas and…"

"And you finally persuaded her as you will persuade me. What's Aunt Aggie going to say when you tell her you're taking her baby? But I'm sure you've worked that out too."

"My immediate concern is how I am going to fit into those beautiful dresses for Camille's parties and wedding. In less than five weeks, my waist has to be at least twenty-one inches. I hate corsets, but I refuse to look matronly. The only time my waist will be large is when I am having your babies, my dearest Mr. Franklin."

"Mr. Isaac?" Aunt Aggie called, tapping on the bedroom door.

"Come in, Aunt Aggie."

"Luke had your horse waiting for near an hour now. He want to know if you still planning to go to town?"

"Sure am. It's very difficult to leave two beautiful women. But, I suppose I'd better take care of business." He kissed the sleeping infant and then Adelicia.

"Do not forget about Haiti," she called.

She watched the baby resting beside her in the crib and thought how joyful it was to be a mother. Pregnancy, giving birth and nursing had been natural to Adelicia—she, who had seemed to school friends and acquaints the least likely to ever enjoy motherhood. Until Victoria, she admitted she had found the company of children a nuisance, but now thought it the most wonderful of experiences. This morning, she had already changed Victoria's lace and entre deaux trimmed dress twice, as Isaac had agreed the blue batiste was more becoming than the yellow.

She did wish Camille could have delayed her wedding. However, she could not fault her for wanting to be with Joel when he attended the congressional meetings in Washington City that summer. His election had been unanimous, and Isaac had been a major supporter.

After Camille's wedding, Adelicia wanted to return to New Orleans, which she had savored from the first moment, and then visit Haiti. This trip to the City of New Orleans would prove far more interesting than the one before her marriage when her entire family had been with her, and Crawford Benedict had been out of town. They had also not visited West Feliciana.

Now that she was Isaac's wife and a mother, she would make serious inquiries into the private girls' schools there. Middle Tennessee had nothing to compare with the City's aristocratic French schools, and she intended to see that her children were enrolled in the best.

"Adie, I'm frightened," confided Camille as she and her future sister-in-law sat in Fairvue's formal garden near the ice house. It was a beautiful May morning, the sun was warm, and a cool breeze blew up from the Cumberland's bank below. "What if I don't like everything the way you did? Joel has had no experience," she blushed. "I 'm glad he hasn't, I suppose, but neither of us knows…have no knowledge of… anything."

Adelicia smiled, "My brother may surprise you. I am certain you will surprise yourself. Remember, I, too, was an innocent. It is the feeling of being loved, of being cherished, of returning love…that makes up for experience."

She was suddenly all too aware that she was having to search for the right words, words that would not tell her best friend that her marriage of less than a year was no longer what she had idealized. Though happy with being a wife and mother, changes were occurring within her that she did not understand, that she hesitated sharing with Camille lest even she would misunderstand.

It was not pleasant to admit to herself that perhaps she had idealized loving Isaac to the point of believing. However, upon examining her self-doubts, their importance quickly diminished and for days were erased from her thoughts all together…most likely, the post-birth downs that Dr. Mentlo assured her were quite normal.

She slipped her hand into Camille's and continued, "Isaac says the oneness, knowing you were a part of someone, they were a part of you, made it different for him, in ways he had not experienced before. Anyway," she said, taking both of Camille's hands in hers. "You and Joel love each other very much, and it will be just as wonderful for the two of you as it was for Isaac and me. Our first night, when I stood in my silk negligee that you and I had taken out of my chest so many times to touch and admire and fantasize over, I was not Papa's little girl anymore, nor the model of a young lady. I was a woman, Isaac's wife. And when he held me close to him, feelings rushed over me that I never knew existed, extraordinary feelings, that tingled and surged through my body, making me strong and weak in the same moment, and when he lifted me to the bed, still kissing me, I wanted all the mysteries of lovemaking that the night could bring. I wanted to be part of the magic of the unknown." She smiled at the remembrance and wished that very night to feel that way again.

"You simply have the pre-marital frights like all young ladies have. Remember how nervous I was when I spent that last night with you and we talked till daybreak?"

"Having babies frightens me too."

"That is the best part, Camille! Victoria was here before I knew it. The pain was like having our time of the month…except just before she came…they were strong when I pushed…but it only lasted for seconds…of course you have heard me tell this before."

"It didn't seem as real then."

"You, my dear friend, have never been afraid of anything! Have you forgotten the pact of Nashville's two most indomitable females? 'Camille Perkins and Adelicia Hayes, born with silver spoons, afraid of neither man nor…'"

"I remember, I remember," Camille laughed, "but you've always been the braver. What happened the great day of the rattlesnake? I panic, my horse rears, I get thrown. You sit Mozzalpa like a knight in armor and stare it down."

They laughed. "The great day of the rattlesnake! We were fourteen. I remember coming home and telling Papa, and no one believed me, then Richard and Joel heard about it and Joel said, 'Well, thank the Lord, Camille at least had the good sense to try and get away.' He always took your side."

"I love your brother and I'll love you always as my best friend and sister-to-be."

"Me too. Now we must behave maturely and stop this sniffling. Would it not be fun if you and Joel could live with us?" They burst into laughter.

"It would be wonderful, except that neither man could bear it," Camille said, wiping away tear drops. "You always get me in the best moods and make me laugh. We are silly, aren't we?"

Della interrupted as they still sat in the West garden, sipping lemonade. "Excuse me, Miss Adelicia, Miss Camille, but Aunt Aggie say it feeding time."

"Tell her I shall feed Victoria out here, Della."

"I done thought of that, and she say the bright sun not good for her baby."

Adelicia laughed. "Tell dear Aunt Aggie to...We are on the way."

CHAPTER 19

1841

A LATE WINTER TRIP TO NEW ORLEANS PROVED TO BE AS MEM-orable, as exciting as Adelicia had anticipated. Although Isaac was accustomed to spending September through May in Louisiana and only the summer months in Tennessee, he had departed from the usual arrangements, desiring that Victoria be older before venturing to the deep-south. Thus, they had spent a delightful Christmas and New Year's with family at Rokeby and Fairvue.

On the way down river, they had stopped in Natchez and gone directly to Isaac's house there, an elegant, low-country mansion with massive columns on all four sides that stood idle most of the year, its heavy, musty odor, proof of its lack of use.

After docking in the early afternoon, Isaac and Adelicia walked over the grounds that lay high atop a bluff overlooking the wide Mississippi River below. She had watched the sun's last rays drop behind the flat lands of Louisiana to the west, fascinated as they cast colored pools, shimmering against the still, glass-like water.

Later, when old Anna served supper on the verandah, Adelicia found it delightful dining outdoors in mid-February wearing only a shawl over her long-sleeved dress. She took an immediate liking to Natchez, and was certain she would find Louisiana, their houses and land there, gloriously wonderful, as well.

The following morning, after Isaac returned from his bank in town, they again boarded *The Tennessee* to travel the remaining fifty miles downriver to their own dock, Routh's landing.

It was difficult for Adelicia to contain her excitement as at last she would see the West Feliciana plantations—all twelve thousand acres of them. She stood on the bow with Isaac, and when they reached the mouth of the Red River where it flowed into the Mississippi on their right, and he began to point out their land to the left, she was astounded. And after making the great loop in the river, and turning east, where the green levees protected their property on either side, it continued for another ten nautical miles. It was difficult for her to believe one person could own so much land with so much access to so much waterway. They were richer than she had imagined!

Alfred and Lucy warmly welcomed Adelicia as the mistress of Bellevue, where congratulations and gifts awaited them from local planters and neighbors. The couple was overjoyed with ten-month-old Victoria, whom Lucy immediately took from Adelicia's arms, exclaiming, "My, my. This finest baby ever come into the world."

It was an old, very large, West Indies-style cypress and log house, with living quarters on the second and third floors. It was not pretentious like the glamorous homes she had seen along the river and was probably built, she imagined, early in the century. She would ask Isaac its history; but right away it felt comfortable and homelike, a feeling that pleased her. She would, however, see to its refurbishing when they went to the City; it was missing her touch.

After two weeks of acquainting herself with the area, riding Samson, who had traveled with them, day after day over the land, seeing the fields under cultivation, the sawmill, the gin house, the grist mill, the livestock, each being managed on separate plantations, seeing the magnificent Lake of the Cross on Loch Lomond, visiting in Bayou Sara and its twin town, St. Francisville, and being introduced to the neighbors, they boarded *The Tennessee* at Routh's Landing, and left for The City of New Orleans.

Gifts and congratulations from Isaac's business associates, friends from the city and nearby parishes awaited them at the St. Charles Hotel, where Crawford Benedict had taken care of the arrangements. Adelicia's pleasure mounted with each gathering where they were royally entertained; the Benedicts were usually a part of the company.

She adored the charming Crawford. He was a few years younger than Isaac, not quite as tall, with strands of barely gray that streaked through thick brown hair, creating a perfect frame for his deep set chocolate eyes. But she did not care for Joanna Benedict. In fact, she loathed the chattering, buxom wife of Isaac's best friend. However,

Joanna was beneficial in introducing her to the right people and giving her entrée to the social prominence she was set on attaining in the Crescent City.

As the wife of a shipping magnate, Joanna was received in all of the circles and constantly asked to support charities and causes with her presence or expertise. But Joanna did not need her husband's prestige for social prominence. She was the daughter of one of Louisiana's oldest American families, and her father, the state's first United States Senator, had made a fortune in sugar cane. She had grown up wealthy and married wealthy, but Adelicia wondered where Joanna's dullness would find itself if it were not for either her father's or Crawford's acquired fortunes. But it was definitely to her advantage to befriend Mrs. Benedict.

In the beginning, Adelicia was uncertain if it were from curiosity or sincerity that she so quickly became a sought after guest of those entertaining at teas or elegant luncheons. Even the French aristocrats, who seldom accepted anyone not of their own affluent heritage, invited her into their intimate circles. But after some time, she felt their acceptance genuine...as genuine as she had felt anyone's with the exception of a few close friends like Camille, Susannah and Margaret in Nashville.

She attended luncheons and afternoon teas and supported their charities, even the Catholic ones. Her superb taste in clothing was rivaled by no one, and she charmed those of French origin by singing in their native tongue.

Adelicia was pleased with Isaac's many friends and associates within the city and reveled in how well known and respected he was along the river. They were courted both politically and socially. Isaac had made considerable donations to charities, and to the Ursaline School for Girls, attended by the French Catholics, and to the LeFare School for Young Ladies, where little Victoria was already enrolled to begin classes at age four.

"Darling, I can hardly contain my excitement!" Adelicia said, pushing her dress in at the waist for Isaac to button. "Our first open house, our first entertaining in this marvelous city! Do you think they'll come?"

"I'm excited too, my darling wife. The entertaining I've done here to fore now, I've been both host and hostess. It will be grand repaying all those in whose homes I've been. And to answer your silly question, yes, everyone will be here from up and down the river to all over town. This is the City of New Orleans."

"And our special guest...he must come. We shall be the envy of everyone!"

Isaac had rented a townhouse for the first half of the year at 50 Rue Royal. The rooms were richly furnished, and for the occasion, Adelicia had filled every available spot with fresh cut flowers and native plants in full bloom. The walkways were lit with lanterns, and candlelight glowed throughout the house.

Beginning at half past eight, carriages lined Chartres and Rue Royal from Canal Street to Esplanade, and well-dressed drivers gathered on street corners to visit.

"Darling, how do I look?" Adelicia asked, as she smoothed the satin rosettes attached to delicate piping, cascading from her waistline to the floor over the ice blue satin skirt of her gown.

"Outstanding, my dearest. This color is my favorite on you," he said, fastening the pearl choker's diamond clasp. "Ice blue and perfect pearls...Mrs. Franklin, you are glamorous indeed."

"Thank you, Mr. Franklin," she said, playfully curtsying, "Shall we go meet our guests?"

The house, as well as the enclosed courtyard, was filled with handsomely dressed men in velvet cutaways and silk shirts, and women dressed in imported silks and laces, sparkling with jewels. It appeared that everyone of importance in the city was a guest of the Franklins. They were pleased that Randal McGavock was down from Nashville. Of course, Adelicia wanted him to go back and tell everyone what a splendid gathering he had attended in her home.

"Who is the elegant beauty everyone is gathered around?" asked Lieutenant Joseph Acklen.

"That is your hostess, my boy," answered Crawford Benedict, standing beneath the curved staircase, "and this scene, you'll see wherever she goes. People, especially men, flock to her like bees to honey. Come, I'll introduce you."

"Not just now. I'll observe a while first." He stood watching, his thick light brown hair falling in disarray about his forehead, as she graciously weaved her way among the guests.

At the height of the evening, Isaac took a position halfway up the spiral staircase. "May I have everyone's attention, please?" he called. The large crowd gradually quieted. "We did not announce this prior to the gathering for fear there would be disappointment if our much honored and revered guest should be unable to attend or for fear we would be mobbed by well-wishers. However, I have just received word that his carriage has arrived, so if the musicians will play 'A Mighty Fortress Is Our God.' Begin softly please," he directed. The front door opened, and the old gentleman stepped forward, leaning on his cane. A hush prevailed. "Ladies and gentlemen, our former President, General Andrew Jackson."

Gasps of excitement and awe filled the room. He had been New Orleans' savior from the British. It had been rumored he was coming to the city, but because of failing health, no one was sure if he would be able to attend the ceremony planned in his honor.

A plot of land directly between Saint Louis Cathedral and the Mississippi River would be named Jackson Square and an enormous bronze likeness of him, mounted on his steed in battle array, would be set into place at its center. But now he was here. Adelicia had accomplished what no other hostess had been able to do. She walked among the guests holding the General's arm, seeing that he did not become too tired, or have too long a visit with any one person.

"It is an honor to meet you, sir. My grandfather, General John Hunt from Alabama, fought with you in two wars."

"Yes, yes, I remember him...a fine soldier. And what's your name, son, and what's your occupation?"

"Lieutenant Joseph Smith Acklen, General, from Huntsville."

"You tell everybody in Huntsville that I was especially proud to meet John's grandson. You seem a fine young man...and I'm not often fooled...you ought to go far." He looked at Adelicia and nodded to move on.

"If you will excuse us, Lieutenant," she said.

Adelicia was propped up in bed, too excited to sleep. "Do you know what the General said to me? He said, 'Miss Adelicia, I'm just sorry my Rachel could not be here to enjoy all this...she would have been charmed by you and likewise...no one else like her,' he said, 'Only one Rachel.' Isn't that romantic, darling? I met her once at the Hermitage when I visited with my father, and the General a second time when he visited Rokeby, but I was very small. Papa thinks there's no political figure who bears comparison to Andrew Jackson."

Gently nudging him, she asked, "Did you know that I was born on the General's fiftieth birthday? It was also the same date that Julius Caesar was assassinated."

Isaac, paying little attention, was trying to sleep.

"Isaac?"

"It's four o'clock in the morning." He reached for her hand and sleepily put his arms around her, "Good night, my dearest wife. How beautiful to have you as hostess. Thank you."

CHAPTER 20

Bellevue Plantation

"GOOD EVENING, WILLIAM," SHE SAID, AFFECTIONATELY GREETING her brother-in-law with a kiss. She liked William. At age forty-seven, he was boisterous, handsome and rowdy, and kept what she considered a harem of women about. One also never doubted where one stood with him. William had traveled briefly with his older brothers to Natchez while in his early teens, and following in their footsteps, foresaw the financial advantages of the interstate slave trade, but he quickly found the business uncomfortable, and also began speculating in land and livestock, soon separating himself from it. He, like his brothers, had stayed near the home place near Pilot's Knob in Sumner County, all of whom had built grand homes on either side of the Nashville-Gallatin Pike.

"We've been waiting for you," he answered. "John Armfield and Crawford are having their second rounds." Adelicia took his arm and walked into the large parlor with its strong masculine appeal and took a seat at the oversized game table as the three men stood.

It was the one room at Bellevue that she would leave untouched. It was so thoroughly Isaac with its heavy wooden furniture, his copies of *Spirit of the Times* strewn about, stout tables where he and his planter friends could rest their boots, and chairs that could be leaned back in without fear of breaking. It smelled of cigar and pipe tobacco and the unmistakable scent of Tennessee whiskey.

She was in the process of redecorating the other rooms. The owner of Mallard's in New Orleans had spent more than two weeks at Bellevue assisting her with fabric, paint, wallpaper samples and the latest in floor coverings. The exterior of the old cypress house would retain its textured informality, as well as the interior, but Isaac had given her full rein to redecorate and refurbish, just as he had at

Fairvue. Mostly, her taste was similar to his own, but he liked her feminine touches.

In fact, he gave her full rein in all areas except in his world of business, about which he remained vague and secretive. And it was only after much persuasion that he had agreed for her to meet with his partners on this particular evening when they would be discussing the investments to be made in Haiti. Her interest had begun on their honeymoon when he had invited her to a few meetings with Rivers Thurmond and Harry Stone. She had listened intently then, savoring the idea of fields of sugar cane. She wanted to own a part of it—a part that would be hers alone. She did not find that too much to ask.

"Thank you," she said to Isaac. "And thank you, gentlemen, for allowing me to join you."

Isaac looked at her, pleased, as he settled into his chair with the elephant hide seat. Adelicia, sitting to Isaac's left, quickly noticed that each man had stacks of papers before him and others were scattered over the large table. "We are happy to have you, my dear."

She found the discussion of dollars and profits fascinating, and was beginning to sip from her first glass of sherry, when Isaac apologized for having discussed business for so long a time, and looking at the mantle clock, suggested that she retire for the evening before they brought out their pipes and cigars. She was so caught up in the idea of additional wealth, their talk of how much control they wanted and expected in the sugar cane market, that she had failed to recognize his annoyance with her presence until he spoke, although it was his typical reaction whenever he thought her becoming too interested in his business affairs.

"Gentlemen, as my husband suggested, I must leave now," she said sweetly, at which remark Isaac smiled approvingly. But still seated, she added, "Before I do, I wish to ask if you would oppose my being a sixth partner in the sugar cane operation? I have funds from my wedding dowry."

Crawford grinned and leaned back on two legs of his chair, while John and William looked at her in shocked surprise. She knew they were awaiting Isaac's reaction, which did not take long. Their graciousness at the beginning of the evening had been obviously to appease her.

"Adelicia, I believe you said it was time for you to be going." Isaac rose to his feet, as did the others, "if you'll excuse us."

She was embarrassed and humiliated in front of Isaac's friends and family, and she hated the pious looks on John's and William's faces. She turned the sherry glass up, draining its contents, and as she set it on a nearby table, the delicate stem shattered on the old marble surface.

Adelicia pushed her chair back, glaring, "I was reared to have more sense than to be an ornament, as perhaps some of you view ladies. I had hoped to be more than that this evening." She tossed her head, her hair flowing about her face, "Have a pleasant evening, gentlemen," she said through partially closed lips. Then, curtsying with mocked graciousness, she left the room.

Three weeks had passed since that disturbing evening at Bellevue, and little more than pleasantries had been exchanged between the two of them. She loved Isaac, their intimacy, and was unhappy by the silence and disparity that now loomed. She simply could not understand his lack of wanting her to have her own venture into business, a small part over which she would have control. However, the trip to Haiti had at last commenced, and she had decided to behave as cordially as possible during the two-day voyage from New Orleans.

"I do not feel comfortable leaving Victoria with Fanny and Lucy," Adelicia said sweetly. "She adores them, but she has just been weaned. It would be better if they had come with us. I would not be surprised if they give her a sugar teat every time she cries. If only Essie were here. What is the doctor's name again?" Adelicia asked.

"Lucas Gee, Harvard man, has a new office in St. Francisville. He's not only the best there is between Natchez and Baton Rouge, he's better. Martha Turnbull told me that every doctor in the area seeks him out for advice, that if anything difficult occurs, it's Lucas who takes care of it. When we get to Haiti, you'll see why I didn't want Victoria to come. It's not healthy, and it's simply as hot as hell this time of year."

"You do not have to be profane about it."

"That happens to be how hot it is."

"If anyone ought to know, you should," she snapped, despite herself.

"Look, Adie, I'm not sure how we got into this. I'm sorry if my language offended you," he said, "You are so touchy, darling. If you didn't want to leave our daughter, we could have waited until late autumn. But you insisted on coming now and in another hour, we'll see land."

She said nothing for a moment, but stared at him in obvious resentment, "I do not like being asked to leave a room," she said. "I might add that it will be best if it never happens again. Lest you forget, I am not one of your women to whom you can give orders."

She despised the look she saw in his face. Obviously, she should have kept the thoughts she had been harboring to herself.

"How long have you been seriously considering becoming a business partner, my love?" She gave no reply. "Even before we were married?"

He relit his cigar and stood looking at her. "Adelicia, I made the assumption that you could live quite comfortably on my income. Unless I'm more deceived than I think, you seem content enough as long as everything we have is a little finer and a little better than whatever anyone else has, and that sort of trifling doesn't bother me in the least. But you are not going to engage in business with me, my friends, or anyone else, now, or any time in the future. And as long as you understand that, all will be well."

He flipped the ashes over the side of the ship. "The property and income in Haiti will be ours. How did you phrase it on our honeymoon? 'Thousand of acres of sugar cane, and all ours?' Or is 'ours' no longer enough for you?"

"The first thing you should learn, Isaac, is to never make assumptions," she answered calmly, as if she had heard nothing beyond his first words. She went to her stateroom, uncomfortable as it was, unhappy that she had allowed her idle talk to again overcome her.

Chapter 21

Haiti

Rivers Thurmond was waiting at the harbor with a carriage and driver.

"I've looked so forward to this visit and seeing you once more," Adelicia said charmingly.

He took her hands in his. "Isaac, marriage and motherhood sure does agree with this gorgeous wife of yours. How was the trip?" he asked her.

"Wonderful! It could not have been better. Could it, Isaac, darling?"

Rivers smiled. "Aside from the balls and entertainment, I've arranged for the Governor's wife, Madame DuMond, to take you shopping and sightseeing."

After Adelicia glanced at Isaac, then back at Rivers, "Of course," he said, "if you'd rather not, but if I remember correctly, you loved seeing the sights every moment in New York."

"I can think of nothing I had rather do than shop and sightsee with the Governor's wife. When do we begin?"

Isaac feigned a congenial smile at her sarcasm.

"Our currency is a French exchange," Rivers said. "But all that's been taken care of. We want you to enjoy yourself."

Everything except for riding horseback through sugar cane fields, planning her plantation house and seeing the *real* Haiti, she thought. She always knew that when she went to Europe, and she would go, she would not have excursions planned for her. She would control her own agenda, her own grand tour, not what someone else decided for her.

"What about the voo doo? You did remember?" she asked as engagingly as she could manage.

"Sure did…If it's agreeable to Isaac, it's on for tomorrow night."

"It is agreeable with you, is it not, darling?" she asked in the same feigned sweetness.

"I'm looking forward to it every bit as much as you, my dear," he answered.

Port-au-Prince was lovely, she thought, as they rode in the open carriage. Brightly colored houses and dark skinned children playing beneath large leafed palm trees, swaying in a gentle breeze, instantly charmed her. Not so hot as Isaac had said, it smelled of soft sweetness, lifting from blooming plants, flowers and ocean air. She wanted to do more, much more than spending her days lunching with the American, French and Creole ladies of Haiti.

"Tell me more about the shopping," she said, thinking to act interested in River's planned activities for her might prove profitable.

"There's a seamstress here who designs clothes for all the Spanish and French aristocrats. I'm sure she'll be on Madam DuMond's list of places...but I warn you, she's expensive."

"Expense is of no consequence, Mr. Thurmond," she smiled, as the carriage stopped in front of a quaint, elegant inn, with sets of large glass paned doors opening onto the street. The native help, all dressed in white cotton and wearing white gloves, stood like sentinels in a row awaiting their arrival. "I must get my rest before the Governor's ball tonight," she said, excusing herself, and following one of the porters inside.

"You're a lucky man, Isaac. I've said it before; I'll say it again."

"There's no such thing as luck, Rivers."

The night of voo doo was as exciting to Adelicia as Rivers Thurmond had promised. The women danced bare-chested with nothing more than brief sarongs tied loosely below their navels. The men wore even less...partial sarongs with their buttocks in plain view. Their movements began slowly in cadence to the low sounds of the drum beats. The motions were quick, sensual, artistic. The beats gradually rose, generating more and more excitement...then total silence. The Voo Doo Queen walked into the center of the group, naked, and began slowly writhing, swaying from side to side, front to back, her long black hair brushing the ground as she dipped and turned her flawless body. But suddenly, she stopped, stretched out her hands, turning her back to the audience.

A sheer woven cloth was immediately draped over her, then a low murmuring, before the chief walked over and told the two white men that Adelicia would have to leave.

"I'm really sorry," Rivers said, as they rode the six miles back into Port-au-Prince. "It took all the maneuvering I could think of to clear it with the chief to bring Isaac. I'd thought by sitting in the back, you wouldn't be noticed in the darkness, Adelicia. White people consult New Orleans' Queen, Marie Laveau, for advice as well as for her gris-gris charms of good and evil, but she, and those from the Saint Dominique line, believe a white woman brings bad luck. They won't dance before one. On the other hand, they believe the one watching will also have bad luck."

"Please, do not apologize. I am most appreciative of your efforts, and greatly impressed with what we saw," she said. "My husband says we can attend a voo doo ceremony at Congo Square in New Orleans, but I shall never forget tonight," she said, putting her hand into Isaac's. "It gave me chills. I never dreamed such things existed! Tales are only tales, until seen. I do not think, however, I shall share my adventure at home. And like my husband, I do not believe in luck, good or bad."

She was enjoying Haiti, despite the ladies' affairs, and she and Isaac were behaving civilly to each other, but she would not be satisfied until she could become a part of his world, the one in which he thought she had no place. Although some plans were altered so that she might ride over the fields and view the land with the investors, she was still doing the things wives were supposed to do.

Adelicia seldom enjoyed the company of females, but she had found Madame DuMond a gracious and charming middle-aged woman who fascinated her with tales of the island and its history. Next to their last day was to be spent with more shopping, followed by a formal dinner that evening.

"You'll love Madame de Bloviere's clothes," Madame DuMond said as she road with Adelicia in an open carriage pulled by two chestnut mares. "She designs everything herself. Even the smallest detail is exquisitely sewn. Her orders are taken three to four months in advance, but it is worth the wait. Ah, we are here at last." They alighted from the carriage, met by a young man, dressed in fine livery and stepped inside the quaint shop.

"Is Madame in, Missy?"

"Oui, oui, Madame Governor, excuse s'il vous plait."

While waiting for Madame, the two women looked around the tastefully decorated room filled with luscious silks, tapestries, French laces, satins, linens and wools...every sort of expensive, coveted fabric.

"Madame DuMond! I am glad you have come. We need one more fitting on the blue taffeta."

"If we may, I shall save that until tomorrow; I have promised my guest that she may have all your attention today."

Adelicia smiled pleasantly at the strikingly attractive design-er-seamstress who, oddly enough, looked familiar. "I have heard only the best about you, Madame de Bloviere."

"Merci. Madame DuMond is very kind."

"Not kind, truthful. Madame de Bloviere, this is our guest Madame Franklin, whose husband is investing with Monsieur Thurmond in sugar cane. What is it Madame? Are you ill? Missy, come see about Madame!"

She waved her away, "No, no, I am fine. Just a slight dizzi-ness, Cheri."

Suddenly, Adelicia knew why Madame had appeared so famil-iar: it was the second time the two women had stood facing each other. Although there had been only one brief glimpse on the stairs at Fairvue, Madame de Bloviere was unmistakably Lona. Neither woman acknowledged the recognition of the other, and it was Lona who spoke first, graciously asking, "How may I help you, Madame Franklin?"

Adelicia blushed. Her heart beat was rapid and her palms, cold and damp. The meeting brought pain, the pain of uncertainty—why Lona's and her paths had crossed once more. Lona's presence was no longer a girlish shock to discuss with friends. Had Isaac known

Lona was there? Was this part of his secret? Had Rivers known and purposefully deceived her? Surely not.

"She is very beautiful, Isaac," Adelicia said as they were dressing that evening for dinner, while a servant packed for them in the adjoining sitting room of their suite.

"The Queen of the voo doo is quite something. I asked Rivers to try and arrange to shock you, but I don't think you're shockable." He pulled on his fine leather boots, a pair Adelicia had selected and given him some months prior, while Adelicia fussed with her hair in the mirror.

"I am not speaking of the voo doo Queen."

"Then surprise me," he said playfully, "and tell me who is beautiful besides yourself."

"Madame de Bloviere."

"And who is the beautiful and mysterious Madame de Bloviere?"

"She owns the dress shop where Madame DuMond took me today, the one Rivers recommended so favorably."

Continuing to tease her, he asked, "How many gowns did you buy? Of course, you just ordered nine in New Orleans."

"She also makes children's clothing."

"You are avoiding telling me how much you spent." He walked to her dressing table, leaned over and put his arms around her as she still sat in front of the mirror. "But you know you may have whatever you want."

She remained cold and unresponsive. "I did not buy anything," she said, looking up at him in the mirror. "I did not tell you all of her name."

"Then please tell me the full name of this rapturous being who has so enchanted my wife before we are late to supper."

"Lona...Madame Lona de Bloviere."

For three years, Isaac had suppressed any thoughts of Lona. He had not known where she was, nor had he tried to find out. He had checked only on Bess and Moriah, asking no questions. Now the past came rushing back, flooding his thoughts. To know she was on the island, to know she was near, gave him a flush of forgotten warmth. He wished to see her, to be assured that all was well. If his thoughts served any purpose at all, they were selfish ones.

The following morning, Isaac instructed Rivers to make good notes when he met with the other investors, and those representing the Haitian Government, to vote him in for whatever would be most profitable for their partnership. Then, he called at Madame de Bloviere's dress shop.

The years had made her even more beautiful, and the look he had last seen in her eyes when she stood before the fire in the house on Poydras Street was undeniably there. As they sat in large wicker chairs in the lush garden room, adjoining her dress shop, Isaac learned that the freighter's first stop had been Port-au-Prince, where she had relatives. Lona reiterated that she had not even seen Chance Hadley on board, that she had done well on her own, as she had vowed, combining her excellent taste with the talent she had learned from her Creole nanny in Natchitoches.

"How unfair, Cheri, for you to have even considered that I would *be* with him, he whom I loathed. But, then, you never knew, or understood a woman's thinking. Few men do," she said. "I was angry. I wanted to do what you would most despise...and when Chance Hadley appeared on Esplanade, I knew that it was he whom I could use to hurt you. I gave him money for passage, to go away. I am sorry for wanting to cause you pain," she said reaching towards him. "You made me feel...but let us speak no more of the past. It cannot return, nor be altered...and every day when I go to chapel to pray, I never forget to ask God's blessings for you and for all whom you love."

Isaac was still seated opposite Lona in a large island chair and not once had he removed his eyes from her as she spoke, nor had he taken a cigar from its case as they sat in the open garden-room filled with bright blooming plants and exotic flowers. "It was how it should be," she said crossing the room. She knelt beside him and placed her hand on the wicker arm of the chair. "Your lady is lovely. I am where I should be, doing what I should do. God willed it so."

"Is there…has there been anyone else in your life?" He was surprised at his own words; what difference it should make to him? Nevertheless, it did.

"Cheri, you will not understand the answer. You do not understand such things. I am a woman who loved once. The love I knew cannot be duplicated. Love from anyone else would be nothing more than a substitute, and I am not given to substitutions. No, Cheri, there has been no one else…"

They drove in Lona's carriage to the opposite side of the island to a small fisherman's cottage belonging to Lona. There they listened to soft waves lap and touch the warm sand and watched the sun drop behind the Caribbean Sea. And for Isaac, the familiarity of many nights ago of holding Lona in his arms was once more a reality, as if there had been no lapse of years. It was a day, moments in time, he knew he would remember for the rest of his life. Moments he knew that he could not, would not repeat. He loved Adelicia. She was his wife, and he cherished knowing that fact. He would hurry back to the inn and quickly dress for dinner.

CHAPTER 22

West Feliciana, Bellevue Plantation

TWO YEARS HAD PASSED SINCE THE TRIP TO HAITI. Isaac's investment in sugar cane was providing considerable profits each year, and although other Louisiana planters were growing cane on their own land and building refineries, he preferred growing cotton on his. He had bargained with neighbors until he owned the entire section from where the cut-off of the Red River flows into the Mississippi, all the way around the great bend as far as the Atchafalaya Bayou, providing him with some of the richest and most fertile soil in the area and more river frontage than any other planter.

James Knox Polk had completed his term as the Governor of Tennessee, and was the nation's first 'dark horse' candidate for president, backed all the way by Andrew Jackson. Some even called him "Young Hickory." It was certainly another milestone for the Old General, and Isaac was actively working for his election in Louisiana.

In Nashville, Adelicia and Camille were included in the circle with Tennessee's lovely first lady, Sarah Childress Polk, with whom they enjoyed a genuine and sincere friendship. Isaac's past was no longer mentioned in any circles, nor did there seem to be gossip concerning him of any sort. Adelicia liked being Mrs. Franklin and felt very much a part of Nashville, as did Isaac. Their marriage, she thought, had proved profitable for each. Life as Mr. and Mrs. Isaac Franklin, Esq. was good, her sugarcane ideas put aside.

Fairvue's new overseer, Branch, a burly, strong man with pleasant manners, but under whose direction the Negroes were becoming increasingly restless, caused Isaac growing concern for the welfare of the plantation and its occupants.

He had mentioned more than once to Adelicia about leaving the management of the West Feliciana plantations in the hands of Jim Clack and making Fairvue their permanent residence. However, she resisted the idea, restating her love for West Feliciana and New Orleans, the latter's importance of providing a gaiety, a sense of freedom that she did not experience in Nashville. She also preferred the mild winters and having all the family come down to spend Christmas there.

So much had occurred in the two years since Haiti, that it was difficult for her to remember the sequence. Victoria had a new sister, little Adelicia, and she was now carrying Isaac's third baby, due in January. Camille had had difficulty becoming with child and was not expecting her first until the end of the month, near Thanksgiving. They were again wintering in New Orleans and at Bellevue, but she now regretted not being in Nashville for the birth of her first niece or nephew. More than once she had reflected on their mid-September departure, thinking that she should have adhered to Isaac's wishes and stayed in Middle Tennessee. Her determined will had gotten the better of her senses, she admitted to herself.

That summer, they had completed Fairvue's new west wing, with its arched brick walkway leading to the modern kitchen, patterned after the ones in New Orleans' townhouses. The extensive entertaining at Fairvue from May to September, had caused Aunt Aggie to constantly complain that she and Della did not have enough space to cook and oversee their helpers, so a kitchen was built twice the size of the old one.

Uncle Sugart remained his dear self, complying with his wife's every command, but was growing more feeble, a fact that greatly concerned Isaac. And Adelicia understood that they were an additional motivation for his desire to move permanently to Fairvue. The old couple seemed so sad each time they went down river and so joyful upon their return, always making over the children, spoiling them.

Bellevue Plantation
November 10, 1843

"*Dear Camille,*" she wrote. "*This letter must again be brief, but I could not let the day pass without writing. I am more sorry than you know, that we cannot be there for the wee one's birth, (I should have listened to Isaac) but, Dr. Gee says I cannot travel until sometime after the baby arrives in January, so I suppose we shall not meet until the* three *of you come for Mardi Gras in March. Camille, you are going to enjoy it so! Not quite the excitement of the voo doo, (which Isaac finally allowed me to see at Congo Square), but tantalizing enough! Everything and everyone is gay and cheerful. It seems the merrymaking will go on forever...you actually feel as if it does...the parties begin on Twelfth Night and continue 'til the big day. Some even begin before Christmas. If I could arrange one year not to be with child, I would like to host one of the balls, do more merry-making and parading. Do you think that possible? Too bad we were not familiar with this in the old days (just teasing).*

The trouble at Fairvue frightens me. I know Branch must have done something dreadful to Caleb or he would never have struck him...it is such a mess...Isaac has been corresponding with Papa about it, and I know Papa is doing all he can. Poor Uncle Sugart and Aunt Aggie, we tried our best to persuade them to come with us. I am concerned that they or the other house servants could be in danger. Papa keeps suggesting that Isaac sell out his holdings here and move back to Tennessee (selfish reasoning perhaps, and fueling Isaac's wishes). There are times he would do it regardless of my wishes, if he could find someone who could afford to buy, but you know Isaac and money...he surely has a knack for making it...if I had my way, he would sell Fairvue and move everything down here, but he won't adhere to that. I hope things settle down soon.

I was watching Victoria and Adelicia at play in the nursery, and for some obscure reason was reminded of a time I spent the night with you so long ago. Remember, we slipped out of bed, and in the moonlight, carved our names "for posterity's sake" on the wall near that large mantle...do you suppose it's still there? I hope it stays forever, as we intended.

I said this would be short, and here I am running on and on, but I must leave off now. I am larger with this baby than with the others...everyone but me is hoping for a boy...Remember, it is as easy as pie, and the second comes more quickly than the first. The Lord only knows if I shall have any warning with the third. I so wish I could be with you, but we both have March to which to look forward... cannot wait to see you and my big brother, come down sooner if Joel can pull himself away...Your friend forever, Adie

P.S. Isaac just came in and sends his love. He also mailed your pack-
ages so they will arrive by Christmas...Hope you like what I sent for
the wee one...love to you all...Adie. Roselawn must be lovely with
snow around it. Perhaps I shall see it next winter, Good-bye for
now, A."

January 1844 arrived cold, damp and bleak in West Feliciana Parish. Victoria and little Adelicia had played indoors most of December because of the unusually cold weather. This Christmas season was different for the Franklin family: no parties had been given, and no parties had been attended, nor had they engaged in any of the festivities of Carnival. The New Year had come and gone. For two months Adelicia had remained despondent. She had been able to do nothing more than send condolences to Nashville. She had not been able to attend the funeral of her best friend, whose precious infant was buried with her.

"There are too many things I do not understand. How can I have what is now almost three healthy babies, and Camille never know the joy of having one?" she asked bitterly as she and Isaac sat in the large parlor before the fire. "And how can a doctor in 1843 let someone bleed to death? The oldest medical practice in the world must be birthing children, and one would think we would be smart enough to prevent such a disaster."

"Sweetheart, for your sake, I hope you can stop brooding over it. If it relieves your sadness to continue talking about Camille, that's fine, but we have our own children to consider, and it's time for that son of mine to be born."

"If you do not want to hear me talk about it, it is not necessary that you stay."

"I didn't intend it that way, Adie,...I'm concerned about you..."

"Isaac," she said suddenly, grabbing the arm of her chair, "that pain was strong."

Two hours later, Julius Caesar Franklin was born. Lucy, Alfred, the entire household began applauding, singing and celebrating, and Rufus rode over the grounds with Jim Clack, seeing that the dinner bells rang throughout the Franklin plantations.

Twelve hours later, both Adelicia and Isaac knew the infinite sadness of losing a child.

"He died of congestion," Dr. Gee had said, and there was nothing that could have been done to save him. But Adelicia could not help but wonder if there were not something, somehow, that might have prevented it. Her precious little one was taken, her son who had fed from her body, and grown and lived inside her for nine months. And then he breathes into the world...suckles her breast...and is no more.

It made no sense to her, as she lay on her back, clinging to the damp bedsheets with her hands, sobbing uncontrollably. The birth had been easy, but Dr. Gee had not immediately put him to her breast as Dr. Mentlo had done with Victoria and little Adelicia. And when he did, the tugging of her nipples had been weak, not demanding her milk as had his sisters. Dr. Gee had then given her a dose of laudamen, and walked down the stairs with Isaac to wait.

Neighbors and servants stood shivering in faintly falling sleet while Reverend Jonathan Haskell read from the Book of Job. "...the Lord giveth, and the Lord taketh away; blessed be the name of the Lord."

"Isaac, do you suppose our baby can feel the cold?" she asked, expressionless, as they watched the tiny wooden casket being lowered into the wet earth by Rufus, who had planed it from oak the night before.

She did not want to have any more children, she thought, as Isaac helped her back to the house and up to bed. God had given her two precious little girls, whom she cherished. They would be enough.

CHAPTER 23

Fairvue Plantation

"OH, AUNT AGGIE, UNCLE SUGART, ESSIE! IT IS SO GOOD TO BE home again. There is no April like a Middle Tennessee April! Let me look at you...you all look wonderful."

She looked up at Isaac; it was the first time he had seen her smile since their son's death. It would also seem to him, that she was sincerely glad to be home.

"Look how my babies have growed," Aunt Aggie beamed, as she and Essie held the children to them. "I thanks the good Lord every day for my health, and that I's still around to see these little uns."

"Come see Uncle Sugart," the old gentleman said, motioning to the girls. Victoria and little Adelicia ran to him quickly and crawled into his lap. "Me and your Aunt Aggie shore proud of you. You gettin' prettier than your mama."

"You looking weary, child," Essie said, observing her favorite of the Hayes' children. "Let Essie get you tucked in bed."

"I am so glad you are here," Adelicia said. "I hoped Papa would see to it."

They slowly climbed the stairs, and Essie helped Adelicia remove her clothing just as she had done in years past.

"I am so tired, so sad, Essie...so much ill has happened..."

"Let me loosen these staves. Child, we gotta work on this waistline! Your mama's never did get thick after she bore any of her childrens, and if you don't work on it real quick like, it'll slip up on you and the first..."

"My waist is not getting thick!" Adelicia snapped. "I am expecting another baby in December." She lay between the cool white sheets with her head lying on the soft pillow, sobbing. "I am tired, dear Essie...very tired."

"You going to stay right here in this bed and sleep and get some rest. There's plenty here to look after the childrens, and while Mr.

Isaac taking care of all the problems and business, I gonna look after you just like when you was a little girl. I won't take no sass, neither." She smiled, watching Adelicia drift off to sleep.

Her recuperative powers proved remarkable, and within a matter of weeks Adelicia was more like her old self and enjoying a beautiful Tennessee spring. Isaac, the children and she took long walks and had tea parties among the tulips and daffodils and made necklaces of clover.

However, she was anxious to have this baby and 'get it over with.' As much as she loved what Isaac had taught her in bed and the things they shared there, she found it more difficult each day to stay on good terms. She faulted him in no way, but practically everything he did made her edgy, sometimes just being in the same room with him. He had apologized for having gotten her so quickly with child, but she sensed that her temperament mattered less and less to him.

Adelicia thought her increasing snippiness was due to her sadness over Camille, the loss of her infant son and the frustration of being with child so soon, but whatever the reason, she seemed unable to control the force within her.

However, she was determined to make a genuine effort to correct things after the baby came. She would gallop with Samson over the grounds, with Isaac on Imposter. The children would ride in their pony cart. Victoria would take lessons in the ring. She and Isaac would give parties, and walk on the lawn and enjoy Fairvue with family and friends. And there would be Christmas at Fairvue with their two daughters and a new baby this year.

The doctor had given her the strictest orders because of the closeness of the pregnancies, but she was determined to ride Samson. And she did, cautiously in the ring with Victoria riding her pony beside her, led by Luke. She did not miss a day walking to the stables to visit the gelding, now pastured back at Fairvue.

Adelicia enjoyed her family's visits from Nashville and local Gallatin neighbors, and a day seldom passed when there were not extra guests for dinner or supper.

As Isaac had predicted, John Armfield married his niece, Martha Franklin, and they had built an imposing home on the opposite side of the Gallatin Pike from Fairvue, near the plantations of Isaac's brothers, William and Albert.

She was grateful her father enjoyed excellent health, and for his position of plantation legal adviser to his friend and son-in-law. Her sister, Laura was now a student at the Nashville Female Academy, Bud, Bliss and Henry were at the Virginia Military Institute, and Adelicia found it difficult to believe that her baby sister, Corrine, was already eight.

Charlotte, Aunt Aggie and Uncle Sugart's daughter born at Fairvue, was officially adopted as the children's nurse, with Aunt Aggie overseeing. Della and Daniel managed the kitchen well with their assistants...all the while, Essie took care of Adelicia. So much for which to be thankful, Adelicia thought as she lazed outside with Victoria and little Adelicia, she rocking gently in a swing, and they in the playhouse Isaac had built, as autumn leaves began to fall.

Only one thing had marred the tranquility of the summer months. Uncle Sugart, feeble and still unwell from a spring cough, had developed pneumonia, and in mid-August passed away. Isaac was more distraught over the old man's death than Adelicia had ever seen him, even the death of their own son. Uncle Sugart had been like a father to him from the beginning, he had told her, and now Aunt Aggie was all that remained of that dear part of his life.

On December 5, 1844, Emeline Hayes Franklin was born, healthy and beautiful with eyes like her mothers and with Isaac's dark coloring. Exactly six years from the day of Adelicia's brother Richard's death.

"Look who's here to see her namesake, Adie." Judge and Emma White appeared in the bedroom doorway with Isaac.

"Come in! Isn't she precious?" Adelicia said as they peered down at the sleeping infant.

"She certainly is. Another beautiful Franklin daughter. See what we brought you, little Emma?" Over the crib, Adelicia's cousin Emma held up an exquisite child's silver comb, brush and mirror set, each one engraved EHF.

"Don't make such a fuss," Judge White said reprovingly. "I don't think she can see the gift."

"She may not have her eyes open right now to see it, but she hears every word. It is common knowledge that babies know what adults are saying from the moment of their birth."

"Bring in the other things." The Judge and Isaac stepped into the hallway and returned with three stuffed rocking animals: a horse, a duck and a lion.

"I want the lion," exclaimed Victoria.

"Then the lion you shall have," said Emma. "Which one do you want, little Adelicia?"

"I want the duck. I have ducks in my pond." Judge White lifted the child onto the yellow feathered duck.

"That leaves the horse for little Emma, and it won't be long before she'll be riding it," said Emma White.

On the day Emma was born, Isaac had taken Adelicia's hand and fastened a beautiful gold bracelet set with four jewels, one for the birth of each child; a diamond, a sapphire, a ruby and an emerald on her wrist. It was a bracelet designed with exquisite taste. She kissed and thanked him for it, sincerely appreciating its sentiment, but she had so much jewelry, in small velvet boxes and large satin ones, for her earlobes, her fingers, her wrists and for around her neck.

Since Emma's birth, Adelicia was taking every opportunity to restore what her relationship with Isaac had once been. She wished to again share the joy and delight of being in his presence, the excitement of feeling close, of being one, of flirting. And with her genuine efforts, she began to discover certain contentment, certain resoluteness, a certain comfort.

It was 1845, and again, they were missing Mardi Gras, as well as James K. Polk's inaugural festivities in Washington. However, Adelicia would be hostess of the most prestigious Carnival ball the following year. Isaac had donated to the right charities, praised and done favors for the right people. Together, they had entertained and socialized with the right groups. One had to be rich and socially prominent, and the fact that they had first awed New Orleans by having its hero, Andrew Jackson, as a guest, certainly did not hurt matters. Theirs was to be an elite ball, attended by the wealthiest, most prominent families, and it would take both summer and fall to get Adelicia's gowns ready for the balls and Mardi Gras Day—after all, she thought, she must have the honor before she was too old to enjoy it, for she would soon be twenty-eight.

It was late when Isaac returned from a long day in Nashville, and he looked fatigued. "This slave restlessness that Branch keeps stirred up has upset every plantation owner in the area. Because of Polk being a Tennessean, they've even got word of it in Washington," Isaac said as he sat in the chair near their bed and slipped off the fine leather boots she had given him. "Branch had seemed a decent enough fellow when your father hired him, but he provokes the slaves to become belligerent towards him. Caleb has struck him a second time. News travels fast, and puts fear into the minds of more overseers and owners than I'd like to think. I'm getting rid of Branch, but I want to keep Caleb...we'll see."

"I'm sorry it's such a strain, darling. Were things any better today?"

"Some, but it's rough!" He finished undressing in silence and sat for some time in a heavily stuffed chair near the west window. Finally turning toward her, but actually not looking at her, he said, "Adie, we must talk. I know this past year has been more than difficult for you, and I also know you've borne four children for me in five years."

She listened, as he paused, seemingly waiting for an answer. "Not just for you, darling, for us."

"I know it's not been easy, and I appreciate your willingness to please me, always, and we have three healthy children, so I wondered how you would feel about..."

"Remaining without union for the rest of our lives?" she interrupted. And did he think it was just to please him, she thought? She had never complained about that part of their marriage.

He went over and sat beside her on the bed, "There is a way," he began, "that people can still..."

"Do tell me about it," she coaxed, moving closer to him.

"Adelicia! What do you know on the subject?"

"Nothing more than some old Indian customs shamelessly whispered to me by Essie."

"You're the shameless one," he laughed.

"You share your secrets with me, and I shall share mine with you."

"Mine were handed down by my French ancestors, a part of the family for hundreds of years."

"I am sure," she said, as she lay in his arms, "we shall arrive at something suitable to our liking. Two great cultures, one uncivilized, the other refined."

He held her close and gently ran his fingers over her face, outlining each feature in the moon's light. "I love you, Adie."

"And I love you, my deaest Isaac. Will you put the bracelet on my wrist, please?"

It was a good night, and she had felt closer to him than she had in some time as she lay snuggled in his arms, but it was not the same. Perhaps it was not supposed to be after almost six years of marriage, but she wanted desperately for it to be. She wondered if he felt the same way.

CHAPTER 24

Gallatin

JUNE 8, 1845, NASHVILLE WAS SADDENED AT THE LOSS OF ITS statesman, New Orleans its hero, and America its seventh president. Andrew Jackson, on whose fiftieth birthday Adelicia had been born, passed away at the Hermitage minutes before Sam Houston arrived, hoping to see his friend, his mentor, his general once more. It was actually the doctor who gave Houston the news of Jackson's death, as the physician was leaving the plantation on his way back out Lebanon Road.

Adelicia and Isaac had gathered with hundreds to mourn the nation's loss and to witness Jackson's burial beside his beloved Rachel in the garden to the right of the mansion.

They had also strolled down the cedar-lined, guitar-shaped drive, the neck of which led to the front portico of the house, her arm in his, remembering a man who cherished his wife even to having the cedars planted in the shape of the guitar she played. It was romance, as she had told Isaac before. Perhaps every woman should have at least a touch of an Andrew Jackson for a husband. He had even fought a duel over Rachel!

Plans for travel in autumn were well underway. The winter of '45 / '46 would be spent in New Orleans and on the plantations in West Feliciana, and this year, both Victoria and little Adelicia would attend Madame LeFere's School. Essie agreed to come with them (although she was unaware of one small detail, purposely left unmentioned), and Charlotte with her cousin, Cora, would also come as nurses for the children. Charlotte's responsibility was for the two older girls, and Cora's for little Emma, leaving Essie to oversee both nurses and still have time for Adelicia. Aunt Aggie had refused to leave Fairvue, or Uncle Sugart's final resting place on earth. Thus,

Della and Daniel were in charge of looking after her, as was her father on his by-weekly visits.

Adelicia was anxious to leave Nashville on this early autumn day and to settle into the three-story brick townhouse Isaac had leased from Lucius Duncan on New Orleans's Canal Street that they would share with Martha and John Armfield. Isaac had told her the house was large enough for three families, that John needed to be there for his banking and land investment business. Adelicia was looking forward to the open house she was planning for early December, an event she intended to become an annual affair, also for her daughters to entertain their school friends.

As they were preparing for bed the evening before their departure, with packed trunks all around them as well as in the wide hallway, Isaac said, "You know, the only bad thing about leaving for New Orleans in mid-September is not being able to see the leaves turn."

"We shall be so busy this autumn, you will forget all about falling leaves."

"Your father really enjoyed himself at supper tonight," he said, changing the subject. "There's not a finer man living than Oliver Bliss Hayes. He's a good friend, a real friend, Adie. Without his help and knowledge, I couldn't leave Fairvue and even be as secure as I am about it. I'm mighty glad to be a part of his family."

"Papa always liked you…not as a suitor, perhaps…"

"I know exactly how he felt," Isaac interrupted, "I'll be the same way with our daughters."

"Are we going to check bloodlines before you permit a caller?"

"Without exception," he laughed. "We need sleep. It's almost midnight."

The *Tennessee* pulled in her anchor and slowly sailed from the Cumberland's banks as the sun had just begun to peer over the hills.

"Wave good-bye girls! See Della?" Aunt Aggie had walked to the dock with them to get a last hug from the children, but Della had stayed on the knoll looking down to the river. Isaac had an arm around each of his older daughters and was looking out to the plot where Uncle Sugart lay.

"Good-bye ducks, good-bye Della, good-bye Aunt Aggie, Uncle Sugart, good-bye house," said little Adelicia. "I'm going to miss my ducks, Papa."

"Good bye, Aunt Aggie," Victoria called. "It is such a pretty house, I think I like Tennessee better than Louisiana."

"Yes, it is a pretty house," Isaac said, "and one of these days, we'll come back here to stay for good. How would you like that?"

"I think I should like it very much, Papa. Of course, when I am grown up Mother says New Orleans is much more sophisticated."

"She…" Isaac paused, then continued. "You always listen to your mother."

As the dock at Fairvue was no longer in view, and Adelicia sat on deck observing the lush foliage on either side of the Cumberland, contrasting with its limestone cliffs, Victoria took her mother's hand and said, "Mother, I've never seen Papa cry."

Adelicia glimpsed Isaac standing near the stern. "Papas don't cry very often, darling."

"He did just now. He had a tear in his eye."

As *The Tennessee* neared The City of New Orleans, Isaac overheard Essie and Adelicia.

"No siree, no siree!" Essie stated emphatically. "I'd give my life to have yours saved. Many a time when you a baby, I sit up with you while your pore mama trying to get some rest…and I look at you and think if the Lord have to take one of us, let it be me, but you can't ask me to live under the same roof with that man!"

Adelicia looked at her, smiling. "You're missing the sights, Essie. There's the top of Saint Louis Cathedral…"

"Won't do no good to try and distract me. You don't tell me one thing about the Armfields going to live with us, and I knows wherever Mr. John is, that Pompy is going to be too. You knows how it is. He don't know class when it stare him in the face and he sure don't have none. I'll tell Mr. Isaac that I just stay right here on this boat till it goes back home."

"This is home, Essie, until late spring," she said matter-of-factly. "The children need you. I need you."

Isaac interrupted, "What are you two discussing so feverishly? We're dropping anchor."

"Essie says she does not want to live under the same roof with 'Pompous' Pompy."

He laughed, "Had you not told her till just now?" Essie sat with her head down. "This house is so large, Essie, you'll never even catch sight of Pompy. But just in case you do see him, by chance, and he upsets you in any way, you tell me. If you don't like it here, you can go back to Fairvue or Rokeby anytime you want."

And I'm the one who is supposed to be the charmer, Adelicia thought. She gave him a glance out of the corner of her eye while he continued to grin, puffing on his premium Havana.

The house was exactly as Isaac had described it and when Adelicia entered the great hallway, her disappointment of having to live in the same house with another family vanished. The size, typical of the 'long houses' in New Orleans, was deceiving from the exterior. The rooms seemed to go on indefinitely. The Armfields took the west wing, the Franklins the east wing, and each had separate stairways leading from the magnificent entrance hall.

Both wings opened onto a central gallery that doubled as a ballroom, and then onto an enormous walled brick patio with work rooms and servant's quarters in the rear. The kitchen, on a lower level beneath the living area, was where the supplies and liquors were also kept. Yes, Adelicia thought, Isaac had not disappointed, but then, he seldom did.

Essie's quarters were much to her liking, a part of the main structure, opening directly onto the patio. She was also pleased to learn that Pompy was upcountry, overseeing some work for John and could be there till Christmas. Also, the excitement over the preparations for the Franklin's December open house was contagious, and she was as busy as the others.

Adelicia thought the location of the house could be no better. From their balcony, she could look onto the grand promenade below, and to her left she could see the steamers docked on the river at the end of Canal Street and the bronze eagle atop the Henry Clay Memorial that stood between New Levee and Chartres Streets. It was a magnificent view.

"Miss Adie, I thought we had some parties before, but this out-does 'em all," Essie said as she and Adelicia stood in the grand hall, observing the "fixins," as Essie called them.

"Is it really that wonderful, Essie?"

"Your mama give some fine doings at Rokeby, and them balls you and Mr. Isaac give at Fairvue is something, and the first one here you tell me about when the General hisself come...but nothing we ever done come near this one, not even near."

"Are the children dressed?"

"They looks just like the little angels they is. Victoria say they practice curtsying in class today, and Madame LeFere say she the most lady-like of all."

The sassiest, too, thought Adelicia. But everyone adored Victoria, and in the few months the children had been in school, their friends seemed to multiply daily.

Charlotte brought the children to Adelicia's dressing room, beautifully decorated in varied hues of light blues and ivories. "My darlings, how divine you look!" She hugged them lightly, as she sat before the mirrored table. "Now you remember exactly what to do, right, sweethearts?"

"We remember, Mother," they chorused.

"Mr. Franklin say the guests beginning to arrive, and he wish you hurry up and come," said Charlotte.

"Tell him we shall be right there."

The children were tucked in by nine after having earlier assisted their parents in greeting the guest. Adelicia was radiant in her pale pink peau de soie gown designed in New York, and as she looked over the crowd at the glittering gowns of the elite, she could not help but wonder if any had been designed in Haiti.

Her Middle Tennessee charm continued to enchant both the men and the women of New Orleans' elite and of the countryside's wealthy planters. The great hall and parlors and receiving rooms on either side were filled to capacity. Men gathered round her to compliment, to ask polite questions and to flatter, and Adelicia loved every moment of it. An important difference between New Orleans and Nashville, she noted, was that here the wives did not seem to mind nor did they gossip.

Everyone was there: Mayor Montegut and Governor Mouton and their wives, bankers, congressmen, importers and shipping magnates.

Madame Octavia Lavert, an international socialite, had come over from Mobile, draped in diamonds and escorted by her friend and companion, Henry Clay, who had recently lost his bid for president. It was an *almost* tradition, in both America and abroad, to include Madame Lavert on all guest lists. It was especially true in New Orleans, as it assured the hostess of having the affair make the society page of the *New Orleans Picayune*. Adelicia, no longer feeling the need for such assurance, liked the beautiful woman who had been reared in Augusta, Georgia, to be exactly who and what she was: a brilliant, universal socialite.

Elizabeth Patterson Bonaparte, the American-born first wife of Napoleon's brother, Jerome, whom Adelicia had previously met on her honeymoon trip with Isaac, was also at the gathering and also draped with jewels. And how pleased Adelicia was with her attendance, as it was a rarity for Madame Bonaparte to accept an invitation.

"It occurs to me that I am always introducing handsome men to you," Crawford drawled, as he caught Adelicia's eye amidst the crowd out on the gallery. "I'd like you to meet Ransom Bennington, a most successful merchant, banker and investor from Massachusetts."

"Actually, sir, I request Mr. Benedict to bring all charming men to my attention," Adelicia said. "I am delighted to meet a gentleman from my father's native state. Are you acquainted with the Hayes or Bliss families?"

Before Ransom had an opportunity to answer, Isaac had diverted her attention and motioned for her to come and speak with Governor and Mrs. Mouton.

"Excuse me, gentlemen, my husband wishes for me to join him. I look forward to hearing your answer at another time."

Ransom Bennington, enchanted, watched her walk away and followed her with his eyes until the crowd between them was so great, he could no longer see her. "How extraordinary!" he exclaimed. "Tell me everything about her."

"That, my dear boy, is not possible," said Crawford. "I'll tell you this. Every man who meets her falls in love, but I'm not sure any man will ever have her, mind and soul, I mean."

Crawford's answer fascinated him the more, "How intriguing!" Bennington replied, but for the remainder of the evening, he was not able to speak with her again.

Adelicia and Isaac walked among the guests, talking and smiling and charming until the last of them had bid their farewells.

"This was the grandest of parties, darling!" Adelicia exclaimed, as Isaac unfastened the diamond clasp of her pearl choker. "It was even grander than the one General Jackson attended! We do not have such guest lists from which to choose in Nashville. Everyone who was invited came, not that I expected otherwise, but everything was perfect," Adelicia gloated. "The fresh seafood, pineapple punch, touched up with your Tennessee whiskey, and dear Uncle Sugart's country ham between Essie's biscuits, the likes of which no one had tasted…all seemed happy and ravenously enjoying themselves! They raved about our children! Just think about all of the parties and balls for Carnival!"

"That's exactly what I don't want to think about. Goodnight my dearest, Adie," he said, pulling her close to him, before they went to sleep cuddled in each other's arms.

CHAPTER 25

New Orleans, 1846

ISAAC HAD BEEN LESS THAN PLEASED WITH THE LETTER HE HAD received from his father-in-law in mid-December of '45, stating that Caleb had completed the job he had begun two years earlier and had now killed Branch. And according to Oliver Hayes' letter, it seemed there would be no way to save him from hanging. In an angry reply, Isaac wrote, "I am considering breaking up the entire establishment and transferring the majority of the hands to my Louisiana operations in the fall," although it was the last thing he wanted to do. For certain, he would not let Caleb, a trusted and talented slave of many years, be hanged, but would somehow bring him to Louisiana.

He loved his land in Tennessee, and Adelicia's indifference toward Fairvue as a permanent residence distressed him. She preferred the children to attend school in New Orleans, where she found the social life, opera, theater, and sometimes the plantations themselves—when riding in a hunt or giving a party—superior to those in Gallatin or Nashville. He, on the other hand, preferred the beauty and tranquility that he found at Fairvue. What each sought was decidedly different, so different that it seemed useless to discuss.

As a husband and father, he no longer sought the style of life that had once intrigued him in Louisiana. He enjoyed being home at Fairvue with family and friends. He recognized their age differences; Adelicia young and much desirous of the gaiety of New Orleans, all new to her; he, a family man, and regularly attending church services, all new to him.

A portion of Fairvue had been an original grant to his father, James, for Revolutionary War services when he, along with James Robertson and others, defended the Cumberland region. Then, in 1784, as one of the "immortal seventy," James Franklin had received title to six hundred and forty acres at Pilot's Knob, by act of the North Carolina assembly. Soon, before his father's death in 1828, Isaac had purchased the portion on the gentle knoll where Fairvue stood from his father, and acquired the additional acres from his older brothers and neighbors, which gave him two thousand acres of one of the finest tracts of land in the area, with direct water access to the Cumberland.

It was true Fairvue presented more problems than all his other holdings combined, but that was partially due to his long absences. Since the plantation's conception in '32, it had seemed next to impossible to hire a responsible and competent overseer in his absence. In Louisiana, he was fortunate to have James Clack, an exceptional man with the qualities of patience and gentle persuasion, so necessary for successfully running a large operation, as well as two foremen who oversaw the individual plantations. In a full day's journey, they could visit all five West Feliciana properties, speak to their inhabitants, and rest assured that all was well.

The care and responsibility of land, slaves, crops and livestock, and the distances involved between Louisiana and Mississippi, Madagascar Bay and Bexar County, Texas…and Tennessee, were taking their toll. Although some relief had come when he had sold his interest in the sugar plantations to Rivers Thurmond, his burdens were heavy and ever with him.

He wished to return to Sumner County and to live there permanently; he would somehow convince Adelicia of that. She never failed to remind him that the profits lay in Louisiana, that the cotton market was skyrocketing, and how foolhardy to sell when the prices were going higher every day. She had consistently insisted that all pressures would be lifted by selling Fairvue.

Adelicia walked over to Isaac's desk, where he sat in his study writing and stood behind him with her hands on his shoulders. "Did you sleep well, dear?" she asked, sweetly. "You look tired."

"How's Emma?" he asked, not looking up.

"You have the worst habit of never answering my questions. Charlotte stayed with her all night after I gave her laudanum for her to rest more easily. She is up and playing, and all the girls are waiting for their papa to come in and see them this morning. Are you feeling well?" she asked kissing him on the cheek.

"I feel fine and slept well," he answered curtly. "I thought we had discussed your giving the children drugs to enhance their sleep. Essie agrees it's not good. Emma's only two years old, and it might not hurt if her mother stayed with her one night instead of..."

"Have you not said enough, Isaac? Since before the holidays, even before that, there has been one criticism after the other. Everything I do displeases you. I came in to ask how you were, and I am reprimanded about our daughter. I enjoy New Orleans and its social life too much. I ride Samson too much. I don't do something else enough. Goshens amighty! I do not know what to do anymore!"

Exhaling, she took a deep breath, then continued, "I do not suppose there has been a decision made concerning Fairvue?" she asked, not waiting for an answer. "Not only is it a problem, that you are quite willing to admit, it's not economical! In truth, it's fast becoming a deficit. We have thousands of acres in West Feliciana, where we can grow corn and raise hogs and sheep and whatever else Fairvue is supplying. Aunt Aggie can go to Rokeby," she said, at last sitting in an arm chair near Isaac, "or come here with us. We can purchase a townhouse in Nashville, and she can live there with Della and Daniel. Times are changing."

Isaac held the quill pen near his chin and gazed out the open window. Then after a time, he got up, walked over and closed the door and lit his cigar, all in a rare silence.

"Adelicia, as of late, it's difficult to remember the good days we shared. I thought you would be able to enjoy Fairvue with me and love it as I do, the way I believe you did at first. Yes, I thought you did, when we first married, the year Victoria came, and the year after when little Adelicia was born, but when I reflect back, you were always anxious to be leaving on the next trip. No sooner were we home than you were planning to leave, or attend the next party. Perhaps I kept waiting to see what wasn't there."

"Why should I share your feelings for Fairvue? I never asked you to love Rokeby the same as I, nor did I expect it. Fairvue is beautiful and grand, but it has served its purpose. It is clear that it is losing money and causing you unnecessary stress."

He was leaning against the window watching her intently. "Have I, too, served my purpose?" He continued staring at her, with a faraway look in his eyes.

"For goodness sakes, Isaac, I just happen not to share you sentiments for Fairvue."

"I'm not sure you're capable of loving anything or anyone—oh, maybe for short periods. You still have love confused with fantasy and intrigue, but to really love..." He stopped short and turned to look out on the garden, thoughts of Lona weighing heavily on his mind.

"Did I not give you four children in five years? Have I not been a faithful and loyal wife, and have I not always been there whenever you wanted or needed me?"

"I'm grateful every day for our children. You've been there, and on my arm as beautiful and delightful as ever. Your charm seems to grow with each passing year, but we're not the same. The flirty, daring girl who so boldly signed her name in my guest book has since been awed by other things." Isaac picked up his cigar and turned it in his fingers, deep in thought. "Adelicia, you love only yourself and what is advantageous for you. There may be one thing you love more, however. Your love of money may even exceed that of yourself."

"Do you really think so poorly of me?" she asked, stunned and teary eyed. "Before you married me, you spent half your time in New Orleans and West Feliciana. Now you wish to spend it all in Gallatin, in your Sumner County. Perhaps the city was more alluring to you in those days with your...?"

"I had my intrigues in Tennessee as well as New Orleans, and elsewhere," he interrupted, "dear heart, but we shant discuss them. When we married, I had hoped to settle down at Fairvue and enjoy life with you and our children in the manner which we could well afford. I had built the grand house with that in mind. I love Sumner County as I do no other place on earth, and I hope my children will feel the same when they are older. I want to be buried at Fairvue and I wish to hear no more about my selling it." He would not even hint to her that in anger the thought had occurred to him after the trouble his father-in-law had reported there.

"Then you shall near no more about it! And I do wish you would refrain from talking about your burial. I do not believe either of us will be passing anytime soon." Adelicia took a deep breath and just before leaving the room said, "I shall have dinner in my room alone, and tonight I shall take your advice and sleep near the children. Perhaps you miss subservient women...like the ones in Haiti?"

The following morning, Adelicia ordered breakfast for the two of them in her room and waited for Isaac to come, as he had done on other occasions when there had been a quarrel. It was not until she was sipping her second cup of strong chicory that she asked Essie to please tell Isaac she was waiting breakfast for him. It was then that Essie told her that he had left the previous evening and had not said where he was going.

When he had not returned by midday, Adelicia's concern grew as she continued to check the mantle clock. She and the children had played outside in the courtyard, running and chasing after a large blue-green ball and playing hide and seek, and she had loved watching Emma totter after her sisters. But her thoughts were on Isaac. If in West Feliciana, it was customary for him to sometimes leave in the early morning to make plantation rounds, or when in New Orleans to conduct business, but either way, he was always back by noon. He had never left in the evening. He had never stayed the night.

She wished to high heaven that she had not been so sharp-tongued nor mentioned Haiti. She had never been foolish enough not to realize how handsome he was, extremely so, at fifty-six, and she had never been foolish enough not to realize that other women found him so, and together with money and the power it brought, she admitted she felt uneasy from time to time. She cared for him deeply and loved him as well as she understood love. Isaac was a wonderful man, so wonderful to her. And she had not dismissed Lona from her mind, not completely, since Haiti. She was sincerely sorry for her behavior the afternoon before, and she would tell him so...she would also agree to making Fairvue their permanent residence.

When Isaac did arrive home just before supper time, she was delighted to see him. He appeared rested, relaxed and briefly mentioned that his brother William was in Natchitoches on business.

Supper was lovely and charming, together with Victoria and little Adelicia—and Charlotte had brought Emma in for good night kisses. Afterward, the girls positioned themselves in a great stuffed chair before the fire while Isaac read to them about the little people in *Gulliver's Travels*. Adelicia was so pleased as she and Isaac sat opposite the children with her hand resting on Isaac's knee, that she believed she could be content for the rest of her life in this ambiance with Isaac and her children. No more harsh words would tumble from her tongue. Their lives would be peace and tranquility, she would see to it. After he closed the book, the children crawled into their laps for delicious hugs before Charlotte came to take them to bed.

When Isaac, yawning, rose from his chair, Adelicia stood and reached for him, nestling herself into his arms. She took his hands and put them to her midriff, lightly kissing his lips as he moved his hands towards her back. His response to her touch was slow, but as she continued to kiss him longingly, he became aroused, and again she took his hands and pressed them to the front of her midriff, guiding them upward, while softly moving her lips over his cheeks and brushing the nape of his neck and curls with her fingertips. He gently lifted her onto the sofa and removed her dress as she unfastened the buttons of his shirt.

CHAPTER 26

ER YOUNGER SISTER LAURA HAD BEEN VISITING WITH THEM since Thanksgiving. Her personality, unlike that of Adelicia's, was introverted and reserved. At seventeen, she had not had a steady beau nor felt comfortable at parties. Isaac had suggested to her father that it would be in Laura's best interest for her to visit with them in New Orleans and enjoy the Mardi Gras social season.

Isaac wrote to Oliver in January, right after the Twelfth Night Ball concerning her welfare: "We are all well except the youngest child, who has a bad cold. Laura is taking polka lessons. She has been attending some parties, and will have an opportunity of attending a good many during Carnival and the opera. She is gradually gaining her confidence, the want of which has been a great drawback on her enjoyments. She is very amiable, and disposed to take advice...I always go with her to take her lessons...If I could leave my family I would come up, but Adie will not hear of it. Give my love to all, and accept for yourself assurances as usual. Laura, Adie and the children join me in sending their love."

Isaac was not enjoying Carnival, and had it not been for his and Adelicia's patronage as host for one of the balls and Laura's presence, he would have attended few parties, if any, even to please his wife. When Mardi Gras was over, he would make major decisions, relieving himself of most of his Louisiana responsibilities and business pressures overall, though there was much to consider.

Each year the parades were becoming more elaborate, almost as elaborate as those in Mobile. Victoria and little Adelicia delighted in catching the trinkets and tasty favors tossed from the colorful floats and from the masked riders on horseback. Essie was thankful for their seats in the reviewing boxes situated where Rue Chartres crosses St. Peter directly in front of the Cabildo, where only the elite and wealthy with special invitations were allowed. The stands were beautifully draped with wide satin ribbons and soft fabrics in Carnival colors—purple, yellow and green.

The February day could not have been ordered to be more perfect. Blue skies feathered with soft wisps of transparent clouds, and a temperature in the low seventies, gave way to festive masked revelers lining the streets and corners, laughing, dancing and singing, donned in bright colorful costumes of every description.

"Aunt Essie, I'm tired," said Emma, "May we go home now?"

"I knew we should not have brought Baby Emma," said Victoria. "She is much too young."

"Now Missy, hold your tongue, little Emma wants to see the parade, too. She just tire out fore you older girls. Cora, you take Miss Emma home. Charlotte and me will stay." Cora lifted the little one in her arms, and Pompy drove them the several blocks back to Canal Street.

"I still think it trouble to bring a baby to a parade. The same thing will happen Tuesday when we ride in the Grand Parade," said Victoria. "I shall ask mother to leave Emma at home."

"Vic, mother has already told us what to expect on Tuesday," little Adelicia said. "Everything is planned. Emma may sleep if she wants, but we are all to be in the parade. It is not for you to say anyway."

"Shush and look," whispered Essie, pointing to the approaching float, "Here come your mama and papa now and Miss Laura. Don't they look grand? They about the handsomest folks I ever did see... and may the Lord forgive me for ever thinking ill of Mr. Isaac. He knowed what he was doing...at times, though, I think the Lord had a little something against him and's making him pay a might. Wave, honey, throw them a kiss...look what they throwed...something for me too... this is some exciting...don't they look grand...I bet this is the handsomest pair they'll ever be...I's so proud."

"When I grow up, I want to do everything just like mother and marry a handsome man like Papa," Victoria said in her prissy air.

"Me, too," said little Adelicia, "but I don't know if we shall find anyone as wonderful as Papa, ever, except, of course, Grandfather."

"Well young missus, the way I's see it, there's quite a few years to go before we be thinking along them lines...but I agrees about your papa and your grandpapa."

"A young lady is never too young to think about her future, Aunt Essie," said Victoria.

On Mardi Gras Day, February 24, 1846, it was raining, humid and chilly. Essie had never understood why no kind of bad weather ever stopped a parade or a party in New Orleans. She had never seen such a "partying" place, and when she had told Adelicia that morning that the parade would probably be canceled because of the elements, her mistress had quickly replied. "Not in New Orleans"—and as she and the children got into the ornately decorated open carriage, their umbrellas in hand, she saw no end to the masked merrymakers on the streets.

The grand parade came to a halt as the carriage bearing Adelicia and Isaac approached the reviewing stand, where they toasted those in the favored seats. In the carriage directly behind them were the three Franklin children, Essie and Charlotte. Victoria, Adelicia and Emma appeared as young princesses in white dresses with scooped necklines slightly baring their shoulders, with matching parasols. Victoria's dark hair was tied with a lavender blue ribbon on top, leaving wide satin streamers to flow down her back. Little Adelicia's ebony curls hung full with a pink ribbon pulled to one side, and Emma sat as angelic as her sisters. Essie sitting near them, looking regal in deep blue taffeta, topped off with a matching bonnet, holding parasols over herself and Emma.

Adelicia thought it a glorious day, despite the rain, and despite the fact that parasols had been necessary for everyone, even the masked revelers on horseback.

The elaborate costume ball that concluded Mardi Gras on Fat Tuesday was held that night in the grand ballroom of the St. Louis Hotel. The embossed invitations had been sent months prior to the occasion to enable elaborate planning by the invited elite.

"Miss Adie, I wish your mama could see you tonight," Essie said, beaming as she helped Adelicia with finishing touches. "Miss Sarah would be so proud. You look as much like an angel as one of God's own. You're prettier than I ever see you...more than earthly..."

Adelicia, still sitting on the satin upholstered stool in front of her dressing mirror, stood up, taking another pose. "There are times I wish I were not earthly," she said reflectively. "Please hurry...check the crown in the back and make sure it is set in my hair just so."

Essie made a minor adjustment to the diamond tiara perfectly secured in Adelicia's dark hair piled meticulously on top of her head. She fastened the sapphire and diamond necklace that matched her earbobs, then went down the stairs where the children were gathered to see their parents leave for the magnificent ball.

Isaac was dressed in white heavy satin with diamond studs in his shirt and cuffs, and a gold cummerbund that held a jeweled handled sword. He comically tossed his matching satin cape from side to side as the children laughed, then bent forward to get a kiss from each daughter, and to let little Emma fasten the loop around the large amethyst stone that held the cape in place.

"You are the prettiest mother and papa in the whole world," said Victoria.

"And my three darlings are the dearest in the whole world," Isaac replied.

"Will you tell us all about it in the morning, and not forget a thing?" asked young Adelicia.

"Yes, Angel, we shall tell you all about it in the morning...and not leave out a single thing. Now goodnight to all of you. Charlotte, the girls need to in bed soon," Adelicia cautioned.

"Mother, it's Carnival night. Can we not stay up later?"

"I think that's a reasonable request."

"Oh, thank you, Papa...how long?"

"Charlotte, how about half past ten, with songs and games and stories. It is a special night."

"That be mighty fine, Mr. Isaac."

"You're the greatest papa of all," chorused the children, as they happily gave him a final hug.

"Isaac, darling. We must hurry. Laura has been there for more than an hour now, and we both know how sensitive she is."

"She's in good hands with Tryon Weeks, and as of late I'm rather proud of the way she's come out. She'll do fine."

"It is our night and I want to enjoy every minute of it."

This was the real truth, he thought, that bore little concern for Laura.

"I'm sure you will, darling, of that I have no doubt."

Adelicia and Isaac waltzed to the evening's first dance. The elite of New Orleans were gathered in the elegant ballroom of the St. Louis Hotel, as well as their 'by-invitation-only' out-of-own guests. All were dressed extravagantly in dazzling, lavishly exciting costumes. She wondered where the grandiosity had begun, Spain, perhaps.

"George, George Shields!" As the waltz was ending, Adelicia happily recognized an old friend from Middle Tennessee walking towards her. "Whatever are you doing here? I did not think anything could take you away from that big farm."

"First, let me congratulate you," he said. "If the folks in Nashville could see you now!"

"You must go back and spare no detail," she said, extending him a warm reception.

"This ball sure is a sight to see for a poor farm boy. Sure nothing back home to compare."

"There is not one thing poor about you, George Shields. Did you know Laura was here?"

"You mean here tonight?"

"I mean here tonight."

"Where is she?"

"I am not sure, but we shall find her. Isaac, darling, you remember George Shields, from Robertson County? We are looking for Laura. Have you seen her?"

"Excuse me, Your Highness," John Armfield interrupted pretentiously. "May I have the honor of this dance?"

"Yes, kind sir, you may." Adelicia gave her hand to John, dressed to a tee like General Napoleon Bonaparte, even to gold epaulettes on the shoulders of his cropped blue jacket with gold buttons down either side.

"Confound it, I hate these things," John complained to Adelicia, twirling her around the floor, "but Martha's having the time of her life as Josephine. Pompy put his hands over his eyes and said he just couldn't look when we left the house."

Adelicia laughed, "I think you are having a much better time than you are willing to admit. I am sure it was not easy for Martha to get you in this garb, however, the Napoleon costume really becomes you."

"Laura's escort is Tryon Weeks, a friend of ours from Natchez, a real nice fellow. What brings you to New Orleans?" Isaac asked George Shields while searching for Laura.

"Some friends of the family from Huntsville invited me down," he answered. "I had actually planned to call on you this week to discuss, I should say, to ask if you'd be interested in any additional corn or livestock for your plantations. I was talking to your father-in-law in early winter, and he made mention you sometimes bought corn and hog sides from farmers here because Fairvue hadn't been supplying enough as of late. I raise a lot of corn along with my hogs and cattle. Fact is, I got near six thousand hogs..." Isaac smiled wondering if Adelicia had had anything to do with his offer.

"Do you see the sophisticated young lady in the pale pink satin, standing beside," he asked, squinting his eyes for a better look, "someone who must be King Lear? That's Laura."

"She's beautiful! Grown up!" George exclaimed.

"Of course, she's beautiful." Isaac led George through the crowd of gaily dressed revelers, to find the fourteenth century, *Juliet*.

"Laura, look who's here from home," Isaac said, the loud music making it necessary to shout.

"Mr. Shields! What are you doing here?" Laura asked blushing.

"You all asked the same question. Am I really that much of a recluse? I do get off the farm every now and then," George answered, not letting go of Laura's hand.

"It's hard to manage though," a man interrupted from nearby. "Please forgive the intrusion, I'm Joseph Acklen," he said, pushing his thick blonde hair away from brown, deep-set eyes. "George is my family's guest."

Isaac extended his hand. "I'm pleased to meet you, Mr. Acklen. Meet my friend Crawford Benedict." Crawford, regally dressed as King Lear, offered his hand. "Do you reside in Louisiana?" Isaac asked. "I don't believe I've heard the name before."

"No, sir, we're from Huntsville, Alabama, but I'm opening a law office in Nashville. We did meet before, though, at your open house when General Jackson was there."

"You must forgive me. There were so many."

"No apology needed, sir, I was honored to be among the guests that night."

"Meet my wife's sister, Laura Hayes, Juliet for tonight, visiting with us from Nashville, and our friend Tryon Weeks from Natchez."

From the dance floor, Adelicia spotted her sister. "I see George and Isaac found Laura." She took a short quick breath. "John, who is that talking with them?"

"I don't know, can't see him that well...everybody's so fluted up can't tell who..."

"Shh, it is a lieutenant from Huntsville."

"Who's he?" John asked.

"I just told you. When the waltz ends, I shall introduce you."

The waltz ended, but it was impossible for her to make her way through the crowd. "I need some refreshment, but the next dance you shall have, Crawford," she said, continuing to weave her way through the myriad of guests in the elegant St Louis ballroom, graciously accepting compliments as she passed.

Finally reaching her sister, Adelicia said, "I see you found her, George Shields. Laura, is it not grand to see our friend from home?"

George turned to the man beside him, "Allow me to introduce my friend from Huntsville, Joe Acklen, the one who got me off the farm."

"A toast to the queen," said Acklen, raising his glass. Adelicia had remembered his light brown eyes.

"I'll drink to that," said Tryon. The group raised their glasses to toast Adelicia, who did indeed look like a queen. A toast to Isaac followed.

"It is delightful to see you again, Lieutenant Acklen. We are pleased you have joined us tonight."

"Would you honor me with this dance?"

"This one is promised to our friend, Crawford Benedict, but the next one shall be yours."

A glorious evening, Adelicia thought, smiling to herself. She and her husband King and Queen of Mardi Gras! She could not sleep, nor could she lie silently brooding beside Isaac. She slipped noiselessly from bed, put on her ivory satin robe that lay across the silk upholstered chaise lounge, and walked onto the gallery overlooking the enclosed courtyard. Everything was still and silent as she felt the warmth mingled coolness of a late February night and the evening's revelry lost in the quiet of early morning.

She walked to the far end of the verandah and peered into the window where Emma lay sleeping with Charlotte nearby. Further down, she stopped by the bedroom where her two other daughters slept, stepped inside, bent over and kissed each of them. Then she cautiously went down the stairs and sat near the center of the courtyard beneath the large oak, the tree on whose branches the children loved to climb and play and swing: "their tree," they called it. "Papa says it must have been planted there especially with us in mind," little Adelicia and Victoria would say. "It's almost as much fun as our play house at Fairvue."

She thought about herself as a little girl at Rokeby...her dear mother...Richard...Camille... Isaac...burying their son who lived so short a time...her three daughters...how precious, they were...then again, Isaac.

As she rested her head against the oak's great trunk, she pondered the one lesson from her earliest teachings that had been as important to her as any other, perhaps more important. Her father had said, "If you are honest with yourself, Adie, fully honest, seeing yourself, and seeing the things and life around you as it really is, you'll be all right. It's the person who tries to fool himself who loses. Never swindle yourself, my darling, daughter." She clearly recalled that summer afternoon he had said it. They were riding side by side, slowly returning to the stables.

Things were not the same now as on her wedding day when she walked down the curved stairway on her father's arm. Feelings change in seven years—in fewer years than that—months—or weeks, or even days, perhaps. Whatever the time frame, she was consciously aware of her change; and she was frightened; holding on to sentimental girlishness of days past while feeling, knowing inside, her cringing aloofness to things that had once seemed so important, her initial enchantment with Fairvue, with Isaac. If only she could pinpoint when it had begun...to know the hour...the cause. She wondered if men had moments like women when they too reflected on feelings and relationships—probably not, she thought, they were too different.

She stood and pulled the robe tighter as the early morning air grew more crisp, uncertain if she would tell Isaac of her disillusionment, or even if it mattered. And as she continued slowly back up the stairs, she decided she would say nothing at all.

The night, the Carnival season had been sheer splendid grandeur. But as she neared their bedroom door, she also knew there was more, much more to come...grander days than those already passed. She felt its certainty just as keenly as the day the monarchs were fluttering around the icehouse at Fairvue, the day she knew that she would return there as its mistress.

CHAPTER 27

Bellevue Plantation

APRIL WAS BALMY AND WARM AS THE FRANKLINS SAILED UP THE Mississippi to Bellevue. The spring green grass on the levees was colored with Delta wildflowers—black eyed susans, periwinkle, blue bonnets and pink clover. Field hands waved at the passing *Tennessee,* and the children delighted in returning the salutation.

They were spending their Easter holiday from Madame LeFere's School at Bellevue and were excited about being back in West Feliciana. They loved the old house with its wide verandahs and great moss-laden oaks, ancient oaks that stood as sentinels to its solitude, so that when one viewed the house from the river it appeared ghostly, almost unapproachable.

"Aunt Essie, Aunt Essie, we are here!" exclaimed Victoria, pointing to Routh's Landing.

"We sure is, sugar lamb."

"Yes, my darlings," Adelicia said, walking to where her daughters stood with Essie. "Is everyone ready to go ashore? What a wonderful week we are going to have."

She swept Emma up and gave her a kiss. "I am so glad we have you. Come children, we are dropping anchor."

Adelicia had been looking forward to spending these special days with Isaac and their daughters. She thought that being with her family at the plantation would be a welcome sedative that both she and Isaac needed. It might be the exact potion to repair her pining. Their love making on the night he had returned from his absence at home had been magical. She was certain it could be again.

"Your papa says it is time to go!" Adelicia said, still holding Emma in her arms.

When they disembarked, workers along the levee and field hands paused to watch the entourage walk up the passageway leading from the river to the waiting buggies that would take them two miles up Tunica Road and an additional one-half mile through the tunnel of oaks leading to Bellevue.

Alfred and Lucy stood waiting on the steps, eager to see the youngsters, who were equally fond of the older couple. Essie and Lucy had fast become friends. With Lucy overseeing Bellevue and its servants, and Essie seeing to the children's nurses, left them time for a satisfying friendship.

The Easter morning worship service had begun early just as the sun's first rays touched the river. The Franklins, Laura and the house servants, sat on wooden benches in the garden west of the main house amidst day lilies, lilacs, daffodils and rhododendron. The other Negroes continued to gather and branch out behind this semicircle and to slowly hum "My Faith Looks Up to Thee," as Isaac stood, and in a tradition begun many years before, began reading from the book of Saint Matthew:

And when the Sabbath was past, Mary Magdalene, and Mary the mother of James, and Salome, had brought sweet spices, that they might come and anoint Him. And very early in the morning of the first day of the week, they came unto the sepulcher at the rising of the sun...and when they looked, they saw that the stone was rolled away for it was very great...

The sun was almost fully risen over the river, when everyone joined in singing, "My Sweet Lord." Communion was passed, a prayer was given, and Brutus, from Loch Lomond, preached a sermon on the crucified and risen Lord.

As the Franklins left the garden and returned to the big house for dinner, the Negroes continued with their hymns as many in the group came forward, took Brutus's hand, stretched their arms toward heaven and prepared for baptisms in the Lake of The Cross.

From the onset of his days as a planter in '28, Isaac had made certain that his Negroes had religious instruction. It was not forced on them, but they were given the opportunity to become baptized Christians. Daniel Turnbull at Melrose Plantation felt the same as he, but some planters in the Feliciana's, such as Bennett Barrow, frowned upon the practice, and had told Isaac it was a deterrent to obedience and gave the slaves cause to unify. In fact, many of the planters refused to let their Negroes organize in any sort of group, no matter how small for fear of insurrection, a thought that was never far from most planter's minds.

As the family sat eating their traditional Easter dinner of boiled ham, snap beans, potato salad and stuffed eggs around the oval mahogany dining room table, young Adelicia asked, "Mother, when we die, will we rise up again like Jesus did?"

"Yes, sweetheart…when we go to heaven."

"I mean, will we be on earth again and know people…like we were before? Jesus knew people when he woke up."

"Jesus was special, sweetheart. He was God's son."

"So we won't come back like He did?"

"When we die, God gives us a long rest, and when we wake up, He lifts us by the hand, and we go to live with Him in heaven, forever."

"And become an angel with wings and halos and golden shoes, like our little brother?" asked Victoria.

Isaac, seeing tears well in Adelicia's eyes, quickly said, "I think it's time we finished our dinner and see what we can find hidden on the lawn."

The children delighted in finding the brightly colored eggs Charlotte and Cora had helped them dye the day before, plus the candy ones purchased in Natchez. Since childhood, Adelicia had never ceased to be fascinated by colored eggs hidden in green grass, and she loved hunting them with the children. In addition to the hunt, Isaac had given each daughter a crystallized sugar egg with a small hole in one end, allowing them to peek inside and see the petite bisque figurine within.

"It has been such a fun day, Papa," Victoria said as her father sat beside her bed that evening. "How many eggs were hidden in all?"

"Oh, about a thousand, maybe more. You think there were enough for everybody to find?"

"My friend Josey found twenty-two boiled ones, and he said he was going to take salt, sit on his cabin steps and eat every one of them at the same time. I bet he does, too."

Rufus and Fanny had overseen the hiding of the eggs, along with Lucy and Alfred, and stood about helping the younger ones, as the children from all five plantations gathered for the service as well as for the big hunt.

Victoria put her arms around Isaac's neck. "Good night, dear Papa."

"Good night, my angel."

Isaac placed a box in the center of Adelicia's dressing table, a medium sized yellow one tied with purple velvet ribbon. Adelicia never ceased to be delighted by beautifully wrapped ribboned packages, and quickly untied the loosely knotted satin bow and lifted out the gilded china egg. "It's exquisite!" She exclaimed. "It is..."

"Look inside."

She lifted the hinged upper half of the jeweled egg and discovered a pear-shaped diamond pendant. "Oh, Isaac! Help me fasten it." He clicked the gold clasp into place allowing the chain's length to drop the diamond to the hollow of her throat.

Adelicia looked into the dressing table mirror. "I adore this," she said, tenderly, touching the pendant and lightly rubbing it between her fingers. "This and the egg are my favorite gifts, ever," she said, teary-eyed. "I shall cherish them for always."

"I'm glad you like it. You've made me a happy man, Adie, despite the disgruntlements and quarrels that I'm sure everyone has. And, most importantly," he said, bending over to kiss the tip of her nose, "thank you for agreeing to Fairvue. "

She picked up the enameled and jeweled egg and held it in both hands. "It is so beautiful." She set it on the table beside their bed, "I want to keep it near." She reached up and put her hands around Isaac's neck, and pulled his face to hers. "Hold me, Isaac...hold me so close." She longed and wished for the feelings of past times, for the magic.

CHAPTER 28

THE RETURN DOWNRIVER TO NEW ORLEANS WAS SPACED BE-
tween clear skies and spring showers. Charlotte and Cora had
found it difficult to keep the children out of the rain; the weather
was warm, they argued, and the fresh water good for them. Isaac
appeared happy and relaxed, as he and Adelicia stood arm in arm
standing on the bow enjoying the children's chatter and the lapping
Mississippi.

And as the *Tennessee* docked in the busy harbor, there was Pompy
waiting with the carriages. Essie had had as little contact as possible
with "Pompous Pompy," as she continued to call him. And though she
occasionally found little niceties done for her here and yon, strongly
suspecting they were Pompy's doings, she remained as aloof to him
as ever. She did admit to Adelicia that his manners were improving.

186 Canal Street was a welcome sight to Adelicia. She had immensely enjoyed Easter at Bellevue and the lovely days with her
family, but she was glad to be back. Isaac would be busier than usual
in the coming weeks, putting business in order after Carnival and the
Easter holidays, and she knew how much he was looking forward to
returning to Fairvue in May, as was she.

They had agreed on a more permanent move to Gallatin. She was
resigned to the idea that January through April would be spent in
New Orleans and West Feliciana, that the children would attend
Madame LeFere's during those four months. But the remainder of
the year would be spent at Fairvue, and a tutor would be hired.

She had not considered her resignation bleak, spending eight
months of the year in Middle Tennessee; instead, her children would
be with their grandfather, uncles and aunts more often. She had also
begun to have a greater respect for Fairvue's importance to Isaac,
not just his will to be there, but who he was, endeared to the land
his father had been granted, then what he himself had acquired long

before she had known him. Perhaps she was becoming wiser. Her trifling she had set aside, and would no longer interfere with that part of him that longed for home. She wanted to please Isaac, to share in the joy of being at Fairvue with him and their children. She would not deviate from her commitment.

Three weeks after Easter, James Clack sent word requesting Isaac to return to West Feliciana. Two of his Negroes at Bellevue had been jailed for public drunkenness while on a purchasing trip to St. Francisville, and three field hands had taken to the woods with some of Ruffin Barrow's.

Barrow's plantation was a good ten miles down Tunica Road from his own, but Isaac's Negroes always knew when Barrow's were heading for the woods.

Clack had immediately posted bail for the two in jail, Lemuel and Chooks, but other problems existed, and he thought it best if Isaac were present. No one in West Feliciana would ever forget the Natchez uprising of '34 when eight white family members had been massacred. Although Louisiana had seen few insurrections, as most had occurred further north, Virginia and elsewhere, white families all over the South were uneasy when a group of Negroes took to the woods.

Isaac was feeling tired when he swallowed a dose of the medicine Dr. Gee had prescribed for his recurring indigestion just before boarding the *Tennessee*. He told Adelicia that if all went well at Bellevue, he expected to return within the week, in time for Laura's voice recital. He was fond of her younger sister, Laura, and pleased with her success after her debut into New Orleans society five months before. He also liked her sharing the by-weekly letters with him from George Shields.

Four days after Isaac arrived at Bellevue, Jim Clack sent word on the morning packet, from Bayou Sara to New Orleans, that Adelicia should come immediately to Bellevue. He wrote that Isaac had been ill from the time of his arrival and was not responding to any medicines or remedies, that he had also sent word to John Armfield who was in Natchez.

When the Negro boy had come with the message, Adelicia was in the morning room reading to the children, sprawled about her on the

Aubusson rug. She later remembered the exact moment that Essie had come into the room. Adelicia was reading from *The Arabian Nights* and had just finished the lines, "The Prince turned the horse toward Persia, and as soon as the Princess had mounted behind him and was well settled with her arms about his waist, he turned the peg, whereupon the horse mounted into the air with his accustomed speed..." It was a favorite passage the children often asked to have repeated, and a passage that Isaac sometimes read to them, never forgetting to mention that that was how it had been between him and their mother on their wedding day.

Afternoon readings were seldom interrupted and when Essie had burst in with Clack's note and with Isaac's unmistakable maroon-bordered stationary in hand, Adelicia was immediately alarmed. She broke the seal, quickly read the brief words, and handed it back to Essie. With one gesture, it seemed to her, she kissed her three daughters, rang for the carriage, and was on her way to the wharf.

And yet too soon it now seemed, she was on the packet's return trip up river to Bayou Sara...the same packet that had brought the boy with the news. Isaac could not be seriously ill, she told herself. But Jim Clack was not an alarmist, he would never have sent for her had he not felt the situation grave. And then there were the words penned by Isaac: "My Dearest Adie, yes, I did love you from the first moment. But how could I have ever told you so? You have brought me the greatest joy a husband could know. Thank you my dear wife, for our precious daughters. All will be well. Take care...of yourself, the little ones, Fairvue...Yours, always, Isaac."

She sat on the forward deck, her hands folded in her lap, watching as the Mississippi's water lapped and sprayed at the sides of the boat. She repeated over and over to herself that Isaac was in excellent health; he could not be ill. Then she remembered how fatigued he had been throughout Mardi Gras, and how restless, knowing he had participated only because of herself and Laura. Yet he had seemed happy and rejuvenated on their return holiday from Bellevue. However, he had felt unwell just before Jim Clack had asked that he return to Bellevue.

Brutus was waiting when the packet let down her plank at Routh's Landing, and Adelicia hesitantly stepped ashore. And as the horse and buggy neared Bellevue, she asked Brutus to slow the mare. She wanted more time. She would stare into the Tunica Hills, watch lizards scamper along the side of the road, peek for alligators in the swamp, pick wild violets in the dense woods...anything to delay reality. But Isaac had to be all right, she repeated, she knew he was. She prayed to God that he was.

The afternoon heat caused Adelicia to dab perspiration from her neck and forehead as Brutus stopped beside the other buggies that stood in front of the large mystical structure, and Daniel Turnbull reached for her hand, with Ruffin and Bennett Barrow and John Sterling standing beside him.

There was no mistaking any of the signs: the neighbor's buggies, the Negroes absent from the fields and already gathering outside the house.

She hurried from the carriage and ran up the stairs to their bedroom, where Isaac lay unconscious. She sat beside his bed, recalling seven years before when she had done the same. She wanted to scream at them all, the neighbors, the servants, the doctor, and ask if they were there waiting for him to die.

She lifted his left hand in hers and traced with her fingertips the outline of his palm, then over each sinew and nail, and over the monogrammed gold ring she had given him on their wedding day. His hands were strong and firm, but so gentle when they had touched her. She lay her head on his chest and closed her eyes after glimpsing his favorite boots that stood in the corner.

It seemed only moments later when Dr. Gee put his arm around her, lifted her up and placed her in Lucy's care, and certainly no more than moments, just as the sun had finished dropping behind the Tunica Hills, that Dr. Gee pronounced Isaac's death due to complicated indigestion.

John Armfield reached the plantation from Natchez an hour later and although outwardly distraught, he sent to Baton Rouge for John Lobdell, Isaac's lawyer and legal advisor for the past twelve years. Before Adelicia had finished dressing the following morning, John Armfield had knocked on her door with a paper for her to sign from Lobdell as to whether or not she would "stand to Isaac's will, or would dissent."

The obituary in the *New Orleans Picayune* read: "On Monday, April 27, 1846, on his Bellevue Plantation, Isaac Franklin, Esquire, left an amiable wife and three young daughters with a large circle of friends to mourn his untimely death. He will be buried in Gallatin, Tennessee at his beloved Fairvue Plantation."

"The uncertainties are the only things that are certain." Adelicia remembered the day when she and Isaac had watched, through a haze of falling snow, the Cherokees board the rafts taking them West, and he had said those words. Now, she and John silently sat beside the wooden box with Isaac's body inside, while Pompy piloted the *Tennessee* toward New Orleans.

Friends, business associates, politicians, merchants, common laborers black and white, had gathered in the house on Canal Street to pay their respects, where Isaac's body lay in a walnut casket at the end of the long hallway, the same hallway in which they had danced. Adelicia had accepted condolences, stood long hours to speak to the many who came to comfort and console. But she had preferred the time at evening's end, when only the house servants remained, and after they, too, and the children and Laura were sleeping. It was then that she could sit in the leather chair at the foot of Isaac's coffin, with a sadness she had never before experienced, attempting to sort out her thoughts...the illusions, the realities. The certainty of death, the uncertainty of life.

After two days of steady streams of visitors, she watched as Isaac's body was removed to an oak coffin and immersed in five barrels of whiskey to preserve it, then put aboard the *Tennessee* for a final trip to Fairvue.

The gray fog emerged thick and silent on the early May 6th, morning as the river boat wound its way west back up the Mississippi. And through its stillness, Adelicia heard the muzzled sounds of distant ships grow fainter, as New Orleans' busy port lay further and further behind her.

The *Tennessee's* flags flew at half-mast, and her sides were draped in black. Passing ships slowed their speed and saluted, and field hands stopped their work and stood along the levees in respect. When they neared the bend of the river, Adelicia stood holding Emma in her arms, the older girls clutching the skirts of her black crepe dress. The veil that covered her face lifted in the gentle river breeze as they passed Loch Lomond, Bellevue, Angora, Panola and Killarney, each of which flew black flags from their widow peaks.

Standing rigid and tearless, she listened to the Negroes uninhibited humming and weeping as they lined the levees to bid a final farewell to their master, as the ship slowly passed the plantations, blew its horn for a final salute, then made the turn north for home.

When Charlotte came to take the children, Adelicia kissed each one and told them to be good girls. She wished to be alone with Isaac's coffin as she attempted to sort out her thoughts and to integrate the uncertainties, the detachment she felt from everything around her, deepened by the vast emptiness within...her husband, the father of her children, forever passed from her life.

All seemed a dream, as she had held the children and told them that their papa was going to be in heaven like their baby brother. Her words had seemed unreal, as were her attempts to read or play with them between their naps and meals.

She was a widow at the age of twenty-nine with three young daughters and God only knew how much land, stockholdings, houses and slaves. Other than knowing there had been no limits placed on her spending, she knew little else about their finances. Had Isaac not always been so secretive, had he not always refused from the time of their honeymoon to share his business affairs, she would not now be faced with dependence on family, or lawyers or whomever for guidance. She had already signed a paper on the morning following Isaac's death. She could not understand, then or now, why the singular thought on John Armfield's mind seemed whether or not she would contest Isaac's will that she had neither read nor heard read.

She hoped that she had not hurt Crawford and Joanna Benedict's feelings when she refused their offer to accompany her to Fairvue. She looked forward to their continued friendship but at this moment she wanted nothing from anyone, and as the sun was setting and the ship neared Natchez, she felt more than ever her sense of right in being alone.

"Adie," Laura called gently, "Charlotte and Cora are ready to tuck in the children. Do you not want to leave this room for a while and tell them goodnight?"

"I'll come," she answered, void of emotion.

She rose slowly, retucked the black veil around her face, and stood silently for a moment before reaching out and touching the oak coffin with its strong whiskey smell, then went below to the sleeping quarters with her sister.

On May 18th, as the *Tennessee* docked at Nashville's wharf, Adelicia stood on deck beside Isaac's coffin, then watched as it was placed in the horse-drawn hearse that would transport it to McCombs and Carson Funeral Parlor to be prepared for burial. Afterward, the body would be returned to the original walnut casket brought from New Orleans, then sealed with glass and lead. She insisted that Laura return to Rokeby with their father.

The sun glistened against the Cumberland as the *Tennessee* continued upriver to Fairvue where she dropped anchor in mid-afternoon. Weary and worn, Adelicia walked up the hill from the landing, holding a child's hand in each of hers. Essie and Charlotte followed, and Cora carried Emma. Della and Daniel stood just inside the doorway with their heads bowed, and Aunt Aggie sat in her favorite chair with a handkerchief to her face.

"Charlotte, take the children to their rooms, please," Adelicia directed. "Mother will see you later," she said, giving them a kiss.

"Essie, speak to Della and give her instructions. Make sure she understands the details and necessary preparations. Please see to Aunt Aggie."

"Don't you want me to stay with you, child? You not looking good."

"No," she answered in the same monotone in which she had spoken for days. "I prefer to be alone."

She walked past the stairway and stood looking into the long double parlors. The furniture filled rooms appeared vast and empty. She looked at their portraits, hers and Isaac's, that hung on either side of the mantle, the ones painted by Earl the year they were married, and at the mantle whose marble filled the room with cold. She walked into the dining room, pulled out her familiar armchair and sat staring down the length of the long table to the empty chair at the opposite end and the empty chairs in between. She recalled the first time she had sat there, when she had looked past her family and wished to be mistress of Fairvue. She remembered when the two had dined alone...the times when the great table was filled with guests...the breakfasts when the two older children sat on opposite sides in the middle and Emma sat in the highchair near her. Memories of past joys were filling her thoughts, but not her emptiness.

She moved slowly up the stairs and into their bedroom. And feeling chilled, she reached for the down comforter that lay across the bed's foot rail, sat in the damask chair and drew the soft down about her before leaning back and closing her eyes, as tears began trickling down her cheeks. Why must she always appear to be strong? Why could she not weep aloud? Even as a child, few people besides her own parents believed that she felt pain. No one knew the insecurities that dwelt within her delicate facade of strength except herself and God. Stunned, she had wept briefly as Isaac took his last breath. She could not weep as they came to pay their respects in New Orleans, nor on the Nashville wharf. She could not weep when they would come to Fairvue, but she could weep now.

But on the morrow, she would again prove herself void of emotion. For two days, the house would be filled with friends and family bestowing their condolences, constantly going and coming. Della and Daniel would see that everyone had food and drink. Charlotte, Cora and Essie would see to the children; John Armfield, William and her father would assist her in receiving. Isaac would lie in the middle of the two parlors, between the black Kilkarney marble mantels. On Friday, he would be taken to the cemetery plot on the West side... the finality...the burial, then the silence of the house.

CHAPTER 29

THE MORNING OF THE BURIAL, ADELICIA WAS STANDING AT THE same arched doorway where Uncle Sugart had stood with the umbrellas the first time she saw Fairvue. She watched as the hearse, with its transparent glassed sides, and pulled by four glistening black horses, slowly rumbled up the winding drive, with John walking behind leading Imposter. William and John were next, along with her family, then Governor Harris Brown, followed by a long line of carriages and men on horseback that completed the long procession.

It was much as she had imagined it would be, as she sat between Victoria and little Adelicia, holding their hands, her father, brothers and sisters on either side of them, while Reverend Edgar, not quite seven years after having performed their wedding ceremony, pronounced the eulogy. It was also only five days before Isaac's fifty-seventh birthday.

She thought of all those who had passed before, and as she heard the scriptures being read, feeling emptiness deep within, her mind wandered to an earlier incident when Isaac had returned late in the afternoon. She could not help but wonder if Lona had learned of Isaac's death.

Adelicia refused to have anyone stay with her at Fairvue that evening, nor would she agree to go to Rokeby. Sarah had invited her to Polk Place, but she declined her invitation as well. She needed the silence that she knew would only come when the last guests had gone, the children were tucked in their beds, and the last candle snuffed out.

When it did come, she, carrying a single taper, wearily climbed the stairs and entered the bedroom she had shared with Isaac, just as the peacocks were making their eerie cries, flying up to their perches. She sat in the ivory damask chair and drew her legs up, wrapping her arms around them, closed her eyes and rested her head on top of her knees. Silent tears fell, that quickly turned to heavy sobbing, just as she heard an alarming clap of thunder and the first drops of a spring rain.

Two weeks from the day of the funeral, Adelicia ordered the wreaths removed from the doors, the black drapes from the windows and asked that the household resume its normal activities, except for dressing in mourning. Aunt Aggie was doing much better than expected, and enjoyed having the children gather around while she told tales of their father's childhood when he was her "baby boy," and tales of Uncle Sugart, all the while having her pipe nearby.

The children brought life anew back to Adelicia, and that first week, when she was not resting, she spent her time with them, walking to the river in May day breezes and gathering wild flowers. In the afternoons when they napped, she went to the plot west of the house where Isaac was buried and sat on the marble bench beside his grave, often holding a clod of fresh earth in her hand.

She did not want to stay at Fairvue without Isaac, nor did she want to return to New Orleans. She had no thoughts of what she did want, but in the meanwhile, she and the children would enjoy the summer together with their cousins, their pets, their playhouse, the fertile countryside, the stability of home in Sumner County. They loved it, much like their father, and life at Fairvue would continue. The plantation activities were no longer stilled...their was work to do.

May passed. Architect William Strickland had completed the design for the enormous granite mausoleum requested in Isaac's will, and it was in the process of being built.

How wonderful, Adelicia thought, that children are such marvelous acceptors, marvelous examples of continued life. She had walked on the lawns with them and ridden in the ring with them. She had cantered through the rich pastures on Samson and was beginning to feel secure in her new world. Emma took such delight in her older sisters, and they loved toting her about the lawn and pulling her in the small wagon that Caleb had made for them, Caleb who had become their protector. Adelicia greatly missed Isaac, but it still seemed almost as if he were away on business and would be returning any moment...until the late afternoons, when reality set in and she would walk to his grave.

Victoria and little Adelicia were elated when she told them of plans to accompany the Armfields to Beersheba Springs, only forty miles from Gallatin. Aunt Essie, Aunt Aggie, Charlotte, Cora and their grandfather were also coming, all avoiding the approaching summer heat. The cool mountain air would be refreshing, she had told the children...they could splash and play in the magnificent falls, an outing their father would have tremendously enjoyed.

"You ought not take the child if she feeling no better in the morning," Essie said as she assisted Adelicia in packing the trunks. "Little Adie's fever come up again this afternoon, and she coughing mighty bad. I stay behind. You send Pompous Pompy back to get us later."

"We shall see in the morning," Adelicia answered. "Dr. Mentlo said there was no danger, just a late spring cold. Are the children's dresses pressed?"

Before retiring, Adelicia checked each child's room and kissed their sleeping eyes, but soon after, she summoned Charlotte to send for the doctor. Little Adelicia was burning with fever and choking as she coughed.

"Cora, get the steam ready. Hurry."

"Essie, dip more cloths in ice water! In alcohol?"

Adelicia gently rocked her feverish little one, stroking her damp curls while tears streamed down her own cheeks. "Oh, God, do not let anything happen to my child," she cried.

But within only moments, it seemed, Adelicia felt the faint, last breath of her young daughter as she drew her even closer, and continued rocking her until Essie knelt beside the chair and asked her to please let her lay the child on the bed. Reluctantly, Adelicia stood and holding her daughter in her arms, ordered Charlotte to put a sheet across the library table in the center of the hallway. There she laid her on the clean white linen and bathed her in cool water, with tears flowing down her cheeks and onto the child. It had happened so quickly. Just that morning, she had played with her sisters.

Adelicia dressed her in the new white batiste with ecru lace and pale blue ribbon entredeau inserts, recently made for her in New

Orleans. She brushed her long dark hair, carefully placing each ringlet around her cherub face and shoulders, then tied in a blue satin ribbon on top that matched the sash of her dress. Then she laid her precious child on the swan tester bed and knelt beside her.

Although Adelicia had allowed Essie to assist by bringing those things she needed into the room, she received no help dressing or doing her daughter's hair. "Never," she told Essie, "will, I be able to do so again."

When Dr. Mentlo arrived from Gallatin an hour after little Adelicia had succumbed to scarlet fever, Adelicia was sitting on the bed beside her, stroking her curls and refusing to leave where she sat. After checking Victoria and Emma, who had similar symptoms, the doctor placed the house under quarantine.

On June 13th, five days later, another small casket containing the body of Victoria was lowered into the ground beside her sister, to the right side of their father. Aunt Aggie's was farther back to the left, beside that of Uncle Sugart's...four newly dug graves in less than a month.

Adelicia was recovering from the same malady that had taken her children's and Aunt Aggie's lives, and had not been rational from the day of the burials.

"Thank God, Emma is all right," someone had said as Adelicia lay in bed, too weak to do little more than occasionally remember.

"Except you become as a little child," Reverend Edgar had read from the *Gospel of Matthew*..."They cannot return to you, but you can go to them," from *II Samuel*. The words fusing together as repetitious phrases from the ministers lips that flashed in and out.

Adelicia saw her children so plainly, but each time she reached for them, their faces faded into a light, a bright light for which she also extended her hands. She lingered between consciousness and unconsciousness, with glimpses of sounds and memories and moments that returned, then vanished again.

July 1846 was coming to its close before Adelicia was able to take short walks on the lawn. Essie had been her constant nurse and companion while Charlotte took care of Emma, and Dr. Mentlo made the six mile trip daily from Gallatin to prescribe and administer to both mother and daughter. After the quarantine was lifted, Adelicia's family and friends, some of whom she thought would not have been concerned, made visits for which she was very pleased and grateful. But as she sat in the garden with her father on this particular, warm, August afternoon, the horrible nightmare of death continued, from which she could not awake.

"You're looking much better, Adie," said her father, "I wish I could persuade you to come home to Rokeby with me, at least for a while. I want to get to know my granddaughter before she grows into a beauty like her mother."

"She will not be two until December, Papa." Adelicia made no further response, and a long silence followed.

"I hope you're not thinking of returning to New Orleans. There are some excellent tutors in Nashville, and I..."

"She is not even two yet! I have one child left out of four. I do not want to plan or think about the future, or have anything to do with it. Emma is all I have left, and I pray God does not take her, too."

Pausing, she took her father's hands in each of hers. "I am afraid to pray, Papa. God does not answer my prayers. Nothing lasts, Papa. Nothing!" She lay her head in her father's lap and broke into loud sobbing, her hands clenched in his.

CHAPTER 30

Nashville

"In The Name of God Amen!"

"I, ISAAC FRANKLIN, OF SUMNER COUNTY, STATE OF TENNESSEE, son of James and Mary Franklin who are both deceased, a citizen of the United States of America, and now residing, for the present, on my estate in the parish of West Feliciana, and State of Louisiana, do make, ordain, and declare the instrument which I have caused to be written from my own dictation..."

The reading of the will...Isaac had never discussed it with her, nor mentioned its contents...and she cared little to know what it said now. All worldly possessions were hers and Emma's, but the financial operations were to be controlled by her father, William and John. For two long hours she had remained aloof to the words being read, and it was William who nudged her to say it was over.

She had listened to, or heard, how everyone was to fare after her husband's death. William, John, Albert, his sisters, nephews, his nieces and his favorite slaves were all remembered, including those in Louisiana. Isaac had seen to everyone when he made his will in May of '41, she thought. She would remain at Fairvue with Emma, Essie, Charlotte, Della and Daniel. She was tired, and did not want to think.

Eleven months had passed since Isaac's death and no one, except the immediate household and her family, had seen Adelicia's face without the black veil.

One of the few visitors whom she enjoyed, to whom she was not just polite, was the country's First Lady, Sarah Polk. When in Nashville, she visited with Adelicia and in Sarah, she found a solace, a sincerity, a friendship, for which she was deeply grateful. And it was Sarah to whom she first spoke about the conditions of Isaac's will.

"I have read and reread it with William and with Papa...with the two of them together," she began. "And with each reading, it becomes clearer that Isaac entrusted nothing to me...nothing at all, Sarah. And before you say so, I know there is nothing unusual about its contents...Papa has told me that enough times. I have learned well enough, it is the abominable way men keep women under their control, even after death. I have also learned that I cannot accept it. Why do men feel such a need to lock their widows into a life of seclusion, a life where they must live according to the dictates on a piece of paper, or have what they have lawfully inherited taken away?"

Sarah sipped tea from a delicate floral china cup as they sat in the front parlor opposite each other on matching ivory silk arm chairs with a tea table between them. And as they spoke, Adelicia carefully watched for any change or expression of concern from Sarah.

"You are right, of course," Sarah agreed. "The will is written in the usual manner. And if the President passed, God forbid, I would have it no other way. But you are different, my dear. You have a spirit, a will, that reaches beyond the bounds of most of us...and I understand your concern."

Adelicia relaxed her shoulders as sunlight filtered through the large window, and moved nearer the edge of her chair, hoping that Sarah did truly understand. "It is true that Isaac has left me, if not the wealthiest woman in the United States, among the few who are in that position when all assets are totaled. But, Sarah, to remain so, Emma and I must make Fairvue our permanent residence and I must live the rest of my life as a widow. If I decide against either of those conditions, the estate reverts back to the trustees, half of which will be held in trust for Emma and the remainder used to perpetuate Isaac's name in a school for young men to be built on the grounds of Fairvue."

"How interesting, Adelicia. That should make Sumner Countians very pleased. Do you know the details of the school?"

The regalness with which Sarah sat as she listened, the assurance of her tone, gave Adelicia confidence, propelling her to continue. "Nothing more than, according to the will, the school is to have the best of instructors and will accept any student who meets the academic requirements, regardless of financial status."

"That is very noble, an honorable gesture. Are you not pleased?"

"Sarah, more upsetting is that the trustees are even to have guardianship of Emma: for her education, support and maintenance! Only one brief line mentions me caring for my own daughter, and I quote, 'her mother is to be consulted at all times.'"

Realizing that she was becoming more distressed than she wished Sarah to see, Adelicia set her tea cup on the oval Louis XIV table that separated them and walked to the rear of the room, from which she could view the river and the cliffs beyond. And suddenly, she hated the sight. She hated the room's lavender flocked wallpaper. The French imported paper she had thought so beautiful now suffocated her. She turned to see Sarah, still sitting regally, as if she were an oil portrait or an artist's subject.

"I apologize, Sarah," she said from where she stood, "I've never spoken these words to anyone, and as I speak, it brings more fatigue than I had imagined."

"You need never apologize to me. Would it be best to continue another time?"

"No, please, I would like to finish, now that I have begun."

She returned to her chair opposite Sarah. "If I leave Fairvue or remarry, all that is left to my keeping are one hundred thousand dollars, the household goods and the servants I brought with me at the time of our marriage. Sarah," she said, lowering her voice almost to a whisper. "Isaac has locked me in...to have it all or to have nothing. Six years ago, he saw to my future... he had no right! Tell me I do not sound like a whimpering schoolgirl. Tell me what you think."

"Adelicia, my telling you what I think right now would not be fair to either of us. I believe things became clearer to you today as you spoke. Doing so, often lets us see beyond that which we have understood before. But let me consider what you have shared in confidence, and we shall discuss it over tea at Polk Place."

Adelicia moved from her chair and knelt beside Sarah and took her hand, smiling.

"No." Sarah said. "You do not sound like a whining school girl."

Adelicia stood in the arched doorway and watched as Sarah's carriage, pulled by two dappled grays, turned onto the pebble drive leading back to the Nashville Pike, grateful for Sarah and for her special friendship. The United States was at war with Mexico, yet this dear lady had time to listen to her.

CHAPTER 31

IT WAS THE FIRST DAY OF SPRING, 1847, AND ADELICIA AWAKENED while it was still dark and the moon had not yet left the sky. The early morning air was chilly when she walked outside Fairvue, snuggled inside her woolen robe, and stood on the rear portico looking across the lawn down to the river. She felt fresh and alive in the pale morning moonlight, and except for the great void that gnawed within from the loss of her children, Adelicia felt nearly like herself again, revived from a reality of events over which she had had no control, events that had been perpetrated years before without her knowledge, but over which she would not succumb.

"Remember," she recalled herself telling Camille, "Born with silver spoons…We'll always soar…"

She wished for her friend once more to share the joys and pleasures they had known growing up and during their marriages, but Camille was not there. She was now a beloved memory of years and times that had forever passed.

Adelicia was alive…so alive on this particular March morning! She was going to become a participant in a game, a wickedly vicious game, and be the victor. There was no reason whatsoever why she should not have it all: to live where she wished, and if the occasion arose, to marry when and whom she wished. Most importantly, she would have access to managing Isaac's estate in its entirety—complete control—to double, triple its assets, to develop it into what even Isaac may not have imagined for West Feliciana!

Admittedly it was unclear exactly how or where to begin, or whom to ask. But it was possible, she thought, as she walked in the peach orchard, stopping now and then to touch the thumb-sized fruit, the future racing through her mind.

The sun was rising over the Cumberland, the peacocks strutting on the lawn picking at last evening's grains through blades of spring green grass before she went back inside, the chill of the air long forgotten.

"Della?"

"Yes, Miz. Franklin?"

"I would like my coffee in the dining room now."

"In the dining room?

"Do not bother me with questions this morning. I said the dining room. Bring fresh fruit, lots of it, a poached egg, steaming coffee, or one of your surprise concoctions that will taste delicious on this glorious day. Please be quick."

"'Please be quick,' Della mocked, as she walked away. 'Don't bother me with questions this morning, I'd like this, and I'd like that.' I still says the only reason Aggie and Sugart ever like her was cause of Mr. Isaac and them pore childrens," she grumbled, hurrying to prepare breakfast.

"What you mumbling about, woman?" asked Daniel, standing at the kitchen table grinding smoked sausage.

"I'm mumbling about that widow in there," Della answered, breaking an egg into boiling water. "One of these days somebody's gonna figure her out. You wait and see. Ain't nobody as perfect as she got some folks thinking she is."

"Good morning, Miz Franklin. You up early," greeted Daniel, as he put her fruit and hot coffee before her on the dining room table. "Your egg's coming next."

"It is a good morning, Daniel. Will you tell Della I prefer her to be better prepared whenever I decide to dine? There is no usual time, and it is her responsibility to be aware. Also, say that when she wants to repeat what I have just said to her, that she might wait until she is completely out of ear-shot."

"Yessum, I tell."

CHAPTER 32

WHEN LUKE STOPPED THE CARRIAGE IN FRONT OF POLK PLACE, Adelicia told him that she would not be long. The majestic mansion stood not from the state capitol, and she smiled as she touched one of the massive columns that surrounded all four sides of it; she had heard that Sam Houston's dwelling in Texas looked much the same. She had not thought of Sam Houston since Andrew Jackson's funeral.

"You are very kind to see me this morning, Sarah. I know how little time you have."

"I'm never too busy for you. Now what is the urgency?" she asked, ushering Adelicia into the morning room, brightly lit by a mid-day sun that beamed into the three sides from floor to ceiling windows.

"I need your advice before I act on the matter we discussed," Adelicia said, sitting beside a tea table opposite Sarah where Dorrie had placed a sandwich tray.

"Often when one asks for advice, that really is not what one wants. Do you wish my opinion to have someone agree with you, or will what I say alter your plans?" She looked kindly into Adelicia's face. "I think your mind is, most probably, already made up. You look like your old beaming, spirited and determined self, but pray tell me about it."

"You know me well," Adelicia smiled, placing a napkin across her lap, "I suppose it is decided. What I need to know is, how will it be received? It has mattered little before to me what people thought, but this is a different concern. Sarah, I have thought it through; it is only right that I have complete control of Isaac's estate. Obviously, I must have the best representation possible, and am aware the case may have far-reaching implications. That is where my uncertainty lies… and, my guilt. So, please, advise me. Tell me what you think."

Sarah straightened the afghan draped over her lap and rang for tea. "Adelicia what I think about your decision is of no consequence. Your mind is made up, and I admire you for it. As for what people may think, who can be the judge of that? Friends sometimes become enemies, enemies have even been known to become friends. I do believe, however, you are going to run into considerable opposition, perhaps from the very ones on whom you think you can rely. You must determine the price you are willing to pay to get the results you desire. You will need the perseverance and endurance of a martyr. When I am in Nashville, I shall always be available to you." Sarah sipped from her tea cup and returned it to the saucer in her hand. "I am your friend, but I am afraid you are going to be very much on your own."

Adelicia looked gratefully at this gracious lady, in some ways like herself, yet so different, but nevertheless, one of the few females who had ever understood her.

"I do not think I shall be remembered as a martyr," she smiled, taking Sarah's hand. "I respect your opinion, and value our friendship, but if it does become worse than I can imagine right now, and the state itself becomes my enemy..." she paused, "You are the First Lady, and I shall understand, if you can no longer be my friend. Thank you, Sarah, for telling me the truth."

Sarah stood and walked with Adelicia into the grand hall, taking her hand, "Let us not have any more nonsense about our friendship. And you may not be remembered as a saint perhaps, or a martyr...but most probably for something just as valuable. Remember that. Good luck and God bless you, dear."

Adelicia stepped into her handsome barouche pulled by four, full of renewed confidence. "Luke, the next stop is Judge White's, and hurry." The Judge would keep her affair secret from her father, William and John, until she had collected the necessary facts and information to present to them. The fewer people involved right now, the better, and even if there were unforeseen problems, as Sarah had suggested, she felt certain of triumphing over them later with the support of her father's and Joel's friends.

While courteous as always, Judge White let her know quickly that he would not be a willing participant in the contesting of Isaac's will. She felt the muscles in her face tighten, and the longer the Judge spoke, the more determined and willful she became. He told her what Sarah Polk had most likely known, and she had not: that James

Green, Balie Peyton, Eli Odum, and other Sumner County residents had already filed a petition with the Tennessee Judiciary Court to incorporate and build the Isaac Franklin Institute on a portion of the two thousand acre estate, just as soon as Adelicia remarried—as they were certain she would.

They had also designated William Franklin, her father and John Armfield as trustees with power to appoint their successors. "Why do you not understand?" the judge asked her, "that Sumner Countians are eager to have such an academy established? The Tennessee Legislature is extremely pleased with the positive effect it will have on our state. After all," he told her, "it is the largest endowment ever bequeathed for an educational institution in these United States."

The Judge insisted that Adelicia would receive little or no support from anyone in Middle Tennessee, and strongly urged her to pursue the matter no further.

"There is no sane reason behind your decision," he said. "You are doing Isaac, as well as the State, an injustice."

Adelicia would hear no more. Feigning gratitude, she thanked him for the information and extended an invitation to him and her cousin Emma, to call anytime to visit their godchild and namesake.

Her original plan had failed. "Take me to my father's office, Luke, and again, hurry." She would never, under any circumstances, have suspected that Judge White would have reacted in such a way to her. Thus, there was nothing left to do but tell her father of her intentions.

Oliver Hayes was at his desk, pipe in hand, reading, when Adelicia hurried into his Union Street office. "What is it, my Adie, you are out of breath? What brings you to town?"

"Papa, I cannot, will not, adhere to Isaac's will," she blurted out. "It is not fair to me…not until recently have I fully understood its impact. I find it difficult to believe my husband would…"

"Adelicia," he interrupted, "it is difficult for me to believe you would consider such a thing! Legally, yes, you may possibly have a point as to property acquired, improvements made, et cetera, since the time of your marriage, but you are overlooking altogether the moral issues involved!"

"Isaac certainly did not overlook anything! Papa, how long have you known about this? Why, you have known all along!" Infuriated, she continued without giving her father an opportunity to answer. "The day the will was read, before the will was read, you have known from the day it was written! If you refuse to help me, I shall find someone who will!"

"For once, be reasonable. Isaac has left you as well off as any woman in this country, and that is not figuratively speaking...that is literal. Yes, I have known since the will was drafted, and I found nothing contrary to what was best for you and my grandchildren, just as I find nothing now to..."

Adelicia tossed her head, defiantly interrupting, "I do not need anyone deciding what is best for my child and me. I shall make that decision." She put her hand on the doorknob, "I do not care what anybody on this earth thinks, and as for the moral issues...!"

Adelicia leaned back against the cushioned seat, numb with disbelief. When she left her father's office, she had asked Luke to make one more stop before returning to Fairvue: at Mr. Perkins' and her brother's law firm. Joel, who had sided with her on nothing in recent years that she could recall, and why she had expected a miracle today from her brother after the morning's futile beginning, she did not know. She would never forget how Joel and Sam Perkins had stood side by side, agreeing with each other on every issue, and disagreeing with whatever she said.

The Judge, whom she had known all her life, her brother, her brother's father-in-law and her own father—the ones on whom she had thought she could rely—every one of them had looked at her as if she were the devil himself, committing the unpardonable, defiling the sanctity of the grave. Each had said so in his own way: "Adelicia, you are still upset over all your losses...go home, think about it...then you will see...you have everything right now...do not meddle with it." Even Sam Perkins, whom she loved like a second father, had used words like "unscrupulous," "unethical," "dishonest."

They had made no attempt to understand her position. Their minds were closed before she even spoke.

Politics! Tennessee politics! The refrain, "No one's going to help you in this," kept returning as Luke drove the horses home at top speed. She would defy them all and overlook any scruple or issues, if that was what it took. There must be someone, somewhere who would help her, or at least advise her so she might begin legal proceedings.

Dusk had settled in when they turned off the Nashville Pike onto the pebbled drive where she had so often galloped Samson. She looked at the heavy boughs hanging over the lane and the land around her. "Damn the ethics, damn the scruples, and damn Fairvue! And you, Isaac Franklin, for the way you have seen so well to my future!

"I shall go to New Orleans, to Crawford, telegram Rivers in Haiti. I shall go wherever I have to go and see whomever I have to see, until I find a way to dissolve the will."

Part II

Adelicia Hayes Franklin and
Colonel J. A. S. (Joseph) Acklen

1848-1863

CHAPTER 33

IT WAS SEPTEMBER 1847 WHEN ADELICIA AND EMMA, WHO WAS not quite four, left aboard the *Tennessee* for New Orleans, Essie and Charlotte with them.

As the riverboat headed south, Adelicia watched the leaves change from amber-bronze shades of' autumn, to the greens of magnolias, then Delta cypress gray. She was glad to be nearing New Orleans, leaving Middle Tennessee and everyone there behind her.

The granite mausoleum requested by Isaac had been completed to the specifications of his will. Not only did she dislike and disapprove of the cold massive structure, she abhorred it. Her precious darlings lay asleep there, the only thing she held dear, or sacred, or abiding about Fairvue, and in time, she told herself, she would move them to another place.

Adelicia had sent a telegram informing Crawford Benedict of her arrival and just as expected, he had carriages waiting to take her entourage to 186 Canal Street. She so hoped the servants had readied the house as she had asked.

Fresh cut flowers filled each room and savory scents permeated throughout. Maison's had also honored her request; Victoria's and little Adelicia's rooms had been redecorated as guest rooms without so much as a trace to remind her of the stark present without her children. Emma's lovely room, adjoining her own, had been done in variegated hues of green, pink and white. Adelicia's suite was exquisite in shades of gray-blues and ivory.

Pleased, and feeling very much alive, she complimented the servants for the special attention given to every detail. And when the hefty bill came from Maison's, she would compliment them.

Adelicia had discarded her black veil and widow's attire in May and had requested members of the household to remove all traces of mourning; a year had passed. The first item on her lengthy list for New Orleans, was to take Emma and herself on an all-day shopping expedition for new "everythings," and to outfit Essie and Charlotte as well. That would be the morrow's agenda, first she must take care of pressing business that evening with Crawford.

Two dresses ordered prior to her return hung in the ornately carved armoire in her bedroom, along with matching slippers. She chose the melon silk for that night, a perfect contrast to the dreadful black.

Knowing she was lovely as she sat opposite Crawford in the private dining room at Antoine's, Adelicia had delighted once more in the awareness of heads turning and smiles of approval as she had stepped inside the door. She was also immensely enjoying the company of a male companion at supper.

In March, she had spent her thirtieth birthday alone, remembering when twenty-five had seemed ancient and turning thirty meant impending old age. But as the year had progressed and her spirits strengthened, she became reconciled to the idea that this decade would be a wonderful one, more than the ones before. It was a new beginning.

"You are beautiful...then, I've never seen you when you weren't," Crawford said. "But tonight, you are especially captivating."

Crawford did not appear as she supposed a widower of only three months should appear. His gay manner had no hint of sorrow, and she decided against expressing her condolences at present.

"It seems eons since anyone has told me I was beautiful, and as for the rest of your statement, you have not seen me at the right times, or should I say, the wrong times?" She smiled. "I need some advice." Adelicia set the wine glass on the table and ran her fingers around its rim.

"You know if there's any way I can be of assistance, you've got it."

"Before you commit," she taunted, "you need to hear what it is. I am led to believe it is quite out of the ordinary, and I might add, the great state of Tennessee wants no part in it."

"Keep me in suspense no longer, fair lady," Crawford replied, as he touched his glass to hers. "Into what foul deed hast thou befallen?"

"The question is whether or not the lady hath fallen afoul. She is befriended by no one save the First Lady of her country. Even her family hath turned against her."

"Ah ha, my chance...at long last...to become thy sovereign and savior and rescue thee from the depths of despair. Tell me more, Dear

Lady. Another bottle of this excellent vintage," he told the waiter. "Now continue, my love."

"Crawford," she began, resting her hand on top of his, "I know you were one of Isaac's best and dearest friends."

The bottle was uncorked, sipped and approved. He made a toast for future evenings, then said, "That is very true. Now tell me what bothers my lady."

An hour later, he was summing up all she had said, making notes and reiterating specifics. Unlike those in Nashville, Crawford had listened intently without interrupting except to clarify an issue, or scratch down a word here or there. And unlike John Armfield and the others, he agreed with her, smiling, admiring—much as he had on the evening, that now seemed eons ago, when she had proposed becoming a business partner.

After she had confided every detail, Crawford sat clicking his sharpened pencil against the table, appearing to weigh and calculate. She sat with her hands folded around the crystal stemmed goblet, observing him. "Are you not going to pass judgment?"

"Judgments are God's business. But I'm thinking we have a case. I'm certain of it. Something's been overlooked; something you nor the Tennessee lawmakers have considered, or if they have, they've avoided telling you. Tomorrow I'll know for sure. Henry Sherbourne's the best lawyer in Louisiana. Yes. We may have ourselves a pretty strong case..."

"You mean you will help me?" This was what she had been waiting months to hear, what she had thought she would hear in the beginning. "Oh, Crawford, I adore you! For goodness sakes, do not just sit there. Tell me what it is!"

"Can't let you know until tomorrow, but if my suspicions are correct...Let me warn you, though," he paused. "It will be a messy business. Think you're ready for it?"

"Please keep in mind that I have no ill will toward Isaac's request for an educational institution. That must be made clear to all ears from the onset. However, the terms of its development, directly affect what rightfully belongs to Emma and me, and I will not have that taken from us. It must be preserved for us alone, and we shall not be beholden to anyone, ever. I shall be in control, Crawford."

As she spoke forcibly, but with great poise, she looked at him with a confidence she had almost forgotten, ones that were so much a part of her. "Yes. I am ready." she stated.

It was four days later before Crawford had gathered the necessary information and returned to report to Adelicia. He had been to the courthouses of St. Francisville, New Orleans and Baton Rouge, piecing facts together for what he considered a tightly woven case. With Sherbourne and Houston Roberson, he confirmed his hunches, although even he had been unaware of the massive extent of Isaac's wealth.

"Let me understand what you are saying," Adelicia said, as she sat opposite Crawford in the front drawing room facing Canal Street, her eyes wide in anticipation. "Because Isaac's will was probated in Louisiana, his legal voting residence is here, and most of the estate is here. Roberson and Henry Sherbourne believe we can take my case to court in New Orleans instead of Nashville...win...including all of the properties...and everything will legally be awarded to me until Emma comes of age?"

"That's about the size of it, although we can't jump the gun and become overly optimistic. Thou must not count thy chickens before they are hatched! It's like I said at Antoine's, this could get pretty messy."

"But you really believe we can win?" she asked, not waiting for an answer. "Goodness gracious, I had no idea how much holdings were involved! Can you imagine how rich Emma and I shall be? Town lots in San Antonio, even property on Third Avenue in New York!"

"And what do you intend to do with so much wealth?" he asked, standing and taking her hand.

"You ask far too many questions, Crawford, darling. I assure you, I shall have a plan for every penny to make more pennies. And no one will ever take it from us."

"I have no doubt," he responded, flirting. "Are you ready to dine with your ardent companion at Antoine's again this evening?"

"Essie," Adelicia called from the front door, "Please, do not wait up. I am having supper with Mr. Benedict."

After Crawford helped Adelicia with her green satin cape, she placed her arm through his, then briefly laid her head against his shoulder. Stepping into the carriage, she said, "I could not have accomplished any of this without you."

CHAPTER 34

New Orleans, 1847

"Miss Adie, Miss Adie." Essie shook her gently. "Wake up."
She turned over, yawning, "It is still dark."

"I sure knows that, but Mr. Benedict just arrive, and he say he have to see you right now."

Adelicia quickly put on her robe and hurried downstairs where Crawford was in the library, puffing on his pipe and pacing the floor.

"You don't look so bad in the mornings either," he said admiringly.

"What is so urgent?"

"Read this." He handed her a telegram from Nashville.

"It cannot be!" she said, slamming her fist against the table, "They went ahead and...the will plainly states they cannot do this! They cannot break ground for the Institute!"

Her voice raged as she rummaged through the papers in her top desk drawer. "We have been over that blasted will a hundred times with three of the best lawyers in Louisiana. Now, you tell me how the Nashville lawyers can do what they did! Where is the will?"

Crawford opened his briefcase and calmly removed a well-worn copy that Adelicia quickly perused until she found the passage she wanted. "Here it is...they cannot extract money for the institute unless I remarry!" She shouted the last statement, causing Essie to come to the door. Adelicia flung the will on the table.

"They've taken the clause about your remaining at Fairvue, and because you've been here for three months, twisted and construed to prove you've broken the stipulations of the contract. As Hamlet doth say, 'Something is rotten in the state of Denmark.'"

She picked up the telegram and reread it, "On this day, December 1, 1847, the Tennessee Legislature passed act incorporating Isaac Franklin Institute...wishing to inform you to prevent delving further into matter...Will post letter shortly containing fullness of enactment. William Franklin, Trustee."

Adelicia rigid, crumbled the paper in her hand. "Crawford, tell me we can still win this case!" she said, giving him no time to reply. "There will be no institute on Fairvue if I have to stay there every day of the year until I die! Somehow, I shall beat every one of them!" She took a deep breath, "This is an issue of control, not the honorable education of young men."

"I agree, my love!" He took her in his arms. "But don't worry. They have no idea what we're doing here." He held her tighter with one hand encircling her waist and the other entangled in her hair, supporting her head as he kissed her lips so hard that the pressure stung her chin.

"I have loved you since the first day I ever saw you," he whispered. Again she felt the sting from the pressure of his face against hers. She pushed away until he held her more gently, and responded briefly to his kisses. "I thought Isaac was the luckiest man in the world, and I watched you, envying him all the while. I want you for myself, Adie. I want you to marry me. I can do more for you than Isaac ever could and love you in a way he wasn't capable of loving." Crawford kept his arms around her, kissing her face and hair. "Say you'll marry me, Adie."

"For goodness sakes, Crawford," she said, stiffening as she pulled away. "There are too many other things to consider right now. We shall talk later, after we have won the case," she smiled, putting her arm through his.

"You've been widowed for more than a year and a half," he continued. "Emma adores me, and settlement or no settlement, you'll be wealthy. You haven't forgotten I own a fleet of ships, I'm sure, and I can make and keep you happy."

"Do not close in on me, Crawford, please, I adore you. You know that I do. But it is too soon to think of marriage. I shant think about it." She stood by the tall window, staring out onto Canal Street already flooded with carriages, driven by exquisitely dressed drivers, delivering passengers to their places of business. "I am not sure I can ever love anyone again...or if I want to be married. Isaac said...," she stopped. "It does not matter now...and as for making me happy...

It is relative, happiness. Not even your Shakespeare can define it. What makes it come and go, and if one is lucky, come again, I do not know…I wish I did."

She looked over at him, who had been watching her intently all the while. "I have said too much. Thank you for helping me and for coming, even before the sun had peeked through." She smiled again, "And I am ready for a fight. See you in four hours." She held his hand to her face, "Thank you, dear Crawford."

"I shall be there with counsel, and we'll plan a case the likes of which this state has never before heard," he answered, as if there had been no mention of a marriage proposal. "And the latter part of our discussion, we'll consider later when you decide you can't live without me."

After seeing him to the door, she returned to the drawing room fire and poked it to make the flames brighter and higher. It was no surprise that he was in love with her; and she felt a gentle comfort in his having said it. In the past few weeks, they had worked on the case together almost daily, lunched together, dined in the evenings together, and taken Emma on outings together.

It was delightful being with him. She loved the jesting, his irony, his love of the "forsooth" of Elizabethan days, and he was quick to make her understand what she did not know about law and politics. She was eternally grateful for the assurance and aid he was so willing to give when no one else would, but none of those things were intended to mean that she was in love with him. He was a friend, a dear and special friend, whom she believed would see the case to its completion regardless; that was Crawford.

She was sorry that she had briefly returned his kisses; the moment would not be repeated; and sorrier that she had allowed, or led him to misinterpret her feelings. She was comfortable with him and she did care for him, but nothing more. Was it only Crawford's desire for her that had led him to come to her defense? She questioned.

He was not her only suitor. Every eligible male with whom Adelicia came in contact was a potential admirer-become-husband of the widowed Mrs. Franklin. It was clear in every expression, every gesture of kindness or sympathy, and indelibly shone in their eyes. But she was not interested in being anyone's wife, or anyone's lover.

Isaac may have been right when he said she was incapable of loving anyone but herself...or money. She hoped not. She did revel in the attention, being favored, being courted, the sheer excitement, but she was certainly aware that she felt nothing more than friendship for anyone and doubted very much there would ever be a time that she would feel differently.

She did adore Crawford. She was somewhat fond of Rivers Thurmond, whose trips from Haiti to New Orleans had become more frequent, at first discussing sugar cane, then speaking of love. But to her, love remained an elusive term, without special sentiment, or feeling where suitors were concerned. Rivers caused her to think of Lona, tempting her to inquire, but never doing so.

There were times when she lay in bed at night that she wished she could know and feel real love, whatever that was. Perhaps it was what she had felt with Isaac. Perhaps there was nothing more. But, whenever she thought about it for too long, the familiar echoes returned: to remain alone and enjoy the advantages of being the wealthy Widow Franklin.

CHAPTER 35

THINGS MOVED QUICKLY AFTER THE TELEGRAM. TENNESSEANS wanted the Isaac Franklin Institute...Sumner Countians wanted it. They considered Adelicia unprincipled, ruthless. "The determinist, orneriest woman I ever witnessed," John Armfield described her in a letter to her lawyer. But she cared little, at this point, for what he or anyone else thought or felt.

Regardless, the official letter came, announcing the establishment of..."The Isaac Franklin Institute, with succession for five hundred years, a seal, authority to make stature for its regulation, the same power of conferring degrees as is possessed by any literary institution in the State, the faculty of suing and being sued in any judicature in the country, and the power of acquiring and holding, for the purpose of its creation, property, real and personal."

In late January of 1848, the case of "Mrs. Adelicia Hayes Franklin versus Mr. Isaac Franklin's will in contest" went into litigation in New Orleans. Adelicia found her excellent advisors invaluable, in obtaining and securing all available and some not so available evidence on her behalf. On the advice of Henry Sherbourne, she sold her life interest in Fairvue and that of Emma's to Trustee William Franklin, represented by Richard Loucks, for thirty thousand dollars. She retained all rights, however, to the rest of the estate and its profits, while she remained in Louisiana.

Because the will had been filed in the City of New Orleans and Parish of the same, and was being contested in Louisiana, construction of no kind could be erected at Fairvue until the final ruling. Thus, Adelicia could live in New Orleans or West Feliciana and enjoy the benefits of Isaac's wealth, securing the profits from investments and improvements on the plantations, overseen by her father and John Armfield, as stipulated in Isaac's will, to whom she had also agreed to pay an annual sum of six thousand dollars each from the estate.

As long as the case remained in litigation, no one had as much control as she. And there was not a lawmaker in Tennessee who could do anything about it. She loved it! A small voice within told Adelicia that when the final ruling was made, it would be in her favor. Judge Boyle in St. Francisville had almost said as much when he had summoned her in February to make her Declaration of Domicile, she stating her wishes to reside in West Feliciana and pursue planting. Adelicia was quite content, for the present, in her process of victory.

In late March, with its windy, rainy days contrasting with sunshine and calm, and early spring flowers and trees budding all around, Adelicia felt a calm confidence growing within her, a marked difference from the desperate anger she had felt the year before when her pursuit had begun.

It somewhat grieved her that John Armfield had forbade Martha to be on more than polite speaking terms, but Martha was Isaac's niece. In actuality, no one in Gallatin was more than polite, especially Franklin relatives who abhorred her.

She and Emma had moved from the large rented house on Canal Street to a smaller but elegant townhouse at 22 Rue Dumaine. It was her first purchase of a dwelling, hers and Emma's, their very own. Essie and Charlotte, Cora, Jedidiah and six other servants moved with them, including Caleb, saved from hanging in Gallatin, and Luke who had come down as her driver. Della and Daniel remained at Fairvue.

Adelicia liked the new three-story house with its green shutters and black wrought iron fence and gates. The brick walled courtyard was lovely, with thick foliage, richly blooming flowers, and tropical plants. The back of the house was U-shaped, and Adelicia liked being able to see all the *workings* from one vantage point. She loved the feeling of ownership and the sense of power that came from that. She named it "La Mouette." Longing, perhaps for the freedom of the seagull.

Her suitors varied from state legislators to French aristocrats, to planters and congressmen from Washington. An evening did not pass that she was not invited for dining, the opera or the theater. There were small dinner parties with friends, large parties and grand balls. Men adored her and envied her escort (who, most frequently, was Crawford). Women just envied, as Adelicia was less popular in their circles now that she was a widow and eligible.

Adelicia continued to be no more than pleasantly amused by the attention. Her quest was set on what she considered rightfully hers, and anything that complicated or diverted her from that quest was of no interest. It was a simple matter of self-preservation, of security. Isaac's will, the courts, and those on whom she had thought she could depend, had proven that. She would not be controlled nor intimidated.

Isaac and her precious little ones had been gone for almost two years. With every day and season that passed, she had become more secure in her new role, more absorbed, and more certain that if she were to ever remarry, it would not be for love. And because it would certainly not be for money, she was more convinced there would be no second marriage.

Upon self-examination, she had difficulty understanding why men were so drawn to her, someone as willful, determined and self-serving as she. Her behavior was certainly opposite that taught at The Nashville Female Academy on acquiring a beau.

Adelicia's closed-in feeling became suffocating, so much so, that she told Emma it was time for them to make a trip to Natchez.

Margaret and Tryon Weeks were among the thimble full of friends from home who were supportive of her efforts to have her inheritance, and had invited them to visit their farm in Mississippi. Margaret was also expecting her first child at age thirty. Thus, she thought it a good time to leave New Orleans' social life behind, as well as the fuss and hassle of lawsuits in the capable hands of Crawford and her attorneys. She wondered if Isaac's former acquaintances in Natchez would know about the will.

CHAPTER 36

𝓘T WAS THE FIRST DAY OF SUMMER, THE LONGEST DAY OF THE year, 1848, and Adelicia had not been on the river since having returned to New Orleans eight months before, eight months of lawyers, depositions and suitors. The muddy Mississippi never ceased to intrigue her, just as it intrigued her the first time she saw it. She stood on the *Tennessee's* deck, looking into its murky depths, letting her hair blow freely in the breeze as they neared Natchez.

When the boat docked at the base of tall cliffs, Adelicia, Emma and Charlotte got into the waiting buggy driven by Ole Pete and headed for Montpier, a low country house, warm and inviting.

Margaret stood in the doorway watching as they came up the drive. In her fourth month, her dress was already tight across the bust and through the waist. "Adie, I'm delighted to see you, so glad you came. You look wonderful," she said, hugging her cousin and friend from childhood.

"I, too, am glad we are here. Look at you, bursting out all over! Do not dare blush! Having babies is as natural as breathing." Then she hesitated, remembering Camille and similar words, "I have forever wondered who the first old biddy was to make it something to be ashamed of."

Margaret laughed. "You're so good for me. I can't say how happy I am you're here." They hugged again. "And look at this precious Emma," she said lifting her up. "How adorable. Phidora will show you and Charlotte to your pretty room upstairs, where cookies and lemonade await."

Emma slid from Margaret's grasp, gave her mother a quick hug and ran up the stairs with Charlotte behind Phidora.

"Would you prefer to rest, or take some refreshment first?" Margaret asked.

"I would love to sit and sip iced tea and relax with you. We have much catching up to do."

They went into a small sitting room where tea was served, making its tempting cracking sound as it dribbled over the ice, and conversation was begun.

Natchez did know! And according to Margaret, gossip and *talk* was running rampant in Nashville. Heretofore, the news that Adelicia and her counselors had received was all court and legal information. Margaret afforded a different perspective: the social one. When Adelicia had said that everyone was against her, she did not know how nearly true that was.

She asked Margaret not to mince words, and her cousin timidly revealed everything she knew or had heard. Every tongue was wagging: old friends, family friends, political friends, political enemies, everyone whose name she knew. How attitudes do change, Adelicia thought. The same people who chastised her for marrying socially beneath herself now favored the interloper. Popular sentiment was, to quote the *Nashville Whig* … "the magnanimous, considerate philanthropist who chose to leave a portion of his great fortune to construct an institute of learning to give young middle Tennesseans the advantages he himself had not had."

How political! The power of money. It buys its way through the opposition, allowing them to forget those things they once deemed so 'important!' It was she, the wicked witch, the widow, who sought to ignore her husband's "kindness and generosity," and selfishly seek to obtain everything for herself.

Margaret also said that folks in Sumner County were certain no court in the nation would award in Adelicia's favor, and that plans were presently being drawn up and the groundwork laid for the institute.

Although Margaret did not say so; Adelicia knew their desire would be that she get nothing in the end. How gratifying to the old biddies, the young biddies, and the men as well, to see Adelicia practically penniless. Well, that was a gratification they would not have!

Later that evening, she laughed to herself as she lay in the soft bed with two pillows propped beneath her head. Solomon spoke of a woman's power. Someday, she would return to Nashville triumphant and build a mansion at its center. Not a country manor, like Fairvue, but one so magnificent, so splendid, that it would be listed among the finest homes in the nation, along with presidents' estates and tycoons in the East. People would come from all over to see its splendor. Then, she wondered, how long it would take for Nashville to forgive her?

Summers were even hotter in Natchez than in New Orleans. Over humid days and humid nights, she and Margaret had stayed mostly in the coolness of the house with its tall octagonal ceilings. For two weeks, they had sipped iced tea, dined on crisp garden vegetables, fresh farm fruits and melon and taken walks in the late afternoon, when the mid-dayheat had lessened.

Emma was enjoying the hot days. It was Charlotte who complained. Ole Pete had hooked up a cart pulled by a large ram, and each day Emma was ready to ride from after breakfast till supper time. After the first few days, however, Charlotte helped Phidora pack Emma and Old Pete a noon dinner and she stayed indoors.

The aged Negro and the young heiress would go out on the little cart, letting the goat rest while they ate their dinner beneath a shady, spreading oak whose limbs stretched over the rock bed creek below the barn. Then they were off again. Emma soon discoverd that although goats will eat anything, Billy favored apples, so along with their bag dinners each day, there was a hearty supply of Mississippi wine saps.

"I am reluctant to see this lovely interlude come to an end," Adelicia said, as she held Margaret's hand. "This has been the most wonderful, relaxing two weeks I have known in a long, long while. I wish you were coming home with us," she continued as they sat, rocking on the rear verandah, dabbing their foreheads with cotton pads soaked in cool water.

"Please stay through the Fourth. Tryon will be home by then, and he wants to have a small gathering. You can meet a few of our neighbors."

"That is almost a week away. My lawyers can only do without me for so long."

"They'll probably get more done without you standing over them," Margaret teased. "Now say you'll stay and help me plan the party."

"All right," she smiled. "I would love to celebrate the holiday with you and your friends, but then we must go home. Emma will be delighted, of course."

Among their "few" neighbors was former Mississippi Governor, Albert G. Brown, and his wife, Roberta, their two nieces with their husbands, Pleasant Williams and his new bride, Amanda; the Camdens, who lived on an adjoining farm, and Colonel Joseph Acklen with his fiancée Catherine Ferrell, who was a sister to one of Governor Brown's nephews-in-law.

Although the noon celebration had been planned for out of doors, a morning thunderstorm brought the party inside. Red, white and blue reigned throughout the house, and small flags bearing the nation's thirty-stars stood in bud vases in each room flanked by small white tissue flowers. A linen runner, reaching from one end of the long dining table to the other, was also in patriotic colors, and the centerpiece of red and white gladiolas had each stalk tied with narrow, blue satin ribbons, attached to tiny flags throughout the silver compote.

After the Governor's prayer, asking for God's continued blessings upon "these United States," they were seated. The arrangement placed Adelicia between the two nephews-in-law and diagonally across from Joseph Acklen, whose face she had not forgotten.

"Mrs. Franklin," began Catherine, "it must be so lonely being a widow."

What a stupid thing to say, Adelicia thought, as she lifted her fork to her mouth to avoid replying.

"I'm sure it has been good for you to get out like this and visit with your cousin," Catherine ran on, "I'm sure it must feel terrible to be older and to be left all alone."

"How old are you, dear?" asked Adelicia, dripping with feigned sweetness and wondering if Catherine ever hushed.

"Eighteen. We Ferrell's always marry older men; Mother is fifteen years younger than Father."

"We older women do enjoy sitting and talking and tatting to while away time," Adelicia remarked. "I remember when I was eighteen." Catherine listened intently, nodding her head sympathetically. "Life was so gay and wonderful. I certainly hope yours can be as exciting as mine was."

"I've always doubted anyone's to be half as exciting as mine, and Joseph adores me so," Catherine said, turning her face to him, batting her eyelids.

"I am certain he does, dear," Adelicia said. "There is nothing more wonderful than to be adored by a handsome man, and the Colonel looks as if he will be a marvelous keeper of so young a bride."

Adelicia, thinking the stupidity of the remarks had progressed far enough, was pleased when Tryon intervened, initiating topics to include everyone. However, Adelicia continued to glance discreetly at Joseph Acklen, whose brown eyes dashed from person to person, but consistently returned to hers.

Conversation became light and cheerful after Catherine's initial remarks, and it was past six o'clock before the table was cleared and farewells were made.

"It was a delight meeting you," Governor Brown said, "and we're equally pleased that you've accepted our invitation for Saturday next along with your hosts."

"Thank you, Governor, for including me. I look forward to your company," Adelicia replied.

Adelicia could not sleep as she lay in the large double bed later that night, and she could not remove Joseph Acklen from her thoughts. She hoped her restlessness would not awaken Emma, sleeping beside her, a special holiday treat.

She lay quietly in the dark with her feet propped on one of the tall bedposts. "This is our third introduction," she had said. "Only our second," Joseph had corrected. "The second time we weren't really introduced." "How flattering for you to remember so precisely," she had answered.

Later he remarked, "Mrs. Franklin, I remember everything precisely from the first time I saw you. There were so many men gathered around, I could barely get a glimpse of your smile as you turned, charming us all."

She slid further down in the soft feathers and propped her feet higher. She adored his directness. His eyes were medium brown, soft and memorable with reflections of what she supposed would be any color he was wearing. She closed her eyes, imagining his. She liked his hair, light brown and uncontrolled, autumn blond mixed with pale highlights that matched his slightly tanned face.

She smiled as she lay there, reminding herself of long ago days when she and Camille day dreamed about imaginary beaux. It was like being fourteen again and recalling every detail about her latest crush. She continued to smile as she thought of Joseph's smile and the way he looked at her. It unmistakably spoke of interest.

She wondered what on earth he saw in Catherine. She was pretty, but obviously simple. Her hair was a shade lighter than Joseph's, too much blend and not enough contrast, Adelicia thought. Joseph was at least a couple of years older than herself, perhaps three. In the morning she would ask Margaret if she knew a seamstress who could have a gown ready in four days.

Daylight was breaking when she finally dozed off, only to be awakened by Emma's kiss. "Mother, it's time for breakfast and to take a ride with Billy and Uncle Pete."

CHAPTER 37

MARGARET WAS SURPRISED BY ADELICIA'S REQUEST. "I KNOW an excellent seamstress, but you have so many lovely gowns with you, I can't imagine why you want a new one."

"Now, Margaret, do you ever remember a party when we were not all having fits for new gowns?"

"You'll never change," Margaret laughed. "As soon as breakfast is finished, we'll be on our way to the seamstress."

The measurements were taken, the fabric and design selected; a pale, pale blue taffeta, off the shoulder, with a vee bodice, that made her slender waist seem even smaller. Delivery was promised for the morning of the evening ball.

Adelicia was not disappointed. The fit was perfect. It was trimmed with a deeper blue satin at the hem, matching the ribbons woven in her hair, which she wore parted in the middle and pulled back away from her face, allowing her thick curls to hang loosely on her bare shoulders. She found it absurd that once married, one was never expected to wear one's hair down. She would continue to wear her hair however she chose.

She fastened a single diamond pendant around her neck and inserted a diamond stud into each pierced lobe. As she slipped her hands into elbow length white cotton gloves and took one last look in the mirror, she thought she looked much like she did on her first coming out party, however, more elegant and wealthier.

The former governor's home on First Street was handsome and spacious. She, Tryon and Margaret were the first to arrive, which suited Adelicia. She was glad for the opportunity to talk with the host and hostess alone, and to be given a tour of the palatial dwelling. When guests began streaming in, she stood with the Browns, whose gracious introductions of her to the arriving Mississippians seemed to fuel her ability to mesmerize those into whose hands she placed her own. This was as obvious as the gossip she began to overhear, even as she stood receiving.

"Franklin's widow," someone whispered. "He once ran his slave trading business out of Natchez."

"Dear me!" another lady responded, "you mean to tell me she was married to a trader? Franklin? Why he was the very one who had that horrible pen right where the Washington Road forks."

"I'm surprised at Roberta having her in this house, although conditions in the pen improved when Franklin and Armfield owned it. Of course it's rumored Franklin still held an interest in it when he died. And look at the men making over her! Catherine, is that your Joseph with whom she is dancing?"

And indeed Adelicia was. She nearly embarrassed herself at how shamelessly she was flirting with him, and momentarily wondered what her hosts would think. But she quickly dismissed the thought as they enjoyed their second dance.

"I hope my clumsiness doesn't offend you," Joseph said, "but I've never been able to keep my feet moving in the right direction for very long."

"You dance divinely."

"I like being flattered, but do try to keep it on a more believable scale, if you please."

She laughed. "Then what if I say you are not the worst who has waltzed me across the floor?"

"That sounds nearer the truth. I watched you dance on one other occasion, when you said the next one would be mine. But somehow I got lost in the long shuffle of admirers and my opportunity never came."

"Will it be too wicked to say I looked for you and was disappointed not to have seen you again?"

"It doesn't sound wicked at all, if you mean it. Of course, I hardly see how you could have missed anyone that evening."

"I do mean it. I was disappointed," she flirted. "I had thought your eyes would probably change colors according to what you were wearing, but now we are both wearing blue and I see speckles of darker brown."

"It's the reflection of your eyes in mine," he said, his hand clasping her waist more tightly.

"What a lovely thing to say, Colonel."

He held her tighter. "I've never seen eyes that reflect so beautifully in another's."

Adelicia continued looking intently at him. "Someone is going to notice how closely an engaged man is holding an aged widow."

Joseph made no response until the music had stopped. Then releasing her slowly, he said, "I must take care of my obligations."

They walked over to a group of ladies. "I do not think I can dance another step, Mrs. Brown," Adelicia said breathlessly. "Hello, Catherine. I have seen very little of you this evening," she said to Joseph's fiancée.

"Forgive my intrusion. Mrs. Brown, you've not danced with me even once." Joseph led Mississippi's former first lady onto the crowded floor as the music began with another waltz.

Mrs. Brown's absence left the two women alone, and it was Catherine who spoke first. "You dance well, Mrs. Franklin. Of course everyone in Natchez thinks I am the best dancer in the state; Joseph certainly thinks so."

"The people in Natchez may have seen very few good dancers. As for Colonel Acklen's opinion, well..." she stopped, thinking Catherine too simple to comprehend. "I suppose I do get along quite well for an older lady."

"Yes, you do! I asked my Joseph to dance with you to cheer you up. I've known him all my life, you know. Our wedding is scheduled for December. Everyone says I cut my baby teeth on him," she giggled, at what sounded like a much repeated line, one she thought quite clever.

"It is a pity, dear, you did not cut your wisdom teeth as well. Now if you will excuse me, I had better sit for fear of exhaustion."

Adelicia had been on the verandah for only a short while when Joseph appeared beside her.

"May I call on you at the Weeks, Wednesday next?" When she made no response, he asked a second time, "Well, may I?"

"I do not believe your bride-to-be would approve."

"I don't intend to ask whether or not she approves. Will you please answer my question?"

"I am sorry. I cannot permit you to call while you are engaged to another woman. My daughter and I are leaving soon to go home." Adelicia rose and courteously took his hand. "I wish the best for you."

"I recall your saying you missed me in a crowd while you were married."

She neither liked nor appreciated his comment, and felt her face flush. "Did I say that? Good evening, Colonel Acklen."

She turned, went inside and danced from gentleman to gentleman for the remainder of the evening, amongst glares from many of the ladies.

Adelicia spent another restless night. What had upset her so about Joseph Acklen's remark? Was it pride, admitting she had been disappointed not to have seen him again that evening at the ball? Or guilt, admitting that she had compromised a value, a principle held sacred to her, the sanctity of marriage? She recalled in anguish the night she sat beneath the large oak, desperately seeking to see and understand herself, almost admitting she was attracted to someone else while married to Isaac.

She sat up in bed, suddenly thinking she had possibly unraveled yet another mystery, aware of why she felt she could never marry again. Love, or loving itself, frightened her. It frightened her when she felt it slip away, it frightened her to know that feelings change, emotions so certain, inevitably followed by others, radically different. The excuses one made to one's self mattered not. Nothing tangible marked the beginning, nor the end.

Perhaps, it was the way Joseph had said it, as if she would be willing to accept a clandestine affair. Or he may have intended it honestly and honorably. Whichever, it was a remark she thought best left unspoken. It was a remark that had brought her pain.

Joseph Acklen was the first man since her marriage to Isaac to whom she had given a second thought, and she found it curious how their paths continued to cross. Dismissing this pondering as useless, she returned to her conviction that she could not love again, and wondered why on earth she was thinking so much about this Colonel Acklen.

Then she recalled what Senator Gottledge, a friend of her father's from Washington, had told her once when they were sitting in her father's study. She was sixteen and daydreaming about her sweetheart Alphonso while listening to the two gentlemen discuss their wives.

Senator Gottledge had remarried, but her father declared he could never do so. The topic of conversation was loving for an eternity, and Adelicia had interrupted to ask how one knew when one was really in love and how one knew it would last forever.

While tugging at his graying beard, Senator Gottledge thought for a moment, then answered by saying, "You know when there is no choice to be made; love makes it for you. You do not ask, 'Do I love him, do I want to spend my life with him?' You do not weigh the idea, and then decide. You have no need to discuss it with friends. There is no turning back. You'll know the feeling one of these days, Adie," he had said. "You will know it is right."

She had forgotten all about the Senator's remarks until this moment. Perhaps she *would* know, love for love's sake. Perhaps she would fall madly in love. Adoring or affection was not love, nor infatuation, flirting and intrigue. How extraordinary if it could happen to her!

The spirit, the strength that enveloped her, propelled her to obtain the unobtainable, to see dreams become realities that by all odds should remain dreams, were a part of her. She at last closed her eyes and slept until almost noon.

On the following morning, Adelicia, Emma and Charlotte returned to New Orleans. "I wish I could talk you into staying longer," Margaret said, as she hugged her cousin and Emma goodbye. "But you do promise to come in November?"

"I promise to be here for Tryon Junior's birth, or little Margaret's," she answered affectionately. "Essie and I shall come before your confinement and stay the week."

"Wonderful!" she said. "Be careful, and try not to worry about the horrid Nashville business and gossip. It will all work out."

"Take care of my dear cousin, Tryon," she said. "I shall see you both in November."

Emma gave Uncle Pete a hug and once last apple to Billy before she and her mother departed, waving goodbye until the carriage turned down the side of the bluff toward the river.

CHAPTER 38

IN ADELICIA'S ABSENCE, HENRY SHERBOURNE AND HOUSTON Roberson, had been feverishly working on succession details of all properties, real and personal, required by Louisiana law. They were also obtaining testimony from character witnesses (many of whom were Sumner Countians) of their opinions of Isaac and Adelicia as individuals, as well as their marital relationship. The proper steps were being taken, as far as Adelicia could tell, and she was confident in her counsel's ability. The succession papers, legally recorded documents of Isaac's entire business entailments, before and after his marriage to her, were a necessity.

She was also gaining confidence in herself as an astute business-woman. She enjoyed nothing more than reviewing the books after they had been audited to see the profit increases. John Armfield and her father were competently carrying out Isaac's wishes for the con-tinued improvements on the Louisiana plantations. In fact, in the two years since Isaac's death, the land itself had almost doubled in value, according to Ruffin Barrow's appraisal, and the price of cotton was continuing to reach new peaks. Although she thought it worth the annual salaries she was paying her father and Armfield, she rel-ished the moment when she could take complete control, when the estate was no longer under the thumbs of the trustees. The costs of their transportation down river from Nashville, lodging and meals at the Saint Louis Hotel while in New Orleans on estate business, was in addition to their salaries. However, she was reaping the profits and reinvesting.

Two new plantations were being added, also according to Isaac's wishes, one for lumber and one for sugar cane. She was delighted to pay James Clack's overseer's salary of one thousand dollars per year, and she would raise it when the time came. Per Isaac's request, Jim had also purchased and planted cane along the river.

A week after her return from Natchez, as Adelicia sat at her desk mulling over the books, she decided that when she gained complete control, no one, positively no one, would have, as Essie would say, "a finger in the pie" ever again. All would be preserved for Emma and herself. They would be dependent on no one.

She opened a letter from Margaret that Essie had delivered earlier. "Dear Adie," it began. "Thank you for the beautiful silver epergne... you need not have done that." The letter continued with casual news from Nashville, nothing of major significance. Then near the end: "I almost forgot. The day after you and Emma left, Colonel Acklen came by. Although he sat and talked with Tryon for some time, he appeared disappointed when he found you were not here. Tryon and I both think he came to see you."

She stopped reading. Of all the nerve, when Adelicia had specifically asked him not to call! He was not someone with whom she could simply flirt, and she had no time for games with Joseph Acklen. If she ever saw him again, she would tell him exactly what she thought of him, as well as his ignoramus fiancée.

It had been fun to flirt with Isaac, to tease, to tantalize, but she had been a mere girl then. In the beginning, Isaac was never where she wanted him to be. He appeared, it seemed, at his own will and often out of nowhere. She had almost driven Camille and Margaret mad those first few months, wondering where he was and why he was not calling on her every day. How different Joseph Acklen was; she was not so certain she liked the difference. Regardless, she was thirty one now, far too old for games.

Adelicia was having supper alone in her townhouse on Dumaine, a luxury she rarely enjoyed. Crawford was in New York, and she had accepted no other invitations. Maison's had done an exquisite job remodeling the twenty-year old structure to her specifications. She found the deep green wallpaper, framed by rich mahogany woodwork and the handsome furniture relaxing, and relished being in the room's quiet elegance. She wished there were more evenings that she could dine without having to make conversation and be able to sip a second glass of sherry while simply thinking.

Most mornings, she breakfasted with Emma, and they often had dinner together, but the little one was well tucked in bed before her own supper hour at eight.

She was about to ring the small crystal bell for the butler when Essie came in, announcing, disapprovingly, that Colonel Acklen was in the drawing room.

Adelicia's first thought was her appearance. She had been dressed since early morning and had not freshened up since dinner. "You want me to say he can come back tomorrow?" asked Essie

"No," Adelicia answered quickly. "Tell Colonel Acklen that I have just finished dining, and that he may join me here for a glass of sherry."

Essie frowned, and Adelicia recognized the familiar expression. She did not think it proper for ladies to entertain gentlemen in their homes unless they were old friends, and then only when a third party was present. Essie most certainly thought this improper—a gentleman calling unexpectedly and then to be invited for alcohol in the dining room! "You sure that's what you wants me to say?"

"I am sure, Essie. I am no longer sixteen, you know."

"That's what I's afraid of." She walked grudgingly out of the room.

Within seconds after Jedediah opened the door, Joseph appeared. "Good evening, Mrs. Franklin. I hope you don't mind my calling unannounced, but I'll only be in New Orleans briefly."

She nodded for Jedediah to pour two glasses of the deep amber sherry. "As you were saying, Colonel?"

"I'll be here only one day. And remembering your busy schedule, I thought I had better take my chances on finding you at home. So, I hope you don't mind dispensing with the formalities."

"Not at all, Colonel."

"May I call you Adelicia?"

"Why do you bother to ask, Colonel?"

"Is it just I, or do I detect a note of sarcasm in your voice?"

"Now why would I use such tones with you?"

"That is why I asked."

She lifted her glass, then put it down again on the gilt topped table. "I thought I made it clear that you were not to call, whether it be Natchez or New Orleans. Or perhaps you need the picture drawn more clearly. You need to learn about pictures, as you will be drawing continuous ones for Catherine."

He smiled a perfect smile that she could not help but return, and simply looked at her for a moment. "I'm no longer engaged to Catherine."

Adelicia wished he could not see the light in her eyes; it was too assuring of her feelings. It was he who broke the silence. "The day after the ball, I knew for certain what I had often felt. For years, it was taken for granted that when Catherine became of age we would marry. Our families go back to the Revolution—seventy, seventy-five years. One of those planned..." He swallowed the dry sherry quickly. "I'm talking too much. Better get on with what I came here to say." He barely paused, "I would like for you to become my wife."

There was something about the way he looked and the hurried manner in which he spoke that made her laugh. "Colonel, Colonel," she laughed, "what idiocy! Three weeks ago you were engaged to your childhood sweetheart, and tonight you are asking me, whom you barely know, to marry you!"

"I know it seems mad, and you may go ahead and laugh. But I know you much better than you think. I know who you are and what you are."

"If you know that, sir, you know far more than I."

"I know the important things."

"How long did it take you to decide this?" she asked coyly.

"Overnight," he replied.

They laughed. "Adelicia, I'd like to kiss you."

"Joseph," she said softly, "I am more than flattered, but I have a regular suitor and more of everything than I can handle. I am not ready for marriage or," she hesitated, "love."

"I know you have every man in the country on his knee to you, and it doesn't bother me in the least. I can wait. As for love, I'll not say more." He rose from the table and gently drew back her chair. "I can't stay any longer. My driver is waiting, and I have a nine o'clock appointment to keep."

He slipped his arm around her waist. "I want to hold you for just a moment." She felt him tremble as he turned her towards him and with both arms around her, supported himself by leaning against the sideboard.

Being held so close to him awakened senses that caused her to tingle. His arms were strong and hands powerful. She laid her head against his shoulder while he kissed her forehead, and as he lifted her lips to his, she felt the world spinning about her.

She did not know how long it lasted, nor how long Essie had been standing in the doorway when Joseph finally released her.

"Colonel, your driver say you done a half hour late to your pointment." She whirled and left the room abruptly before he could thank her.

"I'll be back in the morning," he said, with his hands still touching Adelicia's shoulders.

Consciousness slowly returned, despite her wishing it away. "I shant be here. I shall be in St. Francisville."

"I'll be back in two weeks. Will you be free to see me then?"

"Contact me as to when…I shall see to it."

Adelicia watched him step into the cab then turned to see Essie standing at the foot of the stairs. "For goodness sakes, Essie! Can I not have any privacy?"

"Not when you're sinning."

"Kissing is not sinning."

"That kind of kissing is sinning, and you ought to be ashamed."

"I'm going to bed now, and I have done nothing about which to be ashamed."

"Your mama never kiss your papa till she was married to him."

"Times do change, and besides, I am me."

"I knows that for sure. Times may change, but the good Lord don't."

"Essie, the good Lord did not mind my being kissed. Goodnight now."

Midway up the stairs she called back. "How do you know that about mama and papa?"

"I just knows that's all… I just knows."

CHAPTER 39

HE WEEKS PASSED QUICKLY, AND JOSEPH ACKLEN BECAME A REGular among the suitors of the widowed Mrs. Franklin. Although the War with Mexico had ended in February, Joseph continued at his post in Galveston under General Zachary Taylor's command. And whenever a ship left Galveston's port to make its run to New Orleans, Joseph managed to be aboard.

Since the night Joseph had made his surprise visit to her in New Orleans, Crawford had unrelentingly asked for her hand in marriage. Rivers also continued his pursuit. Whether or not either knew the intention of the other was not discussed. However, she felt dishonest with neither; marriage was out of the question; she *had* told them often enough. While she sometimes found herself wishing to say, "I love you" to Crawford, the words never left her lips. She admired him greatly. He was older, handsome, witty, wealthy, but she wanted her own wealth, one not to be merged with another's. And although advised by counsel not to consider marriage until the will was resolved, Adelicia could not remove Joseph Acklen from her mind.

He took his turn among the suitors, accepting her flirting at parties and suppers, seemingly amused. Once, when they had attended the same party, and she was escorted by Crawford, she glanced over to see him leaning against the newel post with folded arms, wearing that irresistible look of confidence, the one he often wore when they were alone together.

Not since that first evening had Colonel J. A. S. Acklen mentioned marriage. But, each time she was with him, she was more and more certain that if she were to marry, it would be to him. Very soon, she would need to tell Crawford that she was in love with Joseph Acklen, if indeed that was what it was.

In love! Two words…like being touched with a fairy godmother's magic wand.

No matter where she and Joseph were, or what they were doing, it was wonderful. He was a blend of Old World charm and sophistication, but so lacking in pretension one could mistake him for a farmer's son.

She had built many barriers against pain, but fully understood that her greatest fear was that of loving, then losing what she had loved.

In three years, she had lost a husband and three children, two precious little girls and an infant son, losses so terrible that she struggled to push this reality into a private reserve. She was in the middle of contesting a will she felt unfair and unjustified, and the people in her hometown were turned against her.

And she could not erase from her memory the disappointment she saw in her father's eyes when they were last together. He was fulfilling his part as trustee according to Isaac's wishes, not to help her.

Tears always flowed during reflective moments, when she athought about the effect of her actions on her father, violating principles and values he held dear. Her intention was not to be unkind, nor to hurt, and she had asked his forgiveness for her outbursts, but the cruelly spoken words had left their tarnish. She had also asked God to forgive her for the disgrace, embarrassment that she was causing her family, but the course was drawn, and she would follow to its end.

Emma was fascinated with Joseph's storytelling. The three year-old had adored him the first afternoon she met him, and he had been charmed by her. She had put her small hand in his and led him upstairs to show him her new dollhouse, complete with the latest furnishings that her Grandfather Hayes had had shipped from New York. Joseph wondered if she were friendly with all her mother's callers, as he had obviously never seemed a stranger to her.

When they had come down the stairs, her hand still in his, and sat in the small parlor off the drawing room, she had said, "You are just as handsome as my mother said."

Although Joseph had not been around many children, he found it unusual that a little girl not quite four could be so grown-up. "Do you mind if I take your mother to supper?" he had asked.

"I think it's a grand thing to do," she answered.

"Would you like to go with us?" he questioned.

"Oh, could I?" Then she hesitated as if in deep thought, "You are not just being polite? You really mean it?"

"Yes, little one, I really mean it. Go have your mammy get you dressed and we'll surprise your mother."

Emma called back delightedly as she ran from the room, "My mammy's name is Charlotte. I shan't be long."

They had begun with a carriage ride by Lake Ponchatrain and an early supper in the country at a plantation house built by early French settlers that now offered the finest cuisine in Orleans Parrish. Their specialty, oysters baked in a thick brown rue, was served in a bowl with delicious hard-crusted bread on a side plate. It was eaten by dipping the bread into the savory sauce, a delight to Emma, whose mother never allowed her to imitate Essie's, sopping bread in her molasses or gravy.

"Mother," asked Emma, one morning soon after that first outing with Joseph. "Are all of my uncles related to me like Uncle Bliss, Uncle Henry and Uncle Joel?"

Startled by the question, Adelicia asked, "Why, darling?"

"Yesterday, I was naming all of my uncles for some friends at school, and they told me *no one* had that many uncles, that I was making it up."

Never had it occurred to Adelicia the effect her numerous male callers might be having on her daughter. "Sweetheart, Uncle Joel, Uncle Bliss and Uncle Henry are your real uncles," she explained. "They are my brothers and when Aunt Laura and Aunt Corrine marry, their husbands will be your real uncles. Uncle is also a word we use that is less formal than mister when the person is a friend, like Uncle Crawford. It is more familiar."

Adelicia was unsure if she were making any sense at all to Emma. "It is not polite for children to call adults by their first names. For example, you call Essie "aunt," because she is older than you, which shows respect. You would not call her 'Mrs.' because she is a part of our family."

"So everyone who takes you to parties, I may call Uncle?"

What insights one gains from a child, she thought. "How would you like it if from now on, I had only one caller?"

"Then there would be just six uncles, four real ones, Uncle Crawford, and a familiar one." Emma's remark caused Adelicia to laugh aloud.

"Yes, darling, four real ones and a familiar one."

"Could the familiar one be Uncle Joe?" Emma asked.

"We shall see...and I shall tell him you voted for him first."

She was recalling the incident to Joseph on their way up river, aboard the *Southern Star*, on one of her regular runs from New Orleans to Natchez.

A colonel and lawyer from Huntsville, Joseph had no intention, he told her, of compromising anything that could be construed as benefiting from the Widow Franklin's money and assets. If he were going to Natchez with her, he would be responsible for their getting there, and not afloat one of her river vessels.

"How scandalous, our taking a trip like this!" she said excitedly, "even though Essie and Emma are with us."

"It's like this: I'm going on behalf of one of my best friends, who unfortunately, was ordered back to Mexico on official business, to become godfather to his child. You're going to see your cousin who's about to become a mother for the first time, and if anyone wants to make more of it than that, they'll just have to do it. As long as it doesn't bother you, it doesn't bother me."

"I am pleased to know we feel the same. I have never taken a trip with anyone but my husband. It seems scandalous and utterly wicked."

"I've never seen a female so complete with contradictions. You're an example of the perfect mother, devout Presbyterian, with an extraordinary business sense. But you also have devilish thoughts of what you can do next to be wicked."

"And which do you prefer?"

"I'm not sure. I think it must be ninety percent of one and ten percent of the other."

"Which is which?"

"I'll let you figure it out," said Joseph, leading the way to his stateroom below. It was a relief from the cold wind that had blown icy spews of water onto the deck from their moment of departure. Although Emma, Essie, Joseph and she had been enclosed in the sitting area of the *Southern Star* with some warmth from a single wood stove, it was minimal.

"Are you sure you want to marry someone who may be ultra conservative one day and quite the opposite the next?" Adelicia asked.

Joseph looked at her teasingly, his windblown hair hiding his brows. "What makes you think I want to marry you?"

"You did ask me three months ago."

"That was three months ago. I may have changed my mind since then."

She put her arms around his neck, allowing her hooded cape to fall. "But you have not," she said.

He had never kissed her in their brief relationship that she did not feel invigorated, tingly, and for the first time she was returning his kisses. She felt as if she could not get close enough to him, that if he were to hold her until she was breathless, it would still not be close enough.

She gently pulled his hands away and held them to her face, then turned with her back to him, with his arms still encircling her, holding his hands and examining them. "These hands are marvelous," she whispered, "but it is the power in their touch, I cannot resist."

"It may have something to do with their liking what they touch. If you can let go for just a minute, I promise you may have them right back." He turned her towards him and reached inside his shirt pocket. "See if this fits?" He took her left hand and eased a brilliantly cut solitaire diamond onto her finger. No package, no box, no pretty ribbon. He had been carrying a five-carat, perfectly cut stone set in platinum in his pocket.

"How beautiful, darling!" She tilted her head upward to kiss him. "Are you sure you are not afraid of my dual personality?"

"No," he said brushing her lips. "I know which is the real you."

She whispered in his ear, "How long before we can be married?"

"As quickly as possible. My discharge should soon be in order."

Essie knocked on the door and stepped inside. "Miss Adie, we's turning the bend for Bellevue, and you say you want the Colonel to see all Mr. Isaac's plantations," she said, placing great emphasis on 'Mr. Isaac.' "This the first one, and you been in that room long enough to smother."

"Thank you, Essie," said Joseph. "We were just coming up."

CHAPTER 40

TRYON WILSON WEEKS III WAS BORN ON NOVEMBER 15, 1848, healthy and robust, only three hours after his mother's first pain. Adelicia was sad that Tryon could not be there for the birth of his son, as she held the newborn infant in her arms before returning him to his mother's breast. Even when a war was over, its men were detained, its effects lingering on and on. She wondered what war ever accomplished, although this time it was for the annexation of Mexico, Sam Houston's Texas!

Margaret's milk had spilled onto the sheet and with no embarrassment, she allowed Adelicia to dab it up with a linen towel.

"I am so thrilled that you are going to marry Joseph," Margaret said, "that you'll be having more babies. But you must wait until I can travel to Nashville—I mean for the wedding, not the babies." She smiled.

"Do you promise you will be an attendant, along with my sisters?"

"Of course! I am so happy you asked."

"It could not be otherwise. But you must get plenty of sleep, and stay in bed for at least three weeks, perhaps four. It helps with the waistline."

It had been grand to have had Isaac present at each of their children's births, pacing, he had told her, along with the house servants. She hoped that Joseph would be with her when their children were born.

Emma, Joseph, Ole Pete and Billy, enjoyed a week of lazy days. The air was late fall crisp, just cool enough for an extra wrap. Joseph was wonderful with Emma, and Adelicia enjoyed watching them romp outside together and seeing Emma's excitement when her little hands would be filled with arrowheads found in the creek bed.

Adelicia spent her days busy and gay with Margaret, discussing children and marriage, and sometimes making suggestions to little Tryon's nurse. Her nights were spent reading to Emma before bedtime, then sitting in the parlor with Joseph, making plans for their future. She missed babies.

The days were warm and filled with sunshine as they traveled back downriver to New Orleans. To appease Essie, Adelicia and Joseph stayed on deck until each retired to their separate state rooms to sleep. Essie accepted the fact that Adelicia would soon become Mrs. Acklen, and had even told her while at the Weeks, that she was beginning to tolerate the idea. He *was* from an old Huntsville family and planning to open a law office in Nashville, and he had some spunk. Essie also told Adelicia that she hoped it would "settle her down," but most importantly, "would get her own self back to Nashville," which Essie far preferred to New Orleans. The three story townhouse Adelicia had purchased on Cherry Street would be a welcome sight.

Joseph returned to General Taylor's command immediately upon their arrival in New Orleans, and Adelicia was faced with telling Crawford that Joseph had gone with her to Natchez, and that she had accepted his proposal of marriage.

It was not easy being direct when she cared about someone, and she truly cared about Crawford Benedict, but she could never be in love with him, not the sort of love that leads to marriage. She looked at the ring on her hand. "I shall mail a note to Rivers, then meet with Crawford," she said to herself, while musing at her writing table.

After Jedidiah ushered Crawford into the parlor that same afternoon, bringing information on her counsel's progress, she gave him a familiar embrace. Previously when he questioned her about Joseph, Adelicia had been vague in answering. With her consistent lack of confidence in her own feelings towards love, she had feared telling Crawford about Joseph one day, and retracting what she had said the next. Crawford had helped her when no one else would…it was gratitude she felt, a deep sense of gratitude that she would never forget. Joseph would learn to be his friend. Her selfishness, she recognized.

She had patted Crawford's shoulder lightly after the initial embrace, and he seemed to have a sixth sense as she began to speak about Joseph. He put his fingers to her lips, lifted her left hand and ran his fingers over the vibrant stone, saying nothing more than, "Joseph Acklen is a lucky man."

She deeply regretted hurting Crawford, and was almost assured that he felt deceived. But in spite of what he felt, he not only agreed to remain her advisor but insisted upon it. She needed Crawford. She could depend on him, and he had never asked anything from her except marriage, which she could not give to him. It was one of life's inequities, loving and not being loved in return.

Later that day, after completing a letter to Joseph, she sealed the envelope and ran her fingertips over the moist edges, then looked at the stacks of documents and papers on her desk, papers she had read and reviewed many times before. She hoped Joseph would not have to go to war again. However, war separating them was one thing, a will was another, and this will which had kept her bound and constantly searching for answers was not going to keep her from Joseph. She needed him, too.

The news Crawford had brought that morning had astonished her more than she thought possible. "They actually think," Adelicia said aloud to herself, "that I am going to accept one hundred thousand dollars and sign away all rights to Isaac's estate! I fear there will be some surprises for the Tennessee Counsel," she continued, strumming her lovely nails on the desktop.

Luke brought her carriage and in a matter of minutes, she was sitting in Henry Sherbourne's handsomely furnished office. Looking about her at the burgundy leather winged back chairs, thick piled carpet and heavy brocaded curtains, richly draped at the four windows facing Royal Street, she could not help but look at Henry and smile. She liked his office furnishing and his taste very much...and he knew that she liked it very much.

The question confronting her attorneys as they sat around the large mahogany table was whether or not she would accept the money allotted her. If she did, would the acceptance affect her community rights of acquests and gains in the Louisiana estate which would be her title to one-half of the increase of the property since her marriage to Isaac nine years before?

For days, her counselors had deliberated over the will, looking for any loophole, however slight, to further bind the Tennessee counsel.

They advised Adelicia it would be best to marry Joseph after the court proceedings. However, if she were intent on marrying him in the spring, she would have to accept nothing and continue with her present financial arrangement.

They also reminded her that the marriage might be a detriment, perhaps a slander on her character in the courts. She reminded them that as long as the case was in litigation, it did not matter. And as far as her character, that was an area which would have to remain on hold. She would, by law, continue to accrue the profits, and her father and John would continue to oversee the estate, although she would legally own nothing. She would take her chances.

She was intent on marrying Joseph now, and her impatience did not allow for a compromise. It could be months or years before the case was heard and a settlement reached. She loved Joseph Acklen, she was almost certain of it. It was a different love than she had felt for Isaac, and every day without Joseph was one more that she did not wish to spend alone. His discharge would be effective the following month and when he returned to New Orleans, she would make specific plans for their wedding and their return to Nashville.

"Gentlemen," she said, rising from her chair in Sherborne's elegant office, "you have heard my final answer. I regret the problems you feel my decision will bring, but we have been submerged in problems for almost two years. I shall continue with my plans to marry Joseph Acklen in the spring."

CHAPTER 41

New Orleans, 1849

THE TREATY OF GUADALUPE HAD BEEN SIGNED FEBRUARY 2ND, the year before, and the last of the thirty thousand volunteers were at last returning home, one of whom was Joseph. It was a drizzling March evening when he came bearing an enormous rolled canvas to Adelicia's door, and as they unwrapped it together, they were increasingly astonished by the painting's quality and composition. Then he began, how a member of his unit had discovered it partially wrapped around the body of a dying Mexican soldier, asking that it be returned to the cathedral from where he had taken it, but before he could speak the name of either the church or town, he had passed away.

It was an extraordinary work: Mary, bending over her crucified son with legions of angels ministering to Him as streaks of sunlight streamed through dark, yet soft clouds. How Adelicia despised war—its effects on the conquerors, on the conquered, the disruption of lives, the loss of lives. The evil it produced. She and Joseph made a vow to one day, somehow, return the master canvas to where it belonged. In the meanwhile, it would be framed and hung in the drawing room over the mahogany library table, where the family Bible always lay open.

The wedding was planned for May 8th at her townhouse on Cherry Street in Nashville, performed by Reverend Edgar, who had done the same for her and Isaac ten years before. Joseph not only agreed to a prenuptial contract, but insisted on its contents that concisely affirmed that Adelicia and Emma would retain all rights to their inheritance, whatever it might be. However, any children from their union, from monies accrued after their marriage, would share equally with Emma, but from no part of Emma's original inheritance.

That was Emma's. Joseph himself would own none of the properties, nor have any legal claim to them, nor inherit.

Joseph had made it clear that he had no desire to possess any portion of Adelicia's fortune, that he would practice law in Nashville unless it became necessary for him to work with her in securing, procuring and overseeing the plantations. The agreement signed by Joseph, was an additional assurance that her inheritance was not the main attraction.

Her lawyers' supposition had proved true: because she had refused the cash money or any of the goods, the attorneys in Tennessee could not force her hand, even if she remarried. First, because she had sold her life interest in Fairvue, that placed most of Isaac's estate in Louisiana. Secondly, because the will was being contested in Louisiana, where through much research her attorneys had proven it to be Isaac's legal domicile, excepting 1840, when he had voted for Tyler in Tennessee. The important factor being that in 1844, Isaac had voted for Polk in Louisiana.

The more Adelicia understood the law, how it worked, the more she wanted to know. Her father had often said, had she been a male, with her persuasive tongue, she would have been the most successful trial lawyer in the state. The challenge and varied interpretations of the law fascinated her. The power of language fascinated her. One phrase, one word, could be the determining factor. The cleverer the lawyer, the better the chance of winning, and a good attorney was most often why a case was won or lost, not the guilt or innocence of either party. Crawford had certainly sought and obtained for her the best counsel in the state of Louisiana.

She was also marrying a lawyer with an excellent reputation. Joseph had served under four presidents as the United States Attorney from the northern district of Alabama, a position only interrupted by war when President Polk relieved him from office to join the ranks of General Taylor. With the addition of Joseph's counsel, she felt even more secure in victory.

It seemed a reversal, she mused while sitting in front of the drawing room fire with her feet tucked beneath her, sipping a late night sherry. Isaac had loved and spoiled her, but he had also needed her and her family's position in Nashville's society to procure for himself what his money could not buy. And it was no secret that his wealth had obviously been an important factor to her.

Now it was Adelicia who needed to restore her reputation and regain respectability that her money could not buy. Joseph was a young, handsome attorney from excellent family stock in Huntsville. Her marriage to him would prove advantageous, including his Washington connections. She could not help but wonder, however, if he were not dazzled by more than love, as she had been by Isaac, even though Joseph had repeatedly stated his indifference to it all.

CHAPTER 42

"AND THEY LIVED HAPPILY EVER AFTER." ON THE EVE OF Adelicia's departure for Nashville, she read "Cinderella," from *Grimm's Fairy Tales* to Emma. Adelicia closed the book, then moved from her chair to sit beside Emma, sinking into the softness of her bed, looking down at her and smiling.

"What's wrong, Mother? Why are you crying?"

With her fingertips, Adelicia brushed back the dark curls from around Emma's cherub face. "I was thinking of how much I love you and how very precious you are to me."

"I love you too, very, very much." She raised her small arms and put them around her mother's neck, "but I don't want you to cry."

"I am sorry, sweetheart. Sometimes people cry because they are sad, sometimes because they are happy, sometimes because they are sentimental, and, well, sometimes girls just cry."

"Which one are you crying for now?"

"I think it is sentimental tonight. Are you all ready to go to Nashville in the morning?"

She nodded and yawned. "My dress is so pretty for the wedding, and after it is over, I can call Uncle Joe 'Papa.'"

"You surely may. Stay awake for another minute. I promise to be right back." Adelicia returned shortly. "We will not be here at Easter, and I want to give you this now."

"Mother, the beautiful egg!" she exclaimed. Emma held the jeweled, enameled egg in her small hands.

"You do not remember much about your real father. He was a wonderful man, Emma, who loved you and your two sisters so very much. One Easter, when you were just a baby, your papa gave me this egg wrapped in the prettiest box with a velvet ribbon tied around it. I liked it better than anything he had ever given me, and there's not another one like it in the whole world. Just like there is not another you," she said, lifting Emma into her arms.

No matter how hard Adelicia tried, the tears would not stop flowing. "There was also a necklace inside, a pear shaped diamond on a gold chain, that will be yours when you are older. He would want you to have it. It would please him very, very much." She held Emma in her lap and rocked her gently back and forth for a long while, then laid her back in the same cozy spot and kissed her. "Goodnight, little Angel."

"Goodnight, Mother. Thank you for the egg. It is my favorite thing too, and I shall keep it forever and forever."

Forever! And they lived happily ever after, Adelicia pondered as she walked slowly to her room with tears still flowing. How do you tell a child there is no such thing?

She thought of all of the forevers in her life as she undressed for bed...her mother, Mozzalpa, her horsey love from childhood, Camille and her brother. All the forevers of falling in and out of love, crushes and infatuations. Isaac-his death—their infant son—Victoria and little Adelicia, for whom she secretly wept daily, wishing to be able to touch them once more. All these she had loved and all had passed from her.

In some confused sense, both death and love held its element of fear. She accepted the inevitability of death; the one thing from which one could not escape, nor control. Recalling the words of *St. James*, "For what is life? It is even a vapor, that appeareth for a little time, and then vanisheth away." She thought perhaps the word *life* could be exchanged for the word *love*. She accepted the inevitability of love: it too, passed away, could not be controlled. She feared both.

"Only one thing remains constant," her father told her once as they were walking in the woods at Rokeby, "God and those things He has made. Adie, you love beautiful things, dresses and parties, fine furniture and houses and horses—I love them too,—but you see these." He bent down and picked one of the daffodils flourishing along their path among wild violets. "These are the things that are lasting. All the rest can be blown away or burned to the ground. But just as certain as the spring, the daffodils will come forth from the earth again, and the trees will bud."

They walked into a clearing where flowers bloomed in every imaginable shade. "This is what will last," he repeated as they stood looking across the fields, "the things God made. When we are no longer here, these flowers will bloom, the grass will come up and the trees will sprout their leaves. They'll be older, but it's something you can count on just the same."

Her melancholy would not pass as she lay between cool cotton sheets; the past returning, fusing with the present and the future, much like after Isaac's death. Try as she may, Adelicia could not push the thoughts away to a safe place, for later musing.

She had wanted her wedding to be smaller than her first, but that had proven next to impossible. The friends and relatives of the Acklens and the Hunts were coming from Alabama, (some said no one would be left in the state; they were all descending upon Nashville), as well as Joseph's friends in Washington. President James K. Polk and his dear wife Sarah, both of whom had returned home in April to attend a gala political reception, would also be in attendance.

Adelicia felt certain that no one in Nashville would be there on her account, but all the 'right' people's names were on the guest lists, and each would appear out of respect for her father and her family, as well as to gape. Others were not invited—any and all Gallatin residents—whose presence she would certainly not miss, except those of her cousin Emma and Judge White. Joseph's family did not seem to mind her being in the middle of a lawsuit, nor the events leading into it. She would miss Camille, she thought, remembering how pretty she had looked ten years earlier; she would also miss Uncle Sugart and Aunt Aggie.

The past ten years had brought significant changes. Certainly the trials and obstacles she had faced had played their major roles, but the changes were wrought by more than that. Something inside her had changed. She wondered what the next ten years would hold.

"The only things certain in life are the uncertainties," she recalled Isaac saying as they watched, through falling snow, the last of the Cherokees board the rafts. At times she felt that Joseph knew her better than anyone on earth, that he could see what she could not, or what she feared. She felt certain that she loved him deeply, perhaps more than she had ever loved. She wanted to love him completely, fully, unselfishly, without condition. For that she would strive.

Adelicia was radiant as she came down the curved stairs on her father's arm in the 'filled to capacity' townhouse on Cherry Street. She had chosen a pale lavender peau de soie gown trimmed with echelon lace and a matching mantilla that fell even longer than the train of her dress.

The furniture had been removed from the ground level rooms except for the chairs that were tied with ivory satin ribbons. Candles glowed in sconces along the walls, in every window, in every chandelier and flanked the lovely drawing room mantel, creating a spectacular setting for the green and ivory magnolias and gardenias. Corrine's, Laura's, Margaret's and Emma's dresses were in shades of candlelight, which caused the rooms to appear a single spectacle of greens and ivories and glowing light. Essie and Charlotte, beaming, sat with the Hayes family to the left.

The pianist stopped as Adelicia and her father reached the entrance hall. Oliver Bliss Hayes left his daughter standing alone, walked to where Joseph stood with Reverend Edgar in front of the flower draped marble mantel and read from the Book of Ruth, concluding with, "May the Lord deal with me ever so severely if anything but death parts me from thee."

During the reading, hers and Joseph's eyes never left each other's. Afterward, she proceeded into the room, and for the second time her father gave her away in marriage.

For a wedding present Oliver Hayes had, despite their differences, generously given Adelicia sixty-five acres of choice land between Granny White and Hillsboro Pikes, and a few days before the wedding, she had purchased an additional one hundred and five adjoining ones.

Amidst this one hundred and seventy acre tract, her grand house would stand, and construction would begin just as quickly as she and Joseph returned from their European tour. Emma would stay with Essie and Charlotte and a household filled with servants at the fashionable townhouse. Adelicia was pleased that Emma would be near her grandfather, aunts and uncles, who would spoil her terribly; that too, was pleasing.

"Joseph," she said as they were having supper aboard the steamer on their way to Rome. "I intended to tell you this before we were married, but I kept forgetting."

He looked at her with those soft, reflective brown eyes. "I've had so many surprises in the past four weeks, I don't know if I can bear another."

"Would you like to know my definition of the ideal man?"

He laughed, "I'm sure it is I."

"It is one who can spoil a woman, but always maintain control. It takes an extraordinarily rare and powerful man to do that."

He looked at her still smiling with his lips slightly parted, his teeth barely exposed—the pose he took when thinking, while observing her.

"Adie, dear, I've been in control of you since we first met, and I intend to stay in control!" He took both her hands in his and practically lifted her from the chair. "Would you like to go below to our room?" He kissed her in the middle of the dining area, and they walked with their arms around each other to their suite

CHAPTER 43

1850 ARRIVED WITH GREAT PROMISE OF ECONOMIC PROSPERITY FOR Nashville and its populace of just over 10,000. The early beginnings of the frontier town and its hardships were all but forgotten, and the city was fast becoming known for its educational institutions—including schools of medicine and divinity—for mercantile businesses, banking and trade, and as the publishing and printing center of the south. In prosperous, sophisticated Nashville, tales of James Robertson and John Donelson, Fort Nashborough and Indian attacks had merged into heroes and heroic deeds seemingly detached from reality.

The city's location on the Cumberland made it ideal for water commerce for northern or southern ports and its free Negroes, along with Irish, German and Italian immigrants combined to create a distinct and appealing blend of old world cultures. And in early February of that year, when Adelicia and Joseph returned from Europe laden with paintings and sculptures, expensive fabrics and wallpapers, Nashville citizens, old and young, black and white, watched wide-eyed as the precious cargo was unloaded from the steamer and onto ox drawn carts cushioned with bales of cotton, and driven from the wharf up the hill on Summer to its destination on Cherry Street. The newlyweds also brought with them a full set of plans to build an Italian villa.

While in Verona, they had attended a production of Shakespeare's *Merchant of Venice*, and Adelicia, fascinated, instantly decided that her grand house for Nashville would be a villa much like Portia's. She planned for it to be the largest, most luxurious dwelling in Middle Tennessee, to rest on a knoll in the center of the estate and to attract all eyes in all four directions.

She also planned for everything to be of the best quality, the finest workmanship, constructed in the grandest style. Well known Nashville architect Adolphus Heiman would work with her plans and design the splendid structure. Local artisans would complete the project designated to Heiman's specifications.

It was midsummer, however, before work actually began on the mansion, because three months after their return, on May 19th, Joseph Hayes Acklen was born at the townhouse on Cherry Street. And Adelicia was determined to be present as the first shovel of ground was unearthed that began her dream of Belle Monte.

That December 13th, when a steamboat unloaded a locomotive engine at the Cumberland's wharf to the Nashville and Chattanooga Railroad, an additional avenue of travel and trade was opened. Nashville was indeed aglow with promise and prosperity, and 1851 marked its tidings for another good year. It was also the time when eight-month old Joseph Hayes and six-year old Emma accompanied their parents on the maiden, four mile trip aboard the city's new locomotive, when Emma's infectious excitement, finally persuaded Charlotte to sit with her at the engineer's post.

Emma had watched the tinderbox being filled and refilled and had hung her small head from the window to get a better look at the great iron wheels that made the "clackity clack." When engineer Clarence Vick asked if Emma would like to pull the whistle for the round trip stop, she jumped into his lap and held her small hand tightly to the cord until he called, "Pull!" and the train came to a screeching but gentle halt. When Charlotte finally set foot on the ground again, she vowed it was her first and last ride on the "iron horse." Cora, on the other hand, holding Bud (the affectionate name bestowed upon Joseph Hayes by Emma) found it a wonderful invention and declared that when Bud was older they would "ride and ride and ride."

Adelicia felt too happy, too serene. Although her court case was still in litigation, Nashvillians were becoming warmer, her reputation and respectability, resurging. Her marriage to Joseph had proved as advantageous as she had supposed, and she truly loved and cared for him.

"Joseph, darling," she said while dressing in the second floor bedroom of her townhouse, almost a year after Bud's birth. "I do wish Belle Monte were ready so we could hold the grand reception there. What a difference it would make! It is not even half complete. "

"It would make no difference at all. Everyone will have just as gay a time here."

"You know what I mean. I dream at night of having house parties and lawn parties and..."

"...and more babies," he asked.

"Oh, Joseph!" she playfully reprimanded, turning her back to him. "Will you please fasten this hook? I fear the day when my dresses will no longer fit in the midriff. Essie has almost convinced me one's ribcage expands after each child, and I dare not give anyone the satisfaction of thinking my waist to be even a half size larger."

"Sweetheart," he said holding her, "you are as beautiful tonight as I have seen you, and the only place your gown may be tight is where it pleases me," he continued, observing the full cleavage protruding over the neckline of the rose silk.

"Honestly, I believe you think of nothing more!" She gave him a quick kiss on the cheek and hurried downstairs to make sure she would be on time to meet their guest of honor, who on the following evening was giving a concert at the new Adelphi Theater on the corner of Summer and Spring Streets. She and Joseph had heard Jenny Lind sing in New York and Washington, and the singer's reputation proved true: no clearer, sweeter, purer sounds could be heard than those trilling from her voice.

A select group crowded into the townhouse drawing room, sitting in fascinated silence as the world's most popular songstress entertained them with a preview of the melodies she would be singing during her Nashville engagement. Few of the guests had seen her perform before, and as she sang the popular "Bird Song," "Home Sweet Home," and "The Last Rose of Summer," it was obvious why she was heralded the toast of every city. Her grace and charm were as exceptional as her talent. It was truly the "Jenny Lind Era." Furniture was being named for her, and there were those who referred to the manner in which she sat or stood as the "Jenny Lind way." The evening was a great success, their guests lingering past midnight, spellbound, as they mingled and talked with Jenny Lind and P.T. Barnum.

Lind's performances at the Adelphi were sellouts, with some tickets being auctioned for as much as two hundred dollars. And when the Barnum entourage departed a few days later, the Nashville docks were crowded with those well-wishers who had been fortunate enough to see her perform, as well as with those who were straining for a single glimpse of the "Swedish Nightingale."

On summer evenings, Nashville's streets were crowded, some residents strolling the avenues, others leisurely riding in carriages and barouches drawn by four, some on horseback and others in plain buggies—all fashionably dressed. English journalist, G. W. Featherstonhaugh, stated in *De Boe's Journal*, as early as the mid-thirties, that the "frontier town" had the finest dressed populace, and the handsomest carriages he had seen on his entire visit to the continent.

Nashville was indeed a prosperous city in 1851, and Adelicia was proud of it. After all, it was home and she wanted it to be proud of her. She would dismiss Louisiana and its luring gaiety for the serenity she was finding in Nashville as Mrs. Joseph Acklen. Her husband would spend time with Jim Clack in West Feliciana while she saw to her dream—her mansion—Belle Monte.

The rededication of the First Presbyterian Church, partially destroyed by fire the previous year, was an important and meaningful event to Adelicia, whose family, on both sides, had been staunch Presbyterians since the reformation. She had twice been married by its minister and four of her children had been baptized at the church. Dr. Edgar had continued to hold Adelicia in high regard; one of the few who had not openly criticized her opposition to Isaac's will, which she considered a defense, if only by omission. So it was not surprising that she and Joseph delayed a trip to New York in order to attend the Easter dedication services on April 20th. It was also not surprising that she had made a handsome donation to the building fund.

Spring had further rejuvenated Adelicia, as Joseph's frequent trips to the Louisiana plantations brought favorable reports upon his return. And her daily trips out Hillsboro Pike, checking the progress of her new home, found her fascinated with each phase of its construction.

In mid-October, Adelicia and Joseph embarked for New York, in order to view newly arrived paintings and sculptures, commissioned the year before in Europe, and to shop for fabrics and interior decor.

Octavia Lavert, who spent more time abroad than at home, was also in the city and they would attend the grand opera gala she had organized preceding the event.

When Adelicia thought of Belle Monte, she thought of Nashville. The two had become synonymous, and what she built on her estate would bring enjoyment to her city. Her proposed art gallery would be a first, and in it she would house her treasures for everyone to see and enjoy. Belle Monte would become a center of culture and intellectual pursuits for Nashville, as well as for all those visiting the city that was already being hailed the "Athens of the South."

On their fourth evening in New York, while she and Joseph lazily dined in their hotel suite overlooking a magnificent park filled with trees and bright flowers, and aglow with gas lamps, their meal was interrupted by a telegram from Henry Sherbourne, bidding Adelicia to return to New Orleans without delay. It read, "The 'set' has been completed before anticipated. Believe outcome of case predictable in our favor. Timeliness, important."

Elated, Adelicia and Joseph departed New York aboard the *Maple Leaf* two days after receiving the news, and sailed into New Orleans' busy port on a windswept November day. The cab took them directly to Sherbourne and Roberson's office where, amongst a gaggle of lawyers, they reviewed the completed nine hundred and twelve page *Succession of Isaac Franklin*. The case was already one week into trial.

At the end of November, the Orleans Parish Court ruled in favor of Isaac, a move her attorneys had not expected. "Don't worry," Roberson told her, "there are higher courts."

Thus, endless hours of work began all over; this time to discover or upturn a legal loop that had been overlooked. "It is either so obvious, gentlemen," Adelicia said, at a called meeting in Sherbourne's office, "that you have missed it all together, or so minute you have not yet found it…but it exists!" She exhaled. "If you want to be paid the handsome salaries you are expecting, for more expensively dressed offices, or mistresses or whatever else, you had best find the way to win my case." Both Roberson and Sherbourne blushed. "If need be, it will be tried before the Louisiana Supreme Court, nothing short of." She hoped they understood her. She was glad Joseph had not been present. She was glad she had not sworn.

Chapter 44

IT WAS A COLD FEBRUARY DAY, 1852, WITH THE SUN PEEKING through heavy, overcast skies that Joseph, Adelicia, Charlotte and eight year old Emma sat in the plush Victoria and watched as Nashville's first gas lights were turned on around the city square.

"Mama, Papa, how pretty!" Emma exclaimed as she removed one small hand from her brown beaver muff. "Charlotte, we must tell Bud everything when we get home."

Emma was a unique blend of herself and Isaac. Physically, she was a miniature reproduction of her mother, except for the eyes and brows which were definitely Isaac. Emma was also as daring as herself, but had her father's serenity and common sense, combined with a genuine love for everything and everyone. "An extraordinarily beautiful child," all commented.

Adelicia pulled her close, stroking her dark curls. "You are my precious darling. We are going to have gas lights at Belle Monte, and you may turn the one in your room on or off by simply moving a lever on the wall. Then you will not have to beckon Charlotte anymore to light the lamp for you."

"They's getting so many new inventions, pretty soon won't be nothing for me to do," said Charlotte. "Lights that goes on and off, track engines, and them bath things you talk about for the new house, next thing you knows, they'll have something that dresses and undresses the childrens and washes their clothes for 'em."

"Charlotte, I'll always need you. You're my best friend," responded Emma.

Adelicia smiled, remembering favorite scenes of Emma; walking through ankle deep green grass, her black Labrador puppy following close at her heels, so adorable with long dark braids tied with gingham ribbons that bounced over her small shoulders as she skipped between steps. Emma had grown to be so sensitive that the lightest remonstrance of disapproval caused tears to well-up in her deep blue eyes with lashes so long they curled into her brows.

Adelicia recalled a particular day at Bellevue when she had watched Emma coming up the oyster shell walkway from the levee to the house, taking the indirect path. Circling a large oak tree and rounding a stump, she twirled around and turned backwards to speak with a rabbit who sat partially hidden on the lawn beside her…then suddenly, wearing her irresistible smile, she ran with the airiness of March as she neared the front steps, jumping into her mother's arms.

The first of April, Adelicia and Joseph returned to Louisiana. After weeks of new investigations, her counselors, again talking with character witnesses from New Orleans to West Feliciana to Gallatin, the appeal was granted to try the case before the Louisiana Supreme Court. Judge Amon LeCriox in New Orleans had dismissed the relevance of Isaac's voting status. But by proving West Feliciana was his major domicile, as well as from where the major portion of his wealth was generated, Sherbourne believed Judge Boyle would at least "listen."

Thus, the case was reopened and continued into the sixth month of 1852, when on June 22, the Louisiana Supreme Court ruled in Adelicia's favor on the basis that the clause in the will that provided for the establishment of an institute in Tennessee out of revenues derived in part from properties in West Feliciana was **"void on the grounds that it set up a perpetuity."**

An "annuity payable forever" could not be paid out of funds derived from one state to maintain an educational institution in another. William Franklin's attorney, Loucks, had lost. Isaac's attorney, Lobdell, had lost. The estate's attorneys had lost!

Victory was sweet! So sweet! The case of Franklin versus Franklin was over! She would return home to Nashville—triumphant! She would awe them with her paintings and sculptures created by the artisans in Europe, her lavish grounds with their many attractions— her villa—her mansion. She wanted them to adore her, to love her, to forgive her and to understand.

CHAPTER 45

DELICIA AND JOSEPH IMMEDIATELY RETURNED TO NASHVILLE following the victorious settlement. She was expecting again and was quite large, larger than with her five previous pregnancies. However, this did not prevent her from making daily trips from Cherry Street, out Hillsboro Pike to inspect the progress on Belle Monte. She had told Joseph that it "must" be more elaborate than Belle Meade that was also under construction by the Hardings.

It was taken for granted that Adelicia held to few if any conventions, and gossip always found its way to her door one way or the other, especially the frequently whispered that she would be seen in public "up to the very day of birth." Another of societies' foolish rules, Adelicia thought. She abhorred decorum, decrees made by old biddies with little else to do than formulate a code by which they would prefer others to live. All things had their place of beauty, Adelicia often said, and she found something especially beautiful about a mother-to-be carrying her child.

They were sitting on lovely wrought iron benches just outside the Nashville Inn on the town square, awaiting Adelicia's cousin Sally, on her mother's side, and Sally's husband, Dr. Sam Carter and their two children, Rodney and Amanda, who were close to Emma in age.

"Joseph, the Carters are here."

"Mama, must I be nice to Amanda again tonight? Every time we are together, she gets me in trouble." Charlotte put her hand to her mouth to keep the smile from showing at Emma's intellectual righteousness. "She blabs everything to Cousin Sally in her favor."

Adelicia looked at Emma, "I suppose you did not really cut the hole in your new green plaid taffeta dress?"

"Only because Amanda dared me. And the only reason she did so was to blab to you. She enjoys saying horrid things about me."

"Well," said Joseph, smiling, "you must be nice to Amanda and behave the way young ladies should—during supper anyway. And you must refrain from this hideous word 'blab.'"

The two families walked inside the inn together and were seated at a lovely round table with a white cloth and napkins and monogrammed china. And as was Adelicia's custom, Charlotte dined with them. Although some eyebrows were raised when it became popular to eat at public establishments, it was Adelicia's opinion that the nurses ate with the children at home and would likewise eat with them when they dined out. No one had dared approach her to the contrary.

Adelicia complained of indigestion after eating the first few bites and sipped hot tea while the others leisurely finished their meal, enjoying the conversation. As the two cousins stood in front of the inn hugging good-bye, Sally kissed Joseph on the cheek. "Let us know tomorrow, honey, if Adie is not feeling any better."

They watched the Carters step into their carriage, and at Emma's request, the four of them strolled along the lighted square. And although it was almost nine o'clock, businesses were still open and one could not mistake the present air of prosperity. "The fat fifties," Adelicia thought, as they walked with the October wind pushing behind their backs. The alliteration had a nice sound, and she intended to be among those whose fortunes soared. She believed what her father said about being without limitations. Success was how one used what one had; one used what one had to one's advantage.

Her indigestion grew worse as she climbed into the handsome walnut bed with its hexagonal shaped post and elaborately carved headboard. She had fallen in love with the grand piece of furniture at Mallard's in New Orleans and had it shipped by steamer to Nashville. It was a bed exclusively for her and Joseph, the one in which Bud had been born and the one in which she hoped all her children would be born.

"Joseph, send for Dr. Shelby," she said, putting her hand on her abdomen. "I think it is time for your second child to be born."

On October 20, 1852, at 2:30 A.M., Corrina Victoria was born, and ten minutes later, her twin sister Laura Adelicia.

At breakfast, Emma was fascinated with the news of not one, but two baby sisters to fit into the nursery with her little brother. Gulping her milk, as she had been instructed not to do, Emma ran up the stairs and peeked into crib as Joseph held Bud up over it, showing him the latest arrivals. "We're outnumbered in this household, son. We'll have to stick together like glue."

"That boy already more of a handful than ten girls could be," said Cora. "You don't need no worries over that."

The room was quiet by late morning. The infants were asleep in the swan-shaped brass bed prepared for only one. Adelicia gave a smile of contentment as she watched them, listening to their soft breathing sounds, sounds unique to newborns.

She picked up the silver hand mirror beside her, the one Joseph had given her, along with the matching pieces, as a wedding gift. She looked at her cheeks, still full in the 'womanly way.'

She wondered how many children Joseph might want. They had never discussed it, but she was thirty-five years old, and she thought six pregnancies quite enough for any woman. Although she had been lucky in the past, she feared the day when her figure might not return to its natural state and her waist not quickly become twenty-one inches. However, she would see.

She had not dismissed the idea of taking control of the plantation management, just as quickly as she could phase out the present arrangement that still included John Armfield and her father. During her three weeks of bed rest, she would consider those things that must be considered for the welfare of her family and Belle Monte's completion.

May through September—Adelicia lay there thinking, with a daughter sleeping in each of her arms—would be open house at Belle Monte, but the winter months would have to be spent in New Orleans or on the plantations themselves to insure efficiency and productivity. John Armfield and her father would soon be eliminated from the estate expenses, saving a minimum of fourteen thousand dollars annually. With Joseph's assistance, she would be in direct contact with Jim Clack to learn everything necessary for perfecting the operations. No one knew what the sixties would bring; it was of the utmost necessity to make the most of the abundant fifties. There was talk of States Rights…and of Secession.

She wanted desperately to move into Belle Monte before Christmas. Its massive rooms and stately interior columns called for the holiday season, to hold festive balls and parties. Some described her villa as Grecian, others as Italian or French, but no one could deny that she had built a house the likes of which had never been seen in Tennessee. The yet unfinished rooms appeared to have no end: children's rooms, intended children's rooms, servant's rooms, guests rooms, drawing rooms, music rooms, a study, a library, a gentlemen's room, a ladies' room, formal rooms, informal rooms, galleries—and there was the upstairs, reserved exclusively for Adelicia and Joseph, with the exception of a nursery. Each had separate bedrooms; actually, separate wings with closets and baths (the first with running water in Nashville) and an adjoining sitting room between, lavishly decorated with heavily stuffed furniture and a Corinthian design wallpaper in tones of browns, grays and blues.

The furnishings, fabrics and floor coverings had been imported from Europe or purchased in New Orleans or New York. Most wallpaper selections had come from Paris, but some, like that in the sitting room, was commissioned in Rome. With their busy schedules, it was necessary for both Adelicia and Joseph to have their own desk and work area. However, it was definitely understood that her husband, without exception, would sleep with her in their special bed.

She lay in that bed now, waiting for him to come upstairs, thinking how empty it felt when he was not lying beside her! She rubbed her fingers across the cool sheets that had not yet been warmed by his body and glanced up at the molding where the walls joined the ceiling, the egg and dart, life and death. This same motif had been used in the house on Canal Street and in two of the rooms at Fairvue, but she would not have it at Belle Monte; it would be defined by a dove and fruit design, nothing reminding her of death. She had seen and felt enough of its sting; she foolishly wished to never again feel its clutches.

"Are you asleep?" He brushed the hair back from her face, and she recalled the many nights she had gone to sleep in his arms with him gently slipping his fingers through her hair. Not speaking, Adelicia took Joseph's hand, held it tightly and kissed it.

"What's wrong?" he asked, touching the tears on her cheeks.

"I love you," she answered.

She lay with half her body on top of his, clinging to him, revealing the fear and insecurity, foiled by her basic nature that suggested confidence. Only Joseph and God knew how frightened and difficult it was for her at times. "Will you hold me close?" she said

Streaks of morning were criss-crossing the floor when Joseph dozed off, still holding Adelicia in his arms.

Often, mornings that began with drowsy, sleepy kisses and gentle caresses, continued until each was wide awake enjoying, delighting and fulfilling the other.

Her love for Joseph had not waned; their marriage had moved smoothly. All was so serene, she wondered if her vivacious spirit might also be waning. However, when she dwelled too long on this sort of thinking, she concluded that it was at rest, awaiting the right moment to resurface. She did not trust serenity for herself.

For the first time in some years, there were no battles, no obstacles, no deaths, no competition. Nothing besides gossip! But that was nothing new. Any goodwill on her part was dismissed by Nashvillians as selfish ambition, and Adelicia was despised by those in Gallatin, by some in Nashville. Her mention of French schools in New Orleans again raised eyebrows, and the gossipers had also heard rumors that she would send Bud to a Northern boarding school, an idea widely considered pompous, showy.

The plantations further south awaited her direction, but for now she would enjoy Belle Monte, and those who came to see it. She would relax into its world until the twins were old enough to travel with the family to Louisiana.

It was not until the spring of 1853 that the Acklens and their servants moved into Belle Monte. And it was another day that Nashvillians stared in envious disbelief as the oxen drawn carts trudged their way out Hillsboro Pike to Belle Monte laden with the finery of Europe.

People came out of their shops and houses, lining the city streets to gawk at the parade of moving oxen, mules and wagons.

Some remarked that Adelicia and Joseph were living "high and fancy" with her first husband's money—not bothering to take into account the increases made in land and cotton production in the past six years, or the long hours Joseph spent working in the plantation offices in order to keep close and accurate accounts of all transactions.

She was extremely pleased with his ability to manage the burdensome task of twelve thousand acres and over five hundred slaves. It was a responsibility that he performed dutifully and willingly, to the great praise of neighboring planters in West Feliciana. Of course, Jim Clack and his assistants were excellent overseers and managers. And after the peaceful transition from John Armfield and her father, all was now under her watchful eye.

Adelicia's desire to win the approval of the majority seemed futile. Acceptance and approval were separate entities; they accepted her, but she well understood there was little chance of her ever having the townsfolk's approbation.

CHAPTER 46

THE FULL MOON SHOWN ON BELLE MONTE'S OPENING GALA. Adelicia had consulted an almanac before giving the mid-summer ball so that Belle Monte's grounds would not only be illuminated by the colorful Japanese lanterns hung to light the shrubbery and gardens, but from the luminous light of the moon as well. Her guests would stroll through the gardens among the sweet fragrances of eglantine, star jasmine, gardenias, hibiscus, azaleas and lilacs or sit in one of the delicately laced iron gazebos or view the Italian statuary placed throughout the grounds.

Belle Monte was imposing! Awesome! The mansion's two facades faced north and south. One entered the estate from either Hillsboro Pike on the west or Granny White Pike on the east, but whichever the choice, the shell paved drives lined with cedars and magnolias were breathtaking to the beholder.

Dressed in an ivory beaded gown from Paris, Adelicia delighted in introducing her Washington guests to Middle Tennessee residents. It was by far the grandest affair ever given in Nashville, marking a new type of entertaining. It was not simply a gathering for musicians to play for dancing, or coquettish talk, dining on rich food or sipping madeira punch; but for guests to spend time browsing in the columned art galleries, to view paintings by Old World masters as well as originals by contemporary American artists, to observe Italian statuary and hear music from Italian operas.

South of the mansion were three formal gardens, diminishing in size as one walked farther from the house. Beyond was a large white, low-lying conservatory, providing fresh flowers for the tables and rooms throughout the year: roses, orchids, violets, daffodils and over one hundred varieties of tulips. A water tower of hand mold brick, one hundred and five feet tall, provided balance at the end of the gardens. The moat at its base was fed by a limestone spring, and a windmill and a steam engine drew water into storage tanks that fed an intricate system of underground pipes, providing water for the entire estate, the gardens, fountains, orchards and arbors, as well as the mansion itself.

The circle in the center of the largest garden was ornamented by an Italian fountain of Carrara marble, and lush blooming roses graced the third and smallest circle which well informed guests compared to the Petit Trianon of Versailles. The middle garden made up a maze of intricate walkways amongst sweet smelling jasmine.

Four lace-like, wrought iron summer houses that adorned the gardens and paths winding through and around them to the conservatory, were paved with delicate white and pink shells, bordered by planters of boxwoods.

A large building in the Greek influence housed a bowling alley and billiard room, and a smaller building in the southeast corner boasted a small zoo, including pet monkeys, dressed in colorful costumes for the gala affair. In addition, a deer park with three spring-fed lakes, ran behind the estate on the south side. The stables, orchards and grape arbors were all to the left of the mansion near Granny White Pike.

The grounds presented such an imposing spectacle, most doubted that the mansion's interior could possibly equal the grandeur of the gardens themselves. But as guests approached from the south entrance, greeted by magnificent granite lions on either side, then walked between white columns before passing through hand carved walnut doors, flanked with panes of rich, multi-colored venetian glass, there was no disappointment.

Carrara marble mantels magnified each fireplace, further adorned by large gold framed mirrors hanging from rich woven, gold cords. The furnishings were mahogany and rosewood; handsome cut-glass chandeliers provided gas light; imported lace curtains, set deep inside the cornices, dressed every window.

Belle Monte's debut was an evening no one would forget, an occasion that would be discussed over tea and supper for many years to come. Five hundred guests strolled and danced and dined and celebrated until the full moon's brightness was dulled by the sun's first rays. At last, Joseph and Adelicia, exhausted, fell into the large mahogany bed and were quickly asleep in each other's arms.

CHAPTER 47

Nashville 1860

IN THE SUMMER OF 1852 WHEN BELLE MONTE WAS BEGUN, Adelicia began recording each day's events…brief glimpse of life. In a pensive mood one cold afternoon as the month of January 1860 was taking hold, she removed the journal from her desk drawer in the morning room. Lying on the divan and propped up by down filled pillows before a roaring fire, she thumbed through the pages, stopping here and there to remember…The house was quiet. Joseph was in Louisiana and the children visiting with friends. For the opening gala in 1853, she had written: "It was difficult for me to believe how truly glorious last night was. All the planning and preparation was certainly worth it. Belle Monte was more beautiful than anything we saw in France, Italy, etc…more than European splendor…it was like a fairytale…not one person went away without a happy heart…At last I feel we are perhaps gaining the approval of some…

"**September:** I had tears in my eyes today as we left our grand and dear Belle Monte to go downriver to West Feliciana, but we must see to the harvesting and the plantations themselves…

December: What a grand year it has been…this is the best crop since forty-five so all the planters say…ours is abundant…cotton waist-high…rich with boles (thirty to forty each)…The twins are so amusing, being "toted" by their sister Emma and tugged at by Bud… Emma is such a darling…How I adore her.

January, 1854: West Feliciana and New Orleans…The gaiety of carnival is marvelous this year…our first in so long a time…good to see old friends…wish we could have everyone at Belle Monte…of course, most of the planters along the river have enormous mansions… The Randolph's, I am told have seventy-five rooms (one can overindulge)…Joseph says we may plan ours beginning next summer…It will be different from Belle Monte...more "Louisiana," but elegant. Isaac did not live to build the grand house he had planned.

April: Laura and Corinna become more precious each day...they roll and frolic on the playroom floor and toddle about the room... Emma thinks she and Charlotte should have full charge...However, Charlotte is grateful for Jasmine and Biddle...

May: All my life, I have wished to be as happy and contented as I am right now....sitting in the stateroom on our way back to my beloved Belle Monte watching the twins take their easy breaths in sleep...and Emma sitting on the floor working a puzzle...Through the port hole, I can see Joseph and Bud...what a marvelous scene to behold, father and son standing on the starboard side with Bud's hand clasp firmly in his father's...life is glorious!

July: The gates of Belle Monte are never closed…visitors are always welcome...no one is ever been turned away...it seems there are no "overnight" visits...some of our guests and relatives remain for weeks...they stay as long as they please...knowing their welcome comes from a sincere heart. Essie always sees that extra places are set with the greatest of care and ease so that even the latest drop-in will think he is expected.

August: Belle Monte has certainly become known for its hospitality, not a visitor from Washington or abroad comes to the city who does not stop by for either afternoon tea or supper...Millard Fillmore visited last evening (a handsome and charming bachelor)...How I love entertaining when the moon is its fullest...My dear brother, Henry, married Mary Boyd yesterday.

December: Here we are, another Christmas in New Orleans...the plantations take so much of our time, but we are in complete control now...how productive they are!...Our profits have more than doubled in the past three years...the "fat fifties" are certainly as they say...

January, 1855: "The children so enjoyed Kris Kringle...they had placed their stockings on the hearth and were each thrilled with the treasures found inside...Laura and Corinna are the dearest little cherubs...They found the tree most amusing...their first real Christmas... and loved touching the pretty ornaments...Bud and Emma made many of them themselves…she lovingly helped Bud, a precious older sister...The twins are walking and talking well now, of course none of us understand what they say to each other...Emma says it is "twin language."...My sisters, Laura and Corrine had double weddings at Rokeby today. How I longed to have been there. After visiting in the City of New Orleans, they are coming here to stay some time with us at Bellevue. How exciting and grand! We shall have parties and show them off to our neighbors."

..."The twins are not feeling well, especially Laura...ever since the deaths of my first darlings, the least illness frightens me.."

"Yesterday, January 25th, my precious Laura was taken from us...oh, how can I bare it...her dear sister reminds me so much of her.

February: The plantation has been placed under quarantine...scarlet fever...may God please spare my three dear children and Joseph...two of the house servants have already been taken...

The 9th: Little Corrina is burning with fever...have not slept in so many nights...

The 11th: This morning at three o'clock my other precious baby was taken...now God has five of my children...oh, dear Lord, will you take more?

The small coffins holding my Laura and Corrina were put aboard the *The Tennessee* to Nashville and buried at Fairvue. Dear Joseph and I, our hands in each other's, knelt and prayed long after the others had gone, beside the stones bearing all their names, Isaac, Julius Caesar, Victoria, Adelicia, Corinna, and Laura. One day, I, too, will be alongside them. Not one person from Gallatin came to the burial, except for my cousin Emma White. Della and Daniel were there.

March: Bellevue Plantation... "This is the first letter I have been able to write since our return to Louisiana. Oh, Corrine, how I hope you and Laura may be spared the griefs I have known...it all seems a terrible dream...and when I ask, can it be, is it true that those lovely little ones are to gladden my heart no more or their sweet prattle delight my ears...then the horrible convictions that it is so. How lone and desolate feels the mother's heart. It seems nothing can give consolation...and indeed nothing does. We shall return to Fairvue at the usual time...of course, there will be no parties...no moonlight dancing on the lawn...no gaiety at Belle Monte this summer...and perhaps never again...it feels life itself has been taken from me. Give my love to all...Your affectionate sister, Adie...Corrine, I am again with child...October."

August: This has been the bleakest of summers...I cannot even joy in the expected birth...will my heart never be lifted?

September 8th: I gave birth to William Hayes Acklen in that same dear bed I have so long shared with my husband...William is a precious baby...hair like his father and large brown eyes...God is merciful...

January 1856: There was no Christmas celebration at Belle Monte...our first one spent here...oh, the vain frivolity we had planned...Joseph took Bud to Corrine and Bill's at Hillside, to enjoy Kris Kringle with his cousins, aunts, uncles, and grandfather...Jasmine cared for baby Will...My dear, my precious, Emma with her long dark curls was taken from me, diphtheria, the first day of November, and she was placed beside her sisters and her father...I held her until Joseph and Essie, literally took her from my arms...I did not think I could bare another trek to Fairvue, this time following behind sweet Emma's hearse, but strength came, allowing me to see the earth shoveled onto yet another daughter's grave...Dear God, I do not know how much more this heart can bare...five daughters and three sons I have borne, and only two remain...please purge me of all sins and give my heart rest...

March: I no longer like being at Bellevue...I am not content anywhere...I know I must do as Joseph says and be a happy mother to my sons...how I long to touch Emma once more...my babies...It seems if I could see them for only a moment, my heart would be glad...my dear, dear Emma...the longest I had any of my children...

April: A terrible disaster! The Nashville Inn and Court House have been burning since yesterday...we can see the smoke billowing from the north portico...I fear we do not have the equipment or man power to keep them from burning to the ground...William was baptized by Reverend Edgar with water from the River Jordan...How I weep for Emma and my twins each day!

September: We are on our way to West Feliciana to Bellevue...Belle Monte is still in mourning as am I and my husband...life has been taken from me...I only go through the motions...

December: We put up a tree for Bud this year...he and Rufus went into the woods and chopped it down...William reminds me so much of the twin's first Christmas...touching the pretty ornaments and emptying his stocking on the floor to see what Kris Kringle has brought...my smiles, few as they are, only pretenses...

February, 1857: Dr. Kincaid assured me today that I am expecting again in July...have been feeling quite poorly as of late...since the holidays...

March: Visited Madame Octavia Lavert in Mobile for three weeks...she has lost two of her children...

April: Joseph has worked so hard seeing the new crop into the ground...our cotton for the fourth year in a row was judged the best in the parish...to be certain, we have had some fine crops...the Negroes enjoy the contest among themselves for the amount of cotton picked, etc...prize is a five dollar gold piece and one week off after trashing season...

June: Our first large party in some time...everyone was here including some Washington politicians...Nashville is certainly well known...after all, we've had two presidents...more than any other southern city...Belle Monte becomes more beautiful each year...I think this fall I shall hire a tutor and stay in Nashville...New Orleans and its gaiety holds no intrigue for me. Papa was here. He has forgiven me...and has been very kind over my children's deaths, as have my sisters and others.

July: What a blessed event it was. Our third son was born.

September: Claude is so dear at two months nursing at my breast...must speak with my husband about the size of our family... oh, the joys and sorrows that fill a mother's heart...

December: Christmas was as we have long wished it...all the family came for the Eve and awakened early for Liza's special thick creamy eggnog and a breakfast that no king's table could rival...after the men left for a day of hunting...the ladies talked and rested and played with the little ones...the children were so excited over their goodies from Kris Kringle...Bud cannot wait for snow so that he may try out his new ice skates...Ham, oysters, fruits, nuts and pastries of every sort!... and the roast beef seemed tastier than ever before. Mr. Guben said he had saved his prize beef for me...he runs on so...but I must agree it was excellent...conversation and merriment lasted till quite late and everyone retired after sipping steaming hot, holiday brandied chocolate around the fire...Miss Heloise Cemas, our new tutor from New Orleans is a darling...the children love her...she fits right in with the family...what a wonderful day...Papa shot the only buck...

February, 1858: Joseph writes and says the city is filled with carnival revelers...all seems so frivolous now...my dear husband will be home in six weeks..

April: What a remarkable evening! William Walker referred to as the "gray eyed man of destiny," by the press from coast to coast...dined with us tonight...he is indeed captivating with his tales and his quest...he held us captive with his talk of arrest within the states and his arrest, capture, banishment and battle in Nicaragua...he feels the Americas should be our territory, and intends to "take" and become president of Nicaragua...I have no doubt he will succeed...Stockley and Phila Ann Donelson were here, the Randall McGavocks, the Foggs, Berrien Lindsley and others...it was a wonderful, young group...except for papa, but he fits into any gathering...how happy our differences have long been resolved...Joseph carved the delicious roast beef...fresh sea foods, ham, an abundance of Madeira, squash soufflé, fresh green beans with slivered almonds, silibud...everyone, (even the ladies) ate until we could eat no more...William Walker will certainly leave his mark on the history of this country and elsewhere...how I admire his spirit and the force that drives him...the full moon shown on us all evening...

October: Joseph has returned to West Feliciana and we are settled into our routine here at Belle Monte...*Southern Ladies Companion* had a wonderful article today on what the fashions will be for the sixties...I must have some new gowns sent from Paris...

November 15th: My dear, dear papa passed away the first day of this month...three years from the day of precious Emma...how I loved him...no man has been, or will be like Papa...the loss is great... The will was read today at Rokeby, and he was most generous with all his children, as well as the servants...I had my share divided between my brothers and sisters...I have been blessed with so much, it did not seem right to take an inheritance...I chose some personal items that had belonged to both Mama and Papa...I took Papa's pipe and have placed it on my bedroom mantle...a wonderful reminder of him...He is buried beside my dear mother.

December: All the family gathered at Belle Monte again for the holidays...The children especially delighted in the white sugar, cone-shaped loaves that had been beaten in a mortar with pestle...Papa's absence was felt heavily by everyone...It seems each year there is another empty chair...

January 1859: Thank God for a new year! I am anxious for the fifties to come to an end...yet most thankful for my three healthy sons... although we have prospered in a wealthy market, our family has suffered greatly of the heart...oh to be in poverty with my darlings than have one pence of gold without them...

Joseph and I attended the theater this evening with the Donelsons and took Sally Carter as our guest...she has been out very little...so young and pretty to be a widow...

April: Michael, our Irish gardener, who has been with us since Belle Monte's grounds were first designed, continues to be a wonder...the green house flourishes with orchids, lily of the valley, violets, gardenias, roses and tulips year round...pineapples, oranges and lemons grace our table in the depths of winter...we also enjoy Michael's family and have built them a lovely cottage on the west side of the property.

September: Joseph has gone to Bellevue but will return before Christmas...Our *last* child was born two weeks ago...precious Pauline...and Joseph Smith Acklen knows it is our last...nine pregnancies are quite enough!...I began breathing deeply from my abdomen the day after her birth. My waistline will never be larger than twenty-two inches again! I abhor the thought of giving in to staves! Pauline is such a darling...God has once again given me a daughter...she looks much like her father.

December: Seven years is indeed long enough to record the histories of the times...perhaps the children will enjoy it in later years.

December 29th: A wonderful Christmas was had at Belle Monte! The holidays are quite merry as we bid a decade good-bye and ring in a new one. However, I am quite uncertain about it...there is much talk of secession and war...wish the North would leave well enough alone...Tennessee does not want to leave the Union...I think much of the fault lies with some self-seeking radicals in South Carolina...I have heard the politicians there are so ignorant of the real issues, they have forgotten what the argument of war is about...as for myself, I would not disagree to freeing the slaves...but what would become of them all...

Adelicia closed the journal and rested her head on a pillow that had slipped over to the side...revisited moments...of recorded time. With tear stained cheeks, she held the book in her hand at length, then laid it gently beside the hearth.

CHAPTER 48

A DECADE HAD COME TO A CLOSE. THE PROSPERITY OF THE "FAT fifties" had left few of the larger planters disappointed. Cotton was selling at a premium of ninety-two cents a pound and the Northern and European markets were crying for more, regardless of the price. Merchants, bankers and businesses in Nashville were flourishing just as they were all over the south. Adelicia's Louisiana plantations had more than tripled in production in the previous four years and she had plans to cultivate another two thousand acres to plant more cotton in the spring.

Joseph had not disappointed Adelicia in his ability to oversee her empire. He had proved an excellent manager, and the pamphlet he had written on slavery and planters, published in *De Boe's*, had gained him the genuine respect of other planters, as well as favorable comments from the North. The document, "Rules, Regulations and Instructions for the Overseers and Employees of Plantations," gave just cause for the care and treatment of slaves, including their education and religious instruction. Not all planters agreed with Joseph's reasoning, but who did always agree, Adelicia thought?

And their plans to build an even grander house than Belle Monte on the Mississippi was becoming a reality. They had selected a slight knoll two miles northeast of the Bellevue structure, just beyond the river's loop but still with the enchanting Tunica Hills for background. Adelicia did not want it simply in keeping with those of the other planters, but larger and grander of scale. She would lease the Bellevue house to Jim Clack for life.

But there was no time for building now. There was talk of war, of insurrection by the slaves, and even direct intervention from Washington. Some southerners believed nothing could disturb their world, the only one they knew, speaking in whispered tones of gallantry. But for those wise enough to see what might lie ahead, there was fear. Fear for the wealth they had accumulated with the aid of slave labor, and fear that it could not be maintained without it. Also fear of losing their identity. Fear, Oliver Hayes had believed, was courage still holding on. That through fear, came wisdom.

Adelicia certainly felt there was nothing gallant in war, and that if this one occurred, the one between the North and the South, neither would be the victor, or upheld for its gallantry.

Honor was meaningless when there were families to feed and debts to pay, Adelicia mused. However, if there were going to be a war, there was no reason why one could not prosper from it, and there was no reason why she should not be among those who did. Tennessee might, or might not secede, or for that matter, perhaps none of the states would secede, despite the talk. But if they did, one sure way to be in the winner's circle was to take all payments in gold only, and beginning with her next shipment of cotton, that is exactly what she would do. Her excitement mounted as she lay in bed, thinking about payments in gold.

Joseph was now in West Feliciana overseeing the spring planting for 1860, and although she had wanted to go to New Orleans this trip, the cholera epidemic there had caused her and the children to remain in Nashville. Joseph wrote that the plagued city was under quarantine and although sulphur and tar pots burned every few blocks, and that lime was sprinkled over the hundreds of daily victims, even in the cemeteries, nothing seemed to halt death, the stench or the filth. It reeked on every street corner, in every house.

Bud had reluctantly returned to his boarding school in Lexington, Virginia after the holidays, leaving young William's and Claude's education to a highly recommended Scottish tutor at home.

Adelicia had retired early that evening, thinking of Joseph. She admired and respected her husband and missed not being with him. His few flaws vanished when weighed against his strengths and virtues. He also overlooked her flaws, most of which she was well aware, and loved her in spite of them.

As she lay with her arm stretched over on his side of the bed, she thought of when he had first kissed her, which now seemed so long ago...and that bright glow she had felt then had not diminished in eleven years of marriage. He called her his strength, but it was he who was hers. His tenderness at the twin's births, the comfort and tenderness at theirs and Emma's deaths…yes, she thought, she had grown to depend on Joseph for the serenity, the joy, unique to loving and being loved.

She was dozing into a soft sleep when she heard footsteps on the stairs.

"Essie?" She waited for an answer, then sat up and called to her mammy again just before seeing Joseph's silhouette by the bit of moonlight seeping through the closed drapes.

"Joe Acklen, you almost frightened the death of me! You are not due home until next month." She hugged her husband around the neck, feeling the blessed security of being in his arms.

"Am I not welcome?"

"What a silly question. How did you get away so soon?"

"You won't believe what's been taking place the past few weeks. All up and down the river, everybody's going crazy in one way or another. Some planters are storing up cotton for the south and others are frantically shipping theirs north."

She was wide awake now, sitting up in bed with her legs folded beneath her. "I hope you are doing what we planned with ours."

"England is just as frightened as everyone else. Nobody ventures to take sides, and everybody's looking for a deal, buyer as well as seller."

"But where is ours?" she persisted.

"Loaded so heavy and tight on a boat to England that even a boll weevil would smother."

"You were beginning to make me think you had lost your senses along with the others," she said, reaching up and hugging him.

"My dear, I wouldn't even accept a note this time, and I didn't go through the agent…I was paid in full before it left the dock. Everybody's promising everything, and God only knows what the state of affairs will be from one day to the next. Bishop Polk is a strong influence, and he's very pro south; that could impact a lot of us, for good or bad."

"For now, my concern is making sure the cotton arrives safely in Liverpool…" With a hasty thought, she interrupted herself. "Joseph, we did get paid in gold?"

He laughed and swept her up into his arms. "It was put in our account in London." He laughed again. "Don't worry, not one boll of your cotton was bought with anything but gold."

"I have heard enough business prattle for tonight. I have missed you." She drew him into bed with her, undressing him as she ran her hands beneath his shirt, unfastening his trousers and moving her fingers freely over his body.

Chapter 49

TENNESSEE WAS THE LAST OF THE ELEVEN SOUTHERN STATES TO secede. Although its sympathies were divided, when the final vote was taken in February of 1861, Tennessee cast hers with the Confederacy.

Excitement, tension and fear, combined with vain hopes of glory and victory, hovered over Nashville. Few understood what it was about...even fewer realized the seriousness of secession, or its repercussions. But the newly organized Tennessee Volunteers were ready to form an army for "The Cause." As far as Adelicia was concerned, it was for the cause of gallant southerners galloping off to war against the North whom many considered jealous of the south.

Without complaint, all paid their increased taxes, but when the southern states began to develop into a confederacy, and began to impress the land, both small farmers, without slave labor, and large plantation owners with slave labor, felt the sharp financial pangs. The wealthy were further asked to donate to the cause in great proportion. There was honorable talk that southerners would kill their own livestock, or burn their cotton fields to keep them from the grasps of the Union Army. In reality, however, no one expected a Yankee to ever set foot on Southern soil.

Adelicia found the talk rash, senseless. She had no intention of having her cotton burned. Neither the North, nor the South were going to profit from her land, her livestock or her crops, and she did not believe any planter or businessman in his right mind wanted anything of the sort.

But it was true that Jefferson Davis was asking each state's governor to make an accounting of all landowners with more than a hundred acres in cotton. And for certain, in the state of Louisiana, the West Feliciana plantations would be at the top of the list.

How grateful she was that in the spring and fall of 1860, Joseph had put their gold in London banks. After all, honor was one thing, war was another, and Adelicia wanted her money to be negotiable when it was over. If, indeed it ever began. But if worse came to worse, and the Union Army did tromp into Nashville, she did not intend to be caught with her head turned in the wrong direction. She would play both sides, and work hard to somehow prevent Joseph from joining the Confederacy.

He had not agreed with her position, and felt even more strongly after the first shots were fired off Charleston's coast and eleven southern states no longer belonged to the Union. Still she had stopped him thus far from being one of the first to run and enlist. She needed him with her and the children; she especially needed him in Louisiana. Just when she felt her past sins were at last being forgiven, she was once more becoming a topic of muffled conversation.

"Joe Acklen has given every excuse for not joining the Army," the old biddies were saying. "It's probably her fault." Adelicia would like to tell every last one of them where to go. However, now was not the time, but one of these days she just might do so.

The discomforts and inconveniences of war were all around them and reports of victory for the South were not coming in splendid successions. The close of 1861 brought the return of the wounded, visions of glory gone from their eyes…the return of the dead, who would never know on which side victory lay.

Adelicia, along with her cousin Sally, Sarah Polk, Ada Murdock, Selistine McGavock, Philla Donelson and other Nashvillians, known as "The Ladies Southern Aid's Society," were instrumental in establishing makeshift hospitals to care for the wounded. And Adelicia was extremely pleased to see her beloved First Presbyterian Church become one of these hospitals, where she talked with wounded soldiers, fed those unable to feed themselves and wrote letters home to their families.

Bud sometimes accompanied her, and she strongly hoped his work there would help satisfy his urge to serve the South, that there would no more attempts to lie about his age in order to join the Confederacy. She and Joseph were astonished to learn of his daring to join the troops in Virginia, and grateful the attempt had been foiled by a scrutinizing officer before sending him home. Of course, he was not the only young man vying to join...the war was considered noble by most, and for young boys, believing themselves to be men, it seemed far grander.

It was a soggy-wet and cold January morning when Adelicia sat beside the cot of a young man who looked no older than Bud. His face was swollen and puffy, and his right arm was severed at the shoulder. "Good morning, young man," she smiled, putting her hand on his left arm that lay across his chest.

There was no response except for the clear, deep brown eyes that stared into hers. "May I get something for you, to make you more comfortable or write a letter to your family?"

He turned his head away, and bit his lower lip. "I don't have no family, ma'am."

"What's your name, son?"

"Jakey. Jakey Brown."

"Where are you from, Jakey?"

"I don't have no home. I can't never go home again."

She felt his fingers tremble as she held his hand in hers. She looked at his swollen face set with the dark eyes and could not restrain her own tears as his rolled down both cheeks.

"How old are you, Jakey?"

"Fourteen, ma'am." He looked up at her, questioning, "Will you be my mother, just for today?"

The sudden, unexpected question took her aback. With her handkerchief, she blotted the tears from her own face and from his, "Of course," she answered, "I shall be very proud to be your mother."

She sat beside Jakey for the remainder of the day, after the sun had gone down, after the lamps were lit.

She read from *The Last of the Mohicans* and from the *Bible*. He was familiar with Cooper's tale of Uncas and his father Chingachgook in the virgin woods. He would like to see an Indian, he told her, and go west like Natty Bumpo. But instead of trapping, he would search for gold.

After feeding his supper, Adelicia read from the *Book of Psalms,* "The Lord is my Shepherd, I shall not want."

"Could I say it after you, Ma'am?"

"Of course you may."

"I use to know it by heart, and there's another one too, in the last book, about the city where there ain't no more crying or pain and everybody loves everybody."

She recited the Psalm slowly and clearly, and he repeated each line after her, then she turned to *Revelations*. "Is this the one you mean?" she asked, reading from the Twenty-First Chapter. When he nodded, she continued:

"And God shall wipe away all tears from their eyes; and there shall be no more death, neither sorrow, nor crying neither shall there be any more pain for the former things are passed away... He that over-cometh shall inherit all things; and I will be his God, and he shall be my son... the lamb is the light... and the gates of it shall not be shut at all by day; for there shall be no night there." She closed the *Bible*, and he smiled for the first time.

"Can you come again tomorrow, ma'am?" Jakey asked.

"I shall be here first thing in the morning. You rest well tonight." She bent over and kissed his forehead and gently patted his swollen face. "Rest well," she said tenderly as she reached the door leading into the sanctuary. "Good night, my son."

Adelicia hoped Jakey had rested better than she, for streaks of morning were stretching across the ceiling and she had not known even a twilight slumber. She had told Joseph the story three times, and with each telling, Jakey seemed more tragic. What could a boy of fourteen have done, or experienced to prevent him from going home again? How horrifying those words were to her. She was also curious over his familiarity with the scriptures and with Cooper. She would learn more.

Bud, William, Claude and Pauline sat at their usual places at break-fast, deciding among themselves if the ice were frozen hard enough on the ponds for them to try out their new Christmas skates. The two older boys were complaining about having to take five year old Claude with them and the additional burden of Pauline on her first ice skating adventure. Adelicia and Joseph listening, as they stood in the doorway, suggested that Bud and William go out for a few hours by themselves, then return for the younger ones, a compromise that seemed to please. "We shall be home before dark," she said, walking out into the cold.

Adelicia had insisted Joseph go with her and meet Jakey, well aware that her husband knew she had every intention of bringing the boy home with them, that that was the real reason she wanted him along.

They walked through rows of the wounded and dying, hearing the cries and labored breaths of suffering, cries that made her want to cover her ears with both hands to muffle the reality.

When they at last reached the door of the small room where Adelicia had spent the day with Jakey, the cot on which he had lain was replaced by two army style ones and the men occupying them appeared asleep. Adelicia asked a passing volunteer where the boy had been taken. "I just came in, Ma'am. I've more to do than I can do."

"Wait here, Adie," Joseph said. "I'll go find Dr. Shelby."

"I shall go with you."

Again they walked among the wounded and found the doctor preparing for surgery.

"The boy died this morning, about four. You must be the one he was talking about before he lost consciousness, Adie. He spoke of a beautiful lady, her being his mother for a day, going west, looking for gold in a city without pain. Didn't make sense. Did you know him?" Neither answered. "It's good to see you, but if you'll excuse me, I have to get on with this."

They stepped aside for him to pass, then walked out of doors. Joseph put his arm around her and asked if she were ready to go home.

"No," she answered. "There may be some more Jakeys. I shall stay. You go home and be with the children; perhaps I shall be there in time to skate." Joseph left her standing on the front steps, with her wool hooded cape drawn tightly around her.

"I'll send Luke for you later."

This was only the beginning of a war, she thought, only eight months into it, and God alone only knew how many Jakeys had already died, or were going to die.

Deep in thought, Adelicia left the hospital, hoping Joseph had made good their promise and skated with the children on one of Belle Monte's icy ponds.

On the ride home, she could not remove the horrors of war and the makeshift hospital from her mind. Songs of easy victory were sung no more, and it was rumored that Nashville was virtually unprotected despite the presence of Generals Johnston and Forrest and thousands of troops. War! Adelicia wished she and her family could leave the country, go to Europe and stay there until it was over. Idiots began wars; idiots were the losers; idiots were the winners. "Surely the reason God had said there would always be wars and rumors of wars," she said aloud, "was because He knew there would always be idiots."

But she must not dwell overlong on futile thoughts. Tennessee was part of a newly formed group of eleven states, a confederacy, and at war. She would do what she could for those victims of idiots who needed her.

Chapter 50

S MOG FROM THE BURNING BRIDGE SETTLED OVER NASHVILLE. THE busy arsenals lay silent, the streets were deserted, the city appeared ghostly. Not the barking of a dog, nor the scurrying of a rat broke the heavy silence. Pieces of clothing and household belongings lay strewn about the cobbled stone streets, dropped by those in too great a hurry to stop and retrieve them. Shop windows were smashed and doors stood ajar.

Three days before, on February twenty-sixth, 1862, Nashville had been in chaos, its residents wild with fear, and crime and looting rampant. Carriages, wagons, buggies and carts filled the streets. Residents, black and white, on horseback and on foot, were evacuating after news had reached the city that Fort Donelson had fallen.

Twenty-two days before, General Ulysses S. Grant had moved up the Tennessee River with sixteen-thousand men and attacked Fort Henry, the first battle fought on Tennessee soil. Grant then quickly maneuvered his troops to Fort Donelson, a battle that raged for five days, until Brigadier General Simon Buckner surrendered on February sixteenth. Fort Henry, Fort Donelson and the Cumberland, scurrying with Union gunboats, were under Grant's command. The gates to the Confederacy now lay open!

Confederate Generals Johnston and Forrest had cut the cable and burned the Shelby Street Bridge before they retreated to Murfreesboro and Franklin. And Governor Aaron Brown had fled on a train with other officials for Memphis, taking state documents with him. The city on the Bluff had been without any form of law or order since.

The mayor's lone figure and the click of his horse's hooves provided an eerie ambience as he crossed the Jefferson Street Bridge and made his way to the courthouse. Hitching his mare at the rear entrance, he went inside to wait. Union General D. C. Buell, now just across the Cumberland River to the north, had promised Mayor Challen protection and safety for those Nashville residents who had not fled the city, among whom were the Acklens, the Murdochs, the Hardings and the Dyers.

The sound of distant drums came closer as General Buell and his army of two thousand crossed the river on the one remaining bridge. It was a day no one living in Nashville would ever forget, a Sunday morning when no church bells tolled and no members thronged to worship. Nashville was captured by Union forces just ten months after secession.

Adelicia's mind had sped in a million directions since the morning she learned the Yankees were indeed invading Nashville. No longer an if, or perhaps, Union troops were actually on their way! And if necessary, she vowed that she would entertain every Yankee in town—every last one of them—to protect what was hers. Nashville captured! She hated the thought, the sound of her city being invaded. She hated the war, but if war meant being nice to the Yankees, she would do just that. It was not necessary they know what she was thinking, nor what she was doing behind their backs.

"Adie, if you will please listen," Joseph said sternly, as the family, Essie, Charlotte and Cora stood on the upstairs gallery of Belle Monte. "You must take the children and go to your brother Bliss's. You'll be safer there."

"I shall be safe here. I shall not leave Belle Monte. You have not joined the Confederacy, and for all they know, we could be Union sympathizers. You also have a major business to run in Louisiana, Joseph Acklen," she said, putting her arms about his neck. "I am not leaving this house!"

"You may as well save your breath, Mr. Joe, I don't argue with her atall no more, I done too old for it." Essie was holding Pauline as they stood facing Nashville to the north—all waiting and watching.

"It is a waste of breath, Essie," Joseph replied. "Too hard headed..."

"Is that who Bud takes after?" interrupted Claude, bringing welcomed laughter.

"The reason Essie never argues with me is she knows I am always right," said Adelicia. "Is that not true, Essie?"

"No one answered my question," said Claude.

"There is nothing wrong with Bud. He simply has a mind of his own," answered Joseph, as Cora rolled her eyes up in her head.

Every day, since the time Cora officially became Bud's nurse, she had mumbled to Adelicia and to anyone in ear shot, "...there never been another child like him and never would be."

Although Bud had not uttered a word, Adelicia suspected that he was thinking what fun it would be to drop Claude over the balcony.

Their tension mounted as they strained to hear the ever-nearing beating of the distant drums.

"Mother, will we get to see a Yankee?" asked William.

"We shall get to see lots of Yankees. We may even have a party and invite them all."

"Beg your pardon!" exclaimed Joseph.

"Why not?" she replied, as they waited and listened, still gathered on the balcony.

"Look," William shouted, pointing northward, moments before they heard the first full roll of the drums, whose cadence grew rhythmically louder, and saw the billowing smoke that had risen high enough to be seen clearly pushing upward through the clouds.

Two weeks had passed since the day of the Union invasion, and it was worse than anyone had suspected. The streets remained deserted and the residents were filled with fear. Many homes were without any male occupants over sixteen years old, and those homes who did were under the closest surveillance and scrutiny.

Andrew Johnson, Tennessee's former governor from East Tennessee, was sent by President Lincoln as Military Governor. He lost little time seeking out the wealthy. They were not only asked to donate to the Union cause, but to sign a pledge as well; a pledge of allegiance to the United States. If they refused, they were faced with imprisonment as well as large assessments, sure to leave their families destitute. "Dear me," Adelicia declared, "Scylla and Charybdis!"

So, thought Adelicia, one either gave it all to the South, or all to the North. Obviously, neither side expected anyone to be left with anything when the damnable atrocity was over.

CHAPTER 51

IN THE SPRING OF 1862, AN OCCUPIED NASHVILLE COULD 'FEEL THE screws tightening each day.' The Ladies Southern Aid Society was given permission to continue meeting, usually assembling at Sarah Polk's. As the former First Lady, she had unlimited freedom and was immune from the scrutinizing eyes and ears of the Union soldiers. These gatherings were among the few events the least bit akin to their lives before the Yankee invasion.

"Ladies, it is going to get worse," said the soft-spoken Sarah. "This is the beginning of what I fear will be the greatest disaster our country has ever known, or will ever know. But we must not lose faith. We must be thankful we are allowed to gather in my home and make bandages," she said, cutting a strip of bleached cloth and handing it to Phila Donelson. "And thankful that we may visit the hospitals and minister to those who need us so badly, both physically and spiritually."

"I am not thankful to the Yankees for anything," Adelicia said angrily, ripping a large sheet in half. "It is a disgusting affair."

"I agree with Adelicia." Matilda Dyer was sitting right beside her, folding the precious gauze. "But why on earth, dear, do you have them in your home?"

Not at all taken aback, Adelicia answered quickly and directly. "I shall tell you why. Thus far, we have convinced them, without Joseph's having signed the pledge, that we are neutral, but hinting that if we had a real commitment, it would most likely be with the Union. Sarah understands my intent."

Sarah nodded approval.

"We have made it a source of entertainment to play the game with them and keep them guessing," Adelicia said, handing a pair of scissors to Phila Ann.

"Well, I just cannot have them set a foot in my door, and Ada Murdoch feels the same, do you not Ada?" asked Matilda.

Before she, or the other ladies could speak, Sarah answered, "Some of us have family fighting on both sides. Because a man has taken a position for one or the other does not necessarily make him an enemy. My husband had many friends, some of whom are now here in our city. I cannot close my doors to them any more than I can to my friends and family here Think it over ladies, carefully."

Adelicia did not know if Sarah were coming to her defense, or defending both her and Matilda, but she was grateful that for once, someone had endorsed her logic.

When the meeting adjourned, Adelicia asked Luke to drive home slowly. The April day was lovely, and she needed the four miles to think.

The prize stallions and mares, and the three finest carriages were sent a few miles south to the Hightower's in Brentwood, hoping they would be safe for a time. Belle Monte was reduced to using the two-seated buggy with the black fringe around the top and pulled by one of the few Morgan horses they had kept.

It was not the time for one's livestock to look too plentiful, nor for one to appear too prosperous. From the open buggy, she smiled to strangers who now filled the streets, as she pondered the plan conceived some time before, which now seemed plausible, if she could only convince her husband.

"Essie, where is Joseph?" Adelicia demanded, bursting in the front door of Belle Monte.

"In the deer park with the childrens."

"Pauline, too?"

"Sure nuuf, he sure love 'em all. There something fine about a man who love childrens. You sure picked two good children lovers. Mr. Isaac and Mr. Joe. They both fine. We been having babies so long, seem strange we not be having no more."

"And may I ask why you said that and why this conversation has become so personal?"

"Just saying what I'm thinkin'. There come a time when respectable ladies don't have no more childrens. That's all I'm saying."

"Essie, dear, I shall never get too old to do anything I choose to do, if I choose to do it. Please tell Joseph when he comes in that I am in our sitting room."

It was late in the afternoon when Adelicia heard Joseph coming up the stairs to their sitting room, followed by the three boys. William was the first to jump into her lap, then Claude.

"Ma, don't believe a word of what they say," said Bud. "Father will tell you it's not true."

"Bud chased the deer away all day. Whenever they came to us, he would run them away," whined Claude. "And he tells us creepy things about the war whenever Papa can't hear him, about people who get their eyes shot out and their heads blown off, and he knows it frightens me and gives me nightmares."

Bud—looking innocent, as always—stood erect beside his father. He was handsome at twelve and quite tall, with locks of dark hair falling in attractive disarray around his face. Adelicia glanced at Joseph, whom she suspected was biting back a grin and wondered at the time he must have had with the four of them. "Where is Pauline?"

"Getting her bath before supper," answered Willie. "You haven't scolded Bud."

"I only wish to hear happy tales this afternoon," said Adelicia, "and right now I need to talk with your father. All of you get your baths and dress for supper. We are having guests tonight."

"Are we going to play 'be nice to the Yankees' again?" asked Bud, before leaving the room.

"For a change," she said laughing. "We are not playing 'be nice' to anyone, we are going to have a lovely evening with friends and family. Now run along, all of you, so I can talk with your father."

"Joseph, darling, I want you to sign the pledge." She smiled and motioned for him to sit in the chair beside her.

Astonished she had actually said it, she hurriedly continued, "This morning I learned the Yankees were at the Murdocks and the Hardings last night. Both of those dear men were told they must either sign or have everything they own taken away, or worse yet, be sent to prison or hanged! Everyone who knows you will know you do not mean it. It is just a matter of pacifying the Yankees. It only shows how ignorant they are. Signing a meaningless piece of paper has nothing to do with how one feels."

Taking long puffs on his pipe, Joseph allowed the smoke to slowly escape between his lips and curl into the sunlight filtering through the glass doors of their sitting room.

"Answer me, darling! You will do it?" she asked, putting her hand in his.

He spoke without hesitation and walked over to the mantel. "Adie, I am not going to sign the pledge."

Tears welled in her eyes. "But why? I have always found you an intelligent man. This is madness! What difference does signing a piece of paper mean? You may as well have leapt in with Andrew Ewing, Randall McGavock and the other wild secessionists, and gone off to die *gallantly* on the battlefield, or come home maimed for life and poor as Job's turkey."

"Sometimes, I can't tell if you are more afraid of my going to prison, or of losing your money. I prefer to think it's a combination of the two, and I'll not ask you to sign as to which is the more important, because you just said signing your name to a piece of paper doesn't mean anything."

Her tears were streaming, as she jumped up from the chair.

"Joseph Smith Acklen, you are twisting my words! I do not want to lose money, land or our crops, or anything else. And most of all, I do not want to lose you."

She stood with her hands on her hips, her lips clenched, but this once, he did not laugh, nor apologize, nor come and put his arms around her.

"Let's sit down, Adie," Joseph said, motioning to the matching morocco covered chairs on either side of the fireplace in their sitting room. "A lot has happened since last night. And while you ladies were at your meeting this morning, Union officers went out to Belle Meade and arrested Giles Harding. I've received word they're sending him to a northern prison."

"That is not possible!" she interrupted, her mouth agape. "They are invited here tonight!"

"I'm afraid the arresting officers didn't give your party a consideration."

"What will happen to them, Mrs. Harding, the rest of the family?" she gasped.

"For the immediate future, I'm hoping Mrs. Harding and Selene will come here tonight as planned."

"But what will happen to them after that?" she asked, her anger rising again. "I suppose you think it very noble for Giles Harding to refuse the pledge to protect his precious honor and leave his home and family at the mercy of the Yankees! I am sick of the word honor. As I have said, what is in one's heart may not be for all to see. Mrs. Harding and Belle Meade Plantation would be a site better off had her husband chosen to behave differently than he felt! But if you want to leave us and go off to prison, please do so."

Her thoughts were racing, knowing if she did not think of something quickly, Joseph would do just that—go to prison, or join the Confederacy—and she was quickly losing ground.

"Adie, I'm a soldier at heart. I fought for my country in the Mexican War, two grandfathers fought in the Revolutionary War, and the one on my father's side also fought in the War of 1812 with General Jackson. But you know that. My friends and family in Alabama must be wondering where I am now."

Changing her tactics, she walked over and knelt beside him. "Henry Fogg had two great-grandfathers who signed the Declaration of Independence and where is he now? Lying in an unmarked grave in Kentucky, shot by his own people." She saw a slight change in Joseph's expression, and hurriedly continued. "Yes, it sounds barbarous...by his own countrymen. Just a minute ago, you spoke of defending your country. That country is now divided. This is not like any other war, Joe! Friends are fighting against each other; families are fighting against each other. For which country are you going to fight, or is it for a cause, or an idea?"

Joseph reached into his pocket and handed her a folded piece of paper. "Have you seen one of these?" He began to read aloud: *"I solemnly swear, without any mental reservation or evasion, that I will support the Constitution of the United States, and the laws made in pursuance there of; and that I will not directly or indirectly give aid to any person or persons belonging to any of the so styled Confederate States, who are now or may be in rebellion against the Government of the United States: So help me God...It is understood that the penalty for the violation of this is death."*

"Oh, my God!" she gasped.

"I will not sign it, Adie. I cannot."

She took his hand and looked tenderly at him. "I had no idea the words to which you would have to sign your name," she said, looking at the paper in his hand. "Darling, please forgive my selfishness. We need you, just as I needed you thirteen years ago, but I know you must do what you feel is right. I fully understand now why you cannot possibly sign this horrible pledge."

She laid her head in his lap, and he bent over and kissed her hair and began removing the combs and pins holding it in place.

"We had better get dressed for supper. I shall tell Essie to inform the other servants of what is happening, so there will be as little excitement as possible...just in case."

She knew exactly what he meant. If Giles Harding had been arrested, anyone of them could be next on the list. The Yankees had chosen one of the city's elders, one of its most influential men, perhaps as an attempt at intimidation.

Adelicia rang the bell for Doreen and asked that she send Corinne and Sally to her dressing room immediately upon their arrival. She must speak with them out of earshot of Joseph, then perhaps her alternate plan, her supper charade, would work.

The table was elegant, as were all of Adelicia's tables, even when guests were not present. Joseph announced dinner, and the guests walked in, found their places and stood behind the elegant mahogany chairs while Joseph offered thanks.

Mrs. Harding and Selene did come, as word was sent it would be in their best interest. The Murdochs were there, Sarah Polk, Sally Carter, the Donelsons and Corrine and Bill. Pauline had been put to bed earlier, but the three boys were in their places, listening intently.

Joseph carved the medium rare roast beef, for which Belle Monte was famous, and passed the rose china plates with the hollyhock centers, just as he had on so many occasions. But try as they might for pleasantries, the conversation turned to the damnable things occurring throughout the city, and what was happening to its people. Mrs. Harding's attempt to eat a few choice bites, resulted in her excusing herself in a fit of tears, and was quickly followed by Selene. Adelicia sent Essie to look after them, then gave a nod to Sally sitting across the table from her.

"Joseph, dahling, I'll tell you what you ought to do," Sally said in her slowest drawl. "For the sake of the South, you ought to hightail it to Louisiana and raise all the cotton you can."

Leave it to Sally, Adelicia thought. Sally was the only woman she knew with whom she would compare herself for sheer spunk.

Sally continued, "And when the Yankees get there, and I'm sure they will, honey, you can convince them you are trying to feed 'yore pore starving niggas' with what little livestock them awful Rebels left you. After all, they wouldn't want any poor slaves to starve. You tell those Yankees they will be more than welcome to your cotton for the cause of the Union just as soon as it's picking time. And from what I hear, Yankees will believe almost anything."

Sarah Polk appeared on the verge of laughter. Yes, Adelicia thought, Sally should be on the stage. Her gestures and facial expression would put Maureen Dulaney to shame.

"Yes sir," Friarson Murdoch agreed. "Yes sir, what the lady says sounds good to me."

"Of course, dahling. What I'm saying is the truth. Corrine, don't you and your handsome William agree with me?"

"In all seriousness, Joe, it is a good idea," Corrine said. "That way you won't be forced to sign the pledge, and you will be doing as much for the South as anyone."

"I agree with Corrine," said Sarah, "If you do not protect your cotton, the South may burn it to keep it from the North, or if the North gets it first, they will surely use it for themselves. So everything considered, you would be doing the South a great service."

"If this is such a grand idea, I want to know why Friarson and Bill are not volunteering to do the same thing?" Joseph said.

Bill spoke up, "For one thing, I'm taking Corrine and the children to Bliss's tomorrow. Hillside's not that safe anymore, even with the servants there, and you can't tell which ones will be around the next morning. With my business in town, the Yankees find me useful as a merchant and a teacher, so perhaps our home will be all right, for a while anyway. But I'll feel safer with my family at Bliss's in Williamson County. If it weren't for my business, I might go with you."

Unfortunately, everyone turned to Friarson Murdoch, all realizing it was only a matter of time before the Yankees called at Harpeth

Hall. His sons were already enlisted in the army, and there was doubt if one, or any would return alive.

Adelicia quickly turned the conversation to herself by interrupting, "No one seems to have considered me at all."

"I wondered when you were going to speak up, Ma," said Bud. "It's not often you let Cousin Sally outdo you." From the mouth of babes, Adelicia thought, as she looked at her eldest, then quickly glanced at Sally.

While true that the two women were sometimes rivals, they had always liked and respected each other, although they had not become close until after Adelicia had married Joseph and moved into Belle Monte. Like herself, Sally cared little for peoples' opinions, or for formalities when they were in opposition to what she wanted.

"That is enough," Adelicia said, winking at her son. "Joseph, if you go to the plantations in Louisiana, it means you will be away from the children and me, from Belle Monte for God only knows how long—months, years. And what in heaven's name would the Yankees do to us when they discovered you had gone?"

"Dear heart," he said, looking through the warm glow of sixteen burning tapers. "It would be more like what you would do to the Yankees. And knowing you, I'm sure you can slip back and forth through enemy lines and visit often," he said good naturedly.

"And we'll all go with her," Bud said excited. "We'll put on ragged clothes and pretend to be an orphaned family attempting to make our way back home, which ever direction we are traveling: to father or to Belle Monte."

"I'm not going anywhere." Willie's eyes were large, as he sat ramrod straight in his chair. "I'm not leaving Belle Monte until all the Yankees are gone."

"You won't have to, darling," Adelicia said. "Your papa is only teasing us. It is..."

The conversation was interrupted when the door chimes rang, signifying a late or uninvited guest. In days past, the conversation would not have ceased, but with the curfew placed on the city, and the fact that no one was allowed on the streets unless they were going to or from a specific place, it was most alarming. All was quiet when Uncle Ben stood just inside the great double doors to the dining room, announcing that Captain Reynolds had come to speak with Mr. Acklen.

Everyone stiffened and faces became flushed. Joseph pushed his chair back and stood up. "Tell him I'll be there directly. Ask him into the library."

Uncle Ben never winced. He turned and left the room. Adelicia was thankful Joseph had warned the servants before time, suspecting it might happen that night, or another very soon.

"Adelicia, you give the grandest dinners," said Sarah. "If only my husband were here to enjoy these delicacies. And this beautifully set table." Her next words were spoken in hushed tones. "We must keep up the pretense of gaiety, conversation and laughter. The fact that I am here may be of help."

"How right she is, darling," Joseph whispered. Then speaking up, "If you will excuse me, a gentleman wishes to see me. I should not be long."

"Invite him to join us," Adelicia called, loudly enough for them to hear, "Liza can set an extra place, and there is plenty of food and claret."

Time seemed endless as they kept up the facade of gay, whimsical talk, but it had been no more than fifteen minutes before Joseph returned with three men, Captain Reynolds and two corporals, Watkins and Samuels.

"Liza," he called, "set another place and put fresh china and silver where the Hardings were sitting. We have three more guests for supper."

Liza did as suggested with a nervous twitch, and all the while, Adelicia watched Essie peeking through a crack in the doorway, obviously sizing up the uninvited guests. She remained there for some minutes before coming in to announce it was the children's bedtime, that Charlotte and Cora were waiting. Despite the seriousness, Essie did it with such exaggerated dignity, it was difficult for Adelicia to refrain from smiling. Essie had such disdain for Yankees, she had vowed she would never have been in the room with one, had her mistress not invited them to Belle Monte. And she often remarked that Yankees had a very peculiar odor about them.

Bud, upon his father's request, reluctantly departed the company.

Adelicia was certain as she observed the three men, that not only were these Northerners unaccustomed to finery, but had never been in its presence. Captain Reynolds's table manners were acceptable, but the other two ate much like pigs, especially the one called Samuels, whose ginger hair hung disheveled over his face. They gorged themselves to the point that the food dribbled from their over-filled mouths to their plates, and was rinsed down with claret that Mattie continued to pour before the glasses were even half emptied, just as Joseph had instructed.

An hour passed, and Adelicia's guests continued to indulge the intruders with light conversation...in truth, whatever came to mind to keep them eating and drinking, especially drinking. It was easy to see the beginning effects of the intoxicating claret, but the Captain remained sober enough to insist that they must leave and report back to General Buell that night.

The two corporals leaned against each other as they were shown to the door.

"Mighty fine lookers sittin' at the table," Samuels said in slovenly drunken speech. "So many women folk alone in all the places now."

Joseph would like to have killed him on the spot. The way he said it, the way he looked when he was saying it, caused his insides to burn. But all was going too well to kill a Yankee soldier in his own home, or on the grounds. He pretended to ignore the remark, and reassured Captain Reynolds that he would be at the state capital by nine o'clock the following morning to sign the pledge, expressing his appreciation for not having to leave his guests, one of whom was the former First Lady, and sign that particular night.

The Captain shook his hand, again expressed his gratitude for the fine meal and thanked him for being a gentleman on whose word he could depend.

Joseph closed the door, then stood for a long while looking about him: the Bohemian red glass panels around the doors, the plaster motifs in the tall ceiling above him, and the crystal chandelier from which dangled prisms that caught the gas light's glow. Then he stretched his long arms to either side of the free standing stairway, rested his hands on the newel posts and bent forward, weeping. His tears were angry and fearful, tears shed when trapped without alternative. Doubtful of his decision, knowing that danger lay equally with either…his original one, or the one he had just made…"Scylla and Charybdis," he whispered. He had just lied to a Union officer, assuredly, the first of many. He would not see General Buell on the morrow…he would be far away by then. Joseph dried his eyes and walked back into the dining room where their guests spoke quietly.

No one asked specific questions. In this time, ignorance was truly bliss, and out of respect for each other, unless information were freely offered, none was asked.

Friarson Murdoch held on to Joseph for some time when he said good-bye, as did his brother-in-law, William. The ladies all kissed and wished him well, and Sarah Polk assured him, "One day this will all be over. We shall be one nation, and all our men will be home again. God bless you. I shall help look out for your family and keep you in prayer."

"Remember, dahling, fool all them Yankees," said Sally. "They'll never know the difference, and don't set your eye on any of the Creole beauties while we're up here entertaining the generals."

Sally could have let the last remark pass, thought Adelicia, as she and Joseph stood in the doorway watching the last of their guests step into their buggies.

They walked slowly up the stairs together, arms around each other's waist, and when they reached the first landing where the stairs divide to the right and to the left, they turned right toward Joseph's suite.

Without any questions, any words, they removed each other's clothing. And standing naked together, shivering in the cool winds of April that caused the curtains to flutter against the cornices, he lifted her onto his bed, and with kisses that seared and covered her body, the very essence of her, they made beautiful love. With tears of pleasure and tears of not knowing how long it would be before they would hold each other again.

"I love you, Adie, more than I knew possible for a man to love. You've given me great happiness, just loving you, and when this war is over…when it is over …"

She put on her robe and helped him dress, between kisses…kisses that would have to last. He would take little with him. Whatever he needed, he could purchase in New Orleans, and there was ample clothing at Bellevue.

"That was quite a performance you four ladies gave tonight," Joseph said turning the gas lamp higher overhead. "I must say, Sally was at her best, never missing a cue. You two could have a lucrative business: you writing the script and she performing."

"Joseph, how unfair! You knew all along," Adelicia said, playfully pulling his undershirt over his head.

"Of course, I knew. Unbeknownst to you charming dears, I had mostly decided this is what I had no choice but to do, sooner or later, before joining the Confederacy. It was just ironic the Yankees came right in the middle of your production. Bud had the best idea about the old clothes. See if Luke can find me something," Joseph said, "I'm going to be a stranger to these parts, not knowing from whence I come, or to whence I go."

Adelicia hurried to Luke's quarters on the lower level, but there was no need to awaken him or any of the servants. They were all gathered, busily mulling over the night's dramatic episode.

"Luke, hurry and get some old clothes ready for Mr. Acklen, ragged ones and a hat of some kind."

"Oh, lordy, is he going so soon?" Essie asked, her eyes beginning to water.

"Yes, and tears will not help. Since all of you are awake, make yourselves useful. Mr. Acklen must start out long before daylight. Mattie, make sandwiches, put them, along with fruit and cheese in a tow sack, nothing fancy, in case he is stopped. And hurry! Doreen, tell Luke to get the nag ready, that belongs to him. Essie, you see that everybody does everything they are supposed to do."

"Is Mr. Acklen gonna' take my horse?"

"Good Goshens, Luke! I shall get you another horse, a good one, when the war is over. Furthermore, you ought to be ashamed for saying such a thing."

"Miz Adie," he said with tears welling up, "you know I don't mean it that way. I's honored he ride that old plug."

"I know, Luke. Everyone, please hurry!"

She ran back to their bedroom with the silly attire the servants had thrown together. Joseph wore his own boots, old ones he had never discarded, used years before to walk over the muddy grounds when Belle Monte was being laid out. But the rest of the garb was borrowed: corded pants tied around the waist with a brown leather strap, a red and black plaid, moth-eaten shirt, over an even more distasteful, heavy blue work one, and a broad brimmed hat with holes in it that fit nowhere, bought for Uncle Ben eons before at a rodeo. They believed her when she had said old. Adelicia quickly stitched gold pieces inside the placket behind the buttons of Joseph's trousers. Then they held each other for only moments, before he tied the strap to hold them up and hurried down the stairs.

The horse was waiting on the front lawn, an old knapsack thrown across his back and a tow sack filled with food. Again, Joseph took her in is arms and kissed her one last time before putting his left foot into the stirrup.

She would have to cherish this moment for weeks or months to come, this feeling of being held by her husband. "I love you, my Adie," he said. "I trust it won't be for long."

"I love you with all my heart," she called to him, as he reined the horse south. "I shall love you always."

"Good luck, and God bless you," the servants added.

"Good-bye, my darling Joseph," she said, in a whisper, watching until in the early morning shadows nothing could be seen but the silhouette of the preposterously oversized wide-brimmed hat against a bit of fading moonlight filtering in between the clouds.

CHAPTER 52

JOSEPH TRAVELED ON THEIR OWN LAND UNTIL HE REACHED THE southeast side of the Granny White Pike, then took an old bridle path that led out to the Lea Place into the Overton Hills. He would stay in the woods, following the Franklin Pike along the Columbia route to Lawrenceburg, then to Florence, Alabama, before heading southwest to Columbus, Mississippi, then Meridian, to Hattiesburg, and at last New Orleans, where he would be safe.

Adelicia wept through the darkness of early morning and into the light, tossing and turning, still dressed in the robe she was wearing when Joseph left. Wishing and praying for her husband's safety, she wondered if he knew how much she really cared, if he would ever know. She wished she could tell him. How human to think of a million things that should have been said. Then her thoughts turned to the officers whom she knew would soon arrive.

At breakfast, she told the children their father had gone to the plantations on business and would be home, she hoped, by Christmas. In the meantime, they would be safe as could be at Belle Monte.

She supposed she actually believed what she was saying because she felt no fear, but rather the old conviction that she could and would make it work.

It was half past eleven when the chimes rang and Uncle Ben answered the front door. Adelicia was dressed in one of her prettiest and most becoming gowns, a pale lavender taffeta trimmed in deep purple velvet that just bared her shoulders. In her hair, she had a fresh spray of baby's breath around a gardenia.

Uncle Ben announced to Colonel Ashton, and the two lieutenants with him, that Mr. Acklen was not at home but if they wished to speak with Mrs. Acklen she would receive them.

"Colonel Ashton, how nice to see you again!" Adelicia graciously greeted, "Let me see, I believe it was three weeks ago you had supper with us, or was it four? Time passes so quickly."

Ashton removed his hat and nudged the two with him to do the same. He was handsome in a rugged sort of way, with a full beard just graying along the chin line and deep set eyes beneath thick, dark brows.

"Mrs. Acklen, it's nice to see you again as well, but this time the visit's not a social one. We've come to get—rather, talk with your husband."

The obese man to his left nodded to Ashton's every word. A motion quickly becoming annoying to her.

"I'm very sorry, Colonel. Mr. Acklen is not at home right now."

"Then could you please tell us where he is? Meaning no offense to you and knowing he's a man of his word, he did promise to be at the capital this morning at nine o'clock to sign the pledge in front of Governor Johnson, and when he didn't show, we were sent to bring him in."

"Now I wonder when he did that," she said, as if to herself, "You see, I haven't seen my husband, I mean Mr. Acklen," she spoke as if groping for words, "in some time."

She took the handkerchief in her left hand and dabbed at her red puffed eyes.

"But, ma'am, just last night three men talked with him right here in this house and even with you, and as you know, drank your wine. So much, that when they got back to the barracks the ruckus they caused escaped no one's notice that they were drunk while on duty. All three were thrown in the guard house, and I might add, lost their ranks as well."

Adelicia hoped the handkerchief, still at her eyes, covered enough of her lips so that the smile she was biting back would not be discovered.

"Colonel, there must be some mistake. We did have guests last night, but none of your men, and for sure...." Feigning loss of words, she hesitated, "What I mean, sir, is Mr. Acklen...Did they say he was here? If you must force me to say it, I do not know where he is."

She broke into sobs and invited them into the parlor where she might be seated. Essie brought a glass of water to her mistress and asked the officers if they would like a refreshment, to which they replied some iced tea would be appreciated. The tea was quickly brought by Liza, while Essie stood beside her mistress's chair, attempting to console her.

"Mrs. Acklen, my men had orders to come here last night and bring in your husband. They let him talk them into joining a social gathering and returned too drunk to make sense. That I know."

Adelicia looked dumbly at him. "Colonel, I shall be more than happy to give you the names of our guests last night, and you may check with each of them as well as my servants. There was my sister and her husband, the Murdochs and Mrs. Polk. Please tell them, Essie."

This time Adelicia did not lower her head, but kept her eyes directly on Colonel Ashton.

"Mrs. Acklen always speak the truth, and the truth she has said," Essie replied. "Weren't nobody here but friends and family that sure don't include no Yankees of no kind. And as to Mr. Acklen, he no better than one hisself, no telling which army he with...nothing but woe."

"Essie, you must not be unkind," Adelicia reprimanded. "You must pardon her, she is old and set in her ways. You are more than welcome to search the house or the grounds." She stood up, making a gesture to the hallway.

"Ma'am, if there's one thing I'm smart enough to know, it's that your husband is long gone by now. But when he does show up, he's going to be in trouble."

As Uncle Ben held the door open for their departure and the soldiers were putting on their hats, Adelicia calmly asked, "Colonel, how may a lady get protection for herself, her children and servants? It has been a constant concern for days now. One never knows when someone, anyone, might just—I do not mean one of your army, but there are so many strange people on the streets these days, one can never be sure and without...Oh, I do not mean to bother you, you must have many more stops to make." She watched his expression change, and for the first time she believed he might be sympathizing with her as she stood faintly smiling with a look of total helplessness.

"Well, ma'am, if you or your place here ever need protecting, you can send for me. I'm stationed on High Street below the capitol. You know the name, Jesse P. Ashton, Colonel Jesse P. Ashton. I'll also mention it to Governor Johnson and see what we can do for you. This place is sure a dandy."

"Oh, thank you, Colonel, you are most kind. See, Essie, a gentleman is a gentleman, regardless on which side of the line he is born." She looked up, smiling, "Perhaps you can call again soon."

"It'll be my pleasure, ma'am, my pleasure indeed. Good day to you, and I'm sorry to have bothered you. Takes a mighty fool man to leave a lady like you in the lurks." She put her hand to her mouth, feigning shock at his familiarity, and again he stood begging her pardon, reassuring her he would speak to General Buell and the Governor on her behalf, and that he would ride by personally to see that all looked well, but would not disturb her.

She and Essie watched until they were out of sight. "Miss Sally shore right," said Essie, "a body can make 'em believe anything. But I'm not thinking too much of all that flirtin'. First thing you know we'll have Yankees swarming like a nest of hornets all over the place. I don't like it."

"Essie, dear, if it will protect our cotton and Joseph, all of us, there is no telling how much flirting I shall be doing," she teased. "It's been so long since I flirted, I think I enjoyed it, even if it were with a Yankee! Was I truly convincing?"

"One of these days...one of these days, Mr. Joe need to take you over his knee and wallop you a good un."

"Now, Essie, you do not mean a word of it. You like me the way I am. You know you do."

"Chile, I put up with you 'cause nobody but me and the good Lord would, and He too far away and have too many others to watch you every minute." Adelicia put her hand on her mammy's shoulder and they walked inside together.

Belle Monte
June 8, 1862,

> *My Dearest Joseph, it has been almost two months now since you left, and it seems a lifetime. Even with all the turmoil around us, I could not forget that thirteen years ago today, we were married. I miss you so, my love, and I trust we shall be together soon.*

> *General Buell has moved most of his army east of Nashville, and again the city is left undefended, this time from our own people.*

Rumor has it that Generals Forrest and Morgan plan to recapture it, but Governor Johnson says he will burn it first, and I believe he would do just that.

Barracks, forts and barricades are being quickly built all over. You will not recognize it when you get home. Thus far, nothing on our place has been bothered, but we never know what the next day may bring. So many of the trees are being cut that most of the familiar woods are completely extinct; the children want to know where all the animals will go. My guess is the Yankees are using Negro labor, unpaid at that, which makes this whole thing seem even more an atrocity.

We are faring quite well, and I hope this letter finds you the same. The children send you hugs and kisses and the servants bid you God speed. I must get this into the hands of the carrier or it will take even longer reaching you, if indeed it does. I am staying busy with the enormous work at the hospitals (we have two more since you left) and the ladies organizations.

I almost forgot to mention, I moved all jewelry, some silver and other valuables to Sarah Polk's. Her house is the only one of whose protection we can be absolutely assured from either side. A twenty-four hour guard is posted around it. Your father's sword, the one laid in gold with the amethyst handle, I also took it. She says there is room in her cellar for the paintings as well, but for now I shall leave them where they are.

Again, I hope you receive this, as well as, the others I have written. Hurry home to us, my love. Give Lucy, Alfred, Rufus, Brutus, Fanny and the other servants my regards and tell them to take special care of my dearest.

Yours, Adie

CHAPTER 53

RUE TO THE RUMORS, GENERALS FORREST AND MORGAN LED almost daily raids against the Union weak points around the city...of which there were many. Most residents, however, thought the raids served no purpose other than to rouse Johnson's fury and make it more difficult on everyone.

The truth was, Nashvillians wished the Rebel forces would leave well enough alone, unless they were certain of recapturing the city, a certainty that was highly unlikely. But throughout the long, hot summer, the raids continued. By September, so many of the woods had been cleared for barricades and temporary shelters, it looked like a city that had been shelled or burned, minus the charring.

Food was becoming increasingly scarce, although merchants kept their stores open and advertised their produce. Prices had risen so high that only those of great means, primarily Yankees, could purchase the quality goods available. Most could afford only the bare necessities. Eggs were selling for two dollars a dozen, and chicken, one dollar per pound. Adelicia continued to buy her sides of beef, but was ashamed, even for the servants to know what she had to pay for them.

Disease was another enemy, and Johnson's government proved to have little or no effectiveness toward its cure. Word was, there were as many prostitutes in the city as there were officers, and looting and vandalism ran rampant. Not until Major General William S. Rosecrans marched into the city in late October, with fifty thousand troops, was law and order restored to some degree, and the public houses, inns, taverns and theaters reopened.

When the war began, Nashville had an estimated population of twenty thousand. Now, only one and one-half years later, that figure had soared to well over eighty thousand, largely made up of undesirables: enemy soldiers, prisoners, prostitutes, profiteers, Yankee officials...all the vagrants, riffraff and self-seekers that come with flooding populations...and free Negroes with nowhere to go. The streets were unsafe, and no one was allowed in or out of the city without permission from the Governor himself.

One of the war's greatest inequities, thought Adelicia, were former slaves who fled into the city by droves, seeking refuge from a government that had promised them what they could not possibly comprehend; just like those who had made the rash promises. Although temporary shelters were erected, when Adelicia saw the deplorable living conditions, she thought of her own well-kept servants at Belle Monte and in Louisiana. Once again, she wanted to tell the Union army to go to Hades, this time for making promises they knew they could not keep, and forcing the Negroes to work with little or no compensation.

She had no idea what they would do with winter coming, and so little clothing, and no fireplaces for heat. The United States government did not know what it was getting itself into, and she bet there was not a soul in Washington who would not admit to just that, including President Lincoln.

"Bud, do we need to go over it once more?"

"Ma, you ask me that every time, and every time I say once is enough. I haven't made a mistake yet, have I?"

Adelicia had to admit that he had not, as she stood with her hands on his shoulders, waiting for Uncle Ben to bring his pony. "I know it is not far, and a route you well know. Also, that it is your way of fulfilling your duty to the South, but one mistake is all it would take, Bud."

The twelve-year old had been carrying memorized messages back and forth to Cheatham's Calvary, and had not once been prevented from accomplishing his mission. Yankees had searched his biscuits, even stripped the skins from the fried chicken, but had found nothing. It had obviously not occurred to the Union soldiers that a twelve-year-old could carry messages, important and very exacting ones, in his head.

Adelicia kissed and hugged him good-bye and as always, prayed for God's care. Bud delighted in playing spy, also in taking the same route his father had taken along the Franklin Pike when he left for

Louisiana. Confederates had continued to camp in the outlying countryside, but Bud could not confide his information to anyone, not even his mother.

Astride his pony, he had just rounded the curve on Franklin Pike north of Brentwood, not that far from home, when he heard an unfamiliar, "Halt!" It did not sound like a soldier's order to Bud and for the first time during his journeys, the boy felt frightened. He had never feared the Yankee soldiers, because it seemed a game to him. He slowed the Shetland, that had been traveling at a clipping trot, and stopped just before a gruff, ginger bearded man grabbed at the bit, causing the pony to rear.

Bud immediately grasped the man's ignorance; one did not grab at a pony's bit; they can rear and kick faster than any horse. The ginger haired man jumped back to miss the hooves, falling against a limestone cliff that jutted out of the Brentwood Hills.

He put his hand to his head, then looked at the dripping blood. "All I wanted, Sonny, was a bite to eat. Can't you spare some food for a hungry man?"

Bud sensed danger and thought he looked much like one of the Yankee corporals who had eaten at their table the night the men had come for his father. Unknown to his parents, the boy had watched from the upstairs balcony. He reached into his sack, pitched some biscuits and chicken on the ground and started his pony at a fast gallop.

It was a relief when he was stopped for a second time by two guards not much older than himself.

"Are you a Rebel?" they questioned.

"No, sirs," he answered quickly and proudly. "I don't belong to no army or nobody. I'm a orphan taking food to an old man lives about two miles on down the road."

"Is that so? Just who fixed the food you're a-taking?"

"The man I chop wood for. He sends me 'bout once a week, sometimes twice, and if I don't get the food to the old man, I get beat 'cause he thinks I eat it myself."

Fortunately, Bud was thin, at the growing stage when boys grow taller than they do broad. He was enjoying stretching the yarn but knew not to get so carried away that it would become unbelievable.

"We better take you anyway. Can't trust a Rebel of no kind."

"I told you, I'm no Rebel."

"That don't necessarily mean you ain't."

He followed them to a tent pitched about a mile to the southwest near the banks of the Little Harpeth. He felt sure no one in Nashville knew the Yankees were camping this close, and from what he could surmise, there were a good many, perhaps three or four hundred, and they were not that far from his Uncle Bliss's farm. He repeated the same story to the officer in charge and after searching him, he was released. They could find nothing on his person remotely in the form of a message.

"Always tell the truth, boy," the officer said. "Don't ever forget that."

"Yes, sir," Bud replied. This time they had left the remaining biscuits and chicken intact.

He had much to report to Cheatham's army. It would be of special interest for them to learn that Yankee General Rosecrans was in the city now, permitting Confederate Generals Forrest and Morgan to take up new posts where they were more needed. The two generals were unprepared to meet Rosecran's army of fifty thousand and had departed.

Bud completed his mission to Cheatham's camp—and had remembered precisely, the hospitals, the forts, how many men and where they were, as well as the campsite where he had been questioned.

He returned home by a different route, through back pastures bordering Hillsboro Pike, to the southwest side of the Belle Monte property. He would not mention to his mother about the man who stopped him for fear she would not let him go again. But after his encounter with the stranger, the war took on a different perspective.

His mother was giving a party that night, and he would be anxious to hear the information she had learned from her guests the morning after. All she had to do (so everyone said) was bat her eyelids and smile, and the Yankees knelt at her feet. He believed that even when his mother was one-hundred years old, she would still charm whomever she wished.

Bud recalled how she had become visibly upset with his father once when he told her she would probably charm the angels in heaven and have them kneeling to her instead of the Lord. She had found his remark distasteful and told him so. One thing about his ma, she did not want the Lord spoken of lightly.

CHAPTER 54

March 1862

IT WAS LATE IN THE EVENING WHEN JOSEPH ARRIVED AT THE Bransford's on Bourbon Street. He had made the trip on Luke's horse in ten days, without meeting any major opposition until on the outskirts of Hattiesburg where he was flanked by some of General Bank's brigade. However, he had been so convincing with his tale of hardship: the death of his family and the burning of his house by Rebels, they had let him pass under his pretense to board a steamer in New Orleans for California. He anticipated Adelicia's amusement when he would tell her the story. He also thought that when he posted a letter to Adelicia, he would have her tell Luke that his horse was safely stabled in New Orleans.

John Bransford and his family, Joseph learned, had left for Texas when rumors circulated that Admiral David Farragut was headed for New Orleans with a fleet of ships, but the Bransford servants who remained had fed Joseph a king's feast, and quickly boiled water for his bath. Mary Bransford's old mammy scrubbed him herself and without asking, had thrown everything he had worn outdoors to be picked up by the early morning street cleaners.

It was not until Joseph was lying comfortably in the thick folds of a feather bed, that he remembered the three hundred dollars in gold sewn into the front placket of his trousers and went charging to find Mary's mammy.

"Rusey," he called. "Rusey." There was no answer. "Confound it," he complained to himself walking onto the enclosed courtyard. "Rusey!"

"Yes, sir, Mr. Acklen?" she answered from the door of her sleeping quarters.

"Do you have my trousers?"

She waddled to where he stood in the middle of the courtyard. "Them trousers no good for no gentleman. They full of holes and about the dirtiest I ever saw. I done laid out a pair of Mr. John's for you," she replied, fully satisfied with her answer.

"Rusey, those trousers must be returned...they're very special."

"I done put em out on the street, but I guess I can go looking," she said moving toward the locked gate.

"Please, Rusey, find the trousers and give them a good washing." He looked at her, grinning in the light, as he stood there in her master's undersized night shirt, thinking how peculiar it must all be to her. She gave him a look from head to toe, then went outside to retrieve the breeches.

Joseph was almost too tired to sleep, but when it did come, he did not awaken until past noon. Except for his own freshly laundered pants, gold coins intact, he dressed in John Bransford's clothes that had been laid out for him. After hurriedly eating double portions of eggs, ham, hot biscuits, fried potatoes and oysters stew, he walked the four blocks to board the packet that would take him one hundred and sixty-five miles upriver to Bellevue.

He carried nothing on board with him, save a knapsack, and kept to himself, attempting to look as inconspicuous as any of the river bums who usually traveled alone, seeking work at stops along the Mississippi. He was grateful no one recognized him, that he recognized no one. There were as many strange faces on the river as there were in Nashville, and from what he was able to learn that morning, New Orleans was on edge over its weak defenses. When night came, he lay with his head atop his knapsack, unable to sleep.

Bellevue Plantation was situated precisely in the bend of the big river and only a few miles upriver from Bayou Sara and its twin town, St. Francisville. The Red River's mouth opened into the Mississippi at the exact spot of Angola's wood yard on the west, making the plantations of strategic importance to both Confederate and Union governments. Joseph was certain that each side had already gathered their information of advantageous properties, and Adelicia owned the largest, continuous track of land in the Delta.

He had no idea what he would find at Bellevue and dared not ask the packet pilot to stop farther up at his own landing. Joseph disembarked at Bayou Sara, where in the early morning he hired a horse to ride the ten mile stretch up the Tunica Road.

As the hilly, unpaved road ended, he guided his horse across the top of the levee and looked across the fields, catching a glimpse of Bellevue's roof as dawn appeared between the thick oaks. He raced down the plush green side of the levee, remembering the many times he had done so before, and continued up the crushed oyster shell drive to the house.

"Alfred, Alfred!" Lucy called, holding a lantern. "Mr. Acklen's a-coming! Hurry up man. He by hisself." Lucy had watched from the parlor window, and was now on the porch calling to Alfred, already up and attending to the outside chores.

The stuttering Alfred walked out with his wife to greet Joseph, who had gratefully appreciated their ready acceptance of him after his marriage to Adelicia. Knowing the couple's fondness for Isaac, had made Joseph appreciate it the more. He was quite fond of them.

Louisianans referred to Alfred and Lucy as griffes, defining their fathers as black and their mothers mulatto. Joseph had not heard that term prior to being in Louisiana, and found the distinctiveness of color interesting, a subject, he had thought little about, if ever.

"Mr. Acklen, man, it sho good to see you! Winters ain't right when you not here." Joseph shook Alfred's hand before going inside.

"Tell me what's been happening. How are things along the river?"

"Biggest problem we having is the field niggers. Harvest time a coming, and they hear all about freedom and how the government gonna pay for fighting in de army, and we don't know iffen they'll be any left come picking time," Lucy ran on. "We already late."

"Is it real bad, or just a little bit bad? How many have left?"

"You know how dis woman xaggertes," Alfred answered. "Out of five hundred, Mr. Clack say not more than two or three even mention leaving, and ain't none really left for all I knows."

"Ain't no xaggerating to it. You get a bunch niggers thinking they don't gotta work no more and gonna get paid for not doing it, and you see what'll happen. Next thing I knows, us house servants will be in the fields plantin' cotton and then pickin' it, and my hands won't never get use to such, and what's more they don't wanta get used to such!"

"There the woman go again! She already got us in the fields a picking, when we still at least got four hundred and ninety-nine left."

"I promise you, Lucy, that before I have you picking cotton, I'll be doing it myself." Pleased that his answer had calmed her, Joseph changed the subject and asked the whereabouts of James Clack.

"He over on the Angora place, scuse me, Angola, been there since yestiddy."

"Send for him right away, and have Rufus saddle my horse. This one needs to be returned to Brown's Livery at Bayou Sara. Tell Clack I'll be down by the river on the east side. I know it's difficult to get use to the name change, call it Angora if you want." Alfred left quickly, leading the hired mare.

"How's Miz Acklen and them precious little uns? And why she not with you? She not feeling poly again, is she?" Lucy asked.

"She and the children are fine, but we're living in an occupied Nashville now, and I'm considered a deserter, a fugitive."

"Occupied. Oh Jesus me! Does that mean the Yankees are there?"

"That's exactly what it means, and soon they'll be here. But we have a game to play, and we're all going to play it very well."

Lucy was fanning herself, "Oh, Jesus, have mercy. What about Miz Acklen and them children, how can they be fine? Oh Jesus, they'll kill 'em all!"

"Believe me, Lucy, they are fine. They're much better off without me, and if there's one lady who can take care of herself in a crisis it's Mrs. Acklen. It's me they're after. So calm yourself. I'll spew out my tale of woe to you later."

As Joseph rode among the rows of newly planted cotton, he was reminded how much warmer and more humid March in West Feliciana was than March in Nashville. He had already needed to remove his hat and wipe perspiration from his brow and neck, and it was not yet ten o'clock.

The field hands seemed content enough, and he was pleased there had been few incidents of ill feeling among them. None had ever been struck by hand or whipped and he defied any man to harm them. One of the reasons he had written his pamphlet on plantation management was to unhesitatingly make his beliefs known, that there was a decency, an integrity by which and with which, all men should be governed. And Joseph left no doubt that anyone who worked for him must hold such similar beliefs and be of such character, or his employment would be terminated.

As the rows of cotton closed in behind him, Joseph followed the path into the dense woods that led through Killarney Plantation to the river. As he trotted rather briskly, a covey of quail flew up in front of him when his horse's hooves disturbed their hiding place. And the leaves from the huge trees, set out centuries before by the Tunica and Natchez Indians, touched his shoulders and hat as he rode through.

When a buck leapt across his path followed by a doe, he stopped his horse to observe the beauty around him. Could a war really be in motion while such peace, such serenity still existed? He did not want these woods disturbed by soldiers and guns and bullets. Then a quick remembrance of his last night in Nashville stopped his dreaming, and he knew it mattered not at all what he wanted. The country was at war, and he had to do what he must to save the plantations and himself.

The sun was high overhead and shining directly over the lush levee, causing the water to appear as if it had tips of green splashing against its muddy brown when Jim Clack rode up with two foremen, Bard Young and Strapp Kelly. The men shook hands, dismounted and walked with their horses to a cool spot in the shade, well-hidden from prying eyes.

Hours later, they emerged in complete agreement for plans regarding both the Rebels and the Yankees, the roles they would play, and who would be involved.

The Negroes were strategic to the operation and would serve as major foils in the charade. Rufus and Alfred would take the lead, informing only those whom they could trust about the upcoming events, aiding and deceiving both the Union and Confederate armies and navies. Their wives would have their roles as well.

The sun no longer shone over the levee; all that remained were its orange and pink streaks across the sky. Without a doubt, Joseph had come, as Lucy had said, just in the "nick of time." The Union Navy had their sloops and boats patrolling up and down the Red River, realizing its importance and knowing there was a large mass of land commencing at its mouth and bordered on three sides by the Mississippi. This mass of land, key to the movement of supplies and troops, belonged to Adelicia!

CHAPTER 55

THREE WEEKS AFTER JOSEPH'S ARRIVAL AT BELLEVUE, HE WATCHED as a Union sloop anchored in still waters about three miles south of the mouth of the Red River on the banks of Bellevue. He had observed the Yankee sloop the previous day chasing a Rebel gunboat, before it gave up and settled in at the plantation. Although relieved that the gunboat had escaped, he was now confronted with the first Union ship to dock at the Acklen property and could afford to lose no time informing Clack, Young and Kelly. Joseph reined his stallion, and took off in the direction of Angola's sawmill.

Moments later, Union Lieutenant Lowry lowered a boat to come ashore with some of his men. By the time they reached the levee, they were met by the ordained, happy faces of cheering Negroes of all ages.

"Good afternoon. I'm Lieutenant Lowry of the United States Naval Command, and I have come to inquire as to who owns this land."

"Afternoon, sir. We sure glad to see you. My name Rufus and this Alfred."

There was silence as the two Negroes stood grinning from ear to ear, as rehearsed, looking at the uniformed man with wide, unknowing eyes.

Lowry did not know what to make of it. He was not sure if the motley crowd thought he had come to rescue them from the perils of slavery, or if the smiling were from the sincere pleasure of having a Union officer come to their plantation. But because both ideas appealed to him, he thought he would try again.

"I've come to inquire as to the owner."

"My name Rufus and this Alfred."

Aware of his lack of experience in dealing with Negroes, Lowry knew he obviously was not communicating.

"Good afternoon, Rufus," he nodded. "Good afternoon, Alfred."

Again he nodded, having distinguished them by name, and then nodded to the rest. "Now if you would be so kind as to tell me who your owner is, and who all this land belongs to?"

"Well, Alfred and me, we been here a long time, real long time, and it don't belong to the people it first belong to. Right, Alfred?" Alfred nodded, still grinning, behaving as if he were half idiot. "On the other hand, the mistress is still the same, it's the master that different. Right, Alfred?" Again, the grinning Alfred nodded his head.

Lowry's growing impatience was apparent to his audience as he shifted from one foot to the other. He had heard about southern Negroes never getting to the point, and their ability to ramble on and on, but he had also heard tell they were masters of trickery and deception.

"Look, Rufus, would you just tell me who the present owner is and where he can be found? Then you can all go back to your work."

"Oh, it already quittin' time for us. We gots the rest of the afternoon and evening with nothing to do but scrap up enough food for our bellies for supper and maybe have a little left for morning. It shore hard to work all day on a howling belly, right, Alfred?"

Alfred's composure changed only slightly as he managed to say, "Rrright."

The talk of hunger momentarily sidetracked Lowry, and his sympathy went out to the obviously overburdened darkies who were no doubt cruelly treated by their master.

"That is why you were so elated at my arrival! Will you tell me this renegade's name, who expects you to work unfed?" So the stories he had heard were true. Slave owners worked the poor devils half-fed, got all the work possible out of them and caring about nothing— and all those poor women who were nothing but brood mares, more slaves for the masters!

"You don't understand, atall. He feed us better than some white folks eat. Right, Alfred? It's them awful raiders and Rebels who go against the United States of America. They threaten to kill us and burn us and takes our animals and crops, and they raids in the middle of the night, and our pore master beside hisself for fear for his own life."

At this last remark both Rufus and Alfred dropped their heads as if in sorrow.

Lowry, thoroughly baffled, having shifted his opinion back and forth so many times, had only one question left, his original one. "Rufus, I am sorry for everything. Would you please, please tell me the name of your kind master?"

"Oh, yes, sir! Of course, sir! It Mr. Joseph Andrew Smith Acklen. Most folks just call him Mr. Acklen."

Lowry wiped his brow, thanked him very much and asked, although he was weary of another query, if either of them, or any of them could please tell him where they might possibly find Mr. Acklen.

"Well, you see, there's six plantations here, and Mr. Acklen, he own 'em all."

"That's r-r-right, f-f-far as you can see, all this land, all 'round this river, all 'round the Mississippi, he own it all."

Rufus frowned at Alfred and nudged, at which point Lowry ascertained that Alfred might be the one with whom he should talk instead of Rufus, except for the stuttering which took him even longer to provide information.

"But where is Mr. Acklen now, Alfred?"

"Y-you o-on B-Bellevue. I can't rightly say where Mr. Acklen be r-r-right this minute cause there s-s-six plantations, like Rufus say, and he could be on any of the s-s-six. He could even be on t-this one or he could be on that one," he said nodding to his right. "Or he could be on t-t-hat one," nodding to his far left. "I just don't rightly know."

Lowry's patience had vanished along with any hope of receiving what he considered rational answers to any of his questions. He had been standing for well over half an hour attempting to converse with two idiot-grinning slaves, he mumbled to himself, while the others attentively watched, never seeming to comment among themselves.

But just as Lowry was planning to return to his sloop, Joseph came galloping at full speed, his tan shirt showing great blotches of perspiration and clinging to his body. Panting and out of breath, he appeared frightened to Lowry as he dismounted, but cordially put out his hand. After the introductions were made, Lowry informed Joseph that he was an officer aboard the *U.S.S. Brooklyn*.

"I'm so glad you're here, Lieutenant—you don't know how glad!" He said in short breaths. "Two men just met me a mile or so back while I was making the rounds, ordering me to burn my cotton. Every plantation owner in the parish is under the same pressure."

"Who are these men?" Lowry asked with a great amount of interest.

"I wish I knew—their names, I mean," he answered still panting for breath. "There's a band of guerrillas who hide out in the swamps, the bayous, the hills. They keep watch on everything going or coming. They don't wear a uniform, but we all know it's the Rebel army giving the order."

"Then I may ascertain, sir, that you are not a sympathizer with the Confederate Government?"

"Lieutenant Lowry, I'm a planter. What you see here," he said, motioning with his hand to the fields behind him, "plus a lot more, a hell of a lot more, is the way I make my living. Or I should say *did* make my living, till this hideous war broke out. When my cotton is gone, my income is gone and sir, that's no small matter. My family in Tennessee is in danger of having everything we own confiscated by the Confederate Government. The last letter I received from by beloved wife stated that both she and my children are frightened to step foot outside our own door, and that government to which I swore allegiance," he lied, "which I now know in full was the gravest error, has taken all our livestock, horses, wagons, mules, anything movable, leaving my family with no manner of transportation." At the thoughts of such injustice, Joseph spat on the ground. "I might add, without sounding pretentious, that I own more land than any man between Natchez and New Orleans, and the Rebels are well aware of it. The harassment and threats grow stronger every day."

Lowry was more than pleased to see this poor victim of circumstance pouring out his heart and even over anxious to divulge the extent of his holdings.

"Do you say you have been threatened before, sir?"

"Threatened is not a strong enough a word. The two guerrillas I mentioned said if I did not burn my cotton, they would be back with two or three bands just like themselves, and burn it for me. Not only that, they'd hang me on the highest limb on the place!"

Both Alfred and Rufus, who had not been dismissed with the others, became teary-eyed at the mention of some disastrous deed befalling their master. They commenced their performances with sounds of pitiable sobs and the obvious wringing and shaking of their hands.

"It's all right," Joseph said kindly, "You may go back to your dwellings now. But I say to you, sir, that I have two thousand bales of last year's crop that I shall defend with my life if necessary, and I swear that Jefferson Davis will never benefit from one penny of it!" Again, he spat on the ground.

Intensely interested, Lowry liked every word he was hearing. "Sir, we anchored off your plantation for the night, and I came to ask for provisions, fresh beef and vegetables for which we will pay market value. We're on our way back to Vicksburg and join up with the *Merriweather* and the *Hartford* along the way. We're in dire need of fresh food."

"How I wish I could serve you, even in some small way, but I have five hundred slaves to feed, and every day brings the problem of having no idea where the food is going to come from. The Rebels have taken my cattle, my hogs. I become angry even telling the story." Joseph hoped his lies were not becoming too preposterous for belief.

He lowered his head, then raised it, looking at Lowry. "I had three thousand pounds of pork alone in my smokehouses...all gone, all taken. I tell you, if I ever see Jeff Davis, I'll shoot him on sight! Not a penny paid for it, just a worthless piece of paper, a damned IOU. It happened the one week I went into New Orleans. They watch us all, sir, they know our every move. You're probably aware that they're watching us right now!"

"Sir, I beg you let me station some men here for your protection. I assure you, your private property, your honor and your life will be safe under the protection of the United States Naval forces."

"That would be the worst thing that could happen. My life would not be worth as much as the note they signed. Thank you, sir, but I can't accept what I know you extend in kindness and sincerity."

"But what will happen when these guerrillas return?"

"Every planter up and down the river is faced with the same question. The Rebs don't know about my last year's crop, just what I've planted this spring, and that's what they want burned. The others and I have been meeting once or twice a week to decide what to do… usually in the old sugar house near Bayou Sara, but recently we've been meeting more often. About the only thing we can do is form our own militia, including foremen and the most trusted slaves, and try to stand against them. It's a terrible tragedy, a terrible tragedy."

"With your permission, we'll stay the night anchored off your plantation. Would you suggest we be on guard?"

"Without a doubt, sir. They stay in these swamps and in the rattlesnake-infested hill country back of the river—They know them by heart, every inch of them, and as you can see, with so much land, they can hide on your own property and you never even know it."

Lowry shook Joseph's hand, thanked him for his honesty, commended him for the position he had taken, and wished him well.

"Sir, I've just had a thought. My Negroes raise their own poultry and vegetables. If you'd like to ask them if they have anything to spare, you surely have my permission. Just pay them the market value, but forgive me, I need not remind an officer of your integrity of such. I'm certain they'll be more than ready to accommodate you with whatever they can spare."

"My faith is restored to meet a gentleman such as yourself. We'll do as you've suggested and keep a watch through the night. How would you recommend we approach the Negroes?"

"I'll speak with them. It's the least I can do. We'll meet here in the morning…let's say seven thirty?"

"I'll look forward to the pleasure of your company again, Mr. Acklen."

"By-the-way, do be careful of the alligators in the swamps. The lizards, however, are harmless."

Joseph watched Lowry walk to the levee and amble down sideways toward the small boat waiting to return him to the *U.S.S. Brooklyn.* This was the beginning of a masquerade that, with one slip-up, one miscalculation, could have him tried for treason and hanged. Or maybe not even tried—just hanged. He mounted his horse with its slick black coat and full dark mane, and this time took the direct path back to the house, just in case any field glasses were aimed in his direction. The Negroes had performed their roles to perfection! And Joseph had proved a convincing liar to Lowry; after all, deception was the crucial element.

There had been no time for him to change a scheduled meeting with his neighbors at Bellevue, and if an unexpected visitor came knocking, they would appear to be engaged in a serious game of poker.

Lucy was in a fit when Joseph came in and had already pronounced doom to the other house servants. Why Alfred had informed her about Lowry's visit, Joseph did not know, given her exaggerated, emotional spells.

"Mr. Acklen," she said, as he sat at the large kitchen table eating hurriedly before his neighbors arrived. "Iffen you don't get yourself killed one way, you gonna get yourself killed another! You say you running from the Yankees in Nashville and you making up to 'em here—or pertenning to, anyway. Now, what you think gonna happen iffen they ever get together? I answer for you. Miz Acklen ain't gonna have no husband and them childrens ain't gonna have no Pa. That's what they ain't gonna have!"

There was more than a little truth in what Lucy was saying. Either the Yankees or the Confederates could denounce him as a traitor. But as he had told Lowry, he did not intend to have the Rebel army burn his cotton to keep the Yankees from having it. On the other hand, he had no intention of the Yankees getting it either.

The location of the plantations, with their access to both rivers and the Atchafalaya Bayou, made them ideal for the blockade runners to bring in and take out supplies for the Confederacy, and it would take a legion to search twelve thousand acres—more men and more time than the Union Navy had to spare.

But the patrols were tightening on the river, and it was becoming increasingly difficult for the runners to get through. Just the week before, their coal supply yard had been discovered and confiscated by the Yankees, and at the same time, they had overtaken the *Kimberly*, one of the South's fastest runners. She had been in the wrong place at the wrong time, which was too near the coal yard. Fortunately, most of the crew had fled to the swamps and low hills beyond, but some, including the captain, had been captured and sent to a prison in Indiana.

Joseph's own position was worse. Either side would most likely hang him.

"Lucy," he said, motioning for her to pour him another cup of coffee, "things will be all right. And if perchance a stranger of any sort comes knocking on the doors tonight, you'd better not show one nervous twitch," he teased, "or I'll send you to the fields."

"Oh Lordy," Joseph heard her mumble as she left the kitchen to ready the gentlemen's room. "Please take care of us through one more night and one more gathering!"

The meeting took place without incident. The neighboring planters were all at Bellevue: the ones who had not panicked and fled the year before, sitting in the smoking room on its sturdy, handsome leather chairs and sofas, sipping iced whiskey, rehashing the day's events, planning the next step. A major concern for everyone present was the possibility of an informant among themselves, or among the Negroes.

"We've been friends and neighbors for a long while, some of you for years before I met you," Joseph said. "We all have something at stake, mostly the saving of our cotton and our land. I trust every man in this room, and I trust my Negroes." Joseph reached for his drink. "I trust my foremen. This is serious business, gentlemen. Our futures depend on it."

The men raised their glasses in agreement. Like himself, they had stored their cotton, anticipating the rise in market prices with a war in full swing. "Right now the mills in England stand idle, their laborers out of work, and English manufacturers are begging for the white gold so that more factories will not be forced to close and more men and women put out of jobs. Our northern factories are the same."

What Joseph had told the Yankee Lowry about Adelicia's cotton was true. He had two thousand bales, more than any other man in the room, but whatever the amounts, baled and waiting for shipment, they could name their price and get it on the English market. The time for waiting for prices to go higher was over.

The rumor that England was going to side with the Confederacy in order to put a quick end to the war was nothing but a rumor, thought Joseph, and not a reliable one. The men in the room with him well knew the best plan was to move their cotton quickly, before the crisis worsened.

However, the problem persisted in getting their cotton to New Orleans' busy port without its being confiscated by Rebels or Yankees. For the time being, they agreed that they were safer in the hands of the Yankees than among their fellow southerners.

Although they were aiding the Confederacy by hiding supplies on their plantations as well as giving protection for gunboats and supply packets, the planters gathered in the gentlemen's smoking room that evening knew if they were found shipping cotton, every last boll of it would be burned. The meeting adjourned well past midnight, with the understanding that Joseph would send word to each of them after he met with Lowry.

Although exhausted, Joseph could not sleep as he lay in the half-teester bed—Adelicia had been right, even using theatrical innovations to get her point across. He was glad he had come to Louisiana, that he had not joined the army, that he was engaged in what he was now doing. He did not feel the least bit guilty, nor the least bit greedy.

He smiled, recalling the night that Adelicia's eyes had sparkled upon learning he had shipped her cotton to Liverpool, that spring the secession had taken place. He too saw the irrationalities of the war. As she had said, "Honor is one thing, but mouths to feed when it is over is another." And for certain when it was over, some of those who had been among the most prosperous before '61, would not know from where their next meal would come.

Lying on his back with both hands clasped beneath his head, again he smiled, thinking of Adelicia. Their thirteen years together had passed quickly, with little time to pause and know where one year had ended and the other begun. She had never permitted the children to use the word boring, allowing that people easily bored, were themselves boring. She had certainly seen to it that their marriage was not so.

Headstrong and willful when he married her, he had seen minor mellowing. She had learned to depend upon him, at least in part, which he found gratifying. He saw through her manipulations and charades, finding them as charming and amusing, now as he had in the beginning. As his friend, and now brother-in-law, George Shields had told him, Adelicia always managed to get what she wanted. There was something about a woman with such confidence that few men could resist.

He wondered if anyone other than he knew that the strength Adelicia projected was nothing more than a shield to protect her from hurt. He liked it when she permitted him to be her foil. Lord knew she needed one!

Joseph agreed with her conviction that it was how one handled life's challenges and triumphs that defined one's character, but he never shared her belief that strength and good developed out of disaster. At this moment, he could certainly not fathom what good could possibly come from his role as double agent.

He drifted into sleep, wondering what the morning would bring.

It was an overcast April dawn when Joseph and Lieutenant Lowry stood near the river's bank with the fog occasionally shifting in the light breeze. Alfred, Rufus, Brutus and three or four other Negroes were loading eggs, poultry and sweet potatoes aboard the *U. S. S. Brooklyn*. The cackling of the hens lent a pleasantness to an otherwise dire setting.

"I thank you, Colonel Acklen, for your generosity and the generosity of your Negroes," Lieutenant Lowry said. "I truly believe they have supplied us with all they have to spare, and the United States government will not forget it."

"I'm sorry we have no more to offer you," Joseph replied. "However, I was thinking last night, if the river were opened back up, we wouldn't have this problem. We had thought of trying to obtain an audience with Admiral Farragut. You see, Lieutenant, it was when your Navy began blockading the river that we couldn't get our supplies in and out. And without a doubt," he said continuing to observe Lowry, "supplies of meat and flour and sundries are essential to feed these Negroes. As I've told you, nearly five hundred stayed on. Neighbors all up and down the river also have many who stayed, and have the same problem. Lieutenant, we might be of some real service to you. If I could get my cattle, hogs and sheep shipped in from Texas, and keep it secret from the Rebs, there would be enough left to share with your Navy." He watched for Lowry's reaction. If his hunch were correct, Lowry was believing his story and seriously considering his proposal.

"I sympathize with your problem, but we can't open up the river. We'd have Rebels running their boats in and out, supplying the whole damn Confederacy."

Joseph thought the statement more a matter of policy than one of conviction. Encouraged, he continued. "You forget, these hills and swamps are overrun with guerrilla bands now. They're your enemy as well as ours. They do as much supplying as if you made it legal, stealing and destroying what we have to keep it from you, and salvaging whatever they need for the Rebs and themselves. Think about it. Our Negroes must be fed. You saw how willingly they gave of their own meager means." Joseph added, in apparent disgust, "When I think what this secession has done to our country and its people. I have over four hundred human mouths to feed, and the story is the same all over. Your whole navy will be met with open arms and gratitude such as, if you'll pardon me, only a southerner can provide, if you'll permit open trade on the river. Something else you can tell your superior officer, there's not a man of substance and position who won't be glad when this war's over and our states are united once again under the stars and stripes of the Union. We're all sickened of being robbed and given worthless promises."

Obvious that Lowry was impressed with his plea, he continued. "I can promise you to make a full report of my findings here to Captain Powers and express personal feelings along with them. We'll be in touch as soon as possible."

"One more thing," Joseph added, "if your army wins at Corinth, the Rebs who escape will more than triple the size of the marauders in the hills. Frankly, Lieutenant, I don't know what we'll do."

Before leaving, Lowry offered Joseph a Northern newspaper, which he graciously accepted, containing a report of General Benjamin Butler's proclamation of victory at New Orleans. Then they cordially shook hands and expressed what appeared to be the sincerest of wishes to meet again under more favorable circumstances.

Perhaps, just perhaps, Joseph thought as he galloped back to Bellevue, all would be well. If so, it would sure make it a lot easier to ship in the promised twenty thousand head of cattle for the Confederacy from their property in Texas. Fortunately, the corn growing inland had not been spotted, nor had the other crops and livestock. Everyone had performed well, but if Lowry sent out dispatchers to ride over the land, or if they went to just one of the well-hidden oasis among what appeared to be thick woods, he would be a dead man.

He put the thought from his mind. The Yankees clearly had neither the extra men nor the free time to search twelve thousand acres, he told himself. He did wish, though, that Barclay had not planted his corn so near the river.

CHAPTER 56

Within a week's time, travel and commerce on the Mississippi became less and less a hazard. By midsummer, planters along the river were hiding supplies on their land ranging from sugar cane to cattle and seeing that it got to its destination. At the same time, they were supplying Union ships with a moderate amount of fresh meat and provisions when they asked, neither army aware of the others' good fortune. No Southern officer would agree to feeding Union troops, even if it meant not feeding his own; the Yankees would certainly not agree to aiding and supplying the Rebels.

By the end of August, Joseph had shipped one thousand bales of last fall's cotton to Liverpool via the Atchafalaya Bayou, known only to those planters along the Mississippi who were his closest allies. In the deep of night, they and their Negroes had helped Joseph load his enviable cargo onto barges and move it from Bellevue's banks on the Mississippi to the arm of the Bayou, eventually flowing into the gulf to the open sea—his neighbors were moving their cotton the same way.

For Joseph, payment in gold was assured to arrive in a Liverpool bank, prearranged by a contact in New Orleans...even if the shipment were pirated by either army, or blockade runners, his profit was guaranteed. The British well understood the risk of wartime trade. And when his cotton was picked this autumn, he would have at least three thousand more bales. He chuckled at the notion of hijacking his own ship, a piracy, that he suspected would have occurred to Adelicia.

Cotton was selling at a premium, one dollar and thirty cents a pound; Adelicia would have close to three hundred thousand dollars in gold from this shipment alone! If he survived this war and the dangerous triangle, in which he was now a major participant, he would live out the rest of his life in the joy and comfort of his wife and family...counting his blessings.

Thus had passed a humid summer in West Feliciana, and autumn was rapidly approaching. Joseph, hoping to be home way before Christmas, thought surely the war would soon be at its end. Any fool could see the North was gaining every day, and more and more southern cities going the way of Nashville. However, West Louisiana and Texas remained untouched, still flying the Confederate flag, though Joseph had just learned that the bars and stripes had been lowered in Baton Rouge, and the Union flag raised in its place.

As he dressed to go to the Turnbull's for supper this October evening, he wished to see late autumn in Tennessee and to be with Adelicia and his children.

CHAPTER 57

Nashville 1863

CHRISTMAS OF 1862 CAME AND WENT. MORE THAN EVER, Nashville was a city of strange faces, with new businesses run by a *new* society. The city continued to develop its banking, manufacturing, publishing and other enterprises, but its prosperity now lay mostly in the hands of strangers. Some had signed the pledge in order not to lose their businesses, some to keep their homes and farms; both lawyers and doctors were available professionally to Northener and Southerner alike. Nashville appeared to be settling into its new role, although law and order remained a serious deterrent.

A year had passed since Joseph had stolen away in the late March night of 1862. Letters, Adelicia's only link with her husband, were becoming more difficult to get in or out of the city. Between her and Joseph were approximately five hundred miles, where some of the war's heaviest battles were being fought, especially in Mississippi.

Letters were so scarce and so dear, she read and reread them until they were memorized. Then she would remove them from her desk drawer yet again just to see the words penned in his hand. The last one she had received was dated June 14th, now more than two months old.

She wondered how it would be when he came home. If the North won the war, it was suspected that Lincoln would pardon the secessionists, ranging from those who knew battle to those who fought on neither side; that included Joseph.

It was believed if Washington wanted and expected the states to be reunited, the widespread granting of full pardons would accomplish it most quickly. However, that was only speculation; there was no way to tell what Lincoln would really do.

Thus far, the Union was keeping its promises in Nashville. Adelicia's property had not been molested and was left virtually untouched, although for some time after Joseph's departure Belle Monte had been under close surveillance, until at last the military concluded he was not there, nor returning anytime soon.

Andrew Johnson himself signed a special letter providing protection for Adelicia and her property. And she, like other ladies whose husbands were away, was free to go and come as she pleased inside the city. She continued her daily work at the hospitals, and her ladies' group had been praised by Governor Johnson for its "undying dedication and sacrifice to the wounded."

She and Sally had entertained every high ranking officer of any significance in the Union army, and anyone of importance who came into Nashville. That included the Booths, who had performed their famous roles in both *Hamlet* and *King Lear* over a three week engagement at the reopening of the Adelphi Theater. Both Adelicia and Sally turned deaf ears to the gossip coming from those who frowned on their entertaining. It was the old biddies saying the same old things, "There's nothing Adelicia won't do to get what she wants!" The difference was, the girls with whom Adelicia had grown up were now the old biddies!

People never change, she thought, as she worked side by side with girlhood acquaintances and listened to snide remarks she knew were intended for her ears. That their husbands had been foolish enough to go traipsing off to war and get themselves shot or killed, or were still fighting, was none of her concern. Since childhood, she had been the subject of their envy, nothing would ever change that. Some were already in stages of poverty and did not know from whom a basket of food occasionally came.

They gossiped less about Sally than herself. Sally was at least a widow, although a beautiful one. They gossiped not at all about Sarah Polk, doing what was 'required' because she was the President's widow with a flawless reputation. But she, Adelicia Hayes Franklin Acklen, was a different sort. They thought her to be making merry in time of war, her husband absent, an unpardonable sin in their eyes. The Yankees were her means to a desired outcome. What if it were true, that she would do most anything to accomplish her goals, short of... well, they had never accused her of that, at least she did not think so!

She did find some of the entertaining with Sally enjoyable, never failing to delight in seeing men make fools of themselves over women. Yankees were experts in this area. Northern women must be as cold and prunish as iced raisins, she thought. If she paid a Yankee the slightest compliment, he was literally spilling his claret or dropping his food. All one had to do was smile and carry on the simplest of conversations.

Joseph would not disapprove of anything she was doing—she did not think. Sometimes, she even imagined him as an amused observer, never having failed to gain a certain pleasure from seeing men 'flutter' over her.

How she wished he were there to attend her suppers, carve the roast beef and walk up the stairs with her after the guests had gone, turn to their left at the top and go to her bedroom. But it should not be long...after the fall harvest, she saw no reason why he could not come home, unless there were more cotton than she had supposed, or more work, or complications unknown to her. She hoped the Negroes were still there.

Or perhaps Joseph would need to stay in Louisiana until the war was over—a dreadful thought! Regardless, she wished for it to hurry and end. Most people in Nashville, and she supposed elsewhere, could not care less at this point who won...let either side be named victor, and let their husbands and fathers and brothers and beaux come home, and let life return to normal...A fleeting moment of inane thought; nothing would ever be normal again. All that was would become "used to be."

CHAPTER 58

West Feliciana, 1863

ADELICIA WAS CORRECT IN ASSUMING THAT THE FALL CROP, planted that spring, was a luscious one, full boled and almost ready for harvesting. But she was unaware of the corn and sugarcane planted to supply, as well as, conceal the Confederates. Nor did she know that the week before, the third week in July, Joseph had filled a Union ship with all the mutton they wanted, and would accept no payment. Meanwhile, the Rebel army was using another part of the plantation, where the Ouachila and Red River Landing joined their property near the regular ferry crossing, to land and store supplies.

Admiral Farragut had taken command of New Orleans' Port shortly after Joseph's arrival in March of '62. For a year, ever since Joseph's initial meeting with Lowry, it had been considerably easier to move supplies on the river. But Rear Admiral David Porter, stationed at Vicksburg, had begun to cause new problems. In the short time he had been in charge of the western command, he had consistantly attempted to have Farragut close up the Red River. His police boats were being outrun by the blockaders, but he, or someone high in his command, always double-checked the information Joseph provided concerning the strategic points held by the Rebels. Porter did not trust Joseph, as had Lowry and Powers.

Joseph and the other planters could ill afford to have too much checking, making it necessary to let a Rebel boat be captured now and then, always one of lesser importance, loaded with lesser quality goods, originally intended for the Yankees.

It was no small matter when the news of the burning of Vicksburg and the battle at Gettysburg reached them at the same time. Joseph could feel the circle around him closing more tightly each day, with every move. He had been questioned twice about the Rebel gunner *Indianola* and when his story was checked, he was found not only to be telling the truth, but had been commended for going beyond the basics to provide the most minute details. Although, he had not met Admiral Porter, it was through his command that orders were sent and daily pressures mounted.

July 13, 1863, began humid and muggy at two a.m. for Joseph, Sterling and Barclay. The three neighbors worked side by side with their trusted Negroes and Confederate soldiers on the banks of the Red River where it opened into the Atchafalaya Bayou.

The tenseness of each man was felt all the more keenly in the subdued silence, the silence of fear and determination to complete what had begun, and the silence of hopefulness that they would see the sunrise from their own bedroom windows.

That morning before, two Confederate gunboats, the *Webb* and the *Music,* had been spotted and pursued by the *Clifton.* The Yankee boat had chased them for eight miles and opened fire, but because she had only one boiler, the smaller and faster gunboats had gotten away. For some months, the gunners had been the cover for the landing of troops and supplies on all sides of the Acklen property. They had been spotted and chased, but thus far had steered clear of another vessel coming close enough to fire.

However, this July morning, they had been careless, and as the two gunboats nestled in a cove on the west side of Bellevue, they too felt the silence of fear. The gunboats were critical to the safe movement of troops and supplies from Port Arthur, Texas to the Atchafalaya Bayou, via the Red River, eventually hiding out on the plantations until they could be shipped out.

Confederate army Captain David Carmack wrote on the ledger sheet as the unloading continued, while four supply ships waited their turn to dock precisely where the river was high enough that there was no danger of miring into the muddy bottom. As Carmack wrote, he watched the bridge in the distance that stretched across the Dobey Swamp, where trusted Negroes stood with lanterns and cane poles supposedly vying for an early morning catch. They were fishing from the east side with lanterns lit in his direction. If they moved to the west side, it meant a Yankee patrol had been spotted.

Joseph, Barclay and Sterling also watched the old wooden structure. If the signal were given, there was no alternative but for them, the Rebels and the Negroes, to flee as quickly as possible and abandon the whole operation to the Yankees.

Tension mounted as they continued to watch the bridge. By three-thirty, two of the cattle boats were unloaded, the steers being rustled into the corrals, built deep in the woods. All knew that if there were a Union boat within two miles, the cow's lowing would not go unnoticed. The ledger sheet lengthened as Carmack wrote: 30 wagon loads of lead, 180 barrels of dried beef, 80,000 pounds of bacon, 50 barrels of flour, 2,500 long barrel rifles, and for the last entry, 4,000 head of cattle.

Joseph had promised four thousand head to the Confederate government, and on the ledger sheet that was all that was showing. Another six thousand was his back-up—to feed his Negroes, and, if need be, to share with the Yankees.

As the last of his steers passed onto the wooden ramp and were herded into the woods, the moon slipped behind dark summer clouds, and rain began to fall from a blackened sky. Joseph thought of Adelicia's oft quoted elegy by Thomas Gray. He could not remember the exact words, but he wished the lowing herd would move quickly into oblivion and leave the world to darkness and to himself.

Four-thirty, and all was quiet on Red River except for the sobering sounds of rain touching the water. The lanterns could no longer be seen on the bridge. The men dismissed their Negroes and mounted their horses. Joseph rode slowly, thankful for the protection of the darkness and the rain.

When he reached the house, he left his wet clothes with Lucy. Exhausted, he dried himself off, stretched the full length of the bed, and dozed off listening to the rain fall on the slate roof.

He had just fallen into a quiet sleep when Lucy shook him. "The Yankees are here!" she whispered in a terrified voice. "The Yankees are here! They in the parlor with Mr. Clack, Mr. Young, Mr. Kelly. They gonna get us all. They say they hate disturbing you beings you prob'ly didn't get no sleep last night, and I say you always gets up at six o'clock and yous up here removing your beard."

Joseph hastily began to shave in the cold water left over from the night before. "Get a denim shirt and pants. What did you do with the clothes I had on last night?"

"I drop 'em in the side well, boots, hat and all. They got pore Alfred in such a state he can't say nothing, and the other three is acting like they ain't got a nerve. Please hurry!"

Before she had finished the last sentence, Joseph was looking at his completely dressed and shaven self in the mirror. "How do I look to go to the hanging tree?"

"Dear, Jesus, don't talk like that!" Lucy said, trembling.

"Lucy," he said, with all the composure he could muster, "Stay here. Clean the room, empty the wash bowl, do whatever you would ordinarily do. If they suspect for one minute that you're nervous about something, they're going to want to know what. Everything will be fine. But stay here. I am depending on you." He checked himself again at the door then proceeded down the steps in his usual confident manner.

Three officers in blue stood on the wide back verandah that stretched the full length of the large dwelling. One of the men had pulled wisteria, that draped from the open latticework overhead, and wound it around the pommel of his saddle. Standing near the officers were his three overseers, as Lucy had said, along with Alfred and Rufus and eight more Negroes who sat on the porch steps.

"Good morning, gentlemen. Have you come for more provisions?" Joseph spoke cordially, extending his hand to the officer nearest him.

"I'm Commander Welles of the United States Navy," the Yankee officer replied, responding to the courtesy shown by Joseph but without warmth. "This is Captain Weston and Captain Coles."

"It's a pleasure to welcome you to Bellevue. Won't you come inside? I haven't had breakfast yet, and nothing would please me more than have the three of you join me, along with my foremen, whom you must have met already, Mr. Clack, Mr. Young and Mr. Kelly. Lucy would be pleased to cook for seven hungry men."

"We've met your foremen, Mr. Acklen, and we'll by-pass the hospitality, which I understand you're famous for in these parts."

The tone of Welles' voice made him uneasy, but he continued in his gracious manner. "We are known for our hospitality here, sir. No one is ever a stranger. Won't you come inside? Lucy had said I would find you in the parlor."

"We were in the parlor, but when we asked for some of your slaves for questioning, they refused to come inside, so we felt it would be more comfortable for all concerned out here. Mr. Acklen, I'll get right to the point," said Welles. "I know for a fact that in the early morning hours, ammunition and food supplies were unloaded on your Loch Lomond Plantation, not to mention 4,000 head of cattle. Right this minute, other officers of the United States are at your friends' homes, the two who were with you last night, Mr. Sterling and Mr. Barclay. There's no point in denying any of it, as I have a duplicate of the ledger sheet kept by one of your Rebel officers."

Welles handed him a sheet of paper, and as Joseph's eyes scanned it, he realized it was an exact account of the supplies they had unloaded that morning. And at that moment, he also realized that his fate depended on how skillfully he could act out yet another charade.

"Commander Welles," he answered in apparent ignorance, "if you're suggesting these items were landed on my plantation for the sake of a dying enemy, which to the planters in this Mississippi Delta means the Rebels, you've been badly misinformed. You're more than welcome to search every foot of my land, and anything you find, whatever it is, food, ammunition or livestock, you're welcome to it."

"Thank you again for your generosity, Mr. Acklen," Welles retorted with all the impudence he could spew out, "but I know you were there, as well as these three men." He nodded to the foremen. "And I also know your Negroes were on the bridge as lookouts, not fishing. There's no sense denying any of it. I have proof!"

"Well, sir, let me see your proof," Joseph responded reasonably. "Thus far you have shown me a piece of paper with a list of supplies that you say were landed on my property sometime this morning. These are supplies about which I know nothing, and when I was supposed to have been there, I was sleeping. Lucy and Alfred can tell you that when I retired for the evening I was not feeling well, tightness in my chest. Alfred gave me one of his special liniment back rubs and drew me a tub of hot water. Lucy concocted some of her summer bitter herb tonic, which I drank and went to bed, all before nine o'clock."

"If there's one thing I've learned about darkies since coming to your part of the country, it's they'll tell any type of lie to protect their masters or mistresses or any white folks they feel a loyalty to."

"Massa Acklen, I tell him us niggers don't lie," interrupted Rufus feigning a pleading voice, "I tell him we baptized niggers, and just cause we having a little fun on the bridge last night, the Lord don't hold it against us. They think we not fishing just cause one field nigger don't have no hook on his line, and I tell him you have to excuse field niggers, cause that's why they's where they is, and besides, by the time they patrol come by we's feeling mighty fine, but then I tell em if they tell Massa Acklen, he be mighty upset. I tell 'em you 'low us to slip out there and fish to get extra food for our families, but you don't like the other none atall cause it hard for a man to work when he been sinning at night. But Massa, times is bad and..." Rufus stopped short of finishing his confession and looked at the others as if not wanting to get them in trouble.

"Go on, Rufus," Joseph said sternly, "I've never known you to lack for words, and your story's becoming very interesting."

"Yes sir, I's afraid you'd think so. Well sometimes in the early morning we gets us watermelons. Remember you tells us we can have melons to take out in the field cause it so hot and that sweet juice taste might good to a thirsty tongue. Well, we does that cause you say we can. Course, I just oversees the field niggers directly under Mr. Young."

"Continue with your story," Joseph said, enjoying the yarn spun by Rufus and enjoying his own apparent irritation intended for the Union officers.

"Well, like I say, you say we can have watermelons, and ever now and then, Alfred, he gets a little corn whiskey that we keeps only for medicine purposes, and we makes a hole in the end of our melon and mashes all the juice out of that good pink meat, digs it out and eats it cause it still a might juicy. Then we gets out all the seeds and puts 'em in our pockets. Then come the bad part, Massa—we puts that corn liquor we sposed to use for medicine down in that melon hole and let it set all day in that pink juice, and then we get it out to go fishing at night, you never tasted such good juice in all your life. Weren't no worse than Noah did.

"And last night when the United State of American soldiers come by, we's about on our third melon and feeling mighty fine, and they ask what we doing, and we say fishing, and they ask us who we belong to and I says Massa Acklen, but please not tell him cause he don't like his niggers drinking."

"Mr. Acklen," Commander Welles said, "My men found four watermelons, filled with the pink liquid just like your man described, but we know they were there for a ploy. These men were as sober as they are right now, and although some were fishing, we consider the timing and the location too coincidental.

"The fact is, there've been too many coincidences, too many incidents of falsified information. We have a witness who swore to your whole operation. He named you along with Sterling, Barclay and your foremen. He also gave us the list of which supply boats landed on your plantation. In short, Mr. Acklen, you are under arrest."

Joseph's heart sank. An informer! It had to be one of the Rebels. He knew his men and his Negroes. In the dark, there could have been someone staked out by the Yankees, but he could not recall at the moment an unfamiliar face or voice.

"Because I had not met you prior to this morning, I didn't reveal any information," said Joseph. But because you know now…"

"Perhaps we're getting somewhere," interrupted Commander Welles.

"What you'll find on my land is three thousand head of cattle, one thousand already corralled separately for your army. This information should have reached Admiral Farragut in New Orleans yesterday, indicating they would be ready for your boats tonight. If you want to arrest me, I'll put up no resistance, but it'll delay your Navy receiving a thousand head of beef cattle brought in from Texas yesterday."

Joseph watched as the men looked at each other, and he saw their hesitation. If they had not yet made the search, if Welles men were not searching as he and Welles stood talking—two big ifs—then he could buy time—permitting the Rebels to get their supplies and leave him relatively safe.

Porter was the suspicious one. But these officers were army, not Porter's men. Joseph decided to press his luck. "You can go see the cattle now, or you can send a dispatcher to New Orleans and check my story and wait till in the morning to have the steers loaded aboard one of your suppliers."

He had said "morning," hoping if they fell for the deception, the Rebs could get the cattle aboard the ferry and into Mississippi at dusk.

"It's up to you, gentlemen."

Again, they looked from one to the other, Joseph seeing he had placed enough doubt to cause them to reroute their thinking. If their informer had been wrong, Joseph's arrest could mean breaking up a main supply station to them of which the informer was ignorant. There was also the possibility that Admiral Farragut's orders had not arrived before the officers were sent on their mission. Joseph had told them he sent the message the previous day, and if Welles believed he were telling the truth, they knew enough time had not lapsed for them to have received the information.

Joseph experienced a strange silence as the men, black and white, looked into the distance and then at each other. It was Commander Welles who spoke first with the apparent uncertainty of one who is not sure whose orders he is obeying. "If what you say is true, Acklen, I'll find out in a short while. For security's sake, I'll leave some men here with you so you don't decide to disappear, as some of you along the river have been known to do."

He said nothing more, but motioning to the other two officers, walked between the Negroes still sitting on the steps and mounted his brown cavalry horse.

Clack, Young and Kelly stood with Joseph and watched until they rode out of sight. In their minds, a singular query: who was the informer?

"Joe," Jim Clack asked after some time, as if he were thinking aloud. "Who was there? I'd stake my life it wasn't one of the Negroes. And if it were Sterling or Barclay, they'd be informing on themselves. Whoever it was had to be near Carmack because he was the only one in a position to see the whole operation."

"Maybe it was Carmack," said Kelley. "I never have liked him. Never trust a lady's man. If they'll cheat one place, they'll cheat another."

"It couldn't be Carmack," said Joseph, "he's in as deep as any of us. Your bit of wisdom's not necessarily so. He's a good man. It wasn't Carmack. But it was someone who..."

He stopped short as nine Union soldiers rode up, called a halt and dismounted. The leader, who looked little older than sixteen or seventeen, introduced himself as Sergeant Pat Hopkins and told Joseph he had been asked to post a guard around the house until further orders from Welles.

Joseph welcomed them and invited Hopkins to join them for breakfast. He also included the Negroes because, as he told Hopkins, they had not been in their cabins at meal time and could not do a day's work on an empty stomach.

"Put on the vittles, wife," said Alfred, "everybody gonna eat white folk's breakfast." He turned and rolled his eyes toward Joseph who had walked into the kitchen with him and Lucy.

"I'm sorry I can't give you more than a good breakfast, Alfred. Lucy, we want it all: grits, bacon, ham and biscuits, eggs, fried tomatoes and plenty of chicory. Watermelon wine...my mammy in Huntsville used to keep some in the ice house, and I was the only one who knew her secret."

"Mr. Acklen, we don't have none last night, just sometimes we do. If your mammy have some, do it mean you don't mind?"

"Right now, Alfred, I don't mind about anything except seeing we all come through this with our heads still attached."

"Oh, Jesus, I wish you don't say such things!" Lucy exclaimed, getting more flour on the floor than in the bowl. "I can't stand no more."

"If your mistress knew you were using the Lord's name so loosely, she'd get your head," he offered in jest.

"Iffen there's one thing I knows, it's I ain't loose with the Lord's name. I just calls it hoping and wishing for help and mercy!" Joseph patted her on the shoulders and walked into the dining room.

Lucy seated the Negroes around the large poplar kitchen table; little was said in either room. The only sounds to disturb the silence was the steady rhythm of silver utensils and forks clinking against china plates and the sipping of coffee.

To Joseph, few things were worse than uncertainty, and right now neither he nor the others knew anything for sure. *If* Welles and his officers returned to the ship the way they had come, they may have heard some bawling cattle but would have seen nothing. *If* they sent a dispatcher to New Orleans, it would most likely be the next day before they could receive any word. *If* they did not send a platoon out to search before the Rebel army could move out their supplies—*If, if, if,* then perhaps—just perhaps—they could succeed in this particular run.

With the meal ended, Joseph dismissed everyone, wishing there were a way to know what was happening on the neighboring plantations; but he could ill afford to chance sending a messenger to anyone of them. For that he would have to wait, but just possibly he could get word to Carmack by Alfred. He had asked the Negroes to keep their distance from places where the supplies were hidden, but to report any unusual occurrence to him.

"Member," said Rufus, attempting to cheer Joseph up as he went out the door. "Yankees don't know the difference in a thousand cows bawling and eight thousand."

CHAPTER 59

Belle Monte, 1863

ADELICIA HAD RECEIVED BUT ONE MORE LETTER FROM JOSEPH since the two-month old one in June, and it was dated August first. Although he had said little of actual events, she read between the lines enough to know that she feared for his safety. Her husband was obviously a participant in too many games, on a stage playing too many roles. He could not have three thousand acres of cotton ready for fall harvesting if he were not involved in some dangerous schemes.

How she wished he were home with her and the children. August had begun more hot and humid than she could remember, and as the days progressed, and the heat became even more intolerable, she further wished that she and her family could retreat from the deprivations of war, to flee everything around them that was ugly. Those who had signed the pledge were no better off financially than those who had not, unless they had businesses in town from whom all profited.

September was approaching and another winter that again her husband might not be home. Although the cotton crop would provide more gold stored safely in English banks, the issue of Joseph's wellbeing outweighed the security of greater wealth. She had become even more alarmed with the lack of detail in his last letter, and wondered how he actually was faring in the unresolved political status of West Louisiana. If he could not come to her, she would go to him, she decided.

Occupied Nashville continued to bustle with wartime's quick riches and to overflow with everything except "what used to be." And the soaring population, now at eighty thousand, literally held a dreadful stench. She hated the change in the city that was hers; even her dinner parties were becoming laborious.

Being needed, serving a cause, helping the unfortunate, was also fast becoming a burden instead of a devoted duty. She wished to erase the past two and one-half years and return to the peace and serenity her family had known before the war. She yearned for her life before the gallant Southerners had gone riding off, thinking they would return in three months, parading medals of bravery; before Nashville had become an occupied city; before she had known a young man who could never go home again. But all her wishing made no dent in the course of men.

Miles apart, Vicksburg and Gettysburg had fallen to the Yankees on July 4th, a remarkable date, she thought, for it to have occurred. General Johnston had fled; Grant's army was in complete control of Nashville.

Throughout the stifling August' days, Essie had predicted an early fall, a short Indian summer, and one of the coldest winters in years. Her careful observations of nature had interested Adelicia since she was a child; and this year Essie had noted heavy tree bark, thick onion skins, hornets' nest low to the ground, and the behavior and color of woolly worms. If proved true, it would be a dreadful winter for those without proper shelter; those with no means of wood for fires, Reb and Yank alike, not to mention the freed Negroes.

Adelicia sat in a deep blue velvet chair in her sitting room with her legs curled beneath her, watching the squirrels scurrying on the lawn with their stores of acorns and hickory nuts, preparing for Essie's predicted winter. Some leaves had already changed to shades of orange, yellow and deep red by this second day of September.

The magnolia's thick, wide leaves remained entirely green, of course, but one large oak, the one nearest her bedroom window, was yellow-orange, almost golden, in the sun's reflectinve light. And as she watched its leaves spin and flutter in the breeze, she wished for Joseph. The tree, planted long before even her parents had been born, set out by someone long forgotten, perhaps with no particular plan or purpose, but one whose fruition now gave her great pleasure. She and Joseph had sat beneath it many times, had gathered acorns with the children and had felt the tenderness of its new green leaves in the spring. How she wished him there now to share the autumn.

She would go find Essie and tell her she was going to New Orleans! Surely no one would deny a poor widow from passing through enemy lines to take refuge with Yankee, or Confederate (depending on with whom she spoke) relatives in the Crescent City.

She was determined to be with Joseph—to see him—to know exactly what he was doing—and to, perhaps, join in whatever drama was there.

Chapter 60

Bellevue Plantation, 1863

Again, luck, fortune, or whatever one might tag it, were on Joseph's side. When Commander Welles made the inquiry, he found that indeed a telegram had been sent to Admiral Farragut. Time was also on his side; the Yankees had made no attempt to search the immediate premises or the surrounding acres, thus leaving the Rebel supplies intact. Admiral Farragut was so elated to receive one thousand head of cattle, that apparently nothing was noticed when an additional nine-thousand head were left for Joseph and the Confederates, their distant lowing being foiled by the present bellowing.

Once more, Joseph had escaped the Yankees, and he hoped the word he had secretly sent by way of Alfred to Captain Carmack, had kept the Rebels far enough away that they would not know what was happening with the Union Army.

September 4th. All was well for another day, or at least another morning. But in the future, more caution would have to be taken or Joseph would never see Belle Monte again.

At noon, Barclay and Sterling came over with similar accounts of the previous day. As they dismounted their horses at the rear of Bellevue, they told Joseph a watch had also been posted at their plantations, and the Yankees had remained there until word was received late in the evening that Joseph's story was true. The men continued exchanging ideas until Barclay's foreman, Whit Bowden, rode up with new information.

Barclay had taken none of his Negroes with him on the Rebel supply mission, nor had Sterling, as it was previously agreed that Joseph's Negroes were more than ample. It would also arouse less suspicion if the two men traveled alone from their respective plantations.

However, a relatively new hired hand had questioned Bowden a few days prior to the early morning the cattle were unloaded, stating he had heard rumors among the darkies there was a secret mission about to take place. He insisted upon his hatred of the Yankees and wanted to take part in it. When Bowden declined the offer, the man claimed he could be of great service. There was a peculiarity about him, Whit Bowden reported, that he had not liked, and had found him even more unpleasant that afternoon when he assured the man they were doing nothing secretive and nothing in which he would have any interest.

Whit Bowden had hired the small ginger-bearded man, who called himself Thompson, out of desperation for the coming harvest. The man had given references of having overseen a "fine plantation" outside of Nashville, Tennessee, and of having been in the Confederate Army before being honorably discharged due to illness.

Bowden had inquired of the house servants, the stable boys, and the slaves who lived in the quarters to the right of Cresmon, if any of them had seen Thompson the previous night. For answers, "no one had seen him," but added, "no one ever saw him for long." It was discovered that Thompson was involved in all sorts of mysterious goings and comings, of which the Negroes had assumed their master was aware.

It was Batten, Tom Barclay's butler, who told him that on many nights he had seen Thompson walking on the lawn, or down by the river, or "messing" around the horses in the stable. But on the night in question, Batten had not seen him at all.

Although it was not enough evidence to convict him, it was enough for Barclay to question him. Thompson, he said, had squirmed, mostly staring down at his boots as he shuffled in the yellow-red dust when asked where he had been. His crude mannerisms and shifting eyes told the planter that Thompson was no longer wanted at Cresmon.

Joseph listened intently to the story from Barclay and Bowden. "Tom, under the circumstances, the only thing to do is send for him and see if anyone recognizes him from Tuesday night. It's possible that Sterling, one of my foreman, or one of the Negroes may have seen him."

Thomas Barclay agreed, and Rufus was sent to bring Thompson to Bellevue.

Rufus took the short-cut that followed a small creek running east along the back of the plantation instead of following the river road. He made as much time as possible through the flat bottom land before reaching the hilly Tunica Road and the additional three miles to Cresmon.

Thompson was nowhere to be found, but one of the stable boys told Rufus he had seen Thompson riding toward the north pasture shortly after Barclay had left for Bellevue.

Rufus well knew Cresmon's land. Not only had he ridden on hunts with Joseph to help carry home the game, he had hunted the land, himself, and knew the north pasture led to the river bottom where the corn was planted.

Rufus was an excellent tracker. He sat quietly on the bay mare, with his feet dangling far below where the stirrups would have placed them had he taken time to saddle her. His legs were bowed around her thick middle as he sat erect, tilting his head upward and listening for sounds which might lead to his find. He sniffed the air, still cocking his head, then lowered it bending over the mare to sniff the earth below him. He thought to himself as he trotted right toward the river bottom, that "any white man who leave a trail that easy to pick up ain't smart enough to be no spy."

He stopped short of the spot where he saw a man he assumed to be Thompson talking with some laborers, who were plucking ears of corn. After observing for a minute or so, Rufus rode directly to where they were. "I begs your pardon, but is you name Mr. Thompson?"

He did not know if it were his imagination, but he thought the Negroes with whom the beady-eyed man was talking had looked frightened when Rufus rode up.

"It all depends on who wants to know, and I don't like no nigger acting uppity to me, come riding up like he owns the place and asking my name. What's your business here?"

"My business just say that Mr. Barclay ask me to ride over and find Mr. Thompson so he can talk to him over at my Massa's place."

"And where is your Massa's place?" Thompson asked, mocking him.

"Bellevue. Belong to Mr. Acklen. And your boss man say for you to hurry."

The Negroes were watching closely, their eyes shifting from one to the other, waiting for Thompson's reaction.

"If there's one thing I like less than a uppity nigger, it's a white man sending one to fetch me." Thompson spat tobacco out the side of his mouth and wiped his chin with his sleeve. "You tell your massa and my boss man that if they want me, they can come tell me. Right now I'm tending to my own business, and I'd advise you to do the same and go on back the way you come." His chest swelled as he inhaled the air around him, and spat very near the hoof of Rufus' mare.

Rufus said nothing more but turned his horse and quickly rode away. He had never, he thought to himself, been tempted to strike a white man before.

And in these times, he did not know if those watching would stand in his defense or not. Nor did he know what Thompson was telling them when he rode up, but he knew the man was up to no good. He also knew if he ever met Thompson alone, out where the two of them were far from anyone's prying eyes or ears, he would kill him.

He could see Bellevue's widow's walk now, and he would repeat the conversation exactly as he had heard it to the gentlemen waiting for his return; his thoughts he would keep to himself.

Joseph remained tightlipped as Rufus related Thompsons's words, knowing that Barclay felt the great burden of responsibility; Thompson was his hired hand. The three men still waiting with their horses in the afternoon sun, looked at each other, none doubting that Thompson was the spy and headed immediately to Cresmon, as Joseph went to saddle his horse.

The house servants were in an uproar when they arrived, and because they were all talking at once, it was difficult to discover what had taken place. But they finally understood from Batten, that Thompson had left Cresmon, a fact which no one would have regretted except that at least twenty, perhaps more, field hands left with him and he had stolen two of Barclay's best horses. But foremost, he had kidnapped three female slaves, against their wishes, all knowing the evil designs Thompson had for their future.

Sterling and he stayed for supper at Cresmon before taking their leave past eleven, with the tension mounting around them, paramount in Joseph's mind as he neared Bellevue in the light of a waxing moon.

CHAPTER 61

JOSEPH LAY WEARILY ACROSS THE BED AS THE HALL CLOCK STRUCK midnight, too exhausted to remove his clothing, and with his thoughts running rampant: Adelicia, the children, Nashville, the Yankees, the Rebels, the cotton, the gold, the deceit, the danger. He hoped at that very moment the Rebel army was taking its supplies and its cattle.

He was exhausted, both mentally and physically, and had a flashing thought that he would not care if the Rebels were caught as long as they were far from the plantations. However, his next thought reminded him, that he did care—although for a single moment nothing seemed to matter except for returning home to Belle Monte.

For a year and a half, he had not seen his family. He longed to lie beside Adelicia and hold her so close that he could carry the memory of her next to him until the following night when he would hold her again.

After the cotton was trashed, ginned and baled, which should be by mid-October, he was going home. Except for the money, not a trifling consideration, he would have been just as well off in prison. If necessary, he would sign the damn pledge, and to salve his conscience, donate heavily to the Confederacy. As Adelicia had said when it all began, everyone would know he was a man loyal to the South, and those who did not, he would dismiss.

It was past three a. m. when he awakened, realizing he had slept for some time, unbathed and still dressed. The moon was shining its fullest, causing no need to light the lamp beside his bed. He undressed and washed his face and hands in the water Alfred had brought earlier in the evening, then walked to the window and looked out on the spacious, well-manicured lawn.

Alfred had seen that Adelicia's flower gardens were not neglected, that they had been tended to spring and summer, and that the autumn flowers, asters, chrysanthemums, roses and hydrangeas would be colorful and full through the rest of the season, and in December, the Christmas flowers would bloom crimson red. Adelicia was fascinated that poinsettias thrived outside all winter in the delta and so fond of the variety, she had them planted around the entire exterior of the house.

The moon shone brightly over the lawn, playing tricks on Joseph's mind, causing the tips of leaves, the petals of the flowers, and the oyster-shelled walkways woven in between, to appear as silver. There were no nearby sounds, only a distant foghorn infrequently giving warning on the river. And for a moment, he could almost believe there was no war, that when he returned to the bed and parted the mosquito netting, Adelicia would be lying there waiting for him, and that across the hall the children would be sleeping.

It was past eight when he awakened to sounds of heavy rain and loud claps of thunder, and although thinking he had slept soundly, he felt unrested.

He had hardly begun breakfast when two Union officers were shown into the parlor by Alfred. He took his time, finished a second cup of coffee, then went to meet the callers. They had come to inquire about the *Indianola*, the Confederate gunboat that had been moored for some time near the mouth of the Red River. He had given reports before, and he cordially took this inquiry in style, providing the necessary information to satisfy them without saying anything to damage the Confederacy.

They were interested in knowing about her guns, and Joseph told them she had two XI-inch guns in her casement and two LX-inch aft. He added that if they needed any help in blowing her up, he was sure any of his Negroes would oblige. The officers seemed satisfied, thanked him for his information and told him they might return and solicit the help he had so generously extended. The visit had taken no more than twenty minutes, and Joseph went back into the kitchen for more coffee.

That same morning, Barclay had also reported to the military authorities about Thompson, a hired hand, who had taken more than twenty of his Negroes, he thought against their will. He gave a full description and reported the man as shiftless and one whose word could not be trusted under any circumstances, who would say or do anything to promote himself, protect himself, for financial gain.

The Yankees had never questioned Tom Barclay as intensely as they had Joseph, likely because his plantation was not as strategically situated to the two rivers and the bayou as was Adelicia's. The only thing suspect on Barclay's part was the earlier report from Thompson. However, when they had come to question Barclay, they discovered the corn planted in the river bottom, which was quickly explained as needed for his slaves during the coming winter months. Barclay offered a fair portion to the army, an offer they gladly accepted.

The Union Army had taken no more than offered, still leaving plenty for the Rebel soldiers in Alabama. However, as Barclay, Sterling and Joseph had discussed the previous evening at Cresmon, Porter and his river patrols were becoming wise to their deception. The cattle had to be herded onto a ferry to cross the Mississippi, then onto a large boat via the Atchafalaya Bayou, to the Gulf, to Mobile, then driven into the heart of Alabama.

One more large shipment was due the following Tuesday, now too late to stop, but after that, the men agreed to end their aid to the Confederacy. They would see to their own harvest and salvage what they could for themselves.

Joseph rode his black stallion in the heavy rain to the river where, two nights before, the clandestine work had taken place. He casually looked over the open fields, then rode deep into the interior to seek out the place where the prize cargo had been stored. It was gone, taken by the Rebels, he hoped. The land looked much as it had before, leaving no evidence to indicate the Yankees or the Rebels had been there.

When he returned home, Captain Powers and Lieutenant Lowry were waiting for him in the kitchen. Like himself, they were drenched from the beating downpour and had allowed their horses to be taken to the stables. They were also grateful for a dry place to wait, and for the coffee Nattie, one of Lucy's sisters, had offered them. Nattie, gracious in her serving, was free of the nervousness that characterized her older sister.

Taken aback at seeing the men, as there had been a visit earlier that morning, Joseph had no idea why officers from Admiral Porter's command would be calling so soon.

"Good day, gentlemen. I'm not sure which of us looks more rested." He offered his hand, and they extended theirs. "Nattie, I'll join them for coffee. Would you like anything more?"

"No, thanks. We appreciate the hot drink, but again, this is no social visit, Acklen," Powers said, "I'll get right to the point. Far too many reports have come across Admiral Porter's desk as to your conduct in dealing with the enemy. Amazingly, your stories always check out, so much so that our Army and Navy have hardly considered it worthwhile to carry the matter further. A failing, I should add, on our part." He paused. "You must be familiar with the expression, 'Where there's smoke, there's fire.' Well, where you're concerned, it seems there's a fire. As I stated, because your stories always appear to check out, we've let it pass, although the Admiral has consistently had his suspicions. Even this morning's report concerning the *Indianola* checks. We've had divers examining her in this pouring torrent and everything you said was truth. In your case, it's what you don't tell."

He stopped and beamed at Joseph like a fisherman who has tried for weeks to catch the big one, and at last thinks he has the right size hook to reel him in. "Another report this morning says you're a fugitive from Nashville, a man who neither joined the Rebs, nor signed the pledge of allegiance. Now what have you to say about that?"

"Captain Powers, it's certainly no surprise to anyone that I did not, by my own choosing, join the military service of either side." Powers blushed as Joseph continued, "I wear no uniform, but I'm attempting to keep five hundred slaves from starving, a responsibility, I daresay, your army doesn't wish to undertake. My choices were to join the Confederacy—a cause, incidentally with which I was not in agreement—and lose everything I had, including the very roof over the heads of my wife and children in Tennessee, or I could sign the pledge and lie under oath for another cause with which I do not agree."

Joseph continued solemnly, "Captain, I'm not a secessionist. I was a colonel in the Mexican War. My father was a colonel in the War of 1812 under Jackson's command. My great grandfathers not only fought in the Revolutionary War but the one on my mother's side signed the Declaration of Independence. Therefore, I hardly come from a line of people who are traitors or deserters.

"You must admit that my plantation has been more than just a small service to you, and when you imprison me, or put me before the firing squad, on whose conscience will the starving Negroes be? I need not tell you what has happened to them all up and down the Mississippi whose owners have gone to war or been imprisoned or left the state. You know all too well. They've poured into New Orleans and Baton Rouge by the hundreds. There's no place to shelter them, and there's no extra food for their stomachs. I'm doing your military a great service just being here to see that a plantation gets worked."

Powers was taken aback, not expecting Joseph's ready admission to being a fugitive from Nashville. Nevertheless, his duty was to arrest him. "You talk a good story, Mr. Acklen, but of course you're a lawyer, I understand. Right now, it's imperative that you come with us. Perhaps when you tell your tale to the Admiral, you can be pardoned."

Joseph asked Nattie to get him a dry coat and hat and his rain slicker. The horses were brought up to the hitching area at the rear, and Joseph Acklen left Bellevue amidst a driving rain under arrest.

CHAPTER 62

FOR THE MONTH OF AUGUST, AND NOW SEPTEMBER, THE Confederates continued to use the West Feliciana plantations as a storage depot for receiving cattle and supplies, well aware that Joseph risked his life for them. However, Confederate General Taylor still kept Bellevue, Angola, Killarney and Loch Lomond under surveillance from strategic points in the surrounding Tunica hills. Reports of Yankee visitors had aroused his suspicion, along with numerous details that Joseph was somehow befriending the enemy.

Only moments after Joseph had left with Powers, four Confederate officers rode up to the rear door of Bellevue. Nattie, quickly noting their lack of interest in Joseph's welfare, pretended hysteria, shouting that the Yankees had just come and taken her master away.

"I tell you, I don't know where they take him!" she cried as the four stood dripping in the kitchen. "It was two of em, mean-looking, no it was three, and they took him away. They did, they did. They took my master!"

She wailed so, that the officer nearest her grabbed her by the shoulders and shook her. "I want some sense out of you!" the man shouted. "Now you straighten up and tell me where he's gone."

"Like I say, two come early this morning, then go away. About dinner time two more come. I say Mr. Acklen be back in a minute and sure enough he come back in a minute. And I pour 'em all coffee, and they say they get right to the point. They say he a traitor and fugitive from Nashville, cause he don't sign the pledge, and he admit to everything, and they say he a good talker but they gonna take him anyway. They talk about a ship and a Admiral who not too far away, and they say he can tell him the same story and maybe the Admiral let him go. That's what I know. It just happen, and if it not raining you could see the tracks. I don't know nothing more."

They stayed for coffee, standing by the kitchen fireplace, attempting to dry, while having Nattie repeat her story. They were surprised to learn Admiral Porter had moved the *U.S.S. Brooklyn* out of its cozy spot near Vicksburg and was in nearby waters. He was the only Admiral she could mean, the men counseled, because Farragut was in New Orleans, and to their knowledge there were no others in the Delta.

The Confederate soldiers took leave of Nattie and Bellevue, but not before informing her that they had come for the same reason: to arrest Joseph Acklen for aiding the enemy.

Aboard the *U.S.S. Brooklyn*, Joseph learned, among other things, one choice bit of information that made the puzzle clearer; Thompson was, in all probability, the same enlisted man who had come with an officer, to arrest him that night in Nashville, the one who called himself Samuels, the one Joseph would like to have shot for the remarks he made about the ladies in his home. It fit perfectly: arrogant, ignorant, and tricked to sit at a king's feast, the ginger-haired man had become intoxicated, then dishonorably discharged. Two years later, that same man had shown up for work on a neighboring plantation in Louisiana, either by coincidence or design. Thompson had been spying on his boss as well as Joseph and had been eager to betray both to the Yankees.

"Yes, sir. I knew him in Nashville by another name, or believe it to be the same man, "Joseph told Admiral Porter. "And Admiral, if you'll forgive me, he is not the sort of man whose word one may trust. I am surprised your Navy uses someone like Thompson as a spy and takes his word over that of a gentleman."

They were sitting in the Union Admiral's cabin, from which infrequent shots could be heard coming from the nearby countryside. Porter looked at Joseph for some time, taking long draws from his pipe. "Please continue," he said, finally.

"Sir, I have repeated everything to you, just as I told it to your captain. I did not order this war. I wanted no part of it in the beginning. I want no part of it now. I'm grateful you have allowed us to continue working, shipping, for all our benefits. In return, I've attempted to supply your Navy with fresh meats, staples and vegetables. I can no more be responsible for what might occur on some of my land than you can, sir. It's impossible to watch twelve thousand acres and miles of shoreline. I've given your Navy full permission to do so—I've even requested it—to stake men wherever and whenever they wish. I know of nothing more I could have done."

"Well said, Mr. Acklen. Your story never changes and your speech is as eloquent and persuasive as I've been told. I've reviewed every officer's report concerning you, beginning with Lieutenant Lowry, and find them flawless. However, I still don't trust you." Relighting his pipe as he made the last statement, his lips held a tight smile.

"My grandmother was from Mississippi, and at family gatherings, the story was often told how she wept the first two years after my grandfather took her to Indiana. And it wasn't until after he built her a house to the exact design and scale of the one in which she grew up, did the tears partially subside." Porter took a slight puff from his pipe. "When she and my grandfather traveled and she was asked where she was from, she would answer, 'I live in Indiana, but I'm from Mississippi.' Once a southerner always a southerner; my grandmother would have betrayed her country, but not her Mississippi. That's one of the reasons, Mr. Acklen, that I don't trust you."

Joseph responded with a slight smile, "I understand your grandmother, sir."

"I don't trust you, Mr. Acklen, but I like you. And I wasn't expecting to."

"If I may take the liberty, sir, my sentiments are the same. I suppose this proves that we should never judge a man before we get to know him."

"When this war is over," Admiral Porter said, "perhaps we shall meet again."

"I extend the invitation for you and your family to be guests of Mrs. Acklen and me at Belle Monte."

Porter glanced out the porthole with a faraway look. "We'll all be glad when it's over."

Admiral Porter stood and then Joseph, "You understand that I must validate everything that's been said today." Joseph nodded. "I shall look forward with a great deal of pleasure to seeing you back here aboard ship day after tomorrow."

As the two men shook hands, Joseph said, "Thank you for the trust you've placed in me and for your gracious consideration."

"Day after tomorrow," repeated the admiral.

"Day after tomorrow," Joseph echoed.

He was dismissed to become a prisoner on his own land. He could receive no visitors until he spoke again with Admiral Porter and neither he nor his Negroes could leave their respective plantations. He had given his word that he would abide by the standards they had set, and that he would continue to inform them of any Confederate movements along the river.

An ensign escorted him to a small boat that took him to where his stallion waited by the river's bank in a shed near Cresmon.

The rain beat harder and heavier as it continued to pour from the skies in great gushes that made travel difficult. But Joseph knew the area well, and was able to maneuver his way to the familiar Tunica Road that partially followed the Mississippi a mile or more back from its banks. He was an hour from Bellevue at most, and if he could continue at his present clip, he thought he should be home by suppertime, despite the weather. A warm bath, dry clothes and a rub-down in lineament seemed a heavenly welcome, and to have his horse dried and stabled. He and Adelicia would have a life time of stories to share with each other, with their children and grandchildren. Having her in his arms seemed so near to him, on the one hand, yet so far away on the other.

It would be a good night to rest by the fire, he thought, perhaps removing the chilling dampness, from within and without. The limbs of the trees overhanging the high, muddy cliffs on either side of him made a partial shelter; weighted heavily with rain, they sometimes brushed his shoulders as he rode beneath them down the steep elevations enroute to the levee, and home.

CHAPTER 63

Jim Clack and Strap Kelly had been on plantation business in St. Francisville the better part of the day, and were grateful to be no more than three quarters of an hour from Bellevue. They had just passed Greenwood, Ruffin Barrow's place, the familiar marker for "almost there."

The leather-hooded buggy was not enough to protect them from the torrential rain seemingly washing the road from beneath them. Travel was made even slower, as they tried avoiding well-worn ruts to keep from miring into the thick yellow-clay. The lanterns on either side provided only enough light to steer the horse clear of the gulleys, but as Kelly veered slightly to the right, Clack suddenly called, "Hold up, Strap. That looks like a horse."

"Any horse out in this mess deserves to be left out. You're seeing things."

"Hold up, I tell you."

Strapp Kelly stopped the buggy at Jim's insistence all the while praying it would not mire down. Barely visible in the rainy darkness, yet standing not four feet away was a horse that appeared as dark as the night. "For God's sake!" Clack muttered.

"What is it, Jim?" Before Strapp had finished his question, Jim was out of the buggy and bending over something in the ditch.

"Quick, bring me the lantern! It's Joe Acklen!"

Without further words, the two men lifted him into the buggy, hitched the stallion to the back, and signaled the sorrel mare to continue her journey home.

Lucy had prepared the dinner that evening with Nattie's assistance, as Alfred had convinced her that staying busy was a far better remedy for the calming of her nerves.

Joseph's arrest by the Yankees had not set her aback, as Alfred had feared, but there had been no news since he was taken, and all were on edge. When they heard approaching horses outside, they hoped their prayers were answered, that the Yankees had set him free.

When the door opened, Clack and Kelly were holding Joseph in their arms. "Oh, Jesus, the Yankees has killed him," Lucy shrieked. "They've killed him!"

"Hush, and get some hot water and warm blankets!" Kelly ordered.

They carried Joseph unconscious to his bedroom, where Nattie already waited with piles of blankets and quilts. They undressed him, drying as they went, replacing cold wet clothing with soft cotton underwear warmed by the fire. His breathing was labored, and after wrapping him in blankets, they made a steam tent over his head using a sheet and boiling water.

While Rufus went for the doctor, Alfred stoked the fire and put on more wood to relieve the large room of its dampness. Joseph was pale, his vital signs weak. Strap Kelly felt his pulse, glanced at Jim, then back to Joseph. "Not good," he whispered.

As the mantle clock was striking eleven, Rufus arrived with Dr. DuPree. And after a lengthy examination, he told them that Joseph had a bruise on the back of his head caused by the fall, and had developed pneumonia from having lain in the inclement weather. The doctor hesitantly added that because of the congestion in his chest, he could give them little hope except that Joseph's age and robust health were in his favor, and not to forget the fruition of sincere prayer. He instructed the servants to continue the steam throughout the night, and to awaken him if there were any changes. Then he asked Strap and Jim to join him down stairs in the kitchen.

Nattie poured hot coffee as old Dr. DuPree asked for every detail. Strapp and Jim related everything, precisely, and persisted that a man as healthy as Joseph could lie in chilling rain all day and not become unconscious with pneumonia. As they talked, the doctor was making sketches on the paper before him.

"Doc, are you listening?" Strap asked. He made no reply, and continued with the drawings.

Jim and Strapp looked at each other, before Jim Clack asked, "What's wrong with him?"

"Tell me once more how you found him, the position he was in...exactly." Again, they repeated the story, and again Jim asked, "What's wrong?"

The doctor was still sketching while they talked. He hesitated another minute or two, then spoke slowly.

"Joe Acklen was shot up close in the back of the head. He wasn't bleeding when you found him, the blood had already clotted. The only way we can remove the bullet is to get him up to Natchez, or better, Baton Rouge...if he makes it. I don't have the instruments nor, the ether or chloroform to do it here," he paused. "It's too deep. We'll see what morning brings, go back to where he fell and see if there's any signs to who did this...but that's highly doubtful," he added. "When Joe gets stronger in a day or two, we'll move him and get the best care possible in these times."

Jim Clack and Strap Kelly said nothing, but their expressions of disbelief and shock had mounted to anger. "Damn! Who could have done it?" Strapp asked.

"Anybody...anybody. That's the hell of it...I wouldn't know where to start looking." Jim replied.

The men concluded that Joseph could have lain in the ditch any-where from a half hour to five hours, depending on the length of Porter's inquiry. That riddle, they could solve in the morning when they would report to the Admiral, relating the episode and inquiring as to the time Joseph had left the *U.S.S. Brooklyn.*

They agreed that someone had to have been following Joseph, or waiting for him, knowing the route he would take home; but who-ever it was had known of Joseph's arrest. The person, or persons, had probably followed along the ridge of the cliff from the time he had mounted his horse, waiting for him in the right spot, the right mo-ment. He had been ambushed and left to die in the rain.

Dr. DuPree insisted the two men speak to no one about the wound—the servants, neighbors, no one. Only of his pneumonia, lying in the ditch for hours before being found, how he had bruised his head when he fell from the black stallion. A murder need not be reported: times were too perilous.

Strapp and Jim kept watch with the servants, doing what they could to make him comfortable, but not once did Joseph show any signs of consciousness as morning became visible, only as a slighter gray than the one before. For a second day, the downpour continued, unabated.

By midmorning, however, Joseph's breathing seemed easier, and he attempted to cough. But the hot chicken broth Lucy had prepared sat untouched on the bedside table. She had been unable to force him to take it when she put it to his lips. The kettles were still being exchanged, the steam still aiding his breathing. By two o'clock, Joseph seemed, for the first time, to fall into a peaceful sleep amid the pillows on which they had elevated his head and chest.

After Dr. DuPree felt Joseph's pulse once more, which he reported to be stronger, he told the servants he was going with Kelly and Clack to the spot where Joseph had fallen, then on to the ship.

Foreman Bard Young, who had returned that morning from nearby Clinton, was shocked, at first not believing the news about Joseph when Kelly had met him at the kitchen door. Young immediately ran up the stairs, even more startled at actually seeing Joseph, then told Alfred and Lucy that he would sit with him, suggesting that they and Nattie rest. That he and Nattie's betrothed, Basil, would keep watch.

Alfred came to the bed, lifted Joseph's hand, and held it in his own. "Dear Lord," he prayed, "he too good and too young to die and he got four little 'uns to care for. Please make him better. In Jesus name, Amen."

"Thank you, Alfred, I know he appreciates that," Bard said. "You get some sleep. Doc says he's breathing better now."

Alfred stood for another moment, then clenched the hand he was holding, with tears streaming from his tired puffed eyes.

"He breathing too better for this earth. He breathing in God's heaven now. He gone, Mr. Young," he said, sobbing. "He gone." As Alfred knelt beside the bed, Bard, and Basil knelt with him.

"Sometime the Lord have a different answer than us here wants, "Alfred said, with his bowed head resting against the featherbed.

An hour later, hundreds of Negroes were gathered about the house, rain dripping from their faces. And amid the sobbing and wailing could be heard the plaintive sounds of, "Jesus Lover of My Soul...let me to thy boom fly." They stood their vigil through the afternoon and evening, the solemn singing never ceasing.

Word spread quickly among the neighbors. And as they began arriving, Nattie recruited three additional servants to help her and her sister prepare for the visiting mourners, and hot cider was set out in large kettles for the Negroes.

The news of Joseph's death was carried to the *U.S.S. Brooklyn*, as well as to General Taylor's command. Admiral Farragut in New Orleans was also informed and a request was made to Admiral Porter that a telegram be sent immediately to Joseph's widow at Belle Monte. The request was granted, and the Admiral assured Jim Clack that if the communication wires had no interference, the message would arrive no later than the afternoon of the following day.

The rain ended sometime during the night, and Friday dawned with a bright September sun, drying the muddy puddles and wet earth.

Catherine Barclay and Susannah Sterling were the first to arrive that morning in order to receive those coming to pay their respects, while their husbands who had stayed the night, slept until time for the afternoon visitors. Joseph lay in the front parlor, the one to the right of the large entrance way, the one with the heavily and beautifully carved moldings of the egg and dart. His coffin had been crafted during the night from a single oak, by the skilled hands of artisan slaves. Around him, in tall urns stood freshly picked camellias, dahlias and autumn roses, each lending its own austere beauty and fragrance to the room.

On Joseph's death certificate, Dr. DuPree wrote: "Cause of death, pneumonia."

CHAPTER 64

September 1863

ESSIE HAD REFUSED TO TAKE PART IN ANY ASPECT OF ADELICIA'S proposed trips to Louisiana, repeating her position that they were 'safe and sound' at Belle Monte, even if the city were infested with foreigners, that Adelicia was to "stay put," and leave well enough alone. Adelicia, however, undaunted, by her mammy, had sought Sarah Polk's advice, who also strongly advised against travel, reminding her of the many battles raging in Tennessee and Mississippi,

Adelicia was well aware of the dangers that lay between home and Louisiana, as the military leaders spoke freely in her presence. Governor Johnson had told a gathering that very week about a mother and daughter traveling only from one farm to another, being caught in the line of fire and instantly killed. The *Nashville Whig* had reported a story about three children in Northern Mississippi who, venturing too far into the woods, were shot before either army realized they were not the enemy.

"No, Adelicia," Sarah had advised. "Your husband would much prefer you here with the children than on the road, leaving yourself prey to varmints of any sort, including the military. He will be home soon enough," she had comforted. "You stay here, safe and healthy, for when he does return."

Adelicia was thinking about Sarah's words as she hurriedly dressed this lovely September morning. The lady always persuaded her, in the simplest terms, to see the rational. Sarah was so reserved in her judgment that when she even bordered on adamancy, Adelicia complied. But she had dreamed of Joseph two nights before, and then again that morning. She missed him and would defy them all, regardless.

Her day was a busy one: luncheon at the Maxwell House, followed by tea at Polk Place and then the tatting circle she abhorred but always attended on Friday afternoons. She put on a burnt-orange bolero trimmed with black corded grosgrain around the cuffs and collar, and admired her striking frock as she peered into the heavily gilt-framed floor to ceiling mirror she and Joseph had purchased in London. She tied the black corded half-bonnet to the side of her chin and hurried down the stairs, knowing if she made her hospital visits, there would be no time for breakfast.

Rushing into the dining room just as Charlotte was pouring Pauline a cup of milk, she kissed each child on the forehead, promising to be home in time for an afternoon stroll in the woods.

Luke had the two-seater buggy waiting at the end of the brick walk, and she asked him to hurry so that she might have time to read to the soldiers before luncheon. The buggy and mare were the only transportation left at Belle Monte except for the old wagon their mule Blue had pulled for years. The perfect September day was chilly enough for a wrap in the early morning, but warm enough to remove it as the sun reached higher in the sky.

After an exhilarating yet tiring day, she returned home in time for the promised walk, and began removing her bonnet as Uncle Ben drove her through the last set of limestone columns. However, she was surprised to see buggies lining the circular drive at the front of Belle Monte, and three horses hitched to the nearby post.

"Goodness, Luke, I certainly do not remember having invited anyone for...That looks like Corrine's buggy," she said on closer observation, "And Sally's."

Adelicia walked into the entrance hall, laying her bonnet aside. The children were nowhere to be seen, but she was met by the solemn faces of friends and servants. Corrine took her hand and led her into the parlor. "Adie, darling, while you were out, a messenger came. I am so sorry."

Adelicia's fingers trembled as the yellow paper was placed in her hands.

"Joseph had an accident, darling, and became ill, and he..." Corrine could not continue.

Through the vision of blurred tears, Adelicia read the words, then put her hand to her mouth. She unsteadily sat on the sofa beside Francis Murdoch.

"I do not believe it! It cannot be true! Men die in battle. They do not fall off horses and die of pneumonia—not Joseph! Look at it, Corrine! It says he died of pneumonia."

"I know, darling, I know. It must have been a terrible accident." She had her arms around her sister, attempting to comfort her.

"Where are the children? Do they know?"

"Charlotte and Cora have them upstairs. Essie told them before you arrived."

"I dreamed about him only this morning, that he was here, that we were sitting beneath the large oak when it began to rain."

Tears dripped from her cheeks onto the bolero. It was the first time anyone in the room, except for her immediate family, had seen her weeping.

She appeared stunned as she stood, repeating, "It is a mistake, a major mistake!" She straightened the yellow paper and held it to her chest. "There are many mistakes in war. If you will excuse me," she said softly. "I shall go upstairs now. I should like to be alone."

Six weeks had passed since the news of Joseph's death reached Nashville, news so unexpected, so inconceivable to her, that Adelicia had had great difficulty accepting its reality.

For two years, she had seen the dying and the wounded, a scene as commonplace to her as to everyone else. Now Joseph's death was another wartime casualty, her husband another statistic.

Although she had known much of death—six children, Isaac, her father, friends, nieces and nephews—the struggle, the torment, was no less dreadful. Adelicia thought of the men dying on battlefields, in hospitals, on lonely farms miles from home. Countless others were feeling the intense pain and sadness that she was feeling now. How fortunate Joseph had died in the comfort of his own bed, attended by a physician.

The emptiness she was experiencing was more complex, she thought, than the loss of her husband. Perhaps she was feeling the pangs of all those who had passed whom she had loved, or the deaths on battlefields, or in hospitals waiting to die, for all the dying, for all the suffering. Perhaps a part of herself had also passed away the day they had told her, when she had gone to her room and lain in her bed and dug her nails into its softness, knowing Joseph would never lie there beside her again.

She had had the bed removed to Pauline's room, who delighted in having the handsome bed as her very own, the one into which she had crawled on many mornings and snuggled between her mama and papa. Adelicia had replaced it with one from a guest room, another with tall posts, but with carvings of tobacco leaves. She needed to go to West Feliciana, to see Joseph's grave, to see for herself where he was buried.

As she sat on the balcony overlooking the front lawn on this crisp, October morning, with her shawl and robe pulled closely about her, she felt the intense pain of memory, so intensely bittersweet and haunting.

She thought of the last time she had seen Joseph: on the run, smiling in the oversized hat. She would have no memories of how he looked in death as she had Isaac.

She selfishly thought it better to have never known love's beauty than to have it taken away. Some would not understand her feelings, she judged; they would not have experienced what she had known. Only once in one's life, she thought, did souls come together who truly felt part of another. She would keep her thoughts and memories to herself, perhaps she would share them with her children when they grew older, but most would be kept in her heart.

"Miss Adie?" Essie called softly, watching Adelicia in her now familiar pose of passivity. She came nearer and stood beside her chair. "Miss Adie, they a man downstairs to see you. He got news from Louisiana."

Adelicia raised her head absently. "What did you say?"

"A man with news from Louisiana."

"I am not dressed yet," she said with great effort. "Bring my mourning robe, please. I shall receive him in that."

Essie held the long black broadcloth robe, plain except for the petite tucks across the bodice, and she slowly put her arms into the full sleeves. She took much too long knotting the sash until Essie asked if she would like some help.

"Please go down without me. Say I shall be there shortly."

"Don't you want me to help you?"

"Essie, please do as I ask." Essie went to the door and lingered outside for a moment, uneasy about Adelicia's behavior since the news of Joseph's death.

Adelicia walked to the north balcony, the one opposite their sitting room where she had been resting when Essie called to her. She looked out on the fountains and the black crepe ribbons draped in scallops around the base of each. She saw the columns extending upward in front of her with their black ribbons tied with a bow in the center, and she knew that on the door below, there was a wreath of fresh white roses made up twice each week from the long-stemmed varieties in the greenhouse.

She hated the black, she hated the death that continued to hover over what was hers, what she loved. "Oh, grave where is thy victory? Oh, death where is thy sting?" she cried out.

The sting is to the living. Twice she had been widowed. At the age of twenty-nine when she was left with three small daughters, one an infant...all gone to dark death. And now at age forty-three, with four children between the ages of thirteen and almost three!

She was uncertain how long she had been standing there when she heard Essie call again.

"I am on my way," she answered irritably. News from Louisiana. She had heard nothing since the second telegram from Jim Clack, giving her the details of the burial. Clack reported that the Presbyterian minister from St. Francisville had come and given a graveside service, and how those present, Protestant and Catholic, had sung hymns around the open grave before...She had not wanted to hear about the shovels of earth falling onto his coffin.

Again, she told herself to stop as tears trickled down her cheeks. Joseph would not want her like this. She moved from the window and walked toward the door, dabbing her eyes with her handkerchief, attempting to regain her composure. News from Louisiana, she thought again. Now what can it be?

James Clack stood in the drawing room near the grand piano, his hands clenched behind him, peering out the large windows that overlooked the back lawn and its tiered gardens.

"Yes?" she questioned, upon entering the vast room. "What news is there from Louisiana?"

"Good morning, Mrs. Acklen," he said, turning and offering his hand.

"Mr. Clack, how nice to see you. Why have you made this trip and how on earth did you get here? Was it as difficult as they say?"

"One question at a time, please. It's no easy trip by horseback when there's not war going on. But what I have to say could not be said by letter, even if I could get one to you, so I had to chance it."

Adelicia gestured for him to sit opposite her as she took a chair on the far side of the tall windows.

"Mrs. Acklen, you've got thousands of bolls of cotton sitting there, ripe for picking. And without Mr. Acklen, there's no way—or in other words, we don't have the authority to do a thing with it, once picked. I don't want to see the Yankees get it and I don't want to see the Rebels burn it. And from the politicking in West Feliciana; either is possible. So I'm here to find out what to do. There's also bales not yet shipped."

The cotton! It had not occurred to her! It had been too early, of course, for Joseph to have completed the picking, trashing and baling. She was sure the lure of English gold reflected in her eyes as her mind sharpened to what Clack was saying. "You wish to know what I want to do with it? There is no choice if we do not want either army to have it. We must sell to the British," she quickly blurted out.

"I'm sure glad you see it that way, Mrs. Acklen. Of course, there's the small problem of getting it to the British. You can see why I couldn't write. And while I'm here, we need to make plans to your liking that can be carried out as soon as possible. Every day the ports are getting closer of closing to England and France, and every day's delay is one delay too many, one delay we can't afford. So we've got to act fast to see it through." He looked at her in silence for a moment. "Do you know how much they're paying for cotton right now? One dollar and eighty-nine cents per pound, twenty cents higher than last year. Rumors are it's going higher. There still may not be a way to move it out, but I figure it's worth a try, and as I said, I'm sure glad you think so, too!"

"Almost two dollars a pound! How many bales do we have? How many can we make? We could have a million dollars in gold!" She stood, clasping her hands, smiling—a dramatic departure from her grief-stricken widowhood moments before. She could think of little now, except the million dollars in gold waiting in white, soft fluff.

"I've got to head back tonight," said Clack. "Let's make a plan we agree on, one we think will work. I can tell you what's happened so far in West Feliciana."

"I want to go with you." It had not occurred to her—just as it had not occurred to her about Isaac's will until months later—that she would be left with nothing that was hers unless she fought for it. And that she would do...again. If she failed, her children, her household, would be left without means of any sort. Belle Monte would be worthless. The plantations would turn to seed. There would be no money for taxes. The gold already in her account in Liverpool would not go that far, nor last that long. Her dream, her security would come to its end.

Clack was stunned. "Mrs. Acklen, you can't go with me! It's dangerous enough for a man by himself, you can't imagine what it's like. Just trust me to carry it out the way Mr. Acklen would, the authority to do so. Five hundred miles of battlefield is not to be traveled by a lady like yourself—a woman of no kind. It ought not be traveled by a man either."

"We could pretend I was your wife, hitch up your horse to the old wagon. I must be there!" she exclaimed.

"I told you every day's delay is dangerous. I need to travel alone, and I don't want the responsibility of Mr. Acklen's widow. It's a real war out there! If I can get back the way I came, I can be there in ten days or so and begin on whatever we agree."

She slowly exhaled, thinking he saw it as surrender. "It is treacherous, I know, Mr. Clack. I suppose I should stay within these safe walls," she said, gesturing halfheartedly. "Let us have luncheon and discuss how to ship hundreds of bales of cotton to England."

The sun was full in the sky when Adelicia awakened the following morning. She and Clack had talked through the afternoon, over supper, and into late evening discussing the proposed operation to the last detail. Two thousand bales of cotton would be moved from the plantations via the Mississippi to the Gulf, past the enemy…and put aboard a ship to England to the open sea.

He had partially described the dangerous operations in which Joseph had been engaged, and she had discussed no further, her participation, or the idea of accompanying him. It was true, they could not afford a delay. Each day, each hour was a determinate as to whether or not the cotton was shipped at all. Jim Clack had been persuaded to stay the night, but as Essie noted, he was well on his way before sun up. She hoped and prayed he would have no difficulty reaching Bellevue.

A million dollars in gold! The thought of having so much money and knowing what it would procure, or influence in what remained of '63, and thoughts of '64, was only excelled by knowing its potential after the war, to insure what was rightfully hers and her children's. In contrast with those who would be penniless after the war, she would have one million dollars or more in gold, in addition to her other holdings, which could be worth nothing, or have great value.

This time, her husband's will and testament, she knew backward and forward. All belonged to her and her children…she had complete control.

If she were in West Feliciana, Adelicia thought, feeling much like her old self again, her presence was insurance for success. What man could ask favors like a woman, or play a woman's game?

She would convince Uncle Ben to hitch up Old Blue—a mule that surely no Yankee would want to steal—to the weathered wagon; she would make it happen. She would wear black broad cloth, no jewelry except for her gold wedding band. She would travel lightly, some blankets and quilts and only necessary changes of under clothing.

The idea of traveling with Uncle Ben for over five hundred miles in an open wagon, directly through enemy lines, did not frighten her at all. Taking Bud was out of the question, although she was certain he would put up quite a resistance. He and the other children would be safe with the servants within the walls of Belle Monte.

Three days of mulling over her venture into the world of deception was ended. Pleased, she rose from the chair at her sitting room desk and went to find Uncle Ben and work her charms on the old dear.

It was a formidable task. "No'm, no'm, I ain't about to take Mr. Oliver's daughter, floundering through the Yankees and dodging bullets. It ain't ladylike, Miss Adie, you can't go traveling in no wagon with a old mule to pull you, who can hardly stand up by hisself. I ain't, gonna, that's all. No'm!"

"I suppose if you will not drive me, then I shall have to drive myself," Adelicia said, pulling up one of the pruning stools to sit beside him in the storage barn. "It should not be that difficult," she went-on, matter-of-factly.

"Do Essie know what you planning?" Uncle Ben asked, weakening.

She stood up with her arms folded and the shawl wrapped around her, leaning against the corn crib. "Of course Essie knows," she lied. "It is she who suggested you drive me, after I said that I would drive myself."

Ben looked at her, fumbling with the dried corn, picking at its grains, not shelling it into the bin as he normally would. "Miss Adie, you could slap me for this...but Miss Adie, I just don't believes you."

Her charm was not working this morning, and it irritated her that the old man could see through her scheme. If she could not lie better than that, she would never convince the Yankees of anything, she thought. Her face was scarlet, but after a deep breath, her eyes softened. She looked at Uncle Ben and spoke gently, but firmly. "Uncle Ben, have that nag hitched to the wagon by four o'clock this afternoon." She turned back to him and said, "By-the-way, you have never been slapped by anyone at Belle Monte, ever! Perhaps Essie?" It would be dusk by four, and if she were lucky, she would be beyond Franklin long before stopping for the night, she thought, maybe to Spring Hill.

She walked briskly back to the house through fluttering October leaves, kicking the dried ones out of her path. She would do it alone—no one was going to stop her—not Uncle Ben, not Essie. She would be gone long before anyone besides her children had word of it, including the Yankees. Adelicia's quest, one that she must fulfill, would be explained to Essie after the fact.

She ordered tea and sandwiches sent to her room, busily and secretly preparing for her journey. Within an hour's time, her belongings were together, nicely bundled, unpretentious, black broad cloth dresses, wool blankets, thick cotton quilts, necessary changes of underclothing…and Joseph's revolver.

As she sat to eat in her favorite chair overlooking the south lawn, Essie announced that Sally Carter was downstairs. Although she was in no mood to listen to Sally's endless prattle, she asked Essie to have her come up.

"Adie, dahling." Sally bent over and lightly kissed her on the brow. "How dreadful to be wearing black on such a glorious October day. I know you can't help it and all, but it does seem such a shame. Whatever is that ghastly bundle?" she asked, glancing at the homely package on the bed.

"That dear, is my wardrobe. I am taking a trip."

"Don't keep me in suspense. You're not taking a trip with that, for sure."

"Do not untie it," she said standing to prevent Sally from touching the parcel she had so carefully wrapped. "I am going to West Feliciana…" Adelicia stopped, abruptly. "Sally! Go with me!" That is the answer, she said to herself. "Oh, Sally do!"

"Go where?" Sally asked, looking confused and puzzled before a bit of light shown in her eyes. "Are you really going to Louisiana?" she asked, with interest.

"I am going to the plantations and ship out three, perhaps, four thousand bales of cotton before the Yankees or the Rebels get it. Sally, say you will come with me. Then the Yankees will have two gorgeous, charming women with whom to contend instead of one. Sal, I must do this. Say, yes! I do not expect you to make the journey without compensation. I shall pay you!"

"I don't really expect that," she said, nibbling on a delicate tart filled with chicken salad. Then looking up from where she sat, she carefully asked, "You will take care of all the expenses?"

"Of course. Plus more." Adelicia thought quickly, bribery coming to her mind. "Shall we say five thousand dollars, payable upon our return to Nashville?"

"That's mighty generous, honey. I would love to be of help to you. If you really need me. But it sounds dreadfully dangerous…sneaking across enemy lines, meeting goodness—knows—who. But I suppose so," she drawled.

"There is no time for you to return home. You must send word by one of the servants."

Sally had not moved from her chair, continuing to fill her mouth with delectable morsels.

"Dear me, can I not even kiss my children goodbye? What about them?"

"Sally, let them stay here at Belle Monte! Jusie and Ina can come too, of course," she assured her. "And the tutor. All are welcome. There is room, and everyone will obviously be well fed." Adelicia's tension mounted. "Our children will be company for each other, and the servants will have their friends here as well."

She removed pen and paper from her writing table and handed them to her cousin along with a lap desk. "We should be away no longer than six weeks at most and everyone will be safe at Belle Monte. But hurry! Write! I shall find more widow's clothing and blankets. We must leave no later than four. Two ladies traveling in the late afternoon should not be suspect."

CHAPTER 65

ADELICIA CHANGED HER MIND NOW THAT SALLY WAS ACCOMPA-nying her and would inform Essie of her plans. She announced it in such a way that Essie knew arguing or threatening would accomplish nothing but wasted breath. With a look of disparagement, Essie went to the kitchen, instructing Liza and Mattie to prepare food for the journey and ordering a reluctant Uncle Ben to drive the two women.

"You don't care if this old nigger gets kilt. Well, I cares, and I ain't gonna be sponsible for Mr. Oliver's daughter, nor no other daughter getting catched by the Yankees. I thinks I wants to get liberated. That's what I wants. I's tired of people telling me what to do!"

"If you was liberated, you'd still have to do as I say," said Essie, "and I say you drive them two girls to Louisiana."

Ben insisted that he was going nowhere; he would hitch up the mule but that was all. Essie told him to have the wagon and himself ready by four o'clock.

"Essie," Adelicia said, "I must talk with you. Alone. You must know why."

"Why what?" Essie asked, looking away.

Essie followed Adelicia into the library and closed the door. "Why I am doing this. I did not know until Mr. Clack came that Joseph had been unable to get all the cotton to market, that other things were left unfinished Our welfare depends on it."

"I thought we rich enough," Essie said, picking up a Bible from the table, then putting it down again.

"It will not last that long, what we have. There are many to support, many mouths to feed. Getting this crop out gives assurance on a future where lack of money will not be of consequence, where we shall have plenty for ourselves and plenty to share. I cannot be caught again without my own means. I must go to Louisiana. Please understand, Essie—before I wanted to go to see Joseph, now it is of necessity for all concerned. I cannot, will not, lose what we have."

Tears welled in Essie's squinted eyes, "God'll take care of you. He will. Essie will be here when you gets back." She reached for Adelicia's hand, and held it to her breast. "You take care of you. I take care of the childrens and everybody else."

"Thank you, dearest Essie. Thank you," she said hugging her mammy.

Clouds had gathered since noon, and it appeared much later than half past three when Adelicia sat with her children in the upstairs nursery to tell them good-bye. She hugged and kissed the younger ones, and received an especially warm embrace from Bud, whom she had convinced was the man in charge at Belle Monte. She gave each child specific instructions and promised she would see them long before Christmas.

After Joseph's departure in March of '62, the children had missed him, each day looking forward to his return, especially that December. He would now not be returning this year, nor any year thereafter, making it even more important that she hurry to Louisiana, see to the business at hand and rush back home to her children for the holidays.

She loved them to a fault; no one could deny her that. They were growing up far more quickly than she wished. Bud was thirteen, and little Pauline almost four, the same age as Emma when Adelicia and she had left Fairvue Plantation and made their trip down river to New Orleans. How quickly time passes, she thought, as she carefully examined each cherub face.

She gently squeezed Pauline one last time, then motioned for Charlotte to come and take them to their baths before supper. She blew another kiss from the nursery doorway and hurried down the stairs, as tears dripped onto the bodice of her dress.

It was almost four o'clock when she and Sally, both dressed in widow's black beneath dark hooded capes, dropped their humble bundles into the back of the wagon. Blue's rein was securely fastened to the iron hitching bar near the front walk, and even a blanket was fastened and draped over his back. Uncle Ben was nowhere to be found.

The sky was dusky and the air brisk when Adelicia closed the front door behind her and she and Sally climbed onto the wagon seat. She took the reins and lifted Old Blue's head. The stout mule had been used to help clear the land when Belle Monte was built fourteen years before, and Adelicia had no idea how old he was then. After they reached their destination, she vowed to let him live out his days in peace, to graze on green pastures.

She leaned over and hugged Essie for a second time. "I know you will take care of everything and everyone, as you always have," Adelicia said teary voiced, "and we shall be back before you know it. Do not forget to send the note to Cousin Sally's." Essie nodded, wiping her eyes on her blue checked apron, with one arm around Bud, who stood as staunchly as a soldier.

Uncle Ben had still not shone his face as Adelicia clicked her tongue and tugged lightly on the reins to commence Blue's moving. Slowly, he took a few steps forward and they headed down the winding drive that led to the Hillsboro Pike. Uncle Ben had meant what he said.

Adelicia looked back at the towering mansion and at Essie still standing, waving, until she rounded the bend and could see nothing more than black ribbons fluttering atop Iambic columns.

"What's wrong, lammy?" asked Sally.

Adelicia did not answer, but continued looking back until the turns and foliage rendered it impossible for her to see anymore of Belle Monte.

Sally put her arm around her shoulders, "Oh, honey lamb, we don't have to go. We can turn this old mule around this minute."

Adelicia sniffed and looked straight ahead, biting her lower lip. I shall be back home soon, she repeated to herself, I shall be back to Belle Monte and my children. All will be well. The old spirit, the vitality, the faith, that had sustained her through years of past trials would sustain her now. She sniffed again and gave Blue a single tap with the crop.

"All is well, Sally. Nothing under high heaven could keep me from making this trip. I am doing what must be done," she said thoughtfully. She could not afford to be careless.

Part III

Adelicia Hayes Franklin Acklen
and Sally Carter Leave for
West Feliciana Parish, Louisiana

1863–1864

Civil War

CHAPTER 66

As they headed south on Hillsboro Pike and turned onto a narrow lane leading to the Natchez Trace, the heavy skies became darker and Adelicia prayed no rain would come before reaching a familiar farm or plantation, safe from prying Yankee' eyes and safe from the promising torrent.

But on the far side of Franklin, a steady sprinkle began, one that she tried ignoring until the drops wet her face, blinding her view so badly she had to depend on Blue's instincts to guide her on the familiar path. They had not yet been delayed nor questioned, and Adelicia breathed a sigh of relief when she stopped beneath a large elm to tuck her cape more closely around her and up over her black bonnet.

"Adie, do you think we can trade Old Blue for a faster nag?" Sally looked at the carriage clock concealed in a large pocket beneath the apron of her dress. "In two hours, we've traveled almost no where, honey. Why Robert could be farther than this in half an hour with any number of our horses."

"It is wartime," Adelicia snapped, nudging Blue with the crop to start him moving again. "If we had one of your horses, we would not have made it three steps from the gates of Belle Monte. Please say nothing else so inane."

Sally opened her mouth, aghast, deciding to utter nothing further about trading Blue, or anything further that could remotely be interpreted as discomfort. It must be Adie's time of the month, she thought, and loosened her shawl, holding it further out over her face to keep water from soaking into the bodice of her dress. She had on enough crinolines and petticoats to prevent her from feeling the rain that would surely penetrate her pantalets, but not so much was between the upper part of her torso and the torrent from above.

Blue's reins were loose, and Adelicia tapped him with the crop in rhythm to every slow trot he made. Her hands already ached beneath her doeskin gloves and she wished for a pair of the Negroes' heavy, working ones. She felt the water trickle between her breast and soak into the percale bodice beneath; she also felt the heavy silence as the rain steadily grew stronger. Her hasty choice of inviting Sally may not have been so good an idea, she thought. It had happened so quickly. She doubted Sally would have come at all had it not been for the five-thousand dollars she had guaranteed her.

Although it was storm dark and the lantern gave only enough light to see the road on either side of Blue's wide behind and she was soaked to the skin, Adelicia was thankful for no lightning, only a low thunder rolling up from the Harpeth Hills that now lay behind them. She had long passed the Perkins' place, and thought Jonas Tyree's could not be much farther.

However, the sudden barking of dogs startled both women to rigidness. "Do you think they are Yankee dogs or Rebel dogs?" Adelicia asked, speaking for the first time since her retort to Sally. She was afraid, and supposed Sally to be terrified.

"Are you going to stop and see or keep going?" Sally whispered.

"The barking seems not to be getting closer, but Blue's ears are at attention." she said, just as distant streaks of lightning lit up the southern sky. "We must be near the Tyree Place, but I have seen nothing that looked like the turn off."

"We passed the Spring Hill Road some time ago, lammy. Jonas lives nearer town."

Adelicia wished she could bring the drenched mule to a halt again and slap Sally, but her common sense reminded her that this time he might not start up at all. Thus she slowed him to his natural gait and turned to Sally, furious. "Jonas does live near town! Why did you not tell me you had seen the turn off to Spring Hill? That is what I have been looking for!"

"Darlin, how was I to know you were looking for it? We're miles this side of Jonas's farm, but Montview should be coming up anytime now. I wonder if the Yankees are there?" Then Sally added, "I thought you knew this area 'like the back of your hand.'"

Adelicia had not thought of Montview. And it was true that Yankees could be anywhere. She was surprised they had not seen even one thus far. Must be too bad a night for Yankees to be about, she thought sarcastically. Later, she would remind Sally of her smart aleck remark.

"I think this is the bridge," Sally blurted out. "The turn off is just the other side." Blue clomped across the wooden planks of the short bridge span, and there stood Mount View peeking through two whitewashed gate posts in the rain filled darkness.

"I hope the Carrolls, or a friendly someone is here," Adelicia whispered, looking about her.

All was quiet. Barking dogs could no longer be heard; the thunder had ceased. It was utter stillness but for the rain dropping on and around them. Drawing nearer, they could see a low lamp light in the front parlor, but nothing more. And just as they were approximately ten feet from where a servant would ordinarily have greeted them, taking the mule and wagon, the light went out. As Adelicia slowly pulled up the break, she felt the pounding of her heart. "We have no choice," she whispered, "We need shelter, for Ole Blue, too." She took Sally's hand and gave it a squeeze.

This would be the first performance of their concocted story, part truth and part fiction. She hoped it would not be their last. Adelicia motioned for Blue to start again, but as feared, he refused to budge. She and Sally climbed down, taking him by the harness, tugging and pulling, before finally hitching him beneath a nearby tree.

Soaked and shivering from the damp cold, they waded through slush and mud to the front steps and cautiously moved across the wide front porch. Sally began to turn the chime, but withdrew her hand and looked at Adelicia. Standing still for a moment, she then knocked. There was no response; and she knocked again with more force, but again without response. Adelicia put her hand to the knob but it was securely locked and bolted. "All right, Sally," she whispered, It is time."

"Please help us," Sally cried, "We're lost, my sister and I. We're on our way from Clarksville to Columbia where our dear mother has passed. We're sopping wet. Please let us come inside." They heard footsteps—the unbolting of the door—and finally the turning of the lock, and there stood Amy Carroll Howard. "Amy," they cried in unison to their startled friend. "It's Adelicia Acklen and Sally Carter."

The Carroll's one remaining servant brought their water drenched packs from the wagon, took Blue to the barn, then started a fire for them in the guest room. It was large, with two double poster beds on either side of a deep green Aubusson rug that had a stout octagonal table in the center. The handsome, comfortable farmhouse and Amy Carroll seemed like gifts from Heaven.

They were grateful for the fire, the house, the bed and their friend. The Carroll men and Amy's husband were away fighting with the Confederates, Amy told them, leaving Mrs. Carroll and her elderly father, Grandpa Ewell, Amy and her young daughter to fend for themselves.

After towel-drying their hair by the fire and hanging their wet clothing about the room, Adelicia and Sally snuggled into warm cotton gowns that Amy had brought before gathering around the hearth to sip hot soup.

When the excitement had waned and their tales of camouflage exchanged, the women bid each other goodnight. And at last, when Adelicia lay in the soft feather bed, she thought of her children, and concurrently, that she and Sally were only forty miles from home. It seemed eons since she had left Belle Monte, and yet it had just been that afternoon! Their long trek to Louisiana was just beginning! She turned over on her side, thanking God for their safe journey thus far, and fell into a deep slumber as the rain continued pelting on the tin roof.

The enthusiasm mounted with further explanation of Adelicia's scheme during the five o'clock breakfast. "I don't envy you, and yet I do," Amy said.

Poor Amy, Adelicia thought, the farthest she has ever been away from home is Nashville. "You are welcome to join us. The Yankees would most likely prefer the capture of three Confederate ladies instead of two," she laughed.

Grandpa Ewell did not find it amusing and warned Adelicia of the dangers that lay before them. However, he told her that he knew better than to waste his breath, but did advise them to take the main road instead of the Trace.

"We shall pray for sunny skies and starry nights, and for God to watch over you," Amy said.

Adelicia and Sally, feeling rested and refreshed, hugged their friends good-bye before climbing onto the wagon seat behind Blue, well fed and rested himself, his dry blanket folded beneath the buck-board. Nudging the mule with the crop, they set out on a beautifully crisp October morning.

Ignoring Grandpa's advice, Adelicia had followed the Harpeth River that wound with the Trace, intending to take it all the way to Natchez. They were making excellent time, having already bypassed Mt. Pleasant and Columbia to the west of them, when she turned onto a familiar road that veered to the west. She had come here with her father to ride in the spring and autumn hunts, and she hoped she could remember how to get to Minnow Branch, then take the Campbellsville Road leading southwest into Alabama, avoiding Pulaski all together. The Yankees had already hanged the young scout, Sam Davis, there.

What she did not tell Sally was that she had grown uneasy on the Trace, sensing someone was following them. This route was a short-cut and had more farms along its path.

They went over the first bridge, with its uneven wooden planks, some quite loose, others missing altogether. Adelicia remembered there were three such consecutive bridges before Campbellsville, as Big Creek twisted and turned.

The land, green, rolling and fertile, was as beautiful as any she had seen, and the sky could be no lovelier, not even in pictures, thought Adelicia. It caused her to remember Isaac and his love of a blue October sky. He had convinced her the sky was bluer this time of year than any other. Thinking of Isaac, she wished...she wished a lot, but she would not think of it right now. She would think of it when she was safe in West Feliciana.

"Is that the second bridge ahead?" Sally asked.

"Just one more after that, and we shall be to the Alabama line by nightfall." Jim Clack would never believe, she thought, that two middle-aged widows could make so good a time. After crossing the bridge, they saw the third in the distance. But nearer their approach, it was obvious that nothing was left of the bridge's center, only the iron strips and rails along its side. Adelicia brought Blue to a halt. The banks were low and the creek bed low. And further downstream, she could clearly see the gravel bottom and led Blue to the more shallow spot.

The crossing was smooth requiring only minor tugging to entice Blue through the water and up the sloping embankment, and with that accomplished, they unhitched him and sat resting in the soft grass watching him graze. The sun was warm enough that they removed their capes and shoes and hung their stockings on a nearby bush to dry. They stretched and lay on their backs on what seemed a thick, green carpet, eating fall apples and cheese. "If we can have more days like this one, we shall make our trip in banner time and one day tell our grandchildren how in the 'old days' we traveled five hundred miles by wagon in the middle of a war."

"As long as we are not captured and fed to the Yankees," Sally smiled. "I'm really glad that I can be of help to you, lamby. I really am."

"It is nice to have you." Adelicia replied. "I apologize for being snippy. Much depends on my getting to the plantations, my very welfare." She stretched again, and smiled, "Can you imagine the talk at home right now? I was too exhausted to give it much thought before we left. This is as ludicrous as something Camille and I would have done at sixteen. But," she quickly added in a subdued tone, "The stakes are now very high. And I am forty-six."

"Oh, Adie, we'll be the topic of conversation all over Nashville, at dinner, supper and hearth."

"We must always remember this moment, Sally," she said seriously. "That is what life is made up of you know, moments."

"We always wanted to be a part of ya'lls capers, but you wanted nothing to do with the little ones when you were sixteen and we were twelve."

"Is it not interesting," Adelicia responded wistfully, "how with the passing of years, ages seem to blend together and...?"

"Are you ladies picnicking today?"

Three soldiers in Yankee blue uniforms were standing at their bare feet as they lay in the grass. Startled, the women jumped up. Adelicia quickly recalled stories she had heard about southern women being overtaken by Yankee men. She also glanced over at Blue, grazing near them.

The tallest soldier spoke, "Where you headed?"

"We're on our way to Florence, Alabama,"Adelicia said, straightening her skirt, "to go to our mama's funeral. I'm Isabelle. This is my sister, Sadie, who's not real bright although you can't tell by looking. We've come from Clarksville. Sadie lives with me and my children; there was no one to bury our mama, so we've had to go the trip alone," she added pitiably.

The men looked at each other and then back at the ladies. "You're mighty brave to be traveling by yourselves even if it is to bury your mama, which I doubt, because we've watched you ever since you crossed the creek, and grieving daughters don't laugh and snicker and have a picnic when their mama's just died. But I don't see any harm in what you're doing, and I don't think you're spies so you can go on your way, but these hills and woods are crawling with our men and the next ones might not be so thoughtful."

Adelicia and Sally thanked them, and as soon as they were sure the Yankees were out of sight, they put on their stockings and shoes, hitched up Blue and made him trot. "Adie, they saw us remove our stockings! They said they had been watching us!"

"It could have been much worse, my dear, cousin. Much worse."

Just before reaching the Alabama line, Yankee soldiers again appeared. The obese one grabbed Blue by the harness and began questioning them; Adelicia thought him a sergeant who wished to look good in the ranks as he waved his authoritative air, paying no attention to their story and giving orders to seize the wagon and Blue. They were marched into Pulaski by the three enlisted men and the sergeant, who was certain they had captured two female Confederate spies.

After walking for seemingly endless miles through woods, dirt and semi-graveled roads, Adelicia swore to herself that Sergeant Alex Bender would pay for every step she, Sally and Ole Blue were taking. She refused to answer his questions, deciding to take her chances with the officer in charge in Pulaski. There, she would also mention knowing Military Governor Andrew Johnson in Nashville.

After a two hour march, the last rays of the October sun were behind them when they finally arrived at headquarters on the west side of the town square. Adelicia was indignant as she and Sally were shoved before Colonel Everett Harwell and felt nothing but con-tempt and disdain for the man who had arrested her and for the men with him. During the march, she had concocted a story that Sally was accompanying her to see to the remains of her husband's body and to attend to the welfare of slaves and the plantations. Although Andrew Johnson had not given her leave of Nashville, and she had come this far without his knowledge, she thought he might sympathize with her now, if whoever heard her case in Pulaski did not. However, Johnson had denied her earlier request for safe travel soon after Joseph's death. She would take her chances.

The first words spoken were by Adelicia, standing in front of Harwell's desk. "I demand you send a messenger to Nashville to Governor Johnson. I demand it now!"

"Just what gives you the idea that Governor Johnson would answer your message?" the Colonel asked, somewhat jeering, and perhaps somewhat concerned.

She spoke eloquently, dismissing the country dialect she had spoken with Bender. "The Governor is an acquaintance, and I need not tell these enlisted men my story, nor you for that matter, but especially they."

The Colonel took the chewed cigar from his lips and laid it on a nearby marble topped table, confiscated from the Confederates, no doubt. "We'll see if you're bluffing. Bender, you and the men go back to your post. I'll handle this."

"You are allowing them to leave?" Adelicia protested. "I am under false military arrest. My wagon and mule have been confiscated, my few supplies taken, and you are letting them go?"

She appeared so irritated that Sally, who had remained silent, and who had stood, pretending to weep beside Adelicia, demanded, "You cannot let them leave! It's not fair, sir. These men have insulted us, refusing to accept our word, making us walk till our feet are ruined. I suppose everything we've heard about Yankee men is true," she said, sniffling more loudly.

Her silence had been welcomed by Adelicia, who was certain the Colonel was not much interested in "fair." Adelicia wished she would hush.

"My dear ladies," Harwell offered sarcastically. "I'm sorry you have been inconvenienced, but there is a war going on. Are you willing to admit that you are not traveling under the auspices which you told Sergeant Bender?"

"I am willing to admit that Mrs. Carter and I, Mrs. Joseph Acklen, are traveling to Louisiana to take care of business. I am well aware of the war, sir, because my beloved husband is one of its casualties. He died in Louisiana, and it is necessary that someone attend to our plantations there. The men in my family are either fighting, or serving in some other capacity. Would it please you to know, Colonel, that one of Mrs. Carter's brothers, Dr. John Freeman, is at this moment attending to your wounded and dying soldiers in Nashville?"

When Adelicia saw that an aide was recording every word, she spoke more forcibly. "I demand restitution for all our inconveniences. Further, I insist that a message be sent immediately to Governor Johnson so he may know our circumstances, the Governor who graciously gives my family protection at Belle Monte, who has shown great kindness to us throughout the occupation of Nashville, and who has dined in our home. I demand to be heard by him."

The Colonel picked up his cigar and began chewing again, turning his back to the women. Adelicia looked at Sally, calculating the minutes as they waited, glancing at each other, then peering out the window to the court house lawn across the street that crawled with Union soldiers and few civilians. When the Colonel at last turned around, he nodded to his aide. "Telegraph a message to Nashville. We'll wait for a reply."

Adelicia gave the aide a brief, but informative message imploring Governor Johnson to provide safe travel for Sally and her from Pulaski to their destination. The urgency, she had told him, was to see if any cotton were left on the plantation, to see to her Negroes, who were dependent on her, and to check on a foreman whom she did not trust and from whom she had not heard since her husband's death, and to return Joseph's body to Nashville. She also demanded the return of her mule and wagon, as well as food and supplies.

"Is my mule being fed and sheltered?" Adelicia asked before they were escorted across the street to Adkin's Inn.

"Yes. Your mule is stabled," Colonel Harwell answered, with his cigar clenched between his teeth.

At half past six, Sally, relaxing near the low fire in their room, removed her aching feet from a pan of water to answer the knock at the door. "Guaranteed safe travel to the Angola Plantations, in

Southwest Louisiana," Sally read, "the return of the mule and wagon, the night's lodging, provisions for the ladies' journey and an apology from a reluctant Sergeant Bender." Sally shrieked, "Marvelous!" She twirled onto the bed handing the message to Adelicia. "Guaranteed safe travel. We were magnificent, dahling! Magnificent!"

Adelicia wished Sally would speak faster for once. Even her "marvelous" came slowly and what she meant by "we," she had no idea. But what mattered was they had safe travel and a second night's lodging indoors.

Adelicia was pleased as she lay resting with her legs propped up on the tall footboard, hoping to reduce the swelling in her salved feet. Sally alternated hers between pans of cold and warm water. A late supper was sent to their rooms and after hurriedly eating, they retired with expectations of resuming their journey at daybreak and hoping to make up for hours already lost.

However, simultaneous with the mantle clock striking eight, there was another knock at their door, bringing a message: Elam and Mary Abernathy were waiting in the hotel parlor to see Adelicia. "The Abernathys! How long it has been since I've seen them!" Adelicia said, slipping into her black dress, trying to forget her tired feet. "When I was small, they were at every hunt and chase, great friends of Papa's and Mother's. Do you remember them, Sally?"

"I was too young for those rides, but I've heard Father speak of them."

"Their daughter's name was Susan and had the same birthday as Camille. She was an only child and died of scarlet fever a few days past her thirteenth birthday—Papa said neither parent ever got over it. They own more land than anyone in Giles County. I shant be long, Sally."

"What are you going to say?"

"The same thing I told Andrew Johnson."

The meeting with the Abernathys in a quiet corner of the inn's lobby had been relaxed, enjoyable, informative. She learned the Federal troops had first come into Pulaski in the spring of '62, had withdrawn, then returned that very fall of '63, commanded by General Dodge, who had wreaked havoc on half the population, anyone who had not signed the pledge. Michael Carpenter had been arrested, his house burned, and his family put off their land. The James Hendrix place had also been burned, the two story log dwelling, the split rail fences, the smokehouse and barns, the blacksmith shop, his crops and orchards destroyed, even the still!

Mrs. Abernathy said the tale was the same throughout Giles County, and that many of the Negroes had also run away when Dodge had marched in that September. Some had joined the Union army, some just disappeared, some stayed. Their farm, she said, had been spared. Adelicia did not think it polite to ask why, and neither one had volunteered to give a reason.

Mr. Abernathy remembered when Adelicia was only "this high," he had said, measuring with his hand, how she had sat on his knee, and how lovely she had grown to be when she had ridden in the hunts with Susan.

Fond times remembered laced with sadness, Adelicia thought; life was like that. Mary Abernathy recalled visits to Rokeby and the Hayes' visits to Angus Place, mentioning the children playing and riding together. She inquired about the welfare of Adelicia's family and friends, how the war had affected them. Adelicia's mission remained a secret.

"They are such dear, sweet people," Adelicia remarked to Sally when she returned to their room. "The death of a child is never forgotten. I had Emma until she was eleven; it has been ten years now, but I sometimes still hear her calling my name. And my other precious little ones…how I miss them. They miss their Susan very much." Adelicia paused and turned towards the window, biting her lower lip. "No more of this talk. We have a day's journey tomorrow, and we must be ready for it."

Adelicia found the visit endearing…She would remember to call on them when the war was over. How ironic that a shopkeeper on the square had heard about two women's travail and had told Elam Abernathy who, coincidentally, had come into the store.

Sally was sleeping comfortably when Adelicia climbed out of her bed and went to sit before the fire and stir it with the poker. How much time had passed she thought, how much had passed since the days of sitting on Elam Abernathy's knee and riding in Giles County hunts with Susan and Camille. She recalled visits to the Abernathys with her parents, Camille, and the Perkins; walking over the farm without cares, no children's deaths, no husband's deaths, no wills, no traveling with a cousin and a mule in the midst of a war. Adelicia stared into the fire, envisioning carefree images of her childhood, images reflecting into the shadows on the walls, feeling their warmth.

She thought of Isaac, admitting it was she who had been mostly at fault for the tension in their marriage. Perhaps it could have been different. Perhaps she could have been different. Had he not passed so quickly, so suddenly, perhaps, perhaps…Her large eyes did not move, nor blink as she continued gazing, thinking of Joseph's death of pneumonia. How unlikely that seemed.

It was only after Isaac's passing, after the will, after her marriage to Joseph, that she knew for certain it was her wealth and social position that made Belle Monte the most desired place to be invited for luncheon, for supper or a ball. Except for a small circle of friends, no one had quite forgiven her for her "un-lady-like" manner or her "greedy, self-serving sins." No matter the degree of generosity bestowed, she remained without absolution, and if she were to lose her fortune, the old biddies would think she got just what she deserved.

She moved forward, returning the poker back to its place and folded her arms across her chest, still gazing into the fire. Was it the past she wished returned because she was unhappy in the present? Was it a feeling she could voice? Why the self-examination spinning within her, fusing ideas, confusing, contradicting, controlling her thoughts? Perhaps it was the sudden shock of Joseph's death, perhaps not.

She stood, stretching her arms high over her head, her reflective mood passing almost as quickly as it had come. Leaving Belle Monte had been terrifying for her, but she behaved as if it were a lark, as if she were fearless…Sally would never know otherwise.

She climbed into bed, thinking that on the morrow her old spirit would revive, the intrepid spirit she felt briefly before leaving Belle Monte, the spirit she felt while munching apples in the grass, the spirit that never failed to sustain her, propel her onward. Her quest: to get to her plantations, ship her cotton and add gold to her account in Liverpool, to preserve what belonged to her and her children. She would not be careless again!

CHAPTER 67

ADELICIA HURRIEDLY ATE THE AMPLE BREAKFAST; AN OMELET oozing with rich goat's cheese, grits, milk gravy over hot biscuits, side bacon, preserves and coffee. Sally nibbled on a biscuit and sipped coffee. These Yankees were eating well, Adelicia thought, the food of the South stolen from the Rebels!

"I just cannot eat like you this early, honey," Sally said. "The chickens aren't even up yet. I bet we'll be out of town before the roosters even open their eyes." She yawned. "Did you sleep well? I slept sound as a log."

"All right." Adelicia replied. Sally need not know she had been in bed only a short while before rising.

"Where do you suppose we'll be tonight?"

The Colonel's aide came to the inn's dining area to tell them the mule and wagon were ready. Thanking him, they tucked their belongings safely inside the wagon bed, along with the scrumptious food the Abernathy's had delivered: fried chicken breasts with the wishbones fried separate, bread, cheese, fruit and country ham, plus a two gallon jug of cider wrapped in brown paper to keep it cool.

They thanked the aide who directed them back toward the Trace, but when they had gone no more than a mile, Adelicia stopped abruptly.

"Whatever is the matter, honey? Are we going the wrong way?"

"No, Sal. How silly of me, how could I forget? Andrew Johnson signed a document guaranteeing our safe travel! We shall travel due west to Memphis and take a steamer to Bayou Sara instead of driving Blue. What a diddle that I only thought of it just now!" she exclaimed.

"How far is Memphis?"

"No more than a hundred and fifty or sixty miles. Straight as an arrow. But West Feliciana is close to four hundred. What do you think, Sal?"

"A boat sounds mighty good, honey. If we can hand our orders to the men in blue, smile our sweetest and reach West Feliciana by river, I'll be ecstatic!"

"I promised Ole Blue green pastures for the rest of his days if he got us to our destination, and when we get to Memphis, I shall leave him with the Thornton's. They have a grand plantation, all cotton, near Colliersville, and a townhouse in the city. He is Joseph's uncle on his mother's side. Ole Blue can spend his days grazing." Dear God, she quickly thought, cotton! Remembering her own, she wondered if anything were left in Memphis, or if the Thornton's were still there?

"I'm all for the boat, dahling. Do we have to turn around?"

"We head out the Campbellsville Road, and continue west to Waynesboro, then on to Memphis!"

"I'll surely welcome that boat," Sally yawned, as Pulaski closed behind them. "It's another beautiful morning." The sun was rising over the low, surrounding hills as they watched the first rays reach out and touch the valleys before they turned West.

CHAPTER 68

BY NOON, ADELICIA AND SALLY WERE FIFTEEN MILES ON THE FAR side of Lawrenceburg and less than ten miles from Waynesboro when they stopped by a branch on Big Creek, watered Blue and let him graze while they walked and stretched. Sally bent down to rinse her hands in the cool stream and dabbed her face with water. "Cold spring water is excellent for the skin, keeps wrinkles and lines away," she said, strolling back to the wagon and unpacking their lunch. She handed Adelicia a cup of cider.

"Thank Thee, oh Lord, for this bountiful food, our safe journey and for our many blessings," Adelicia prayed. "In Jesus name, amen."

"This is scrumptious!" Sally exclaimed, eating a ham and biscuit, then looking about her, quickly added, "Adie, have you ever felt like someone is watching us? I've felt it all morning."

"Most likely, you have the jitters from yesterday," she said, unwilling to alarm Sally.

"I first felt it right after leaving Belle Monte, as if someone were following us. I'm dying to do the necessary, but just when I started to the stream a while ago, I felt as if someone were staring."

Adelicia laughed. "You have to go sometime. Rumor is, the Yankee ladies in Nashville think we are immune to such frailty. When we finish eating, I shall go with you and stand by with the pistol, armed to fire."

Although she spoke in jest, Joseph's forty-five caliber was well hidden and cocked beneath the wagon seat. Their Pulaski intruders had returned it, along with the bullets, and Sally's fears gave further alarm to her own suspicions. She had not sensed Yankee intruders, but something more eerie. She would not panic, but be watchful, and say nothing to frighten Sally the more.

"Make fun if you like, lammy, but my feelings are usually not wrong."

"Let's go to the stream."

Doing the necessary went without incident. They stretched again and mounted the wagon for Waynesboro, with hopes of reaching

Savannah by nightfall. But when they had gone no more than five miles, they heard distant gunfire. At first, the shots seemed to be in front of them, then almost instantly, as if they were surrounded. "This may be the excitement Essie and Grandpa Ewell warned us about. 'In the middle of gunfire and you both get killed.'"

"Let's keep going until we see something," said Sally, surprisingly, seeming more excited than fearful.

"What do you think we are doing? I had no plans to stop in the middle and wait on them." The closer to town, the louder the shots became.

And then they witnessed their first battle. To their right, in the hills and leas between, they were close enough to see firing guns, men running, scrambling, falling. It was unclear from the shouting if it were coming from the wounded, the dying, or the victors, whichever, Adelicia gave Blue a stiff whack with the crop. Whether he was afraid of the gunfire, frightened of the whip, or felt his and his passenger's distress, he trotted faster than Adelicia thought him capable.

Waynesboro smoldered from fires and gun blast; its dead lay in the streets amidst the wounded who had not yet been taken inside the shops or houses in front of which they had fallen. Searching through the smoke, Adelicia pushed her hair back from her face and hitched Blue to a post at the deserted blacksmith's. Sickened, she walked between corpses two doors down to the inn.

"Battle lasted three days," an elderly man told Sally. "Fought on all four sides of town, in town, too. Darn Yankees took us." The outcome recorded another fortress fallen to the North, Adelicia thought. Waynesboro also smoldered under military jurisdiction.

"I despise this," Adelicia said, standing with her back against the door they had just entered. "The devastation! Ruined, all ruined!"

"Let's leave, honey," Sally pled. "I can't stand it. I'm suffocating."

"Just as soon as I ask for information and get grain for Blue. Excuse me," she questioned the innkeeper, "how far is it to Savannah?" The man in worn overalls paid no attention, but continued ministering to a wounded soldier sprawled on the divan, looking as if he had been placed there with great speed and little care. The sofas and chairs in the modest lobby were filled. The floor was covered with the wounded and the dying, moaning, pleading amidst cries of agony.

Sally tapped the man on the shoulder. "Sir, will you please tell us how far it is to Savannah?"

He glanced up quickly, then down again. "Bout thirty mile, but it's worser there than here." Saying nothing more, he continued his ministry.

"Sir," she said, again tapping his shoulder, "what do you mean it's worse there?" He stood up and hurried toward the kitchen opposite them, as if he never heard the question.

Adelicia turned to Sally. "I can stand no more of this. We must leave."

"But what if it is worse?"

"We shall take our chances. We can waste no more time. Memphis is still a long way." Adelicia, putting one hand up to shield her eyes from the smoke and the dying, returned to the blacksmith's. After searching for a proprietor and finding no one, she took a half-filled sack of feed for Blue and left a half-dollar gold piece beside the anvil on the work bench.

There was no way to move at a faster pace. The roads were so rough with rocks, and the debris so thick from the vast devastation, the wagon wheels were in danger of breaking. Oddly enough, no bodies lay along the road, but in the fields to either side of them, awaiting burial, she supposed. That is where they must have fallen, Adelicia thought, perhaps in their own fields, the ones they had worked and plowed.

"We saw too much of this in Nashville," Adelicia said, more to herself than to Sally, "for too long, the dying in makeshift hospitals, seeing wounds heal grotesquely, the maimed putting on their uniforms, anxious to return to battle. It makes no sense. I want to live in a world where I shall never see men dying—or war," she said, suddenly angry. "I am sick...sick of it all," she cried out.

"I'm glad you don't feel guilty either about not staying to help," Sally drawled. "We have completed our duties."

"There is nothing we could have done in Waynesboro. I feel no guilt."

"How blessed it will be when it's over, really over and we can all be sane again. Do you think it will ever be like it was?"

"No. But a few smart ones on either side will still have money and have a good life, but 'used to be' will exist only in our memories, as memories go." Another mile was behind them when Adelicia said, "Not many things are ever the same, anyway."

The air was permeated by the acrid smell of battle, the skies were no longer clear, the countryside no longer calm and rich. Charred ground, felled trees and clods of earth filled once serene pastures. "Adie, what do you think about Savannah? If it's worse than Waynesboro, I don't want to stay here."

The fighting now lay behind them. A solitary gunshot cracked through the stillness from time to time, but nothing more. "I do not want to leave the main road," Adelicia said. "If we can get through Savannah, perhaps we can make it to Selmer by dark."

"Sounds fine to me, lammy. But with the road so bad, I don't see how we're going to get anywhere very quickly."

Even though they were moving slowly, they were still being jolted and jogged with every turn of the wheels. Adelicia's hands stung, even with the protection of laborer's gloves over her own; her shoulders ached from holding the reins; her breast ached from the jolting. Because Sally had confessed to never having driven a buggy, much less a wagon, she was relieved of taking the reins. However, she saw to the provisions, prepared their meals, cleaned up and put away. In truth, all duties except the driving were Sally's, and Adelicia felt no guilt.

CHAPTER 69

CONTRARY TO WHAT THEY HAD BEEN TOLD, AS THEY APPROACHED Savannah, the Tennessee River town did not appear nearly so devastated as Waynesboro, although Union soldiers in tattered blue filled the streets and square, along with their military horses, wagons and armory. Adelicia cautiously but confidently moved her wagon along the gutted road to Buckley's Inn and hitched Blue to the post, ignoring staring, inquiring eyes. This time, the keeper was behind the desk, but before they could ask for a night's lodging, they were quickly informed that all rooms were filled, and overfilled, four to a bed. No one in town could take them in. If they were not housing the Union Army, they were housing the wounded...of both sides.

With no further conversation, no further questions asked, Sally and Adelicia wearily walked outside, unhitched Blue and headed for Selmer, another eighteen miles.

A half-hour outside of town, they stopped to rest and let Blue graze on the sparse splotches of green grass. While Sally poured the cider, Adelicia stretched and lay back on the wagon seat to relieve her tired arms and shoulders. Glancing over at Sally, she noted a peculiar look on her face.

"Adie, I definitely feel someone is watching us. I'm really uncomfortable," she said, nervously slicing the cheese and bread.

"It is your imagination," Adelicia responded, eyes closed. "I am still savoring the last bite of the wishbone from morning, by far my favorite cut of any fowl or hoof. How much country ham do we have left?"

"Adie, sit up a minute, please. I'm serious. Someone is watching us. If I take the reins and let you eat, can we not get closer to town?"

Adelicia opened her eyes reading the concern on Sally's face, wondering if she, herself, were so tired that she was momentarily numb to an outside fear, not sensing present danger as keenly as did Sally. She also found no wisdom in causing her further distress. Adeicia's position was to behave prudently and to be watchful.

"All right, Blue, rest time is over," Adelicia said, climbing back into the wagon seat "We have to make it a few more miles before you can be unharnessed, old boy."

They had gone only a short distance when Blue stumbled on his left front leg and abruptly stopped, causing both cups of cider to spill on Sally. Adelicia climbed down to discover he had lost a shoe.

"What is it?" Sally drawled, not moving.

"He has thrown a shoe. Maybe picked up a stone. No wonder, with the roads as they are "

"Heavens to be! Honey, what will we do?"

"We have no choice but to walk alongside the wagon and hope for a place to stop."

"If I weren't so frightened, I wouldn't mind. I'm certain someone is watching us."

"Sally, I do wish you would stop talking about that. You are still frightened from Pulaski. Why would anyone be following us? What would they want? They know we are not spies."

"Adie, if I knew what they wanted, most likely, I wouldn't be afraid. On second thought," she added, "I might be more so. Regardless, it has nothing to do with Pulaski. I told you, I've felt it since shortly after leaving home."

"I admit to feeling uneasy, but we cannot allow fear to overcome us."

They walked down the pitted road, Adelicia leading Blue, and conversation diverting to novelties and trivia.

Adelicia's fears had grown since Savannah, and Sally's continuous chatter was having its effect on her. She felt the heavy burden of protecting them, and Blue's limp had slowed him to such a pace that by half past four, they were still miles from their destination.

"There is no way we can make it to Selmer before dark, Sal, and something has to be done for Blue's foot."

"Men are so necessary. I wish we had four each right now, one to take care of the mule, one to carry each of us and the other five for bodyguards. We've not seen a house since Savannah. We should have stayed."

"Where, Sally? We shall find a place," Adelicia declared confidently. "There is at least another half-hour of daylight."

At five-thirty's deep dusk, they spotted a cabin cradled between two low lying hills, smoke rising from a propped up stone chimney as its only sign of life. Adelicia and Sally tied Blue to one of the posts supporting the front porch roof. Limping, themselves, from blisters and aching feet, they stepped onto a large stone, where steps would have been, and onto the wooden front porch with its random, missing planks.

Sally tapped at the door, waiting for an answer. "Someone has to be here. Listen," she said, standing with her ear to the door. "I hear movement." She knocked again while Adelicia went to the window, glossed over with what she supposed to be years of accumulated grime.

"I cannot see anything, not even the fire," Adelicia said, straining to peek through.

"Shh, someone is coming."

They heard a wooden latch scrape against the door-lift and then a second one. Slowly, the door opened and an elderly lady, appearing to be in her late seventies, stood in its way, wearing a print flour-sack dress and shoes far too large for her small feet and frail body. Her gray hair fell softly in disarray and her steel blue eyes stared directly at them. Motioning with her crooked fingers, she said in a surprisingly genteel voice. "Come in."

Adelicia and Sally gratefully stepped inside to a room filled with the barest of necessities; a homemade wooden bed that was nothing more than four legs, braced by boards and nailed together. But it was fastidiously made up with stacks of quilts on top of a featherbed, all supported by a taut rope.

The wood fire was small, and a straw-bottomed rocking chair sat in front of it, still moving slowly, back and forth. On the mantle were items in contrast to the rest of the room, a fancy French clock, ticking away the minutes, and next to it, a bisque figurine. On the other side of the ornate clock was a Sevres' vase…obvious remnants from another time…another life. A cupboard in the corner held a mixed assortment of dishes and cups, and near it was a large wood-box filled with split logs, placed squarely behind a small unlit stove. "You're welcome to sit on the bed, there's only one chair."

Adelicia and Sally looked at each other and gratefully sank into the bed which was as soft as it had looked.

"You are very kind to invite us in," said Adelicia. "Our mule is lame and we have walked for two hours or more. Our feet are sore. We do not wish to be a bother, but may we rest here for a while?"

"It's not ordinary to see womenfolk alone in these parts. Rest your feet, take off your shoes." She gazed at them, with a peculiar faint smile and sat in her chair near the fire.

Sally and Adelicia simultaneously bent forward painfully unlacing the tiny slippers that bound their feet, slippers with pointed toes intended for walking on polished floors and imported rugs.

Adelicia's feet were so numb she was unable to move her toes; when the feeling returned, so did the pain. Both she and Sally crossed and uncrossed their legs, stretching their toes forward and backward and curling their legs onto the bed to massage their feet.

"Adie, my feet sting and burn. They'll never fit back into those," she said, motioning to her slippers on the floor. "Never! Look how swollen! They weren't even healed from Pulaski."

Adelicia agreed that from appearances, neither of them would ever again fit into a size four. Blisters had developed within minutes after the removal of their slippers; their tender feet and ankles were swollen to the point that it was impossible to see bone or sinew. The old lady, slowly rocking in her chair and being most attentive, seemed to understand about tiny feet and fancy slippers that had danced in the long ago.

"Do you have anything in which we can put water and soak our feet?" Adelicia asked. Their hostess slowly stood and walked over to the corner cabinet, reached underneath the gathered skirt and removed a bucket and an enamel pan.

"Take these."

She took a black kettle from the same cupboard, went to the other side of the room and poured water from a washbowl into it and set it on the fire. "Water will be hot directly, but I'll need to get more."

As she prepared to go out, Sally spoke up, "Let me go. I have to care for the mule anyway. Does the well work?"

"The one in the front's dried up, but another one to the side is where you draw water. Not as fancy, but it works."

"Ma'am, I am sorry to bother you again, but do you have any old shoes I can wear? Maybe some work boots?"

"Reach under where you sit."

Sally felt beneath the bed and pulled out a pair of low-topped leather boots caked with mud into which she slipped her stocking feet, looking all the while as if ready to scream at the thought of a bug being in either of them. Cautiously shuffling to the door, she removed the wooden bar.

"I shall come with you," Adelicia insisted. "Do you have another pair?"

The woman pulled a worn, faded box from beneath a small table near her chair and carefully removed wrinkled yellow paper. She unwrapped it with great care, until she held a pair of handsome satin, lavender slippers. The toe was not so pointed as the day's fashions nor the heel so high.

"They are lovely, but I could not possibly wear them," Adelicia said.

"My foot was never quite as small as yours, but maybe because of their present predicament, these will fit." She held them out.

"They must have been for a very special occasion."

"They're the only ones I own, except what's on my feet and those on your friend's. Please take them."

Adelicia would not wear a memory into the mud and dust. "I cannot," she repeated. "You are most kind, but I must not."

The woman laid the shoes aside, unbolted the rear door and returned with two tow sacks from the back porch. "Wrap your feet in these."

Adelicia wrapped her feet in the course burlap and tied them with even courser rope, reminding her of games played years before on the lawn at Rokeby.

Pain shot through her feet and legs as she stepped from the porch onto the rough stones; both she and Sally grimaced with each step as they first unhitched Blue, then went to the well.

"My feet hurt so badly, I had forgotten how thirsty I am," Sally said.

The well, an open vat with boards lying across the top, had a bucket fastened by a heavy rope that Sally repeatedly lowered then pulled back up. After watering and feeding Blue, they wearily led him behind the cabin where they hitched him near some splotches of grass to bed-down. And, again Sally lowered the bucket for water.

They returned to the cabin, whose only light came from the fire place where the old lady was heating the kettle, each carrying a bucket of water and the remaining portion of the Abernathy's gift, now reduced to cheese, apples and a few slices of country ham. They poured a portion of the well water into the pans and sitting by the fire, doused their aching feet.

The elderly woman soon poured bubbling water into each tub, then set the kettle back on the fire.

"How marvelous it feels," Sally sighed. "I know my feet will never be the same. What about Ole Blue?"

"There is nothing we can do until morning, then we shall see how well I perform as a smithy. Our hostess says it is seldom anyone comes by except for a stray from one of the armies. I believe I prefer repairing it ourselves."

"It's not safe for womenfolk around here nowadays. Have you et?"

"Around noon. We brought what we had left in to share with you. We do not wish to take your food."

The woman toddled to the cupboard, brought out six sweet potatoes and laid them on the hearth's edge, nearest the hot embers. "Spuds are what I have, and I welcome you to it."

An hour passed, and Sally and Adelicia became sleepier with each ticking of the clock. The fire, keeping the metal pans and bucket warm for their pained feet, the dimly lit room, the consoling aroma and sound of hissing baking sweet potatoes, acted as an effective laudanum.

The woman, turning the potatoes from time to time, at last hooked one onto the poker and handed it to Adelicia, who graciously accepted, then to Sally, then to herself, "Lord, we thank Thee there's food to eat and some to share. In Jesus name, amen."

Adelicia thought it the best sweet potato she had ever tasted as she pulled back the peeling and nibbled into the warm, deep golden flesh, savoring every bite. When Sally began to gather the peelings, the old lady handed her a sack and asked her to drop them inside. "It's for the animals."

"Adie, I hear someone outside," Sally whispered.

"You are imagining again. Go back to sleep."

"I can't sleep. I hear something."

The scraping noise suddenly became louder and both women sat up startled. "See, I told you I heard something."

"Shhhh." They listened intently. The fire had died to a few burning embers lending little light, not even enough for shadows on the wall.

They had insisted their hostess sleep in her own bed. And whether it was exhaustion, the warmth of the cabin, or both, the homespun pallet on the floor by the hearth felt luxurious. It was a struggle mentally and physically for Adelicia to tiptoe to the chair where she had laid her stockings and to remove the revolver lying beneath one of her garters.

"What are you going to do?"

"The scraping is coming from the back porch," Adelicia whispered. "Stand by the door while I go out the front and come around."

"Adie, don't be a dummy. You cannot go outside!" Sally shrieked, holding tightly to Adelicia's wrist and to the poker.

"Do as I say." She left Sally crouching by the back door as she unbarred the front. No sooner had she stepped onto the porch, than there was a clanging, then a gunshot, and Adelicia was quickly back inside, bolting the door.

"What happened?" Sally asked shaking, still holding the poker in a raised position.

"Nothing but a raccoon that came barreling from beneath the house, upsetting some pans. The gun accidentally went off. There is nothing to worry about."

"As quickly as you left the room, the scraping stopped."

"It was a coon, as Essie would say. We shant hear it again," Adelicia said, laying the gun aside. "We need sleep before it is time to get up. I fear the gunshot may have awakened our hostess."

"I've been awake since the first whisper. Heard it all. Night to you."

Adelicia and Sally looked at each other, smiling warmly. "Good night to you."

Nestled in front of the embers once more, Sally slept peacefully, but Adelicia lay awake, frightened by what she had seen outside. True, an animal, possibly a raccoon, had run from beneath the porch, but she had not told Sally about the man she had seen run from behind the house. In the darkness, she had seen nothing but his back.

She hoped the shot she had fired into the air had frightened him away, but she wondered if Blue, or the wagon would be there when morning came.

They were awakened by early sunlight seeping through the glazy east window and the smell of coffee grounds being freshly brewed.

"Morning to you," their hostess said.

Adelicia's and Sally's feet were more swollen and sore than the night before as they made their first attempts to stand. Dabbing their faces with water left over from their last trip to the well, they sat back on their pallets, wondering what to do about Blue and their feet.

"Here's coffee," the woman said, handing them hot brown liquid in cracked cups. "Sorry it's not fresh, but it's all I got. We'll drink it with the spuds." They sat before the fire, drinking coffee made from left-over grounds and cold sweet potatoes, both of which tasted delicious.

"It is a lovely breakfast," Adelicia said. "I hope you are able to get fresh supplies soon. We are so appreciative of your kindness and hope you will enjoy the cheese and ham. The apples should last a while"

"I do unto my neighbor, like the good book says. Though mine is gone. It was took by the Yankees when they raided my place. Heaven only knows why they wanted my Bible. Took my chickens, my cow, all the vegetables in the storehouse, canned goods too, then they come in and took everything they saw. I put the things on the mantle in the chamber pot, or else they'd be gone."

"I am so sorry. I wish we could get it back for you," said Adelicia, rising at last in her stocking feet. "Would you mind if I took your sacks with me to use for shoes?"

"You're going to need them. You'll need some, too," she said nodding to Sally. "Wear the shoes you had last night. They're heavy, but you can't walk in the ones you wore in."

"That will leave you with only one pair," Sally said.

"Don't need but one; you take the boots." She gathered up the cups and insisted she go with them to look at Blue's foot. Adelicia had watched their blacksmith shoe horses and remove stones since she was a child, but it was the elderly woman who took the hoof between her knees for them to examine it. "Nothing but a stone," she quickly said, "plus a lost shoe."

Adelicia took a small paring knife from the wagon and removed the obstacle imbedded deeply in the crevice of the tender frog, touched it up with turpentine, then tightly wrapped Blue's foot in tow sacks and tied them around his ankle.

"Old boy, you not only lost a shoe, you had a stone as well; our feet match," she said, patting him on the shoulder. She turned to the woman, "Do you think we can make it into Selmer like this?"

"You can make it, but it'll be a slow twelve miles."

Adelicia and Sally hitched Blue to the wagon, then walked him up to the well where they had first stopped. "We cannot thank you enough for your hospitality," Adelicia said. "We are most grateful for your kindness." She handed the woman her own Bible that she had taken from the package when she had gotten the paring knife. "I want you to have this. It is a nice one, bound in leather. Please accept it."

She put out her arthritic hand and smiled with a sweet, but sad expression, "Thank you, child, thank you."

"And here," Sally offered, holding out a gold coin. "Do you have a way to get into town for supplies?"

"Some folks in Selmer come every other week or so and bring me things, but I can't take this money, wouldn't be right."

"Of course, it's right. Take it," Sally said, folding the crooked fingers over it. "It is yours." Climbing into the wagon, they began a slow twelve miles into Selmer, Sally in the large boots, Adelicia in her tow sacks, and Blue in his.

CHAPTER 70

THE MILES WENT WITHOUT INCIDENT, AND FOR THE MOST PART, Adelicia and Sally were quiet, Adelicia reflecting on the man she had seen running from behind the house. The occurrence is one to which she would have given little thought, had it not been for both her and Sally's strong feelings of being watched. However, as she attempted to shrug it off as coincidence and direct her thoughts toward Selmer and shodding Blue, she was still troubled.

"Adie, we don't know her name!" Sally said suddenly. "We never introduced ourselves!"

"How strange that neither of us asked. I think we were too weary, our concentration elsewhere."

It was mid-morning when they brought Blue to a halt in front of the livery stable that had at least one attendant. The smithy, appearing to trust neither of them, promised to have the shoe in place within the hour. Amazingly, Selmer appeared untouched by war; just an ordinary, slow-paced country town, oblivious to anything outside its own perimeters.

Adelicia and Sally walked across to the telegraph office. "I would like to send a telegram please."

"Where to?"

"Nashville."

"Can't promise it'll get through. What you gonna say?"

"Tuesday, October 21st, Aunt Sally and Mama having nice trip. All is peaceful. Now in Selmer on way to Memphis to catch boat to plantations. Much love to my darlings, Mama."

"That'll be two dollars."

Adelicia paid him with coins from her pocket purse, then went next door to a small inn. The hot coffee and muffins with strawberry preserves tasted delicious, but not as good, she thought, as the meal earlier that morning.

"Do you think we might purchase some shoes in town?" Sally asked the waiter. They had ignored the stares from those who had first noticed the clumsiness of their steps before having glimpsed their foot ware. The waiter glanced at the heavy boots on Sally's feet, then at the tow sacks on Adelicia's. He continued glancing back and forth between the two of them as if waiting for an explanation, but finally answered that they might go across the street to Taylor's, three doors down. Leaving the waiter with his unasked questions, they hurried to Taylor's.

The choices were few, a size too large, plain brown and made of course leather, shoes that in good times their house servants would not wear, but on this particular day, they were well-pleased to rid themselves of burlap and heavy boots, and thankful to have shoes on their feet and thick laborer's socks for padding.

"What size are these?" Sally asked, holding up one of the boots she had just taken off.

The salesman measured it by some he had on display. "About an eight."

"Do you have any more like them? In a seven?"

"That's an old one. A real old one."

"Do you have any similar?"

"I can see. Won't be quite that heavy. In these times, can't get the heavy boots." He returned shortly holding two pair, one black and the other dark brown. "These the only two I got near that size."

"We shall take both pair if you can send them to an elderly lady, twelve miles east of town. She lives in a small cabin, a well in the front yard, but no other buildings. She gave us lodging last night when our horse threw a shoe. Do you know her?"

"Don't know her, but know of her."

"Do you know her name?"

"Waters, I think."

"Can you get the boots to her?"

"A delivery goes out of here twice a month. I can see they get on it. She probably won't wear them if she's like everybody says."

"How is that?"

"Say she hasn't changed anything, or bought anything new since being widowed over thirty year ago. Say she gave up, didn't want to go back east where she was from. Some say from a well-to-do family, just wanted to stay where he loved it and where he was buried. Sold off most the land through the years to get by."

They paid the storekeeper, then gave him ample funds for food supplies, staples and whatever else he thought appropriate for Mrs. Waters along with the boots and coffee. When Sally asked if he might also deliver some chickens and a cow, he laughed. "Ma'am, first, there's none to buy, second, all it would do is feed the Yankees again, or the takers on either side. No, ma'am, but the staples, I'll see to myself."

"I just remembered," Adelicia said, "My name is in the Bible I gave her, 'Mrs. Adelicia Acklen.' "Please address the parcels to Mrs. Waters, from Mrs. Acklen and Mrs. Carter."

Wearing their new shoes, they purchased necessary items from the grocer and returned to the blacksmith's. Once on the road again with Blue well-shod and fed, Adelicia felt reassured and confident. In two days, they would be in Memphis.

"Sal, we are going to drive forty more miles today. That will put us at Grand Junction, and by nightfall tomorrow, we will be in Memphis! And, the first thing I want is a two hour bath, then new dresses, pantalettes, stockings, sachets, all fresh and clean. Memphis should have someone who can do our hair. Dear me," she said look-ing at her callused hands. "I'll be gloved for weeks."

"My mammy would say I was dirtier than a wallowing sow from head to toe," Sally said in her slow drawl. "I want to sit in a tub all night, having warm water poured over me. Maybe there will even be a nice hotel at Grand Junction. Seems eons since I've slept in a bed with sweet smelling sheets and soft feathers."

"Grand Junction may not have anything. Did it occur to you why Selmer still had goods to sell? It looked as if the Yankees had just passed it by."

"It's hard to tell, honey. Maybe the Yankees had friends there."

Or maybe informers, or sympathizers, or whatevers, Adelicia thought, still tense and tired from the night before.

The day had been beautiful, sunny and warm with a breeze so soft they needed only their shawls about them, and the time had passed quickly without incident. But as the early evening air grew chilly, and the light from the lantern lit up the flat lands to the west before them, they were grateful to have arrived safely in Grand Junction. It, too, appeared untouched by the Yankees.

At a small hotel, they were offered a room with two single beds, and gratefully, wearily followed the innkeeper up the stairs. Bathing in a tub was out of the question, he explained, but there would be plenty of fresh water for the bowl on the washstand.

"I am too tired to bathe, even if I could," Adelicia said collapsing into the first chair she saw.

"I'm washing my face one last time with well water," said Sally. "Surely, we can purchase cream in Memphis. My skin may be forever ruined. What do you think, lamby?"

"Your skin will not be any more 'forever ruined' than will mine. I should like to rub cream and oil over my entire body, soak in warm lavender water, then oil all over again, but for now, I am…"

Their dreams were interrupted by a knock at the door. A lovely young girl with long dark braids brought in two pails of water: one steaming hot, the other cold. She carefully set them beside a plain white bowl and pitcher, saying she would return with wood for the fire.

"Who is first?" Adelicia asked.

"If you don't mind, I'll hurry," Sally said, unfastening the tiny buttons of her bodice and stepping out of the black dress. She loosened her petticoats and let them fall to the floor as she stood at the washstand mixing cold and hot water, naked from the waist up and with the draw string of her pantalettes loosely tied.

"The water is brown from just washing my hands. I'll need three baths tomorrow in Memphis."

"It will probably take that many to get us clean," Adelicia responded, not really engaged.

The girl returned shortly with the wood, taking great lengths to stack it perfectly on the grate. She lingered briefly at the door, flashing her bright blue eyes about the room, then at Adelicia and Sally before curtsying slightly and leaving the room, without ever turning her back to them. "How odd," Sally said, "An unusual looking servant girl with unusual behavior."

"I was not paying that much attention. I am weary, Sal, weary. In four nights, I have not slept as much as one normally."

Within an hour, both Adelicia and Sally had washed and were in their feather beds, propped up on semi-soft pillows, munching a light supper of buttermilk, cornbread and wine saps.

"It's been a good trip despite the difficulties, adventures we can embellish to our grandchildren. But a riverboat will be a sweet sight. I don't know how much longer I could sit behind Old Blue's wide behind and swishing tail," Sally drawled.

"As I said before, you and I are the only ones insane enough to have tried it," Adelicia answered sleepily. "I never possessed what the old biddies refer to as 'sound judgment,' but somehow or other, I find the seeming lack of it useful to making things happen. I once thought reaching a selective age was instantly granted maturity, and that reasoning and discernment were granted along with it. I now know differently." She hesitated. "I suppose people rarely change, if ever. Basically, our natures remain the same."

"Behaving the 'traditional way' has forever been boring," Sally commented. "Lack of some maturity can be a good thing."

"I am sleepy and so very tired," Adelicia said, yawning. "Tomorrow is a long day."

"I did not feel as if we were being followed today. Maybe the phantom retreated."

"There never was a phantom," Adelicia said, as if she meant it. "You imagined it all."

"Memphis tomorrow! I am so glad breakfast is not until six-thirty."

"A good night's sleep will benefit both of us," Adelicia said. "Good night."

"Lammy, we will never be old biddies. Age doesn't make you one; it's the thinking. Do you remember the long lists my mother had for things a 'lady never did,' or 'things she never wore' after the age of eighteen? Goodness! Ribbons in my hair, or short puffed sleeves! Why, I would have looked like an old maid."

Adelicia, indifferent to Sally's prattle, fell into a sound sleep.

"What's that?" Sally asked, sitting up in bed, just as the mantel clock marked its one-thirty chime.

"Someone is at the door. It is also raining." Adelicia climbed out of bed, gathering her chemise around her with one hand and holding the forty-five in the other. "Who is there?"

"The girl who brought the water and wood," whispered a frightened voice. "May I come in?"

Adelicia unfastened the door and the small framed girl with stunning deep-set blue eyes stepped inside. "I am sorry to disturb you at this hour, but I have need to ask something of you."

"All right," Adelicia said sternly. "Ask."

Without hesitating, she said, "May I go with you to Memphis tomorrow?"

Adelicia and Sally, who was also out of bed by now, were taken aback.

"Why?" asked Adelicia. "Why do you want to go to Memphis?"

"It is not to go to Memphis. I want to go to Natchitoches, but if I can get to Memphis, I think I can find passage from there."

"Why Natchitoches?" asked Adelicia.

"Possibly, my mother may still be there. If not, there is family who can help me."

The girl appeared intelligent, well-educated, speaking with a slight French accent; and it was obvious she would not willingly offer information.

"Why are you here and your mother in Natchitoches?" Adelicia demanded. "If you want to go with us, we must know the reason."

It was four-thirty in the morning when Adelicia glanced the mantle clock as the girl finished her tale of being apprehended by two slave trader bondsmen when she and her mother were visiting relatives in Natchitoches. It had happened quickly, she had said. They were on the main street along the Cane River when her mother had stopped the buggy long enough to make an inquiry in a shop. One moment she was waiting for her mother, the next she was in the hole of a riverboat.

The two white men had been frightened by Union soldiers, she thought, who questioned them that same night, because they had bound her feet and hands and tied a cloth about her mouth. They had kept her in the ship's hole without food or water until they reached

Natchez, where she was traded to an illicit dealer, who in turn sold her to the couple who owned the inn.

Although she had not been violated, she told them, she knew their original intent was to take her North, because she had overheard them laughing, discussing the high price she would fetch. When Adelicia told her that she could not be held against her wishes, the girl, who introduced herself as Morri explained that the owners of the inn only appeared to be sympathetic with her plight, refusing to help her even after she had told them that her mother was a free person of color.

At first, the proprietors stated there was less danger of Morri being harmed or confiscated if she remained with them until the war's end, assuring her of her safety, but after continuing to solicit their help, they informed her that she was expected to work off the amount they had paid for her, in addition to proposed travel funds. She fully understood, she told Adelicia and Sally, that she was their investment, their purchased servant.

Morri continued that when she heard the two 'fine ladies' mention Memphis, she had observed them and trusted them to hear her story. Then she hesitantly volunteered that her mother was a lady of position and would repay them for any expenses she might incur and that her father had been a gentleman planter.

"But Morri, your skin is white," Adelicia said. "The innkeepers cannot hold you against your will. Slaves have been freed! Regardless, you were never a slave. Legally, you may leave."

"They paid money for me, Mrs. Acklen. I trust no one at the inn and have no place of safety. I fear being kidnapped again or sold. My mother must be very ill from worry."

Adelicia looked at Sally, then back at Morri. "This tale is ludicrous!"

Again, Adelicia looked at Sally, "If my cousin agrees, we shall take the risk if you will be responsible for hiding yourself in the wagon until we are safely out of town."

"I fully support Mrs. Acklen," Sally said. "It is our desire and our duty to see you safely to Memphis."

"Please understand, Morri," Adelicia said, "if you are apprehended while still in Grand Junction, we shall behave as if we know nothing of the affair." Her concerns were already great enough without hiding a stowaway.

"We should be starting out at eight-ish," Sally said, putting her arm around Morri as they walked to the door. "Be careful, dear. We are happy to help you."

Adelicia and Sally had barely dozed when they were awakened at six-fifteen. After freshening their bodies with the previous night's water, she wondered about Morri, if she only worked the night shift, or had her absence already been noted. They hurriedly dressed and went down to the dining room with their homely bundles and ate a hearty breakfast of poached eggs, blackberry jam with flapjacks and coffee, their first real meal in two days. When the waiter apologized for not having any sort of meat, Adelicia assured him they were more than pleased with what they were being served. And after second cups of coffee, they picked up their bundles, paid their expenses and thanked the desk clerk for a pleasant night's lodging.

It was just past eight o'clock when they drove away from the livery toward Memphis into the wake of the previous night's rainfall that had made the roads muddier, and into a heavy October sky promising more. Underneath their parcels and old feed sacks lay a cargo known only to them. Morri was drawn into so small a knot that the most trained eye could have detected nothing askance.

A short distance from town, the rain began; first noticeable by a few small drops, then by a steady drizzle that turned into a downpour. Morri wiggled from beneath her wrappings and peeked over the buckboard seat. "Would you like a sack to cover your bonnets?" she asked.

"We are safe now, I think," Adelicia said. "Were you frightened?"

"Yes, ma'am," she answered, handing them each a sack. "But I am so happy. I hope my mother is still in Natchitoches."

Adelicia, pensive for a moment, asked, "Would she be elsewhere?"

"She may have returned to Haiti, or to New Orleans."

"How old are you, Morri?" Adelicia asked, suddenly feeling uncomfortable.

"Eighteen."

She had not looked eighteen, although her body was well proportioned for her small frame. Her face, beautiful and innocent, and set with sky blue eyes, was framed with long dark brown hair, and her lovely, flawless skin was no darker than her own. She had no Negro features except for her elegant nails, darker than a white girl's would have been, with milky white, well defined moons. Adelicia had seen someone who very much resembled Morri on two occasions: once at Fairvue, and once in Haiti.

"You did not mention Haiti last night," Adelicia said, trying to retain her composure and still the rapid beating of her heart. "Where do you actually live?"

"We have homes in Natchitoches and in New Orleans, but our main residence is in Haiti, where I was born."

"What does your mother do?" Adelicia asked, in a voice so low she barely heard herself speak.

"What's the matter, lammy?" asked Sally, "Why so many questions?"

"She owns a dress shop, three dress shops," said Morri. "She does only the buying. My uncles and aunts take care of the business. My mother is the dearest of ladies, and is fondly admired by everyone. People come from great distances to buy from her."

"Adie, it's drenching! I'm soaked to my pantalettes, right through my petticoats. Don't you think we should stop?"

"Where, Sal?" Adelicia responded, jolted back into the present. "We have not seen a dwelling since leaving Grand Junction. It is better to move, dreary as it is, than not move at all. Think about Memphis and the Clarendon Hotel."

The roads were becoming increasingly hazardous as the crevices and ruts continued to fill with water, and the wind grew stronger. Adelicia was shivering from the cold and from her suspicion of the girl's identity. She also felt fear.

Morri took a dry sack on which her knees had been resting and held it over Adelicia's head. "This will be of more help," she said.

Adelicia hoped the burlap sack wrapped over and around the hood of Sally's cape, and the sound of beating rain, was enough to muffle the sounds of her and Morri's voices.

"Is your mother married?"

"She has had many proposals," she quickly offered, "But my mother believes that when you love with all your heart, like she loved my father, you love only once. Anything short of that, she says is not love. Her friends know that a part of her has always been with my father, who passed away before I was born." Morri paused, "My mother attends many socials on the island, but keeps her distance from marriage."

"What do you know about your father?" Adelicia's words seemed mechanical to her, as if they were someone else's. It was as if Blue were driving himself, as if she were absent from the reality of movement.

"My mother speaks mostly of her love for him, how he was the one chosen by the gods. She speaks of his goodness, his generosity. He must have loved her very much," Morri added. "It was not possible for them to marry, but it would have been impossible for him not to have loved her."

Adelicia no longer felt the pelting rain soaking through her undergarments, nor the chill, nor did she know how many miles they had traveled. Only the jolting of the buggy when the right, rear wheel grazed a large stone, then mired into the red brown clay, did her senses return to her immediate surroundings.

"Well, honey, I believe we are stopped now and without a house or tree in sight, just West Tennessee cotton land," said Sally. "Shall we see what we can do? The wind is horrid."

Two hours later, soaked, with bruised and bleeding hands, Sally and Morri climbed back into the wagon, while Adelicia tugged on Blue's harness through the sludge, encouraging him to move, before taking Morri's outstretched hand to help her back onto her seat. The rain had softened to a slow drizzle, as it had begun, but dark, thickset clouds made it appear much later than two o'clock.

"Lammy, you don't look as if you're feeling well; I can drive, if I must." Adelicia thought that for certain she must look very ill; it was only the second time Sally had offered any assistance from their original responsibilities. She also cringed at the idea of Sally's driving.

"I am fine, but the delay means we shall be later arriving in Memphis and driving in total dark."

"I don't mind, honey, but you really don't look well. Maybe we should stop at the first place we see and settle in for the afternoon."

"I shall be happy to drive the mule," said Morri. "I have often driven, not a mule, but a pony cart, and sometimes drive my mother, instead of a servant, when she permits. Please allow me." Morri held out her hands to take the reins, but Adelicia persisted.

"Adie, do not be a hard head. If the girl wishes to drive, let her. You need the rest, lammy."

"Please. It is a small token for your kindness."

"All right, you and Mrs. Carter exchange places." Morri climbed onto the seat and Sally got into the back, as Adelicia scooted over and put the reins in Morri's hands.

How could I not have imagined last night, Adelicia, asked herself? It was obvious; New Orleans, Natchitoches, gentleman planter, quadroon mother, wealth and position, beautiful, well educated, French accent. On the other hand, why should she have?

When had it happened, she wondered, when Adelicia was in Haiti with Isaac, when he had gone there without her? When he had gone to Texas via Natchitoches? Had Lona come to New Orleans? *Lona.* She had not thought of that name for many years. Perhaps Isaac had always loved her, had seen in Lona what Adelicia could not give: herself. How wildly ironic that she was now sitting beside his child, returning her to her mother.

"…The tangled webs we weave." The intertweaving of past and present was indeed a mysterious journey. It seemed eons ago, or perhaps only yesterday, that Adelicia had seen Lona graciously stand and ask, with flushed face, if she would like to have a fitting. Numb to her feelings, Adelicia wondered if it were Providence…or merely happenstance.

CHAPTER 71

"IS MY DRIVING ALL RIGHT?"

"You are doing far better than I," Adelicia said, offering Morri a slight smile. "Wrap these cloths around your hands. They will at least take away the sting."

It was six o'clock and fully dark when they arrived in Colliersville and stopped at a small inn. Changing into dry clothing was a God send, Adelicia thought, even though it was more black mourning dresses, that had been tightly secured beneath the driver's seat. "My dress fits you tolerable well, my mammy would say," Adelicia quipped, "but you are much too young and pretty to wear black."

"It fits to a tee, honey," said Sally. "Mrs. Acklen will be envious that another girl has a waist so small as her own. She has never forgiven me for having one, one-half inch smaller," Sally drawled, clasping her hands in a circle around her own tiny waist.

"In Memphis, we shall have the seamstress measure us," Adelicia said good naturedly, then added, "Mrs. Carter will most likely not eat her evening meal."

They entered the small, plain dining room, knowing the inn was, "obliged to serve you supper, but not a room, nary a one left...can't make one neither."

"We left our wet clothing in the water closet," Sally told the waiter. "You may give them to one of the servants, or dispose of them however you wish." He nodded and told her clothing was a scarcity with many farm families about town; he was certain of finding good use for them.

With the meal finished, the rain having stopped and Blue fed, Adelicia felt in better spirits and judged they should be to Memphis within the next two hours or so. Not only there, but checked into the Clarendon with its soft beds, hot water and servants.

The kerosene lantern they had purchased in Selmer hung just out-side where Morri sat driving, its wick turned high, lending a nice, soft glow to the gray clouds and the surrounding night. Another hung on the back of the wagon, where Adelicia watched the road fold into the darkness behind them as she lay stretched out in the wagon's bed with her blistered hands tucked gently beneath her head, her cape pulled tight. Although the night air was nippy and she was being jostled about, she felt comfortable and warm cuddled between two blankets, one underneath, and the other covering her from chin to toe. "This is not the worst of ways to travel," she said. "I know why the children preferred wagon rides with their father to the landau."

"Honey, after the war, we shall take all the children overland to Memphis, using this very wagon," Sally babbled. "What a time they will have! When I say we, of course I mean, you and I shall depart Nashville by riverboat, while three, or four servants follow our same route with the children and meet us at the Clarendon."

It was nice, thinking about after the war, but not until Adelicia had accomplished all that she must do. She would certainly not attempt traveling to West Feliciana by land again. The arduous journey had already taken more time than expected, and there was cotton to be shipped, Confederates and Yankees with whom to deal and only the good Lord knew what else.

However, lying in the back of the wagon, thoughts of Morri dom-inated all others. If Lona were not in Natchitoches, if they could not locate her relatives, they could not leave her stranded behind. Morri would need to travel with them to Bellevue until other arrangements could be made. So many matters pressing, and they were at least forty-five minutes from Memphis and a two day trip down river to Bayou Sara, providing there were no mishaps along the Mississippi. After the war! After it was over!

"Is anything the matter, Mrs. Carter?" Morri asked.

Adelicia peeked up to see Sally pulling her black cape close around her shoulders.

"I can stop for a moment, if you like?" Morri offered.

"No, please, don't stop," Sally answered quickly. "The air is chilling— you might step up Ole Blue a bit, though. We've not seen a dwelling of any sort on this desolate road since we left Colliersville. One would think there would be some evidence of life; houses, people, animals on a main road leading into Memphis. Adie, are you asleep?"

"Do you really think I could sleep right now, Sal?" She liked the sound of Sally's childhood nickname. "I am thinking of all there is to do and becoming anxious to do it."

"Do you suppose we took the wrong road out of Colliersville? We've not passed anything alive or with any resemblance of being alive. And the road is becoming more dense and narrow."

Adelicia lifted her head, reclining on both elbows, looking to either side—it did appear desolate. The stars were hiding behind clouds, and only occasionally did the upturned moon slip through, briefly lighting the road ahead and illuminating the heavy foliage around them. Beyond the scant light of the lanterns, there was only darkness. Even the trees nearest them that sometimes brushed the sides of the wagon were not definable except for the heavy limbs that draped over their heads.

"Stop for a minute, Morri," Adelicia said.

"No, do not!" Sally blurted. Morri slowed down, not knowing which request to heed. "I feel uneasy. Keep going, honey."

"I suppose stopping will not help," Adelicia concurred. "Keep Blue at a good trot, while we look for some sign of life…there was no other road to take. I am certain of it."

"Adie!" Sally gasped. No sooner had the words left her lips than Blue reared, then angled the wagon backward into a ditch.

"What in heaven's name?" Adelicia called. It had happened so quickly; she said nothing more but lay deathly still, listening, with her heart beating so rapidly and her fingers so shaky that she was having great difficulty locating the revolver concealed in the pocket of her cape. She felt first in one, then the other, suddenly remembering she had tucked it underneath the seat. As Adelicia's hand cautiously slipped its way under the buckboard seat into the small box beneath, Sally screamed her name again. There was a loud, shattering noise. Then silence.

With her face pushed flat against the buckboard, Adelicia could see through a small crack, the shattered globe of the lantern. And just as her hand touched the revolver, she heard Morri cry, "Please! No!"

A man stood with his hand on the back of the seat, the other on the footrest, holding the reins loosely between his fingers.

"Please, do not touch me!" Morri pled.

He moved his hand from the seat back to her shoulder and then around the hollow of her neck digging his fingers into her flesh.

"Take your hands off me!" she demanded again, reaching for the crop that stood between her and Sally, who lay slumped unconscious beside her.

The man grabbed both Morri's wrists and pulled her from the wagon not letting go.

"You can get that high and mighty look off your face, Miz. Franklin Acklen. Your first man done me a wrong turn, your second one, too. And you done the same. They both dead as dead now and you ain't gonna have no need for another one." He spat on the ground and wiped his mouth on his upper shirt sleeve.

Adelicia gasped and froze. She thought she recognized the voice, but could not place it. In the dark, whoever it was had mistaken Morri for herself, obviously not knowing anyone else was aboard.

"Miz Uppity," he mocked. "I wanted his nigger but she wouldn't have nothing to do with me, even after he give her up for you. Ordered me off his place like I wasn't good as him. Then," he rambled, "you Acklen folk made fun of me, got me drunk and a dishonored discharge. Seen your spy boy on the road once, too. Chance Hadley don't forget a wrong done him." The repellent man spat again.

"I done paid your last man on a rainy road in Louisiana," Adelicia heard him say as she gasped, holding her breath. "Course they paid me to and I's glad to oblige." He held Morri by the throat and waist and began running his hands over her body. "I'm gonna pay you now and that only leaves his nigger I still gotta pay."

Morri screamed as he moved one hand to her throat and ripped the bodice off her dress with the other, exposing her breast. "I always wondered if a uppity woman does it any different from a whore." Morri's hands quickly gauged at his eyes, but as she kicked at his groin, she lost her balance and fell. Hadley laughed aloud and began unbuttoning his pants. "You missed, Miz. Franklin Acklen. You gonna get it now, more'an you ever got before."

Enough moonlight filtered through the darkness for Adelicia to aim and point in the right direction. Just as Hadley's trousers dropped to his ankles, she cocked and fired twice. Blue neighed and reared, pushing the wagon into a deep crevice.

CHAPTER 72

TWO HOURS LATER, ADELICIA, WORN AND TREMBLING, BROUGHT Blue to a halt for the last time beneath the awning of the Clarendon Hotel on Bay Street. Her hair, disheveled and frizzed from the damp night air, hung in disarray about her face. The skirt of her dress was mostly pulled away from the waist and the hem of her skirt, unraveled.

Splattered with mud, she and Morri had shoved and pushed and tugged at Blue while Sally lay unconscious, until at last they were back on the road, losing no time heading for Memphis.

And not until they were well on their way did Adelicia remember the front of Morri's dress was lying somewhere in the darkness behind them along with Chance Hadley, a name shrouded in fear and unknown to her.

Sally had lain in the wagon bed with her head in Morri's lap, her shawl wrapped around Morri beneath Adelicia's cape. Only when they were within sight of the gas lit lamps of Memphis did Sally vaguely recall what little she remembered, and not until the three tattered women were safe in their spacious, but modestly furnished hotel room, did she understand the events as Adelicia reported them to her.

Adelicia could not tell Sally that it was obviously Hadley who had tracked them from Nashville and that after leaving Selmer, realizing the road they would take to Memphis, had gone ahead to wait in a spot he thought most ideal to rape and kill undetected. Because he had not seen them leave Grand Junction, he was unaware of a third passenger, and in the darkness, had mistaken Morri for herself. The very thought terrified her: a danger had surrounded them since leaving home—not a Yankee, but an enemy far worse. And it was she whom he had wanted.

Sally, in her first stage of consciousness, stated that she had known all along that someone was following them, and repeated it until exhaustion and sleep overtook her.

Knowing the identity of the man, whom Adelicia supposed was the same man she had seen run from the elderly woman's house, meant nothing to her. As she washed her face and hands, then lifted her tired feet onto an ottoman, she recalled his atrocious table manners, the sneaky eyes, the ginger scraggled hair at Belle Monte. It was the man who sat at her table, and whom she anxiously wished to be rid of. Looking about the sparsely furnished room, she felt too tired, too bewildered, too exhausted to think clearly, but when morning came, she would make a decision.

She would never mention the attempted rape of Morri, the attacker believing it was she, herself, but wearily pondered if she should tell the authorities that a man lay dead on a road some fifteen miles outside of town, that that same man had killed her husband.

Her pondering was brief. Why not let the story remain as reported: Joseph died from pneumonia after falling from his horse and lying for hours in the rain?

As her aching body lay restlessly on the soft bed, she was more certain no purpose would be served by revealing that Joseph's murder had been avenged, and that it was she who was the avenger. It was a secret she would take to her grave.

When the doctor came the following morning to attend the bruises on Sally's cheek and head, she would remind Sally that she had bumped her head from the jolt of the wagon wheel slipping into the ditch. Sally would never know that she had been struck in the face by Hadley's fist, nor anything more that happened that evening. And as welcomed sleep came, Adelicia wondered why the probability of telling anyone what had actually happened had ever been unclear. She had somehow known that Joseph could not possibly have died simply from the complications of pneumonia.

Adelicia slept so soundly, it was Morri who awakened her when the maid knocked at the door. The hotel keeper had given explanation upon their arrival, that the servants were gone for the evening; that they could only provide a supply of warm water and fresh towels. Thus, the sun was well into the one o'clock sky by the time their bath water had been cleared away for the third time, the doctor had come and gone, and they sat with freshly shampooed hair, clean pantalets and bodices, purchased from the ladies' salon next door. The shop had readymade dresses that would be brought to their rooms, and Adelicia would also ask for gloves to hide her calloused hands.

"Will my face ever look the same again?" Sally whined, looking in the hand mirror. "Look at it! The left side is blue, purple, black and swollen. The ice hasn't helped. It's much worse than last night. Anyone could have done more than Dr. Whatever His Name did. Why he acted as if it were nothing at all, like he sees women looking this way every day. I can barely see. My eyes are so swollen, and my mouth so sore, I can hardly eat."

She stood to observe herself in the large dresser mirror, first from one angle and then another. "The only reason he gave this salve was to pacify me, I know it was. 'Just rest and keep ice on your head and face and it will be gone in a week or so,' he said. A week or so! I could get brain fever! People do develop brain fever from concussions. I've heard my doctor say so."

"You will be fine, Sal. Bruises heal." Adelicia held out her own marred hands, then put her arm around Sally. Had she only known what really happened, Adelicia thought. "By the time we reach Bellevue Plantation, you will have Yankees and Rebels alike falling at your feet with no sign of a bruise; every man who is not falling at mine. However, my hands, I shall keep gloved."

"You can joke about it! It's not your face!"

"Lie back down. Rest until supper and try to sleep. You too, Morri."

"Have you forgotten the maid is bringing up gowns for us to try?" asked Sally.

Adelicia smiled, half-hearted, "For once, I had forgotten about dresses. Let us nap until they come. Every muscle aches from my neck to my toes."

She stretched across the foot of the bed on her abdomen and brought her legs up behind her, knowing she must continue her charade before Sally. All was not well, and she felt pressed in a thousand directions. Too much had happened too soon. Learning that Isaac had a child by Lona, that that child had saved her life, was with her now, that she had shot Joseph's murderer.

She must talk with Morri—it was not a conversation to which she looked forward. Morri had begun to ask questions, questions not intended for Sally's ears, questions, Adelicia was unsure how to answer. The pieces did not yet fit. Although Adelicia had never heard mention of Chance Hadley, he obviously knew Isaac, as well as Lona. He had also been aware of Isaac and herself. She supposed he knew Joseph from the one night in their home. She could not imagine how the man had been responsible for Joseph's death. If he *were* paid to do so, by whom? Or was it strictly revenge?

Had he actually seen Bud on one of his spy missions? If so, was it by accident, or by devious planning? How mortifying! A man who would hold and seek such revenge! A man who had tracked her to Memphis! It seemed nothing was by happenstance.

Lona would have been his next victim; Adelicia had saved Lona's life! Morri had saved hers! It was tangled, despairing. How had Hadley known she was leaving Nashville, why had he hated her? "John Armfield," she said in a whisper. "Or Crawford. I shall ask one, or both. Hadley had to have been an acquaintance of Isaac's long before I met him. I shall wire John," was her last whisper before drifting into sleep.

No sooner had she done so, it seemed, than Morri gently tapped her; the proprietress from the dress shop had arrived with two servants, bearing new clothing. Aquas, maroons, violets, yellows, greens and blues lay across the bed where Morri had been napping. The fabrics were inferior, the gowns not that well made, but they were a welcome sight nonetheless, a dramatic contrast from the drab black that Adelicia had been wearing since the first of September.

After making their selections, a seamstress promptly came to fit them. Adelicia purchased a black taffeta for boarding the *Annabelle*, and for her arrival at Bellevue. Sally and Morri chose lovely fall colors. Adelicia would put on the soft yellow she had selected after her first night at the plantations.

"The lady does not fit so nicely as my mother," Morri said later while Sally slept.

"Your mother is a fine and excellent seamstress. I met her once, I think."

"You have met my mother?" she asked, astonished.

"Yes, in her shop once on a visit with Madame Dumonde. Everyone raved about her handwork and expertise, her beauty, as well. I found they were not exaggerating."

"How do you know it was my mother? This is as mysterious as the evil man on the road saying my father's name and mistaking me for you. Please help me understand."

Adelicia and Morri spoke quietly on the adjoining gallery that ran the length of the wide inner hallway, and she found selecting the appropriate words to tell Morri of the past extremely difficult.

"I learned on a visit to Haiti," she began, "that the seamstress about whom everyone raved had been your father's friend before meeting me. But it was not until we were in the wagon, leaving Grand Junction, that I recognized from things you said, that you were his daughter. I, too, was astonished and remain so."

"I do not understand."

"Dear child, I am very pleased to be of help, but I am displeased that you have had to learn unpleasant things, that you were harmed on my account. I am indebted to you." Adelicia took a deep breath. "I am your father's widow," she said. Seeing the girl's astonishment, disbelief, she took Morri's hand, "I do not wish to cause you pain. I am sincerely sorry about your separation from your mother, the ordeal through which you have gone, Morri," she said in a whisper, "my cousin, Mrs. Carter, must never know of the events of last night. It must be kept a secret."

After a lengthy silence, Morri looked up at Adelicia, "My first impression was that you and Mrs. Carter were fine ladies. Now I know that to be true."

The longer the discourse between the two, the greater Adelicia's dismay. She was surprised at her own remorse. Why such tender feelings for Morri and why such warmth for her mother, a woman she had glimpsed on the stairs so many years before, then met by circumstance in Haiti? Her husband's lover before their marriage; obviously, her husband's lover after their marriage. She had no answers, only that remarkably, she felt a sincere appreciation and admiration for Lona, and found her daughter exceptional. Adelicia also found herself trying to spare Morri's feelings as she gave soft explanations about the past.

She had reached out to a girl about whom she knew nothing, to a girl who had known nothing about her. Yet their lives had already been set, woven into a fine web.

"Morri, there are many things I do not understand," Adelicia said. Evidently, Chance Hadley was at Fairvue Plantation in Gallatin, Tennessee, when your mother visited there. When it is possible, I shall inquire of a friend, a former business partner of your father's, questions I would like to have answered."

"You are most kind. My mother spoke of no one in her past except my father, how handsome, how generous and kind, never omitting her love for him. However," she added, "she did not speak of him often; it seemed to bring pain and make her sad, so I asked few questions." Morri's soft, pleasant voice was an easy sound. "I like you, Mrs. Acklen. You were kind to me when you did not know whom I was, and you are kind to me now that you do. You are a lovely lady." With tears brimming on her long lashes, she put her hands on Adelicia's shoulders and lightly embraced her. "I trust I have not hurt you with my words."

"I am glad we have met, my dear. And whether, or not you are aware, you saved my life. Had you not been with us, the man called Hadley would most likely have killed me, and possibly Mrs. Carter. I can never repay my debt to you. In life's odysseys, this seems a chapter of an ordained plan. When coincidence or fate like this occurs, I cannot but wonder if these sorts of things happen to everyone, or just a select few."

"Mere believes what is meant to be, will be, not in coincidence. Although we are Catholic, we also believe that spirits guide and protect us. It was meant for us to meet, Mrs. Acklen."

"How far back in time do you suppose the spirits planned for this? How far back in the scheme?"

"Mrs. Acklen, I am most serious about the spirits. I would like to know about the man who attacked me, believing it was you. After speaking with my father's friend, I hope you will help me to also unravel the mystery."

The mystery! thought Adelicia. She so wished she could make the necessary connections to satisfy herself, but there was no time to bother with further suppositions. She would attempt to contact John Armfield, who had been wise enough to sign the pledge, and was most likely at this moment enjoying the mountain freshness of Beersheba Springs with Martha, nieces, nephews and friends. He had built his family a lovely cottage there, and developed a profitable hotel where Nashville residents could escape the summer heat. Of course the Yankees could be there too—but she doubted that.

There had been few meetings between her and John since the Supreme Court ruling, but she felt there would be no opposition to his providing information concerning Chance Hadley.

"I shall, Morri. I shall also ask my friend in New Orleans, and when I hear, I shall write to you. Remember," she reminded her, "we shall never speak again of what happened on the road outside of Colliersville. We shall never share our story, our secret with anyone. Do you agree?"

"Yes," she nodded.

"Not even your mother need know. Tell her whatever else you wish, but do not tell her about Chance Hadley. It would only grieve her the more."

"I shall only speak of you and Mrs. Carter. Perhaps you could visit with us on the island and tell me in person what..." Morri paused as if she wished she had not spoken. "Forgive me, please, I should very much appreciate a letter. Perhaps we shall meet again one day in New Orleans."

"We shall see," Adelicia said, "and again I remind you not to speak of this to Mrs. Carter. She was unconscious throughout the ordeal and knows nothing concerning the matter, nor your identity. It is best to never unravel what she has no notion exists."

"It shall be our secret."

"Also, Morri, I think it best that you go to West Feliciana with us. Your father named each of his adjoining plantations there, but the entire tract he called Angora, was later named Angola. The big house and the largest single tract is Bellevue, and from there I can think more clearly about contacting your mother. With the times being as they are, unless we can be certain your mother is still in Natchitoches, I would not feel comfortable sending you there alone, and will certainly not leave you in Memphis. Time is critical to my business at the plantations."

"Have ya'll been talking all this time?" Sally yawned, looking at the mantle clock, speaking in a tone that appeared to reprimand Adelicia. "Should we dress for supper?"

"I am going down shortly to make arrangements for out departure," said Adelicia. "Why do we not dine in our room? A luxury, indeed, not to mention the ease of not dressing."

"How silly of me. Of course, we shall. I shall, anyway." Sally put both hands to her swollen face. "I'd forgotten about this. I slept so soundly, I forgot I had been disfigured."

"You are not disfigured, Sally Carter. Temporarily bruised, perhaps."

"Perhaps? Look at this," she said cupping her face with both hands.

"Perhaps Morri will listen to your tale of disfigurement while I am gone."

"Adie, may I speak with you first?" she asked, making an obvious motion with her head.

"I shall take a walk in the gallery, if you will excuse me." Morri rose from the fireside chair and drawing her shawl about her, quickly went out the door, closing it behind her.

"What is it, Sal?"

"Are you not being too familiar with a servant? I'm amazed, talking for what must be hours on end, as if she were one of us. She shares our room! Our friends, even our mammies would be appalled. When I agreed to help, I was sympathetic with her predicament. I believed she would be going as far as Memphis, no farther. To be more definite, that we would instantly leave her here to go to her mother. How can you possibly find so much in common?"

"Did your mammy not sleep in your room when you were small? Does a mammy not sleep in the room with your children? Have we not left our precious ones in the care of Negroes while we make this trip? Do we not trust them with our homes, our possessions, our lives?"

"That's different. We don't *socialize* with them," Sally quickly responded.

"It is not so different. Had it not been for Morri, most likely neither of us would be here." She paused. "She is from an excellent family and I suspect quite well to do. Morri speaks of the governor of Haiti and his wife as if they are close friends. I suspect her mother is as socially prominent in Haiti as we are in our world," Adelicia said. "Wherever we are."

"That doesn't change the strangeness of having a person of color sharing a room with us, dining with us, treating her as an equal."

"Let us not forget that person of color saved our lives on a lonely road outside of Memphis. I believe the shot I fired to frighten the man you saw jump in front of Blue, frightened the mule the more. Also, do not forget I could not have gotten the wagon out of the ditch by myself, that you, dear, were rendered unconscious when your head hit the wagon brake. The intruder could have killed the both of us." She spoke kindly, but firmly, "I think we need not repeat this discussion."

Adelicia was sorry, on the one hand, that Sally did not share her sentiments for Morri, but on the other hand, she could not care less. She need not defend herself to Sally Carter. There was little Sally could report about the incident at Colliersville; how she interpreted the events as she perceived them when they returned to Nashville mattered not at all. Sally had lain unconscious while Hadley revealed moments of the past, that she, herself, did not even understand. There was nothing to fear, as the worst Sally could report was the initial attack. Sally, nor anyone, but her new found confidante, would ever know the truth about Joseph's death, nor the fate of the man who killed him.

"Do you think we can be on our way in the morning?" Sally asked cordially.

"That is exactly what I am going to find out."

Morri was standing at the opposite end of the lengthy hallway, peering out the window on the Union troops marching below.

Memphis had surrendered only four months after Nashville, after its citizens had stood on the East bluff and watched the Confederate gunboats engage in a hopeless battle with the Union fleet, anchored north of the city. And after only an hour and a half, Mayor John Park was left no choice but to surrender. The entire Confederate fleet, with the exception of the *Van Dorn*, had been destroyed, and the *Memphis Appeal* had loaded its presses on a boxcar and fled to Mississippi.

Adelicia had long tired of blue uniforms, although politically, she did not feel a strong allegiance to either side. However, she was a southerner, and she preferred associating with her own people;

Yankee officers and their wives would never belong; Yankees, of any kind—would never belong. They would remain outsiders, no matter how much wealth they accumulated, nor how long they stayed. They would never be Southerners!

She stood beside Morri with her arm lightly around her shoulders. "Perhaps we shall see some gray uniforms where we are going; we have seen precious few since the first months of the war."

"Will it will be over soon, do you think?"

"Soon, I hope, but it is only a wish," Adelicia said, observing the soldiers below. "The war that 'should not have happened' could, perhaps, be said of any war, but for sure, this one will have no victor. I am going down to see about booking our passages and sending a telegram. Mrs. Carter is in the room; you may sit with her if you like."

"I prefer to wait here in the gallery for your return. Is it all right?"

"Surely, I shant be long."

The lobby was busy, not with guests, but with the scurrying of all sorts of people from soldiers to seamen to stragglers, people who would not be permitted in the hotel had it not been wartime. Adelicia blended well in her black muslin dress, her hair pulled back into a chignon, and her face without the slightest trace of color, except for her extraordinary hazel eyes and thick dark brows.

"I would like to send a telegram to Nashville, please," she said, approaching the front desk. "Is it possible to get through?"

"Sorry, ma'am," the thin man with spectacles on the tip of his nose answered. "There's no way to get out unless it's a death, and we ain't sure of getting it through then. It ain't a death, is it?" he asked leaning forward.

She thought for a moment. "Yes and no," she answered. "My two friends and I also need passage to my plantations in West Feliciana, fifty miles south of Natchez."

"You want a lot, little lady. But I might can help you with the last request. Might can."

"But before we depart, I must get word to my children that all is well. I also need to be advised by a friend. It is very important. I am in mourning, and on my way down river to see if there is anything to confiscate before the Yankees, or Rebels take it. My dear husband passed away there some eight weeks ago, and I need to inform my family of my safety. If you can help me, I shall be eternally grateful."

He glanced at her over his spectacles, quenching his white brows and tapping the counter top with all his fingers. "Sounds reasonable, but can't promise it'll get through. But I might can try. Write down what you want to say."

"Dear Children, Cousin Sally and I spent last night at Clarendon Hotel, Memphis. Tell Luke, Blue being turned out to pasture at Uncle John Thornton's farm today…they are doing well. We continue trip by river tomorrow. Much slower than expected. See you in few weeks. Give love to all. Mother."

Making an inquiry to John Armfield would have to wait.

"All done?" he asked looking at the words she had written on the paper. "Sorry the cost is so high. May not get there, but we'll try." Three, four, five dollars and twenty cents, Adelicia counted. "Thank you, ma'am. Hope it goes. Now let's see what we can do about gettin' you and your friends to Luziana."

"Do you suppose," she asked spontaneously, "we can try another one, this time to Natchitoches?"

"You don't know what you're asking, ma'am."

"It is just south of Shreveport, not all that far."

"Little lady, don't know anyway of gettin' there, death or no death. Be taking your money for nothing."

She had wished to let someone know that Morri was safe, but that, too, would have to wait. They were booked aboard the *Annabelle* for the following day.

CHAPTER 73

THE MORNING WAS CHILLY AND DAMP WHEN THEY BOARDED THE *Annabelle*, a makeshift paddle-wheel that looked as if she had not been in for repairs or cleaning since she was built. Their quarters were cramped, but far superior to the wagon and the perils of driving Blue another three hundred miles, not to mention the luxury of a private room—although with barely enough space for Adelicia to pull on her stockings and not bump her feet against the wall.

How different the river looked stocked with battleships and gunboats—Yankee ones, instead of graceful paddlewheels. Adelicia supposed it would be the same all the way down river, now that Port Hudson and Vicksburg were both under Union control.

She had not anticipated their stopping at every landing: Helena, Rosedale, Greenville, taking on additional cargo and passengers that appeared to push the steamboat's capacity. The heavy fog hovering over the river made moving slow, and although the denseness had lifted by midday, by early dusk the low clouds rose from the base of the high cliffs to their east, stretching across to the flat lands in the west, making visibility almost impossible. It sickened her to see the busy, war-torn ports, one after the other, and frightened her as well. She hoped the Yankees had not harmed Bellevue. There seemed to be no end.

On the third morning, Adelicia spotted the familiar river's bend that marked the beginning of her plantations. How good it was, yet how melancholy. Never had she imagined that she would be arriving in West Feliciana alone, twice widowed. It was the bend Isaac first showed her, and then said, "For the next ten miles, it is all ours." He had loved the land, the river, the unpretentious Bellevue. Joseph had enjoyed and respected it, and had proved a valuable asset for its improvements and maintenance in the finest manner. It was also the bend her children had learned to recognize when very small as being "almost there." Too horrible, yet too wonderful; memories. How different this trip than the many before, yet the same river, the same path.

"Captain," Adelicia asked, "Do you know Row's Landing? Can you let us off there?"

"Micajah Row's landing was there even before my time. Sure thing. Stop after this one."

"Thank you very much." Row's Landing must still be intact then, she thought, the captain would know, and with luck, there could possibly be someone there to take them home.

"Sure you don't want to go on down to Bayou Sara?" he asked.

"No, sir!" she said, elated as they approached the familiar sight. "This is it."

All was still except for the wake of the *Annabelle*, and no one in sight, as the three women stood looking up the long avenue of oaks beyond the levee to the house. "We shall walk and send Rufus or Alfred back for our things."

Sally looked at Adelicia. "Walk?"

"For goodness sakes, Sally," Adelicia quipped, "it is no more than a mile."

As they reached the top of the levee, Jim Clack rode up. "Mrs. Acklen!" he said, astonished.

"Surely you did not think I would miss out on seeing to my cotton, Mr. Clack?" she said extending her hand, as he got off his horse. "May I introduce my cousin, Sally Carter, and our friend Morri." Adelicia hesitated, never had she thought to ask Morri's last name, nor had it been mentioned.

Morri quickly spoke and extended her hand to Jim Clack, "Morri de Bloviere, sir."

"Words can't say how glad I am you're here, although shocked," he said. "Problems surround us at every turn. Wait here and I'll be back directly with the wagon." Adelicia and Sally looked at each other at the mention of 'wagon.'

Clack left at a fast gallop and soon returned with one of the farm wagons, pulled by two stout mules; Adelicia dared not ask about the carriages.

The one thing that was the same, Adelicia thought, as they approached Bellevue, was the excited faces of Alfred and Lucy, anxiously waiting on the porch. How good to see them! How difficult Joseph's death must have been for them.

Everyone was soon settled into their rooms with fresh linens, water and copper tubs. Adelicia had been given a bath and a massage by Nattie, Lucy's younger sister, helping to relieve the aching, the pain throughout her body, but not in her heart. As she dressed in the dark green velvet evening robe from her armoire, she had a brief feeling of luxuriousness, but she was too exhausted, too burdened, to feel beyond the stressful moment, even ignoring her rough hands and callused feet.

"I was bringing coffee and croissants to your room and here you are already out of bed and down the stairs."

"Thank you, Lucy. Take some up to my guests, please. I shall have mine in the breakfast room."

"Speaking of guests, Miz Acklen, I been in this world a long time. Now tell me what a colored doing in the guest room." Adelicia was startled. The old lady's powers of perception never failed to surprise her.

"We shall speak of that later. There are more important things at hand." Keeping her eyes focused on the table, she asked, "Where is Mr. Acklen buried?"

"Near the rose garden," Lucy answered, as if waiting for the question. "Near where little Julius Caesar was fore you move him."

Nothing more was said, and after a second cup of coffee, Adelicia walked to the right of the house toward the garden, pulling her thick velvet robe tightly around her in the late October breeze.

Before her was a reality she would like to have avoided all together: a newly dug grave, that of her husband. The grass had not yet had time to cover the narrow rectangular space, where the brown earth had been shoveled, she standing, staring at the moist clay, before sitting beside it clutching her knees to her chest. Adelicia had only been told her that Joseph was dead, but not until this moment, knowing he lay beneath the mound where she gazed, had it seemed real. She reached out and touched the soil with both her hands then brought them to her face as her tears blended with the earth. Her thoughts of love, of missing, of desire, of heartfelt memories, were overwhelmingly embroiled with great sorrow, causing quiet tears to gush down her cheeks as she rested her hands back on top of his grave as the evening sun set.

CHAPTER 74

"I'T'S A REAL MESS," JIM CLACK SAID THE FOLLOWING MORNING, AS he and Adelicia sat at the breakfast table where he had often sat with Joseph, sipping coffee, discussing the games played in war. "We can't get the cotton out, can't get it ginned. Mr. Acklen had agreements with both sides about our shipping it, but all that's changed. I've done everything I know to do to keep the Rebs from burning and the Yanks from taking. Mr. Acklen dealt with some agents, but mostly we made direct contact ourselves, although that, too, has changed. Either side might take it any day. It's tight."

"What kind of agreements, Jim?" she asked, astonished. "Both sides?"

He pushed back in his chair, fidgeting uncomfortably. "Agreements that let us ship cotton."

"That does not answer my question. I must know what you are doing, what you did, if I am to take part. Now," she said, looking directly at him, "tell me the agreements, every detail."

It was past noon when they finished talking and planning, and as she felt the weariness of her soul, she felt its excitement as well. The lack of clarity remained, unanswered questions, answers that perhaps Clack did not know, or perhaps did not yet reveal. According to him, Joseph had stayed on the good side of both armies and navies. She surmised that the bargains Clack had reported may have been the cause of Joseph's death, as she thought of Hadley, left lying along the road outside Memphis.

"I believe it will work, Mrs. Acklen," Clack said, after Adelicia had further revealed her own ideas and plans, so different from that of her husband's.

"Do you really believe so, Jim?" Adelicia asked, motioning to Lucy for more coffee.

"Yes, ma'am. I'll ask the men here for supper. Trust me, no one will bat an eye about not accepting the invitation to dine with two lovely ladies. You will direct the evening from there."

"Goodness! I am nervous and excited at the same moment! Your confidence and help is invaluable. I shall make the necessary preparations."

After he showed her the official report of pneumonia, similar to what she had received in Nashville, she had not questioned Jim Clack about Joseph's death. She would give it more thought, more time.

And when she had inquired about sending a telegram to Natchitoches or Haiti and mentioned the name Lona, Clack had not winced. However, he had told her that getting a message out of either St. Francisville or Bayou Sara would be next to impossible, that she would need to wait until New Orleans. She wondered what Jim Clack knew about Isaac's life before her. He had to know the real cause of Joseph's death, or so she supposed.

The longer she pondered, while resting before supper, the more she felt that Joseph's murder was due to one of the two sides having discovered his deception, and that Hadley had somehow placed himself in the position to be the one to expose him. It was a dangerous game that she too, would need to play. At least Hadley was dead.

She had had no idea what to expect when she arrived at Bellvue, but it was certainly not what she had imagined. It would be a different game than the one in which Joseph had been a participant, quite different, as she and Jim had discussed, but still one of deception. If it worked, and she saw no reason why it should not, she would be shipping her cotton out of New Orleans and on to England, just as Joseph had done. With luck, Adelicia should be home for Thanksgiving, for sure by Christmas! Women and men playing the same game, play it very differently.

Adelicia was forty-six years old and her soft, smooth skin was as flawless, as radiant, as when she and Camille giddily planned their lives at fourteen. Her hands and arms were void of brown spots commonly associated with aging. Her waist was still a measurable twenty-one inches, and her face without a trace of lines except for slight, smile ones at the corners of her eyes and lips. And when she smiled, those blended to compliment her overall perfection. Her breast and buttocks were firm and the only gray in her dark hair was limited to a few strands spaced intermittently around her face, however, parted so that little of it showed. All in all, she looked nowhere near her age; most would assume her to be years younger.

Isaac had told her she was among those rare women who would remain beautiful and alluring no matter her age, and as she looked at herself in the mirror that early November morning, before donning her velvet robe, Adelicia agreed. Sleeping late and being pampered by Nattie had most assuredly agreed with her, and the homemade cream that Nattie measured into her hands was a miracle in itself. If her dramatic plans succeeded that evening, she and Sally would be hosting a lovely dinner for the Confederates. Twelve officers, known and trusted by Jim Clack, were invited, and she was confident of their being well entertained.

She was dressed before seven, well prepared for her camouflage, making sure all was as she had ordered it. Fall flowers filled each room and delicious aromas permeated throughout. The china, silver, crystal and linens were in place, and Nattie had been asked to mind the handsome music box, playing it continuously, so there would be no lapse of soft sounds while they dined, sounds only produced from the finest German made boxes.

Adelicia, beaming and lovely, was embarrassed for even Sally to know how delighted she was to be giving a party again, and her a widow of only two months, quite apprehensive at appearing too excited over the prospects of entertaining twelve Confederate gentlemen. "Sally, you are ravishing."

"Adie, are you nervous?" Sally asked, primping at the ornate dressing table in her room. "I'm making sure there's no trace of my bruising."

"Some," Adelicia answered, sitting on the edge of a small chair so as not to wrinkle her organza gown. "It is the first time since this dreadful war began that I feel as if I am really giving a party, and this time for a cause. I do feel some guilt, however, they are our boys," she said, "and I do not relish the idea of deceiving them." She hesitated, "I think Joseph would understand it is a performance to save my cotton. Is it too disgraceful that I take some joy in it?"

"Adelicia Acklen, you'd not care if it did. I'm just as excited as you. When you're sixteen you think that anyone over twenty is ready for the grave and unable to possibly enjoy life, but I think it's even better, dahling."

"Now we know what we are doing, or behave as if we do," Adelicia added. Then suddenly she stood up and walked to the window, her back to Sally.

"Is anything the matter, lammy?"

"I never want to love again," she said seriously, "My heart is too heavy, but I must keep my quest in focus and have it over rule my heart." She turned, facing Sally, "I am simply reminding myself of my responsibility." She paused, "I do enjoy the company of men. They are ever so much more interesting than women."

"Thank you very much!" said Sally. "You know if word of what you're doing gets out, you'll be banned from Nashville."

"What *we* are doing. You agreed to this."

"Only to help you out, honey."

"Sally, I have not been 'overly loved' by any of the old biddies since I married Isaac. I have also found little favor in anyone's eyes, save a very few, so another shocking incident should not have so great an effect."

"Honey, it wasn't marrying Isaac. Nashville took to him, you know that. It was the events afterward. You were blamed for wanting your children in a New Orleans' school when Isaac wanted to stay in Tennessee. You were also blamed for wanting to run back and forth between the two cities, not to miss a social season." Sally hesitated, then ran on. "There were also those who suspicioned you knew Joseph before Isaac..." She stopped abruptly.

"Please continue. They thought I was taken with Joseph before Isaac's death?" She looked at Sally decidedly, "You never mentioned this before."

"And then you disputed the will and built a house and grounds that everyone referred to as lavish and ostentatious. Honey, you were blamed for Joseph not fighting in the war and then his death and now, you just know they're all saying: "the two of them traipsing off to New Orleans, to do no telling what."

"Let them say, dear Sally. I am the villain, the sinner. I need not be reminded. Nashvillians have made me the topic of their conversations for years. When people envy, and one is measured by their self-righteous yard stick, it is hardly worth discussing. If I do good, if I do ill, either will be expressed negatively. I cannot dwell on it."

"But, lammy, this is not the same. I agree, you do some things differently than others would, but, Adie, this is tall cotton; you'll never be forgiven by the North or the South if the deception is discovered. And for sure, someone will find out."

"How? You'll not tell. All will be well. I promise." She turned quickly, then added, "If by some ill chance it is discovered, I shall say you had no part in it, that it was strictly my affair. I no longer pay attention to the babblings of the envious. When they are penniless after the war, there will be plenty who will wish they had been wise enough to at least have tried. And Sally, that is how it will be. Most are going to be left with nothing but a dwelling, if even that. You will see."

The downstairs hall clock struck half past seven. "If you prefer not to participate, to go home, I shall understand," said Adelicia. "I had no idea what to expect when I invited you to come with me. I agreed to pay you for making the journey and to assist me in the venture. If you have changed your mind, please tell me now. After all, it is my quest, security for my children and me, for all who depend on me. You may leave on the morrow. You are bound to go no further," she said in a staccato manner. "I shall pay you the agreed amount, less the extended time. And why, may I ask, have you waited to reveal *the talk* about me right before this important gathering? Why not along the way, when there was ample opportunity? Your choice of time is rude and thoughtless."

"Not for the world. I am here to help complete your mission. I simply felt I had to remind you, if anyone at home ever learns of this. I meant no harm."

"And I felt I needed to remind you." Adelicia's authoritive voice softened, "Enough of this prattle for now. We must be ready for grand appearances." Jim Clack, nor Joseph had entertained the Yankees or the Rebels, she thought. She would begin with the Rebs.

Jim Clack was elegantly dressed. Had his manner of speech been that of the educated gentry, he could have been mistaken for one who had spent his life as a reader of books in the finest libraries.

"How handsome you are tonight, Mr. Clack. Please introduce your friends," Adelicia said, looking from one peering face to another, and wondering if these were the same Rebels who knew of Joseph's operations. They had gathered in the wide entrance hall just off the sweeping verandah, and stood talking among themselves as Nattie passed the drinks in heavy pewter Jefferson cups. As introductions were made, she recognized the name Carmack, but none other.

Sally was striking in rose taffeta, her blonde hair set in soft ringlets pulled back on the sides to cascade over her shoulders. Adelicia, who never thought she would wear black again, had found an old organza gown while rummaging through the armoire in her bedroom. She had worn it only once before and Joseph had found it stunning. It fit much better than the ones made in Memphis, and she had had Lucy pressing and mending it all afternoon.

She felt stunning! The plunging neckline revealed her full breast as it draped off her shoulders, coming to a vee in the back where the small covered buttons began. Her curled hair was loosely drawn up atop her head with fresh sprigs of plumeria encircling in a crown twist, allowing her hair to poof just enough to give fullness around her face.

"Ma'am, you're outstanding," Jim Clack said, taking her hand. "May I introduce Major Hanson," he said, nodding to the gentleman on his left. "And this is Captain Carmack."

"We are so delighted all you gentlemen could join us this evening," Adelicia said, one by one, taking each of their hands. "You cannot imagine how beautiful it is to see men in gray. Indeed, the sight is exhilarating. Do meet my cousin, Sally Carter," she said, gently touching Sally on the back. "We hope you can relax for a few hours, enjoy some home cooking and pretend this war is not even happening. I could hug each and every one of you with the sincerest gratitude of heart."

While Hanson and Carmack talked with Sally and Jim, Adelicia met and chatted with the other ten, each a First or Second Lieutenant, until Lucy rang the bell announcing supper. When she and her fourteen guests walked into the candlelit dining room, with its masculine appeal of paneled walls set with pictures of seafaring ships, the soft, seductive sounds of the music box began.

The evening progressed smoothly. The entrees were delicious: seafood gumbo, fried chicken, mutton, and fresh vegetables and fruit, each served with a different wine. After the seven layer cake was devoured and coffee poured, they retired to the handsome drawing room for after dinner liqueurs, where the men looked comfortable sitting on both leather and thick velvet covered chairs and settees.

David Carmack was handsome, a West Point man from Virginia who stood over six feet tall, with dark, curly hair, hazel eyes and lovely tanned skin. Adelicia found him charming; it was obvious he was smitten by her. She guessed him to be much younger than she, ten years or more, but she would not introduce the subject. She loved his Virginia accent. They discussed their home states, traveling and families. She and Jim had agreed that all conversation must be directed away from war.

At eleven o'clock, Major Hanson announced that they must return to their posts, the where abouts of which had not been disclosed during the evening. He gave compliment after compliment to the ladies, the food, the hospitality, the evening. Carmack lingered near the front right column, standing on the first step below the porch where Adelicia stood.

"Will you call again?" Adelicia asked. "I know there is a war. But it was so pleasant to pretend for a short while."

"May I?"

"I would not have asked, had the answer been anything but, Yes." She looked into his eyes with the glow of a schoolgirl, and she watched his pupils dilate with little other color visible.

"When?"

"Come for luncheon tomorrow. Twelve thirty-ish."

"We never know what to expect from one day to the next, however, there's been no action in the area for a while. If I cannot be here by noon, or shortly thereafter, I'll send word."

"I shall anxiously await your visit, Captain."

"Good night, Mrs. Acklen." It did not bother her that she and Carmack had delayed the others, or that she was perhaps making him uncomfortable. This was a first step in fulfilling her purpose, and it had not been nearly so difficult as she had imagined. Flirting and charming had been quite natural, even after so many years. The deception was weaving its way.

"It was delightful," Sally drawled, as they started up the stairs. "When will you know about the cotton?"

"It has just begun, Sal, but it has to be soon. My Negroes began picking again two weeks ago, but we are still way behind. By the end of the week, something definitive should be in the making for the two thousand bales already waiting patiently to be shipped."

"The food was excellent," Adelicia called down to Lucy from the top of the stairs. "Please tell Alfred, Nattie and the others how wonderfully they performed their duties. I am most proud of you all."

Lucy reveled in compliments, but she knew she was being praised for a job performed exceptionally well. "I tell 'em, but I still don't like it none. Tell me one thing. Are you planning to have Yankees in this house?"

"Lucy, I promise you everything will be fine."

"That's what Mr. Acklen say but..."

"Good night, Lucy."

"Did you enjoy your supper tray?" Adelicia asked entering Morri's room. "I am sorry you could not join us, but we know it is best that you not."

"My meal was delicious! I think the cook excellent, so much so that I am overly filled. The sounds of laughter and conversation wonderfully reminded me of home," she said sweetly. "Was it a good evening for you and Mrs. Carter?"

"Yes, dear. All went well, but there will be more evenings necessary like this one," Adelicia said, moving closer to Morri. "So far, Mr. Clack has been unsuccessful in getting word to your mother. I think we should wait until New Orleans, where I feel certain my friend Mr. Benedict will be able to contact the consulate in Haiti."

"I understand. It is best to make direct contact. I worry so about my mother."

As Adelicia lay in bed, she wondered if David Carmack and Joseph had been friends. Jim had revealed Carmack's position in shipping the supplies and the cotton. She wondered what Carmack knew about Joseph's death and what he thought of her flirting after so short a time in mourning. But she could not concern herself with that now. All involved were helping serve her purpose. It was, however, an additional advantage to have someone with whom she could enjoy the repartee, and she could enjoy it with David Carmack. He was a valuable asset, and after the shipping, she would return to Tennessee, and after the war, he to Virginia. Joseph had entertained neither Yankee nor Rebel, but for her it was a must.

Carmack sent word the following day that he would be able to call briefly in the afternoon, and further announced that Major Hanson would like to call on Mrs. Carter. Adelicia never doubted that anything short of death would have kept him from calling, and after an early morning business meeting with Clack, Bard Kelly and Strapp Young, she had begun preparations for his return to Bellevue. Still, she had not asked Jim Clack any further details of her husband's death.

When the two officers arrived, they were entertained in the morning room, a more intimate and feminine space, decorated in shades of sea green, soft ivory and damask upholstery. After Nattie served coffee and shrimp filled croissants, Adelicia invited them into the drawing room, where she and Sally took turns singing and playing the piano while the men sipped rare brandy.

It was the first of many visits from Carmack and Hanson. When it was warm enough, they strolled in the garden, engaged in frivolous conversation and parlor games, singing and playing the piano.

It was on Carmack's fourth visit that he discussed his knowledge of Joseph, volunteering his shock—and that of the Confederate Army, of all who knew him—over his untimely death by pneumonia. He also took the opportunity to express his condolences. Adelicia took the opportunity to inquire about having her cotton shipped, suggesting there was no reason that the work her husband had begun, supplying the Confederate Army, should not also continue.

"I must get my cotton shipped, Captain Carmack, I cannot be left penniless after the war."

"I understand, Mrs. Acklen. However, there are many risks, too many for a lady."

"I am willing to take the risks. Too much is at stake!" she said as he stood to leave. "Will you be, can you be, of the same assistance to me that you were to my late husband?"

"Yes, ma'am, if that is what you wish, but it is dangerous."

"We shall talk about it later over another fine supper," she said. "I also need to know whom we can trust."

Adelicia had made her cotton appeal with urgency, and he had listened. The plan was unfolding. But what pleased her most was hearing Major Hanson mention that Bishop Leonidas Polk was in southeast Louisiana! The Polks of Columbia, and her family had long been acquaintances; Adelicia had learned before leaving Nashville that he had given up his bishopship to become an officer with the Confederate Army, but she had no idea that he was so near, nor a Lieutenant General. She was unsure if he were the chaplain.

"Major, do you think it would be safe for my cousin and me to travel to New Orleans?"

"It will be good for you ladies to go into the city, and as charming as you are, my dear Mrs. Acklen, it would not surprise me if you could even charm old Silverspoons himself. Why, you could make the Yankees believe anything."

How prophetic, she thought. Little did this unsuspecting Rebel know that was exactly what she was planning to do. To use every feminine persuasion to get the assistance she needed from the Yankees and to use the same persuasion to get what she needed from the Rebels.

"Do you think we can board a packet, Captain Carmack?" Adelicia asked. "They come by almost as often as before the war."

"They probably don't even know a war's going on in New Orleans," Sally said excitedly.

"Oh, but they do, Mrs. Carter. I can assure you of that," Carmack replied.

"Yes, we must not forget there is a war, although the company of these gentlemen in gray has certainly helped alleviate some of the anxiety," Adelicia said, gently putting her hand into David Carmack's folded arm, smingly cunningly. "Do you not think we would make good spies, Captain?"

"The best, the very best."

"Morri," Adelicia asked later, entering Morri's room. "Would you like to go to New Orleans, day after tomorrow?"

"May I begin packing tonight?" she asked, jubilant.

"You may begin whenever you wish, dear."

CHAPTER 75

O N MONDAY MORNING, ADELICIA, SALLY AND MORRI LEFT ROW'S
Landing aboard the *Lucas Belle,* all the while Adelicia wondering
if the Yankees had confiscated her townhouse, and if the servants
were still there. Regardless, upon docking, they would take a cab to
the house at Number Four Rue Dumaine.

The river looked much the same: lovely, enchanting, except for
the military patrols moving slowly through its brown rippling waters. It was far better than their passage from Memphis down river.
However, as they neared New Orleans' crowded harbor, Adelicia
was astonished to see the reality of military fleets, ships of every
dimension and style, instead of the usual loading of cotton, indigo,
sugarcane and rice.

But the vendors were still out, selling their fruits, vegetables
and pastries. Overflowing shrimp nets were being hauled up from
the small boats, and Negroes, dressed in bright colors, peddled
their wares. The aromas were magnificently enticing, and Adelicia
could not wait to dine on succulent oysters, crab and scallops.
They took a waiting hack and proceeded to the address on Rue
Dumaine.

The two mile drive through the Vieux Carre passed quickly and
Adelicia was exuberant at the sight of the town house unmarred.
Mossy with one foot in the doorway and ready to go back inside,
turned to see who was stopping in the cab.

The old servant put her hand to her eyes to see more clearly
through the bright afternoon sun, but their baggage stood on the
sidewalk, and they were approaching the iron gates before she exclaimed, "Lawsy me, good griefs, Miz. Adie. We didn't know if we'd
ever see any Acklens again."

She came running to the gate, nervously unlocking it. "Me and
Jacob, we kept hoping for some kind of news, but after Mr. Acklen
gone, we not heard nothing. Where the childrens?"

"The children are home in Nashville," Adelicia said. "These are my guests, Mrs. Carter and Miss de Bloviere. The house looks wonderful, Mossy. You have done well. I trust the funds have been adequate. Have your boy take our luggage upstairs, please."

It seemed strange not to be with her family as she walked inside with Sally and Morri, and even stranger as she glanced around the rooms. Even through the bustle of luggage coming in, and exclamations made, an eerie silence hung over the house, its every crevice.

Mossy and her sister, Fancy, hurried to prepare a delicious evening meal, taking great care setting the elegant rosewood dining table with its finest. Jacob had rushed to the French Market to purchase fresh seafood, and there were warm crusty breads direct from the oven. In the morning, she knew Jacob would return for fresh baked, delicate pastries and fruit for a late breakfast.

Adelicia's mood, however, deepened to one of melancholy as she sat at the table with Sally and Morri, picking over the delicious delicacies of an early supper. Their company was not enough to push aside the pangs she felt within. It was the same table at which she had sat with Joseph and their children, and she missed their laughter and joy. She pondered whether anything or anyone could ever fill the void or erase the emptiness she felt for longer than a brief frivolity.

Conversation was cheerful as they discussed the river trip, planned shopping, the Confederate officers, and Morri's reunion with her mother. But Adelicia's jubilance was feigned. She could not wave away her sadness, her feeling of isolation, nor her longings. Joseph would never again dine with her at that table, would never again be in her bed upstairs. It weighed heavily upon her, as she looked at the pleasant faces of Sally and Morri, wondering if she were forever doomed to feel these sudden changes of mood. She had pretended when she entertained the officers in Nashville, when Joseph was still alive, just as she had pretended at Bellevue, although she had momentarily enjoyed the company of David Carmack.

But the longer Adelicia sat looking at the vacant seat at the opposite end of the table, remembering, the more empty she became. "If you will excuse me," she said at last, "I am retiring early this evening. In the morning, I shall go into the city to make arrangements for you, Morri." She rose and bade them goodnight, touching Sally on the shoulder as she walked past and stooping to kiss Morri lightly on the forehead.

Despite the warm glow from the fire, the bedroom felt as cold and deserted as did she. In this house, she and Joseph had lived a part of each year. And although Adelicia had spent nights alone in their bed before, she had always known Joseph would be returning from the plantations and that her children were sleeping just down the hall. Standing, she gazed out the window overlooking the walled brick courtyard. There was the garden in which Emma had taken such delight when they first moved into 'their' house.

How strange, she thought. As a woman grows older, she wishes to remember everything, while at the same time, wanting to forget. Her memories seemed sharpened, as if the very walls around her spoke with voices, haunting voices, whispering "Remember." "I cannot stay in this room," she said to herself, "Not tonight, at least. It is suffocating." She rang for Mossy. "Do we still have the carriage?"

"They ain't took nothing—not yet. But word say, General Butler going to take everything he get his hands on soon as he find the time."

Adelicia knew how right she could be. "Have Jacob ready the carriage. I am going to the St. Charles Hotel for the night."

"Miz Adie, you can't do that, not by yo'self, you know you can't. Why you not want to stay here? It bad on them streets."

"It is too painful, Mossy," she answered softly. "Tonight anyway. I shall be safe. They know me there. Tell Mrs. Carter and Miss Morri that I went into the city. Say whatever you wish."

"Yes'um, I do what you say 'cept you ought not go."

They were crossing Canal Street when she asked Jacob to turn around and head back into the Vieux Carre for the St. Montaigne, a new hotel on Rue Royale about which she had heard. Why she had ever considered the St. Charles, that held memories of both Isaac and Joseph and her children, she had no idea. As instructed, Jacob made a complete turn in the middle of the wide boulevard.

The French Quarter was lovely with gas lamps lit all along its narrow streets, though the Yankee blue uniforms were imposing, almost black in the darkness except for the brass buttons that reflected in the soft light. Civilians were as plentiful as soldiers; men strolled the streets with lovely ladies on their arms. Shops were open. From first appearances, one would hardly know there was a war in New Orleans. The city had been captured soon after Nashville, but everyone had obviously settled in to enjoy themselves, both the residents and the invaders.

Music resounded from the doorways; as remembered, marvelous music. How good it was! She had missed this city and its charm, an enchantment that had held onto her from her first 'meeting,' that continued to hold her in its grasp.

Three blocks in from the river, the St. Montaigne was elegant and gay with laughter as she walked into its plush lobby. She marveled at the exquisite, expensive décor, its stylish furniture, and the hordes of non-uniformed guests inside. Hardly an occupied city!

"Thank you," she said to Jacob when he gave her bag to the doorman. "I shall send word in the morning. And Jacob, tell Mossy not to worry," she said.

As she walked into her room, she thought what a contrast to the Clarendon in Memphis. It was lavishly furnished in Louis XV, almost too lavish. And what a contrast from her melancholia, she thought as she changed into one of the gowns she had brought from the armoire at Bellevue. But as she looked in the mirror and recalled the lovely fashions she had just glimpsed downstairs, she knew one of the things she must do the following morning was to shop at her favorite venues and purchase a new wardrobe.

However, she was satisfied for now with the lovely salmon-colored chiffon, even though it had been mended in any number of places. And as she draped the matching shawl around her shoulders, she was convinced that Joseph would not have wanted her to remain in mourning attire.

As she had already dined, she went downstairs to do she had no idea what. Perhaps she would have oysters on the half-shell with a glass of delicate sherry. Perhaps she would pretend there was no sadness to remember. She had enjoyed dining alone at home. Why not do so at a hotel restaurant? There were no old Nashville biddies to make comments.

Without a plan, she ventured into the crowded lobby, then into the restaurant, where she requested a table for one.

"I am sorry, Madame, we have no tables. As you can see, the dining area is completely filled." New Orleans! She had forgotten how much she missed it. At half past nine in Nashville, unless there were a party, everyone was bedded down for the night. Yes. She would pretend.

"Sir, I wish a table for one, and if there is no table available, please make one."

The maitre'd looked at her in apparent disbelief, and repeated, "Madame, we have no tables."

"Where is the proprietor?"

"Madame, there is no table!"

"I requested the proprietor. Would you prefer I locate him myself?"

Adelicia knew the maitre'd most likely found her impertinence a sign of ill breeding, and he had every reason to think it; however, she had a need to be seated, as she had begun to feel self-conscious and awkward, thinking her idea not such a good one after all. She refused to be dismissed, though, as her only option was to return to her room. Experiencing the ambiance was a nice salve, and she would not dare to step outside the hotel door alone.

"Madame, I..." he said in frustration, "I shall see what I can do." He returned shortly to inform her she could be seated at a table reserved for six who were a half hour late, but when they arrived, she must give it up. That was the best he could do.

"No thank you," she said, whirling so quickly that her hoop underskirt brushed against the heavy, ornate drapes. "I wish to see the proprietor," she demanded at the front desk.

"I am sorry, Madame, he is not in. Perhaps I can handle the problem for you."

"I hope sincerely, sir, that you can. I wish a table for one."

"Madame," the manager charmingly responded. "If the dining room is filled, it is filled, however, if you would be so kind as to wait for one of our tables, I shall be delighted to prepare a comfortable seat for you in the lobby."

The results were no better. "I shall take the table offered me earlier, reserved for the party of six," she relented, "but, I shant move."

After being seated and ordering a choice white wine and oysters, she smiled to herself at her unmerited haughtiness, suddenly finding that she no longer felt awkward or uncomfortable dining alone in public. How annoying it would be, she mused, if she did refuse to move when the party arrived, who, according to the clerk, was now forty-five minutes late. She wondered about the importance of those for whom the table was reserved.

No sooner had she been served than the waiter, not the maître' d with whom she had had her confrontation, came to say that a table had been set for her and asked if she would be so kind as to move to it; the intended party had now arrived. The nervous waiter seemed more than pleased when she pleasantly agreed, and moved Adelicia to a small round table nearby spread with freshly pressed, pale pink linens and an arrangement of magnolias in the center.

She watched as the staff hurriedly made ready the table she had just vacated, then seated the guests with great pomp. The ladies were elegantly dressed, although, none were exceptionally attractive, she thought. The men were older, but quite handsome. She glanced over, then quickly took a second look that caused a flush and a smile to fill her face.

Sitting to the right of her table was Crawford Benedict! Amidst the stares of an unescorted female dining alone, the lady with him had apparently pointed her out, as he had turned to see the exquisite, inviting face of Adelicia. In his mid-sixties, Crawford was as attractive as ever.

"Adie, Adie, I don't believe it!" he exclaimed, stumbling from his chair. "A wonderful, wonderful surprise! No one in the world I'd rather see." Her old friend and beau stooped down to embrace her, stood back, then bent forward, embracing her again. "What are you doing here alone, of all things? Will you join us?"

"I could not intrude upon your friends."

"My dear, you are never an intrusion. Waiter," he called, "move Mrs. Acklen's things here, quickly." The confused waiter immediately set about to do as directed, but Adelicia insisted that she remain where she was; she wished to observe from a distance.

However, Crawford's relentless persistence eventually won and after being seated for the third time, and after the introductions were made, Adelicia quickly sized up Valencia Benedict and wondered why on earth Crawford had married her. It must be her beauty, alone, certainly not her charm or cleverness. He never managed to marry charming women, she thought.

It proved to be a lovely evening, and Adelicia was grateful for the company of make-believe. She immensely enjoyed Crawford, his "forsooth" of Shakespearean days, and there had been no mention of war, just polite exchanges of pleasantries. She had made every attempt to be careful and engaging, but her thoughts definitely lay with Crawford. She had no idea that he owned the St. Montaigne!

The path looked clearer as she later lay in the soft, plush bed. She was meeting with Crawford the following morning at ten. The two would see to Morri's safe arrival in Haiti, and Adelicia to her cotton being shipped.

Chapter 76

ADELICIA WAS AT THE FRONT DESK BY NINE LEAVING A MESSAGE for Crawford, extending her gratitude while asking if he could see her later that afternoon. She then made haste to Madame Duvall's on Chartres, to see what could be designed and completed for her by three o'clock, the cost of which was of no concern.

After selecting a simple but elegant pattern for her meeting with Crawford—pale lavender, high necked, with a ruffle reaching beneath her chin, matching the ones around her wrists—she chose fine taffetas, poeu de suoi, chiffons, silks and cottons. She appreciated the coolness of cotton in the summer and its adaptability when woven into heavy brocade in the winter; that made her lists as well. Madame Duvall's seamstresses were capable of producing a new dress per day for her, and her fitters were excellent. As Adelicia's mother had instructed her when she was very small, "The mark of a good seamstress is in the fitting. Many can sew, but very few can fit properly." The dress in which she would meet with Crawford would fit perfectly through the bodice, then taper into a vee at the waist before flowing into a full gathered skirt in the back.

She watched the cutting and stitching begin on the lavender as she made other selections: pantalets, silk stockings, garters, kid shoes, fabric shoes, underskirts, waist cinchers, corsets, bodices, handkerchiefs, gloves and hats. It felt delicious to be newly outfitted from head to toe, delicious to feel soft fresh undergarments against her skin. There was little that equaled the feel of fine silk against bare skin. And the impression she wished to make could not be accomplished in clothes three years old.

Sophie, who had often done her hair in New Orleans, combed it into a lovely bouffant that poofed around her face, and Adelicia, admiring the soft scent of Madame's exquisite lilac perfume felt stunning as she stepped out of the shop onto Chartres. And when she arrived at the St. Montaigne just past three-thirty, she was shown to the dining room where Crawford had ordered a late luncheon of fruit, champagne and crusty bread.

"My dear, when I encountered you last evening, it was like breath to my body, music to my ears."

"You still sound like a sixteenth century poet," she laughed. "You will never change."

"You, however, grow lovelier with every year."

"Please say something that does not sound as if it is directly from a text?" she teased.

"Adelicia, you are a remarkable woman. How's that?"

"Better. Tell me about Valencia, your family, what you have been doing since the war. I could not believe my eyes when I saw you last night."

"Before I talk about myself, I'd like to talk about you. And I am sorry, so very sorry about Joseph. I went up for the wake. A tragic loss."

She put her hand lightly on his arm. "Thank you so much for going. The deaths of two husbands and six of my ten children are losses from which I shall never recover nor heal." Adelicia paused and took a deep breath, "And for last night, I thank you for conversation that briefly allowed me to pretend it was a different time.

"I relied heavily upon Joseph," she continued, "to manage the plantations. I had never felt a great need of dependence before, except for Papa and John Armfield for a few years after Isaac's passing." She lowered her eyes, then said softly, "Remember when I introduced you to Joseph at a party, and when we sat at the first council meeting, the three of us talking till late hours, and you agreeing to continue as an advisor with legal counsel?"

"I remember. I also remember how jealous I was—again."

"There are other things of which we must speak, for instance, why I am in New Orleans."

"Let me guess. You tired of Nashville and came here to shop in the middle of the war. By the way, that dress is outstanding."

"Be serious, please."

"All right, I shall be serious. You want to continue what Joseph was doing. You want to ship your cotton to England."

Of course he would have known! How inane of her—the shipping business! That is how her cotton would leave the docks. "Was Joseph using your ships?"

"Not my ships. Most of them are being used by the United States Navy. The Rebs used them first, now the Yanks."

"Then how do you know about it?"

"There are other ships, my dear. Although I wish I owned them all, there are others—inferior, of course, but they float."

"Will you please tell me what you know about my late husband's affairs?" she said, filled with excitement.

"You must first sip some of the delicate nectar from French vineyards and partake of the fruit and bread. Then I shall tell you."

"Okay, I shall. But I also need help with another matter before I need the cotton shipped. I need to have Morri de Bloviere returned to Haiti, Lona's daughter."

Adelicia never ceased to be fascinated with the element of surprise and shock. She watched as Crawford almost choked on an oyster. His face flushed brilliant red as he washed it down with the remainder of a half-filled glass of champagne. She thought about Jim Clack, who unlike Crawford, had not blinked an eye when Adelicia had introduced Morri to him. Either Clack had not known of Lona or was perhaps a better actor.

Crawford listened closely as Adelicia recounted meeting Morri, omitting the harrowing events on the road outside Colliersville.

Crawford had not thought of Lona for some time, and thoughts of her brought melancholy. He recalled her beauty, her selflessness in loving Isaac. He also remembered the hellish weeks of Isaac's agony before telling Lona about Adelicia, how she had gone missing, and after finding her, believing she was leaving New Orleans with Chance Hadley. Isaac's long bout of drinking ensuing.

As they dined, Crawford took great caution when speaking to Adelicia about Isaac and Lona. He made no mention of Isaac's trip to Haiti in October of '45, or Natchitoches in January of '46. It was remarkable to him: the meeting of the two, Adelicia and Morri. How it would play out eventually, he would term more than just interesting, perhaps a saga of great proportion.

As he later sat musing in his hotel office, Crawford admitted to himself, that most probably he would always be in love with Adelicia; most men were, once they had met her. He had invited her to dine at his table that evening, an invitation she had declined, saying she must return to the townhouse and give Morri the happy news that a wire had been sent to the consulate in Port-au-Prince. Adelicia did not know that he had actually sent it to Rivers Thurmond.

Crawford planned to see as much of Adelicia as possible, despite their differing perspectives: Adelicia saw their meetings as a business venture while he chiefly took pleasure in her company.

She had returned to her hotel room more joyful than she had been since leaving Nashville. Crawford's manner had put her so at ease, restoring her confidence. Part of the burden she faced seemed quietly lifted. What a dear he was; she had admired, trusted and loved him as a friend for years. Now married again with two young children, she wished him great happiness. And, of course, on his ships or his arrangement for other ships, her cotton would be shipped to England.

Speaking with John Armfield was no longer a pressing matter. Obviously, Crawford had been well aware of Lona. He had known Isaac as long or even longer than John. Of all people, why had she not have assumed he would have known? She was shocked, however, that he was also aware of Morri.

Soon, Morri would be safely home with her mother, and Adelicia would, most assuredly, ship hundreds of bales of cotton to England, returning home to Belle Monte, her quest fulfilled.

Chapter 77

Ecstatic with the anticipation of going home, Morri embraced Adelicia at the townhouse in her gracious manner, repeatedly expressing her gratitude.

Walking into the front parlor, Adelicia told Sally that she would be returning to the St. Montaigne for the remainder of the week, stating that only with time would she become reconciled to sleeping in the house without Joseph. Sally assured her that she understood.

However, as they were taking tea in the lavender-papered sitting room before the fire, Sally insisted that she go to the hotel with her. As Adelicia had supposed, the idea of not being amidst society was too much for Sally's patience, but she managed to persuade her cousin to allow her one more day to herself. An old friend, she told her, was working diligently on behalf of shipping her cotton. Sally reluctantly agreed after Adelicia invited her to the hotel for supper on the following evening.

Morri, still unable to contain her jubilance, gave Adelicia yet another endearing embrace. "It is difficult to believe that I shall soon see Mere. Oh, I hope very soon!"

"You will my dear. It should not be long now."

As Adelicia approached the crowded dining area that evening, she was met with smiles of recognition, on this occasion graciously greeted and escorted to a small table reserved for her dining pleasure. What a pronounced contrast, she thought! The table was distinguished from the others by an arrangement of pale pink roses instead of magnolias; also there was a note lying folded and sealed on a silver tray.

"My Dearest, Adie. Just in case you change your mind and choose to dine here tonight. I deeply regret I cannot be with you, but have seen to your pleasure as best I can in the absence of my charming self. I should like to meet with you for luncheon tomorrow...one-thirtyish, as I have talked with friends concerning matters at hand. Forsooth! Another mysterious and intriguing encounter with the beautiful Mrs. Acklen. Again, I trust you will find everything to your pleasure...I already look forward to the morrow. Fondly Yours, C. B."

She smiled as she folded the note into her small umber beaded bag. Although she had not really expected him to join her, as she had told him she would not be available, the lack of certainty had been engaging, and she had nevertheless hoped to see him.

It was an evening of elegant dining; everything pre-ordered and set before her in six petite courses: turtle soup, Russian romaine salad, oysters Bienville, Pompano, pheasant smothered in a heavy wine and cream sauce and strawberry mousse, each served with fine, aged wines. Time escaped her as she sipped, enjoyed, and ate alone, observing the boisterous crowd amidst the elegance. When the large foyer clock struck eleven, Adelicia was surprised to find she had been gorging herself on the delicacies for more than two hours. She did not know when she had delighted so much in a meal, and when the maître 'd saw that she had finished, he pulled out her chair and escorted her to the stairs.

In her room, closing the door behind her, she dropped her clothes wherever they fell, a luxury she had not known since before the war. The servants in Nashville and West Feliciana had more than enough to do without waiting on her. It was a luxury she enjoyed, burdens were lightened, and Crawford was the reason for it! She felt his influence more than previously, and wondered what kind of games he was playing with the Yankees and the Rebels. Owning hotels and ships must be nice commodities in wartime.

She slipped on the ice blue silk gown she had purchased that morning, and slid beneath the soft covers. The shop had promised another dress the following day, one of deep blue moiré. Madame had called it storm blue, the latest color from Paris, and it did look like dark blue-black clouds gathering just before a storm. Adelicia closed her eyes in a peaceful sleep; she, too, was looking forward to the one-thirty meeting.

Breakfast was served in her room at ten, just as she had ordered, and on the serving tray was a single pink rose with a card that said simply, "Good morning." She smiled and settled in bed to enjoy the sumptuous food, feeling much younger than her years. She would return to Duvall's on Rue Chartres, check on her dress and perhaps make more selections.

Later, when she descended the stairs, she felt elegant. "I'm amazed," said Crawford, slipping up behind her and taking her arm. "You're on time."

She had been so anxious to see him, to dine with him, to learn more of the internal business of wartime New Orleans, but after the lapse of an hour, when the conversation continuously alluded to themselves, she felt herself amidst a charade from which she must escape. Being courted by the married Crawford was certainly secondary to getting her cotton to Liverpool, or Morri to Haiti. It was not part of her agenda, though she found herself surprised by her own feelings of lukewarm and cold. Perhaps it was her idea of "ideal reality," the moment, the extended moment that existed in neither past nor present nor future, but somewhere outside any reference of time.

Crawford was treading beyond where he should. Tiring of the innuendoes, she interrupted him by asking what he had discovered about shipping her cotton and of Morri.

"What's wrong, darling, am I boring you with memories and wishes?" he asked.

"You are married. We—I—you are behaving as if...Please forgive me."

He looked sternly at her, she thought, a look she did not recognize.

"Crawford," she responded, "I must know about my cotton. My cousin Sally has made the trip with me, and I purposefully kept her at the townhouse today so that we might talk in private. She only knows of my plans to ship, not how! I must know what my chances are. My cotton must get to England."

"And it will, my dear, it will," he said as if there had been no previous conversation, using a tack he had perfected. "It's a matter of how, on whose ship, and when."

"Crawford, if I knew the answer to those three suppositions, I would not have needed you," she said before realizing. "I did not intend that," she quickly apologized, resting her hand on his wrist. Visibly upset, she continued. "I must deal with the North and the South; a complicated, complex task. There will be an end to how long I can continue the charade I have begun. Please continue. I am sorry." And she was. Crawford was an insider, and she would not foolishly jeopardize their relationship with self-righteous outbursts. Although she had prayed for it, her patience had not matured with age.

Adelicia settled back into her chair, poised and relaxed. Although Crawford's table was in a secluded corner of the hotel's dining area, she in no way wished to appear out of sorts.

"I'm friends with the Northern houses, with the officers, even Old Spoons Butler, and Military Governor Shepley and General Banks. They come to my hotel, especially the room not admissible to the ladies, where strong liquor and smoke and gambling is allowed, as well as loose talk," Crawford said, motioning to the waiter. "I propose to persuade the Northern houses to store your cotton until we can arrange a shipment to Europe. This is quite different than what your husband did the first part of this year. Two coffees please," he said to the server. "It can be done, however, and I hope to clear it by week's end. In other words, when the cotton arrives here under guard, it will go to Northern storehouses to await shipment before being loaded onto ships that I will provide."

"Can they be trusted?" Adelicia asked, nodding for steamed milk to be poured into her coffee.

"We really have no choice, but I say, Yes."

"Crawford, I am not going through the trials to get my cotton this far and have it confiscated by Yankees."

"I can promise that all within my power, nothing will happen to your cotton. Nothing ever happened before."

"And were you directly involved in that?" she asked.

"I knew the Acklen cotton was shipped safely out of port, as I told you yesterday. Yes, I knew about it. You ask too many questions."

"What about this General Butler of whom everyone is so frightened?"

"He's just a lot of wind—not being disrespectful, actually easily handled. I like the man but his reputation got out of hand—quickly. If he were still in the city, I'd arrange for you to meet him, but he's been gone for almost a year. An interesting sort of fellow, for a Yankee. People here still speak of him as if he's just around the corner, especially the women."

"What shall I do next?"

"Be sweet to me."

"Crawford, I am exhausted. Be serious."

"I am serious. But to please you, I'll give you a briefing. First, Morri must be brought safely to her mother. She departs Saturday morning for Haiti."

"Crawford, dearest, the arrangements are made? Oh, Crawford! You are wonderful!" She leaned across the table and kissed him on the cheek.

"By that time, I am also hopeful to have arranged for the storage of your cotton. Next step is to find a way for your cotton to be protected during picking, trashing, baling and getting it here."

"I am working on that with some Confederates. Actually," she corrected, "setting the stage."

"If you set the stage, my lady, I am assured of a major production. And as always, I shall be one of the players—never the star, that's your role."

"I have set up preliminaries," she said with a twinkle. Then she proceeded to tell Crawford about entertaining the Confederate officers and about David Carmack, whom she had invited back more than once.

"Do you want more coffee, my dear?"

"No thanks," she said, "One cup is settling, another is too much." The waiter cleared the table and returned the bouquet of white camellias to its center.

"Your husband did it differently, sweet Mrs. Acklen. He did not entertain the military." Crawford did not need to say the obvious: he did not approve. Nevertheless, she would continue what she had begun.

Adelicia changed the subject, asking if he would find time to meet Sally the following day. It was then that he took her hand and asked why she had refused the invitation to his home for the following Thursday evening.

She pulled away from his gaze. "Perhaps because I did not want to spend an evening pretending, or just perhaps. I do not know. I honestly do not know."

"Let's take a stroll, look in the shops. It was once one of your favorite pastimes."

"It seems I must protect both our reputations. What would the good ladies of the city say if they saw you strolling with someone other than Mrs. Benedict?"

"You know I've cared little for what people say, much like yourself."

"I really cannot, Crawford. Our relationship must be business. I apologize for having been forward. I just so enjoy your company"

He looked at her, then placed his hand over hers. "Tell me something, lovely one. If I were not married, would it be different, this time?"

"That is not a fair question. How can I answer what is not?"

"You're right, I suppose," he said, removing his hand. "Would you like me to escort you to your boudoir, or canst thou make it alone?"

She laughed. "I think me canst make it alone." He walked with Adelicia to the foot of the hotel staircase. "I shall recommend the St. Montaigne to my friends," she said. "I shall tell them, that pale pink roses adorn the tables in the evening for dining, and that each morning, a single pink one adorns the silver breakfast tray." She looked up, with her arm still locked in his, "Thank you, dear, dear friend," she said, then tip toeing, kissed him on the cheek.

As she had promised, Adelicia sent a messenger inviting Sally to the St. Montaigne. She wished to tell her cousin of the latest plans, and prepare her for Saturday evening when the Benedicts would host a party at the hotel after the theater. The affair would be attended by New Orleans' elite, which now included Yankee officers—a grand opportunity, she thought, for her and Sally. They would have an early shopping spree before meeting Crawford.

At half past eight, Adelicia recognized Sally's knock at the door. There she stood, looking lovely in the bright blue, "Memphis special."

"Come in, come in," Adelicia said in delight. "You look wonderful. Not a trace of your so-called 'disfigurement' remains."

"I don't feel wonderful," Sally drawled, "nor New Orleanzy in this frock. Oh, look at you! The lobby is filled with ladies in gorgeous gowns. First thing tomorrow, I'm going to your Madame Duvall's "

"Of course you are, but, Sally, you are so attractive no one would know if you were not wearing a Paris original or a hand-me-down. As I always say, it is the one in the gown who makes the difference."

"You also 'always say' 'The apparel oft proclaims the man.' You need not bother to flatter me, Adie. You've probably purchased dozens of new gowns by now."

"I left some fabric for you," she laughed. "Madame is expecting us in the morning."

Adelicia was almost ready for supper except for slipping into her dress that she asked Sally to hook in the back. "It's stunning, honey, simply stunning."

Adelicia was wearing the pale lavender with a single strand of tiny mother of-pearl shells with matching ear bobs, the same she had worn the day before. She knew Sally would never go downstairs with her had she donned the more pretentious green dress delivered that morning, which was quite revealing. "Madame is a wonderful designer," she told her cousin. "Her seamstresses have completed two for me and have seven more to finish. You'll need a very special one for the theater Saturday evening."

"What theater?"

"I shall tell you while dining."

The following morning, Jacob delivered a message from Morri thanking Adelicia for the beautiful gifts that had arrived the afternoon before, expressing her delight with the lovely dresses, the matching accessories. She had first put on one, and then the other to have Mossy see her in each. "I shall wear the aqua taffeta to meet Mere," Morri wrote. "I am also so very fond of the yellow one."

Adelicia, greatly pleased, had guessed at Morri's size. Of course, Madame insisted she come in for a fitting if needed.

Adelicia and Sally had requested their breakfast trays for eight, and planned to be well into a fitting by nine. "Good morning, dahling," Sally said upon entering Adelicia's room through the adjoining door. "Did your tray have a pink rose on it today?"

"Did yours?" Adelicia asked, trying not to reveal her surprise. Nothing gets by Crawford! How on earth did he know her cousin was next door? She smiled. How could one not admire a man who thought of everything! The morning was clear and cool, and they strolled the four blocks to the seamstress instead of taking a hack.

CHAPTER 78

CRAWFORD HAD ASKED THAT LONA WIRE HIM WHEN SHE RECEIVED the message about Morri. However, at half past ten that morning, Lona was sitting in his office, lovely and regal as if the years had made her beauty even more enviable. Taken by surprise when his secretary announced her name, he had barely had time to rise from behind his desk before she was standing in the doorway. "Do you have news of my daughter?" she asked without a trace of familiarity.

"Lona," he said extending his hands. "Rivers obviously made haste getting my message to you, and you made haste arriving from Haiti. It's been a long time. You're simply ravishing. Some ladies never change. You are even lovelier than..."

"Mr. Thurmond was kind to arrange a hurried trip," she interrupted. "What is the news of Morri?" She did not move, nor did she take his extended hands.

He stepped back behind his desk, asking her to take a seat in the deep brown leather chair to his right. She sat erect, on the edge of the seat with the calmness and refined coolness he had remembered. Her elegance and beauty had weathered in no way.

"Morri is hearty and well," he told her. "I haven't seen her yet, but she couldn't be in more capable hands. She's with a friend of mine, an acquaintance of yours."

"I wish to see her now and take her home. I do not understand. We have no mutual friends or acquaintances."

"Lona, need you be so hostile? I have always been your friend and held you in the highest regard. Please stop behaving as if I am the enemy."

"Mr. Benedict, I greatly appreciate your help, sending the wire to Mr. Thurmond. I have had detectives, the police and politicians, such as they are, searching, but to no avail. It is the time of war, and it is very difficult for anyone to find a kidnapped child. I have been sick, almost to my death, over my daughter whom I cherish more than life itself." Her words trailed off... "I am grateful to you, I shall repay you and the ones who have found and cared for her, any amount. Money is no object. I have been blessed. Greatly blessed…alive and well… my Morri is safe, how thankful to God, I am! Please, when may I see her?"

"I'll have my driver take you now if you wish, but there are facts of which you should be aware. Will you agree to come to the dining hall to talk over coffee? Afterward, I promise to... No," he said, reconsidering, "we'll have Morri come to the hotel."

"May we take coffee here?" Lona asked.

He rang for his secretary and asked that a message be sent to number four Rue Dumaine, and to inform him immediately upon Morri's arrival.

Within minutes, coffee was brought and served. Crawford stood looking out the window at vendors, shoppers and soldiers passing by.

"Our Haitian coffee never tastes quite so good," Lona said. "Whenever I visit New Orleans, I take many pounds home with me."

"Are you here often? I do hope you'll stay in the hotel when you come, as my guest."

"I come infrequently to select and order fabric for my shops, those that do not come from Europe. It is increasingly difficult to get shipments at present."

"Why have you never called? I would like to have seen you."

"Mr. Benedict, when a part of your life is no more, one that you held dear and sacred—when it cannot return—it is best to have no association with any part of that life. You are a memory. It has been only the past few years that I could bring myself to visit the house on Esplanade. I have had it looked after these many years and kept it partially staffed. I wish Morri to have it. She will have no unpleasant memories there. I hope she will cherish it as did I. I pretend to her that all was happy with her father, as it was for a time..."

Lona lifted the china cup to her lips, but looked down quickly, brushing away quiet tears. She then lifted her head with a soft smile, her eyes directly meeting his. "It is a grand house, the finest on Esplanade," she continued. "Acceptance is a role all must play. I have grown to accept and can therefore abide being in this city, even in that house, but Mr. Benedict, time does not heal all wounds. The scars are forever. When Morri was taken from me, I thought my life would end, that the gods were punishing me…my faith, only, kept me alive. I have said more than I have realized," she said, putting her cup and saucer on the tray. "I ask you to forgive me. Please tell me about my daughter. Will she not be arriving soon?"

Crawford proceeded in his typical, dramatic manner to reveal Morri's tale as he knew it. The chance meeting in West Tennessee, the escape, the harrowing trip to Memphis, and the passage down river. He paused, took a deep breath, then continued. "They docked at Bellevue Plantation, Adelicia Franklin Acklen, her cousin Sally and Morri." Lona's hand went to her mouth as she gasped, then paled. Crawford rang for the attendant to bring water and smelling salts. "Drink this," he said holding the glass in her hand. "Are you all right?"

She nodded, "How long," she asked in a whisper, "has she been with her—them?"

"Morri can tell you more than I can. Probably some four or five weeks. It was a freakish accident, or providence or whatever name you want to tag it. Lona, Morri knows."

Again she paled, and the attendant poured her a second glass of water at Crawford's signal.

"I'm not sure what, but something occurred that made it necessary. Adelicia has taken care of Morri, treated her as her own."

"It is too difficult to comprehend—all of it—any of it. I cannot imagine! Morri with Mrs. Acklen, Mrs. Acklen with Morri? It is, it is…"

"Please don't cry," he said tenderly.

"I am sorry."

"Don't be sorry either." He reached across the corner of his desk and took her hand. "Morri should be here soon, but before she comes, I have one question. Did…?"

"Isaac never knew about Morri," she said sternly, without emotion. "It would not have been right. I respect marriage. Once, my love for him was stronger than my faith. God has forgiven me. But when I understood that possibly I had lost my cherished daughter, I cannot tell you of my thoughts…"

Lona took a delicately laced handkerchief from her bag and put it to her eyes. "It is very difficult to speak of Isaac's death. I saw him for a brief moment only when he came that January, and in that moment, I almost told him."

Obviously then, Crawford surmised, Lona was unaware of the trust Isaac had set up with a local banker for his "child" when it came of age. It must have been Rivers who told him. And all these years, Crawford had assumed it was Lona who had shared the news of her child with Isaac.

"Mere!" Morri burst into the room. "Mere!" She ran to her mother, embracing, kneeling beside her, clinging as Lona pressed her to her breast and caressed her hair.

Lona lifted Morri's face and pulled her closer. "You are safe, you are safe...Cherie, Cherie, oh, how I love you! How I have missed you. Thank God, you are safe," she said, weeping.

Crawford found himself caught up in the moment's emotion, as scenes passed before him, scenes of Isaac that he remembered in the flash of an instant. "Now," he said, clearing his throat, "let me take you to a room. You two have much to talk over in private."

"Forgive me, Mr. Benedict. This is my daughter, Morri."

"She is almost as pretty as her mother."

"Thank you, sir, that is the finest compliment I could receive," Morri answered smiling through her tears.

"Thank you, Mr. Benedict," said Lona, "but we shall go to our house on Esplanade, and in the morning we shall leave for home, if nothing interferes, on the eleven o'clock."

He escorted them to a waiting hack and watched them drive away. Life's strange twists, he thought. Who could have ever imagined it? Morri reminded him of Lona when he had first met her years before; she had been about the same age, sixteen or seventeen, except Morri's eyes were blue. Adelicia, with Isaac and Lona's daughter! Shakespeare could not have dreamed that one up, he said to himself. He left a message for Adelicia, asking her to get in touch with him the moment she arrived.

The afternoon chill called for the servants to build a fire in the parlor where Morri and Lona sat on a small settee, embracing and holding hands. Morri told her mother all that had happened—from the time she had been kidnapped to the time of her escape with

Adelicia and Sally and their adventures along the way, even the horrible night when a stranger accosted them along a lonely road. She told Lona about the Angola plantations and New Orleans, of her fondness for Mrs. Acklen and her appreciation for her cousin, Mrs. Carter, carefully omitting the attempted rape and Mrs. Acklen's murder of the stranger.

"They have been wonderful, Mere. Mrs. Acklen selected two lovely gowns for me with matching bonnets and gloves. I chose this lovely taffeta to wear to meet you today. You would like her very much. She is a great lady much like yourself."

Lona smiled sweetly at her daughter. "I am certain she is, and I can never repay her for having brought you back safely to me. I do not know what to make of it."

"It was meant to be, Mere, I feel it."

"Perhaps you are right, my Cherie. We must get your things," Lona said, "and be on our way in the morning. I thank God you were not harmed before you met Mrs. Acklen. Morri, Cherie, I prayed for you continuously, night and day; our friends prayed and the bishop. You are so beautiful, my Cherie. I want the best for you always—I am sorry you had to know—I am sorry it was not I who told you."

"Mere, it is all right. You loved my father; he loved you. I love you, and I would have loved him. Mrs. Acklen is a lovely lady, but not nearly so lovely as you. Everything is fine, Mere, wonderfuly fine." Morri rested her head on her mother's comforting shoulder as Lona held her tightly. "Mere, I would like to tell her good-bye. Will it be painful for you to see her?"

"My Cherie, I should think it will be painful for Mrs. Acklen as well. I am sure she will not want to meet. She has been kind and good to you. That is enough."

What Lona did not express was her surprise at Adelicia's kindness. She had thought her a cold, self-centered woman who cared for no one else. "Moriah will drive us to Mrs. Acklen's to pick up your belongings, then we shall stop by the hotel if it pleases you, where you may see your friends before our departure. I do not want you out of my sight."

Morri smiled. "I shall do as you wish, but it is late. We must leave right away."

Within minutes, Lona and Morri were in the carriage enroute from Esplanade to Rue Dumaine. At the townhouse, Morri, wearing the aqua dress and a black velvet wrap of her mother's, embraced Mossy and Jacob, thanking them for their kindness as Moriah hastily put Morri's luggage in the carriage. Then they headed for the St. Montaigne. However, when Morri was told that Mrs. Acklen and Mrs. Carter were out, Lona agreed to take a room where they might wait.

Forty-five minutes later, Morri spotted them from the gallery window, Adelicia and Sally stepping from the hack, laden with boxes and packages. Hurrying down the stairs, she met them at the lobby door where the bell boys were scurrying to get their purchases loaded onto a cart.

"Morri, I was sending for you this evening to join us for supper You must have read my thoughts," Adelicia said excitedly. "The dress is beautiful on you. Thank you for your kind note. You must have been up at daybreak for Jacob to have delivered it so early."

"It fits perfectly, as does the bonnet. It is far too much, you should not have done so." She hesitated. "I am here to say good-bye. Mere has come for me and our driver is waiting. Mere is so grateful and happy. She is going to send you beautiful fabric from Haiti, fine silk and brocades. She says she can never repay you."

The words stung with an odd sort of pain. Unaware that Lona was coming to New Orleans, Adelicia thought she would see Morri off that Saturday morning. Perhaps, it was the abruptness, without time to consider Lona's presence there. Her fondness for the child was as real as if Morri were her own. Her four children by Isaac were gone, yet this daughter of Lona's survived, a part of him. For whatever the reason, the pangs were deep.

Perhaps she had loved Isaac more than she had realized, perhaps, this is how it was when one grew older, realizing gradually that love is a combination of all things. Adelicia had missed Isaac—and now she wanted to hold onto his child. How improbable, she thought, how inane; no one would ever know of her feelings, among the many things she would take to her grave.

"It is I who must repay you, Morri. You saved my life and that makes me indebted to you forever." Adelicia hugged Morri, warmly. "Do you think your mother could join us for supper this evening?"

"I shall ask."

"It would please us very much," she heard herself saying without bothering to acknowledge the look on Sally's face, wondering if she should exclude her all together. After all, Sally was unaware of the complicated relationship, not that that would dare be mentioned.

Adelicia, wondered if there were anyone who might still recognize Lona when they dined at the hotel that evening. She had never known New Orleans to be, "gossipy" like her native, Nashville, although the former wife of the deceased, dining with his former mistress would make gossipy gossip for any city.

Thus far, she had seen none of her and Joseph's friends, nor any of her and Isaac's with the exception of Elizabeth Patterson Bonaparte and Crawford. There were many, Adelicia was certain, who had known Isaac before she was his wife. However, that was a quarter of a century ago, she surmised. She would forewarn Crawford of the invitation extended to Lona and Morri.

"We shall dine at ninish," she said, "I hope to see you this evening."

Morri kissed Sally lightly on the cheek, "Thank you for your kindness, Mrs. Carter."

"If you ask me, you should have left well enough alone. I just do not understand you. Her mother was obviously trying to save you embarrassment, putting you in an embarrassing situation. Asking a woman of color to dine with us in public! I certainly hope no one in Nashville hears about this. I just don't think I can do it."

"I am sick to my death of hearing what people in Nashville will think," Adelicia raged. "You volunteered to come with me, I shall add, for a price, and you seem grandly fulfilled entertaining at Bellevue, charming the men collapsing around you. And you have served as a good companion on our arduous trip. But your inability to accept being with those who have color in their blood amazes me. Most Haitian aristocrats are mixtures of French, Spanish and Creole. Morri's mother was reared a free person of color, educated in French schools," Adelicia said, barely pausing for a breath. "She has obviously excelled on her own, more than can be said for most women with whom we are acquainted. Haitian aristocracy is not necessarily based on color, but on accomplishment. I am pleased to be seen with Morri, or her mother.

"I suggest you do some very special praying when you attend church on Sunday," Adelicia said, pointing her finger at Sally. "Had it not been for Morri, you nor I, most likely, would be here—need I again remind you that you were knocked unconscious when Blue reared and the wagon wheels rolled into a ditch, that I shot twice unsure if there really were someone there who spooked Ole Blue, that I could not have gotten the wagon out of the ditch alone? For all our sakes, you will behave civilly, and I will not speak on this topic again."

Adelicia finished in a rage, slammed the door to Sally's room, and went into her own. She rang for a maid and left a message for Crawford, asking him to make the arrangements for the proposed supper that evening. She looked through her wardrobe. Madame Duvall's had completed two additional dresses, plus matching hats, gloves, bonnets and more lavender toilette water. The exclusive shop, now heavily patronized by the wives of Yankee officers, and Yankee officers for their mistresses, had just received a shipment of new undergarments when she was there, both pink and white silk that she could not resist, and she had purchased four of each.

A bath in Epsom salts never sounded very romantic, she thought, but it left her skin marvelously smooth and soft. After splashing in rose water, she patted her body dry with the large towel, lotioned and oiled it entirely, then wrapped her ice blue satin robe around her before briefly lying on the bed to relax before dressing. No sooner had she lain down, however, than Sally knocked at the door.

"May I come in? I'm sorry, Adie. I'll get dressed now."

"Okay, Sal."

"I've not been around anyone of color except for servants. It's new for me. But often, the new is for the better. I am sorry," she repeated.

"We must hurry. It is almost eight-thirty."

"I'm looking forward to the theater on Saturday and to the affair following. You say that parties here are so different from the ones at home."

"It is the people who make them different. You will love it."

Did Sally really believe she had convinced her of her penance? She had obviously weighed matters and reasoned it better to dine with someone unfavorable than to possibly miss the big event and its opportunities on Saturday evening.

"How do I look?" Adelicia asked, as Sally came into her room.

"Lovely, dahlin, lovely. Gray silk draped off the shoulder like that is wondrous!"

"But missing are my pearls. That would make it complete. Papa always said beautiful women did not need jewelry, but I feel naked without my pearls."

"The ladies can say how beautiful your dress is, or how gorgeous you are instead of talking about your gems. Besides, that elaborate hair plume makes up for lots of jewels, dahlin."

Adelicia's hair piece was rather lavish, she admitted, set with cabochon sapphires, and gray ostrich feathers extending from the comb, that flipped over her head from the right side. "We shall go down and be there to greet them," Adelicia said taking another glance in the mirror.

"I'm ready," Sally said sweetly.

As they were shown to their table, Adelicia caught a glimpse of Crawford.

"Mrs. Carter is just as lovely as you said," he remarked, almost by her side by now, and taking Sally's arm. "The message was late in coming, but Morri and her mother will not be joining you. I know you are disappointed. However, you are both so elegantly dressed and lovely, what hindereth us from supping together?"

Adelicia could not mask the disappointment that must have shown in her face. "It appears," Crawford continued, "that the joy of having Morri safe, plus the months of anguish, had caught up with the lovely Madame Dubloivere, rendering it impossible for her to join you. But she expressed her sincerest regrets, believing that you, dear Adie, will understand. She also asked for me to say that you would hear from her upon her return home."

"How kind," Adelicia answered, somewhat aloof. They were the only words she could think of as her mind raced into myriads of flashbacks. How foolish of me to have thought Lona would desire to come into town and dine with her. "She addressed the note to you?"

"Yes, dear heart."

"I am starving," she said abruptly, "Let us make a table for four a table for three. And to have the charming Elizabethan actor in our company is indeed a blessing."

"The sinews of Dante's Hell could not prevent me from the company of you sumptuous creatures," declared Crawford.

Adelicia, with pretended laughter, took one of his arms as Sally took the other.

Supper had been pleasant, with Crawford complimenting and flattering and keeping the conversation light and gay as only he could do, perhaps considering her disappointment. But Adelicia ate less heartily than usual, nibbling on the three courses served with different wines. The dessert she had enjoyed, remarking on its deliciousness: thick, rich chocolate sauce poured over four flavors of meringued ice cream pie, served with stout black coffee.

It was an evening of performance on her part; feigned laughter, feigned conversation.

After good nights had been said to Crawford, Sally went to Adelicia's room and excitedly flung herself onto a stuffed chair. "He is enchanting, dahling, simply enchanting. How long have you known him?"

Adelicia was changing into her robe; her performance over at last. She looked at Sally and spoke as tired as she felt. "He was a good friend of Isaac's. And he is a good friend of mine."

"How good a friend?" Sally asked, teasing, "Is this why you wanted to keep him all to yourself?"

"For goodness sakes, Sal, he has been a friend for years—nothing more than a friend," she said. "Crawford is married, with a family. I knew you would adore him, everyone does. I am tired. We shopped all day. More discussion of Mr. Benedict tomorrow."

"I've never known you to tire from shopping. Where's the old Adie?"

"I am not sure. She appears from time to time, then disappears, waiting. Since Joseph's death, the trip, the pressures on me now; it is a difficult time. But you may set your bonnet, that the old Adie will resurface. Ever since Joseph left Belle Monte, nothing has been quite the same. Do not worry, cousin, all will be well."

Sally walked over and took her hand, "I'm sorry, honey lamb, I was only teasing. I guess I forget you have feelings too—get tired, I mean. Good night."

Adelicia, happy to be alone in her room, sat in the stuffed chair and propped her feet on the ottoman, brooding, watching the flames flicker against the shadows of the hearth. Sally had said it, although unintentionally. It was true: no one thought Adelicia felt like others, as if she were oblivious to pain, unknowing it was pretended gaiety while weeping inside.

Adelicia would be on the wharf the following morning to see Morri and Lona off. She did not know what she would say nor how it would be said, but she knew she must go. Lona surely understood the debt Adelicia owed to Morri.

"Holy Father," she prayed. "Please forgive my sins both past and present. They are many. Continue to grant me Thy favor. Stay with me, Lord, through all the tomorrows…especially in the morning. In the Name of Jesus, amen."

Adelicia had asked to be awakened at eight, requesting no breakfast, and by nine-fifteen, she was in a hack on her way to the wharf. She walked to the edge of the steep bank then stood for a moment, watching the activity on the river, military ships, patrols, cargo, tugboats, barges—all interconnected with the sounds of horns, toots, sloshing water and blended voices.

She smiled as the brisk breeze from the river lifted her taffeta tan skirt, causing it to rustle. And as she stood holding the matching hat with her left hand, she felt radiant against the backdrop. The tan suit coat fit perfectly in the waist, flaring snugly over her skirt, proper attire for the occasion, she thought. The cuffs fit snugly around her small wrist. The tall collar and the border of her skirt trimmed in deep, black-brown velvet, matching the hat and small covered buttons of her jacket, made for a splendid look.

She quickly walked the short distance to the pier where the ship would depart, leaving for warm Caribbean Seas, and saw Morri and her mother on deck with their backs to her talking with another passenger.

"I request permission to come aboard, sir," Adelicia said to the captain, who stood at the bottom of the gangplank biting into an apple, purchased from a nearby vendor.

"Don't stay too long," he nodded. "We're pulling out in twenty minutes."

She hurried up the boarding plank, hoping not to be visible until she was much closer. But suddenly she felt frightened, reluctant that she had come as she watched the acquaintance walk away just as she was within range to say, "Excuse me, I hope you do not mind, I feel a need to say good-bye."

"Mrs. Acklen!" Morri said in surprise. She embraced her with girlish delight, "Pardon me, Mere, this is the dear lady who brought me to safety."

"I can never thank you enough, nor repay your kindness. If there is anything I can ever do for you, please ask," Lona graciously offered, taking Adelicia's hand.

Adelicia felt neither joy nor pain in her soul, but an uneasy feeling impossible to describe. Here she was standing face to face with Lona again as if she were an old acquaintance—but that—she was not. She hoped her nervous words would sound soft and pleasant and tumble out in the manner she intended. Thank God, supper had gone as it had. Lona's beauty was unmarred by time.

"On the contrary, your daughter saved my life. Had it not been for Morri, when we were on the road near Memphis, perhaps neither my cousin nor I would be alive today."

"Morri, you did not tell me of this."

Morri's face reddened.

"It does not seem as dreadful now that we are removed from it," Adelicia lied.

"Shall we sit?" Lona asked, motioning to a deck bench.

"Thank you."

Adelicia had smiled near the end of her story, successful in erasing its seriousness and successful in releaving the stress still evident on Morri's face.

"So you see, Madame, I am indebted to your daughter for my life. I shall return the proposal. If there is anything I can ever do for you or your daughter, please ask," Adelicia paused, then continued. "And it will be a great pleasure for me if you will allow Morri to correspond from time to time. Mrs. Carter and I have grown quite fond of your lovely daughter, whose sweet countenance has graced our days..." Pausing, she added, "I must go, or I too, shall be bound for Haiti, and I shall not get my cotton shipped."

Adelicia gently embraced Morri then took Lona's hand. The two women looked into each other's eyes...much different from the startled look of over twenty years before on the staircase at Fairvue.

"I shall cherish this visit," said Lona. "May God bless you, Mrs. Acklen."

"And may God bless you—and Morri," Adelicia said, holding Lona's gloved hand between both her own, while wondering what Morri, who stood to the side, must be thinking as she observed her and her mother. Reaching the end of the wharf, Adelicia looked back, holding her arm high overhead, waving good-bye.

Blinking back tears, she walked directly to the Cafe DuMonde and sipped hot blended chicory. She had needed the good-bye; she hoped Lona had not found her visit intrusive. Adelicia would sit until her melancholy passed, then return to the hotel and make excuses to Sally as to where she had gone so early in the morning. Later she would meet with Crawford, and make firm plans for the cotton. One thing for certain, she thought, as she sipped her third cup of the creamy liquid, one never knew with whom one's life would interfold. One needs to expect surprises, she thought. Life's surprises—the Providence of God!

CHAPTER 79

"ADIE, I FEEL GLAMOROUS, SIMPLY GLAMOROUS, THE MOST glamorous I have felt since before the war, but are you sure it's proper for us to go to the theater unescorted? Even if this is New Orleans?" Sally, outstanding in pale pink satin, Adelicia most compelling in an off the shoulder ivory tulle, stood admiring their gowns.

"My dear cousin, we are both widows who want to attend the theater, and, yes, it is proper, at least according to my standards. Do you suggest we not go?"

"Never! It does seem 'different,' however."

Adelicia had borrowed jewelry from her old acquaintance, Elizabeth Patterson Bonaparte, whom she and Isaac had met years before at the Virginia Springs. She was nearer Isaac's age, and although eccentric then, and pushy, on behalf of her grandson, Charles Joseph, Adelicia had become very fond of her.

The countess was seldom seen in New Orleans' society, and held a serious disdain for men. After her unfortunate involvement with Jerome, she vowed to never trust another male. He had agreed with his brother, The Emperor Napoleon, that she must return to the United States, rendering it possible in Paris to annul the marriage as if it had never existed, even though she was the mother of his son, Jerome Napoleon, "Bo." Still lovely in her late seventies and quite wealthy, Elizabeth had lived as if she were expecting poverty to befall her at any moment, even when she traveled between the continents.

On her third day in New Orleans, Adelicia had overheard the dressmakers speak of sewing a dress for Madame Bonaparte, and she was delighted to find the grand old lady joyous when she called on her that same afternoon. While discussing the theater, Elizabeth had insisted Adelicia wear some of her treasured jewels and to, "wear them proudly."

"I shall guard them with my life," she had told her. Adelicia counted herself fortunate to be in Elizabeth's good graces, as few people were. She neither liked her daughter-in-law, Susan, nor the *ordinary* way her son was living his life. She favored the younger of her two grandsons far more than the other, thinking he had some promise of *style*.

Adelicia could not have been happier than to be wearing the Countess's diamond necklace, with matching ear bobs and bracelets, and as she slipped one of them over her white kid glove, she thought she looked much like a countess herself.

Adelicia and Sally stepped from the carriage and entered the old Spanish theater on Rue St. Peter and went directly to the Acklen box seats, seats Adelicia had held for many years. She was well aware that most every head had turned upon her and Sally's entrance.

"No one," Sally whispered, "would venture to guess we're at war."

The curtain rose and Adelena Patti, a favorite of New Orleans, brought everyone to their feet at the end of her first number. Her splendid half hour of song was followed by an excellent performance of *A Mid-Summer Night's Dream*, and a most deserved standing ovation. Meanwhile, Adelicia peered into the other boxes looking for familiar faces, remembering the courting she had observed through the years during intermissions. It was where the best of casual introductions were made. And where 'those that be' made certain their sons and daughters met.

How good to be part of society again, she thought. She had been widowed for a second time and isolated in Nashville for almost three years. Would that not cause change in anyone who loved life? She felt marvelous—without a trace of the scenes that had recently upset her. She would spend this evening fully in the moment of a time. "Let us celebrate," Adelicia said giddily, leaning over to Sally after the last curtain call.

"And what do you suggest?"

"I suddenly feel that all is wonderful."

"I'm surely thankful to hear that, dahling."

"And what are two lovely ladies doing unescorted in this town of sinful, lurking, evil men, awaiting to devour?"

Adelicia had no need to turn around to recognize Crawford's unmistakable voice. She admitted she was glad to see him. "And where is Mrs. Benedict tonight?" she inquired.

"In the powder room. I'm requesting the two of you join us for a 'late night supper,' I think you call it in Tennessee, this evening."

"Thank you very much," said Adelicia. "Have you forgotten, you had previously extended the invitation? "

"I'm especially looking forward to it and to meeting Mrs. Benedict," Sally echoed in one of her syrupiest voices, definitely intended for Crawford's ears.

"May I get a cab for you?" he asked.

"Now, Crawford, darling, you should know we would have our own driver for the theater. Jacob drove us in. And it is he will deliver us to your grand palace hotel."

"I should have known." He laughed. "I'm glad to see my eloquent speech has been an influence on you."

The three walked down the curved stairs together into the courtyard and out to the waiting carriage. "I shall see you fair damsels in a short while," Crawford said.

As Adelicia had foretold, "everyone" was at the Benedicts gathering. She found herself among a few old acquaintances, but mostly strangers, and she was in a mood to enjoy them all, even Valencia Benedict. Later in the evening, she realized she had not seen Sally for some time; she was too busy buzzing from person to person herself, delighted with the evening, and suspecting her cousin was doing the same.

The handsome ballroom was set with elegantly dressed round tables for dining wherever one chose, and it was an affair, with only one belle, as far as Adelicia was concerned. A miraculous spectacle, indeed, considering she was well past forty, to see young and older admirers alike pass over the younger damsels to focus their attention on her.

The secret must lie with the fact that beauty and charm, accompanied by common sense, intelligence and experience, was much preferred to simpleton beauty and charm, not discounting, of course, self-confidence and poise. Most women, she thought, for example Crawford's wife, who was years younger than she—begin imagining at thirty-five that old age has settled upon them. It was an inherent truth that none of the above need be wasted on any age. All years are fair game!

"Excuse me, my dear Adelicia," Crawford said. "Mrs. Shepley," he nodded to the governor's wife, with whom Adelicia had been conversing at the special table done in exquisite decor. "The General has been urging me to make an introduction for the past hour."

As she had walked with Crawford to where General Bennington stood, Adelicia felt an extraordinary anticipation of meeting him. He was handsome, tall, with a large frame, deep-set dark eyes and thick dark hair blended with gray that touched his earlobes and the nape of his neck. She had noticed him earlier in the evening as he mingled with guests and had wondered how long it would take for him to come to her. Longer than she had anticipated. He also looked familiar.

"General Bennington, the lovely, enchanting Mrs. Acklen," said Crawford.

"It is my sincerest pleasure to meet you, Mrs. Acklen," he said, taking her outstretched hand and glancing at Crawford. "I've been observing you since your arrival."

She grew even more fascinated as he spoke, his voice deep and mellow, unlike that of most Yankees she had heard. It sounded like New England, like the accent of her Grandfather Hayes.

"It is a pleasure for me, sir. Do you have a name other than General?" she smiled.

"Forgive me, my dear Mrs. Acklen," he said bowing, "the name that goes with this stature is Ransom Bennington, from Massachusetts, United States."

They laughed together. "A handsome name, General, that becomes you."

He blushed. "Why is it that southern ladies pay compliments with an irresistible charm that causes one to blush?"

Her retort reflected her disdain of being grouped with other ladies. "Charm is not a respecter of geography. Anyone may possess it. Charm, however, is measurable, depending on from whose lips it comes—proving sincere and fascinating, or no more than a blowing wind."

"I take the reprimand in earnest. You are charm itself. Shall we dance?"

"But it is not a dance...no one else is..."

"It doesn't matter," he said, taking her hand.

"If you will excuse me," Crawford said, bowing.

The General took her in his arms and onto a small portion of floor not crowded with tables or skirts or feet and slowly waltzed her to the strands of "Laura Lei" played by the three piece ensemble. It was a beautiful moment into which she was swept, tuning out the chatter around them and those moving to clear their path.

"Sal, it was so wonderful," she said later, collapsing into bed. "He is one of the most interesting men I have ever met. He talks so like Grandpa Hayes. I love hearing New Englanders speak."

"It's not been two days since you said you would never marry or fall in love again and you are behaving like..."

"No one," Adelicia interrupted, "has said a word about either love or marriage—he is exciting, unforgettable, unlike any..." She stopped abruptly. She did not want to think about Joseph or Isaac or any man she had 'ever met.' She had loved Alphonso, Isaac and Joseph all so differently, and she had no thoughts of love. Ransom was simply exciting, witty, intelligent...sincere.

"I agree he's handsome and charming," said Sally. "Is he married?"

"A widower. The reason he never remarried, he says, is because he is looking for perfection. I wanted to say he had found it. However, because I shall never marry again, I looked at him and simply smiled. Besides, I am not sure perfection is ever what we perceive to be."

They were laughing as Adelicia stretched the full length of her bed and yawned. "We have an engagement for supper tomorrow evening."

"So do I, with Colonel Nicholas Pauche. We chatted off and on throughout the evening. His father was the famous General Pauche from Rhode Island, War of 1812, a friend of President Jackson's. So far, he's not as exciting as he is strikingly handsome. But I'm working on that," Sally added. "I also spent time with Crawford. He's truly magnificent!"

"Sal, the connections we have made!" Adelicia said excitedly, ignoring Sally's last remark.

Adelicia spent most of Saturday afternoon preparing for her evening with Ransom Bennington. She had heard Elizabeth Patterson tell the story of how she and Jerome Bonaparte had fallen passionately in love with each other on their first meeting. Although interference, adhering to his brother's wishes caused him to desert her, money and position being powerful contenders, she somehow felt the depth of Jerome's love long after they were parted. If Adelicia allowed it, she knew that she could care deeply for this New England aristocrat. Without pretension, he had mentioned Queen Victoria as casually as if she were his relative.

She wore her new emerald green velvet, trimmed around the low-cut neck line with old ivory lace that hung softly over her shoulders and the tops of her arms. Her hair was done up in braids with gardenia buds woven in at the crown. Again, she donned her borrowed jewelry, and again she viewed herself in the mirror as being a most elegant and beautiful woman.

She could not remember a time when she had been unable to take her eyes from a man's face but from the moment they were seated at Antoine's, Adelicia could not stop looking into Ransom's eyes. She was awed by him.

"We've met before, you know," he said.

"Where?" she asked, fascinated. "I was certain you looked familiar."

"Many years ago. During Mardi Gras. I never had my dance with you, so last night I was determined to take no chances."

Adelicia smiled, then asked, "Was it Crawford who introduced us? Wonder why he did not mention it."

"I requested that he not. He and I have become better friends over the years. I do a great deal of brokering with him, or through him. I never thought I'd be wearing a uniform that would show our country divided."

"Tell me about yourself," she said.

"At Mardi Gras of '46, Crawford introduced me as being from Massachusetts, and you had asked if I were acquainted with the Hayes, Bliss or Chauncey families, but before I could answer, Mr. Franklin called you away. So seventeen years later: yes, I did know them."

"Ah," she laughed, "your memory excels! Now I wish to know much more about you."

"I chose to seek my fortune in America. My grandfather, Duke Bennington, returned home to Kent, unharmed, after fighting with the British in the Battle of 1814—here in New Orleans, to be exact. My great grandfather had also returned home unharmed after fighting during your Revolution, two losses, I fear, for Merry England. The tales of lush greenery, clear skies, dense forest and opportunity that I had heard since my birth, fascinated and lured me to your Eastern shores. After Cambridge, I set up shop in Massachusetts, banking, investing. I've been blessed, as my faith in the United States had foretold."

"Then you married an American?"

"Yes," he answered, before abruptly changing the subject. "I thought you a most interesting, fascinating woman, and I have hoped for many years to see you again."

"What an enchanting man you are."

"I'm in love with you."

She was unsure of her sensation, whether embarrassment, conscience or shock. Her need for words, or...She lightly touched his hand that was stretched across the elegant square table. "I have been widowed for only a few months, not quite three. I should not be here with you. I should still be dressed in mourning." Tears welled up in her eyes.

"I had not intended to upset you," Ransom said, removing his hands from the table. "Nor did Crawford tell me it had been so short a while since you were widowed, nor do I know the circumstances. Please forgive me. But you are here, and the words I spoke were not said in haste."

She asked to be taken back to the hotel, disappointed in herself and guilt ridden. But as the carriage neared the St. Montaigne, she tilted her head up towards him "I am sorry," she said. "May we go to Jackson Square and walk in the park?"

The horses were given rein. And no sooner, it seemed, had the order been given than they were sitting on one of the granite benches near Andrew Jackson's statue, the cathedral and Cabildo behind them, the Pontalba buildings on either side and they facing the river. Gas lamps provided a soft glowing light for them to see each other as they talked, and when he took her face in his hands, she quickly moved them to the space on the bench between them.

"When I was first introduced to you, I was a widower," he said. "My precious young bride was taken when our son was two, our daughter, an infant. I never believed there would be anyone about whom I could feel as I did Ellen. I still believe that." He took a deep breath, exhaling slowly. "Expecting two feelings of love to be the same is to lose love altogether. I was smitten the first time I saw you, but I knew you were Mrs. Franklin. I never thought I should see you again, but I also never forgot you. I was taken aback when I discovered you were in the City of New Orleans, and widowed."

She considered his thoughtful words, then continued with her own agenda, "My life has changed drastically during this war. I shall not go into the details now, but I must be honest with you. I am not in New Orleans to attend plays or parties or go to supper. I feel guilty, mostly, for enjoying them. You are correct when you said that I was with you now—I am with you."

She looked steadily into his eyes. "I feel guilty for the feelings I have for you so soon after my husband's death, so soon after meeting you," she heard herself say. "And I am most sorry about the early loss of your wife, and I thank you for sharing that with me." She reached for his hand and held it between her gloved ones.

"Ransom, I am here on a mission. I need to have two thousand plus bales of cotton shipped to England. Another eight hundred acres has been picked, mostly, and the Negroes are in the process of trashing, ginning and baling. It must be removed from my plantations in West Feliciana Parish to New Orleans and onto a cargo ship bound for England. Crawford Benedict will make my ship connections and help in other areas as well. He has friends in all places, it seems. But I need assurance that the Yankees will not confiscate the cotton for their own use. I intend to be wealthier when this abominable war is over then before. My children's welfare—their future, and mine—is dependent upon it. Most of our friends and family have had everything they own taken, or have donated it to the Confederacy. I intend for neither to happen. I am in 'the hot seat,' as my mammy would say—frightened to death that the Yankees will steal it or that the Rebels will burn it."

The look in his eyes never changed. He asked only one question, "Whose side are you on?"

"Was that intended as humor?"

"I asked you a question."

"Neither!"

"That was honest," he said matter of factly. "I have nothing to confess to you. I have been a widower for many years, and I'm a general in the United States Army. I wish there were no war."

"I told you as a friend. I trust you. I realize you could seize my crop or put me in jail. Admiral Farragut thinks I have just a few acres in cotton. It has been difficult, to say the least, as his and Porter's boats patrol the river that flows through and beside the plantations twenty-four hours a day. Thus far, I have been lucky. For all I know, the Rebels will have it before I return to Angola."

Ransom had gently lifted her left hand into his, as if he had heard nothing to upset him.

"I enjoy your company—more than I wish to admit," she said, "and I did not want you to think I was..."

"Using me," he interrupted, "to get your cotton safely to New Orleans, then to England?"

"Yes. If we are to have a friendship of any sort, it must be an honest one."

"Agreed. I am glad you enjoy my company," he said as if teasing her. "And I am happy to see what I can do to arrange safe storage for your cotton, whatever Crawford doesn't arrange. I feel certain it can be accomplished. I am sincerely sorry about your husband's death. And I apologize for having been overly familiar. Perhaps war causes one to say things that ordinarily would be left to later times, other times. I hope you will accept my apology."

She allowed her hand to relax in his. "You are an interesting man, General Benedict, and I accept your apology. I am hopeful we shall see much of each other."

He stood, gently took her in his arms and kissed her tenderly on the cheek. "Would you like to walk to the Cafe Dumonde for coffee and beignets?"

She nodded, and they walked toward the river, stepping closely, with her arm through his, as the damp thickness of the Mississippi's fog closed around them.

CHAPTER 80

IT WAS NOT UNTIL ADELICIA WAS COMFORTABLY SITUATED IN BED that she heard Sally's key in the lock, and then the knock on their adjoining door.

"Are you asleep, dahling? Oh, he is divine, simply divine! Nicholas Pauche is divine!"

"You must have had a wonderful evening." Adelicia yawned.

"Men are such adorable creatures, aren't they? I'm certain God created them simply for our pleasure."

"Tell me," Adelicia asked, fully awake. "Did you discuss anything relevant to *our* mission?"

"First, let me tell you about the evening, then I shall come to that."

After an hour of exclamations, Sally hardly drawing a breath, she told Adelicia that with the connections of Nicholas' late father, and his own, he felt he could be of much assistance in securing the cotton.

Adelicia could not return to her relaxed state prior to Sally's entrance. She would ask Ransom if Nicholas could be trusted, if so, she would reveal more information. Ransom's and Nicholas's connections, along with Crawford's assured success from the Union. Now she must obtain that same assurance from the Confederates. Considering that not so difficult a task, she eased her mind with the thought that all was working to her advantage, that her mission in West Feliciana would soon be accomplished. On the other hand, it was seeming too easy. She had never trusted easy.

It had been almost two years since she had seen Joseph, but she had been widowed for only three months. Not long enough to be infatuated with someone else when she had been so in love with her husband, or believed so. She disliked doubting her feelings for Joseph were real, as real as feelings could be, just as she had disliked doubting her feelings for Isaac. She fully understood, as Ransom had so eloquently stated, that each love in one's life was different from the other. She was dismissing 'love' with Alphonso; then she was only seventeen.

What she most disliked was doubting herself. Her father had told her, "Never doubt yourself—once you begin, it gradually seeps into everything you do; it is the beginning of confidence never regained."

Who had set the time limits on widowhood? On feelings? On love? Opinions! Traditions!

Those, she could do without, would do without, and no longer concern herself. I shall see Ransom when it is convenient, and when the war is over, she reasoned, he may call at Belle Monte or I may visit Massachusetts, or both. He may even choose to open a bank in Nashville. Of course, she had no idea when that time would come or if she would still be attracted to him then, or if it were the war, this city, or the times that was causing her these rash thoughts. After her cotton was shipped, she would have more time to think before going home.

Adelicia fell into sleep, dreaming of grand things to come, while missing her children terribly. It seemed eons since kissing their cherub cheeks, since hearing their laughter and holding them to her, but soon she would be with them; all was going well.

Rain had poured from heavy skies all day on Sunday, so instead of the planned drive to River Road and picnicking on the levee after mass at St. Louis Cathedral, Sally, Nicholas, Ransom and Adelicia went to Boudro's for brunch, then to the townhouse. Mossy and Jacob unsuccessfully attempted to conceal their shock at seeing their mistress and Sally with two blue-uniformed Yankee officers. And after Adelicia had shown her guests into the parlor, she asked to be excused. "Mossy, control yourself. The two gentlemen are going to help get our cotton to England."

"Is it General Butler?" Mossy asked, frightened.

"No. It is General Bennington and Colonel Pauche. You may remember the Pauches," she said comfortingly. "His father was a guest in our home some years ago. Now stop being a silly, get Jacob out of the cupboard and serve some hot tea. Also, have him build a fire in both parlors."

The next two hours went uninterrupted except for Mossy's entrance to bring the requested tea, which Adelicia poured and served, and the building of the fires by a reluctant Jacob.

After having spoken with Ransom about Nicholas, Adelicia trusted him, as she trusted Ransom. And that afternoon, before the warm fire, they discussed the most efficient, logical route for Adelicia to successfully execute her plan. A strategy that sounded to her much like a strategic military operation.

After the initial business, they chatted on various subjects throughout the dark and damp afternoon, with Ransom rekindling the fire from time to time. The most memorable, as far as Adelicia was concerned from what she considered sheer prattle, was that of the Catholic mass, a first for both her and Sally. Similar to an Episcopal service, with exceptions of communion, creed, et cetera, Nicholas had commented. But it was far from the Presbyterian ones to which she and Sally were accustomed, and Adelicia made it clear, she was pleased to have been reared Presbyterian.

Time passed too quickly, it seemed to her, for the hall clock was soon striking eleven. Mossy had not winced when Adelicia asked her later in the day to set two extra places for her guests, and had prepared a sumptuous meal of chicken and dumplings smothered in heavy broth. And as they stood in the wide alcove beneath the clock, Ransom took Adelicia's hand, saying, "It's been a week end I shall not forget."

"Nor shall I," she said, looking wistfully into his eyes. He kissed her hand lightly and left with Nicholas.

CHAPTER 81

ADELICIA AWOKE REFRESHED, HURRIED WITH HER BATH AND toiletries then quickly wiggled into her undergarments and silk stockings before breakfast at half past seven. She intended to be on time when she met Ransom at Governor Shepley's office.

"Good to see you, General," Governor Shepley said, extending his hand to Ransom. "Is this business or pleasure?" he asked, acknowledging Adelicia.

"Business, unfortunately. May I present Mrs. Acklen. You met, I believe, at the St. Montaigne last Friday evening."

Adelicia smiled, extending her gloved hand. "I need your help, Governor."

After hearing Adelicia's plight, the Governor assured her there would be no restraints placed on her, or the shipping of her cotton so long as he had her solemn oath that the Confederate Army would receive no part of it, nor the money she received from it. Because there was no Confederate Marshal in East Louisiana, it would be easier for Adelicia to avoid handing over her crop to them, or its proceeds, he openly acknowledged, but he had asked her about West Louisiana and Shreveport, where the state government had been moved after Opelousas had fallen.

"Governor, my neighbor's horses are being impressed as well as their tools, harnesses and wagons. For two and one-half years, they have been given script, which has proven useless, and I see nothing to make me think it will be otherwise. Neighbors up and down the river are strained to pay their bills and to feed their remaining Negroes after having given the Confederate Government money and supplies. It is a pathetic scene to behold. Some are already ruined, have left the state, unable to pay their taxes. Thus far, I have been spared. Many of my Negroes are still with me, but I must feed and clothe them, keep up the buildings on the plantations, my townhouse here in the city and my estate in Nashville. I give you my solemn oath that the

Confederate Government will never reap any rewards from the sale of my cotton. The proceeds are for myself, my children, for our future survival and independence, and for those dependent on me. I think it better that I care for my workers than make them your wards. You already have enough hungry mouths to feed, as does every other southern state, and you do not need five hundred more. One might say I am doing you a favor."

The governor puffed on his pipe while listening to Adelicia's rhetoric and her self-imposed logic. From the looks of the almond colored velvet suit she was wearing, the matching hat, gloves and slippers, her manner, her voice, her presence, caused him to chuckle to himself. He knew she was accustomed to the finest and had no intention of being without it, either now or after the war. He was also aware, as was Ransom Bennington, that there was much activity engaging both sides in and around the Acklen plantations, and on Red River. Still, he would trust her.

Governor Shepley promised her Union wagons and mules on which to load the bales of cotton and that when they arrived in New Orleans, her cotton would be stored and secured in Union houses until it could be shipped. Crawford would see to the shipping, that was his department.

"May I have your word, sir, that you will not confiscate my cotton after it is stored in your houses?"

He stood, smiling. "Yes, my dear, you have my solemn oath."

"I was told to never trust a Yankee, but it seems I am surrounded by them and have no choice. Of course, my father's family is from New England, but I do not think that is considered, Yankee." He chuckled aloud and took her hand.

"I shall confer with General Bennington and Mr. Benedict. Do not be troubled. All will be well. And I hope to see you again under strictly sociable conditions."

"And I, you, sir. Thank you, thank you very much."

The December morning was crisp. The previous day's chilling rain had brought with it a delayed cold front. Adelicia turned up the velvet collar of her cape and put her hands in the matching black muff as she and Ransom stepped from the hansom and walked into

Crawford's waterfront office, where additional arrangements were made and concealed.

It seemed to her that everyone knew everyone, whether Army, or Navy, Yankee or Rebel and most amazingly, everyone did everyone favors. All were interconnected, woven into a mysterious and intriguing web. She was watching it; she was living it. She felt certain the history books that would attempt to record this war for future generations would never report it accurately, report what had really transpired, and no one would know what it was really like, what really took place. Perhaps it was the same with all wars. She supposed so.

Adelicia and Ransom met Sally and Nicky—as Sally now called him—for luncheon at the St. Montaigne with Crawford. She and Sally would return to West Feliciana with expectations of the arrival of Union wagons and mules. An order of safe conduct from Confederate Lieutenant-General Leonidas Polk would protect her cotton from being burned by the Rebels, and a military guard would insure its protection.

"I must telegram home," Adelicia said.

"Come up to my office, you can do it from there,"Crawford suggested.

"Dearest children, how I do miss you and long to touch your sweet faces. Cousin Sally and I have known many delays but plan to have our goals accomplished in another week, no more than two. Cannot wait to hold you in my arms and tell you of our adventures. Give Essie and all my love. Cousin Sally sends her love, as well. She is also sending telegram...will see you before the Merry Holiday. Your loving mother.

Two days later, Adelicia and Sally were boarding the *Lucas Belle*, Ransom arriving early to take them to the wharf. She quickly bid Mossy and Jacob good-bye, promising to see them before returning home to Nashville.

"How, I wish I could go with you, my dearest," Ransom said, holding Adelicia's hands in his, "but duty demands that I return from my leave tomorrow. Keep these papers in a safe place," he said, tucking them into the pocket of her cape. "It's highly unlikely we could come by them again—orders from Lieutenant-General Polk, Governor Shepley and General Banks! And as you play the enemy sides, don't forget that I am in love with you."

"Take care," she said, "and I shall never forget."

She was unhappy to be leaving Ransom, who in so brief a time had revitalized feelings she had not believed possible to have again, recaptured the tenderest thoughts of love, even as she understood there was no assurance she would ever see him again. He must return to duty, and she to the business at hand. That was the way with life.

Nicholas Pauche, General Bank's aide, was remaining in New Orleans. His secret could never be told. That would mean treason for Nicholas, for it was he who, through a Confederate friend, had obtained the signed papers from Lieutenant-General Polk on Adelicia's behalf. Knowing her and her family, and sympathetic with her circumstances, Polk had readily signed the order.

"You know, Adie," Sally said when they were well on their way up-river, "if someone wrote this story, from the time we left home until now, no one would ever believe it. Cooper, Dickens' and Eliot's tales are at least believable."

"Have you read *Moby Dick?*"

"Goodness no, it's too long and boring unless you want a lesson on whales, whaling and the sea."

Adelicia smiled. She had read Ahab's quest for the white whale through twice, and had studied some chapters at length, fascinated and intrigued with the lessons learned, a spirited text.

"I have no idea how often I have read Cooper's 'Tales' to the children. Bud recently read *Uncle Tom's Cabin,*" she added, "and remains shocked at the superb reviews it received. Bud says Stowe writes on pre-school level, infantile. Of course, it is only the Northern sympathizers, the Northern papers exalting it."

"Have you ever wanted to write a play or a novel?" Sally asked

"In school, when we wrote poetry, I considered it...never seriously though. I probably liked living tales rather than telling them." Adelicia laughed.

"We should write our adventures."

"An excellent idea, but as you say, no one would find them believable. You write the novel…but, Sal, do change the names."

They were enjoying the peaceful, playful revelry aboard the *Lucas Belle* when Sally suddenly asked, "What are we ever going to do with Major Hanson and Captain Carmack?"

"There will be no changes. We shall proceed exactly as before."

CHAPTER 82

THE DECEMBER DAYS WERE PASSING QUICKLY. ADELICIA HAD ALready missed Thanksgiving with her family and now the Christmas holidays were approaching. Everyone on the plantations was engaged with the cotton: ginning, baling, then loading it on twenty wagons pulled by mule teams sent up from Baton Rouge. She had ridden Promise up and down the Federal and Confederate lines, requesting and securing their cooperation with her maneuvers. To General Taylor of the Confederate Army, she had shown the authorization from Lieutenant-General Polk, to which he added his own signature. To Union General Scott, she had shown the papers signed and co-signed by Governor Shepley and General Banks.

In total, it amounted to having a guard of sixteen Confederate soldiers, under Captain David Carmack's command, overseeing the safety of Adelicia's cotton while on the plantation, and to its being loaded onto Union wagons pulled by Union mules.

She felt certain that no one really understood the operation from the highest to the lowest in command, but it was working. By the tenth day of December, she sat on her five-year old, molasses brown gelding and watched the last wagon pull out of the gin house guarded by David Carmack, to begin the thirty mile trip overland to Bayou Sara. The shipment would cross the Mississippi by ferry then be transferred to a Union escort until it reached New Orleans. Upon arrival, the cotton would be stored in Union houses until it was shipped to Liverpool. Her mules and wagons would return to Baton Rouge.

The smoothness of the operation was as amazing as it was unnerving to her. Shelling and firing exploded up and down the Mississippi and in the surrounding Tunica Hills, but amidst it all, two thousand bales of last year's cotton was in route to New Orleans.

Adelicia thought she must have provided the entire Confederate army its meat supply that autumn, not omitting her neighbor's corn, ground at her mill. She had promised the South her continued aid through 1864. She had promised the North nothing, except that the South would not benefit from the sale of her cotton. But, of course, she was still seeing to Yankee' welfare with cattle and goods, just as she was the Rebels. Indeed, a task within itself.

Sally was aware only of the basics known by Ransom and Nicholas, nothing of the deeper, interior deception. She was totally unaware of the extent of Adelicia's illicit dealings, the internet of supplies, by whom, to whom, the deals made between the two sides, or who did what. All three knew about the orders from those high in command; only Adelicia and Jim Clack knew the complexities of those orders as they entered the scene.

Well you did it," Jim Clack said, standing in the parlor at Bellevue with his hands on his hips, looking like a satisfied man.

"Let's not forget, you were the strategy planner that took each of us working and playing our part for it to have happened. You also commandeered the home front. I cannot thank you enough for all you have accomplished." She smiled. "I shall be thanking you with more than words when I make a draw from the bank, after returning to New Orleans."

"It's not necessary, Mrs. Acklen. We've done something I bet no one else has ever done, or will do. It was as challenging as it was frightening—even the entertaining!"

"That, it has been."

"You know ma'am, we only shipped a few of the new bales already, along with last years. Anyway, there's at least another two thousand to go if you think we can make one more run for it," Clack said, taking the chair opposite her.

She said nothing for a moment, and neither did he. A smile broke on her lips, "I have actually thought of the same thing."

"Hot damn!" He threw his hat into the air and stood up. "Oh forgive me, Mrs. Acklen, but the excitement is—if you stay through the spring planting season, it will be better. There's another load to ship, like I said, as much as this time. And if we get the fall crop in the ground by March, we can plant and gin at the same time. You've done it different from Mr. Acklen, and there's not been any trouble. Of course, there wasn't any trouble the first few times with him. What do you say?"

"I want to see my family, Jim, I miss them, and it will soon be Christmas. I have never been away from the children at Christmas. With neither mother nor father present, it would not be very happy for them. Of course, Essie can see to the necessary shopping and baking, and perhaps see to their parties as well. Corrine, Laura and Sally's children, all their cousins, are there, so they really would be with family. Yes, I..." Suddenly realizing she had been thinking aloud, rationalizing, convincing herself, she was embarrassed that Jim had heard her mental deductions. "Yes, I suppose I could stay. When do we ship? When do we plant?"

"If the market does what I'm hearing, next fall's crop might bring double this one. Never thought I'd see $1.89 per pound, and this shipment will at least bring that, probably more!"

"Do you think that's possible? For the autumn?"

"That's the talk."

"Double! I did not think the market could go higher! How extraordinary! I shall take the children, Essie and the nurses to Europe just as soon as the war is over. I shall build a library! That is exactly what I shall do. I must hurry back to New Orleans, send telegrams, go to the bank. I shall leave in the morning and return at week's end." She had also stored away the idea of making certain that all two thousand bales were safely ensconced in their temporary housing, and that the mules and wagons were again available to Bellevue Plantation.

Adelicia and Sally were aboard the early morning packet down river, she to complete the necessary business, and Sally to resume her relationship with Nicholas Pauche. She had not mentioned her discussion with Jim Clack to Sally. She would give it more thought.

"Dearest Children, Mama cannot be with you this year at Christmas. Our plan worked perfectly, but it is necessary that I stay and help Mr. Clack manage the plantations and complete the shipping, as did your papa, and see to planting the autumn crop in the spring. It seems so long a time since I have held my darlings. Tell Essie when the war is over, we shall take a trip to Europe and perhaps

meet queens and kings. Ask her and your nurses to take each of you shopping and for Essie to shop some by herself. You may send mama letters to Bellevue Plantation, although few get through. Let me know what Kris Kringle leaves for you. Mama misses her precious ones and shall be thinking of you all on the Holiday as I do every day. Give your aunts and uncles my love. Sending you all of the hugs and kisses possible until I can be with you once more, Mother. Never forget your prayers."

Handing the lengthy telegram to the operator, she dabbed the tears flowing down her cheeks, and hurried to the Bank of New Orleans, arriving minutes before closing time. After making a large withdrawal, she headed for the townhouse. "I shall only be here over night," she told Mossy, "but I kept my promise to return."

She sat with Mossy and Jacob around the kitchen table, giving them tales of the plantations. She had purchased a gift for each and after placing them under the tree, put a ten dollar gold piece in each of their hands. "You too good, Miz. Acklen, you too good. Thank you," Mossy said.

"Not as good as I would like to be," she said going up the stairs. She meant that in more than one way.

"Mossy," she called down. "Bring a dinner tray to my room, please. I am staying here tonight. Mrs. Carter is dining out."

"I spose with the Yankee?"

"Colonel Pauche. She will not be returning with me to the plantations in the morning."

"Lausy, I almost forgot," she called out. "In all the citement I did, but on the blanket chest is a package, a big one."

Indeed, it was a "big one." The supreme joy in opening any sort of parcel remained constant, and she excitedly tore into the heavy brown paper wrapped securely around the box. Inside was some of the loveliest fabric Adelicia had ever seen: ivory brocade, ecru lace, deep blue velveteen, and four spring colors of silk. The box itself was as large as a wardrobe. From a smaller box within, she removed a sea green tulle gown with exquisitely sewn mother-of-pearl beading down the front panel and on the off-the-shoulder sleeves. It was extravagantly beautiful. The note with it read: "I can never thank you, nor express my feelings of gratitude enough for the kindness you extended my daughter. May God keep you in His care. Lona de Bloviere."

She was awed by the loveliness of the fabrics, the delicate handwork on the dress. When she had hung it in the armoire and placed the gorgeous fabric in the highboy, she went back through the packaging and the boxes, thinking perhaps she had overlooked a letter or a note from Morri, but to her disappointment, there was none, and no return address for her to send a reply of thanks.

Jacob soon had the room rosy warm, and she curled up in bed with a copy of *Julius Caesar* that she read until supper. "There is a tide in the affairs of men which taken at the flood leads on to fortune…" She very much liked the sound of that line.

She was still no more comfortable with the idea of sleeping in her and Joseph's room at the townhouse than when she had first arrived. But she had done so twice now and would do so again, just as she had done so many things because it was necessary, things that could appear strange or cold to others, but that to her meant survival. With a heavy heart, she closed her eyes.

The river appeared icy cold as the *Lucas Belle* made her way back up the Mississippi that December morning. Adelicia was pleased that Sally had stayed behind in New Orleans. She could think better when alone and remained uncertain as to how she would share the news of extending her stay in Louisiana until spring. She had told Sally they would only be delayed by a few weeks.

Jim Clack met the boat and drove swiftly to the house, she, happy for the foot warmer on the floor of the buggy. She asked Lucy to place the boxes of wrapped packages that Jim had brought in beneath the tree, then put a ten dollar gold piece in her hand. "Alfred and Rufus will receive the same," she said. The Negros would have their Christmas and New Year's celebrations as usual, gifts, scrumptious, plentiful food, fiddling, dancing, whiskey, and two weeks off—a tradition begun by Isaac that had not been altered. Work would resume at the beginning of January.

To Jim, she handed a package for his wife and an envelope for him. "Do not open it here," she had said. "Wait until you are home. Take the remainder of the day. You deserve it and your family will be happy. Also, please give these to Strap Kelley and Bard Young," she said, handing Clack two yellow envelopes.

"That's mighty kind. See you first thing tomorrow." She watched through the window as Jim rode away to home, two miles upriver to Panola Plantation, just above where the Mississippi makes her arched bend.

He was a good man. She remembered her first meeting, just after her marriage to Isaac, when they had come to New Orleans for the winter. He had remained the trusted and competent overseer of all the West Feliciana properties through the years, and had referred to her just as easily as "Mrs. Acklen" as he had "Mrs. Franklin."

The gnawing emptiness, already filling her, came with thoughts of the approaching holidays; to be absent from her children further deepened the great void she felt and weighed on her heart. She put her cape back on, muffed her hands, and told Lucy she was going out for a walk, knowing Lucy was aware of where the walk would lead.

She knelt beside Joseph's grave with its new growth of sod. *"This is the third Christmas, we shall not be spending together...I remember the last one...it was Pauline's first. You held her up so that she could put trimmings on the tree, and when we finished, we gathered to sing carols before having a sumptuous dinner, and that night, after the little ones were tucked in, we crept down the stairs and filled their stockings. You picked me up just as we were finishing the last one, waltzing around the room, holding me close. It was a beautiful moment...When we went back up the stairs, you said what fun it would be when we were doing this for our grandchildren one day, and I laughed and said I did not want to think about being a grandmother. The next morning, after taking all the little goodies from my stocking, I found the beautiful strand of pearls that are now at Sarah Polk's...They were the most perfect ones I could imagine...I thought we would have a thousand Christmases after that one. It is not the same without you...I wish the season to hurry and end...No matter how the future unfolds, I shall always love you, miss you, dearest, Joseph."*

She leaned her head forward on her knees, knees she had been clutching close to her with interlocked arms, and wept the tears she had wanted to weep for weeks. When she at last went inside and up to her room, she cried herself to sleep.

Her eyes were puffed and swollen and she felt tired. It was a morning she would have preferred to stay in bed. She had awakened early to a sound she had found melancholy since a child, the sound of quails making their quick, but plaintive "Bob White." Adelicia put on her robe and opened the doors leading onto the gallery and stood looking below as a covey of quail pecked between blades of thick green grass. She watched as they continued to slip from the taller grass behind them, until there were thirty or more stopping to listen, then running with their heads against the ground to eat the select morsels.

In her haste of shipping cotton, there had been no time to remember, nor miss, nor feel, but with the first shipment complete, all was quiet. The Negroes were absent from the fields, taking their two weeks holiday before the machinery and other maintenance needed attending and before the planting, ginning and baling began again. She felt tired, drained, and she did not want to spend the season without her family alone at Bellevue, nor with Sally at the townhouse in New Orleans. She longed to be home. However, she had made a choice, and if she were to accomplish what that choice entailed, she would not see Nashville, nor her children, until mid-spring.

She had hardly noticed the cold until she closed the double, glass paneled doors behind her, when she suddenly felt a chill and went to stir the fire and sit before it. Picking up a hand mirror from the table beside her chair, she looked at her red, swollen eyes.

Adelicia pondered over how to tell Sally that she must make the planned trip home on the eighteenth without her. Civilians could now travel safely via the Mississippi, and Sally would be fine without her. She went back to bed and wept some more before ringing for Lucy to bring her breakfast tray.

"I shall rest in my room for the remainder of the morning," she said.

"Yes'um."

As she began eating the aroma-enticing hoop cheese omelet, brown rice and fruit, she thought that lying in bed might help relieve the pangs of self-pity in which she felt engulfed.

She dared not ask Sally to stay, even though her companionship on the overland trek had been comforting, and from time to time she did enjoy Sally's company. She had also proven most competent and useful. However, she had served her purpose, and was being handsomely paid for her participation. Sally, although unaware of the greater scheme, had played her part well upon their arrival, but now that was all in place. As Adelicia sipped her strong, chicory coffee, she thought of Ransom, wondering where he was, how he was. Setting the cup aside, she rang to have the tray removed, then cuddled up to the thickly stuffed pillows beneath her head.

Soon after, it seemed, she awakened from a dream that had frightened her. Life, events, objects, people, were swirling about her. She was in the center, not knowing the way, nor how to exit the circle of mass confusion. Trapped and smothered, she recognized nothing. Her soul was restless as if it were trying to escape her body and spin into the swirling.

Wide awake and frightened, she sat up quickly and rang for her bath, but after Lucy had cleared it away, she returned to bed with a copy of Walter Scott's *Lochinvar*, feeling more weary than when she had first awakened. She did not wish to return to the city the following day, to encounter Sally or anyone else. She pondered remaining in bed for the week, something she had never done except when her children were born. Then, perhaps, she would feel relief from her troubled state.

She rested peacefully this time, and it was half past six when she awakened, the book still clutched in her hand. Going downstairs, still in her dressing gown, she saw an envelope addressed to her lying on the dining room table.

"When did this arrive?" she asked Lucy, who was hurrying to put her supper before her.

"Right after breakfast."

"Why did you not tell me?"

"You say not to disturb you, so you not disturbed," she answered, continuing to serve the meal.

It was from Crawford, informing her that John Armfield was in New Orleans for three days only, that he would be pleased to see her.

"I am in no mood to hear more of that situation," she said aloud to herself. But, she had asked for it, and would return to New Orleans to meet with John. Slipping the note into the pocket of her robe, she found she was not nearly so hungry as she had been in the morning.

And after forcing a few bites of the beautifully prepared meal, she bid the servants good night and asked to be awakened at four a.m. She would board the early morning *Southern Star.*

Thoughts of talking with John Armfield, with whom she had had no conversation since Isaac's death, except in the strictest business manner, stressed her the more. She propped her head on the pillows, leaned back against them, and again picked up Scott. Upon turning a page, a piece of pale blue stationary fell out, penned by her hand, but spoken by Solomon: "The race is not to the swift or the battle to the strong, nor does food come to the wise or wealth to the brilliant or favor to the learned: but time and chance happen to them all." *Ecclesiastes 9:11*

She considered the passage for some time before closing the book, then puffed the pillows beneath her head, blew out the lamp and in prayer, fell asleep.

CHAPTER 83

$\mathcal{I}$T WAS A CRISP COLD WHEN ADELICIA STEPPED FROM JIM'S RIG and boarded the packet. She pulled the merino wool cape about her and fastened the hood closely at her neck, wishing she had layered heavier clothing beneath. When she had bid good bye to Lucy and Alfred, wishing them happy holidays, Lucy had said, "Miz. Acklen, I know it not easy...there's tolerable trouble sometimes, but you come back and spend Christmas with old Alfred and me."

"You have a wonderful one," she answered, reassuring them. "It is a blessed and hopeful time. Hope is a good thing."

She would not celebrate the twenty-fifth at Bellevue while Joseph lay outside and her children absent. Perhaps she would spend the holidays with strangers in New Orleans, she had no idea.

It was mid-evening by the time Adelicia reached New Orleans and she went directly to the St. Montaigne. "A pleasant surprise my dear, a pleasant surprise," Crawford said, giving her a warm kiss on the cheek, as she signed her name in the register, requesting her usual suite.

"You are not surprised at all. You knew I would come."

"John's at the St. Louis," Crawford said.

"How did you know he was in town?" Adelicia asked.

"A strange and wondrous occurrence happened in the Old Absinthe Bar, the one where Isaac and I, and infrequently, John, would sit for hours in the long ago. Monday night was one of those melancholy ones, and who should walk through the door but the former trader himself, dressed, as always, in black from head to toe and would you believe Pompey is still with him? And neither of them looking a day older. Needless to say, we closed up the bar and then came here. Like all good patriots, John signed the pledge and is engaged in a government contract, artillery. I told him you were in town, had spoken of him recently, and would like to see him. Seemed all too pleased, to oblige."

"I wish I were in a better mood to discuss that now."

"And what kind of mood are you in, my dear?" he asked. "You may answer after you freshen up." Crawford watched her glance back over her shoulder as she followed the bellman up the stairs.

Seated at Crawford's table amidst the gaiety of laughter and voices, Adelicia asked, "Is there any news of Ransom's unit?"

"Nothing atall. But don't you think you would hear before me? You can rest assured that no news will come from those Alabama woods until a major battle is fought. Word is, Sherman, Grant and Buchannan are moving in to take everything south of the Tennessee line, so General Bennington will not be seen by any admiring females for some time. Would you like a glass of sherry, my dear, before supper? Settles the nerves. John will meet us here."

They were sipping a very fine Amontillado when Crawford asked, "You think much of him, don't you?"

"Of whom?"

"Bennington, who else?"

"This seems like a conversation we have had before."

"The difference being, I was a single man then."

"I like him very much. I admire him very much. I do not know him that well, of course."

"He won't disappoint you. He's had the wildest of reputations with the ladies since he was widowed. The story goes that he eloquently courts beautiful women, then leaves an elegant trail of weeping hearts behind him. But I've observed him with ladies here, and I've observed him with you; there's a major contrast. He's quite taken with you, as are we all," he said, motioning for the waiter.

"Does he really have such a horrible reputation?"

"You sound like a schoolgirl, my lovely Adie. Every word's been the truth. Ransom won't disappoint you, though. He is true blue. Well, look who's here."

As Crawford had said, John had not changed in the least: same beard, same physique, same weight, same look, only the black attire from hat to polished boot appeared new. He bent forward and took her hand. "It's a pleasure, Mrs. Acklen."

"Have a seat, John," Crawford said.

"Will do," he said, carefully placing his hat in the chair beside him and sitting to the right of Adelicia.

"It is nice to see you," she said smiling, and she meant it.

"Tell me about you and the family, what you have been doing since the war broke out, why you are here," John asked, stretching his arms behind him. "I was surprised when Crawford said you were in the area."

"I would prefer to hear about you and Martha and the Beersheba Springs' project." Adelicia had forgotten how meticulously John ate. One would think him a graduate of a men's manner's society. Thus went a heartily eaten supper with light conversation until Crawford timely excused himself. It was then that she told John about her encounter with Morri.

John Armfield portrayed not even a flicker of emotion. She had forgotten how stern his facial expression could be. She had also forgotten, in her haste with words, that he could embellish the story and spread whatever all over Middle Tennessee.

Adelicia had not expected the kindness and gentleness with which John spoke. He had not known about Morri, and appeared touched when she questioned him about Lona. He had neither seen nor heard from Lona since the autumn Isaac returned with her to New Orleans. Thus, he began the story of Isaac and Lona as he knew it, from the time Isaac first introduced her to him. And when he had finished, there was nothing more Adelicia needed or wanted to know.

She did not want to stay at the hotel and asked for a hack to take her to the townhouse, feeling sorrier for herself than she had the day before. Lona was eighteen, only a year older than Morri, when she had met Isaac at one of the quadroon balls attended by the most beautiful and rare of the young women. Isaac had provided a house for her in New Orleans, as well as at Loch Lomond. That explained, she surmised, why he never wanted her and the children to stay there, a place Adelicia had liked from the onset because of the beautiful Lake of the Cross in its midst.

Isaac had at last taken Lona to Fairvue, against John's and William's warnings. While there, Chance Hadley had insulted her, resulting in an altercation between him and Isaac, and in Isaac's ordering Hadley from the premises. After meeting Adelicia, Isaac had returned to New Orleans with Lona and left her with servants at the house on Esplanade. Hadley had somehow found her there, and for a reason unknown, Lona had reportedly left on a boat with him. There was where John's remembrances ended.

Adelicia better understood a number of things now: Isaac's absences after they first met, the distant look in his eyes. He must have cared very much for Lona, she thought, as the great churning within caused her stomach to feel as if it were in knots.

The same Chance Hadley had returned to Tennessee from wherever he had been, joined the Union army and ended up at her dinner table. After being dishonorably discharged, blaming it on Joseph, he had found the opportunity to become a spy in West Feliciana and unmercifully killed her husband. His hatred for Adelicia must have come from his fury at the two men she had married. It was more than unnerving to think of the revengeful plans he had long held for those whom he had blamed, and the calculations necessary to know where she and Sally were and how to get to them. His having followed Lona to New Orleans, was obviously his way to 'pay' Isaac. But why Lona left with him, if it were true, remained a mystery to Adelicia.

She was furious with herself for having revealed the story, in part, to John Armfield. She should have questioned him more cunningly, but certainly hoped he would carry the tale no farther. Fortunately, his wife Martha was not a gossip.

Mossy and Jacob were delighted and surprised to have their mistress return that evening and pleased she would be there for the holidays. Mossy complained that she had missed "all the fixings and the doings" that had been the custom at Christmastime with the children and guests, and although she understood the festivities would be limited this year, she expressed excitement, nonetheless.

Adelicia was glad her presence made them happy. However, she had hardly removed her hat until she asked Jacob to take her back into town. He stopped in front of Carveles, where she rang the bell for the proprietor, whom she was certain had long since retired for the evening. In his night robe, he unlocked the door. She purchased a piece of jewelry for each of the children: a gold, but not extravagantly expensive, pocketwatch for Bud, sterling and bone handled pocket knives for William and Claude, a small gold locket and chain for Pauline and a cameo brooch for Essie, items small enough for Essie to slip into their stockings and that John Armfield could take with him and deliver. They hurried to the wharf where she quickly ran to the shipping office and left the gifts with Pompy. Surely John would not mind delivering them to Belle Monte. She had also slipped in a twenty dollar gold piece for Essie. "Let us go home now," she told Jacob.

Sally had sent a message to Mossy that she was dining with Nicholas Pauche after the opera, which meant she would be returning late, and for that, Adelicia was thankful. She had far too much thinking to do. She wished for her energy to resurge, the energy that once burned inside her. Tired and weary of heart, she also wanted a peaceful, night's sleep.

It was daylight when Sally awakened her by tapping on her door. Adelicia yawning, sat up. "You are up early," she said stretching. "Or did you just come in?"

"Honey, it's you who's sleeping late. It's almost eleven-thirty. I was elated when Mossy told me you were here! She says you're not feeling well. I've really missed you."

"I am sure you have," she answered in jest. "Will you join me for breakfast?"

"Some coffee, perhaps." Adelicia rang for Mossy. "I have sincerely missed you, honey."

"Sal, I cannot go home with you on the eighteenth," she blurted out. "I must stay for the spring planting and ship the remainder of this one. I gave Jim Clack my word. All goes more smoothly with me present, he says. I am sure it is his way of conning me. Nevertheless, I am also uncertain how long a plantation can make a profit with the owner missing. Joseph did an excellent job managing, but after the war it may even be necessary for the children and me to move here, with the exception of the summer months."

"I agree wholeheartedly, honey," Sally responded, appearing sympathetic with Adelicia's plight, showing neither surprise nor disappointment. "If you're shipping what's left, then you certainly need to stay and make sure the cotton gets out safely, just like this time. So, if you're staying, so am I. I shant leave you here alone, not at this season, and we'll go home together in the spring."

Sally may never leave New Orleans, Adelicia thought, so long as the wealthy Nicholas Pauche remains her constant consort. She wondered if he did anything at all for General Banks.

"I am sorry, Sal, I cannot keep you indebted to me any longer. You were sweet and kind to come with me when I said we would be gone no longer than six weeks; that has already turned into eleven. You must return home to your children."

"I've never considered having you indebted to me. I came as a relative, a friend, and I shall not take more payment than first agreed, nor have you responsible for future expenditures, with the exception of my passage home. I choose of my own free will to stay, so don't think for a moment you're imposing. You must remember that you're feeding and caring for my four children and servants along with your own, all the while, and I'm grateful for that. In Franklin, Mama and Papa have been ransacked and raked over the barrels like most of our friends. Goodness knows what could have happened by now, or what will happen. As long as the children are safe, I'm happy. I'll telegram them today. I shall stay right here with you, Honey Lamb."

Adelicia had not forgotten, and thought Sally's reasoning sound. Belle Monte was safe.

"And Colonel Pauche?"

"Adelicia Acklen, I consider that rude and common." Sally had risen from her chair so quickly, she had almost stumbled. "At least he is a southerner," she snipped.

"A southerner gone Yankee you mean?"

"I shall not stay in this room a minute longer." She almost knocked the silver tray from Mossy's hands as they opened the door at the same time, in different directions. "Excuse me, Mossy."

"Sally, I was teasing you. Stay and have breakfast with me."

"You better stay," said Mossy. "I fix fresh fruit and cream for two and coffee. Miz Acklen been feeling poly, and she need it. You could use some too."

Reluctantly, Sally sat in the overstuffed chair again. Adelicia moved to the one opposite her as Mossy set the tray on the table between them. She poured thick rich coffee from the sterling pot into petite china cups. Everything was silver: the tray, the bowl laden with fruit, creamer and sugar bowl, the spoons, the forks. Even the small bowls from which they ate were silver. The fruit, was a rainbow of colors, all shades of greens, purples, blues, reds and pinks, yellows and oranges. "How beautifully presented, Mossy," Adelicia said, "elegant enough for two queens."

They ate in silence until at last, Sally told Adelicia that she was sorry for her outbursts. Then plans were made to stay at the townhouse through the remainder of December.

"You do need me, don't you, Adie?"

"Sal, I would not have asked you to come in the beginning had I not needed you."

"Can you imagine the reputations we'll have to live down when we do get home?"

"I can imagine, but I shall not concern myself with it now."

CHAPTER 84

ECEMBER TWENTY-FOURTH DAWNED BEAUTIFUL AND UNSEA-
sonably warm. Adelicia had been invited to parties and dinners
by Crawford, to dine with Elizabeth Patterson Bonaparte, and was
also asked by Sally to join her and Nicholas, yet she had accepted no
invitations. She had resolved to spend Christmas Eve and Christmas
Day working at the hospital, cheering the wounded, and not least,
comforting the dying…and comforting herself.

She had gone on a regular basis for five consecutive days, days that
had proved fulfilling and satisfying. "Serve God and others," were
her mother's words. Perhaps she could become more like her mother,
Adelicia thought, a legacy that lacked selfishness all together.

The hospital was never without shortage of help, but especially
during this season when everyone wished to be home with their families, what was left of them. Thus she had volunteered for eight hours
shifts on both the twenty-fourth and the twenty-fifth.

The New Orleans' Ladies Volunteer Society was better organized—she thought, while dressing that morning—than the one in
Nashville, or perhaps it was the personalities of the ladies. All ran so
smoothly, everyone congenial and pleasant.

She was almost to the bottom of the stairs, when she heard the
door' chimes. "I shall get it," she called to Mossy. She took the telegram, then put her hand to her chest, "Dearest Adie. They assured me
you would receive this. I have been wounded, but not seriously…am
in the hospital on Levee Street. Blessings on your day. I miss you. I
love you, Ransom.

"He must have arrived after I left yesterday. Jacob, hurry, please
hurry!" she called. "I miss you, too," she whispered.

The day suddenly smelled fresh, looked brighter than before, and
felt even warmer…She was going to see Ransom! Be with him on
Christmas Eve, even Christmas Day! "A merry heart doeth good, like
a medicine." How blessed she felt.

General Ransom Bennington's wounds were serious, not as he had fabricated. He had been shot above the left knee, shattering his knee-cap. He had also been wounded in the right side of his chest, directly below the clavicle. "My darling," he had said, soon after her arrival. "I did not want to frighten you. I shant be able to walk again without the aid of a cane. Will you want a crippled Yankee for a future husband?"

His last words stunned her. She leaned over and kissed his forehead in the midst of an audience. "It matters not how many canes you need. I shall carry an extra one for you as long as you are alive and safe, my dearest Ransom. And, yes, my darling, I will marry you." The words had come easily, smoothly, so that she commenced to repeating them over and over in her thoughts. And not until Jacob arrived with two baskets filled to the brim with all sorts of Christmas goodies, did their giddiness momentarily cease.

Adelicia sat beside Ransom on the iron bed, enjoying Mossy's delicious morsels, taking one bite herself and feeding him the next, while they smiled into each other's eyes.

Mossy had included enough plum cake, chocolate tarts and sugar cookies to share with other wards as well. And when all had finished eating, Adelicia stood and read the Annunciation scriptures, from the Gospels of *Isaiah* and *Luke*, then offered a prayer for peace. As she held Ransom's hand between her own, she looked over the room, listening to the voices of those who were able to sing from where they lay, time tried carols. There were no dry eyes, and she was certain it would be a Christmas Eve forever etched into the memories of everyone there.

The following morning as Adelicia dressed early to return to the hospital, she thought of her children, how she missed them and wondered if they were opening their gifts, peeking into their stockings at that very moment and prayed for their safety and her own, happy the children were with family.

The second week of January, Ransom was released to Adelicia's townhouse to recuperate. He left on crutches amidst good-natured jeering from the men on his ward: "Not only a private nurse, but one with whom he was going home." Doctors' orders were for him to stay in bed, with an additional warning of not delaying necessary surgery when well enough to travel, reminding him of the possibility of losing his leg.

Ransom was given a guest room where he lay on a bed of eiderdown, a masculine room decorated in bold gold and crimson. And he avowed to a stream of visitors that he felt as if he were in a king's room in a king's bed. Adelicia wondered if there would be a king's ransom to pay.

Mossy and Jacob were actually taking a liking to the "Yankee officer," proof of her father's adage: "If you want to know a man's true worth, ask one of the darkies; they have the proper senses, intuitions of humanity, that never falter."

Adelicia, continuing her work at the hospital, was sometimes joined by Sally, for four hours each weekday. They had also taken on the task of gathering bleached and unbleached cotton cloth from all over the city to be used for bandages, sheets, whatever the need. Mornings and evenings she spent with Ransom.

December's events had been bittersweet to her, blending extremes of happiness and sorrow. She had spent New Year's Day at the hospital with Ransom, and when the church bells rang in the tidings of 1864, Adelicia had wept.

The morning before, she had watched her cotton loaded onto the *Heppleberg* bound for London, and stayed until it pulled up anchor and left the crowded dock. If the blockaders did not interfere, she was assured of having one-half million dollars in gold deposited into her Liverpool account. Still nothing replaced being at home with her children and family for Christmas.

It was the last of January, and she had neglected her cotton for long enough. The Negroes had long resumed their work and her place was there. Although she was unhappy to be leaving Ransom behind as she boarded the packet for St. Francisville; having a Union General at Bellevue would not set well with the comings and goings of the Confederates. Ransom, nor the Union Army, knew that Adelicia was supplying the Rebels with cattle from Texas, though by a different route than Joseph, nor that she was also supplying sugar, sheep and grain milled on the plantations to both armies.

Adelicia did dwell in some fear of being discovered by either 'enemy,' as Jim Clack had termed them…regardless, her course was set. She aimed to send one more shipment of her white gold to England before heading for home.

The South was unaware that they had only two of Adelicia's four riverboats. The North was unaware there were more than two. She had kept her promise to the Army of the United States that the Rebels would not financially benefit from the sale of her cotton. The Union had kept its promise of storing her cotton. Crawford had seen to its leaving the dock.

Behind the sugar cane, whose tall stalks rustled and rubbed in the river breeze, corn grew, corn intended to feed the army and the navy of both the Confederate and Union governments. It was frightening as gunrunners continually patrolled the rivers and bayous, searching for evidence of someone giving aid to the enemy. But neither army or navy had control of West Louisiana, and the flag of the Union did not fly there. In fact, it was intriguing to see ships on the Red and Mississippi Rivers, sometimes very near each other, one flying the Confederate flag, the other flying the Stars and Stripes.

Mostly, the planters were able to convince the Yankees and the Rebels that aid was given only out of fear of having their crops, houses or buildings burned, as both armies allowed the Louisianans to continue their planting and harvesting as usual. However, many in the area were no longer there; they had either joined the army or fled the state, like Ruffin Barrow, who, financially ruined, had left all behind and taken his entire family, as well as some slaves, who chose to go, to Texas. With each brief absence from Bellevue, upon her return, the area offered up greater and greater changes and challenges, more and more deserted plantations.

Adelicia's quest was an awesome one, but the pangs in her heart told her, that after this shipment, she would not see to the one in the fall. Jim Clack could handle it for her and receive a hefty commission. Of course one's mind could change, she thought.

CHAPTER 85

By the second week in March, the cotton was, for the most part, in the ground; barring and tending having been overseen by Clack, Young and Kelly. For five weeks, Adelicia had continued her Open Houses, Sally's and her charades with nearby Confederate and Yankee officers. Lucy and Nattie prepared excellent evening meals for her guests. No longer nervous, Lucy had finally accepted Yankees in the house, if it were, she said, for the cause of shipping cotton and saving their homes.

The most frequent callers had remained David Carmack, whom Adelicia continued to adore; the Virginia charm and his youth not having lost their appeal, and Brett Hanson. Less frequently, Confederate General Taylor, a charming gentleman of sixty, called and also Yankee Colonel Michael Adams, though certainly on different evenings.

All was well on the fifteenth day of March 1864, when Adelicia returned to New Orleans. It was her forty-seventh birthday.

On that same evening in the townhouse parlor, she found herself settled into the warmth of Ransom as they sat in front of the fire, leaning back against the curved velvet sofa, talking very little. She was happy, as she knew happiness; perhaps she was in love with this New England gentleman. She believed he was in love with her. She would, however, be cautious with her words.

She understood her feelings little more than she had from the onset, when Crawford had introduced her to him at the post theater affair, a time that seemed eons ago, not a matter of months. She felt as naive as if she had never been kissed. When she looked into Ransom's eyes, or his fingers lightly brushed her shoulders, or she felt his breath touch the nearness of her neck, a warm flush filled her with emotions long suppressed; a passion that led her to press her lips to his, arousing unexpected sensations. His response, automatically returning hers, so defining a bliss, that there were no thoughts to blot out her feelings of euphoria. It was God who had designed the ultimate relationship between men and women. God had to have planned passion along with love, as well, she thought.

Her children would approve of him, she felt certain. Even though a Yankee, he was a New Englander like their grandfather, and would make an excellent stepfather. There would be no babies from this marriage. He could help her with the plantations after the war, or he could open a bank in Nashville. After the war... how many times had that phrase been spoken or thought? Too many. So much depended on it.

March developed into memorable, airy, frivolous days and nights. She and Ransom dined for hours, never missing his not being able to dance. She could talk and laugh with him hour upon hour, sometimes serious, sometimes playful. They took short, slow walks along the lake front, and carriage rides in the countryside. When weather permitted, they rode in an open carriage, their hands always touching, and she, leaning into him for tender kisses as gusty winds blew the spring grass and budding blossoms about them. At night, she lay in his arms. Unforgettable days and cherished nights, for always.

On the second of April, Ransom received his requested orders to return to headquarters in Alabama, despite the pain and unpredictable swelling in his leg. He would not go to New York for surgery. His men needed him, he told her—the Union Army needed him—his surgery would wait. Although she had tried to sway his decision, she greatly admired his desire to be with his men. She found his quest honorable, gallant, virtuous. A true general, a soldier at heart, a patriot.

Adelicia had also run out of precious time; she would return to Bellevue where duties and the purpose of her trip awaited, interrupting the tranquility that had been hers for a time. However, this interruption brought reality, the greatest purveyor of all.

Their plans were to meet in Nashville, for Ransom to be her guest at Belle Monte, as soon as the Northeast Louisiana campaign was over, which Ransom did not believe would be long in coming. Surely, she would be home by that time, she whispered aloud, whenever that time was.

Her cotton would be shipped at the latest by mid-May, and if the Lord would bless her this once more; she would soon be with her children, and perhaps with Ransom, forever—a word she was learning not to fear. She had experienced enough of partings.

As she and Sally made the trip back upriver, Adelicia still doubted Sally's intentions, wondering if she wished to be of help to her as badly as not wanting to miss any possible excitement. She also wondered if in later years, that it might be said that had it not been for Sally, "Cousin Adie would never have gotten her cotton past the first corporal." But too much of her frivolous thinking would surely be termed paranoia in Cullins' newest observations, and Adelicia would not concern herself with such, although she found the idea plausible.

CHAPTER 86

HE NEW COTTON CROP WAS BLOOMING INTO A LUSCIOUS ONE, with large bolls appearing almost ready to burst into white fluff. For a number of years they had planted Highland cotton developed by Bennett Barrow in the early forties, and had not been disappointed in its productivity. Jim Clack, as usual, had performed his task exceedingly well. Not only was the crop extraordinary, there had been no disturbances. Nothing to bring disquiet to any of the plantations; nothing to even cause alarm to Alfred, Rufus or Lucy.

For some weeks, Captain David Carmack stayed on guard with fifteen or more enlisted men, all camping on the plantation, not eating army rations, but food from Adelicia's kitchen. Carmack and a host of officers dined with her and Sally on the evenings when the Yankee officers were not present. Although the Rebels were well aware of the presence of the entertained Yankees, the Yankees remained unaware of the dining privileges of the Rebels.

By the end of April, the remainder of the past fall's cotton, all one thousand acres of it, was in the process of being ginned, baled and loaded onto the wagons. And again the Negroes had worked around the clock, laboring as if time would, in all reality, run-out.

Questions, however, had begun to arise, first among the Confederate soldiers encamped at Bellevue, as to why Mrs. Acklen's cotton had not been burned like that of their own back home, their families and friends. David Carmack, nor his superior officers, could do anything other than make excuses. The lack of harmony that had crept its way in greatly troubled Adelicia.

The Yankees felt more secure, not minding the Rebels guarding the cotton to be loaded onto their wagons. They had phrased it "a bunch of ignorant southerners, fooled into guarding cotton they think is going to aid their losing cause." It also kept the Rebels from active duty, and they assumed it was being shipped to their Union houses in New Orleans for the use of the Union.

It was the Confederate Army who commenced on the first day of May to attempt to unravel the mysteries and rumors concerning Mrs. Adelicia Acklen and her friend Mrs. Carter.

Colonel Frank Powers was asked by Assistant Inspector-General George B. Hodge to head the investigation, seeing if indeed it were true that, "Yankee wagons were hauling Mrs. A's cotton." He was to also inquire if the same circumstances had prevailed in the late fall of sixty-three. When information was brought to his Whittaker Springs' camp that Yankees were hauling Adelicia's cotton, he sent Sergeant William Doherty with twenty men to ascertain the truth of the accusation. If it were true, he would see "every last boll burned."

When the sergeant and his men arrived, they saw exactly what Colonel Powers had suspected, extraordinary amounts of cotton being ginned and baled, and indeed, Yankee wagons standing by for the purpose of hauling it. What they did not expect, however, was one of Brigadier-General Taylor's staff officers, Captain Carmack, not only guarding it, but showing him orders from Lieutenant-General Polk, countersigned by Colonel Dillon and Brigadier-General Taylor, to the effect that Adelicia was permitted to remove her cotton to a point on the Mississippi, preparatory to shipping it to Europe, and that no Confederate officer or soldier should in any manner molest it.

Not understanding and taken by surprise, as well as being out-ranked by the Captain, Sergeant Doherty quickly departed in disbelief of what he had seen.

Upon receiving the report from a nervous and confused Doherty, Colonel Powers soothed Doherty's fears, as well as his own, with the explanation that both Colonel Dillon and Brigadier-General Taylor most likely had orders to sell cotton for munitions of war, and because a Confederate officer was guarding it, he assumed it must be a government contract, although he was still uncertain about the Yankee wagons. But, he amused himself with the idea that if Mrs. Acklen's charms were as effective as rumors indicated, perhaps she had charmed the wagons away from the unsuspecting Yankees—though he doubted that anything so preposterous could actually occur.

Circumstances placed Powers in the presence of Brigadier-General Taylor two days after Sergeant Doherty's report, and it was then that he casually mentioned the absurdity of sending his men to burn cotton that was being guarded by Captain Carmack under the General's orders. General Taylor replied that Carmack was in no way—no way—he emphasized, working under his orders.

Shocked and embarrassed, Colonel Powers proceeded to relate the entire incident, as reported to him by Doherty, then took his leave. He immediately ordered a Captain Terry, of his regiment, escorted by a squadron of cavalry, to go to the plantation, to arrest Captain Carmack and all others concerned. Further orders directed the seizure of the teams and the wagons, property of the Union forces that would be put to excellent use in their own army. Also, his men were to set fire to Mrs. Acklen's cotton, and the gin as well.

"An ill wind blows," Adelicia thought as she undressed for bed that evening. She liked not at all what had happened—having her affairs checked into by a Confederate sergeant. She was satisfied that the lanky country boy had been perplexed by what he had seen, and after viewing the orders had most probably cast it off as another anomaly of war. But she was concerned with his superior, the one to whom he would report. He might not believe the bizarre setting as willingly as the sergeant. The attitudes of her daily guests, except for David Carmack and Major Hanson, also seemed changed, an agitation often apparent in their voices. The men on both sides had obviously talked among themselves, she speculated, that had sown suspicion. Perhaps enough had been overheard, that spies had developed among them.

Adelicia well knew that her cotton could be either confiscated or burned. However, she had not come this far to lose what she had begun. She would be independently wealthy, beholden to no one and—secure. She would be wealthier after the war than before, much wealthier than Isaac had left her, and accomplished by her own stratagems. This time, no one other than her children, her heirs would share in it…what was rightfully theirs, and under her control.

Recruits for the South were coming in daily from Texas and crossing into Mississippi via her plantations, where they were fed and hidden by the Negroes until it was safe. Others waited until

Confederate gunboats could take them aboard, outrun the Yankee ones, then reinforce the Rebel troops in Mississippi and Alabama.

The Confederate *Webb and* the *Pierce*, and the Union *Marrietta* and the *Glover*, had been playing games on the river for months, but thus far the Union gunboats had been defeated by the swiftness of the *Webb* and *Pierce*. Cattle were still crossing at the same points on the Red River that she and Clack had devised in the autumn; corn was growing undetected, destined to reach into the heart of Alabama for distribution to the Confederacy. Alabama's defenses remained strong. Montgomery meant to the South what Nashville now meant to the North.

Adelicia considered it all, knowing if they came a second time, she would probably be summoned and must feign ignorance of anything but her cotton. In her own mind, she was well within her rights to have it shipped.

It was a beautiful May morning, warm and fresh when she stood and watched over five hundred bales of newly pressed cotton being borne away on the long wagons, each pulled by six Union Army mules. What a sight! She stood and watched until she could see nothing more than distant movement, silhouetted against the wispy, cloud-touched blue sky. Peace and serenity shown on Adelicia's face—her task, her charade was almost complete—another one-thousand bales, give or take, and she and Sally would be on their way to home.

Perhaps she would return in the fall, she thought. Another one-half million dollars in gold certainly would be welcome, and if the money were well invested, she could possibly leave a financial legacy for her great-great grandchildren, their children after them. She hoped the war would be over by autumn and the demand for cotton just as great. The journey had been a long, arduous one, a quest almost completed, one to ensure, preserve her future and that of her children.

"Jim," she asked, "how much longer until we are finished?"

"End of the week. We ought to be through with the ginning by late tomorrow and have it baled and loaded by Friday, Saturday at the latest. No way to go any faster. The Negroes deserve two weeks off after this. I'll sure be glad when it's gone. Something unsettling in the air."

"I feel the same," she said, "I am anxious to get home. The Negroes certainly get two week's rest, with extra rations. Are you paying them wages, as well?"

"Twenty-five cents a day," he nodded.

"Double it," she said. "Mrs. Carter and I shall be leaving as soon as Mr. Benedict can clear passage for us all the way through. What is unsettling, Jim?"

"Questions are being asked," Clack answered. "May not amount to anything more than caution on their parts, but it makes me uneasy. We'll talk later."

Adelicia stood on the back portico watching as Jim rode away; she had never seen him this apprehensive. Leery of all, she walked into the parlor where Sally sat sipping lemonade.

"Honey, are you sure Crawford can get us through? I mean, I sure don't want to travel by wagon ever again. And why on earth is Jim Clack uneasy? About what?"

"Were you eavesdropping by any chance?" she asked Sally, who seemed taken aback.

"Crawford will take care of us. Do not concern yourself, Sal." Adelicia walked over to the window and looked out over the sprawling land beyond. "People are still traveling," she said turning back to Sally, "although it is more difficult. Jim is simply tired and worn out, as are we all."

The following morning, Adelicia had ridden back to the house on Promise, pleased with the operation. David and Jim had lunched with her and Sally, Carmack gaily elaborating on how dull it would be "after the fair ladies had gone." Clack, goodheartedly commenting that life would become much easier without the social comings and goings of officers from both armies, not forgetting the Navy. He would settle into supplying small amounts of supplies and harbor for both armies, and troops for the South, a task, he commented, that had once seemed complicated, but was now trivial in comparison to the past months.

It had been a pleasant, somewhat relaxed mid-day meal. As Lucy removed the last of the cups, Sally retired to her room, and Adelicia requested that Promise be saddled and brought back up from the stables.

"We're taking another ride, my boy, a long one." She paced him at an even trot until they reached the crest of the levee, and rode slowly along, till past dusk, observing the movements along the river, the movements of forces from both North and South.

Upon her return, she patted her molasses brown Promise and nuzzled her face against his before Rufus led him back to the stables. All had seemed peaceful along the river, but she wondered if spyglasses were not pointed in her direction.

CHAPTER 87

"M IZ. ACKLEN, MIZ. ACKLEN, COME QUICK! THEY SAY THEY gonna see you now. They in the kitchen."

"Gracious," she said sitting up, yawning from a morning nap. "Who is in the kitchen?" she asked Lucy.

"Rebels."

"What is so terrible about that?"

"They come to get you, the cotton, everything." Lucy was twisting her shaking fingers and her eyes were wide with fright. "Oh, Dear Jesus! They may get us all!"

"Did you recognize them?"

"Never a one. They done rested pore Captain Carmack and been talking awful to the others, and Mr. Clack not nowhere to be found, and now they say they gotta see you before they burn everything down—the house, too! Dear Jesus help us! You gotta come quick!"

Adelicia was well out of bed and taking a quick glance in the mirror, touching up her hair, dabbing perfume on the nape of her neck. She was frightened, and as she straightened her dress before descending the stairs, she thought of *The Trojan Women*, the Greek Tragedy she and Camille had sneaked and read so many years before. She would neither surrender, nor sacrifice her cotton.

"Delay disturbing Mrs. Carter just yet," Adelicia ordered. "And, Lucy, please gain control of yourself. Where's Nattie?"

Moments later, she stood in the kitchen where Captain Ham Terry was holding David Carmack under arrest; meanwhile approximately twenty enlisted men mumbled among themselves out on the gallery.

"May I ask what you are doing in my home and why you arrested this officer and friend?"

Saying nothing, Terry handed her the orders he had received. "And who, may I ask is this Colonel Frank Powers?" she indignantly inquired.

Sally had just walked into the kitchen smiling, then gasped at the wrist bound Carmack. "My poor dahling," she interrupted. "Whatever is the matter?"

"Captain Terry has some absurd orders from an absurd Colonel, and he has of yet to open his mouth. I am Mrs. Acklen and this is my cousin from Nashville, Mrs. Carter. And may I inquire again, what you are doing in my home?"

"You've seen the orders and who they're from. And if you don't have some papers of proof that the goings on here are legit, meaning that the cotton we see is going to the Rebs and not to the Yanks, I'm setting fire to it and every building on this place."

When Lucy screamed, Adelicia nodded to Alfred, who took her from the room. She abhorred Terry's insolence and right away decided he had just enough education to make himself feel important, the worst of inadequacies.

Portraying no fright at all, Sally drawled, "Legit, Rebs, Yanks, why I never heard such language—whatever do they mean? Where are you from?"

"Obviously, from none of the areas or families we know. Captain Terry," Adelicia said matter of factly, "you are burning nothing, and I shall show you no papers. There is no place for insolence in my home, nor for captains who come barging into it making rude demands. And as for your Colonel, you may report that he may come himself if he wishes to see the orders from his superiors, that state nothing on my plantations is to be touched. As for yourself, I strongly suggest you leave my property immediately, taking Captain Carmack with you, whom I shall have released by morning, or I shall have my people here, who far outnumber yours, to hold guns on you all. You may also tell your Colonel that I prefer an officer with manners."

Terry had just turned and pushed Carmack ahead of him when he saw Colonel Powers ride up with ten additional men. Stepping around Carmack, Terry quickly ran out the door, and after saluting, expressed his gratitude for the Colonel's presence as he could do nothing with the senseless woman inside, he told him, other than arrest her, which was his intention, because she had threatened an officer of the Confederacy and belittled him in front of his men. He also hurriedly told Powers that the female with her was just as ornery.

Colonel Powers looked up to see Adelicia and Sally standing on the long gallery, listening, looking as perfectly lovely as he had been told. "And which of you is Mrs. Acklen?" he asked politely, dismounting and walking towards them.

"I am Mrs. Acklen," said Adelicia offering her hand. "You must be Colonel Frank Powers," she said hospitably. "This is my cousin, Mrs. Carter. May I help you, sir?"

"Since Sergeant Doherty was here last week, we've had some contrary reports, not good ones, I fear. Will you be so kind as to take me to your cotton?"

"I shall be happy to, Colonel. Rufus, saddle Promise for me." Minutes of small talk passed until Rufus brought the saddled horse, and she and Powers, with four of his men, rode down to the cotton gin where a myriad of white fluff lay bagged, with more still in the process of being baled.

Colonel Powers looked over the situation, observing the bulging tow sacks, the piles still unginned, and of course, the wagons and mules with the insignia of the United States Army stamped on them. "Do you have any questions, Colonel?"

"Is this all the cotton?"

"It is now, sir."

"Was there more?"

"Yes. There was." Her fears were lessening. Obviously, the cotton that left that morning had gone undetected.

"Where is it now?"

"Sir, I hope on its way to England."

"Under whose orders have Carmack and his men been working?"

"Why, under General Taylor."

"I spoke to General Taylor yesterday evening, he told me that Carmack's presence was not under his orders."

"Colonel, you must be mistaken. All of those high in command obviously know what is happening. Sir, you take away my guard, and the Yankees will have my cotton."

"Why are we protecting your cotton?"

"I am not at liberty to say. I do not think it prudent."

"Is it true that your cotton is going to a Yankee house in New Orleans?"

"It is true. And from that Yankee house, it is being shipped to England."

"Is the South prospering from the sale of your cotton?"

"Indirectly, sir."

"Can you explain that?"

"Colonel, am I under arrest?"

"I'm sorry, Mrs. Acklen. This has to be cleared up. It doesn't make sense to too many of us, and the protection of this operation is demoralizing to all who see it, especially the enlisted men. A full explanation is in order."

"Often things which make no sense on the surface make the most sense in the end."

"Then perhaps we need to get to that part. We have ignored rumors, persistent ones, for some time. And to be honest, I had a spy checking things last fall when the reports first started, but his findings never created enough suspicion to merit further investigation. But a lot of us are wondering why your cotton is not only protected, but gets shipped out, as well. You admit it goes on Yankee wagons to Yankee houses. You must agree, Mrs. Acklen, this is not the usual."

"I shall admit that. Would you mind walking alone with me for a moment?"

He asked his men to wait as they walked a short distance from the gin where the activity had presently ceased. She told them to resume their work, and the Colonel said nothing to counter her request.

"Colonel, you appear uninformed as to what is being done for the Confederacy by my plantations. It is not prudent that I tell you. But I shall say that if General Beauregard in Montgomery wants his army to have beef, and if he wants more troops to arrive from Texas, he had best inform his officers to leave me alone. Of course, if the Yankees have spies, this investigation will prove advantageous for our cause. Here are my orders."

From her pocket, she retrieved a cream-colored sheet of paper that enjoined every Confederate officer not to molest any of her properties or her cotton, signed by Generals Taylor and Polk. She did not reveal the ones from General Banks or Governor Shepley.

He held it for some time, reading it over and holding it up to the light as if to see if the signatures appeared fraudulent. He looked at the paper, seemingly embarrassed, and then back at Adelicia, believing, yet doubting, and not wanting to be tricked for a second time.

"Mrs. Acklen, the orders look good, but they also looked good to my sergeant last week. You're not under arrest and I won't burn your cotton today. I want to believe you. But I'm going to take your wagons and mules. They can be put to better use in our army than hauling your cotton."

"Colonel, they are not yours to take."

"Are they yours?"

"Yes."

"May I ask what favors you are doing for the Yankees in order to have gotten them?"

"That question I resent, and consider crude. Take whatever you like, but I promise you I shall get them back.—Colonel, what if I told you I stole the wagons and mules?"

They rode back to the house in silence, the four men trailing by five or six paces. He unloosed Carmack's wrists, but ordered him to report to General Taylor, under arrest. After bidding Powers good afternoon, Adelicia stood watching the entourage of Captain Terry, thirty enlisted men, twelve wagons, and forty-eight mules depart.

She watched until they were out of sight, then quietly said to Rufus, "Keep Promsie saddled."

"Where on earth are you going?" Sally asked.

"To see General Taylor."

"It's almost five o'clock!"

"He's no more than two miles this side of Red River. You stay here and help calm Lucy."

"You know I hate to miss it, lammy...also the General is so handsome."

Adelicia had slid off Promise so quickly, she tripped as her shoes touched the ground before handing the reins to a stable boy.

"General Taylor," she demanded, bursting into his quarters, "how dare you tell Colonel Powers that Captain Carmack was not acting under your orders!"

"Mrs. Acklen, when I agreed last fall to protect your cotton and honor the request of General Polk, I was not informed that Yankee wagons would be hauling it to Yankee houses in New Orleans, nor did I know there would be another shipment. I thought it a one-time operation. There is a war going on, Mrs. Acklen, and men are needed elsewhere to save what is left of our South—we've none to spare to guard cotton shipped to only God knows where, nor time for women playing secesh games. The entire Confederate Army is being made to look like fools."

She listened intently, "I would suggest, General, that you become more concerned with what is actually happening than how the army *looks* to the uninformed. I would also suggest that if you can get a message through to Montgomery, to do so. I am feeding your army and supplying it with troops from Texas. I want my wagons returned tomorrow. The ship leaves in three days for Liverpool, and I intend for my cotton to be on it. And, General," she said upon leaving, "please quiet down this talk that the Confederate army is being fed, supplied and reinforced through my efforts. Do not forget my life is in danger from the Yankees— because of my aid to you. Now, sir, if I am free to take my leave, I shall expect to hear from you tomorrow. Good evening, General." She kept Promise at a nice clip back home

That woman's life could never be in danger, the General Taylor said to himself. It had been a well-kept secret from the masses of enlisted men, as to the aid Mrs. Acklen was giving the Confederacy, for fear of Yankee spies who seemed to turn up in all places, discovering the ferries and crossings, and putting a halt to one of the biggest supply operations in the South, the largest by far by a private citizen—a female at that! However, he had been unaware of the use of Yankee wagons and Yankee store-houses. Carmack had not been given orders directly from himself. In truth, the past autumn, he had ordered the Captain to put a guard at the plantation without a lot of explanation, only that it was aiding the Confederacy. He had assumed, however, the Captain was now resuming his duties elsewhere in the war.

General Taylor, surmising that Carmack found the assignment quite agreeable, had kept the situation well in tow with his confidant, Major Hanson, and had not bothered to report to him. It was a matter in which blame could be passed from one to the other, and a matter in which everything was understood on the surface, and nothing understood more deeply.

It was necessary that he be emphatic to Colonel Powers, who appeared totally ignorant of all endeavors. He also wondered if any high-in-command officers knew the entire operation—or if they only knew in part, as did he. The thought occurred to him that Mrs. Acklen might also be aiding the enemy, although he did not see the probability of it and would not pursue it. He would clear matters with Carmack and Powers so that everyone's mind would rest more easily, and the pompous Mrs. Acklen could ship her cotton to England. Regardless, he was grateful to have the wagons and mules and that seemed favorably good to him for the time being.

However, two days later, General Taylor received an order signed by General Lee, himself, to return all confiscated wagons and mules to Mrs. Acklen and to see that neither she, nor any of her properties were molested in any manner. General Taylor reluctantly released Carmack to return to his post at the plantation. He and his men would resume protecting Mrs. Acklen's precious commodity. With Carmack's resumed position went the wagons and mules on their return trip to Bellevue.

Carmack and his men rode in the wagons with their horses hitched to the back on the six mile journey. General Taylor, although unsatisfied, would not question the authority of the Commander-in-Chief. Perhaps Lee was the only one who knew the entirety of Mrs. Acklen's operation. President Davis, according to General Hodge, certainly did not. General Taylor wondered to what degree rumors would persist after the war as to the how's of Mrs. Acklen's methods. He well knew the role he had played, and he thought that story enough to tell as he reread the order, then laid it aside to be placed in the files for May 10th, 1864. He wondered if anyone would ever know how it had all happened, other than the sheer gumption of Mrs. Acklen.

Rear Admiral David Porter, in charge of the Union Mississippi Squadron, knew about Adelicia's cotton being hauled to New Orleans in return for supplies, information and harbor. He had received a request from General Banks, as well as Governor Shepley, that she would be detained "in no manner" while hauling her cotton to New

Orleans. He had thought Joseph Acklen a gentleman, a man of integrity. He had nevertheless not trusted his widow, whether it be her beauty, her rhetoric, or her charm.

Yankee gunboats continued to be captured on the Red River, no matter how tightly they patrolled, and Rebel reinforcements continued to emerge from first one place, then another. And just two weeks prior to the damning report having come to the Admiral—that all the while their wagons were hauling Mrs. Acklen's cotton, and a Confederate guard overseeing it—two of their fastest gunboats had been captured, *The Marietta* and *The Glover*.

Union Lieutenant Commander Breese reported that from the information he could gather, "Mrs. Acklen had been playing a very secesh game"…that although her cotton and wagons had been stolen by doubting Rebels, they had also been returned, perhaps as a ploy. It was even rumored that she had received new wagons, mules and harnesses from the Union Army, and he further reported to the Admiral that this was the talk at Red River, that they were convinced, "Mrs. Acklen was still a very good Rebel." As a widow, they had wished her no harm, and in good faith, had allowed her to ship her cotton, but it was stated in their records that she had "belied their trust and was aiding the enemy."

Admiral Porter, however, was not at liberty to report that she, as well as Joseph, had given food and supplies to the United States Army and Navy, that she had "loaned" them two river boats, that she and Joseph had given them harbor, permission to bury their dead on her property, had always been helpful and courteous to any men or officers with whom they came in contact, and that the government was receiving three percent of the gross sales of her cotton. As the screws tightened, Crawford had advised her to cut the latter deal soon after the first shipment—*insurance*!

The Admiral assumed that she was aiding the enemy—how, he was unsure—but he would soon be compelled to close the Red River to all traffic, thereby securing the position of the Union. Knowing the planters would be greatly affected and suffer the ruin, it was a necessary precaution of war. However, no further inquisition would be made into Mrs. Acklen's affairs.

CHAPTER 88

FRIDAY, MAY 16TH, THE LAST OF ADELICIA'S COTTON LEFT WEST Feliciana Parish enroute to New Orleans, laden on Union wagons that would return to the army, along with forty-eight mules. An awesome sight to behold, she thought. Weary and worn, she wondered as she watched the last bale being loaded and ready to be pulled away by fattened mules, if she would attempt another shipment of the partially boled, waist-high cotton in the autumn. Most likely, she would not.

She had thought there would be a celebration, invite the neighbors, military confidants, a party for the Negroes, but now she felt no need or desire for celebration. She had simply done what she set out to do: ship the bales left behind by Joseph, plus an additional one thousand acres unpicked when he had passed.

Dueling feelings of great joy and deep melancholy caused the turmoil to deepen within her as she sat on Promise, teary eyed. She watched until she could see nothing but the rear of the wagons appear as small specks against the light blue, May sky. Her purpose for having come to Louisiana was at its end, a journey that had unfolded as she could not have dreamed. Eight months that seemed a lifetime. She was blessed beyond what she could have imagined, and now it was time to go home.

Two days later, when she had gone to the barn with Rufus and nuzzled her face against Promise's velvet brown neck, she looked at Rufus, with tears trickling down her cheeks, asking him to take care of her gelding. From the time the colt had been foaled six years before, Rufus had groomed, cared for, and ridden him in her absence. She hoped that none of the Yanks, nor the Rebs, had cast their eye on him to conscript after she were gone. "I will bring you home to Nashville one day soon, boy, perhaps we can convince Rufus to come with us." She walked away from the barn, glancing back at Rufus and Promise, then looked about her, struggling with the gnawing within.

The ginning press was still, and the fields absent of workers, now enjoying their rest. All was somber as Adelicia walked into the house for supper. She ate alone, and when she went upstairs to make final touches to her packing, she instead walked onto the verandah, observing the vast beauty around her, intermittently interrupted by the sounds of gunfire coming from the Tunica hills beyond. Soon she would be with her cherished darlings and family. She could only imagine what had happened to Nashville in her absence, though she was confidant Belle Monte was safe. In all this time, she had never asked Jim Clack about Joseph's death

She and Sally bid farewell to West Feliciana on the morning of the 20th, waving a last good-bye as Jim guided the buggy around the bend down to the river landing. Safely aboard, they departed on a steamer up the Mississippi for home, but between Natchez and Vicksburg, their vessel was stopped by the military and ordered to return from where it had come. They were informed that civilian lives could not be risked, that dangerous battles were commencing on every side, both land and river. So on the evening of the day they had left, they returned to Bellevue to await the morning packet for New Orleans.

On the 22nd, Adelicia and Sally again embarked for Nashville, this time from New Orleans, on a medical supply ship bound for New York. Crawford had made the arrangements. She was disappointed he was not there to say good-bye, only a note stating he and his family were away.

It was not the most comfortable of arrangements—far better, however, than overland on Ole Blue. She and Sally shared a small room with cots squeezed so tightly together, turning around was difficult. There was no room for luggage except for a small toiletry bag and Adelicia was hopeful their trunks, somewhere above, would arrive with them.

Enroute, they were neither shelled nor stopped by any patrols—North or South—but travel was slow, sloshing through murky and rough waters. Not only were they the only females on board, they were the only civilians, and it was with grateful hearts that she and Sally set foot on the pier in Manhattan. Seemingly, they were quickly whisked away to their hotel, luggage in tow, compliments of the St. Montaigne…Crawford!

It felt eons since she had been in New York with Joseph, staying overnight before sailing for Europe. And it was so very long ago that she had visited the bustling city for the first time on her honeymoon with Isaac. It too had been touched by war—rioting and looting at its beginning, and with an uneasy stock market weighing each day's outcome. But the lights shone brightly upon uniformed troops and immigrants, its people going about their regular business, posted notices of events and political promises of victory. As always, New York appeared to have more of everything.

On June 1st, 1864, after two nights at the Fifth Avenue Hotel in separate rooms with plush beds and hot baths, where Adelicia had found herself too happy to sleep and too exhausted not to, she was at last able to book passages via train, stagecoach and boat, for home.

Part IV

Adelicia and Sally return home to Nashville

1864

Civil War

CHAPTER 89

ADELICIA AND SALLY ARRIVED AT THE UNION FORTRESS ON THE Cumberland exhausted, anxious, yet elated and satisfied. Nashville appeared no more than a shadow of its former self, of its "used to be." Gutted roads and trenches marred once majestic lawns. Schools, churches and hotels were now Federal Hospitals. Elegant homes stood empty, stripped of their finery, burglarized, or headquarters for Federal troops. General Harding's deer and buffalo had been slaughtered, first as sport by the Yankees, then for the necessity of food—trees had been leveled. Where they once stoutly stood were stone and wooden forts, protecting the city from being invaded by its own.

Many of Nashville's wealthiest had come to financial ruin— the Hardings, the Ewings, the Overtons, the Basses, the Weavers. Although Dempsey Weaver had retained his position as the president of Planter's Bank, as had John Kirkman of the Union Bank, they were not dealing in southern currency. Some homes were used for wounded Confederate prisoners being nursed back to health through the aid and expense of their owners. The McCalls, the Buchannans and the Russells, all on Cherry Street, each cared for at least fifteen of the wounded and were held responsible for their return when the patients were well enough to be imprisoned. Guards were stationed at the houses, admitting no one without a pass.

The littered streets reeked of foul odors and cast offs of every sort loitered there and in alleys. The main arteries leading South— Franklin, Hillsboro, Murfreesboro and Nolensville Pikes—were dug out and dirt thrown up around them for barricades. Fences had been burned, fruit trees ravished or disfigured—vegetable gardens depleted—rose gardens trampled and grape vines crushed. Once wealthy merchants who remained were in bankruptcy, men from the North daily taking their places.

As she and Sally stood waiting for a driver, unnerved by the dramatic changes in the city, they spied the tent strewn Capitol lawn, grass replaced by mud and litter. Adelicia wondered what she would find at Belle Monte. Who would be tromping over her grounds?

After an hour's wait sitting atop their steamer trunks and having seen no familiar face, they at last contracted with a Yankee driver to take them in an obsolete hack pulled by an animal who would have made Old Blue look like a champion. The buggy slowly treaded, cracking and creaking, through deep ruts and pits on once smooth, cobblestone avenues out Union Street, left onto Cherry, then right onto Hillsboro Pike. Foul odors reeked from homes, churches and warehouses, odors characteristic of the sick and dying, and the smell of fresh blood.

Union officers hurrying past on horseback added an additional impact to the sickening, disheartening scene, not foreseen by the 'gallant,' a southern city after its capture, or after its battle, Adelicia thought. It had all been a vision—a vision of glory and life everlasting, based on pride and ignorance, pride of not considering the reality of war—ignorance of not realizing that states could not separate from the main and fight against an organized, well equipped Army and Navy of that main, not discounting that a people will not stay suppressed in a civilized society, that change is the inevitability that must come and be touched by all.

Adelicia gasped as they turned between the enormous granite post onto the pebbled drive up to Belle Monte. It still stood majestic—not manicured, not well maintained, but unmolested. Governor Johnson had honored their agreement, the one he had signed that seemed much longer than two years before. There was her villa on the knoll, appearing unharmed. Both she and Sally, weeping, hurried from the hack and up the granite steps.

Adelicia turned as the driver yelled, ran back, and put the fare in his hand and again bounded up the steps. The doors were locked, a custom unfamiliar to Belle Monte or of any southern family of genteel birth. She rang the bell and peeked through the cranberry etched glass side panels, but saw no movement. Sally was equally unsuccessful. "What on earth do you think has happened?" Sally drawled, her body tensing. "Where are the children?"

Adelicia did not bother to answer as she ran to the stables. No one—not one horse remained. She went to the greenhouses, every plant gone. Belle Monte felt ghostly, all seeming as if she were awakening from a nightmare. Unnerved, she remembered her father's words, "Never panic—the panicked do not think—always think, Adelicia, always think through everything, no matter the trial, no matter the pain, how small or great." Though tears streamed from her eyes, she would not allow herself to panic.

"We shall return to the house and try to find an open window. If need be, we shall break the panes. There must be a note, a clue of some sort!" They tried the windows that could be reached on the front and all they could reach on the back to no avail. Nothing budged. The house had been fastened tight. Breaking one of the cranberry glass panes flanking the door would not help. Only a key would unlock it from the inside. Her only choice was to break the panes around the lower left window that opened into the music room.

Tossing small stones, they broke one pane and then another until Adelicia could reach the latch that held it fast. She removed a blood streaked arm from a broken pane, but with a triumphant look, as she and Sally pushed up the heavy window and crawled through. She was home, and she would not be outdone now.

The furniture was exactly as she had left it. The women hurried from room to room, finding nothing out of place, until Adelicia suddenly gasped as she noted the paintings, art objects, silver and European antiques were all missing. Amazingly, the kitchen below was particularly well stocked.

"Sally, someone has taken the children and the servants—the valuables, most likely to their home. There is nothing else to do, but walk back to Hillsboro Pike and if we are fortunate, hire a ride back into town."

"Why in town? Can we not go to a friend's home?"

"What friend and where? How do we know what we would find? They may all be like this." She stopped short as they heard movement on the stairs above them. The startled women froze as the footsteps continued, then they saw the gray head of Uncle Ben peering down. "Uncle Ben!" Adelicia exclaimed. The old man hurried down as fast as his rheumatic legs permitted. "Where is everyone?" Adelicia asked.

"They gone, everybody but me—I say I not going nowhere."

"But where, where have they gone?" she asked, hugging him.

"They all go to Miz. Polk's."

"Thank God," she and Sally said in unison. "When?" asked Sally

"When they find out the Yankees coming to Belle Monte and the General gonna live here. Essie say she not gonna have the children live with no Yankees, and she sure not gonna."

"When was that? What General?"

"They go yestiddy, and I don't know what General, they just say General."

"Uncle Ben, we must get into town. Is there anything alive that will take us?"

"The horses we sent to Mr. Henry's all been took by the Yankees or ussens, one of the which." Adelicia gasped, her finest mares and stallions!

Damn the war, she thought, but dared not swear in front of Uncle Ben, thankful that he and Sally could not read her thoughts!

"Ain't nothing living on this place but ussens."

"Then we shall walk to the road."

"Old Ben's legs not much for walking any distance."

"You cannot stay here. We shall walk slowly with you. Come," she urged, taking him by the arm.

On Hillsboro Pike, the scenery was the same; officers in blue and strange faces. Anyone familiar would appear an outsider, she thought. Two disheveled women dressed in semi-finery, holding onto an old Negro between them was not a common sight, and before they had gone but a short distance, they were stopped.

Their plight, taken into consideration by an officer with some sympathies for mothers attempting to locate their children, asked them to wait. He returned shortly with a driver and team that looked somewhat better than the one that had brought them from the wharf. They climbed aboard and headed for the corner of Union and High Streets.

The wrought iron fence at Polk Place stood intact, the first she had seen unmolested; around the palatial mansion, even the trees had been spared. And the children playing on the spacious lawn were her own and Sally's.

With tears streaming, Adelicia paid the driver, then ran through the gate with Sally trailing close behind; all before Uncle Ben had climbed from the hack. He had spoken no words to the Negro driver who, wearing a blue uniform, was a sight Uncle Ben could not abide.

"Darlings, darlings," she cried tumbling over with them on the grass. "Oh how happy I am to see you, to hold you. Where are Claude and Bud?"

"Mama, Mama," Pauline and Willie cried falling into her arms, "You're home! You're home!" At that moment, the older boys came running out with Sally's younger two.

"Mother, I thought we would never see you again," Claude cried, running into his mother's arms.

"I did not want to leave, Mother, but Essie, governess and nurse forced me. I wanted to stay and take care of Belle Monte like I promised," Bud said hastily.

"You did the right thing, Bud, darling. We are safe here. Let me hold my eldest son," she said, pulling him close to her for a long embrace. "How you have grown. How all of you have grown!" She lifted Pauline and swung her into the air, and amidst more hugs and kisses, they went inside. With Pauline in her arms, she and Sally sat on the carpeted floor, hugging one child and then the other. A pleased and gracious Sarah Polk welcomed them as a disgruntled Essie watched.

"Essie, why such a frown? Are you not glad to see me?"

"That a silly question, but them Yankees come two days ago and tell us they gonna use Belle Monte for a fortress, and Yankees gonna live in it, and I tell em they not gonna sleep in your bed or Mr. Joseph's bed or the children's beds, or my bed, and they not gonna use our dishes or none of our stuff, so they may as well not come. They look at me real fierce and say they gonna be there, and if I know what good for me and the childrens, we better be gone by today cause that's when they arriving. So we come to Mrs. Polk's cause I don't know where else to go. General Beatty done at Hillside, and Miss Corrine and Mr. Bill gone. They broke, Miss Adie, cleaned out. And

General Hood camping at Traveler's Rest. Generals everywhere!" Essie shrieked.

Adelicia gasped in astonishment. They had gotten to Corrine. She hoped Laura and George were still safe in Alabama.

"So I send Bud and Mrs. Polk tell us to come, and here we be."

"You did well, Essie," Adelicia said, standing and putting her arm around her old mammy. "You have taken care of us for so long, all of my life." She looked at Sarah. "We cannot impose on you any longer. There must be fourteen of us. I shall go into town to see what I can do. There must be a way to keep them from invading Belle Monte."

"Shall I go with you?" Sally asked, tightly holding her youngest.

"No. I shall go alone, first thing tomorrow," she said. Eight months was long enough to have been with her cousin, and she did not want to impose on Sarah Polk any longer than necessary. Sally was blessed with a large, endearing family, well able to accommodate her, her children and servants. And Adelicia had paid her handsomely before leaving New Orleans. She would do well.

Sarah, generous to a fault, quickly said, "You are welcome to stay as long as you like dear, all of you, until the war is over. Adie, you are strong, but you must not keep this pace—taking on and doing what ten men could not. Stay here and rest. There is enough room and plentiful food." Sarah continued, interrupting Adelicia's thoughts.

What about clothing?" she asked addressing the children. "Did you bring any changes?"

"Some," they responded.

"Then I shall return to Belle Monte and get our clothing," remembering that her and Sally's bags were still where they had left them, but quickly asked, "Where are the valuables?"

"All safely here," Sarah reassured her. "We added the paintings and other art collections to your silver and jewelry. All is well. Come dear, you and Sally take tea and tell us eight months of happenings."

"Did you ship the cotton?" Willie asked, anxiously.

"Yes, darling, we shipped it all to England."

It was comfortable sitting in the green velvet chair, behaving as if it were a social gathering, but Adelicia was no more than halfway through her second cup of tea when she felt the day's excitement begin to wane into exhaustion. She had dreamed of the moment, being back in the safe arms of Belle Monte and having Essie once again turn down her bed and lull her to sleep with the soothing whispers she cherished, and to hold her children in hers arms. Now here she was, exhausted and weary, in the home of a friend, who was hosting her entire family and the servants as well.

"I am more tired than I suspected," she said. "Perhaps I should lie down before supper." Pauline took her hand and led her to the room they would share. And after washing her face and hands in a bowl of freshly poured water, she lay down and quickly fell asleep in the poster bed.

Following a pleasant supper of cold cuts, garden vegetables and one of Essie's cream filled torts, everyone gathered to hear the experiences of the past eight months. Adelicia, Sally and Sarah, sipping iced tea, sat in deep green velvet parlor chairs, while the children gathered around them on the settee and floor. The servants stood listening in the doorways. Bedtime was not mentioned, and it was midnight when Adelicia finally returned to her room, with Bud carrying Pauline, who was fast asleep.

After she had pulled Pauline's nightgown down over her head and laid her on the smaller of the two plush beds, she removed her own clothes and slipped into a soft white cotton gown, borrowed from Sarah. Adelicia knelt to pray. "Dear God, do not take my strength from me. Continue to bless and care for my precious children, the servants, Sarah, Sally and her children, and all my loved ones. Please keep Ransom safe. Thank you for life and for the blessings bestowed throughout my journey and for every day. And in the morning remember me when I go to see Governor Johnson. In Jesus name, Amen."

Tears dripped onto the sheet as she stood and suddenly turned to see Essie in the doorway. "You should be asleep, dear soul. How long have you been standing there?"

"That's where you ought to be." Essie came to the bed and sat on it, like in times past.

"Oh Essie," Adelicia cried like a child. "I hate this. I want to go home—I want the war to go away." She wept with Essie soothing her, gently rocking her shoulders, cradled in her still, strong arms.

"Everything gonna be all right, baby, everything gonna be all right."

CHAPTER 90

GENERAL THOMAS J. WOOD AND HIS OFFICERS MOVED INTO BELLE Monte on the same morning that Adelicia went to see Governor Andrew Johnson.

"Thank you, Governor," she said extending her hand, "for the kindness you showed to Mrs. Carter and me during our travel to Louisiana, and again, for protecting my property and home while I was away." He motioned for her to take a seat.

"We were pleased to do what we could, Mrs. Acklen." She observed that he was not in the best of moods, and his words mere courtesies.

"I am here because some days ago, my children and servants were ordered from Belle Monte. The document signed by you, providing protection to my estate and my family, has remained with me ...."

"The document," he said, interrupting her, and taking a seat behind his large, over-sized desk, "lasted as long as was possible, longer than most. No more promises can be made or papers signed. I am sorry."

"But Governor Johnson, you cannot let your army come in and take our homes and belongings! Does your government have no honor? Do you not know there will be nothing but hate, coupled with revolt, if you continue such practices?"

"Mrs. Acklen, in case you've missed it, there is a war—a hellish war that I don't like any better than you. There have been many changes since we promised you and others protection. We believe there will be a major attempt by the Rebels to retake the city. We cannot permit that. It could and would change the course of the war; Nashville is our strongest artillery base. It is necessary that we use every means to prevent such a disaster. Our officers are being quartered in strategic spots throughout the city. Belle Monte's excellent location on the knoll, with a water tower for a lookout makes it choice property. I am sorry. I truly am, but few, if any, remain who've not been touched by the war. Your friends, your neighbors have all, or most all, left their homes—and not just your Rebels, Union sympathizers have had to concede just like everyone else. As I said, we must use every available resource. At the war's end, adjustments will be made for damages, but for now your home must be used. There is no doubt, you know, the North will win."

As he talked, she sat across from him near the left corner of his desk—listening and thinking. "Where do you expect the families to go? How will they manage?"

"I can answer neither of those questions."

"My family and servants cannot continue to stay with Mrs. Polk." She was becoming unnerved by the small talk and hearing his words, projecting the war's outcome. "Are we allowed to leave the city?" He nodded. "The country?"

"As far as I'm concerned, a widow and her children may go anywhere they like. I know you've helped us in the Deep South, been a primary contributor. I've also heard other rumors." He hesitated, "You are free to go wherever you like."

"When do you expect this attack?"

"You ask a lot of questions. I wish I knew the answer to that one." He stood, "Good day, Mrs. Acklen. You've been lucky."

Instead of returning to Polk Place, Adelicia went directly to Belle Monte. Already, amongst her marvelously designed gardens and fountains and statuary, Union soldiers—three hundred or more, she estimated—were setting up tents, their horses eating whatever appealed to their appetites. She put some money in the driver's hand, stepped down, and stood watching, angry, infuriated, helpless—"Damn, damn!" she said under her breath.

"May I help you?" asked a voice from behind. "What were you saying?"

Startled, she turned to see a short and stunningly handsome General Wood. Flushed with anger as well as embarrassment that he may have overheard her swearing, she turned and calmly said, "I am Mrs. Acklen, the widow of Colonel Joseph Acklen."

He bowed and took her hand, "You are the mistress of this grand house then?"

"Yes, General, I am mistress of this grand house," she answered bitterly.

"Your mammy may have told you that we had your art treasures and other valuables sent by wagon to Mrs. Polk's, thereby preventing their molestation in any way."

She was taken by surprise. It had never occurred to her that it was he, the new occupant of Belle Monte, who had seen to her valuables.

"No, sir, I was not aware it was through your thoughtfulness. I have been away, having just returned yesterday, and had asked no details, as I found it horribly shocking to return after so long a time to find my home and grounds deserted. Only because a faithful servant had remained did I discover the location of my family. How long do you plan to be here?"

"Mrs. Acklen, I am certain it will be no less than three months, perhaps a year or more. I cannot say."

A year, she thought, Yankees, men alone in Belle Monte for a year.

"Will care be taken with my home, or will you ravage it, perhaps even burn it?"

He gave a brief laugh and looked at her over the top of his glasses. "You've heard some tales, haven't you? And some, unfortunately, are true. Mrs. Acklen, I can promise to treat your home and its contents as if it belonged to a best friend. My officers and I shall be staying here and the enlisted men camping on the grounds, or in the outside buildings. I promise no harm will come to any building on the estate by me or any of my men. I can make no promises about its being shelled by the enemy. I can make no promises about the grounds. We must dig trenches for fortification purposes, at least on the south portions along both sides of our lines. I am sorry," he said compassionately. "I wish it could be otherwise."

She felt easier, even though he had just told her the grounds would be dug up. She both trusted and believed him. He seemed as concerned as if it were his own wife asking the same of another general in another place. "Sir, may I come tomorrow and get our clothing?"

"Of course. Anytime."

"General Wood, I believe you to be a gentleman and a man of honor. I leave Belle Monte in your care. I shall consider you as a guest in my home, assured that you and your staff will behave accordingly."

"You are a most gracious lady," he said taking her hand. "I shall consider myself your guest, and no harm will come to your grand house."

"Thank you, sir," she said, standing in the large doorway encased with cranberry venetian panes over the top and on either side. "I shall come tomorrow for our clothing."

She had reached next to the last step when she suddenly turned and said, "I have changed my mind. I should like to pack the trunks now. Do you have someone who can assist me?"

"Certainly." He spoke to an officer nearby, who in turn went to fetch extra men. In a short while, they had helped her put all the clothing she conservatively thought they might need, in five large trunks, then loaded them onto the wagon General Wood had provided.

"Again, sir," she said, as she stood at the front door, "I bid you good day. If perchance we are to meet again. I hope it to be under more favorable circumstances. I leave my home in your care."

She did not want to return on the morrow, nor at any time when Belle Monte was occupied by strangers. Nor did she want time to stand and ponder over the pieces of furniture that she loved—the spacious rooms—or to walk from window to window—to touch and feel those things, those spaces she held dear—nor did she want to return to an occupied Belle Monte.

Not once had it occurred to her in Louisiana that she would return to find the Union Army encamped in her home. For sure, she, Essie and the children would go to Europe and remain there until the war was over. And when they returned, she would walk into Belle Monte as mistress, just as before. And whatever the Yankees or Rebels had touched or harmed, she would rebuild, redo—and she would have the means with which to do it!

CHAPTER 91

"I DONE A LOT OF THINGS WITH YOU, BUT I AIN'T GOING OVER NO ocean on no big boat to no foreign country. I am not. The Mississippi is a big a water as I want to be on. I don't see no need to take the childrens either..." Essie stopped short of further ranting, and asked, "If there no fighting in New York, like you say, then why don't we just go there and wait it out?"

"So you will go to New York and be surrounded by Yankees?" Adelicia teased.

"There ought a be some place in these states we can go away from fighting Yankees?" Essie unfolded, then refolded items from the trunk of clothes, haphazardly putting them inside an armoire in the room Adelicia shared with Pauline.

"We could go west and prospect for gold, live in tents, surrounded by outlaws and Indians, but," Adelicia said defiantly, "we shall go to England, just as soon as I can make the arrangements. We cannot continue to impose on Mrs. Polk. The children will love it. Joseph and I often spoke of taking all of you there. It is settled, and do not try any of your devious tricks to talk me or my darlings out of it." She pondered as she helped Essie with the unpacking, "I think we shall hire an English nanny while in England and a French governess when we tour France. That is what I think we shall do."

'Devious tricks!' Essie thought. Adelicia appeared in almost too good of spirits, the best Essie had seen since 1861, and she wondered if it had anything to do with the Yankee General Bennington whose name had materialized into that of a family member!

"Miss Adie, you not planning to take no gentleman along are you?" Essie demanded.

"Whatever gave you that idea? No, dearest Essie, but the war will not last forever," she said, holding up a lovely pale blue nightgown. "But I have been thinking how enchanting it would be for General Bennington to join us in Europe. We could even be wed in Italy, in the charming Thirteenth Century Duomo, with which I fell in love in Verona. Then, after the war, we could all return to Belle Monte together. Do you not think that a wonderful plan?" Adelicia was enjoying the lighthearted teasing with her Mammy. However, the random thoughts were taking on new dimensions.

"I know something was different. I know my tuitions was right. You gonna marry a Yankee! My baby is gonna be wed to a Yankee!"

"Essie, he is the most wonderful man."

"I done heard them same words before."

"But this time, Essie, I love him just for the sake of loving him. I ..."

"You not been a widow for even a year," Essie interrupted. "No ma'am. You not marrying nobody yet. You done lost all your senses, and I'm not moving one foot outside Nashville."

The following morning, Adelicia received a letter from Ransom, delivered by courier from Belle Monte to Polk Place, formally proposing, and asking if there were someone with whom he should speak for approval, for example, her eldest son. A true gentleman, she had smiled to herself. She would remember to conceal the magic she was feeling. As Essie had amply explained, she could marry no one, not now. It was a lovely thought, however, and she was enchanted with the possibility. Much was still at stake—much yet to complete. She wondered if God really did have a design for her future, if it included Ransom.

She would inform him of the conditions in Nashville, at Belle Monte, that it was in her best interest to leave for Europe, that they would meet, as planned, at war's end and begin the lasting relationship about which they had spoken, for which he had asked...for which she yearned...that she hoped possible for her.

Sally, who had not stopped raving about her Colonel and the social engagements in New Orleans, had decided to wait out the war with her children in either Lebanon or Beersheba Springs. She could certainly not go home to Franklin, where only God knew what would be occurring there, as Confederate troops were gathering and organizing to retake Nashville. Sally had arranged to leave at week's end. She would now make her own plans for Europe before the onset of Autumn.

Essie burst into Adelicia's room just as she dipped her pen into the inkwell to begin her letter.

"I don't think nothing about 'all' returning to Belle Monte together—nothing at all about 'all.' Miss Adie. I'm not going to Europe, and that's 'all.'"

She looked at her old mammy, smiling, "I was only teasing you," she said with a warm hug, "I always want you with us, but I know you prefer to be here. You must promise, however, to be waiting upon our return, and Essie, I shall not have a husband with me." Both, teary eyed, Adelicia sat beside her mammy on the settee, the unpacking still not finished.

The following morning, Adelicia went to Governor Johnson's office to inquire about passage from Nashville to New York, the route she and Sally had taken a few weeks earlier. She was told by him that it was not a prudent time for her to be traveling to Europe, no matter how self-sufficient and independent. However, upon her persistence, he would provide her protected leave.

The children, long fascinated with tales from their parents of "across the waters," were excited at the prospects of foreign travel. Bud and William, well read in the classics and in geography had a good knowledge of the continent. Claude told his mother that he preferred to go West and prospect for gold, however, the next best thing would be to cross the ocean and see where the unfortunate queens had been decapitated.

Adelicia chose the late afternoon in the side yard of Polk Place, to tell the children about her friend, Ransom Bennington. She began by showing them the small miniature of him in her locket, beside that of their father as they sat on white wrought iron benches, balancing glasses of ice water, beneath thick branches of a shading elm.

"Yes, darling," she said to Bud, "he is a Yankee, but being a Yankee or a Rebel does not make one good or bad. Many families are divided, fighting on different sides because they believe differently. I have no answers as to why this war started. I wish it had not." She set Pauline on her lap. "You were only three when your father left for the plantations two years ago. I think you will enjoy meeting General Bennington. I believe all of you will."

"If he is your friend, we'll be happy to meet him," Claude said, walking over to hold his mother's hand.

Willie and Bud concurred as their mother continued, "He is a very nice person, a good person, whom I met at the hotel in New Orleans after attending the opera with cousin Sally."

It felt good to share her story of Ransom with her children. "The general is someone to whom I can write while we are away. Perhaps he will visit us upon our return home, or even join us in Europe. However, he was wounded, and must have surgery and recuperation time…so we shall see. Mostly, I want you to know that his friendship is very important to me."

They had, to her surprise, and joy, acted quite pleased. Adelicia had not stopped to realize before, that like Emma, Pauline had seen little of her father before his death. She felt that she was deeply in love with Ransom. He would be good for her children, good for her. He did not need her money, nor her social status. That he had. His bloodline was purer than that of her own. Perhaps he was the first person to enter her life who would have no need to use her. And perhaps this was at the very core of her fears. Whatever, the force within that drove her, perhaps deceived her, that kept her from fully loving and accepting love, remained. She would guard her thoughts.

With the passing of days, Adelicia realized that Essie could not have made the trip, had she even wanted to do so. She had believed her eternally young, the Essie of her childhood, but Essie was old—not feeble, but slow in step. She had watched as Essie climbed the curved stairs at Polk Place, thinking how she had aged in the eight months she had been away, or perhaps, she had just not noticed before.

Sarah agreed to house the servants, as many who wished to stay, for as long as necessary. Uncle Ben, Essie and all would be safe there.

Adelicia would tour the continent with her three sons, one daughter and one servant, and would hire a governess in England. In the meanwhile, their mammy, Cora, would be sufficient to attend Claude and Pauline during the journey. Essie, she hoped, would be waiting for them at Belle Monte when they arrived back home.

The mid-July morning was hot, humid and with temperatures already reaching ninety. The servants had lazed inside, or in their quarters or in the coolness of the cellar, the children were lazing on the large back porch shaded beneath the arms of a spreading oak, without energy to play, not even the board games. Adelicia sat indoors with Sarah, using a paper fan, thinking if she were at Belle Monte, she would remove her undergarments, ridding herself of clinging underskirts, roll her sleeves above her elbows, and lift her dress to just above the knees, baring her legs without stockings and unbutton her dress to just above the point of indecency. But here she was dripping with perspiration, sipping iced tea, laden with layers of unnecessary clothing, and the sun was not even near its mark of full day.

"I shall get the door," she lazily told Sarah standing as the chime rang and discovering that even in walking, no comforting breeze soothed her face.

"A telegram for me," she said after resuming her stifled posture in the Wedgewood blue upholstered chair. She fanned herself briefly with the envelope before unsealing it.

"I regret to inform you, that General Ransom Bennington of the Army of the United States, was killed in action near Cullman, Alabama on the first day of July, 1864. My sincerest sympathy to you. Mark Shepley, Governor of the State of Louisiana.

"What is it? What is it, Adelicia? You are ashen," Sarah asked, taking the telegram from her hand that barely clung to it. "Oh, my, this is your General Bennington! I am so, so sorry, my dear."

How cold and impersonal the telegram was, just like the one she had received, not even a year before about Joseph! Ransom had been dead for almost three weeks! Oh, dear God, she questioned, does everything I care for die? Is there nothing to which I can ever hold? Nothing that will ever last? My children—my husbands—my love? Then the inevitable answer: no, not even her wealth. How many times had she spoken to God of her losses? However, she could not dismiss, that she was still blessed with four of her ten children. And it was kind of Governor Shepley to have notified her, very kind, she thought.

"Oh, Sarah," she sobbed. "I must leave here, leave as quickly as possible—I do not want to see the South or the North—I do not want to see the war or fighting or death—I do not want to see it or hear about it, or talk about it. I hate it! I despise it," she sobbed piteously, burying her head in her lap and clutching Sarah's hand.

CHAPTER 92

ON AUGUST 10TH, ADELICIA BOARDED A PASSENGER-CARGO TRAIN for Louisville with her children and Cora. Essie, Uncle Ben and Charlotte had gone with them to the Cherry Street Station, and as the train pulled away, the children leaned their heads from the open windows, waving until they could see nothing of their old friends but three small dots.

The railroad between Louisville and Cincinnati, still incomplete, had them first transfer to a stagecoach pulled by four, then to a mail packet on the Ohio. The children had been in awe since boarding the train in Nashville and never ceased exclaiming the wonders as they at last arrived at Bennet House in Cincinnati.

Disheartened and weary, Adelicia was pleased that Cora's daring permitted her to take the children for an outing in the park and on their first streetcar ride. Adelicia had engaged three rooms at Bennet House, one for herself, one for the three boys and one for Pauline and Cora. It was the arrangement they would continue.

Still devastated, bereaved, night passed, morning came, and Adelicia was unsure if she had even moved from her original position when Pauline tiptoed in to awaken her at half-past eight. Reluctantly, she rose. She would need to hurry to arrive at the depot and be en-route to New York by noon.

The startling news of Ransom's death had met her at a time when she had believed that nothing could block her path to happiness, when all had seemed in place. She was certain there would be no other for whom she would ever feel the sheer passion she had felt for Ransom. This time, she would remember about love, and not allow its presence to enter her heart again.

She was more convinced than ever that her decision to travel in Europe was best for her and her children. She would meet with her banker, Harry Stone, who unfortunately was not in New York, but at his residence in London.

New York in 1864 was a city far removed from what she had first seen with Isaac in 1839, and far removed from 1855, when she and Joseph were last there. She had only glimpsed it two months before, a brief encounter with Sally. Today she saw it as more magnificent, busier, more sophisticated but tame, despite the rabble-rousing, diversity and the influx of immigrants who flocked its port daily with hopes of achieving their dreams. The war had driven its industries upward, and business flourished, despite the closing of most of the cotton mills. War had made it richer. No wonder there were political outbursts here, she thought, people like Pauline Cushman speaking at museums and theaters, keeping things stirred up.

And as they drove along Fifth Avenue between the fashionable rows of three story brownstones, she thought it might be a wonderful place to live, or at least visit more often. Brevart House on Washington Square was the most aristocratic hotel in the city, and it was here she had reserved a suite for them. Lavishly decorated in the latest Victorian décor, Adelicia felt at home in the room of pink and lavender satin. It was an elegance she loved, in which she felt comfortable, the elegance she had known at Fairvue, in New Orleans, at Belle Monte. It was an opulence she intended to enjoy despite a life forever void of her beloved Ransom.

The children dined in their rooms with Cora that evening, and she dined alone in the luxury of her handsome bedroom. She took a miniature of Joseph from her bag and placed it on the table beside her bed after carefully admiring the lock of his hair on the opposite side of his picture. She held her locket in her hand, the one with both Ransom's and Joseph's pictures, then carefully unwrapped a small, velvet lined box and from it took a silver framed miniature of Isaac. She would not involve herself with love again, she whispered sadly, remembering her earlier words. She would enjoy the beautiful, good things, with family, with friends, with acquaintances, with life. The men she had loved, to whatever extent, had all vanished from her life, from life. She would hold her reserve from everyone except her children, and God forbid anything should happen to them—for then her strength would surely fail her.

The children immensely enjoyed their three weeks in the city, as they awaited their departure. They shopped on avenues that Cora declared "too big and too busy for respectable people to set foot on," visited museums, the theater, puppet shows, rode horse drawn buses that rocked from side to side with hay strewn on the floor, and visited old acquaintances with their mother.

They had especially delighted in an Italian organ grinder who stood on Washington Square morning and afternoon, across from Brevart House, with his small acrobatic monkey, dancing and soliciting tips from bystanders into his red velvet cap, a cap visited each day by her children. Cora's most frequent complaint was the general attitude of the people, especially the shop keepers, whom she considered sassy, so different from the ones at home, even the Yankee ones.

Adelicia's wait for their London departure had been made more pleasant by running into her old friend Octavia Lavert, also a guest at Brevart House. Their renewed friendship gave Adelicia an additional introduction to the Bonapartes in Paris, from where Octavia had just returned, and where a reception by Prince Napoleon Bonaparte, called "Plon Plon," and a ball by Countesse Marianne de Walewska, had been given in her honor.

Octavia's introductory letter, along with the one from Elizabeth Patterson Bonaparte, should propel her European tour into an unforgettable experience. Octavia's energy, intellect and poise melded with her flightiness. The woman fascinated Adelicia, and she looked forward to seeing her again upon her return to America, when she would invite the celebrated, worldly aristocrat to Belle Monte.

The children and Cora waved until the New York Harbor faded behind them, and all that was visible was the spraying and sloshing of lukewarm Atlantic waters.

PART V

Adelicia in Europe and return to Nashville

1864–1866

CHAPTER 93

The *Nova Scotia,* a paddlewheel commandeered by a Captain Perkins, had small cabins and no private baths. Her live poultry and milk cows gave off an unpleasant odor that prevailed at all times, and barnyard sounds awakened everyone aboard, well before most would like to have been awakened. Yet despite the inconveniences, the Atlantic crossing was without major turbulence or inclement weather—"a calm sea," Adelicia reported. However, there was no one not elated at the first signs of land, anxious to set foot on the dock in Liverpool.

Their days in the musty city were mercifully brief; never had they seen such squalor and filth. From their hotel window, Adelicia had observed two women fighting, hitting and scratching each other in front of a cheering crowd. The food was barely edible and she refused to allow her children to drink the water unboiled. And after they had been served sour milk one morning with breakfast, she insisted they only drink hot tea for the remainder of their stay.

The chill and misty weather did not permit outings and while Adelicia attended to business and her bank accounts, Cora stayed indoors with the children, not daring to go in the streets. And when the train pulled out of the station for London, she and the children cheered.

Adelicia had notified Harry Stone of her arrival. Isaac's old friend and president of one of the largest banks in New York, also held interest in four British banks where Adelicia's funds were in safe and capable hands. She had not seen Harry for many years, not since she and Joseph had called on him on one of their New York trips. She wondered if he were as handsome as ever and if he had the same mischievous twinkle in his sky blue eyes, the one she had seen when Isaac first introduced her in the summer of '39.

A carriage drawn by four, a lovely surprise, whisked them away to the Langham Hotel, while a cart followed with their luggage.

Waiting at the entrance of the fine establishment was Harry Stone. In his late sixties, the passing years had not diminished his imposingly tall frame. And although his gray hair was thinner, it still curled on the ends and waved back over the tops of his ears, only one spot at the crown bare enough to see his balding. His excellent nose was framed by silver brows, set in a winter, tan skin. "Mrs. Acklen," he said in a strong voice, rushing to take her hand. "How pleasant to see you again, and in Europe! I trust your trip was as favorable as is your bank account," he exclaimed, bending to kiss her cheek.

"Mr. Stone, please call me Adelicia." She suddenly felt safe, a much desired feeling, reminding her of something warm from her past, pleasant to recall, like seeing a childhood mammy after a long absence, or recalling days and people from an era long passed.

Almost absentmindedly she said, "Meet my children. Joseph, who is fourteen, William, ten, Claude, eight and little Pauline who is six and their mammy, Cora." He spoke with each child and Cora, then gave orders for the luggage and trunks to be taken to their suites. As the children followed the bellboy up the stairs, with Cora trailing close behind, Harry took Adelicia's arm and asked her to be his guest for dinner that evening. She thanked him graciously, but feigned fatigue from the arduous trip, then added that she hoped he would extend the invitation for another time.

How happy she was to be residing at the Langham Hotel overlooking Portland Place. She marveled at the excellent arrangements, as she soaked in soapy lavender, before stepping into a second tub filled with rose water. Then draping a towel about her, she powdered her entire body before slipping her pale pink silk gown over her head. Sinking into a down feather mattress, she slept.

Adelicia awoke refreshed, looking forward to another bath. The previous evening's had been her first in four weeks.

Her first full day in London began with a trip to the bank, where she checked her accounts, as she had done in Liverpool, to see for herself that all was as it should be. She was a millionaire, and no one would take it from her. Harry had explained that she would be referred to in London as "the Lady Acklen," a distinguishing mark of wealth. She was rich, and would become richer, but never hoard it. She would enjoy it, share with those in need—she would have total control. And while in London, she would make every effort to enjoy the historic city, despite the sadness heavy on her heart.

That same evening, she attended Shakespeare's *Othello* with Harry, who, after the theater, introduced her to Baron Rothschild and his party. The Baron then asked her to attend the opera as his guest the following evening. She suddenly thought of Crawford, wondering if his ships came to London, remembering she had not yet thanked him for her passage home to Nashville, nor the carriage at her disposal in New York.

"Baron Rothschild must remember you from a previous visit." Harry said, as they walked to their waiting landeau.

"Is this all one does in London?" she asked as they returned to the hotel. "Attend the theater, the opera and dine?"

"The social whirl has just begun, Lady Acklen. Baron Rothschild does not invite just anyone to sit in his opera box. Be ready for teas, parties, late dining, hunts, balls, more theater and more opera. I hope you'll do me the honor of allowing this old bachelor to be your escort."

"How extraordinary! Do you think the Baron favored us?"

"You, my dear, not us. I've been his acquaintance for many years."

"I must go to the dressmaker's tomorrow."

"I'll direct you to the best."

"Harry, do you think we might see the Queen? When Joseph and I were presented at court, she and Prince Albert were on the Isle of Wight."

"Queen Victoria remains in mourning, even though it has been more than three years since Prince Albert's death. She sees very few socially. But if you wish, I'll inquire."

"It will be the highlight of my trip."

"Your trip, Mrs. Acklen, has not even begun."

The children spent their mornings taking lessons with an English governess, Miss Birdie, recommended by Harry Stone, and their afternoons on outings, with Cora tagging after, grumbling, much like Essie, Adelicia thought, when the Hayes' children were all young.

They delighted in sitting atop the double-decked horse buses, hearing the driver call out in his cockney accent: Westminster Abbey, St. Paul's, the Tower of London, London Bridge, Big Ben, Madam Tussaud's a Wax Works, Parliament House. They saw hundreds of statues, "More than Mother has at Belle Monte," Bud had coyly remarked, and the houses of famous literary figures. Having read Thackeray, Dickens and Johnson, Bud and William had developed a mental picture of London prior to their visit. However, William and Claude's special interest was on the green where two queens and Sir Walter Raleigh had lost their heads.

It was during Miss Birdie's morning lessons, that they were taught proper pronunciations and informed that one of breeding *never* spoke in any other manner, *never*. However, the children remained fascinated by the Cockney sounds that they were instructed never to use, finding them far more appealing than 'proper' English.

Carriage rides around the city meant seeing men going about in top hats and frock coats and taking afternoon airings in Hyde Park, where coachmen waited in long lines with carriages, while their mistresses strolled in fine gowns, holding gay parasols among elegantly designed flowerbeds and green turf.

Adelicia attended few of their outings. That was left to Miss Birdie's discretion and Cora's grumbling. She was in a social whirl, one in which she wished to remain. Dining with the British aristocracy, attending their balls—one at Buckingham Palace, although disappointed once more that Her Majesty was absent—she did not have to think. She did not want to think because when she did it was of Ransom, of partings, of death. Illusions were her preoccupation; at least she recognized them as illusions.

Baron Rothschild's opera box was at her disposal, and he had seen that her name was on the society lists. Although Harry Stone continued to be her formal escort, it was obvious that the twice married Baron had eyes for the American, Lady Acklen. She found it necessary to avoid the charming, wealthy Baron whenever possible, accepting no gifts other than the availability of his opera box, invitations and small favors to the children. It appeared that in English society, the wives of noblemen, who seemed cold and aloof to her, cared little, or bothered little, as to where the affections of their husband's lay. Ironically, a permissive yet prudish society, Adelicia thought.

London's December was bitter cold, and their thickest woolens did not deter the wind's chilling bite. But the holiday spirit abounded, and her children were accepted and invited into the societies of young people of their age and breeding. Harry Stone, the children and she had attended Dickens' recitation of his "Christmas Carol." A more charming man she had never encountered, and when they met him after the performance, and after he had signed a copy of *Great Expectations* for her children, Adelicia found him even more attractive, wishing to spend more time with him. However, she doubted he would find interest in the societies in which she presently found herself.

The Christmas season was a gay one for the wealthy, a desperately sad one for the poor. She saw more real poverty in London, on the very streets of the homes of the affluent than she had ever seen or imagined; the slums were unbearable. England would support whichever side won the war, but for a British statesman or journalist to write of the perils of slavery—as Featherstonehaugh had done in the 1830's, when their own people were literally starving, ragged, living in hovels, the streets, in debtor prisons, or workhouses—was abominable. Her Negroes, and those of her family, friends and neighbors, were housed, clothed, warm and fed. They were not begging, like the poor children they had witnessed, for half a sixpence in the snowy streets, shoeless and scantily clad, scenes by which she and her children were appalled and horrified. It was certainly no argument for slavery, but it was an argument for foreigners casting the beam out of their own eye before casting the mote out of another's.

As a family, they had delivered food to debtor's prisons and orphanages, the sights of which had affected their joy with what the Season had to offer in London. In one orphanage, on the East side, they found no semblance of the holidays, and that some of the youngsters had no idea that Christmas was even approaching. Adelicia and her children had ordered a spruce tree, and had taken ornaments to decorate it. They had also shopped for each boy and girl and had placed the gifts beneath it. However, there was no assurance that after they had left, that the gifts would not be taken by the greedy 'keepers.' Londoners dwelled in a major caste system.

Had Dickens' "Carol," written in '43, made no impact with its universal message: "Mankind is my business." She could not imagine how conditions for the poor could have been any worse then than what she witnessed now, although supposedly, there had been reforms. No wonder to her that immigrants poured into America every day!

On Christmas morning, the family attended Holy Eucharist at St. Paul's with Harry, the Rothschilds and other acquaintances. Afterwards, Adelicia, her children and Cora enjoyed a scrumptious meal in the hotel dining room. Although Kris Kringle had visited on the Eve, there were also gifts for everyone at supper, and on the following evening, Boxing Day, they would go to Westminster Abbey to hear a special performance of the Boys' Choir.

However, amidst the festivities, Adelicia's thoughts were never far from Belle Monte, wondering if General Wood and his officers were celebrating Christmas in her home. What was happening to the rest of her family and Essie? As Christmas memories flashed to mind, she recalled the December Day that she had persuaded Essie to ride into town with her in order for her to telegram Isaac, the telegram that reappeared in her father's hands! But oh, the thrill of being on the snowy streets that morning and feeling the excitement in the air. And how beautiful Rokeby had been that year! Before dear Richard's passing.

Later that Christmas evening, when all was quiet, teary-eyed and missing home, Adelicia wrote letters to her family, to Essie, to Sarah Polk, to Margaret, to Sally, wishing God's blessings for the New Year and a prayer for the war to soon be over. She asked that they write to her in care of Harry Stone, who would forward her mail to wherever she might be. She told them of the delights of England, not of its poverty, about the children's activities, little of her own.

It was after she had fallen asleep, after having tucked each child in bed, even fourteen year old Bud, that she awoke sobbing, missing home. She was longing for the familiar, for those whom she had loved who were no more, and for Belle Monte that was much changed. She felt very alone despite the glamour and bustle about her, and she decided that on the New Year, they would continue with their journey to France—away from the fog and rain—perhaps just—away.

CHAPTER 94

ON DECEMBER 29TH, NEWS ARRIVED FROM HOME STATING THAT Nashville remained an occupied city. The Confederate Army had failed in its final attempt to capture it and the Battle of Nashville, the one over which so much speculation had been drawn, on whose outcome so much had depended, had finally been fought, and lost—a decisive battle—the decisive one. The Union was at last assured there would be no major defeats. Nashville held the largest arsenal on either side. All was a matter of time—a matter of waiting—a matter of more lost lives.

The news troubled Adelicia's heart all the more; on the one hand, causing her to yearn desperately for home, and on the other, feeling relief that she was absent from it. She had seen enough of the wounded and the dying, although she would never have the visual perceptions, nor feel the impact of battles fought in her own city like those who had actually witnessed it.

She could only imagine what had happened at Belle Monte, not knowing if the Rebels had advanced that far, or if the lines were held farther back. The ill-fated attack had begun in Franklin, on December 15th—how many must have fallen between there and Nashville in deep snow and ice—most likely poorly clad—a disaster for the boys on both sides, and many were just boys, a little older than Bud. She could not conceive of anything ever happening to her home and she would try not to think about it. The cablegram from her brother-in-law, Bill Lawrence, had served its purpose. Christmas must have been bleak all over Middle Tennessee. Hood's Army was in full retreat.

"Must we go, Mother?" the children had asked almost simultaneously, as Adelicia and Cora continued packing.

"Paris is beautiful in the spring. You will make new friends and have a French governess."

"When are we going home?" asked eight year old Claude.

"Do you want to return home? Amidst the war?"

"I miss my things at Belle Monte, but I should like to see Paris," he answered.

"Good, my darling." she said, motioning for him to sit beside her on the small tapestry divan at the foot of her bed, "I want you to see all the sights while we are there. It is not often that entire families can travel about Europe together, and who knows when it may happen again. And for Bud," she said looking up at her eldest and taking his hand, "I have arranged a six month study in Switzerland."

"Can we not all go?" asked William.

"Yes. But not until the end of Bud's term."

"Is Miss Birdie going, too?" William continued.

"No darling. I just told you, I have already engaged another governess for France. We shall see Miss Birdie upon our return to London."

"Is Cora going to stay in England, too?" Pauline asked jumping onto the divan.

She smiled into Pauline's pretty face, "Of course Cora will be with us, she is family." Hugging both Pauline and Claude, she asked them to wait with their mammy while she made one last check of their rooms.

Two nights before their departure, the Rothschilds, Lord and Lady Lonberry, Lady Montcalm, the Count and Countess of Marlton and Harry Stone gave a farewell dinner in Adelicia's honor, with a promise of seeing her in Paris and asking that she rejoin their society upon her return. The stay in London had been lovely, but when she and her children boarded the channel boat for Calais, Adelicia had no regrets about leaving. With the cliffs of Dover folding behind them and the approaching magnetic France, bright and sunny, so opposite from England's dreary fog and mists, her heart grew lighter. It was a new year, and at its end, she would be home for Christmas.

CHAPTER 95

PARIS OF 1865 WAS EVERYTHING A CITY COULD BE, EVEN IN ONE'S dreams. Its public gardens were even lovelier than she remembered. Paris itself seemed one enormous garden—flowers along the boulevards, in the center of the boulevards, along the banks of the Seine, from the balconies above every shop and townhouse and sold on every corner. Music swelled from its doorways, and hopeful artist applied paint to their easels along the avenues.

Nashville, its troops and gunsmoke, seemed far removed as the carriage drawn by four white mares stopped in front of the Hotel Bristol at the corner of Rue Castiglione and the Place Vendome.

In her scrumptious room, Adelicia spun and fell onto the ice blue eiderdown duvet, delighting in the elegance around her, in the magic of Paris she had felt once before when she was there with Joseph. The outside cold felt warmer as the roaring fires in their rooms glowed. They were occupying the same suite of rooms that had been used by the Kings of Holland and Greece, and Edward VII when he was Prince of Wales.

Magical Paris was like so few things that were actually better than remembered. Twice, she had missed the Queen of England; she wondered if her fortune might change, and that possibly, she might meet the Emperor and Empress of the French.

She had heard persistent rumors about the Empress Eugenie, as well as read what in America, would never be printed about a lady. Still Adelicia was certain of liking her; the tales portrayed a daring Empress, unmindful of tradition and the dictates of others. Adelicia's favorite rumor was of Her Majesty riding bareback through the streets of Spain in her native city of Carablanchel, dressed like a gypsy, her long red hair flowing behind her.

Adelicia had also heard of Eugenie's suicide attempt at seventeen over a lost love, a similarity they did not share, as the man did not exist over whom she would consider taking her life. It may or may not have been true, but it provided the grounds for very interesting gossip. She was certain about the Spanish and the French; when it came to a beautiful woman, one might as well be prepared for gossip and rumors and learn to enjoy them. She had also heard that the Empress made it a point to never comment as to the truth or falsity of the reports.

Adelicia's children were also caught up in the glory and flavors of Paris with their German governess, Miss Verta, who took them to parks and museums, Notre Dame, the site of the Bastille, and of course, to the Place de la Concorde, Claude's favorite, informing his mother that seeing where Marie Antoinette and many others were guillotined, was far superior to the simple beheadings in London.

Adelicia saw to their continued reading of Defoe, Scott, Stendhal, Dumas, as well as contemporary writers, such as Hugo and Flaubert, nor did she neglect their daily Protestant lessons from the King James Bible. In London, they had attended the Church of England, but were now in the midst of Catholics. She was happy that Miss Verta was saturated in Protestantism, Lutheran though it be.

The enchanting and lovely Champs d' Elysees was inviting to the children, where they sat along its rows of brightly painted benches and watched marionette shows with Miss Verta and Cora. Sweets and hand carved toys appeared from vendors and shops along its long strand, and Bud reported that the grandeur of the ladies strolling along the boulevard in their elegant gowns made those in London appear homespun in comparison. Her children, it seemed, were seduced by Paris as well.

Once, when they were touring not far from the Arc de Triumph, the driver made a wrong turn, or so he had told them, down a street where women paraded with painted faces and too fancy of dresses. As they motioned for Bud, who was riding on the outside seat of the open carriage, to come, Cora had put her hands over his eyes and gave most definite instructions to the driver to, "Set his horse on the right tracks, fast!"

Adelicia was certain that Bud had found it as intriguing as he had the very vitality of Paris, and her son was no doubt embarrassed at having his mammy with him. She thought to herself that he most probably would like to get away for a second look before being sent to Switzerland. And had Cora not reported the excursion to her that evening, saying that she had never seen anything like it in all her days, and that Paris was "a wicked and evil place to have her children," he probably would have found a way to have done so.

"Paris," she said to Cora, "was a city of leisure and pleasure, and in truth, catered to entertainment of all sorts, even to decadence. Here one must choose, as one was compelled to do wherever one might find one's self, between good and evil." Adelicia would not blame Paris.

CHAPTER 96

ADELICIA WAS ABSORBED IN THE WHIRLWIND OF PARIS, ITS GAIety, its leisure, its strictest formality. It was on her tenth day in the City of Lights that she received the coveted invitation to a ball hosted by the Emperor and Empress at Tuileries! Her pleasure was unparalleled, and her preparations to attend exceeded those of any ball heretofore. The society in which she found herself was unparalled. She would be shamelessly striking, shining in its magic.

It was Pieugot who designed a gown made from her own sketches, intrigued, himself, with the American lady who knew what she wanted and how she wanted it, so different from the French ladies who entrusted everything to their designer. The gown contained forty yards of the finest Lyons ivory silk and gathered from the vee-cut waist to the hem in small bunches of seed pearls, giving an illusion that the entire skirt was smocked in pearls. An off the shoulder neckline was cut much lower than Adelicia's American dresses, with seed pearls sewn around it and around the shoulders, coming to a vee in both the front and back, making her waist appear smaller, and her breasts larger, all of which was enhanced by her flawless skin.

It had been on her third day in Paris that Adelicia called on American Ambassador John Bigelow and his wife, with a letter of introduction from Harry Stone. They seemed pleased to meet her, and it was through them and the Rothschilds that her round of invitations had begun. She had not even needed the letters of introduction from Octavia and Elizabeth. The Bigelows had introduced her to French Ambassador, Emile Cologne, and she had been escorted by the Bigelows to a dinner party given for the Consulates in Paris, a gay affair where parlor games were played, lasting until dawn, with champagne, caviar and rich pastries served all the while.

After those introductions, she quickly perceived that she was expected to receive other engagements on her own—the groundwork had been laid. It seemed a return—almost—to the '30s, when every man she met ogled over her. And it did not take long for her to discover that marriages and mistresses in France were far different from those in America. In France, mistresses were openly accepted in society and Frenchmen thought nothing of blatantly asking a lady to become his lover, most preferring married ones. In America, it was done with more finesse, behind the facade of pious Christianity and the auspices of genteel breeding, never forthrightly.

The *Paris Courier* had made mention of her name in the society section after the Consulate dinner: "...the lovely and widowed Mrs. Adelicia Acklen from Louisiana, Tennessee and New York..." In her most fanciful dreams, she could not have imagined her European tour to be anything like this!

The night of the Emperor's ball at Tuileries, Pauline sat in the armchair of her mother's room, observing as the French maid twisted Adelicia's hair high atop her head and pinning it with a fluttery ivory feather clasp. She had called Pauline over to look into the mirror with her, "How precious you are," she said, pulling her daughter close. "I remember watching my mother as she dressed for fancy occasions. She always allowed me to come into her room, and I would sit in fascination. Your grandmother was very beautiful," she said, giving her one last hug. "Now you must be tucked in bed."

"Good night, my darlings," she called, before descending the curved stairs to the hotel's grand lobby below.

The Tuileries was splendor from a fairytale, truly breathtaking. French in every respect. The Emperor and Empress stood to the left of the ballroom on a dais covered in rich, deep purple velvet, trimmed with ermine along the edges. And as Adelicia stood in the receiving line with Harry and the Bigelows, observing those before them, bowing and curtsying as they passed, she got her first full glimpse of the royal couple. She found the Empress dazzling, confident, beautiful. And she found the Emperor earthy and handsome, with a twinkle in his eye designed for all the ladies who passed. She liked him without even having heard his voice, and she was instantly envious of the Empress. "The Lady Acklen," she heard Ambassador Cologne say, and she graciously curtsied before them.

It was not just her imagination—it had happened too often before—the Emperor had his eye on her. A word was not spoken, but she knew instinctively, as an observant woman always does. The Empress, too, had glanced her way throughout the evening—fondly—Adelicia thought, and she secretly wished that she could have the honor of a private audience with her. She had no doubt they would have much in common.

She was well aware that many of the ladies were inquiring about "this American," most probably, she thought, not out of concern for their husbands, but out of concern that she might be chosen as mistress by one in an elevated political position, in preference to themselves. In Paris, that seemed the primary concern of most ladies in the society of the elite; the more prominent the position, the more honored the lady.

The glamorous evening had been dined and danced away, and after she tiptoed into the children's room and gave each a kiss, she undressed and lay in her bed unable to recall the number of gentlemen with whom she had danced throughout the night and into the morning. More than two each were with Emile Cologne, Harry Stone and Baron Rothschild. She was so enraptured with the evening, she was not even disappointed at the inability to be anywhere near the Empress or the Emperor after her brief introduction.

Life was even more exhilarating at forty-seven than at sixteen. She felt marvelous, filled with renewed energy and desirous of life, confident that she looked marvelous as well. She thought no one in the room that evening would have dared venture a guess that she was a day past thirty-five. All unpleasantness and brooding she had willed from her mind to the extent that it seemed not to have been there at all. This was Paris! Everything was enchanting and gay.

After a late luncheon with her children, when all had retired to their rooms for a nap, she was dozing when her maid knocked at her door. Adelicia had received, by royal livery, the most coveted of invitations—to attend the Imperial Ball at the opening of the National Assembly. Clinging to it, she took a deep breath, twirled about the room, then read it again.

She would ask Pieugot that very afternoon for the gown of all gowns—perhaps a pearl satin, lavishly designed. She rang for the servant girl assigned to her suite, sending a note for Monsieur Pieugot stating that she would arrive at his shop no later than four o'clock, to have the finest fabrics laid out from which she might choose. The girl hurried, as she was told, and soon after returned with a reply that Monsieur would be delighted to receive the Lady Acklen.

When she dined the following evening in a group with Harry, the American Dukes and Palmers, the Boulwares, the Dumas and the Bigelows, Adelicia could not divert her thoughts from the ball, still six weeks away. Her dinner companions spoke at length of government affairs, politics, both local and abroad, and only as an aside mentioned the Emperor's long association with the Countess Castiglione. Adelicia was not interested in what was happening in Mexico or Austria or anywhere else at that moment. She was only interested in hearing about the Emperor's mistress. "Do tell us more about the Countess," she insisted. "We do not have such tantalizing tales at home."

"Lady Acklen is becoming more and more French, and I might add," Baroness Elise Dumas said resting her cheek on the back of her hand, "it is most becoming."

"Is it possible to live in Paris, or enjoy an extended visit and not become French?" Adelicia asked.

Frances Bigelow frowned at her remark, however Baron Dumas commented, "I thought American ladies' ears were too delicate to hear about the tete-a'-tetes of the opposite sex."

"Our ears, Monsieur, have never been delicate," she said glancing around the table, giving special attention to Francis, "For the sake of convention, we must pretend to be uninterested, or shocked over what is later whispered behind closed doors. Do you agree, Mrs. Bigelow?"

"Do not look now, ladies," Baron Dumas interrupted, before Francis Bigelow could reply, "but it is Plon Plon himself who is being seated two tables from us with a few cabinet members."

Prince Napoleon, a nephew of Napoleon Bonaparte, and unaffectionately called Plon Plon by the French, was quite obese, Adelicia quickly noted. He was dressed in the contemporary three piece suit of the day, much like those worn by New York bankers, with a large gold chain extending from the vest and stretching over his large middle into the watch pocket below his bulging waistline.

"We shall give him time to order, then make our presence known. We would not want the Lady Acklen to miss such an opportunity," the Baron said, winking.

Adelicia was unsure of his intonation. On the other hand, she did not want to miss the introduction, regardless. It was another adventure to record in her journal. She was certain the French were most familiar with women opportunists and from the brief accounts she had read, all the Bonapartes had kept at least one mistress, often two or three in most fashionable settings. The children from such dalliances were made Counts or Countesses and given land. She supposed if one desired that sort of life, it was one's own business.

However, she found it far more honorable and satisfying for a lady to become wealthy by her own merits, without giving of her charms, instead using her mind and cunning. Then she need never depend on, nor acquiesce to any man. Adelicia's daring, her fearless determination, had taken wealth and developed it into greater wealth, riches that afforded her pleasure and extravagance, if she chose, as well as benevolence. Her wit and manner, not overlooking her appearance and good taste, allowed her introductions in which she took great delight and enjoyment.

After the initial greetings had been exchanged, Baron Dumas asked, "May I persuade you to come to our table so that I may present the Lady Acklen?"

Prince Napoleon cleared his throat and coughed as a bit of red wine dribbled over his chin, then stood and walked with the Baron to their table. "How pleasant to see you again, Lady Acklen," he said, taking her hand, "You are the lovely American lady who attended the ball at Tuileries, and about whom, I may add, there is much discussion." Then he made great formal sweeping gestures of bowing to kiss her hand.

Although she felt her face flush at the mention of "much discussion," she replied, "May I be so forward as to ask how I missed meeting so charming a gentleman?"

"American ladies never think themselves forward—they are extremely crafty," he replied.

"You are familiar with American ladies, then. Do you distinguish them by the regions from which they come? For instance, Southern American ladies?"

"Baron, your party must join us. It will be only a matter of fuss for the waiters, which is of no consequence. Do you not agree?"

"How gracious of you, but we are in some haste to arrive on time for the opera," responded the Baron.

"In that case, you will all come to the Palace Vendome for libations and delicacies after the performance."

"It will be our pleasure," he answered.

Through the remainder of the meal, the Prince steadfastly glanced over at Adelicia. It seemed he took his eyes off her only long enough to put a bite of food to his fork. Occasionally, she returned a glance with a smile or nod, grateful when it was time for the ladies to retire to the powder room to freshen up for the opera. It was then that she told the Baroness, who burst into laughter, that she could not possibly go to the palace that evening.

"The poor man is beside himself. He hardly knows what he is eating. He fumbled over his silverware more than usual, not mentioning the spills of wine and water. You, Siren," Countess Bouleware teased, "will do quite well in Paris."

"She is doing quite well in Paris," spoke up Baroness Dumas.

"Indeed she is, indeed she is," Francis Bigelow agreed.

The following morning, long before Adelicia had even thought of rising, messages had been left at the hotel desk. And not until almost noon, when the maid tapped on her door with the usual tray of fruit and coffee, did she know that Prince Napoleon had been sending messages on the hour, each time asking that she not be awakened. After a few sips of strong coffee, she opened one of the notes and read: "Your absence last night was felt by all, especially myself. Will you dine with me this evening?"

She laughed aloud while sipping more coffee. She was certain that when the tales arrived in Nashville, and for certain they would, while greatly exaggerated, that she would not be any more loved nor endeared.

She rang for the servant girl to take her message: "How kind are your words. I had asked the Countess Boulware to express my regrets. Again, I ask your acceptance of my sincere apology. I cannot dine with you this evening. However, I am free for Tuesday next, if it pleases you. I fervently await your reply."

Not only did the reply come within the hour, but with it came an enormous bouquet of mixed flowers, followed by a basket of confections for the children of the Lady Acklen.

It was a small dinner party given at Prince Napoleon's townhouse on the Champs d' Elysees. Harry Stone had returned to London, and the Prince had sent his carriage for her at the Bristol. The Count and Countesse Walewska were there when she arrived, and they were soon joined by the Count Marlboro and the Countess Leviana, the Boulwares and the Dumas.

It was also the Eve of Valentines, 1865, and everything was done in gloriously variegated shades of pinks and reds, touched and melded with white. So this is how a prince entertains, she thought, as she glimpsed around the lavishly decorated rooms, her gaze passing from here to there, then resting on the heavy, ornate pieces of glistening silver and heavy cut crystal on the dining table. The room looked as if an artist had taken his brush and painted it, as if it had been designed for the evening to honor her; even the chairs were tufted in pink satin that matched the lace placemats set with pure white china and Louis XIV sterling pieces. Adelicia was dressed in white grosgrain, with pearls around her neck, both wrists and dangling from her ears. Her hair, puffed loosely, was brought to the crown of her head and held by a pearl clasp; the simplicity of all white and soft pearls was the effect she desired.

Most of the conversation was directed toward the National Assembly and the ladies chit chat about what they were wearing and who would be designing. Spring hunts were also discussed, conversation to which Adelicia listened intently, wondering if the hunts were the same as at home. She found herself in very different company than that to which she was accustomed; far more worldly, far more sophisticated. And she was acutely aware of Plon Plon's focus on her every move as she read the faces of those in this new society.

She was the only American present and thoroughly enjoying herself among the French, who spoke with her in their language as well as English. Balls, princes, emperors and the prospect of riding at Fontainebleau! Ah, she thought, while listening with great care; splendid surroundings and splendid personalities, but after all, they were only men and women with titles, often bestowed as gifts: was not all of humanity basically the same without the exterior trappings?

The following morning, she received an elaborate Valentine designed with the finest alcyon lace, along with pink and red roses. Plon Plon also asked, in a separate note, that she join him for a private dinner. Oddly, there had not been the slightest reference to his wife or children in any conversation. Baroness Dumas had told her that his wife and he were seldom seen together in public, and that she was away from Paris much of the year.

Adelicia replied with a brief but cordial note, thanking him for the elegant bouquet of roses and expressing her regrets of being unable to dine with him.

If Plon Plon wished to be her consort, it was not a wish that she desired. To make a favorable impression on the Prince was one thing, anything more was not on her agenda. Her fascination lay elsewhere.

CHAPTER 97

THE CARRIAGE ARRIVED AT EIGHT, LIVERY AND FOOTMEN IN TOW, as Harry Stone stepped out to escort Adelicia to the grand ball. Feeling much like a princess herself, swathed from head to foot in pearl-white shimmering satin, she greeted Harry with a gentle smile. Nothing could be seen except for her face concealed beneath the hood of her long flowing cape, its lining of the same quality satin, but emerald green, matching her heeled slippers. Her steps were small and deliberate as she descended the curved marble stairs into the hotel lobby, took Harry's arm and stepped into the gilded carriage.

It was not until she and Harry were ready to be announced that she unfastened the tiny clasp that held her hood in place and let the cape fall from her bare shoulders into the hands of the waiting servant. Nearby, Plon Plon appeared breathless and within moments, all those near Adelicia had paused from their conversations, turning and positioning themselves to admire the elegant American guest.

Momentarily, it was her turn to go before the Emperor and Empress. Ladies pulled their full skirts aside so that she and Harry might pass, and Adelicia knew without question that no one could rival her appearance, nor her manner. The evening belonged to her.

It was a moment in time, in which a woman feels a calm, a confidence, that transcends reality itself. It was she who felt like an empress as she took Harry's arm, knowing all eyes were upon her. She graciously curtsied before the royal pair, the Empress warmly commenting on her loveliness and her pleasure that she could join those assembled for the occasion. The Emperor said nothing, simply acknowledged her presence with a smiling nod, but Adelicia felt his eyes on her long after she had passed, and afterward, glancing at her as she danced with the Minister of Foreign Affairs to the first strains of Chopin's "Polonaise."

Plon Plon had come to her for the second dance and made it apparent that he wanted her within his grasp for the evening, an intent contrary to her own. However, she had to take into account that he was the nephew of Napoleon Bonaparte and the first cousin of the Emperor.

After Plon Plon, she danced the difficult Sir Roger de Coverly with Ambassador Cologne, well aware of being stared at and whispered about, and she reveled in it. Nothing she had previously experienced rivaled the splendor of this evening, and she did not believe it possible, all seeming a dream from which she did not want to awaken.

She felt herself the most magnificently dressed woman at the ball. Her gown, made from fifty-five yards of pearl white satin and gathered around the extensive skirt bottom in scallops, exposing the ecru alcyon lace beneath, was astonishing even to Parisians, who felt they alone were the experts on fashion. Whispers rose throughout the crowd that surely she must have called in a designer who kept his fashions secret from the French. They were guessing Rome, Vienna, Leningrad, unaware it was their own Pieugot who had created a design that Adelicia, again, had primitively sketched, an idea fashioned from a fairy tale dream.

White satin draped from her shoulders into full sleeves that fit tightly around her dainty wrists, upon which she wore slivers of emerald and diamond bracelets; her neck and chest, baring skin that was soft, smooth and flawless. Tiered diamond ear bobs dangled from her ears, a single strand, diamond choker sparkled around her neck. In her bouffant hair was an elegant, but simple tiara set with clusters of small diamonds.

When she had shopped at Cartier's, she had intended to rival every lady at the ball, even the Empress. She had succeeded. "Extravagance," she had told a new acquaintance, "was spending what one could not afford. I have never been extravagant."

As the great hall clock struck its last chime of midnight, everyone gathered onto the ballroom floor. And after a portentous silence, the orchestra began to play the French National Anthem, grand and impressive, as French patriots attentively paid honor to their country that had so long been torn and ravaged by wars and leaders of wars. They stood as one, with allegiance to the concept of France, although many were in disagreement with the Emperor, in whose presence they were. But a singleness of purpose, thought and heart prevailed for a time. She wondered if anything this patriotic and impressive were done in Washington, or would be done after the war, as if her country were never divided.

After the cheering that followed, the orchestra played a fast polka, the Emperor and Empress twirling and dipping about the floor to the smiles and applause of all those gathered. The music did not stop, but the dancers did when Eugenie stretched her hand in the direction of Maximillan, who bowed and joined her to the rhythm of the polka. Napoleon III walked near to where Adelicia stood, sipping champagne and talking with Harry and Plon Plon, and extended his hand. She was so unnerved, she did nothing more than stare up at the Emperor until she regained enough wit to put one hand in his, while Harry removed her stemmed flute from the other. She did not miss a step and found him the smoothest of dancing partners as they glided and stepped together for what seemed an eternal moment, till everyone joined them on the floor.

Too quickly, the music ended, and she heard the Emperor ask, as he escorted her back to where Harry was standing, "May I have the pleasure of another dance before the evening ends?"

"It will be the second honor I shall have received tonight, Your Majesty," she answered, smiling up into his face.

"I shall look forward to it with great pleasure, Lady Acklen." He nodded to Harry, "If you will excuse me."

He was quickly out of sight, but as the orchestra began a romantic waltz, she saw him dancing with the Countesse Walewska, as Adelicia had her second dance with Harry.

"Is it customary for the Emperor to dance with each lady at the ball, Harry?" she asked. "I do not remember his doing so at the Tuileries."

"He'll slow down after a while. It's good politics, notwithstanding the eye he has for the ladies. But I shall answer your unasked question. He presented you with the place of honor, when he asked you to dance the first one after the Empress, following the anthem. Aha! I see your overweight admirer returning."

"And how do you know it is I for whom Plon Plon is returning?"

"Don't be coy with me," Harry admonished. "By the way, Plon Plon and the Empress do not get along, so any attentions the Emperor may give you will probably anger Plon Plon. It is rumored that he sought the Empress' attentions and was turned down. However, he could find it amusing to see the Emperor have a look in his eye for you in order to irritate Eugenie."

"The Bonapartes and Paris are so filled with rumors. Do tales circulate about everyone?"

"Even about me, my dear."

They laughed. "You are remarkable, Harry," she said. "Do you think the Emperor is really attracted to me?"

"The Emperor is attracted to all beautiful women. Smile, dear, Plon Plon is approaching."

She did smile, and put both hands in his as an American polka began. At least she had no need to be close to him, only holding hands while skipping and turning. She flattered the Prince, appearing absorbed in his verbal anecdotes, and he let Adelicia know how honored he felt that so many men wished her for their dancing partner. He must assume, she thought, that after one innocent, cordial note thanking him for the roses, that future contacts were eminent, that she was his. She found it odd that he was accompanying no one that evening, that his wife would miss so important an occasion.

Plon Plon was easy prey, and if she had need of an escort, she could count on his being at her disposal. His wife, she learned, was on an extended stay in Capri, where it was rumored that she had an extraordinarily handsome young lover, the Italian Count Berantello. Adelicia's mind was set on the Emperor.

Long ago, she had once desired to be the First Lady of Texas. Empress of the French was a far stretch—a very far stretch from her girlish dreams.

It was not until mere minutes before the carriages were to arrive that Napoleon III asked her for a second dance. She gave the glass from which she had been sipping champagne to the nearby attendant and fell into a fast paced quadrille in which both partners displayed their expertise, laughing as they gaily tripped from one side of the room to the other, changing partners, then together again, much too out of breath to speak. Again, too soon, she thought, the music ended, but the Emperor signaled for another, a waltz.

"I was unaware that one learned such graces in the backwoods of Tennessee," he said jokingly, between breaths.

"And I, Your Majesty, was unaware that Corsicans made such delightful dancing partners." She had said it, looking into his eyes with all the softness and coyness she possessed, waiting. He was looking deeply into hers as she spoke, and she detected an expression of surprise. She also saw it soften until he smiled.

"A clever woman you are, Lady Acklen. I shall refrain from erring again concerning your homeland." He slowed their pace and asked if she would come for the stag hunt at Fontainebleau, two weeks from the coming Sunday, as he understood her to be an accomplished equestrian.

"And from whom do you understand that?" she asked.

"I have been told that all southern women of the aristocracy ride well."

"I do not believe you answered my question, but I shall let it pass for now, and Your Majesty, we have no aristocracy in Tennessee. It is called good breeding." She paused. "I shall be filled with thoughts of nothing but the hunt until Sunday next."

As the music was ending, he led her to the Empress. "I have asked the Lady Acklen to ride in our coming hunt."

"I am pleased, Lady Acklen. We have need of new equestrian skills, perhaps some that will be a match for my own. I shall look forward to seeing you ride."

"Your Majesty, the honor is mine," she said curtsying. The two women met eye with eye, and Adelicia admired what she saw: a confident, amused expression. Then the Empress asked, "Will you join us for luncheon day after tomorrow at St. Cloud?"

Adelicia was taken aback. "Thank you, Your Majesty. Once more, the honor is mine."

"One o'clock, shall we say?"

"I shall arrive at one o'clock."

The orchestra had continued to play after the first signal from the Emperor, and as the Empress finished speaking, Prince Mecklenburg walked to where they were standing and asked the Empress to dance the fast polka with him.

Adelicia was alone with the Emperor, feeling more uncomfortable than she wished to admit, or ever remembered, except for her first meeting with Isaac.

"Lady Acklen, I shall count the hours with great solicitude until you visit St. Cloud."

"So shall I, Your Majesty."

The following morning, the servant girl, as usual, put a copy of the *Paris Courier* on her noon breakfast tray. Adelicia turned to the society column and saw in bold print: "Lady Adelicia Acklen, the charming American, visiting our country while on an extended European tour, attended the Grand Opening last evening of the General Assembly. She was received with marked courtesy at the Imperial Ball by Napoleon III and the Empress Eugenie. In social circles, she is universally admired. Her beauty, grace and courtly manners, with her rich and tasteful dress at all times, and the superb style in which she lives has created a sensation in Paris."

She loved it! Every word! She would have it framed, along with her invitation to the Imperial Ball! "A sensation in Paris," the fashionable, fun-loving city of the world... "her rich and tasteful dress, her courtly manners, the superb style in which she lives..." how she loved it! How ingratiating!

She stretched and yawned, looking at the small marble clock on her dressing table. It was almost one, and she had promised to go with Pauline, Claude and their governess to the zoo. She quickly rang for the servant to draw her bath and lay out the clothes she had chosen—a stylish maroon merino wool suit trimmed in stark white grosgrain, with a matching hat of the same fabric topped with a white egret's plume.

There was no time to waste. They must make a stop at Pieugot's and see if, by working through the night, he could create another sensation for the luncheon. Of course he could, she decided. Not only did she ask for a deep melon raw silk for the occasion, she selected a deep green velvet for her riding habit trimmed in black corded file for the hunt. Then she and her children were off for a wonderful afternoon's outing to the zoo.

The luncheon, with the Emperor and Empress had been more enjoyable than she had imagined, yet filled with anxious searching of her soul. She had felt stunning in her dazzling melon frock. The Empress, six years younger than she, was equally stunning in sage blue. Conversation, ceaselessly interesting and lively, reinforced Adelicia's idea that the three had much in common. She and the Empress even laughed over daring youthful pranks, in which the Emperor appeared delighted. He made no reference to anything personal, nor did he show any sign or hint of a sign of interest towards her, other than that of a well-meaning host.

They also discussed the war at home: France's sympathy lay with the South, as they saw slaves and serfs a natural part of agricultural and economic growth for the agrarian sections of both countries. When she recounted her trials with the cotton, trials from which Adelicia now seemed so far removed, it was as if she were telling a story from the distant past, the Emperor and Empress laughing in disbelief at her daring, then toasting the Lady Acklen's cleverness.

They spoke of the futility of the war in America, expressing wishes for its end—the three knowing, that without Divine intervention, the South would lose, and soon. She asked about Waterloo and told of her plans for Brussels, of her older sons interest in the great battle.

It had been a wonderful, exhilarating occasion, unpretentious and charming. Adelicia could not remember a time since arriving in Europe that had been as invigorating, yet relaxed. She was made to feel comfortable, not as if she were dining with royalty, but as with old friends, a hospitality few hosts could claim. She was even more in awe of the Empress! She found her exciting, adventurous, intelligent, sincere. It was seldom she found women anything but a nuisance. She liked and admired the Empress.

She also liked and admired the Emperor, handsome with dark eyes, thick mustache and goatee. His hair, thinning on top, was full and black on the sides with daring hints of gray. She liked his meticulous manner of dress; his hands were strong, but mostly, she was enchanted by his flirtatious, sparkling personality that she found endearing. He spoke with a gentle, yet strong voice, a characteristic she found most becoming in men, and he seemed to say exactly what she wanted to hear, even in the presence of his wife. Perhaps part of Adelicia's attraction to him was knowing that he had had many mistresses, and presently had one or more. It was fascinating to ponder why so many women were so desirous of one man.

She was far more attracted to this married Emperor than was decent. Never had she dared flirt with a husband, perhaps Crawford, but more or less in between his marriages. Her respect for the bond of marriage, and herself, was sincere. And it bothered her deeply that she had looked forward to nothing, as long as she could remember, as to the hunt at Fontainebleau, well aware, it was not the hunt itself.

During the interim, at parties, luncheons and afternoon teas, her singular thought was the hunt, with which came the desire to again see the Empress. But her heart knew, that her real desire was to see the Emperor of France, to ride fearlessly for him at Fontainebleau.

Chapter 98

THE BAYING OF THE HOUNDS COULD BE HEARD FROM GREAT DIS-
tances as they chased antlered buck and fawn colored doe over
luscious grounds of forests and pastures. She felt splendid in her
handsome green velvet riding habit, its skirt flowing, and her black
plumed hat, nodding in the wind. Adelicia rode naturally, dauntlessly,
with an ease most riders would never feel, not even once.

It was an extraordinary gathering of royalty and French aristocracy;
but it was she who rode so magnificently, she who rode with such abandon that the Emperor declared her the finest rider he had ever seen.

Afterward, when Adelicia stood with the Emperor and Empress
on the east balcony, sipping warmed brandy while looking onto the
marvelous gardens and lush countryside so favored by Millet and
Roseau, she spoke of hunts in Tennessee, the fox, the deer. She talked
of riding purebreds and thoroughbreds, of Tennessee walking horses.
When Eugenie told the story, the one Adelicia had heard rumored,
of riding through the streets of Spain bareback and astride, in a dress
of gauze when she was fifteen, Adelicia laughed, saying that she regretted not having a similar one to share.

She was given a partial tour of the Twelfth Century Palace,
the apartments of Marie Antoinette, of Napoleon Bonaparte, the
Gobelin tapestries and the room where Napoleon had signed the
abdication papers. Never had her eyes feasted upon such grandeur,
and she wondered if ever again, she would be content in the less ostentatious rooms of Belle Monte.

And when she was shown the stables, she was captivated by the
extraordinary golden palominos, and could not help but make references to them during the elaborate evening meal, where she was
seated completely out of view of the Emperor. The guests dined on
roast pheasant, vegetables in rich sauces, cherries marinated in heavy
cream and liqueurs, breads and champagne, all of which enamored
her senses, making her giddy.

And through all the conversations and teasing, Adelicia wondered if she could become someone's mistress—in particular, the husband of the Empress whose friendship she most desired.

With subtlety and cleverness, it seemed to her, Louis Napoleon had arranged to be alone with her on the gallery overlooking the grand canal long past midnight. It could not have been coincidence. In the chilled, breezy mid-March air, he said, "Your riding is magnificent."

"As is yours," she replied. "And the Empress is superb."

"Let us say, we are all riders of exceptional quality, but you 'got the fox.'" The metaphor was unmistakable, and the look in his eyes was unmistakable. "You are a beautiful and fascinating woman, Lady Acklen. It is not often that women come with all the traits that make her so desirable; most beautiful women have some, but few possess those like yourself. Are all American Southern women so well possessed?"

"Only I, Your Majesty," she answered engagingly. She was close, close enough for him to touch her. She looked into his flirtatious eyes, "You are very kind, with your remarks. I had no idea that a trip to Europe to rid myself of the turmoils and trials of home would find me in favor with the Emperor of France." She wanted him to kiss her, and she felt herself shiver as he put his hands to her waist and she tilted her face upward toward his.

"May I see you alone—at my chateau in Deauville? We may take a week if you like, or whatever time pleases you."

Having partially regained her composure, she answered, "You must be careful with your words, Your Majesty. What if I should ask for a lifetime?"

"The way I feel at this moment, I should grant it to you without so much as blinking an eye. Will you join me there?"

"When?"

"The day after tomorrow, Wednesday. It is already Monday morning. I cannot arrive until late evening, but I shall arrange for you to go by way of the Imperial train that morning. The servants will see to your comfort," he said moving closer, close enough for her to feel his breath touch her face, "I shall count the seconds between now and Wednesday evening," he whispered, sliding his hands from her waist to hold both her hands in his.

"And I," she answered nervously as they walked back into the grand salon, where she received, amidst much pomp, the customary gold pin designed in the shape of a hunting horn with the head of a hound protruding where the horn curves, presented each year to the one judged to have ridden most skillfully to the hounds. The honor, without question, was Adelicia's.

Although the sun was rising as she at last slipped between warmed sheets, she was not sleepy and wished for laudanum to ease her into a heavy slumber. She doubted whether she could go to the Normandy seaside. She also doubted if the fluttering of her heart would allow her to stay away. Of flirting, she was surely guilty, of immorality she was not, but at the moment it seemed unimportant. Among the wealthy in France, it was a way of life and no one would ever know, except God of course, and for the moment, the desires of her heart were overruling her logic, her common sense, and making the proposed affair to seem good and right. She would go to Deauville. Her appetite indeed overruling her reason.

She would lie there until the shops opened, then hurry to Pieugots, or Worth's, or perhaps both to select fabrics for new riding habits, day and evening dresses and exquisite night wear. What could not be completed in two days could be sent. Her heart was pumping far too fast for her to sleep, and she wondered if the Emperor's were doing the same.

Before ten o'clock, she was on her way to the designers, after having left instructions with the governess that she would be lunching with the children at one.

When she returned to the Bristol, there were two notes awaiting her, both stamped with the Imperial seal. One, from the Empress asking her to dine with her the following evening at St. Cloud. "The Emperor will be away for the remainder of the week, and I should enjoy more delightful conversation, comparing youthful pranks and daring."

The second was from the Emperor, stating he was able to leave a day earlier than expected, expressing his desire to send for her the following morning, but if not possible on short notice, they would take the Imperial train together on Wednesday, as early as her pleasure allowed. While at Deauville, he continued, they would visit his stables, where she might select the finest of his Spanish palominos for her own. "I affectionately await your reply, LNB"

She hurried up the stairs with her heart racing, and into her suite where the children were dressed, waiting to go on their outing.

"Mother," asked Claude, as they lunched on the Champs d'Elysees. "Are you listening at all today?"

"Be quiet, Claude," reprimanded William, "Can't you see Mother is thinking of home?"

"Of course, I am listening, darling," she answered. "Now tell me once more your very favorite acts at the circus."

It was a lovely day, and after luncheon, they had walked along the boulevard, exclaiming once more over their previous week's visit to the zoo and the rare species that they had not seen in New York. But Adelicia was there in body only, commenting when it was appropriate and laughing on cue. For the children's sake, she hoped it was a convincing facade.

Her mind was fencing between carnal desires and moral goodness—the choices of right and wrong—of good and evil. How beautiful and divine temptation appeared, the bliss of momentary evil, that her strict Presbyterian upbringing refused to allow her to dismiss. She even wished to be like those who knew no way but to follow fleshly desires that appeared so rewarding.

It was the choice from her internal agony, the conflict in her heart that would bring redemption and salvation, or utter damnation. How difficult to take the first step, contrary to her teachings, contrary to her long held values. And once having done so, would it be easier the second time, when her passion had become slave to her reason, and damning sin?

Pauline and William fell asleep while the governess read, and Claude and Bud retired to their room to read their assigned studies of Balzac and Voltaire before supper. On the morrow, the older boys' March holiday would be over. Bud would return to his school in Lucerne and William to the academy in Neuilly.

Adelicia hoped the Empress had received her note of acceptance when the carriage stopped in front of St. Cloud, the magnificent chateau on the banks of the Seine, waiting for the gates to be opened for her visit.

"Her Majesty will receive you on the terrace," the butler stated, then took her wrap and led the way.

"Thank you for inviting me, Your Majesty," she curtsied. "It was a surprise, a delightful surprise." Eugenie's dark auburn hair was pulled tightly back from her face, making her dark brown eyes sparkle the more. The simple strand of pearls around her neck and matching earbobs complimented the sheer elegance of her beauty.

"Please be seated, and do call me Eugenie, as I requested before. I am not overly fond of formality. Before contradicting myself, however, I thrive in the pomp and circumstance of parades and balls, of parties and dinners, of court, but I like to live casually and be like the simple folk, to quote the Scottish Burns, so much so, that in my youth, I went to great lengths to be like the children of the servants and of those who worked on the estate. I suppose I wanted both and still do." She smiled. "At times, I should like to dress as a peasant woman and shop in the market places unnoticed, to ride a cycle down the boulevard in a simple skirt and blouse, or go dipping in the waters with nothing more than the briefest clothing."

Adelicia returned her smiles, identifying with each word, and much to her own surprise, she heard herself say, "Let us do it. Let us ride down the boulevard. I have never ridden a cycle!"

Eugenie laughed. "It is not so easy anymore. Too many queens of France have been guillotined and with the uncertainty of the times, guards are with me wherever I go. I would have to be in complete disguise and slip out of the palace."

"You speak as if you are serious."

"I may be."

Their conversation was stimulating, pleasing and amusing. Eugenie first spoke of the scandalous gossip that had surrounded her before coming to court, even that she was illegitimate! Additional rumor had declared her to have led a wild and decadent life, including that she wore a red wig because her hair had fallen out after her attempted suicide! The more they laughed and talked and shared homespun gossip, the greater the similarities Adelicia saw between them; the dominant contrast being, Eugenie was the Empress of France, Adelicia an untitled citizen of America.

Adelicia found Eugenie so genuinely tender when she spoke of her sister Paca. She had written to her between the interim of the civil ceremony of her marriage to the Emperor, and the one at Notre Dame when she was first called, "Your Majesty," telling her she felt as if she were in a play that she and Paca had directed as children when her role was that of the queen. Eugenie's great love for her sister, for Spain, for humanity, was made more endearing by her humility, evident to Adelicia in her every word.

Eugenie spoke of her husband's nobility, his generosity, how he had married her despite the objections of his ministers, courtiers and the powers of Europe, who preferred a stronger political alliance. That the wives of the above had snubbed her from the moment of her first appearance, and she lightheartedly told Adelicia how drastically the stock market had fallen the day after the official announcement had been made of their forthcoming marriage. Eugenie was the choice of Louis Napoleon, not of the people, and she, a pious Catholic, had added that her faith in God, her immense desire to help the less fortunate and her unbounded faith in her husband to do what was best for France, had brought her greater happiness than she had expected. The hordes who had blamed him for the outcome of the coup d'etat that he imposed in 1852, was a highly unfair judgment, she protested, greatly misunderstood and exaggerated.

The Emperor, she had said, based on the romantic chivalry with which he treated the women he loved, was indeed a man. That, she told Adelicia, she had exclaimed by letter to Paca, soon after her marriage, "He is a man!"

The Empress of France and the American socialite chatted like schoolgirls on a lazy afternoon. It was after a light supper on the terrace, or perchance when the conversation began to turn more serious, that Adelicia remembered this beautiful, enchanting woman whose hospitality and companionship she was enjoying, immensely, was the wife of the man in whose company she was planning to be at his country chateau in Deauville.

She had unconsciously divorced herself from that idea, that fact. The extraordinary, exhilarating Empress, was in Adelicia's mind, separate and apart from the Emperor—and from her reality.

"Eugenie," she said, "I fear I have overextended my stay; I have kept you far too long a time."

"Please do not apologize, but if you have an engagement," Eugenie said rising, "you must not delay."

Adelicia was unsure if it were her imagination, or if indeed there were a glint of recognition on Eugenie's face when she spoke. Regardless, it made her uncomfortable.

"No," she answered, hesitating. "I have no appointment."

"Then stay, and we shall venture into my salon and muse over our past darings and plan the bicycle ride down the boulevard." She smiled and took Adelicia by the arm as they walked into a lovely emerald green room with white brocaded fabric on the chairs and settee, and tapestry covered walls by Beauvais.

The coachman drove along the Seine, still lit by the gas lamps, their reflection glimmering upon the river. A few hours before, Adelicia would have engaged herself in the scene's romance, but now she pondered over her evening, listening to each hoof beat along the quiet, cobblestone boulevard.

Only God knew why she slept so soundly that night, whether exhaustion from the evening and day before, or whether from the serenity and truth that had come while visiting with Eugenie, or another element of her decision left unexplored. She awoke refreshed, and not until she recognized the reality of the time, that it was the day before the intended rendezvous did she feel the strain of agony return to her cheeks.

She wondered if a friend, or one of her sisters had been faced with a similar situation, quickly concluding not, and just as quickly, changing her mind. Surely it happened to most women, the agonizing pain of wrong seeming right, or attempting to make it seem right. On the other the hand, she admitted, that perhaps other women did not place themselves in that position. Not even in her wildest rationale could she reason that meeting the married Emperor in Deauville was right to do.

She wrote on the embossed hotel stationary and signed it in a large penned hand: "Mrs. Joseph A. S. Acklen," above the hotel address and rang for it to be delivered to his Majesty's offices. She felt the easing of her facial muscles, the heaviness leaving her heart, and while commending herself for having made a prudent choice, she checked her self-praise as she picked up a folded note lying on the bedside table, whose message she already knew. It was an apology from Claude, for having praised himself for being good and finding his mother harsh when punishing him for what he considered a small wrong. She had told him that one did not commend one's self for doing what was right.

After she had sealed the envelope and was dressing to take luncheon with Elise Dumas, her ardent prayer was that the Emperor would indeed receive her note, that it would not pass into enemy hands. Surely he was at his offices, where he had said she could get in touch with him, directly. Surely he had not gone ahead of her to Deauville, certain that she would arrive. The Empress had said he would be away.

"I find it difficult addressing the Emperor of France by hand on this misty March morning. I also find it difficult to write that I must obey my reason, and not my heart, that longs for Deauville. I should prefer to say this in the warmth of your presence, perhaps, however, this is how it should be, lest I change my resolve upon seeing you. It is my desire that you understand my thoughts as I have penned this note with great concern for all. Affectionately, Adelicia."

Relieved by her decision, yet admitting deep regret as well, she handed the envelope to her maid...reasoning that its basis was not her goodness so much as her fear, fear of the cost, fear of herself. It was not the fox of which she was afraid: It was the shadow of the fox.

CHAPTER 99

IT WAS NOT UNTIL A DINNER PARTY THAT SATURDAY EVENING, that she heard the Emperor had returned to Paris after a shortened holiday She was unsure if she blushed, but she was certain of her joy in having dined with the Empress that eventful evening.

The dinners, luncheons, teas and balls continued, and Paris continued; one elaborate party, day and night, a gaiety unknown, she thought, in any other city in the world. Her lovely friendship with Eugenie had permitted her to entertain the Empress at the Hotel Bristol, and they had ridden in the countrysides together, always with guards following, exchanging pleasantries and discussing those things that two women, born into different cultures, on opposite sides of the Atlantic, surprisingly had in common: literature, art, antiquities and being a woman.

On her visits to St. Cloud, she did not see the Emperor, nor was there conversation of him except for an occasional remark by Eugenie, referring to something trivial, or a brief mention of matters of state. France was on the verge of major changes and upsets, as was America, and its politics and government becoming increasingly fragile.

Adelicia felt there would never be another woman whom she would find more spirited, more entertaining, or whom she would more admire than the charming Empress Eugenie. She put other women to shame, for sure.

She neither saw nor heard from the Emperor until April 11th, when she was summoned to his offices in Paris by a most formal note suggesting an urgency. The American and French Ambassadors, along with others, had arrived before her, and as she entered the room, the closed circle opened and she was informed that two days prior, April 9th, General Lee had surrendered to General Grant at Appomattox Court House in Virginia.

Startled, yet knowing it must be, she was unprepared to hear of Lee's surrender. Quiet and somber, all those gathered had chatted briefly in the Emperor's formal office, taking coffee before scattering to a line of waiting carriages.

That evening she told her children and by the following morning, it was heralded in the Paris papers. "Civil War in United States Ends. South Loses." Although a desire for the war's end had been on everyone's heart, it was devastating to hear, especially so far from home. Adelicia had not thought she would want to be there for its end, but now there was a deep longing of melancholy and regret, as if she were needed and had shunned her responsibilities in Nashville. Those longed for words, **"When the war is over,"** were now reality.

The Confederacy had lost, as she and Joseph had supposed, and she wondered at how great the losses were on both sides, and at the amount of ruin and desolation that lay in all the states, the families, what was left of them, those without homes, the women unnecessarily widowed, the children unnecessarily fatherless. The senselessness of a war that should not have been, a country divided, the South devastated by its presupposed gallantry, brother against brother—father against son—friend against friend—all without cause. She wondered if it were not for the deadly sin of pride that all lay wasted.

Her reverie was interrupted by a knock at the door; a letter from her brother-in-law, Bill Lawrence, written three weeks prior, stating that Corrine and Laura, all her family were safe and well and that General Wood still occupied Belle Monte. "Thank God," she said aloud, leaning back against the tall post of her bed, rereading the words. Her family was safe; Belle Monte was safe; she had trusted General Wood to keep his promise, and her mansion went unmolested. She wondered for how much longer he would need her home. How soon would it be before it and others would be vacated by their invaders? She was certain that Polk Place was secure.

Although Adelicia was far from the only American in Paris, she was, at least in her circles, the only southerner. Notes arrived daily from her French and British acquaintances, expressing their concern, and she was most appreciative of each one.

Within a matter of days, she was again summoned to the Emperor's offices, this time with the astounding, devastating news that President Lincoln had been assassinated at Ford's Theater on the 15th, by John Wilkes Booth. She had watched as Booth played Lear at the Adelphi in Nashville! Assassinations did not happen in America! In ancient Rome perhaps, to kings and queens in England or France or Russia, but not to presidents in America! How dreadful for the country so newly united. This meant that Tennessee's former Governor Andrew Johnson was now the seventeenth president! "Oh, dear," she said aloud.

Each day found her longing more deeply for home and feeling the war's futility, and the void within her returning. Her money was secure and she would return to her war-torn country and help rebuild. However, Ambassador Bigelow convinced her of the imprudence of returning home at this time, encouraging her to complete her European tour.

Heeding his advice, she sought solace in May in Paris, riding at the hunts and making the society rounds. She took trips into the countryside with Claude and Pauline, visiting peasant villages and farms, returned to the Louvre time after time, toured ancient castles, and patronized the fashionable shops—always aware of the Emperor—and the uneasy gnawing within the depths of her heart.

By sheer coincidence when she, Cora and the children had taken the train to Deauville for a brief holiday, and their luggage was being loaded onto a cab, she saw the Imperial train further down on its private track. Her heart froze, wondering if the Emperor could possibly have known that she was coming. However, when she checked into the Grand Hotel that opened directly onto the sea, there was no mention of a message. Admitting feeling a tinge of disappointment, she asked, if perhaps, one had been left for her, committing a breach of etiquette so unlike her. There had been no oversight.

The hotel was lovely, and she felt warm amidst its elegance and fresh saltwater breeze that filtered through the open front doors to the back terrace. And while the maid did their unpacking, Adelicia and the children walked long the seashore, leaving Cora to take in the scene from the pale pink stone verandah.

No sight in France had enchanted, nor captured her heart more than the sheer beauty of Normandy. They took open carriage rides to nearby farming villages whose lush pastures were dotted with gorgeous 'Norman' cows that produced the richest and most delicious cheeses made...an undeniably, exquisite taste. The trees were laden with apples, and she could only imagine how it would appear at autumn harvest, the orchards filled with peasants picking, juicing and readying the drink for the vats, from which would come the intoxicating Calvados. She wanted to return here one day—to the villages and to the sea.

On the morning of the sixth day, when they boarded the return train for Paris, Adelicia saw that the Imperial train was no longer there, and its absence caused her melancholy. She questioned if she were so enamored with her own self-righteous goodness, that she thought all would have been well had she accidentally run into the Emperor, had he invited her to dine. She also questioned if that were not what she had wished, expected. She hated admitting once more, that her fear lay in the shadow of what would follow, the consequence.

CHAPTER 100

IT WAS MID-JUNE WHEN ADELICIA AND HER CHILDREN LEFT FOR Italy to complete their European tour. Her French acquaintances were also leaving Paris for the summer, many going to Italy as well. The Emperor and Empress would be at Biarritz, Eugenie's favorite of their palaces, and the nearest to her native Spain.

A dinner party was hosted for her at the American Embassy by the Bigelows and attended by those in whose circles she had been engaged while in Paris. Noticeably absent were the Emperor and the Empress—and noticeable only to herself—was her missing each of them, but for very different reasons.

She had written to Corinne upon their departure, *"We cannot enjoy moonlight and have the advantage over nature, as with almost everything in Paris, although we have loved it well. I am hopeful that you and Laura will receive my letters, knowing things are not back to normal at home. I was thinking this morning on awakening, for I have been dreaming of home, how very far away I have gotten from you all; the longer the absence, the more you are in my thoughts. Last night, I dreampt we were in the greenhouse at Belle Monte, but when I reached out to touch you, all vanished. I do miss and love each and everyone of you."*

"Your affectionate sister, Adie"

"Yesterday, I continued my travel journal," Adelicia wrote, "desiring to remember details of places and events, perhaps forgotten if not penned in ink. The lack of local railroads in Italy, causes us to travel by carriage, and because the papers publish weekly reports of robberies by the brigands who run rampant; the talk among locals and travelers is frightening, stories concerning females, reminding me of Papa's warnings of the Natchez Trace so long ago. My jewelry is well concealed in the bosom of Cora's undergarment, and my larger pieces are sewn into the second layer of my petticoat, though bulky and uncomfortable, are well concealed. The Hotel de Russie in Rome is comfortable enough, and the July heat not yet exhausting."

"My melancholy returned as I reconsidered calling on the Emperor and Empress in Biarritz, but using my better judgment, refrained. 'I need not flirt with disaster,' she said aloud to herself while peering onto the Spanish steps from her writing desk at the hotel window. 'I must think on Deauville no more.'"

"Today, I purchased works from some American sculptors studying and working here—had them shipped directly to Belle Monte, via New York, never doubting that they will not arrive safely. Ives,' "Sans Souci," Randolph Roger's,"Ruth," and Mozier's, "Peri" were among my choices. There is something mysteriously wondrous about "Peri." I shall place the angel in the center of the ballroom. I also commissioned Rinehart's,"Sleeping Children," in memory of my precious twins, Laura and Corrina. How I miss them. A mother's heart remains empty for her lost children."

"Tomorrow, we visit the Vatican. I am anxious to see again Michaelangelo's, "Pieta" and the Sistine Chapel. How fortunate to have my children with me."

"On July 14th, I am reminded of the revolution of America against the British, and today that of the French Revolution, fewer than a hundred years before," she wrote in her journal, "the desire for independence, I find to be buried in the depths of each man's soul. Italy itself is just now in the throes of becoming united, its city states strong with pride and courage. With my thoughts in tow, I returned to the studio to see the sculpture of "Peri," the penitent angel, inspired by Thomas Moore's, *Lalla Rookh*, that again captured my heart. The goblet holding the patriot's blood in one hand, three tears of repentance, shed for all mankind, held gracefully in the other, the face and body so immortally beautiful and captivating. I slipped my fingers over the hard, smooth marble feeling the mounds and hollows formed by the artisan's hands. And from the disgruntled look I saw on Mozier's face, I felt I had insulted him when I asked again for "Peri" to be shipped with special care."

"The sun shone brightly," Adelicia entered in her journal, "as our carriages left Rome for Naples where Bud joined us on the last day of July. Cora refuses to go with us to visit the ancient sites. She prefers Florence and complains about the heat in southern Italy being unbearable and vows not to go 'touring.'"

"We are enjoying Florence, where I have taken an exquisite villa, fully staffed, that appears to be built directly into the hills of Fiesole. Cora is extremely pleased, and asked if we might stay 'put' until time to go home. The villa is near one occupied by the Empress Eugenie for parts of the year.

"I find Italy more romantic than any other place...perhaps the most romantic place on earth...as well as the most spiritual. Romance and spirituality are somehow closely linked. However, I think no more of romance, nor do I wish to be caught up in its guises, or its enchantments, but I do wish to feel again the deep spirituality that was once so much a part of me."

"Giotto's magnificent fourteenth century bell tower fascinates me, as do his splendid frescos. My favorite artist from all periods to date, except perhaps for Duccio whose alter piece in Siena causes me to weep. Fortunately, most of these master's works are 'attached' to Duomo walls, or are alter pieces, otherwise I would have them at Belle Monte...only dreaming, of course, Italy is where they belong."

"The children were fascinated by the walled medieval city of Siena. It is like no other. They especially enjoyed the Piazza el Campo, and quickly made friends with a local shop keeper who invited us for an outdoor meal at his home...then to participate in one of the contrade parades. Spectacular! Even Cora got into the spirit and marched with us. How gracious was our host and his family. How gracious are the Italian people...I wish for Corrine, Laura and me to take this trip together one day.

"I must put away ink and pen. Our bags are packed and soon our coaches arrive to take us to Venice, as we continue on our way to meet Bud in Lucerne...most anxious to see my eldest son."

"We are at last in Lucerne after a brief visit to Milan and with the children viewed Leonardo's, esteemed, "The Last Supper." On the opposite wall is Donato Mortorfano's awe inspiring, "Crucifixion." We were in the small room for more than an hour...comparable to a religious service."

Although a guide led the entourage from Lucerne to Basel, Bud took great pleasure in presenting himself as head of the family. After a brief visit to Geneva, they traveled to Verney, where Adelicia extended their stay at the Hotel Three Crowns, in order to make excursions to Chillon and Montreox.

One morning, while breakfasting on the balcony, with its exceptional view of Lake Geneva and the snowcapped Alps, Adelicia surprisingly met Mrs. Andrew Polk and her daughter, Antoinette, from Tennessee. And just as surprisingly, Adelicia was asked by Mrs. Polk, if indeed she had met the Emperor. Adelicia considered the question rude—no telling what they were saying or thinking back home, she said under her breath. However, she simply smiled and later requested to be seated at a different hour from the Polk's for the remainder of her stay.

"Autumn is lovely in this beautiful city," Adelicia wrote in her journal from Strasburg, "lovely and appealing. Oddly enough, our suite of rooms has just been vacated by the Emperor and Empress. I have made every attempt to dismiss Louis Napoleon from my mind, as I cannot deny how flattering it was to have been courted by the Emperor of France. Does the woman exist who is not drawn to such power? And does the Emperor not embody that? I cannot help but wonder how many mistresses there would have been after me and how many there were before. How foolish and vain to be thinking in such a carnal manner. (I must remember to strike this from my journal, any mention thereof.)"

"Last night, I lay amidst disturbing dreams until the light of morning allowed me to ring for an early breakfast of steaming tea, light cream and fruit. But, the out of season delicacies remained untouched when I rang for more strong tea that I sipped, off and on, throughout the morning, during my bath and shampoo. And as the hotel coiffure towel dried my hair, my thoughts wandered to decades before when my mother had dried my own hair in the same manner and how I repeated the tradition with my precious daughters, Victoria, little Adelicia, Corrina, Laura and Emma. Now, there is Pauline's lovely hair, that seems to dry effortlessly."

Adelicia knelt beside her bed and prayed, "Dear God I am thankful that I have four of my ten children, one daughter out of five, still with me, safe and well. I could not endure another being taken... Thank you for the blessedness of children."

"Wintering in Strasburg," she wrote to Laura, *"was yet another Christmas spent away from Belle Monte. But Miss Vicey joined us and we enjoyed a lovely holiday season, not that far removed from ones at home...outward appearance...snow upon heaps of snow...carolers, readings of Dickens' Christmas stories, decorated trees in the shops and homes...Our hotel was quaint and beautifully furnished and for the season, booming with festivity...On the Eve, Kris Kringle visited with laden stockings and gifts beneath the tree, including ones for Miss Vicey and Cora...Bud had taken the younger children shopping and purchased a lovely scarf for me...one I shall treasure, always...greetings came from England and Paris...But the most meaningful ones came from home, from my dear family. All was bright and gay...outwardly. I was desperately melancholy...but appeared happy as a buzzing bee. It will not be long, sweet sister, until we are united once more…summer will come, after all.*
Your loving sister, Adie"

"The coming of the New Year, 1866, in Paris was a gay occasion, and I found myself feeling less melancholy. I attended a small dinnr party in the company of the Bigelow's, the Dumas', the Bouleware's, the Rothchild's, the de Veres and Plon Plon, whose proposal to join me over the holidays I had declined. We have two lovely suites at the Hotel Scribe.

"Spring finds Paris over run with Americans," Adelicia jotted into her journal. "Either touring Europe on money well invested before the war, or money well invested during the war, or borrowed in hopes of marrying their daughters to Europeans with rank and position. Some are expatriates...I cannot imagine giving up one's homeland. None of the 'new comers' have been invited into our circles. Surely none of them are from the South. Am extremely pleased to have renewed my friendship with the Empress, who greeted me as an old friend. However, much is different...politics are changing daily, not in favor with the Emperor.

"Last evening I dined with Harry Stone, in Paris on business, a truly charming gentleman. I was bold enough to ask why he had never pursued me other than for friendship. He openly revealed that upon meeting me in New York, with Isaac, he decided that a man would never have to compete with another man for me, but with life itself, and that, he said, was too big an order for any man. I must say, the answer astounded me. He is a wonderful person, a man to be adored and admired. I am very comfortable with him.

"Spring," Adelicia continued to write, "has also found the Emperor enjoying the hunts in which I ride, avoiding me, it appears at all cost. There is no game playing, and never 'manages' to find himself alone in my presence. The parties are fewer, however. In the course of a year, the court has changed dramatically, taking on a more serious identity. It is rumored, the regime as the French know it, is nearing its end...and with it, the ousting of the Emperor and Empress. That greatly saddens me. The Emperor's belief that Maximillan's position in Mexico is secure, gives the world much concern...interesting how quickly the tide may turn."

"The Paris of 1866," Adelicia continued, "no longer holds the intrigue as did the Paris of '65. Perhaps it is I who has changed, perhaps I have become wiser, perhaps I am no longer awed by the pomp of power, perhaps I have become dull. I marvel within myself, how two springs in the same place, can appear so vastly changed. Perhaps the intrigue is gone...what intrigues today, most often holds no intrigue tomorrow."

"It is next to my last day in Paris and am extremely pleased to be alone, filled with the anticipation of home. The going away festivities have been delightful and many, certainly rivaling those described by Octavia Lavert. Louis Napoleon attended none of the parties...not even the luncheon given by the Empress. Plon Plon missed none.

"I am penning this entry at midnight on a lovely May evening lit by the full moon: This morning, I dressed in the lovely green silk designed by Pieugot, and took a cab to Sainte Chapelle, where I have often gone to pray. I climbed the stairs to the upper portion, and walked its length to a small alcove to the left of the apse, my favorite spot to kneel in prayer. Sunlight streamed through the massive stained glass around me, so much so, I felt as if it were actually touching me. Alone in the quaint Chapelle, I began praying silently, then aloud, for forgiveness, for mercy, for redemption. I wished to once again feel the nearness to God that was lost amidst the whirlwind, the frivolity, in which I engaged when first arriving in Paris. I do not fool myself entirely, for tis true the illusions helped mellow the loss of Ransom, whose love had been instrumental in not dwelling on Joseph's death, the war, and those who held me in disdain. But for me to feel peace, my heart must be in harmony with God, and despairing, recognizing my foolishness and folly, my selfishness, my desire for greater wealth, my weakness in wishing to be with Louis Napoleon, I asked for the strength to secure those things I hold sacred and dear...my children and family, my home. The past rushed before me, separately at first, then fusing as one, until my own weeping startled me into the present, as I sought to feel God's absolution and peace. It seemed appropriate that it was here that I tell Paris good-bye."

On May twenty-fifth Adelicia and her children crossed the English Channel to London, and two weeks later, were at last sailing for home. And later that evening, after the farewells had been made to those who had come to see their departure, and all were settled into bed, Adelicia wrote, *"Dearest Corrine, as the ship slipped from the harbor, the same one on which we had arrived, our same dear Captain Perkins was with us; also the cows, the poultry and the odor. The children commented that my jubilance of sailing for home, appeared greater than that upon our embarking. Pauline is thrilled to have regained her front teeth, and is most anxious to smile for her aunts and cousins. No one is more grateful to be leaving 'foreigners behind' than Cora. She has been packed for three days. I shall stay in touch with Harry Stone, and when he is in New York, shall invite him to visit Belle Monte. I long to see you and all our family.*

Your loving sister, Adie."

June was a lovely month, Adelicia thought, to be sailing across the Atlantic, and with the exception of a few rough seas, it had been a good crossing. Tears trickled over her cheeks as she stood holding

Claude and Pauline's hands, when through the fog she glimpsed the bright colors of the American flag with its thirty-eight stars, fluttering in the breeze at the tip of New York's busy pier, then the outline of the shore.

Looking up at his mother, Claude asked, "Why are you crying?"

"We are home," she answered. "We must always recognize when it is time to go home."

They arrived at the lovely Fifth Avenue Hotel overlooking Madison Square, quite rural and surrounded by shrubs and flowerbeds, and the first hotel in the city to boast elevators. "How exhilarating," she announced to Cora, the following morning, "to have fresh clothing and baths after our sea journey...to have our clothing done up."

"Dearest Laura," Adelicia wrote. *"We are still awaiting our passage home…last night saw My Awful Dad, starring Leslie Wallack, most talented actor…most enjoyable performance. At luncheon in the dining room of our hotel today, we were introduced to General Butler, ('Spoons') the terror of New Orleans, the one Crawford thought 'harmless.' Interesting. The war was not mentioned, of course.*

"I declined Octavia Levert's insistence that the children and I go with her to Saratoga for the month of July where the "posh" of society will be. I did not say so, but feel I have seen enough "posh" in the past two years to last for some while.

"The children and I attended a devotional with another Presbyterian family, our first Protestant service in some time. The children are grand, Laura. Every day I thank God for them and do not know what I would do if just one were taken from me. Oh, how I miss all of you and home and counting the days until we arrive. How often I have wondered what you are doing, and try to picture you in your rooms doing those daily things that are joyous to a wife and mother, those things we have always admired. Give all my love, and hug the little darlings for me.

Your affectionate sister, Adie.
P.S. We shall be here another week or so, then home to my blessed family, Belle Monte and Nashville. How I long for it. I would not

give one week of the society of true friends and dear kindred, for years of the heartless and gay life of such a metropolis as Paris."

"This is my last entry into this journal that I shall remember to destroy, at least in part. I believe it best not to leave one's thoughts in print. Much can be removed from the context and be misconstrued. We shall arrive soon at my beloved Belle Monte."

"Yes, my darlings, it will not be long before we begin our journey home," she said as the porter put their newly purchased packages into the elevator.

"Madam," the desk clerk interrupted, taking an envelope from behind him. "My apologies, please. This arrived more than a week past."

Adelicia opened the letter stamped with the Imperial seal. "Mrs. J. A. S. Acklen: four palominos from the Royal collection are enroute to New York as a gift from the Emperor and Empress. Their Majesties are hopeful the horses arrive for your viewing pleasure before your departure to Nashville, and wish you every happiness. Sincerely, Leone Dupre, Secretary to His Majesty, Louis Napoleon."

Obviously, I am forgiven, she whispered softly to herself, stepping into the elevator.

Chapter 101

The War Between the States had been over for more than a year when Adelicia stepped off the train at Nashville's Cherry Street Depot with her children and Cora. Among the peering heads and searching faces, Adelicia first spotted Bill, then Corrine waving beside him. Suddenly everyone was running and greeting, hugging and weeping.

"We've tried to get Belle Monte ready just as you asked," Corrine said as the sisters walked with arms locked around each other to the wagon that Adelicia recognized as one once used for hauling. Drawn by two yoked oxen, the driver would first deliver them to Belle Monte, Bill told her, then return for their trunks.

Seeing Corrine's dress not only showed wear but was conspicuously patched, Adelicia felt embarrassed as she glanced at her own fine gown. She could not wait to take her sister for a complete outfitting. "How are my nieces and nephews, Essie and Uncle Ben, Charlotte, all the servants?"

"They're waiting for you at Belle Monte," said Corrine. "Laura and George are safe and well in Alabama, and Bliss and Joel will be up tomorrow. The money you sent has been more than adequate. I hope you're not disappointed."

"I could never be disappointed with anything my baby sister did. You are as beautiful and sincerely good and sweet as our mother," Adelicia said, pulling Corrine close.

"Most of us have been ruined, Adie," she said softly. "You cannot imagine the state of devastation everyone and everything is in. I often think you were right." She whispered, getting closer, "What the Yankees did not take, the freeloaders and carpetbaggers did, from land to livestock, not to mention the new taxes and no money to pay. But Bill does not dare let me speak it. He will not hear of such talk. He believes everyone not in rags is a traitor."

So that is how it is going to be, Adelicia thought. If Bill's opinions were that of the majority's, as they usually were, the problems she would face would be paramount.

"We shall discuss it later, in detail. I want to know everything about you, our family," she said hugging Corrine again. "I love you, dearest sister, with all my heart. I have missed you all so very much. Look children, we are almost there." Adelicia reached behind her to boost Pauline so that she might see between her and Corrine's shoulders. Belle Monte was just ahead, standing splendidly against the summer sky, amid its barren, molested grounds.

Adelicia could not stop the mammoth of tears gushing over her cheeks as they turned off Hillsboro Pike and onto the rutted drive to the mansion. We shall replace the trees, she thought, set out new plants and shrubs, exotic ones from all over the world! Belle Monte and its gardens will be even grander than before. Chopped trees and gutted roads can be mended. I shall see to it all.

As the wagon stopped, she jumped out and ran smiling through her tears to Essie's waiting arms. The children, close behind her, tugging Cora by the hand, ran from room to room, shouting for each other to come and see home.

How wonderful to be surrounded by the dear and familiar, to have her worldly treasures returned to their respective places. Corrine and Bill had indeed accomplished a major feat setting her house in order. How good it felt to be home and together again!

It was late when the gathering of family and friends departed. Knowing it would take weeks or months to hear Essie's tales, Adelicia suggested to her beloved mammy that they not begin that evening. She wanted to adore her Belle Monte alone.

Thoughts of sleep were far removed as she sat starry-eyed in the lovely tan and turquoise sitting area between her and Joseph's bedrooms looking across the moon-streaked lawn, remembering how it had once appeared, imagining how it would appear again. She was home, and the glamour and lure of Europe seemed distant and terribly insignificant, as she tucked her feet up into the stuffed chair and rested her chin on her knees.

Nashville's Union forts stood vacant and ghostly, and the streets were congested with vagrants and carpetbaggers—varmints, Adelicia called them. Many residents were back in their homes, such as they were, unkempt, bearing treeless lawns. She soon found the government's attempt to make reparations for property damages and losses insufficient. How could it be otherwise, she questioned? It was not even in the realm of possibility. Money could rebuild, but not replace; money could not restore lives.

Adelicia drove about the city's outskirts and within its perimeters in her newly acquired Handsome, pulled by the four golden palominos that had arrived safely from New York. Although the Emperor and Empress had known of her admiration for the Spanish breed and vaguely mentioned her having a pair in America, she had dismissed the offer as a pleasant gesture. Though she wondered when Louis Napoleon had invited her to Deauville, if he had not intended to make her a gift then of the gorgeous, glowing foursome. The animals were grand, fine specimens of horse.

After penning a lovely note of thanks to the Empress, along with a photograph of the palominos in pasture, and inviting her and the Emperor to visit Belle Monte, she had walked out to the stables to view and make over all of her recently acquired fine horses. Since a child, she had found them her elixir for solitude and serenity.

Not only did Adelicia travel about Nashville in this self-proclaimed, showy manner, she also rode astride on her magnificent white gelding, Perchance, purchased in New York at the same time she bought the carriage. What should she do, she pondered, ride in a rickety wagon, hide her wealth, be ashamed of what had been acquired? Disturbed by the times and mood—she questioned if the past were simply a remembered illusion, if everyone had adopted an insanity denying how they had once thrived, lived.

Her desire to bring excitement and prosperity back into a city still under Union control and in the throes of Reconstruction, was frowned upon, unwanted. Friends, as well as some family members appeared to enjoy the 'new poverty' so popular among the old establishment. It was honorable to be poor! Disreputable to have money! The less one had, the more one had supposedly contributed to The Cause.

She rode Perchance along the perimeters of Belle Monte, visiting nearby plantations and farms, checking on the welfare of her neighbors and her family, offering assistance to any who would accept. They were few. Her brother-in-law, Bill Lawrence, had spoken for all.

She was shocked by the situation to which she had come home, and would have no part in what she considered sheer foolishness. Adelicia intended to enjoy her riches; the wealth for which she had toiled, had planned, had sought—self-preservation, and if those she loved continued to reject her offers, she would become reconciled to that fact. Her brother-in-law, had made it clear that his family would accept none of her charity. And in the short time she had been home, she was already being criticized for making an "extravagant display of her excessive wealth." The gossips were also questioning if she had ever been in mourning for "poor Joseph." They had heard otherwise.

It was a lovely October day, 1866, when Adelicia stood on the rear balcony of Belle Monte watching the construction taking place, reminding her that three years before she had looked out from that same balcony onto serene gardens, the day she and Sally had left for Louisiana. That now seemed a lifetime ago. The servants, with few exceptions, had stayed or returned. With them and others she had hired from the Freedman's Bureau, in addition to her new Irish gardener, progress slowly came, restoring the grounds to a more elegant fashion than before. Marble sculptures and oil paintings, purchased in Italy, had been unloaded from the dock the previous day, and the three wagonloads had been nothing short of a sensation as they trudged out Hillsboro Pike, creating additional gossip of Adelicia's "unbridled flamboyance" that even circulated among the servants, who bragged among themselves that they were part of the Acklen family, some born into it. Her European treasures were being stored in the outer buildings until they were ready to be displayed.

The mansion's exterior wood trim was freshly painted, and the interior's elaborate woodwork, cleaned and shined. Floors were waxed, furniture and silver polished. The remaining valuables stored at Polk Place were returned to their original places, and the heavy draperies were either replaced, laundered or cleaned, depending on their condition. A sofa was reupholstered with an exquisite tapestry she had purchased in Nice, as well as two armchairs in the sitting room to the left of the entrance way. European fabrics were used throughout the mansion wherever there was a need, wherever Adelicia sought a change in color or appearance. Essie continued to oversee the household, obviously pleased to boss about the younger servants as she stood with arms folded, seeing that all strictly adhered to her orders.

Much to the chagrin of the old Guard, it was undeniable that Belle Monte was being re-groomed as a showplace. It was also undeniable that Adelicia was quite caught up in the Victorian desire for gaudiness, as her additional pieces of sculpture were added one by one to the lawn and grand hall within. But she loved it; loved asserting her newly acquired European taste combined with traditional ones. "A nice blend" or "a nice touch," she would say as she observed the renovations from room to room.

It was Mozier's, "Peri" that stood in the center of the grand hall, from where the angel's exquisite beauty would be seen and admired by all.

CHAPTER 102

$\mathcal{I}$T WAS A BRILLIANT FULL MOON WHEN ADELICIA ENTERTAINED for the first time upon her return. Her family and friends had accepted invitations along with General Lucius Polk, brother of the now deceased "fighting bishop," Leonidas, who had generously supported her cause during the war, and was a first cousin of the former president's.

Her guest list was composed of old and new—the latter, Northerners who had stayed and now prospering in Nashville. She never doubted for a moment that anyone invited would stay away. Surely, all would unreservedly understand her sincerity, lay aside their envy, and further understand that she had aided The Cause, in a different manner albeit, and to a greater degree than most.

She looked down at the enormous sapphire that she had begun to wear again on the third finger of her right hand soon after her return home. She was glad it had been kept safe. She had placed it there from time to time since Isaac's death, and it seemed to enchant her now as much as when she had first received it, perhaps even more so, as she moved her hand, watching the diamonds on either side reflect off the warm October sun. "Essie," she called from the sitting room, "Please have Liza hurry with my breakfast tray, and Essie, make sure everything is perfect for tonight."

Later, moving down the stairs amidst the preparations, she reminded Essie, "I want flocks of flowers everywhere, two or three arrangements per room. Do we have all the candles we need? I want them well spaced on both dining tables, and did you personally see to the dessert and do the cream yourself?"

"Adie, child, you know it's too early to make the cream and keep it standing, and you know I done looked to everything. I never seen you so anxious over a supper," she said, finally putting her head in the door where Adelicia was searching through the cupboard for candles and counting them. "Everything will be just like you want it. I promise you."

"Essie," she said, turning and smiling with candles in both hands, "It is very important that everything be sheer elegance for my first supper party at home in four years." It had to be perfect. She had to be perfect.

Adelicia greeted her guests warmly in the entranceway, apologizing for the exterior remodeling, the inconvenience it imposed. But when they entered the great house, the delicate floral scents of jasmine and gardenias, the reflecting candle lights, the glistening finery, was a glorious stepping into the past, a grand reminder, if not more refined.

It delighted her to entertain friends, family and acquaintances in a manner that only a few years before had been the custom. She had instructed the servants to serve the best and to behave as if there had been no war. And as the evening progressed, conversation and laughter peeled throughout the rooms; everyone had warmed to the occasion. Surely they were pleased, she thought.

Adelicia had asked Sally Carter Gaut, recently married for the third time, not to Nicholas Pache but to a Yankee nevertheless, to sit at the head of one of the two tables, each set for sixteen, to steer away from any mention of war or reconstruction.

General Lucius Polk, from Maury County, sat to Adelicia's right at the fastidiously prepared table and Sarah Polk to her left. Not only was Lucius quite handsome and had managed to retain and maintain Hamilton Place Plantation, he proved an excellent conversationalist, witty and charming. Diagonally across from him was his married daughter Susan, whose husband was in Virginia. A lovely girl, Adelicia thought, attractive, in a simple way, with long brown hair pulled back away from her face. Adelicia's guests seemed to enjoy themselves immensely, and she delighted in the echoing laughter that filtered through the rooms. She was also enjoying herself.

After supper, Adelicia asked Susan to play the grand piano while they sipped warm cider, steeped with cloves and cinnamon, in the great hall near where "Peri" stood at its center. She thought Susan's songs sweet and well chosen, and after Sally and Adelicia played and sang respectively, her guest gave gay, lengthy applause, requesting more. And as the evening drew to its close, those attending repeatedly remarked about the joyfulness of the occasion, that surely Adelicia had outdone herself.

Lucius' daughter was talented and somewhat charming, Adelicia thought, as she bade her and Lucius good night, but she had astutely observed that she did not approve of the attention given her father.

October was engaging, filling her with exuberant energy that caused the seduction of autumn to appear rich and lustful. She wished for parties, gatherings, excitement and began by hosting weekly Thursday morning teas, to which old and new acquaintances came. For her children and their friends, a Tuesday afternoon party was held, filling the great hall with laughter. Saturdays, were family outings, including visits to orphanages and houses for the indigent. After Sunday morning services, all the family gathered at Belle Monte, feasting until they could not eat another bite. With the rebuilding and remodeling of her beloved First Presbyterian Church, and the enormous activities in Belle Monte's interior and gardens, it was a busy, exciting time. Adelicia was happy to be home. All was well.

One week after her superb supper party, she received a note from General Lucius Polk thanking her for a well-remembered and charming evening, and expressing a desire to call on her the following Sunday. After some thought, she penned a note of acceptance addressed to Hamilton Place, Columbia, Tennessee.

She hurried Essie and the children from the services on the day of the intended engagement, wishing throughout that Dr. Shipley would shorten his lengthy sermon. She needed a refreshing nap before her guest arrived.

The hour of four brought with it a soft North wind and a ringing at the door. Adelicia received Lucius Polk in the morning room to the left upon entering the mansion and after a half hour of unrestrained conversation, they walked in the gardens, her arm in his, then sat in the gazebo to the right of the pebbled path that led further into the gardens. There, Liza served them steaming tea in delicate china cups.

Yes, she thought, after he had gone, the two of them could have a mutually sincere and satisfying relationship. Marriage and its complications would not be a consideration. She was too content and fulfilled exactly where she was, and she would not have that interrupted. However, Lucius would make the perfect gentle-man friend and escort. The Polks owned major properties in Maury County, original land grants from North Carolina. She had attended a number of parties at Rattle and Snap, George Polk's plantation, but she had never visited Hamilton Place.

Susan was married to Campbell Brown, and her younger sister Mary to Colonel Henry Yeatman. It was well known that the General had doted on his daughters before and after he was widowed, and had it not been for them, Adelicia knew her plans to have Lucius as her friend, on her terms, would have moved without incident. However, she quickly learned that both girls had carefully 'watched Father' since that first night when Susan had dined at Belle Monte.

On that particular evening, Adelicia had thought Susan's attentions to her father no more than that of a proud and protective daughter. However, in the interval since that occasion and since the lovely after-noon in the Gazebo, she had discovered through Sally, who never failed to have her ear tuned for gossip, that the girls were furious and consistently corresponded between Virginia and Tennessee, terrified that "the worldly Mrs. Acklen would lead Father astray."

Twice, Adelicia was invited to Hamilton Place, and twice she had been furious upon leaving. On each occasion, at least one daughter had been present to meander among the guests, holding onto Lucius, and on the second visit, Mary had introduced a young widow to her father as he and Adelicia stood talking.

It was on that same evening that she also felt the distinct snob-bishness of Maury Countians. Not only was Susan icy, the whole of Lucius' family and friends, although presenting themselves cordially, remained decidedly impersonal.

When Adelicia attempted to speak with Lucius about his daugh-ters' behavior, he excused it as how adoring daughters react to their father's attentions to a lovely, charming lady. But when he came call-ing the following Friday, asking her to keep steady company with him, not only was Adelicia surprised at the proposal, but also at his insistence that the rudeness displayed by his daughters was a matter with which she should not be concerned. The idea of an enduring friendship with General Lucius Polk ended.

He had even refused to acknowledge their continued spreading of rumors, the ones for which they were directly responsible. The most frequent of which were: "She definitely had her face enameled in Paris." Or, "She had flaunted over Europe with a sundry of male companions, one of whom was Napoleon III." Another: "She placed her children in boarding schools to rid herself of any responsibility towards them."

Their sources were reported to be relatives of a cousin in New York, who had told them that the scandalous stories were true. With such *knowledge*, Polk's daughters had publicly referred to Adelicia as "an extravagant, worldly woman, whose preference it was to make a public display of her wealth...and far too worldly for Father."

The matron Emily Dyer, still devastated by the death of her second beau, and who had taken a sacred vow to never have another love, had told Adelicia as blatantly as when they were schoolgirls, that Susan Polk Campbell had personally revealed to her the story of Adelicia's face enameling, then boldly asked Adelicia to explain, "the secret of how 'those people' in Paris were able to take an older lady's face and make it look young again."

To add to her dismay, Sally, now back in Franklin, and friends with a number of Maury Countians, was careful to listen whenever "Mrs. Acklen's" name was mentioned. She told Adelicia she thought it in her best interest for her to know the tasteless scheming going on behind her back. Sally informed her that they also spoke of her having accepted an invitation to attend a ball in New Orleans, probably given by Yankees with Yankee money. "A woman who would do so," the Polk sisters had repeated, "was not respectable, and furthermore, no one could have the fortune that Mrs. Acklen flaunted, unless it were obtained through illicit means."

The hints and chatter were dropped, purposefully intended for Sally's ears, Adelicia thought. Sally also revealed that Susan had told her acquaintances in Nashville that her father would never marry such a woman although she might try everything in her power to win him. "Mrs. Acklen does not like being without a husband," Mary had reportedly said. Sally further mentioned that when Adeline Perkins had told Mary how nice it was to see her father enjoying himself again, she had become furious and left the room.

Marriage to Lucius Polk had never been a consideration, and Adelicia had no idea from where he had conjured the idea of a proposal. Regardless, having weighed what she had heard and seen, she felt Lucius' friendship would not be worth the effort, or the energy it would take to convince him of Mary and Susan's ill will towards her. Being the dear soul he was, he would not believe ill of anyone, especially his own daughters.

As they talked that late November afternoon, and as she listened to him begin once more to speak in their defense, she rose and walked over to sit beside him on the maroon velvet upholstered divan. The fire was roaring and the smoke puffing heavily up the chimney when she warmly took his hand, and after listening for no more than a few seconds, said, "Lucius, I had hoped for a lasting, abiding friendship, satisfying to us both."

"But, my dear, I want you for my wife," he said, taken aback.

"No, Lucius, even if I were disposed to marry again, I would not find myself trapped between two other women vying for their father's attention and affection." She kissed him lightly on the cheek, "I cannot accept your proposal."

"My dear, Adelicia, perhaps you will change your mind. May I hope for that?"

"No, Lucius, I must bid you good day…without the assurance of friendship. I wish most sincerely, it could have been otherwise." She spoke tenderly, but without deep emotion.

He rose and walked slowly to where Uncle Ben stood waiting with his top coat and hat, "Good afternoon. Thank you for your company which remains without comparison, enchanting and exhilarating," he said, still holding her hand in his.

"Good day, Lucius," she said, withdrawing her hand.

General Lucius Polk was so unaware, she thought, even more oblivious to reality than she had supposed. Adelicia recalled the events of the past week as she sat near the fire on an early December afternoon addressing invitations to a ball given in honor of Octavia Lavert, who would be arriving in Nashville in less than three weeks. She remembered how she had walked from the room that day, gracefully bearing the hurt within her, the willful damages controlled by gossips. How she had asked Uncle Ben to show General Polk to the door. And as she made out her guest lists, there was not a Polk on it, except for Sarah, whose late husband was only a cousin to the Mt. Pleasant' Polks.

Because her skin was clear and radiant, because it did look years younger than most women's her age, why must it be from enameling? Why could it not be the way she had cared for it? She would teach Pauline the simple facts her mother had taught her. Plenty of fresh air and exercise, daily cleansing with ground oat powder, and egg white masks twice weekly, kept the skin young and smooth, free from wrinkles.

The upcoming ball in New Orleans to which the gossips had referred, was being given by her dear Crawford, whom she had not seen in more than two years. Although it was tagged The Governor's Ball, not a dime spent would be Yankee money. Crawford, too, had outwitted the odds and was identified as a man of astonishing wealth, who widowed for a second time, had invited Adelicia to serve as hostess for his part in the gala affair. And a guest that no one in Nashville knew, or would ever know, would be attending: Morri. The ball was not even until the New Year. How news does travel, Adelicia thought! She had tired of attempts to defend herself.

CHAPTER 103

ADELICIA'S POSITION AS DOYEN OF NASHVILLE WAS ESTABLISHED on the night of December eighteenth, when Madame Octavia Lavert was her guest of honor, and it was a title challenged by no one, so long as she remained Mistress of Belle Monte.

When *The Cincinnati Belle* arrived at the Cumberland's wharf, Octavia and her two daughters were met by Adelicia's handsome landau, outfitted in fine leather and adorned with expensive, tasteful accessories, grandeur Adelicia knew would impress Octavia who had traveled the continents, wining and dining with royalty. She was certain her guest would recognize the four palomino mares with tails and mane like moonlight to be Spanish imports. The two on the left had riders, and Luke, dressed from head to foot in scarlet trimmed with gold fringe, held the reins of the majestic animals, donned in silver mounted harnesses. With such trappings, Adelicia was also certain the mother and daughters would marvel over what they would find upon their arrival at Belle Monte.

The Laverts had visited no inland cities as they were considered far too provincial by Octavia's standards, the exception being her own hometown, Augusta, Georgia, on which she alighted from time to time to recuperate, as reported in the newspapers. Adelicia's objective was that as Octavia rode in the splendid carriage and sunk into the down stuffed leather, that she might question as to whether or not she had been too haughty in her opinions of the inland South.

It was a sunny, December afternoon, warm enough that they needed only a light shawl to protect them from a mildly chilling breeze, when Adelicia and Octavia walked among Belle Monte's Italian statuary set amidst lush foliage. As Adelicia strolled with Octavia, arm and arm, they spoke as old friends, Octavia commending Adelicia on structuring a 'showplace' for all of Nashville to enjoy. They visited the bowling alley, the billiard room and the former monkey house now being transformed into a tea room. Touring the grounds and buildings, all in the process of being restored, Adelicia pointed out specific varieties in the greenhouse and newly designed beds, assuring Octavia they would be abloom in the spring with azaleas, roses, star jasmine, eglantine, camellias, japonica and gardenias. The orchards and grape arbors, she explained, were from both new and old cuttings, the latter of which had been mostly destroyed by war.

Octavia applauded the art gallery, a first for Nashville, and the stables that housed fine blooded horses, including her palominos, and her white gelding, Perchance.

As she was restoring Belle Monte, she told Octavia, she wished to assist in restoring Nashville, the city for which she had yearned from across the sea. However, she did not say it was the place in which she still longed to be admired and accepted, and would do all within her power to succeed in striking down the barriers that prevented it.

To date, the ball in honor of Octavia and her daughters was the most lavish ever to be given in Nashville, and Adelicia wished there were facts to prove that nothing of this magnitude had been accomplished in her Southland, before or after the war. The invitation read:

RECEPTION
MRS. ACKLEN
WILL RECEIVE ON THURSDAY EVENING
DECEMBER EIGHTEENTH
AT EIGHT O'CLOCK
COMPLIMENTARY TO MADAME LAVERT

Belle Monte was decorated throughout for the holiday season. Deep red velvet ribbons held bunches of holly and spruce and fir; garlands draped each mantle complimenting silver epergnes holding fresh fruits blended among the greenery of magnolia leaves and bright red holly berries; silver bowls filled with nuts and sweets were placed throughout the rooms along with bouquets of prized white roses that donned silver and crystal vases, (at least three or four per room.) The aromas of nutmeg and cloves and cinnamon melded with fragrant roses, hickory from fire places and popcorn and cranberries strung by her children and their friends. And when Adelicia

The friends and acquaintance of Col. J. R. S. Acklen and wife, and the late Isaac Franklin, are invited to attend the Funeral of EMMA FRANKLIN, at the Family Vault at Fairvue in Summer County, on Sunday the 4th of November, instant, at 4 o'clock, P. M.

Divine Service by Doct. Edgar.

FRIDAY, Nov. 2, 1855.

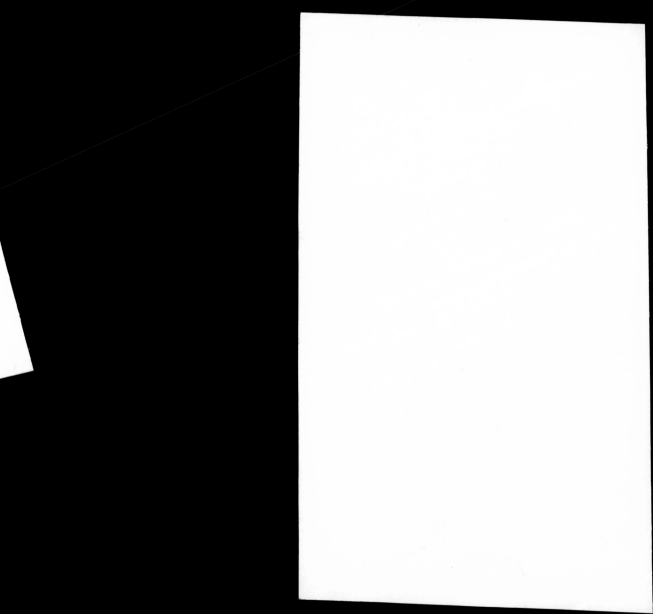

descended the stairs, placing her hand on the right newel post, surveying the house and its dressings, she thought the finest estate in Europe had never looked nor smelled so extraordinarily heavenly—not even Fontainebleau, with its gilt and glitter. And this was home.

She was satisfied that this night was the ultimate of Belle Monte's glories. Never had such a magnificent scene been set! She walked into the dining room to a table laden with French and Italian confections, with slices of roast duck, tender roast beef, leg of lamb, oysters on the half shell, crab claws, lobster tails and frog legs. Essie's mouth-watering rolls would come from the oven at the right moment so that those gentlemen with more hearty appetites, might place some of the delectable meats between the browned and buttered halves.

Candlelight glowed from the tables and in each room, the gas chandeliers burned softly, shimmering upon the silver and crystal. Hot spiced cider laced with Tennessee Whiskey, filled large silver bowls in each of the summer gazebos, where a servant waited to pour the mouth-watering drink into pewter Jefferson cups, warming both body and gloved hands, as guests would stroll through the gardens and into the Greek Revival art gallery, or to the stables, or to simply linger in the December air amidst marble statuary, gleaming and white beneath the torch lights, the heavy skies and the full moon.

She intended to see to her guests every comfort, indoors and out, and to make lasting, positive impressions on friends, family and out of town guests from Memphis, St. Louis, New Orleans, Mobile, New York, Mississippi and Louisville. She slipped noiselessly back up the stairs to await Uncle Ben's ring of the bell, announcing the arrival of her first guest.

Adelicia had presented Octavia and her two daughters each with a personal maid, as they were traveling without servants, which she found highly unusual. She sent Charlotte to inform the assigned maids that it was seven forty-five. She intended for the Laverts to do what they did all over the world: charm and entertain, to bewitch the locals of Nashville, and those from out of town.

Octavia's international fame was unsurpassed. She was praised and applauded in newspapers around the world. She had been reared, as she often stated, by her mother to speak intellectually, but with great charm, to give much concern to her beauty, her skill of languages, to powerful conversation, to stay abreast of the world, whether political, or cultural and to be confident and competent to speak on either. Her mother, from a prominent Augusta, Georgia family, had married a physician and had doted on her only daughter, believing a woman needed nothing more than the curriculum she had devised for Octavia.

She had studied in the finest schools in Paris, Rome, London and Lucerne and spoke five languages fluently. She had even spent six months in China learning their culture and language.

Adelicia, well aware of Octavia's lavish wardrobe, decided she must wear the gown in which she had been presented the first time to the Emperor and Empress at Tuileries, in order not to look 'foppish' standing beside Octavia in the receiving line. And when she looked in the long pier mirror in her dressing room, she again congratulated Pieugot on the magnificent gown. She did not doubt that Octavia and her daughters would be wearing Paris originals.

She hoped Bill and George had not objected to the gowns she had had made for her two sisters and their daughters. If so, Laura and Corrine had said nothing to the contrary. Pauline and her cousins would assist in receiving and were dressed in deep green velvet with long lavender satin sashes.

The bell rang, and with its vibration the recognition that in a matter of moments, Belle Monte would be transformed by its three hundred invited guests. Once more, Adelicia looked in the mirror to admire the lovely pearl satin dress, then touched the coronet of diamonds nestled in her hair to test its being securely in place. On each arm were two diamond bracelets, and around her neck she wore the diamond choker that matched the dangling ear bobs, all from Cartier's. She lifted her skirts and proceeded down the steps, shortly before Octavia Lavert joined her wearing a lilac antique moiré with a Grecian headdress. Her daughters respectively wore a rose satin gown trimmed with Brussel's lace and silver cording, and a lime green lace over satin, trimmed in corded black velvet, each with tiaras crowning their poofed hair.

The chill of the December night went unnoticed, Adelicia thought, as she observed guest lingering, conversing and strolling in the gardens. While inside, the pianist played old ballads, post war music and the new sounds from New York as the receiving line formed, seeming to have no end, in the grand hall. It was half past ten before Adelicia, Octavia and her daughters, Laura and Corrine, Sally and Margaret could join her guests.

On Adelicia's lips was the smile of success, the success of having introduced a new look to Nashville, as she watched the ladies and gentlemen hover about the lovely Octavia, enthralled. No one took leave before two a.m., and it was well past four o'clock in the morning before the last guests departed into the mid December chill. The lingering remarks were music to her ears: "It was the grandest of parties." "... Could not be duplicated, nor rivaled." "Only you, Adelicia could give such an affair."

No one would have guessed the temperature had dropped to thirty-five degrees. The horses wore their blankets and the waiting coachmen had been fed and warmed inside the cellar and stables, but the bite of the wind had suddenly turned bitter as night grew into morning.

The sky was changing from December dark to streaks of gray and yellow, before Adelicia sank into the soft feathers of her bed, praying that all might have a safe journey home. She had established her place! They had accepted and enjoyed her hospitality! Everyone seemed cordial, warm and inviting, even her brothers-in-law seemed to revel among the opulence. Emily was most gracious as were the Murdocks, the Perkins, the Caldwells and the Hardings, and of course, the lovely, enchanting Sarah Polk.

Perhaps she was forgiven, for however her egregious sins had been interpreted. Adelicia had never understood the trespasses involved in conquering one's quest, nor did she find her steps Machiavellian. She would never be forgiven in Gallatin, that she accepted. The Polks had not appeared to have had too loyal a following, as no one who had received an invitation in Maury County had stayed away.

The following morning, December 20th, the *Nashville Whig* reported: "The reception, 'Complimentary to Madame Lavert,' preparations for which caused no small excitement in the business streets of Nashville. The observatory, groves, and parterres were illuminated, and the effect of the light among the statues, shrubbery, and flowers with music from the portico, was fairy-like...this is the forerunner of a new regime of entertainment, combining intellectual and artistic enjoyment with perfect taste."

Oh, how Adelicia liked the sound, the very nature of the words as she repeated them aloud: "...the forerunner of a new regime of entertainment..." This was superior to the applause of Paris! This was Nashville! This was home!

CHAPTER 104

A FREEZE IN LATE DECEMBER BROUGHT A SNOW FILLED, CRISP January. And 1867 had arrived as a year of great promise for financial gain, Adelicia thought, to those willing to pay the costs.

Andrew Johnson was President, and another East Tennessean, 'Parson' Brownlow, was governor and had used his influence to have former Union officer, Augustus Alden, elected mayor of Nashville. The new regime reigned in full array, one that was set to dissolve what was left of the old elite ruling classes, and intending to bring about a resurgence, a rebirth to Nashville in its process of recovery.

Health and education were major factors. Schools would be constructed for all, regardless of economic status or race. In the past year, more than one thousand people had died of the cholera. Stronger laws for health regulations were being enforced for the welfare of Nashville's citizens; physicians and nurses were in great demand. Everyone would pay a price to rebuild the city, its homes, farms, businesses, its land—the price of death lingered, its heavy grasp having taken its toll on all. It was called, "Reconstruction."

Earlier that morning, the children had hitched Bullie to the sled, and the Shetland pony had pulled them over the grounds and onto Hillsboro Pike for a two hour ride. Upon their return, Adelicia had watched from her sitting room window as they gave Bullie a pail of rewarding oats before throwing snowballs, she laughing as Claude, Pauline and Wille turned somersaults, making shadowed valleys in the deep snow, before rolling and packing the white crystals into a snowman.

Later that afternoon, sitting by the warm fire sipping hot chocolate, Adelicia read from *Oliver Twist*, Dickens describing those parts of England that they had witnessed. It was the third time she had read Dickens' late '40's novel to the children. It was a favorite with its happy ending, Claude and William still persisting that the servants in America were much better off than the street urchins and poor in England.

Pauline had listened intently, and after her mother completed an hour's reading, she asked her to begin, for the second time, *Great Expectations*, the copy signed for them by Dickens. Like her mother, it was also her favorite. *A title I like very much*, thought Adelicia, as Pauline ran to fetch the book from the library shelf, then sitting beside her on the Aubusson rug. Thumbing through the lovely illustrated pages, Pauline asked her mother whom she would prefer her to be, Estella or Biddie. Adelicia smiled, thinking of the great expectations she had for her children, as well as for herself.

Bud had returned to his preparatory school in Virginia, and the other children were being taught again by the remarkable Miss Cevas. How dear, she thought, as she observed the scene: two sons, and one daughter, witty and bright and physically handsome, and the eldest son preparing for Harvard where his fifth great grandfather, Charles Chauncey, had been its second president. Life is indeed glorious and wondrous, she thought, as she kissed the children before Cora called them for supper. Her quest was fulfilled. Her fortune intact.

She could not help but believe that all would indeed be well with the world. She was content: she could ask for nothing more than what she had at that moment. Life had become what she had supposed it to be, thought it should be. In a few months, she would be fifty!

The holidays had been the best Adelicia could remember since before Joseph's death, and the inclement weather had not prevented all her family from gathering at her comforting Belle Monte. They had come by sled for Christmas Eve and stayed through Christmas Day. There had been laughter, small gifts and sumptuous food. Bud and William had gone hunting with their uncles and cousins, had ice fished in the ponds where all had skated to the music of a local Italian accordion player, Pauline displaying her exceptional skills on ice. Except for a luncheon on New Year's Day for the children's friends, the rest of the holidays had been restful and quiet. Adelicia had put the episodes of the gossipy Polk daughters away and had welcomed the tidings of the blessed New Year.

If the river were free from ice, she would make the proposed trip to New Orleans in just ten days to attend the Governor's Ball. It was pre-Mardi Gras season as well, and there would be parties to attend. She looked forward to seeing her old friend Crawford and anxious over Morri. Perhaps the reason for her not having written would become clear.

CHAPTER 105

W HAT A BALL IT WAS, AND HOW FLAMBOYANT AND DIVERSE THE guests gathered in the grand ballroom of the St. Montaigne on this February day of 1867. But most importantly, how pleased Adelicia was to see Morri, after four years' absence and to meet her charming beau, a young Creole, Kinnard Boudeau, a student in Morri's first year class of medical studies at The University of Louisiana. She must have followed Elizabeth Blackwell's lead, Adelicia thought, America's first female physician, the one who became so well known in Paris. Perhaps Morri wished to visit Paris, study there.

Morri was beautifully dressed in soft black silk, wearing no jewelry, elegant and sophisticated. They had warmly embraced when Crawford escorted Adelicia to where Morri stood with Kinnard. The beautiful young woman had shown no surprise at her presence, and Adelicia quickly felt the old warmth of former days as they laughed and chatted and sipped Madeira punch together.

She observed Morri's gaiety as she danced with Kinnard, so poised and gracious, far removed from the naïve young girl she remembered. She could not help but wish that she was the mother of this child of Isaac's. Her last of his daughters, her precious Emma, had been taken at age eleven. How blessed Lona was to still have Morri.

Lona, a reappearing enigma, an image set from that first glimpse at Fairvue, one that flashed before Adelicia from time to time. A lingering shadow that never disappeared entirely.

It was a tender goodbye when Morri and Kinnard excused themselves early in the evening, with explanations of a curfew and study. "May we take luncheon one day," Adelicia asked, "or perhaps dine with both you and your handsome beau?"

"Thank you, Dear Mrs. Acklen," Morri said taking Adelicia's hand in hers, "My days and evenings are filled with study. I intend to graduate at the top of my class. I cannot disappoint Mere's wishes. That calls for long hours of study and the strictest discipline. When Mr.

Crawford informed me you would be attending this evening, I did not want to miss the opportunity to see you once more."

"I have no doubt that you will not be at the top of your class, and in addition will receive grand awards. How could it be otherwise?" Adelicia paused. "I hope your mother is well, and that I shall soon see you again." They embraced quickly before Morri and her beau stepped out into the February night.

Filled with melancholy, Adelicia lay in bed pondering over the evening. There had been no mention of another meeting or of correspondence, but quite the contrary. She wondered if there were cause for Morri's distance. She could not imagine what, unless the effect of whom they were, their mottled past, had worn itself into a distance.

"Crawford," she asked, while dining at Boudro's the following evening, "What are your predictions for this year of 1867? Will it be profitable, despite the horrors of reconstruction?"

"It will, my dear, but before my noteworthy predictions, let us seal and sustain the New Year with your becoming my wife."

Crawford had been widowed for a second time, only four months before, but she was not surprised at the question; his loyalty, nor devotion to her had ever wavered. Perhaps he did love her, she thought. He, the one person who had stood with her through so many trials, the one who had been there, always, and the one to whom she had turned in every crisis. Like Ransom, Crawford did not need her money or her position. But as before, none of the reasons, whether enjoying his company, or adoring him for the grand person he was, was cause to marry. She had never been in love with him.

"Crawford," she laughed, "you are not serious. Do you propose to move to Nashville? You know that is where my heart is now."

"My dear Mrs. Acklen, for you I'd leave the city of my birth and go with you wherever and whenever. I am certain I could learn to love your Northern city almost as much as you."

"My darling, Crawford," she smiled. "You would never be happy away from your river and ships and hotel, not ever. No, my dear, we are fated to dwell in our separate cities, and live our separate lives, meeting betwixt times here and there. I shall always love you, Crawford, dear Crawford," she said sincerely, "as my friend. It is not the time for marriage."

"I shall not give up," he said, then quickly segued, "I haven't told you in person how sorry I was about Ransom. You truly loved him, I believe. In fact, I was more jealous of the General than anyone before him. He was also a good friend, a good man. Like Isaac."

Adelicia glanced at the sapphire on her finger, "Thank you," she said, kissing Crawford on the cheek, "all that seems worlds ago." She reached for his hand across the table. "There are times when every detail of my first visit to New Orleans seems like yesterday, and times when it seems so distant, I can barely remember. Much of my life has unfolded and refolded with you in one way or the other. Love is perceived on many levels, always enveloped in mystery and never definitive. For me, anyway. Thank you for remaining my dearest friend."

The following morning, as she dressed in her luxurious suite to meet Crawford for luncheon, she chose an emerald green velvet gown with long pleated sleeves and her diamond earbobs. She remembered the apparent disappointment in his eyes the night before when she had again refused his proposal. He had not pressed the issue, knowing her well enough to understand that her guise of teasing about cities and ships, was her way of saying that she would never become Mrs. Benedict. He had quickly turned the conversation to the number of ways in which his wealth was daily increasing, of his jubilance in having seen it escalate throughout the war, the pleasure of continuing to outsmart the Yankees, even General Sheridan and the Warmouth-Dunn regime, now exploding over Louisiana. What a good feeling it was, he had said, to be getting richer from their money. It was his daily elixir.

"For once, my dear, you've not kept me waiting but half an hour... me doth think the lady hath learned to be more prompt," Crawford said, taking her arm, walking her to his table in the hotel dining room. "Claret for Mrs. Acklen," he told the waiter, "and bourbon for me."

"If you are partaking of strong drink before four o'clock, this must be a special occasion."

"A serious talk is in order, my dear...one I would prefer to avoid. For once, I cannot figure how you will react."

"So, in the past you have always predicted my reactions?" she asked coyly.

"Without fail."

She smiled. Perhaps he had only wanted to see her reaction to his marriage proposal last night, she pondered. "Whatever can be so serious and confounding?"

He moistened his lips with the last sip of his bourbon and ordered another. "Lona has passed away."

"No!" She whispered in a soft gasp. "I am so sorry, so very sorry," she said lowering her head, as if in prayer, then lifting it to ask in the same tone, "When? How? She was still so young."

"October," he said sipping the second glass of bourbon. "Morri was here, at the university. Lona's maid had gone to awaken her, finding it unusual for her to be in bed so late in the morning. She had obviously succumbed during the night in her sleep...cardiac arrest."

"Dear Morri, poor Morri. She worshipped her mother. But why the two glasses of bourbon?" she asked, observing Crawford's search for words. "If it is a question of money, I am only too happy to finance Morri's education, or to provide for her financially until she is prepared to return as a physician to Haiti or elsewhere." Adelicia paused. "You are behaving strangely, dear one. Are you ill?"

"No, no," he said, gesturing with his hand. "When she enrolled at Louisiana, I helped with that enrollment, the application. Has it not occurred to you that she is in an all-white school?"

Adelicia was taken aback. No, it had not occurred to her, and she felt her face flush. Her joy in seeing Morri had deleted any thought of questioning why or how.

"Four years ago, soon after Lona and Morri returned to Haiti, she wrote, asking that I become Morri's legal guardian. This past August, Lona came to New Orleans, and in my office, told me of her omen of death, but made me swear not to mention it to Morri. She purchased a newly furnished apartment near the university, thinking the house on Esplanade too far way. Lona's joy of seeing Morri move into it was a touching moment, one even moving me to tears. Her request, Adie, was that Morri grow up in the America of her father. That she be known as Morri Franklin. That is the last time I saw or heard from Lona."

Adelicia felt a warm flush rush over her as she listened. She was stunned. Crawford had arranged, agreed to give Morri a new identity, papers that lied, stating she was orphaned in Charleston, by French Huguenot parents during a fever epidemic, that he was her bene-factor and legal guardian. After completing her pre-med courses in New Orleans, she would apply to medical schools in the Northeast, Harvard, all of those now accepting women. Morri's wish, he had said, was to practice in Washington or New York, but planned to first further her education in Paris. It was also her mother's wish.

And all this transpired while I was touring Europe, she thought to herself. She had been elated to learn that Morri had chosen a profes-sion to help her people in Haiti or Natchitoches, and had taken for granted that she would return to one of the places. A medical school for Negroes had just opened in Nashville, though she understood Reconstruction had changed the enrollment policy wherever. Why, after having lived almost half a century, had Adelicia taken for grant-ed anything when it dealt with human nature? The human condition? The news was unsettling, and she would need to ponder over it for some time.

The Morri whom she knew from Haiti she envisioned as a warm and beautiful child of Isaac's. This Morri had also saved her life. But changing her identity, changed other things as well. It was unaccept-able in society, although in Paris, there were many affluent people of color, just as there were in New Orleans. As Crawford had sat explaining that he had already completed the arrangements, that he, like her mother, agreed that this was best for Morri, she suspected that Isaac, too, had wished it. She felt deceived, yet again.

"Adie, you must agree, and it will never be spoken of again."

"I shall agree to nothing that I find so absurd. It is shocking, unfair to Morri."

"Adie, my love. I could not have shared the information with you at all. Whenever you asked about Morri, I could have lied and sloughed it off, but I wanted you to know, and Morri wanted you to know, thinking it would please you. Now I'm sorry I told you."

"At this moment, I could not care less about anyone's wishes. If you will excuse me," she said, rising.

An hour later, Crawford summoned Adelicia by note, requesting she come to his office. Two hours later, when she had still not ap-peared, he requested that the maid temporarily leave 'Mrs. Acklen's' suite. Crawford buzzed the bell outside her room, and upon opening her door, quickly blurted, "Why can you not understand what your acceptance and silence will be giving Morri?"

"How dare you come to my room! How dare you order the maid elsewhere!" Adelicia said, slamming down the top of her trunk, clothes partially dangling from its sides. "Morri and her mother lived very well on the island, elegantly, tastefully, in lush surroundings, including excellent friends and family. What will they think—that the dear child disappeared? What do they think? Will she turn her back on them? Deny a part of her heritage? I shall not keep silent about something so preposterous! Do you know what you have done? What you have created?

What will happen to Morri when someone discovers her heritage?" She continued, "The scenario applies for New York, Philadelphia, or wherever she chooses to be, or wherever fate may take her. Have you considered her future husband, her children? What will be accomplished by this proposed deception?"

"That will be her problem, not ours."

"How unkind, how unfeeling…*her problem, not ours.*"

"She wants to grow up in the America of her father, and I'm seeing to that. If your cousin Sally inquires about Morri, it's unnecessary to say that Morri is anywhere but on the island. No one here, nor anywhere, need ever know her Haitian heritage. It is a secret we shall keep until our graves."

"I have always admired and trusted you, Crawford, but something is amiss."

"Why so abrupt a change towards Morri? I was unsure of your reaction, but I wasn't prepared for this. Please stay. Think it through. We'll discuss it at supper tonight."

"I booked passage on the *Sentinel* for in the morning, and tonight, I am dining with old friends. But I shall consider it and meet you for a late cup of tea. Is eleven thirty convenient?"

"Eleven thirty, it shall be. Adie, you need not be so formal," he said, standing in the doorway. "Do you think there's a possibility that perhaps there's an octoroon in your circles? In many circles?"

"This comes as an unexpected revelation, one that carries serious complications. I am well aware of the political thoughts…such as they are…the movement. But I am thinking of Morri, of sparing her disappointment, embarrassment, hatred. I ask that you please excuse me."

Crawford quickly closed the door behind him and hurried down the stairs to take his afternoon bourbon. After Adelicia's display of anger, he felt more uneasy of ever revealing to her the provisions Isaac had made one month prior to his death, that he had drawn up a signed legal document requesting that when his child by Lona became eighteen years of age, that Crawford, (if Isaac predeceased him in death) would act as benefactor, to see to the child's proper education in America, to having a European tour, and that he, or she, grow up in a white America, if the child and her mother so chose.

Crawford was sitting alone in the empty dining room as the clock struck twelve, mulling over a large leather folder of documents. How many years it had been since first being introduced to Adelicia by his best friend. However, now he was no longer sure that even if she had accepted one of his proposals to be his wife, even when he had been serious, if he would have known what to do with her. Perhaps Isaac had not known either. Her reaction concerning Morri had been an unexpected disappointment, although he had doubted her somewhat ready acceptance.

He had wholeheartedly agreed with Isaac when he made provisions for a child that he would never see. He agreed now. If he had to stand in opposition to Adelicia, he would.

She was wearing an elegant rose taffeta gown when she stepped into the private dining area of the St Montaigne, looking as fresh as if she had just stepped from her dressing room, and it was almost one a.m. Adelicia's face was free from any trace of anger, and her irresistible sparkle had returned. He seated her and poured steaming tea into the china cup as he waved the waiter aside. Crawford did not know that all the while she had been in her hotel suite, pondering.

"I shall go along with your scheme," she quickly began. "However, there is a condition. Tell me the truth."

"My dear Adie…I have told you the truth. What more wouldst thou have me say?"

"Shh." She put her fingers to his lips. "Tell me the whole story."

"What story?"

"The part Isaac played." She hoped Crawford had partaken of enough Bourbon not to omit a single detail, although no matter the number of drinks, he always remained sharp and astute. Interesting, she thought, he did not even appear taken aback by her request.

"All right, my dear, I shall tell you, but you'll probably wish I hadn't."

It was two-thirty before he finished talking, revealing facts he seemed to actually enjoy recalling, perhaps because Isaac had been happy in the planning and the making of them, she surmised.

Adelicia had listened intently, all the while feeling the sharp pangs of inwardly crying. Not only had Isaac made it financially difficult for her if she remarried, even entrusting the care of their children to the trustees, he had made extensive provisions, as well as plans, for his illegitimate child's future, separate and apart from his original will, the will about which she knew, the one she had battled in court and had trusted his best friend who had so eagerly come to her defense. She felt wounded, deceived and empty. She was surprised that Morri chose to be a part of the charade. Lies and deception! Adelicia wondered if she really *knew* anyone, if anyone ever did.

"Thank you for sharing the truth of Isaac's wishes," she said rising. "If you say another word, or ever mention it to me again, I hope you understand I shall expose you, the scheme. I do wish we could have spoken of pleasantries after so long an absence. I have been betrayed, once again. Good-bye, Crawford."

"I wish you would forget this day and stay for Mardi Gras."

"Forget? I have no interest in being in New Orleans, nor in this hotel. Remember, Crawford, much of life is engaged in lies and in deception. There is no need to live a pre-meditated one—false to the core."

The incident with Crawford served as one more turning point in Adelicia's life. Had Isaac ever loved her, or was it only her social position he had desired? Was Crawford's love always a pretense? Had the proposals been a game to him? Had she been a game to him? To

Isaac? Joseph had certainly lived well on her fortune. She now questioned if all had not been a deception—an allusion she had readily accepted, she being the pawn for whatever the reason. It was not Morri, she now understood, but the deception that angered her, reminding her of her father's and Judge White's opposition in 1847...her father having been a witness to Isaac's will when it was written, perhaps he had known of this one as well. There was much to consider, changes to be made. She must begin life anew, apart from the past.

She bid New Orleans adieu, as the *Sentinel* pushed up river toward Bellevue where she spent three days looking over her plantations, seeing that all was in order before making the return trip to Nashville. Jim Clack, with Strap Kelley and Bard Young had kept up the land and dwellings extraordinarily well; all was unmolested. The livestock was replenished, mostly from the properties in Texas. The fields were freshly plowed, ready for planting and for sure, they were expecting a good fall harvest if the "flood gates of heaven would cease," to quote Jim, "and let the earth dry out."

More than half the Negroes had stayed and were earning small wages. Some resided in their old cabins, some built new ones from the surrounding timber, on the two acres each family was given. They were certainly better off than the former slaves in New Orleans or Nashville, Adelicia thought, living on the streets, penniless, not benefiting from futile Yankee promises, and suffering amid a meager, futile job market.

It pleased her immensely to see everyone well—Alfred and Lucy, at Bellevue, happy that the war was over, that the Yankees were gone, for Adelicia to know they had a choice to leave, but preferred to stay. She felt fortunate to have them there. So much of the South was devastated and its people gone, both black and white. The small farmers were still able to make a reasonable living, as most had never used slave labor, but for the most part, the larger tracks of land lay barren, devoid of crops.

Adelicia was saddened to learn that on the day after Christmas, Rufus, the lovable old gentleman, had passed way. He had been buried beside his wife, taken many years before, in the plot for the house servants, fifty yards east of Loch Lomond. Jim Clack told her there had been a tremendous outpouring of folks for his wake that had lasted for days. She would miss him. He had been there from the beginning, when she first came to Bellevue, along with Lucy and Alfred, to whom she assured that she would return in the fall.

Jim Clack had made the arrangements to have Promise shipped to Belle Monte, her Promise who had not been stolen, nor taken by the Yankees, nor the Rebels, whom she imagined Rufus had protected. How Promise must have missed him after his passing! And as Adelicia nuzzled her face against his strong jowl and stroked his glossy mane, she whispered into his ear how happy he would be grazing with her other fine horses at his new pasture in Nashville. Clack drove her back to Bayou Sara to board *The Sentinel* for home.

CHAPTER 106

DR. WILLIAM ARCHER CHEATHAM, A WELL-KNOWN SURGEON who had been commended for his heroism during the war, was speaking at an afternoon gathering of ladies who had been instrumental in aiding the Confederacy, making bandages, caring for the wounded, among other duties. The organization, "Ladies Soldier's Friends Society of Nashville," a branch of the one in which she had been secretary and Sarah Polk, president, in 1862–'63.

The early February snow was seeing its first stage of melting, and as the horses' hooves made their sloshing sounds along the roadways, Adelicia repeated to herself that it was a good year, that she would allow nothing to interfere with her positive thoughts. She vowed to put the past behind her, and to some degree, she had dismissed the unpleasant events in New Orleans from her mind, except for Morri, with whom her emotions were wrapped and tightly bound.

She stepped from the carriage in a maroon velvet suit trimmed with black braid, sporting a matching hat, as she slightly lifted her stylish skirt to free it from the slush beneath her feet. A rush of cold air caused her to tighten her hands deep within the ermine muff while waiting for the door to be opened. A pity, she thought, as she observed the peeling paint and neglect, what a grand mansion Harpeth Hall had once been.

Emily Dyer greeted Adelicia in her unmistakable shrill voice, "Oh, you're back from New Orleans. You go on so many adventures, one never knows whether or not to expect you."

"Yes, darling, I am back after a lovely visit. Hello, Katie. Yes, I am home. You dears must go down river soon or up river. A change of scenery is always good for the health and the spirit."

They stirred hot spiced Russian tea with hard crystal candied sticks and sipped from china cups, making chit chat while waiting for the guest of honor, already a half hour late. When the doorbell rang at last, in walked a stately gentleman, much younger than Adelicia would have suspected, although, in truth, she had given the speaker little thought one way or the other. His hair was thick, blonde, curly. He was handsome in a particularly soft, pleasant way, that she hoped would make the proposed speech more interesting. Sarah Polk introduced Dr. Cheatham to the group of ladies, mentioning they would be able to speak with him after his address.

Although she consistently tried, Adelicia could find him nothing more than dull. His voice was strong, but not engaging. He rambled at some length about "the boys in gray," a phrase she had heard all too often since returning home, and glories of the South for having believed in a cause, how wonderful these ladies were for having given their time, means and support, linens from off their very beds to care for the wounded and the dying. How melodramatic, she thought.

She put her hand to her mouth so often to conceal a yawn that she felt conspicuous when she cautiously peeked into the time piece, concealed behind gold gilt in her jeweled bracelet.

She managed to feign a semblance of contentment and interest until at long last Dr. Cheatham concluded, once more thanking them for their "wondrous deeds, fostered by goodness and loyalty."

"How wonderful!" "How sweet of you to praise us so!" "You are the one who did our boys so much good!"... they cackled in turn with syrupy tongues. She did not know how many of these gatherings she could abide attending. Indeed, Dr. Cheatham's name had become immortalized during the war, laboring long and tedious hours in both Tennessee and Kentucky.

Standing and continuing to sip her tea while observing, Adelicia could not help but feel a twinge of anger, that in the seven months since her return, no one had spoken of Joseph's contributions, nor on his behalf. She was not at all impressed with this man who had attained fame, she thought, by having performed a duty that was his profession, and as for spying, his profession placed him in a particularly good position to do so.

"Meet Mrs. Adelicia Acklen," Susanna said drawing her into the circle.

"It is a pleasure, Mrs. Acklen. I have long looked forward to this meeting," he said, taking her hand.

"How kind of you to speak to us today, Doctor," she replied.

"How nice to be among the hospitable and beautiful ladies of Nashville."

"Excuse me," she said, turning to Emily, "Luke is waiting, and I must hurry. It was a lovely meeting, Emily. Do come and visit Belle Monte at any time."

Adelicia put her hand into her muff, "Good day, sir," she said, nodding to William Archer Cheatham

Although, telling herself not to become "a cynical old biddy," she found herself sickened by the honey-eyed ladies and their flowered comments to Archer Cheatham. In Europe, ladies spoke on more important subjects than flighty flatteries and snitty comments. The men were also—she would think no more on comparisons, except that Dr. Cheatham was a disappointment. She was happy to be out of reach, out of sight of those whose conversations she had just witnessed, the drippy words, the stuffy house and discussing nothing but the past, a past that could not be altered. It was the present—the future—where the focus must lie.

Why was such pleasure taken discussing the War and the "horrors of reconstruction," nothing concerning the present, about which something could be done? Nothing concerning exciting prospects for the future as a result of the present? Adelicia would like to have given them her answer: the pleasure derived in watching, complaining, basking in days, wishing for days that would not, could not return—was their sedative for doing nothing.

Again the disturbing thought occurred, that not one word of praise had come to Joseph, nor to her, not even from her own sisters or brothers-in-law. Joseph had risked his life, day after day supplying the Confederacy with its greatest source of contraband, and she had continued what he had begun. Obviously to Nashville's old guard, there had been no self-sacrifice on either of their parts—none. To them, their actions were probably perceived as greed.

She was glad when the carriage turned onto the freshly graveled drive, glad to be back to her haven with, yes, its pleasant memories, but also with a bright future.

It was the week after Valentine's Day when the widower William Archer Cheatham called at Belle Monte for the first time. One week later he came to Sunday dinner with his two children, Mattie and Richard. Adelicia had warmed to him on his initial visit, finding him sincere and genuinely interested and concerned when she had blurted out her feelings about her late husband's sacrifices. And he had proved kind and considerate, a good friend.

After dining, they took coffee in the morning room before a roaring fire, speaking mostly of philosophies. Her interest had been sparked, and she had not realized that two hours had passed since dinner until their children came in from ice skating and bowling. It had been a comfortable afternoon, and as Archer Cheatham took his leave, he asked that he might soon call again.

He was three years younger than she, with graying blonde curly hair and soft brown eyes, eyes that she thought had known and felt much sorrow, but eyes that were extremely pleasant, intelligent and quick. He was the same age as Isaac when she had first met him and she so much younger—Isaac, her flamboyant pirate, not a noted surgeon from a well to do, prominent family.

She had accepted Archer's invitation, and thus began bi-weekly engagements in her home, in addition to social gatherings. When he had leaned forward to kiss her on the evening of their fourth outing, Adelicia had resisted, saying she was not ready for more than friendship.

Amidst the warming winds of March, when the ice and snow was no more than a memory, Adelicia stood with her children on Church Street, and presented a bell for the tower of her First Presbyterian Church. The great bell, cast in Philadelphia, weighed four tons and cost in excess of five thousand dollars.

It was a magnificently glorious day, with the nearby cherry trees freshly green with bud and the daffodils peeking through spring's new grass. She was happy, and felt as young and radiant as a bride in her fashionable pastel blue three piece suit trimmed in blue/black braid.

She had bestowed a gift for her city and for her church—a bell that would toll for the decades and the centuries to follow—for those whom she would never know—for her own grandchildren and her great, great grandchildren.

She was praised by Mayor Alden, Reverend Bunting and the elders and members of the congregation, just as she was praised by those who had benefited from her generosity in the rebuilding of Nashville and the grand plans for its first public library. It was one of the most memorable moments of her life, one never to be forgotten, nor ever dismissed. Not the praise, not even a thank you was necessary, but her joy and satisfaction in seeing the great bell hoisted upward from the oxen drawn cart and positioned in the church steeple, then hearing its glorious tones peel throughout the city. Heads bowed for a prayer offered by Reverend Bunting, and remained bowed, listening as the church doors were opened and the great organ piped "Amazing Grace." Heads were lifted, applause followed.

Adelicia, dabbing her tears, returned with her children to the carriage drawn by four and hurried to the wharf. Promise was arriving, and she would be there to welcome him home.

Four days following the dedication of the bell, on the afternoon of her traditional Thursday tea in the grand hall gallery, she overheard a conversation not intended for her ears, one that waxed sorely against her heart.

"Why should she not? She certainly can afford it"

"She feels guilty, that's what it is, for having confiscated all that money during the war."

"She did it for show. She's always had to take the bows."

"It is another of her monstrosities, a smaller and less expensive bell would have been far more appropriate."

There they sat, receiving her hospitality but exposing the thoughts that were surely the gossip behind closed doors, in the privacy of their distressed homes. It was, as Adelicia now understood, it would always be. She had not expected their heralding, she had expected to be seen as sincere and generous, without motive.

Her thanks was the polite snobbery of the elites, 'that were,' in their shabby post war establishments, wearing and living the remnants of the past. It was the same prevailing, smothering cloak of self-righteous bigotry that had hung over her like a shroud since she was a child: not fitting the mold, not doing the expected, the accepted, deviating and falling from grace—not God's—theirs!

The ambiguity: invitations to Belle Monte were top priority among the old guard, important they be on *The List*. Adelicia found the new establishment sincere, genuine, and most importantly, seemingly unconcerned with trivia and prattle. They were busy working, restructuring their lives and what made up their lives, accomplishing and building. But to those with whom she had lived and shared and loved and laughed and wept and danced, she would forever be the Adelicia for whom everything was easy and undeserving, and whatever assistance she gave, would be nothing more than "what she should have done," or what she "had not done."

Fully realizing and feeling the axiom, she made the decision to open Belle Monte, as was already the custom, but to go a step further and make it the social center for Nashville, for Tennessee, for the South, to visitors from afar. She would give them something to write about, talk about, gossip about, to keep their unbridled tongues wagging. She would entertain on an even grander scale, dress even more elaborately, perhaps flamboyantly. She would ride to church with her livered driver and footmen pulled by four. She would extend her art galleries, bringing an even greater sense of tasteful refinement and culture to the city.

She would travel, spend more time in Washington and New York, where she owned a city block of lots, perhaps tour the West, to Texas, where she also owned vast amounts of land, fifty to sixty thousand acres here, fifty to sixty thousand acres there, all stocked with fine cattle. The children would like that. And San Antonio, where numerous town lots were still in her possession. She would return to Europe, after a while, perhaps travel to Russia, the Far East, perhaps South America.

With these thoughts in tow, she hurried to her dressing room, donned a well-worn riding habit and went down the back stairs to the stables. Alone, she saddled Promise to the jealous neighing of Perchance, and raced across the back pasture, her hair full flowing in the warm March afternoon. She stopped to let him drink from a small stream and patted his strong shoulders. "I am happy you are home, old boy," she said patting him again, "Pauline will be your new mistress, she needs your gentleness, but I am always here," she whispered, leaning over towards his left ear.

What a grand sight it had been that afternoon, the same day as the tolling of the great bell, when she and her children had watched Luke lead him down the wooden plank. He had neighed immediately as she walked towards him and pawed with his right front hoof. Welcome home she had said, with teary eyes, then hitched him to the back of her carriage enroute to Belle Monte…what a blessed day that had been.

Three proposals she had had in less than a year, if she could count Crawford's. What of it all, she thought?

"A prophet is not without honor save in his own country." She would never again attempt to fit in, a position she had sought throughout her life. And just perhaps she would have her lawyers draw up a prenuptial agreement and marry, to the chagrin of most, Dr. William Archer Cheatham, who well knew of her life, its joy, its struggles. He had his own fortune, not comparable to hers, but enough. A husband would lend a nice dimension especially one so admired and praised and sought after by every available female. She was comfortable with William Archer. He was a kind, intelligent man with whom she could enjoy sharing parts of her life. After all, the delights of a woman change with the years.

CHAPTER 107

A SMALL BUGGY PULLED BY TWO HONEY COLORED MARES MOVED slowly between the stone pillars at Fairvue. A decade had lapsed since Adelicia had driven up the winding lane leading to the country mansion, and that had been to bury her Emma. The walnut trees along its path were unscarred and full with leaf, its pastures, minus of thoroughbreds, but thick with tall corn. Around the second bend, Adelicia drew the horses to a halt and stretched out her hand to an aging Daniel. Removing, his straw hat, he helped her from the carriage.

"Thank you, Daniel. It is good to see you looking well. I hope that Della is over her head cold."

"Yes'um, she is. She got dinner for you."

"Thank you," she said, handing him the reins and unhitching Promise from the rear. "I appreciate your taking such care," she said pointing to the mausoleum. "Unharness the mares, please."

Adelicia took Promise by the bridle and led him to where Isaac and her children lay beneath grassy earth, once rounded mounds now flattened by time. For two months, the gelding had enjoyed the pastures of Belle Monte. Today, she would introduce him to those at Fairvue. She stroked his molasses brown coat and slipped the bridle from his neck. "Do not go far," she said, "We shall ride later, yet another pasture."

Adelicia stood before, then sat beside Isaac's grave, picking up and holding a clod of rich Sumner County soil in her palm. "I have been wearing the ring you gave me for some time now," she said, "It feels the thing to do. I have never known what to say to you, and often wonder what you would think about this or that. So many things I do not yet understand, some I understand better." She sprinkled the soil around a lingering daffodil and pressed it about the root. "I well remember the first time I saw Fairvue. However, the enchantment is not the same today, seeming as if it were all a dream; its master no longer presides." Her sobbing was loud, and she could not hear her voice above its pain.

"I shall move you and the children to Mount Olivet one day, where we shall be together in a grand mausoleum, not as fine, but similar to this one with vaults stacked one atop the other enclosed behind a wrought iron gate. The cemetery is on a knoll, much like Pilot Knob, surrounded by rich pastures and fine country houses."

She glanced about her, as if waiting for a reply, when her eyes rested on two small plots to the right of Isaac. Little Adelicia and Victoria, asleep beneath the stone that bore witness to their names. And next to them, the tiny grave of their brother, who breathed so short a time. "Oh, Dear Lord," Adelicia cried when she knelt beside the stone to the left of Isaac, her precious Emma, and next to her, the twins. "How can it be?" she asked as she lay across the width of the three graves, weeping, clasping clods of earth in each hand—it seeming as if she were experiencing anew the losses of her children. She rose up on her knees, stretching her arms toward Promise who was nudging her gently with the softness of his nose. "Okay, old boy," she said sobbing, pulling on her gloves, "we shall ride."

She had wished to be alone at Fairvue with her memories, despite her children's pleas to see the farm about which they had only heard. That visit would wait for another time, when Pauline would cantor through the fields on Promise and she on snow white Perchance.

She galloped to where the fine brood mares and thoroughbreds had once been stalled and then to their pastures, now void of horse flesh...now in hay. And the headstone, "Samson, 1836–1858." The beautiful creature whose reins young Luke had held, and she had ridden in early autumn, 1839. "What a magnificent animal and friend you were, a beloved companion." Tears dripped down her cheeks as she attempted brushing them aside with the backs of her gloved hands. Nearby, "Imposter, 1832-1857." She nudged Promise, and raced him down to the river.

"Thank you," she said, as Della put a plate before her with sliced chicken breast, fresh fruit and cream. "And how nice to know the manner in which the house has been tended."

Adelicia had no idea how well the servants who had stayed on, drawing small wages, had looked after Fairvue, although funds were readily available to her overseer-manager, Houston White. The mansion and grounds had gone unmolested, though void of their grandeur—too long without a mistress and master to love it. She would need to sell it one day, but not this day, nor the next.

"Dinner was delicious," she said, sipping iced tea, while finishing her dessert. "Aunt Aggie never did give Essie her recipe for spring pound cake, 'lots of butter, lots of fresh cream, lots of sugar.' The recipe is safe with you. The best I have tasted." She enclosed Della's hand in hers, and asked that she speak to Daniel about hitching up the mares. "I shall wander the grounds a bit more before heading for Nashville."

She had eaten in the breakfast room and was tempted to walk into the other great rooms, to view the long elegant dining table, the music room, the bedrooms upstairs, but that reminiscing would wait for another time, if ever, she had visited all the memories she could bare in one day.

Sitting astride Promise, Adelicia would make one last stop before leaving Farivue. She would return to where she had begun to take another look, this time beyond where Isaac and the children lay, to say good-bye to Aunt Aggie and Uncle Sugart.

She had wanted to speak with Isaac about Morri, but the words would not come to her, later perhaps it would be clearer...perhaps Morri would like to see her father's grave, to visit Fairvue, perhaps stay for a while...she would think on that.

Adelicia could not forget that Morri's unexpected appearance into her life, had saved her from a horrible death. And she fully recognized that was not a coincidence, but an event filled with mystery of too great a magnitude for her to dismiss.

Removing Promise's saddle, deep in thought, she rubbed him down before hitching him to the rear of the buggy where Daniel waited, an empty bag of oats crumpled behind him.

Retuning to Belle Monte in the afternoon's dusk, she drove slowly, seeing little traffic along the way, her thoughts calm, subdued, restful. She would do what seemed best. Her youngest, and only daughter, was eight; Claude ten, would soon join twelve year old William at boarding school. Bud would soon enter Harvard.

Spring became summer and she had alternated days riding Perchance and Promise, until the day that Pauline, in a delightful, exaggerated ceremony, was given Promise as a gift by her mother. And Promise behaved as if he were the care-taker of Pauline, stepping carefully as they rode in Belle Monte's pastures, seemingly avoiding trouble spots of any sort that would endanger his young mistress. Adelicia would look over at the pair and smile, remembering Mozzalpa. The days were lovely and long, mild thus far.

Her life had been filled with loves, two to whom she was married, others for brief spans, each different. At age fifty, she would begin anew. It was a good year. Much put into its place, much dismissed, much to set right and much to which to look forward. A lengthy series of putting away—and clinging too. Life was like that, she thought. Sitting astride Perchance, Adelicia trotted down into the valley below and onto the Natchez Trace.

Author's Note

THE CHALLENGE OF WRITING THE STORY OF ANYONE'S LIFE, IS with the profound knowledge that it is seen through the eyes of the story teller.

I walked the streets of Paris, seeing those places where Adelicia had trod and visited and stayed, the Place Vendome, St. Cloud, etc; Fontainebleau, where she rode 'fearlessly' for the Emperor, again following footsteps to visualize and imagine, perhaps to see what Adelicia had seen or experienced.

There were numerous trips to St. Francisville, Louisiana and her twin sister, Bayou Sara, now a remnant of her former self; trekking down the Tunica Road, still unpaved and desolate, interviewing locals and driving the back roads, simply enjoying.

The first time I saw Fairvue, I felt much as did Adelicia, breathtaking! I spent days at a time marking the roads of Gallatin, Tennessee and driving and walking over Fairvue Plantation, until recently, still intact with five hundred acres. Researching there was fun-filled discoveries, one after the other.

For some time, I made daily visits to Belle Monte Mansion, (now the focal point of Belmont University), as well as making repeated trips to the Acklen Mausoleum at Mount Olivet, in Nashville, where Adelicia is entombed along with husbands, Isaac Franklin and Joseph Acklen, and nine of her ten children. The penitent angel, "Peri," stands in the center, where it is easily visible by the light that streams through.

I fully enjoyed discovering the sites of Adelicia's home-place, Rokeby, the sites of her sister's and brother's homes, one of which remains intact as Brentwood Country Club, Brentwood, Tennessee, wonderful days of driving the roads of Nashville, imagining how it once appeared, rich, unspoiled farm land, cattle grazing and meadows filled with purebred horses.

In New Orleans, I felt much at home when I began my search, quickly discovering the exact locations of homes and hotels where

Adelicia lived and stayed while in the City of New Orleans. Those
streets and places, mostly in the French Quarter, from Canal Street to
Esplanade, I now have memorized. The recent experience of taking a
paddle wheel down river was fascinating! Rounding the Mississippi's
bend soon after Natchez and St. Francisville, a sight for this river rat
to behold, was the same scenery and landings Adelicia experienced.

All the above were for glimpse into the life of Adelicia; within
those glimpse, some became historically accurate to a fault, others
embellished by the author's imagination, while staying true to the
basic story…after all, what we see of each other are only glimpse.

The family is still in possession of the pin, a hound's head, protruding through a hunting horn, given to Adelicia by Emperor Napoleon
III for her superior equestrian skills exhibited at Fontainebleau.

Adeicia signed her name, Ade, in letters and notes to friends and
family. For the reader's convenience, the author has used the name,
Adie, for a better sense of pronunciation.

Adelicia's mother, the beautiful Sarah Clements Hightower, did
not pass away until 1871, the author electing to have only the father
involved. All other dates of family births and deaths are authentic.

Adelicia's friend, Camille, was actually Marietta Perkins. The
Perkin's house on Del Rio Pike, Franklin, Tennessee, where Marietta
and Adelicia signed their names on the wallpaper, is still occupied
and well maintained. The story about Camille (Marietta) in the text
is primarily fiction.

Three main characters introduced early in the novel, Lona de
Bloviere, Chance Hadley and Crawford Benedict are fictional.

The terms dinner and supper are the way meals are identified in
this novel, as they generally were in that era. Dinner is what we now
refer to as lunch; supper is what we refer to as dinner.

The dates of all historical events are authentic with the exception of the scene in Part I with the Native Americans. Although the
Cherokee Tribe did move through Middle Tennessee at this time,
the scene itself is purely fictional.

This novel is set during the period of slavery and reconstruction,

1838–1867. Slaves are referred to as Negroes, servants or my people, primarily. This conclusion is drawn via research and oral tradition.

Although many events are fictional, the reader is given a brief glimpse into the life of Adelicia Hayes Franklin Acklen through the above mentioned years, beginning at age twenty-one through age fifty. She changes much, as do we. There is a sequel for the following twenty years, concluding with her death in 1887.

The Civil War years in West Feliciana are literally based on the official logs and journals kept by officers for both the Confederate and Union armies and navies. All officers' names are correct, with few exceptions. It amused the author, while researching, that one woman could baffle/confuse so many men.

Some plantation owner's names are authentic, some are not. There is no intent on the part of the author to develop a personality, etc. for any of these persons.

Sally Carter Gaut is the cousin who traveled overland with Adelicia to the West Feliciana plantations in the fall of 1863. Although Mrs. Gaut is a real character, her personality as depicted is purely fictional.

The name, Adelicia, is from Adeliza of Louvain, Queen of England, 1121–1135. The name, Adeliza, is often referred to in England as Adelicia. The name is taken from the "Rose of Brabant."

The names of all African American characters are purely fictional.

Ransom Bennington, Nicholas Pache and Morri are characters of fiction.

Among the most interesting discoveries from my research is the correspondence between Rear-Admirals, David G. Farragut and David D. Porter, regarding Adelicia.

The color of eyes, or the color of hair in the description of characters, may or may not be factual.

Adelicia's beloved Downtown Presbyterian Church, on the corner of 5th and Church in Nashville, holds regular weekly services, and the pews marked "Hayes" and "Polk," still bear the original brass nameplates. The church's interior is a striking Egyptian revival motif. The bell that Adelica donated in 1867, tolls each day.

There is no reliable documentation for dates of Adelicia's European trips.

Martha Franklin and John Armfield were married previous to stated in text.

The author acknowledges that there are many anecdotes not included at the time of this printing.

Acknowledgments

I WISH TO THANK ALL THOSE WHO HAVE SO GRACIOUSLY SUPPORT-ed me during my research and the writing of this novel of historical fiction, based on the life of Adelicia. It is with deep regret that some of those who were there in the beginning are no longer with us. I would so love to say, "Thank you," one more time.

Dr. Mack Wayne Craig, from whom I first heard the story of Adelicia at age sixteen…"Let me tell you about a lady with whom I have been in love all my life. She married once for money, once for love and once for fame…" The late William Price Fox, Writer-in-Residence at the University of South Carolina, who, upon hearing my, then, brief story of Adelicia, encouraged me to put it in writing. To the late James Dickey, Poet-in-Residence, at the University of South Carolina, "Although, not my favorite genre…" encouraged me in the writing process. For my immediate family who encouraged and believed in me through the *many* years: my daughters Brandilin, Bitsi and Blair; their precious sons and daughters, to whom Adelicia is a household name, Virginia, Keltner, Graham, Ella, Gunnar and Barrett; to my children's father, Bob Blaylock.

I am most grateful to all those who have supported and believed in me in later years; my husband, Steve Wood, a major source of confidence; Rosemary James, President and Co-Founder of the Faulkner Society in New Orleans, who has been unwavering, 'pushing' me to get this book out; readers, Jane and David Wright, of Gallatin, Tennessee, for their expertise in 19th century history; my dear friend and editor, Dana Isaacson, with whom I agreed almost always, "There is a diamond in this manuscript;" Those agents and editors who did not take me on, but who were kind, gracious and encouraging; author Karen Essex, who has, from the beginning, been an encouragement not to despair; cover and interior designer, Bill Kersey, who has worked endlessly to 'get it right;' to the late John Seigenthaler, who encouraged me sensibly and earnestly to "get it finished," to "get it out there."

Mike Sibley, Natchitoches, Louisiana who helped 'dig up' old documents related to the Civil War; Williams Research Center, The Historic New Orleans Collection, New Orleans; encouraging words from author John Jakes during the filming of *North and South*, counseling me, "Remember, you're writing a book of history, you have to get it right;" Angola State Prison, for allowing me to spend a day with the warden and his wife, who graciously invited me for lunch and gave me a tour of the grounds, searching for foundation ruins relating to the plantations, such as, Bellevue; Mrs. Oscar Noel Senior, (Granny Noel, Adelicia's granddaughter, and the daughter of Joseph Hayes Acklen), with whom I had many wonderful, memorable conversations. At her home in Nashville, on Hillsboro Pike, I sipped afternoon sherry from Adelcia's sherry glasses, now in the collection of Belmont Mansion. Mrs. Ellen Wemyss, another remarkable lady, whom I visited many times at Fairvue Plantation in Gallatin, Tennessee; Executive Director, Mark Brown, Belmont Mansion, Nashville, (built by Adelicia in 1852), a gracious host, who has lovingly led the restoration and preservation of the mansion; The University of North Carolina, Acklen Museum, and Rare Papers Collection, Chapel Hill, North Carolina; University of South Carolina Library, Columbia; Louisiana State University Library, Special Collections, Baton Rouge; Nashville Pubic Library, Special Collections, Nashville; Giles County Court House, Old Records Department, Pulaski, Tennessee; Gallatin Historical Collection, Gallatin, Tennessee; and Old Records, Alexandria, Virginia, Archives.

Alden Cohen was the first New York agent to see those first fifty pages of *Adelicia*. I am grateful for her sage advice, "You have created two excellent supporting characters, do not let them go." She, seeing what I did not, is the reason for their survival.

To the many not mentioned with whom I had interviews or were given insights along the way; to the friends who have listened through the years to my ramblings about Adelicia, as often, I could not free my mind, completely, of some aspect of her legendary life. To my author friends…all an encouraging fraternity.

Many times, when wanting to give up, long ago words would return, "You can do it, Mama!" Or, William Price Fox and James Dickey's similar refrains, "You're a good story teller, keep going."

While standing on a street corner, facing the Arc de Triomphe, Paris, 1995, a stranger handed me a piece of candy and then a greeting card that said, (I was thinking at the moment, that when I returned home, I would scrap the manuscript all together), "If you would see your Dream come true, be true to your Dream…this you must do. And never, never, *never* give up." This card remains a treasure, a reminder on a shelf in my study, the wrapped candy, too.

This work of historical fiction, *Adelicia*, would not have been possible without the sincere kindness, generosity and encouragement of so many others, so invaluable in a work of this magnitude. Most importantly, it would not have been possible without God, who continues to fill my life with blessings.

**The author acknowledges, that the reader
may very well find errors within.**

BIBLIOGRAPHY

Succession of Isaac Franklin, a nine hundred and eighteen page record of the proceedings in the Seventh Judicial District Court, holding Session in West Feliciana Parish, Louisiana, 1851.

HOUSE OF REPRESENTATIVES, 49th Congress, First Session: Number 1009.

A History of Pointe Coupee Parish, Louisiana, Bryan J. Costello, Margaret Media, Inc., 2010.

Slave Trading in The Old South, Frederic Bancroft, Frederick Ungar Publishing Company. New York, 1931.

Plantation Life in The Florida Parishes of Louisiana, 1836-1846. As Reflected in the Diary of Bennet H. Barrow. Edwin Adams Davis. Columbia University Press, New York, 1943.

Isaac Franklin, Slave Trader and Planter of the Old South, Wendell Holmes Stephenson, Louisiana State University Press, 1938.

The Bonapartes, David Stacton, Simon and Schuster, New York, 1966.

Napoleon III and Eugenie, Jasper Ridley, The Viking Press, New York, 1979.

Naval Forces On Western Waters...ORN I 26, ORN I 24.

Correspondence, Etc. Confederate, Va., Ky., Tenn., Miss., Ala., West Fla., and N. Ga., ORN I 52, Chapter LXIV.

Frank Powers, Col. C. S. Army.

West Gulf Blockading Squadron, U. S. Navy, ORN I 18, ORN I 28, ORN I 20.

Louisiana Civil War, 1864

The Miskick Krewe, Perry Young, Carnival Press, New Orleans, 1931.

The Historical New Orleans Collection, 533 Royal Street, New Orleans, Louisiana.

New Orleans, The Glamour Years, 1800-1840, Albert A. Fossier MA. MD., Pelican Publishing Company, 1957.

Williams Research Center, The Historical New Orleans Collection, 410 Chartres Street, New Orleans, Louisiana, 70130

Tennessee Historical Quarterly, Spring, 1979. Volume XXXVIII, Number One.

Tennessee Historical Quarterly, Summer, 1979. Volume XXXVIII, Number Two.

Tennessee Historical Quarterly, March, 1944. Volume III, Number One.

Tennessee Historical Quarterly, June, 1944. Volume III, Number Two.

Tennessee Historical Quarterly, Spring, 2011. Volume XXVIII, Number Two.

The Mind of the South, W. J Cash, A Vintage Book, Random House, New York, 1941.

Music in New Orleans: The Informative Years, 1791-1841, Henry A. Kmen, Louisiana State University Press, Baton Rouge, 1966.

THE HISTORIC, Blue Grass Line, A Review of Davidson and Sumner Counties, James Douglass Anderson, Nashville-Gallatin Interurban Railway, Nashville, Tennessee, 1913.

The Queens of American Society, Mrs. Ellet, New York: Charles Scribner and Company, 1868.

LALLA ROOKH, An Oriental Romance, Thomas Moore, London: Longman, Orme, Brown, Green and Longmans, 1838.

The Life of David Glasgow Farragut, First Admiral of The United States Navy, Journals and Letters, Loyall Farragut, New York: D. Appleton and Gregory, 1879.

So Great A Good, Hodding Carter and Betty Werkin Carter, the University Press, Sewanee, Tennessee, 1955.

Manuscript of Division Update, Papers Relating to Antebellum Louisiana, Volume, XII, 1993.

Colonial Natchitoches: A Creole Community on the Louisiana-Texas Frontier, Helen Sophie Burton and F. Todd Smith, 2008.

The Forgotten People, Gary B. Mills, Louisiana State University Press, 1977.

NASHVILLE: The Faces of Two Centuries, 1780-1980, John Egerton, Plusmedia Inc., 1979.

The Greater Journey: Americans in Paris, David McCullough, Simon and Schuster, New York, 2011.

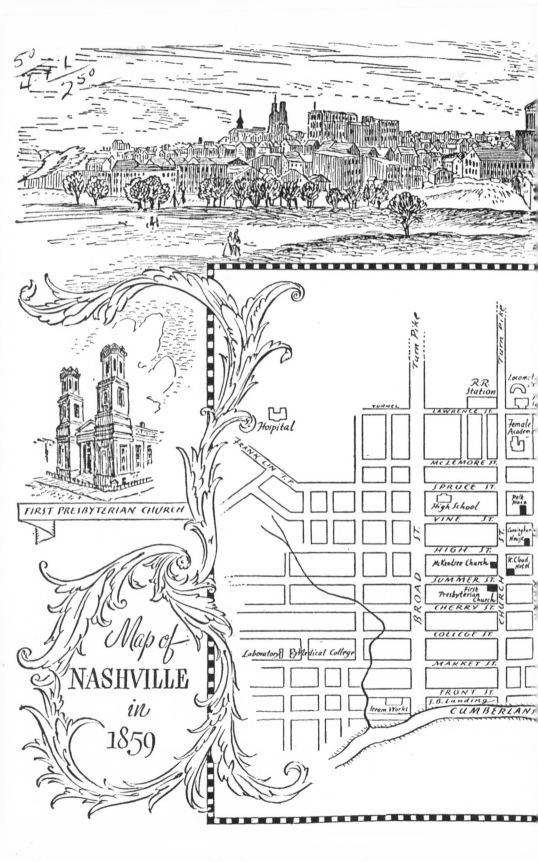

FIRST PRESBYTERIAN CHURCH

Map of
NASHVILLE
in
1859

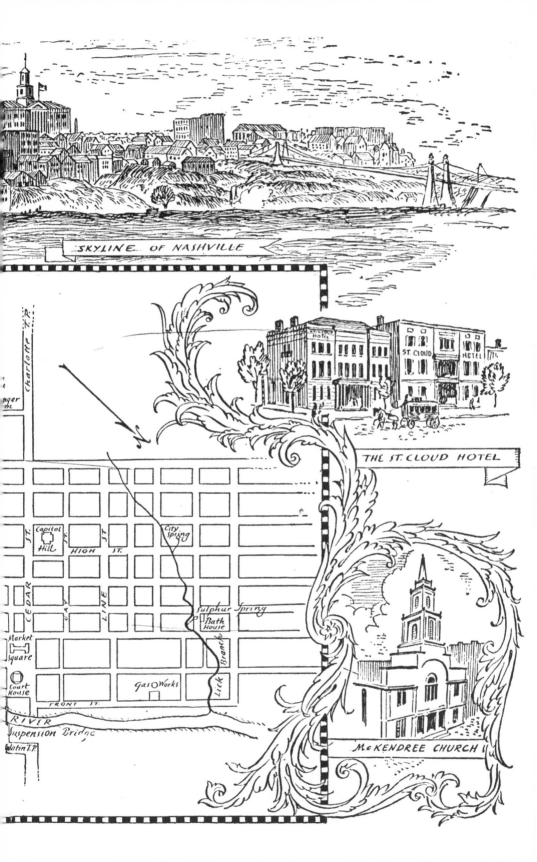

SKYLINE OF NASHVILLE

THE ST. CLOUD HOTEL

McKENDREE CHURCH

Charlotte T.P.

ST. CLOUD HOTEL

ST. CLOUD HOTEL

N

Capitol
Hill

City
Spring

HIGH ST.

FT. ST.

Sulphur Spring

Bath
House

CEDAR ST.

GAY ST.

LINE ST.

Market
Square

Lick Branch

Court
House

Gas Works

FRONT ST.

RIVER

Suspension Bridge

Galotin T.P.

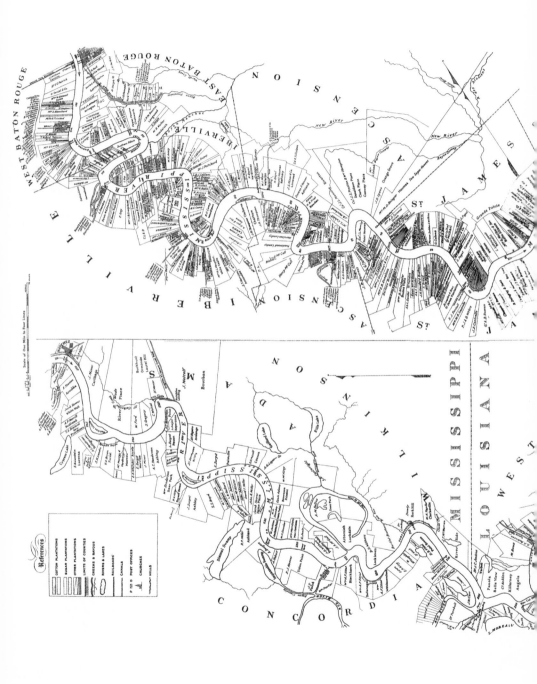

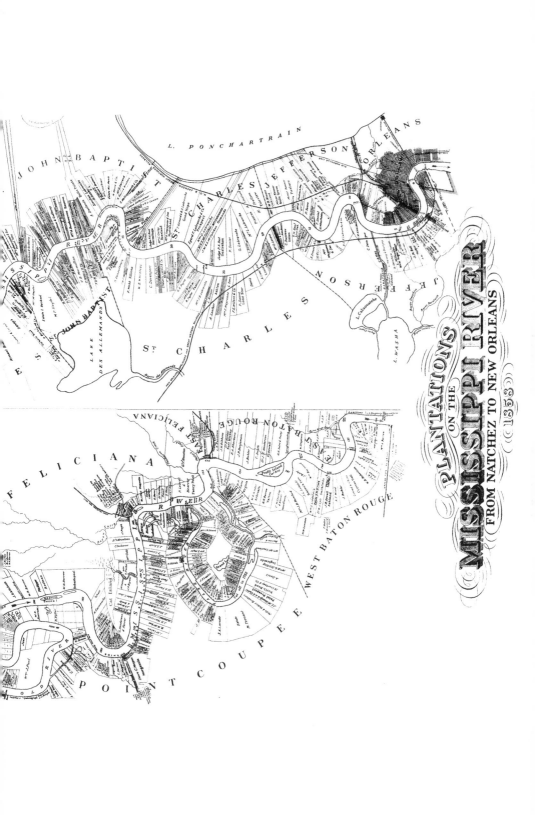

PLANTATIONS
ON THE
MISSISSIPPI RIVER
FROM NATCHEZ TO NEW ORLEANS
1858

CLARIFICATION OF PLANTATIONS

ROKEBY PLANTATION
Nashville, Tennessee
The Hayes Family
Uncle Ben, Essie, Liza, Uncle Bob, Uncle Will

FAIRVUE PLANTATION
Gallatin Tennessee (thirty miles Northeast of Nashville)
Isaac Franklin
Aunt Aggie, Uncle Sugart, Della, Daniel, Charlotte

HOUSE ON ESPLANADE
New Orleans
Isaac purchases for Lona
Bess and Moriah

BELLE MONTE
Nashville, Tennessee
Essie, Luke, Uncle Will, Liza and Caleb

The following are the plantations in West Feliciana Parish, Louisiana, owned by Isaac Franklin, a large parcel of land where the Mississippi River makes its greatest loop before heading East to New Orleans.

LOCH LOMOND
Brutus and Fanny

BELLEVUE
Lucy, Alfred and Rufus

KILLARNEY

ANGORA
(Later called Angola)

LOANGO

PANOLA

The following listings are to aid the reader in identifying the locations of the plantations and the names of the main players.

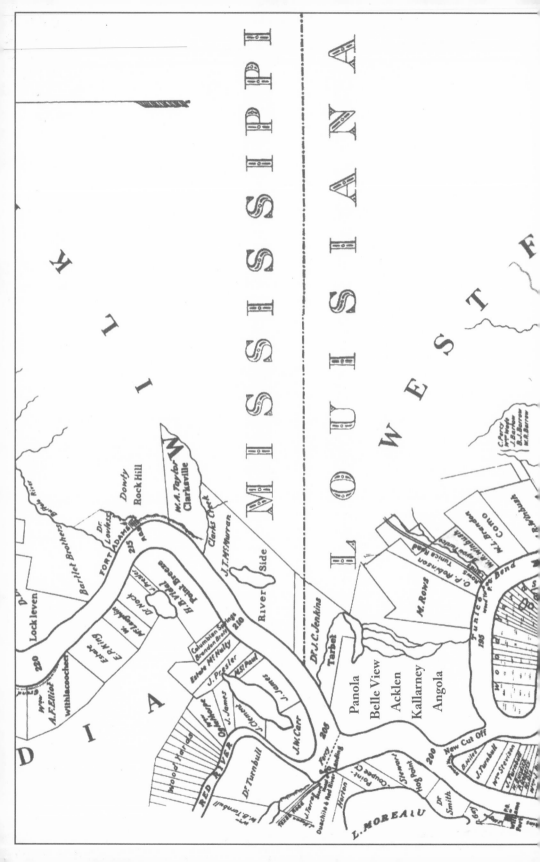